the complete series

claire
goodnite

USA TODAY BESTSELLING AUTHOR

JENNIFER REBECCA

Tell Me a Story | Copyright 2017 © Jennifer Rebecca
Tuck Me in Tight | Copyright 2018 © Jennifer Rebecca
Say a Sweet Prayer | Copyright 2018 © Jennifer Rebecca
Kiss Me Goodnight | Copyright 2018 © Jennifer Rebecca

This book is a work of fiction. Names, characters, places, and incidents are the product of the author's imaginations and are used fictitiously. Any resemblance of actual events, locales, or persons, living or dead, is coincidental.

Unless you are the boys from 'Bama who mercilessly killed my baby girl's dragon in Minecraft. Regardless, of whether or not it was a "bad" dragon, E loved it. She cried for an hour when it didn't come when she called it and for that you had to pay. Thank you for being such good sports about it and willing to laugh when informed you would die. I am forever grateful. But not for killing Ellie's virtual pet.

All rights reserved. Except permitted under the U.S. Copyright Act of 1976, no part of this publication may be reproduced, distributed, or transmitted in any form or by any means, including photocopying, recording, or other electronic or mechanical methods, without the prior written permission of the author.

Cover Design by:
Alyssa Garcia

Editing by:
Stephanie Atienza

For more information about Jennifer Rebecca or her books, visit:
www.JenniferRebeccaAuthor.com

table of contents

Tell Me A Story..1

Tuck Me In Tight..138

Say A Sweet Prayer..268

Kiss Me Goodnight..396

VOLUME 1 OF THE claire goodnite SERIES

tell me a story

dedication

For my mom who thought it was totally normal to read *My Last Duchess* and *Rebecca* to a little girl. She gave me her creativity and a little bit of her crazy.

And also for my dad. It takes a strong man to raise a daughter to believe she can be anything in the world she wants to be. And an even stronger one to keep watching and encouraging when it takes 33 years for her to figure it out.

risk either this job or my family. For anything. Got it.

I push away from my dented metal desk and stand up. I make a move toward my BFF, also known as the coffee maker, and pour myself my 988,473,729 cup of the day. Well, not really, but it feels like it. Sometimes, I wish I could just get an IV tapped so that I can mainline caffeine the way that I need to in order to keep moving today.

Again, not really, because that would probably get me fired or thrown in jail and that place is gross. I'm tough and all, but I am not a fan of peeing in front of other people. No, thank you. I take that first hot sip and it burns all the way down. I sigh to myself just before I'm startled out of my daze.

"Goodnite," my brother shouts and I'm embarrassed to admit that I jump a little. "My office. *Now.*" I roll my eyes. It's definitely different having my big brother as my boss. My dad was the Captain of this station when I was a little kid. Liam has been working towards filling out old man's shoes ever since he got back from a stint in the Navy alongside his buddy who I'm avoiding for the rest of my natural life. It sure keeps things interesting.

We've always been pretty close even though he's eight years older than me. I used to follow him and his best friend, Wes, around all the time hoping they would let me play catch or hunt bugs with them, but they never did. I never lost hope though.

Then they had to go and get girlfriends and that was the most embarrassing show I have ever seen. So, when I finished college and Liam had just come back from his last tour overseas to join the local Police Department, I followed him there too. He was not real happy about that one, but I didn't let that deter me.

"Any day now, Goodnite!" he barks. Sheesh.

"Alright already!" I holler back as I chug half of my coffee and roll my eyes.

"And don't roll your eyes at me!" he shouts.

I pause and look around. There's no way he can see me. He's just guessing. I take a deep breath and start walking towards his office, but not before I shout back.

"Oh, are you going to run and tell mom?" To the tune of snickers all around the bullpen as I saunter into the Captain's office. I wink at the guys before I shut the door.

"Do you always have to be so ridiculous and insubordinate?" he asks me. I pause to look him in the eye.

"Is that seriously why you called me into your office?" I mean really, does he know me at all?

"No," he sighs and runs his palms down his face. By his body language alone, I know the case is a bad one. But what he tells me next, explains everything. "If you weren't the only available detective I have, I wouldn't even be having this conversation with you," he says looking me dead in the eyes. It's creepy the way he does that, but I don't flinch.

"Thanks for the vote of confidence," I droll.

"I'm serious here, Claire. I don't want you on this case."

He doesn't actually want me anywhere near this department so I don't let his comments hurt my feelings. I have no room for that kind of negativity in my life.

"Thank you," I sigh. "So, give it to someone else," I taunt. I don't really want him to do that though and he knows it.

"Everyone else is working another stack of them. You just wrapped up the domestic, so technically, you caught this one," he tells me on another grunt.

"What exactly is it that I caught?" I ask Liam, but by his reticence, I already know.

"A little boy, six years old, was reported missing by his parents when they came home this evening from work," I hold my breath. "If there was anyone else available . . ." He squeezes his eyes tight.

This is hard for him, I get it, but this is me. This is my life and the past is in the past firmly where I buried it under six feet of dirt and two feet of concrete. Metaphorically speaking. It is not open for discussion. With Liam or *anyone*.

"I get it, you'd choose them over me," I sigh, not even surprised anymore.

"It's not like that, Claire, and you know it," he says exasperated.

"I don't care anymore, Liam. Not even a little," I say. "Can I have the case notes? Who called it in?"

I reach for the file on his desk, eager to get this little meeting over with. He opens his eyes, the same violet ones fringed in thick, black lashes as mine. On me, they are unique, on Liam they stop you in your tracks. I can see he is firming his resolve to bully me off this case.

"It's not good for you to handle these types of cases, Claire," he says softly.

"Why don't you let me decide that for myself," I respond just a little too sharply. Making a statement and not asking a question.

"It's not good for me to have you on this case . . ." Liam starts, but I can't let him finish that thought. I hold up my hand to stop him.

"Don't . . ." I say, but it's too late, he's on a roll already.

"Damn it, Claire! I can't protect you out there." He slams his hand down on top of his desk so forcefully that his stacks of paper topple over and his coffee mug rattles.

"I don't need you to," I say softly.

"What about what I need, Claire?" he shouts as he jabs his thumb back into his own chest. I shake my head and close my eyes.

"It's my life, Liam," I say softly, opening my eyes but not quite meeting his. "You know I love you, right?" But he ignores me.

"What about Wes?" he presses on and my spine automatically stiffens.

"This has nothing to do with Wes," I snap.

"He was there that day too . . ."

I know what he's thinking. Wes can calm me down. Wes can reason with me. Wes knows my past and thinks that I can't handle this case or be in the department either. But Wes doesn't get a say and neither does Liam. I was going to catch a case like this some time. Better sooner than later, right?

"Enough, Liam." I slice my hand through the air to silence him. "This has nothing to do with you or Wes or even me. This has everything to do with a little boy who is missing from his family."

Liam looks at me just a little too closely, he sees too much and I have too much to hide still. I know if I looked at his eyes, I would see just a little too much sadness. I can't handle that. I can barely live with the consequences of that day. The day I made so many stupid, immature choices. Childish choices that robbed me of the rest of my childhood. Not only do I get to live with the consequences, so do Liam and Wes. So, do my parents. Everyone's lives changed that day and there is no one to blame but me. So, I reach across his desk and take the file that sits there before turning on my heels and running like hell.

chapter 2
what it's like

THE DRIVE TO 1312 Orange Drive is not a long one, but one fraught with a storm of thoughts twirling in my head. I hate fighting with Liam but this is unavoidable. He can't keep throwing my past in my face to keep me from living my life. Using it to hold me back.

It was hard enough being the weird girl in school. The kid everyone knew about but no one talked to. That was so much fun. Everyone has their opinions about what really happens when someone gets kidnapped. News flash, they're all wrong.

Girls pretended to be my friends to get the inside scoop. Boys wanted to date me because they thought being kidnapped meant I must be easy. Because if the monster had raped me, then I wouldn't have my virginity to worry about protecting anymore. Liam and Wes set those morons straight. And then there was everyone elses's parents who claimed they wanted to mother me and protect me. They didn't. They just wanted something else to brag about at their bridge socials and PTA meetings.

I shake my head side to side like an etch-a-sketch hoping to shake the dark memories from my mind. I'm going to have the dream again, I know it. Fuck, I hate those dreams. Dreams that are likely disjointed memories.

I pull up to the house where the missing child lives. Red and blue lights dangerously twinkle in the darkening sky of the late afternoon. The black and white units line the street in front of the house. I watch uniform officers canvas the upper middle-class neighborhood, knocking on doors and talking to neighbors. Hoping the little boy just wandered down the block. By the scowls on their faces and the tension in their shoulders, they know that is not the case.

I park my Tahoe a little down the way and head to the front door. My badge is clipped to the belt on my jeans, but it wouldn't matter, most of these officers know me and see me around regularly. But they also know my background and by the looks on their faces now, they think this is a mistake. Maybe it is, maybe it isn't, but one way or another it's happening.

"Hey Claire," Jones greets me. He's a nice guy about my age with a girlfriend and a baby at home. "You catch this one?" he asks.

"Sure did, Jonesy," I say softly.

"Sucks," he says, nodding towards the house.

"They all suck."

I walk into the house and take in a clean, modestly decorated living room. There are well kept sofas, nice, but not brand new, a large flat screen television, end tables, and a coffee table. Coordinating curtains hang over large windows.

On one of the sofas sits a well kept woman in her fifties. She has blonde hair streaked with gray and her tasteful makeup now runs down her face as she cries into a soft looking, linen hanky. She is wearing beige slacks and a white poplin blouse with a light blue cardigan over it. The whole thing is topped with a string of pearls and matching earrings and ends in low beige leather sling backs with a pointed toe.

"Mrs. Ascher, I presume," I say as I walk towards her. "I'm Detective Goodnite," I tell her. Hoping to ease her into telling me everything.

"Claire Goodnite?" she asks me. The well-dressed man in navy slacks, a blue striped shirt and tie tightens his arm around her as they sit together on the sofa. There's something there I can't put my finger on. Something is off.

"Yes?" I ask distracted.

"I remember when you were taken," she says softly. I feel the breath in my lungs seize but I force a benign smile onto my face.

"Honey, I don't know if this is appropriate," Mr. salt and pepper hair and wingtips tells me something I already know. It's not appropriate.

"She'll find him," she whispers, putting her hand on top of his on her arm. "You'll find him, won't you?" She says to me.

"I'm going to do my very best to find out what happened to your son Mrs. Ascher," I tell her hoping to defuse this bomb.

"But you're going to succeed because you know what it's like to be taken," she tells me. "You know what it's like," she chants, over and over.

"I do," I say firmly back. "Now, time is of the essence, what can you tell me about your son?" I ask.

"Anthony, his name is Anthony Donovan," she tells me. "His sister, Kasey, was watching him. She doesn't know where he is," she says with a sob.

"Kasey watches him after school until his mother and I get home from work. Then we have dinner and they do their homework," Mr. Ascher tells me.

"And you are, Sir?" I ask. I know who he is, but I need him to tell me everything.

"Jonathan Ascher," he states firmly. "Anthony's mother, Elizabeth, and I married six months ago. The children have lived here with us ever since." Honest and to the point. I like that.

"Thank you. I have to verify everything," I smile softly at him.

"Absolutely," his eyes soften but he does not smile. He may have real affection for the children. Time will tell. "We just want him found," he says. Interesting he didn't mention safe. Not home safe.

"Where would Anthony have gone other than here?"

"That's the thing, he wouldn't," Mrs. Ascher tells me. "He *knows* he is only to go with Kasey," she stresses.

"And where is Kasey?" I ask.

"Up in her room. She's just beside herself," she tells me. I would be too if I had just lost my baby brother.

"May I speak with her when we're done here?" I ask softly.

"I don't think today will be good," Mrs. Ascher says, flooring me. She just said she wanted her son found and now she won't let me interview the last person that saw to him safe. The shock must show on my face because she quickly recovers.

"I really do need to speak with her, Mrs. Ascher," I implore. "It's imperative."

"She's having such a hard time right now," she hedges. "Every time she lost a pet, Kasey took it so hard. This is her baby brother we're talking about . . . maybe tomorrow."

"Tomorrow then," I say softly, not wanting her to become defensive. "How often does she watch Anthony for you?" I ask.

"After school when we're at work and any other time we might need a sitter," Mrs. Ascher tells me.

"And how old is she?"

"She's sixteen."

"Does she drive?"

"Yes, her father bought her a car for her birthday," she shares on an eye roll.

"Do she and Anthony have the same father?" I ask.

"Of course." She narrows her eyes on me.

"Where is he now?" I ask in the same tone.

"Probably off with one of his floozies," she snaps. So, there is no love lost between the

former Mr. and Mrs. Donovan. Good to know.

"Can you tell me a little bit about Anthony?" I ask, changing directions. Her face immediately softens letting me know that Anthony is the beloved baby of the family.

"He is such a precious boy," she says softly, her eyes brightening. "Anthony is so sweet and so smart. He gets straight A's in school. He loves trains, cars, and trucks like all little boys do. He loves mud and climbing trees. He wants a puppy desperately," she says sobbing.

"We were talking about getting him one for his birthday," Mr. Ascher adds.

"That's nice," I say before changing directions. "And how about his friends. Who are they?" I ask.

"He plays with the Johnson boy down the way," Mr. Ascher informs me.

"Jason and Mark are his friends from school," Mrs. Ascher states.

"Can I have you write down their parents' names and phone numbers, please? Addresses will help too if you have them."

"Of course," she sniffles. "Anything to find my baby boy."

I am about to make motions to go talk with their daughter when there is an outburst at the front door.

Yes, today is going to be a *very* long day.

"Where the fuck is my son?" A large man bellows from the front door as the wood panel crashes open and slams against the wall. "What did you do to my little boy?" he cries. I look at Mr. and Mrs. Ascher, their faces have gone equally hard.

"Mr. Donovan," I say softly. "Can we talk privately outside?" I ask as I stand up from my seat in the living room, making my way to the front door.

I look around and see all the uniform officers are frozen solid, with their muscles forced loose, waiting to see what Mr. Donovan's next move is going to be.

"Who are you?" His eyes narrow on me.

"I'm Detective Claire Goodnite and I'm here to investigate your son's disappearance," I say softly. Hoping to not rile him up more because it's already been a shit day and this is not helping me find his son.

"I just want my boy back," he breaks down, nodding. I move to him and gently put my arms around him, guiding him out the door.

"Then help me find him," I say softly, with my head bent towards his. "Talk to me, give me the information I'm missing to find out what happened to him," I implore. I can tell my pleas got through to him when he lets out a soft sob and nods his head again.

I look up to find Marty, one of the uniforms I know and move to ask him on my way out to get the grief officer down here to the parents. But when I look up, it's right into eyes burning so bright they can only be described as true Irish whiskey. Unfortunately, those gorgeous eyes are on the face of my worst nightmare, also known as Special Agent Wes O'Connell with the FBI. And Liam's best friend to boot.

Fuck me, it really is going to be a long day.

chapter 3
dirty laundry

"I CAN'T IMAGINE WHAT would bring you into my jurisdiction, Agent," I snap looking into those God damned amber eyes.

"One would think with a missing child, you would do whatever it is to find him, exhaust all resources, and not sit on your high horse, Claire," he growls.

"This is not the time or place, Agent O'Connell." I respond baring my teeth.

"Let me take over," he says softly, but you could hear a pin drop. Everyone knows. Everyone is watching. And I absolutely fucking hate it. It's as infuriating as it is humiliating to have my big brother's friend here to take over the case that no one thinks little Claire Goodnite can handle. I'm not afraid to admit that it stings.

"Liam called you." I sigh. "So that's how it's going to be is it?"

I motion for a uniform to take the boy's father and put him in the back of a black and white to take him to the station. He needs to be questioned and not on the front porch of the home of his ex-wife and her new husband. I look up at the window of the second story and see the curtains flutter. *Interesting.*

"Hey Mickey, can you escort Mr. Donovan back to the station for me?" I smile sweetly at one of my favorite guys. "I'll be there as soon as I wrap up what I need to here."

"You got it, Goody." He smiles softly to me before he walks Mr. Donovan to his patrol vehicle.

"Don't you think it's just a *little* unprofessional to flirt with every officer?" Wes snaps and I lose my mind.

"Excuse me?" I bark back. My head snapping around to stare at the big bastard in disbelief.

"You heard me," he growls, leaning towards me. "It's unprofessional the way you flirt with everyone." My jaw opens and closes. Then opens again before snapping shut.

"I don't flirt with anyone!" I shout. "it's just your *little* ego and *tiny* dick that can't handle the fact that I don't flirt with you." I let those words hang in the air between us.

"You, of all people, should know that my dick is *anything* but tiny," he shouts back. I gasp. If I thought you could hear a pin drop before, now, the air was still. It was frozen, charged with the coming storm between Wes and me.

"You asshole!" I scream before launching myself at him. I don't get the chance to make contact because strong arms wrap around my waist and pluck me out of the air.

"Both of you, back to your corners," one of the older officers in the department growls. "I know the Captain thinks your shit is golden, *Sir*, but I'm not so sure he'll be thrilled when he gets the report on what just went down here with not only one of his Detectives, but also his sister. Think on that," he says. Still not releasing his hold on me.

I stand there glaring at Wes. I can't believe he went there. I feel the tears sting the back of my eyes but I beat them back. I won't let him see me cry. Wes doesn't deserve that. I knew he would want me off this case as much as Liam, but to air our sordid history stung. I have worked hard here to be treated as an equal. I busted my ass to make it as far as I have. Plus, the way he said it makes it sound like we're having an affair, not one stupid night twelve years ago. Fuck my life.

"Yes, Sir, I understand," Jones, the officer behind me, says into his cell phone. "Yes, Captain, affirmative," he says before disconnecting. Fuck. My spine goes straight at hearing he's talking to my brother.

"Would you do me a favor, *Officer*, and kindly take your hands off the Detective before I remove them from your body," Wes growls.

"Are you fucking kidding me right now?" I yell back.

"Both of you shut the fuck up," Jones snaps. "You are both to haul your asses into the Captain's office. He is not happy. Thanks for the ass chewing, by the way."

"I'm sorry, Jonesy," I say softly. Unable to meet his eyes through my own shame.

"No worries, Detective, a good ass chewing is good for the soul," he winks at me.

My jaw hangs open as I stare at him. I don't think I have ever seen him wink. Let alone at me. He's serious and never jokes around. I mean never *ever.* I close my mouth and nod once, then head for my department truck.

I beep the locks and step in, closing the door firmly behind me. I look over my shoulder out the window where Wes and the officer are leaning into each other, obviously having heated words. As if he senses me watching, Wes looks up and his bright gold gaze locks with mine.

I'm not proud to admit that I jump a little bit and quickly avert my eyes when I see that stupid ass knowing grin spread across his stupid handsome face. Fumbling with my key, I finally fit it into the ignition. I refuse to look back at him but know he's watching. *Me,* he's watching me. I put my truck in drive and peel out heading towards the station.

The drive is not nearly as long as I wish it was. Before I know it, I am pulling into the parking lot and isn't it just my luck, there is a space opening up right in front of the building. I wait for the other vehicle to pull out with my turn indicator on. Once they take off, I pull into the spot and put my truck in park, turning off the ignition. I sit there for a moment with both of my hands on the steering wheel, just staring ahead at the brown brick building that I really don't want to enter.

I watch a pair of detectives I know walk out of the building, clap eyes on me sitting in my Tahoe and then turn around to walk back in. I know what those assholes are doing. A bunch of *Benedict Arnolds,* they are. I sigh and bang my head against the steering wheel between my hands once, twice, three times for good measure. I pick my head up and open my eyes. And there is Liam, my brother, my boss, holding the door open and staring daggers at me.

Unless I am mistaken, that is not a happy look on his face, and I am definitely not mistaken. He raises his hand and extends his index finger, pointing directly to me and then jerks his thumb angrily over his shoulder towards the doorway he is standing in before walking inside, the door slamming behind him.

I sigh one more time to myself wondering why I couldn't have been a stripper or a carhop instead of a cop, it probably would have made our relationship more copacetic. Then pull my keys from the ignition and open the door to my truck. I step down and shut the door behind me. I stuff the keys in my jeans pocket and walk towards the door with my head hanging and my shoulder slumped. *Defeated.*

I will never let those two assholes know that they got to me, so just before I open the door to the station, I roll my shoulders back and lift my chin high looking everyone in the eye that thinks they can get to me with the knowledge that Wes aired some old news at a crime scene. They don't scare me and they know it. Until my dumb brother breaks the silence with his shouts, making me jump.

"Get your ass in here now, Goodnite!" He bellows.

"You've done it now, Goody," the guys jest.

"Nah, it isn't the first time I took a swing at a fed, it probably won't be the last time," I wink.

"But I bet it's the first time you boned his buddy," someone says softly.

"Yeah, there is *that*," I admit.

"Better luck next time."

"Yeah, thanks assholes."

I can't deny it so I just shrug my shoulders and head towards the Captain's office. I raise my hand to knock but Liam's shouts beat me to it. Again. Jesus, how does he do it? I think before crossing myself in the hopes that our very Catholic mother didn't just hear me say the Lord's name in vain. In her mind. She's crazy like that.

"Jesus! Just get in here," he shouts. So, I walk in the door and shut it firmly behind me.

"So . . ." I hedge. "You wanted to see me?" I ask.

He just glares.

"So, I need to follow up with the officers at the scene and interview the dad . . ." I trail off. "So, if you don't need me . . ."

"Sit down," he says, softly menacing.

"Liam," I whisper, his purple eyes cold and menacing.

"I said, *SIT DOWN!*" he roars and I do just that. Without putting any thought into it, I sit down in one of the chairs in front of his desk. Folding my hands in my lap I lock my eyes on them, not willing to meet his eyes.

Liam runs a meaty hand down his face before slapping the top of his desk. Hard. He hits it again and I jump a little at the bang. *"God damn it!"* he shouts.

I sit there silently, saying nothing. Nothing good can or will come from confessing all my sins to my older brother. I was a naive little girl but I have left her firmly in the past. That girl is gone and she's not coming back.

"When?" he asks softly when he opens his eyes and looks at me.

"A boy, Anthony Donovan, age six, went missing sometime between the hours of three and six this evening . . ." I start to report on the case he assigned me.

"No." he silences me. "When did you fuck my best friend?"

"Twelve years ago. You were both home on leave . . ." I start but stop when Liam hurls his coffee mug that was resting on his desk across the room and into the wall, smashing it for good. He drops his face into his hands, his elbows resting on his desk.

"Did you love him?" he asks when he sits up again, looking at me.

"Liam, this doesn't have anything to do with what's happening right now."

"It fucking does if he's bringing it up at an active crime scene in front of all of my officers twelve years later!" I just nod. He straightens himself. I can see him physically forcing himself to calm down. "Did you love him?" he asks me again.

"I was young," I say softly, not wanting to admit that Wes was the only man to ever really hold and break my heart.

"How young again?" *Uh-oh.* He tilts his head to the side and narrows his eyes on me.

"Eighteen. Barely," I add because it's the truth. My brother growls under his breath. Shit. Wes just might be a dead man. I hate that. I never told him because I didn't want to poison their friendship even if I could never look at Wes the same again.

"You didn't answer my question," he states. And no I didn't.

"I don't want to."

"Claire," he sighs, rubbing his palms down his face.

"Liam." He stares at me, his eerily purple eyes burning into mine, and I feel myself waffling. "Fine! *Yes,* I thought I did. *But I don't.* It was twelve years ago so cut me some slack!" I throw my hands up dropping them harshly to my sides.

"You loved me?" A voice I can't bare to hear asks from behind me and my spine goes straight. I look up at Liam, that betraying bastard, who is looking over my shoulder at what is no doubt the one person who will unravel my whole carefully constructed life. With a God damned smile on his face. My brother is the biggest asshole! No, he's the second biggest. Wes still holds the number one spot in my book.

"I gotta go," I say standing and Liam's smile grows wider.

"This is going to be fun," he says as he claps his hands like a dancing circus bear.

"No, it's not. It's going to be nothing," I snap at him, flipping him off.

"God damn it, answer me!" Wes thunders, making me turn to face him. "You love me?" he asks again.

"No," I lie, wondering how I'm going to escape this office with Liam at his desk and Wes blocking the door. I know the windows don't open and I need to get back to Mr. Donovan.

"Bullshit!" he clips out. "I want her off this case right now," he says to Liam. I don't hear anything else due to the blood roaring in my ears.

"Don't you fucking dare!" I shout. "This is my case." I'm breathing heavily, my chest rising and falling as I turn to take down Wes. His eyes dart to my chest for a bit too long before he looks in my eyes.

"I mean it. She's gone as in yesterday," he says to Liam while looking at me.

"Don't even think about it, Liam," I growl, not turning around.

"You and I both know she should not be on the Donovan case. Let me take it over and put the full resources of the FBI behind it," Wes implores.

"You can't be serious."

"She's too close to this," Wes pleads.

"I am not."

"She was in this kid's shoes," he says.

"Not likely," I harrumph.

"You don't know that." Wes looks back at me.

"Actually, I do. The longer we sit here arguing the more likely it is that he's dead."

"She's not rational."

"That's it. I'm gonna shoot him," I declare.

"See?" Wes says.

"Oh, stuff it, you old blowhard," I growl.

"I see you've really matured," he says as he shoots me the side eye.

"Can I please shoot him?"

"NO!" they both shout at me.

"Alright, alright. I get it. No shooting the Fed. Cool. I'm cool. I swear," I placate with my hands held out in front of me in mock surrender.

"See?" Wes rallies. "She cannot be on this case. She's too close with her past. She can't see this rationally."

"And what about you two?" I ask. "Do you really think you both can see it rationally? Our shared past, my past didn't affect you at all?"

"No," he growls.

"No, it didn't?" I ask.

"No, it didn't." Wes folds his arms over his chest.

"Not even a little bit?" I shrug my shoulder.

"No," he scowls.

"So, there was no reason to bring up our shared past in front of my colleagues for any reason than to humiliate me?" His eyes widen when he realizes where I'm going with this. "I knew it!" I shout.

"I did no such thing!" he growls. "You are insane if you think that time in my life, those days, those hours, those minutes you were missing did not affect me. But it didn't happen *to me.*"

"That's right it happened to me," I snap back.

"And I am trying to protect you. Your brother is trying to protect you!"

"I don't need anyone to protect me from anyone except you two overgrown gorillas. And you are not going to take this case from me!" I shout. I toss my long, black hair over my shoulder for effect as I make my way to the door. "Don't worry, boys. I don't take candy from strange men anymore. At least not the kind that comes in wrappers!" I shout as I slam the door behind me.

Shit! They make me mad. I cannot believe that those two idiots think that they are going to protect me. Like I need to be swaddled like a baby. I am not a baby!

I start to storm my way down the hall, away from stupid Liam and his stupid office. I hear the door open and slam shut. Shit! I need to get out of here. Where am I going to go? I start to pick up the pace when a strong hand clamps around my upper arm.

"Oh no, you don't," Wes growls as he backs me into the wall. "No men. No strangers. No one but me," he snarls just before his mouth crushes down on mine.

I gasp and the back of my head hits the wall behind me. Wes needs no flags, no ticker tape, nor neon signs to proceed. His tongue licks into mine. There's an aggression. A need.

Wes's hand on my arm moves up and into my hair. Gripping it tight. Pulling. His other hand pushes me back at my belly until my back hits the wall and I'm trapped, pinned, by a big hunk of angry man. As he deepens the kiss further, his hand at my belly slides around my waist and down. Down. Down. Where he palms my ass cheek and squeezes it in his strong hand, Pulling my hips towards him. Wes groans into my mouth as the hardness of his cock connects with my body.

"You're mine," he kisses me again. "You've always been mine."

"Wes . . ." I whimper on a gasp as he squeezes my ass again, pulling me against his hardness. I moan into his mouth as he kisses me again and again.

"You were always mine," Wes says as he kisses me again. "I'm just surprised you capitulated so easily." He smiles against my mouth.

"Wait, what?" I ask again as the fog begins to clear. Wes kisses me again, but this time I'm not into it. Wes doesn't seem to notice.

"I'm glad we see eye to eye here, babe," he says softly. I'm babe now? What is happening here. "I promise, I'll take good care of this case. You don't have to worry."

"*My* case?" I ask even though I know. I just freaking know.

"Yeah, I'm taking it over. I can't believe you're being so agreeable about it, Claire."

"That's because I'm not!" I shout as I shove him back. "This is my case."

"Yeah, but now that we're together, I want to protect you. I need to protect you," he tells me.

"No, you need to back the fuck up. This is my case, Wes. And if you really cared about me, you wouldn't try and shit all over my job, a job which I happen to love. This just goes to show that we can't be together," I say as I duck under his arm.

"We'll see about that, Claire. We'll see about that," he growls. "You are mine, babe. Your body knows it and so do you."

"I can't hear you . . . la la la la," I shout with my fingers in my ears as I walk away. I always walk away.

chapter 4
ghosts

I'M SO FREAKING MAD. I'm sure there is steam shooting out of my ears as I stomp down the hallway to my desk. I grab the notes on top that let me know that Mr. Donovan is in *Interview Room #4*.

I roll my shoulders back and meet the eyes of every detective and officer in the bullpen that dares to look at me and pass judgement. They do not have the right to because I have not given it to them. I atoned for my sins a long time ago, vowing to live my life only moving forward.

I am not a small child who needs to be swaddled in cotton and tucked away in a safe place. Nor am I the little girl who took a candy bar from a stranger who said he needed help finding his dog because she was so mad at her brother and his friend for not letting her hang around them. I do not need to be *protected*. The word causes a bitter taste to take up root in my mouth. I want to spit it out but I can't because it's not real. Just like I tell myself every day that my old ghosts aren't real. *But they are.*

I scoop up my case file and notes. Then make my way down the hall to the interview room. I knock twice before pulling open the steel door and stepping inside. I shoot Mr. Donovan a sweet smile hoping to both placate him and catch him off guard—*I'm the nice police lady, tell me all of your secrets and lies*—before sitting down in the metal chair across from him, nodding at the uniformed officer standing in the corner.

I flip the switch under the table that starts recording the conversation by both video and audio. It's not always admissible in court, but I want to have it so I can run it by a body language expert I know. Something is just *off* with this case. I am also aware that Wes would have those people at his fingertips with all of his fancy pants FBI resources but I'm still too steamed to talk to him. The sad part is, he's right. I'm going to have to pull him in on this case for Anthony's sake.

"Mr. Donovan." I dim my smile to a sad one directed at him. "I am so sorry about your son. I promise that we will do everything that we can to find him."

"I don't know what to do," he sobs. His face buried in his hands.

"Can you think of anything that you think might be important?" I ask him. "Anything at all?" He just shakes his head. Tears streaming down his face.

"No," he cries. "Anthony is such a good little boy."

"Can you tell me about the people in Anthony's life?"

"Me. He lives with my ex and her perfect husband. His sister. He's got some friends. He goes to school. Plays ball. I guess he knows a lot of people," he whispers. My guess, he's realizing we're now trying to find a needle in a haystack, before it's too late.

"Was there anyone that just seemed off to you?" I ask.

"No—" he starts. "Well, Liz's new guy is weird, but I figured that's just because he's married to my wife and that burns," he says honestly.

"Can you tell me why you and Mrs. Ascher divorced?"

"What does that have to do with anything?" he barks.

"I'm just trying to put all the pieces together so that we can find Anthony," I tell him calmly.

"I slept with my secretary. One time! One freaking time and Liz found out. She couldn't pack her bags fast enough. She was living with that douche by the end of the month," he snarls.

"I'm sorry, that must have been very hard for you."

"It was. But not bad enough to hurt my son!" he shouts. "Those kids . . . those kids are all that is right in the world. Those kids are my entire world," he sobs.

"Can you tell me if there was ever anything that gave you a weird vibe?" I ask. He starts to shake his head no, but I need to see if I can shake something loose in his brain. "Did you see the same car over and over? Bump into the same person again and again? Feel like someone was watching you? Watching the kids?"

"No," he cries. "I should have been there!"

"Did your kids ever seem like something was off or bothering them when you saw them or talked to them on the phone?" I ask. My questions coming faster and faster to try and make him give me *something*. Really anything that might help us catch a break in this case.

"No!" he shouts. "I didn't know. I didn't notice anything because I wasn't there. I didn't protect him!" he screams before dissolving into a broken puddle of snot and tears. He drops his face down on the metal table, and pounds his hands away on the metal slab as if it will offer up some answers about his son. Unfortunately, I can see that the answers aren't here.

I put my hand over his on the table and lean in, whispering in his ear that I will do everything that I can to bring his son home to him.

"One way or another, Detective?" he asks. His watery blue eyes meeting mine. He grabs my hand tight, to the point of bruising. "Bring him home. Even if he's gone. Don't leave him out there in the cold."

"I will," I say. Knowing that we should never make promises like that. But unable not to. One way or another, I will bring Mr. Donovan's son, Anthony, home.

I walk out of the interview room and head to the kitchenette in the office. I grab a bottle of water from the fridge and pound it back. But it can't wash away the weight of this case on my shoulder.

I pour myself another cup of coffee but I can't make myself choke it back. I look out the window and see that it's dark. It's later than I realized. I am so tired. So exhausted. So weary that I don't hear Liam sneak up behind me.

"Go home, sis," he says from behind me placing his hand on my shoulder. "There's nothing more you can do here today. Get some rest and tomorrow you can hit it again."

I nod because he's right. I'm useless right now. My stomach growls and I can't remember the last time I ate. Maybe a burrito on my way into work this morning. I dump my coffee down the sink and turn to head out for the night.

"You know I love you, right?" he asks softly when I reach the door. I just nod.

"Yeah, Liam, I know," I tell him. "I love you too."

• • •

I walk in the front door of my apartment and lock it behind me. I could probably buy a house if I wanted to, but I don't think I'd like being alone in a big space. The solitary lifestyle of my one-bedroom apartment is just right.

I drop my keys on the kitchen counter and toss my coat over the back of my couch. I'm not the neatest person, but the only person who has to live with it is me so I don't care. I open the fridge and grab the carton of fried rice and the leftover egg rolls from last night. Or was it the night before? I shrug and grab a fork from the drawer, happily eating my cold leftovers as I kick off my boots.

I set my carton down on the counter and take a bite of my egg roll. I chew it as I unbutton my jeans and drop them to the floor. I put the egg roll back in my mouth like a cigar and reach under my shirt to unhook my bra and pull it out through the arm holes of my tee.

I grab my carton and continue to eat as I sit down on the old corduroy sofa and grab the remote. I flip through several channels, but the late-night news is covering the disappearance. My service picture—my face so fresh and bright straight out of the academy, no one would see the secrets that hide behind my eyes, but they're there—flashes across the scene with my name announcing my lead role in the investigation.

I'm glad when my fork scrapes the bottom of the carton, because the news has spoiled my appetite. I toss the cardboard in the trash and the fork in the sink. I pull a water bottle from the fridge and down the whole thing, tossing the bottle in the trash.

I pull my long hair up into a messy bun as I make my way down the short hallway to my bedroom. I pull the covers back and flop in face first. I'm asleep before I stop bouncing on the mattress, not even bothering to pull the blankets up over my body.

• • •

Wes and Liam are so mean! I can't believe they won't let me hangout with them. I bet they're just afraid that I'll tell mom and Mrs. O'Connell about the magazines they're hiding with the girls in bikinis in them.

I'm stomping through the woods behind our house. I don't need those gross boys to have some fun. And those boys are gross! They smell weird and put on too much stinky spray stuff when they think I'm not looking.

I just make it to the street on the other side of the trees from our house when a white van pulls up next to me. I hear my mom in my head telling me not to talk to strangers. I feel my eyes going wide as he steps out of the van.

"Claire!" he says and I wonder how he knows my name. "There you are. I need your help!"

"What do you need help with?" I ask.

"I'm so glad you asked, Claire," he says my name again like he says it all the time. It's weird but I don't think too much about it. "My puppy, Millie, got out. She's missing. Can you help me find her?"

"I don't know. I should probably go back home . . ." I say.

"No!" he shouts and it startles me and I jump a little. His eyes widen when he notices my reaction. "I need you to look for her while I drive around. I'll give you this candy bar if you help me . . ." he offers, holding up my most favorite kind. I instantly grab for it, but he pulls it back.

"Okay, what does she look like?" I ask.

He smiles a creepy smile showing all of his teeth, but I open the front door and get in the van. He hands me the candy bar and I realize that I don't even know what his name is . . .

"She's little and fluffy and white . . ." he trails off as I dig into the sweets my mom never lets me eat before dinner. Ever!

All of a sudden, my head feels funny and my ears feel full of cotton like last summer when I got an infection from swimming too much. I open my mouth to tell him something is wrong, but my words don't work. They won't come out! I turn my head to look at him, a scream stuck in my broken mouth. He just smiles his big, creepy smile and everything goes black . . .

When I wake up I'm on an old, yucky blanket on the floor of a dark, smelly house. It's not my house. I know that. I rub the side of my head, it hurts so much. When I look up, the strange man is leaning back in an old torn chair, his feet spread wide and there's a strange bump in the front of his pants that he keeps rubbing his hands on. He smiles when he notices that I'm awake and for the first time ever, I'm scared.

"Hello, Claire, I'm glad that you're awake," he says to me in a scary voice. I just sit there staring with my eyes big. "You may call me daddy."

• • •

I sit up screaming, pulling the gun that I tuck under my pillow each night and pointing it at nothing. The ghosts have won again. But then, I knew that they would. I have to focus to slow my breathing. Sweat rolls down my spine in waves.

I'd like to say that the old Chinese food brought on the nightmares, but that would be a lie. It was the Donovan case, I know it. That and the haunted look in Mr. Donovan's eyes when he realized that his son might not come back.

The ghosts old and new have me in their grip. I know what I have to do even if I don't want to. I grab my phone with the hand not currently holding a gun. I look down at the cold, black steel in my hand and wonder, not for the first time, just when those ghosts will finally claim me for good. When will they come for me with such a frequency that I crave the bite of my own bullet to silence them. It happens to more good cops than anyone realizes.

Will I be the next?

I stalk to the bathroom and place my gun and my phone on the counter. I fill up the glass that sits on the counter from the tap and chug it back. I stand there and sweat and shake, over and over again, waiting for the effects of the dream to loosen its grasp on me until I turn and drop to my knees in front of the toilet and empty the contents of my stomach. No, the ghosts that I can't quite beat back won this round.

I wipe my mouth on the back of my hand before standing up on shaky legs. I run my hands under the faucet again and cup water to my mouth to rinse it out. I splash a little on my face hoping to cool down my overheated skin.

I stand there for who knows how long, looking at my reflection in the mirror. Always hoping that the image changes. One day, I want to see a beautiful, carefree woman who has smile lines in the corners of her eyes instead of red rims and bloodshot pupils. Maybe she'll be fat and happy with a baby in her belly and a gold ring on her finger. Or a little silver streaked in her jet hair and the knowledge of forty years with the same good man by her side.

But the woman in the mirror and I both know that will never be possible. The glint of the steel and the black glass of my gun and cellphone catch my eye. No, I won't be falling in love or having babies. I won't grow old with Wes or any man. Those dreams were all stolen from me twenty-four years ago. My only role now is to find the bad men and to make them pay, no matter how unhealthy those goals may be.

But before that, there's one thing I need to do. I pick up my phone, the metal and glass cool to the touch in my overheated palm. My thumb presses the circular button and unlock the screen. I open my call log and dial a number I know by heart now.

"Claire?" A voice husky with sleep asks when they pick up the phone.

"You were sleeping," I say realizing how late it must be. "I shouldn't have called. I'm sorry."

"Claire," she says before I have a chance to hang up. "Claire, you called for a reason."

"Yes," I whisper.

"You had a dream again, didn't you?" I hear sheets rustle and know that she must be getting up to take my call and turn it into a middle of the night session.

"I did."

"Which one?" She asks in her soft melodic tone. I clench my eyes tight and my hands into fists before I can answer.

"The one—" I have to clear my throat and start over. The rock in my throat is so thick I can't get my words around it. "The one where he takes me."

"And how does that make you feel, Claire?"

"Stupid," I say for lack of a better word because I was. How stupid do you have to be to willingly get into a car with a stranger. "Weak."

"Claire," she sighs. We're getting into dangerous territory. My regular sessions with Dr. Anna Chandler were one of Liam's many demands before I could sit for the Detective's Exam. Somewhere along the way, Anna became more than my shrink, she's a friend and confidant. "You were six years old. At some point you have to realize that you can't sit as your thirty-year-old self and judge the mentality of child you from the past."

"I know," I sigh. "I know it. I do. I just . . ."

"You can't let go," she says softly.

"Yeah."

"It's been a couple of weeks since you last had one of the dreams," she states. I know where this is going and brace for it, physically and mentally. "Has anything changed since we last spoke?"

"Yes."

"Are you going to tell me what it was?"

"I don't want to," I say petulantly.

Anna laughs. I sigh.

"Come on, Claire. Tell me. You know you want to . . ."

"Fine," I huff. "I caught a new case."

"What kind of case?"

"A missing person," I say honestly, feeling a little lighter.

"Hmm," she muses.

"It's a child," I confide. "A boy, a six-year-old boy."

"That's an interesting age," she muses.

"It's definitely a pretty big coincidence."

"I have to admit, I'm surprised Captain Goodnite gave you the case."

"He didn't have a choice," I sigh. "It's been a busy week. I had just wrapped up a domestic. He could give me someone else's case and bump me from the new one, but he'd have a lot of explaining to do."

"Interesting . . ."

"He did spend a great deal of time trying to convince me to hand the case over to Wes willingly if it makes you feel any better."

"And how is the cold and calculated SAIC?"

"Not so cold and calculated," I mumble.

"What was that?" Anna perks up.

I sigh.

"I said he's more . . . warm . . . passionate maybe than cold or calculated these days."

"And why would you say that?"

"He kissed me outside of Liam's office."

"Shut up!" She squeals like a sorority girl just asked to the spring social by a big idiot named Biff.

"Yep." I pop the p from my mouth.

"Tell me all about it," she shouts. "Shit. I need a cigarette."

"I'm not sure you're the consummate professional Liam thinks you are," I tell her.

"Sometimes, I think what Liam doesn't know after hours won't hurt him."

I hear her click her lighter and take in a deep drag from the cancer sticks that will surely kill her one day. But I guess when you hear all the shit she does, you need a vice.

"I couldn't agree more."

"I take it he still wants you to quit the department?"

"Yeah, the fucker."

"It's because he cares," she tells me.

"Something like that."

"You know it's true. He just doesn't have a healthy way of showing it," she sighs.

"Yeah."

"Wes does too."

I snort.

"Oh yeah, he really cares." I roll my eyes but she can't see them. "He has a funny way of showing it if he does."

"He does," she argues.

"Yep, and he showed it when he announced to all of the officers and the victim's family at an active crime scene that I handed him my virginity on a silver platter like a moron."

"He didn't," she gasps excited for a juicy tidbit.

"He totally did."

"How did Liam take it?" I can see her rubbing her hands together with glee in my head.

"He was pissed for about a nanosecond and then he decided that this would be fun. Now their group goal is to get me to quit because he can't legally fire me." I sigh.

"That bastard!" This is why I adopted her as my friend. Really, she's one of the best. Anna and the ME, Emma, are my only two female friends. We're an odd group, but it works.

"Yeah."

"You think you can get back to sleep now?" She asks.

"Yeah, I do. Thanks, Anna."

"Anytime, babe."

And then she hangs up.

chapter 5
non-negotiable

BEEP... BEEP... BEEP...
My alarm is blaring on the bedside table next to my head as I lay on my back, staring at the ceiling. I groan out loud but there's no one here except the ghosts of my past to hear me. Mornings like this are hard. I hate being alone after a night of the dreams, after a visit from the past.

My skin is cool, the sweat from my panic during my nightmares has chilled on my skin making my t-shirt stick to my breasts and my back. My legs are tangled in the sheets where I finally stopped tossing and turning, but my foray with sleep didn't last.

Without turning my head to look I silence my alarm, but I can't silence the ghosts in my head. Maybe Liam and Wes are right about me being on this case. But I'll be damned if I let them know it.

I roll out of my bed and head for my bathroom, not even pretending like I'm going to make my bed. Because I'm not. I turn on the water as hot as I can stand it before stripping off my panties and tee, tossing them into the pile in the corner.

I hiss when I step into the scalding stream before forcing all my muscles to relax one by one. I make quick work of washing my hair and my body. Every time my thoughts stray to Wes and his kiss in the hall my skin heats and that makes me angry.

I don't *want* to want Wes. I fell for his charming song and dance years ago and learned really quickly that is not something I want to do again. It goes like this: get sucked in-sleep with Wes-get burned badly when he bolts. And he *will*. No, I already got the thanks for playing t-shirt and I don't need another one.

I shut off the water and step out, toweling off. I do manage to put the towel back on the rack before combing out my long black waves and then heading back to my room to dress. I pull on a lacy bra and panty set, which are definitely *not* for anyone specific. Then my usual work uniform of skinny jeans and tall boots. I like my boots a little loose so I can slide my drop gun and its holster underneath. Then a white, long sleeved thermal t-shirt with little buttons down the front exposing a light blue tank top underneath.

I head back to the bathroom. My building is old, really old, so I have to wait for the steam to clear from the mirror. I twist my hair up into a bun at the crown of my head, not because someone always loved my hair long and free. Then I slap a little makeup on my face like I do every day with a little blush, mascara, and a berry lip gloss.

I head down to the kitchen and pour myself a cup of coffee and make myself some toast. I give the bread a sniff as I pop it into the toaster because I can't remember when I bought it. I lift my mug to my lips, but freeze as I stare into the toaster and remember the morning Wes woke me from a nightmare…

• • •

"Jesus, what is that?" I hear Wes shout over a scream. It's then that I realize the screaming is me.

I back up against the headboard of his bed, as far away as I can get when he's looking at me like that. I pull the sheet up to my neck. I'm naked underneath. Bare. Vulnerable. I squeeze my eyes tight as I remember last night. What we did, Wes and me.

"Answer me," he thunders and I snap my eyes open. I open my mouth but the words won't come out. I clear my throat again before I can speak.

"Nightmare," I tell him.

"Do you have them all the time?" When I press my lips into a thin line instead of answering, Wes narrows his eyes at me. "I see."

"It's not a big deal, Wes," I whisper.

"I think it is," he says softly.

"Wes . . ."

"No," he closes his eyes. When Wes opens them again, I know that I've lost him. "This was a mistake. I'm going to head out for a bit. While I'm gone, you need to get home," he says quiet but firmly.

I bite my lip to keep it from trembling and nod my acceptance. Wes thinks it was a mistake to be with me. I have loved him my whole life and until recently, he thought of me as a burden. The annoying little sister of his best friend. Last night, I was something else. Something special. Someone that he wanted. But now, now I'm just a mistake. Well, that makes two of us. I won't be making mine again.

"I'm s—" Wes starts, but I steel my spine and don't let him finish.

"Don't," I say sharply. "I'll just be going." I say as I stand up, for once unashamed of my nudity and start pulling on my clothes. I open the door and I'm almost to freedom when Wes speaks again.

"Claire," he starts, the pain evident but I don't care. I won't ever care again.

"I thought I said, 'don't,'" I say and then slam the door behind me, never looking back.

• • •

My toast pops out of the toaster shaking me free of one more trip down bad memory lane. I grab a plate from the cabinet and place my now butter and jam covered toast on it. I take a bite, but it might as well be sawdust. I take another bite knowing it may be the last thing I eat today.

I sip my coffee and hear in my head the sad way Wes said my name all those years ago, but I can't. He doesn't get to break me and then show up twelve years later asking for a do over.

I think about the way he kissed me yesterday and how I caved. *Again.* I'm secretly not sure I will ever be able to stay away from him for long. And I hate it. I had very little left of me that I liked after I was taken, Wes stripped me of the last of it twelve years ago. I see red and hurtle my mug at the wall across from me in the kitchen. I dump my toast in the trash can. I am no longer hungry.

Yep, the ghosts are out in force today. *All of them.* All set to ruin the life that I have carefully constructed for myself out of the rubble. This is why I can't have nice things. So, I clip my badge and my sidearm to my belt and head out into the day, locking the door behind me.

• • •

I park my Tahoe and walk into the station feeling the weight of an already shitty day on my shoulders. I head to the kitchenette and pour myself another cup of coffee, psyching myself up to go to my desk and get to work.

"Goodnite, my office. Now!" Liam bellows from the doorway to his domain.

"Fuck," I say as I let my head hang down from my shoulders. My hands braced on the old laminate countertop. "What now?"

I push away from the counter and set my coffee mug on my desk. I briefly consider locking my guns in my desk in case my brother does something monumentally stupid and makes me want to shoot him.

"What's up, Captain?" I ask as I walk into his office.

"Wes and I have come to an agreement," he states. I raise my eyebrow in question.

"Oh, you have, have you?" I sneer.

"Yes," he says calmly. Too calm. "Wes is going to observe the case as it progresses. Any time we feel like it's too much, we're pulling you out."

"The hell you are," I grumble.

"Yes, we are. And be warned. This is non-negotiable. And the best offer you're going to get from me," he says, his purple eyes burning into mine.

"Fine." I pout, folding my arms over my chest.

"Good, now get out and find that kid." He smiles at me as I stand and start to walk out of his office. "I love you, Claire."

"I love you too, Liam." I smile at him over my shoulder. And I do.

"Just . . . hold onto that feeling over the next twenty-four hours," he says cryptically.

I just shrug and head out into the bullpen and sit at my desk. I flip open the file and am looking at the reports of businesses near the house that might have video surveillance, when I hear a chair shuffle and a throat clear. It's then that I notice there is no other sound in the building. You could hear a pin drop. I look up to see what has caused a stir and right into the whiskey colored eyes of none other than my FBI arch nemesis . . . and fall right the fuck out of my chair.

"God damnit," I shout when my ass hits the floor. That's going to leave a bruise for sure. "You have got to be kidding me."

"Nope, no kidding here," he rumbles in his deep, sexy voice. "Let me help you up." Wes offers me a hand to pull me up.

I reach up and grab his outstretched hand and I am electrocuted. Not really, but it feels like it. Like being struck by lightning. Or when you have to get tasered before you can carry one on patrol. It feels like that. By the widening of his dark eyes, Wes feels it too. I want to slap that stupid, sexy smile right off of his handsome fucking face.

I stand up and wrench my hand free from his. I sit at my desk and the bastard casually walks around to the other side of the partners desk I'm sitting at and sits right the fuck down.

"Umm . . . what are you doing?"

"Getting ready to observe." He smiles sweetly.

"Why are you sitting there?"

"Because this is my desk."

"No, it's not," I counter.

"Okay, it's my borrowed desk . . . *For now.*" His eyes twinkle.

"No, that's Harriet's desk," I inform him.

"I know that, but Harriet is on maternity leave for the next six weeks, so the Captain said I could sit here while I help out with the case . . . and *observe.*" I don't say anything. Okay, I might have growled. And yes, I definitely should have shot Liam.

"Don't do that. I'd miss you if you went to prison," he says still smiling, this time indulgently.

"What?" I ask.

"Don't shoot your brother. I'd miss you if you went to prison," he says, quieting his voice. "I can't kiss you if you're in prison . . . Or do other things to you . . . *With you . . .*" he trails off. I think I might be having a stroke because all I can do is groan and maybe drool a little bit. I shake my head to snap out of it.

"I don't know what you're talking about." I huff.

"You do, but I take it that you didn't mean to say it out loud." He chuckles. I just glare at him before returning my gaze to the file in front of me on my desk.

I start making a list of all the places that I need to check out before calling some of the responding officers to follow up. Then, I'll head out and start looking for creepy vans or bad people who might be looking to snatch a little boy.

"Don't you think we should interview the neighbors or the parents of Anthony's friends before we go looking for a creepy guy in a van?" Wes asks. I just look into his eyes and glare.

"No," I growl. "And what makes you think I'm looking for a 'creepy guy in a van'?" I ask.

"One, you wrote on your notepad, find creepy guy in a van," He ticks off on his fingers. "And two, I think we should do more interviews and find out if there even is a creepy guy in a van," he logics. Fucking logic. But I'm already too far gone with my irritation and angry that Wes and Liam ambushed me first thing this morning.

"Look, I don't show up at your work to slap the dick out of your mouth and tell you how to get shit done, do I?" Before I sigh. "Fine, asshole, we'll do it your way. Get in the car. Let's go interview some people," I say. Hoping to God that I don't feel the need to shoot him.

"I heard that!" he says and when I look up he's walking at a pretty fast clip towards the door. "And I'm driving!" he shouts as he breaks out into a run. The hell he is. Game-set-*mother effing match!*

chapter 6
determination

"GET BACK HERE YOU asshole!" I shout as I sprint through the front door of the station, only to see him grinning like a lunatic from the driver's seat of my department vehicle! "Oh no you don't. Get the fuck out," I say as he turns the key and starts the ignition.

"Are you going to get in or what?" He laughs as he buckles his seatbelt.

"I'll kill you," I seethe.

"No, you won't," he laughs. "You can't fuck me if I'm dead. Now get in." I hear a feral scream and I'm pretty sure it's mine.

"I do not want to fuck you, you stupid shit. Conceited much?" I ask as I climb in the passenger seat of my car. And the big idiot just turns his head and winks at me before backing out of my spot and heading towards the Ascher's home.

"You do too, but that's okay. I'm ready when you are," that fucker winks at me. I feel the growl rumble up from deep in my chest and he just laughs. "Come on, let's go find some bad guys and interview some witnesses." I just glare at the side of his head as he peels out of the parking lot and heads towards the neighborhood of our missing boy.

• • •

The trip to Orange Drive is not long but it feels that way. It feels like years have passed as I sit in silence with Wes. Wes, who has always been magnetic. His energy doesn't pour off of him it radiates out and pulls you back into him. I'm feeling it vibrate off him now.

Wes doesn't try to make small talk with me. He doesn't hum to pass the time. And he isn't overall annoying. And I wish he was. This new Wes has me reeling and I don't know what to do about it. I should be focusing on what I'm going to say to the Johnson's and here I am trying to force myself not to think of Wes, to lean into Wes, to give in to all the temptation that is Wes. He's leaving me alone on purpose. Intentionally leaving me to my thoughts knowing that they would stray to him. Knowing that I love him. That I loved him when I was more girl than woman. That fucker.

Before I know it, he pulls up to the curb a few houses down from the Ascher's home. Wes kills the engine and then turns to me, his face open and honest. I don't like this Wes either. This Wes scares me. This Wes makes me want to believe that I can trust him and I know, I know that I can't.

"I thought we could we could start with the Johnsons," he says, mirroring my thoughts. I just nod, still not looking at his face. "Hey, look at me."

"No," I whisper. I hear the click as he unbuckles his seatbelt and the sounds goes off in the quiet truck like a bullet from a gun. Before I know it, his hand is gentle on my cheek as he turns my face to look at him. "I agree. Let's go talk to the Johnsons." I say softly, my eyes downcast towards his shoulder.

"I said look at me, Claire," he says softly. He waits for my eyes to meet his. "It's going to be okay, Claire. I'm not going to hurt you. In any way." I close my eyes against his words. His face.

"No," I whisper.

"I'm not going to hurt you. I'm going to help you. I'm going to protect you. From bad guys, from yourself, but I am going to keep you from protecting yourself from me. I'm not the same man, Claire, and you have to recognize that." I just nod and wipe my nose on the back of my hand before unbuckling my seatbelt and leaping from the truck.

"Claire," he calls after me, but I just shake my head.

"Not now, now I'm working," I say as I march up the front steps of the Johnsons place and stab at the doorbell button.

I look over my shoulder to spy on Wes, but see the upstairs curtains of the Ascher place flutter as I scan past. I turn back forward as the dead bolt in the door turns. Mrs. Johnson, I assume, opens the door.

"Can I help you?" she asks, her full lips smiling wide and seductive over my shoulder. Fantastic.

"Yes, ma'am." I barely refrain from rolling my eyes and kicking him in the shins. "I'm Detective Claire Goodnite with the George Washington Township Police Department. We're here to ask you a few questions."

"Sure sure." She winks again over my shoulder. "And who are you, handsome?" I grind my teeth and press my hands into fists, my nails biting into the skin of my palms.

"I'm Special Agent Wesley O'Connell with the FBI." And I hear the mother effing smile in his voice.

So, now I see what the game is, he doesn't want me, he never freaking did. He was trying to woo me over so that he could get me off the damned case! Ugh. And now, he's trying to see if he can make me jealous. Angry even. So that I'll storm off and leave him to prove he can handle my case better than I can. Emotional maturity and all that bullshit.

"Oh, a *Special Agent*, well come on in. I hope you have to use your cuffs." She winks and I hear him start to choke. I smile. She's not just a cougar, she's a freaking man eater. This. Is. Awesome. He overplayed his hand. And I couldn't be happier. I want to clap with glee.

"Yes, let's go inside," I say. Mrs. Johnson looks over at me like she'd like to tell me to take a hike, but knows that she can't. This is awesome. "I promise, we'll be real quick and then I'll leave you in the good hands of Special Agent O'Connell." I smile sweetly.

"What are you doing, Claire?" he growls in my ear.

"Getting you out of my hair so that I can get some real police work done while you do what you're good at." I wink at him.

"And what exactly is that?" He glares.

"That should be fairly obvious," I grin. "You are a manwhore. You just can't help yourself." I whisper back. His eyes are gold and glittering, probably a sign I should apologize and back off, but I don't. I pat him on the chest twice and the turn and follow Mrs. Johnson to the living room.

"Thank you for speaking with us, Mrs. Johnson,"

"Of course," she says sweetly. "Anything I can do to find that little boy."

"And what do you know of Anthony Donovan?"

"I know that he is a darling little boy," she answers. Pausing to gather her thoughts. "He's the same age as my son, Scott. They have played together in the neighborhood since the Aschers moved to town a few months ago."

"And what do you know of the Aschers?"

"I know that Jonathan is the vice president of the local bank. His family has owned it for years. And I know that Elizabeth works there, but I'm not sure in what capacity," she says. I find that interesting. Her knowledge of Mr. Ascher is lengthy, but what she knows of Mrs. Ascher is sorely lacking.

"And what about their daughter?" I ask.

"She's alright. She's always hanging around with her boyfriend when she's supposed to be watching her little brother. I've been meaning to say something to Jonathan."

"And what's her boyfriend like?" I ask.

"Do you know his name?" Wes chimes in.

"I don't know his name. But he looks decent enough." Fantastic. Not helpful lady, stop making moon eyes at my brother's annoying ass friend.

"Can you describe him?" Wes asks.

"He's pretty tall for a boy, muscles." She winks at Wes and I think I throw up a little bit in my mouth. "Blond hair. Always in polo shirts and jeans. Tennis shoes." Well, that was decent enough.

"That helps, thank you." Wes smiles his damn charming smile. The fact that it is directed at someone other than me is a nice reminder that he can't be trusted with my heart or my lady bits.

"I'll do anything to help you," she breathes as we stand to leave. "I know you'll catch who ever took him. I know all about you. I read you saved her when she was taken," she says as she wraps her hands firmly around his bicep. Wes tries to disengage when I ask for a private moment.

"Why don't you go on and bang some information out of her," I say quietly as I smile and nod towards Mrs. Johnson.

"What the hell does that mean?" he growls.

"Nothing, nothing," I placate him with my hands up. "I just think you'll get more information out of her without me here." He seems to mull it over for a bit before nodding. I look to Mrs. Johnson.

"Thank you so much, Mrs. Johnson." I smile. "I'm leaving you in the capable hands of the FBI." I wink at her before making my way out the door, clicking it closed behind me.

I walk down the steps and head to the truck to compile my notes. Glad I picked Wes's pocket when the nice neighborhood hoochie was pawing all over him. I'm not jealous or anything.

I climb into the driver's seat of my truck and start going over my notes, making more in the margins and lining up my questions. I look up at the Ascher house through the windshield and see the curtains flutter again. Someone is watching.

I tap my pen against my bottom lip and think who would be secretly watching. The Ascher's want their son found. Mr. Donovan had to be sedated last night because he was so distressed by his son's disappearance. *Kasey.*

It has to be the sister, Kasey. The sister much older than the little brother. Much like Liam and Wes are much older than me. Liam and Wes who are still so torn up about my own disappearance that they would do anything to pull me from this case. But Liam wouldn't have hid when the cops came. That take the bull by the horns attitude is what made him a great operator in the Navy and a great Captain with the police department. Liam is about as opposite of a shy, sixteen-year-old girl as you can get.

I'm lost in my thoughts of Anthony and Kasey, of Liam and me, and even Wes. The parallels are uncanny. My eyes stare forward at the Ascher house, unseeing, my mind trying to puzzle together the facts. But the past and the present are getting to jumbled together.

I jump when there is a knock on my window. I shake my head to loosen the facts bouncing around and shake free the memories that have nothing to do with now. I look up into those whiskey eyes that suck me in every time.

"What do you want?" I ask through the window. He looks . . . *sad*.

"We need to talk, Claire," he says softly. I shake my head again.

"No, I need to find a little boy," I say firmly with more bite than I meant but I brush that off. I'm still shaken from the dream, the memories, all of it just bubbling at the surface. "What you do in your spare time and with whom isn't my problem." For a second, if that, I see defeat flash across his golden eyes before resolution and determination harden there.

"Shall we go interview the sister?"

"That was my plan," I say sweetly.

"Then let's go," he says as he pulls open my door. I step down and tuck my notebook into my coat pocket. Together, we walk up the steps of the Ascher house and I can't help but feel like everything is about to change.

chapter 7
loved and cherished

THE WALK UP THE curb is slowly maddening. I can feel Wes behind me and my anger climbs to new heights with each step. My palms are sweaty and my hand shakes as I reach out to jab the doorbell, all while hoping that Wes doesn't notice.

"Hello," Mrs. Ascher says as she opens the door. "What can I do for you, detective?"

"I'm here to speak to Kasey," I tell her gently, not asking permission, but also not demanding aggressively.

"I'm not sure that now is a good time..." she trails off before she notices Wes over my shoulder.

"Ma'am, I'm Special Agent Wessely O'Connell with the FBI," he says over my shoulder. "I'm sorry to say, but there is no good time when there is a missing child. We need to speak to her," he finishes softly.

Mrs. Ascher just nods sadly and opens the door for us to enter. We follow her into the living room where we will question the young girl.

"Please, have a seat. I'll go find Kasey," she says. We both nod and sit down. Wes on the smaller sofa, me on one of the arm chairs across the coffee table.

The sounds of soft footsteps padding down the carpeted tread of the stairs draw our attention. And I have to say, I could not be more surprised by what I see. Kasey Donovan is the polar opposite of her sweater twinset and pearl wearing mother. She stands tall in light wash skinny jeans and a snug white, vee neck t-shirt that showcase Jessica Rabbit curves on a fairly young girl. She has a black and red plaid flannel shirt tied around her hips.

Her hair is dyed black by the show of light roots at her scalp. And it's flat with no shine, I think uncharitably. I have always wondered why someone would choose this color, but who knows. Kasey has a matte, red lipstick smeared across her full lips. Silver piercings twinkle from both her right nostril and her tongue which she flicks as she winks at Wes. *Uh-oh. Danger, danger, Will Robinson! Jailbait dead ahead!*

By the furrowed brow on his face, I see that Wes notices it too. It's weird. Mrs. Ascher is sitting there with a blank look on her face like she doesn't see it. I still the shudder that's creeping up my spine.

"So, I hear you wanted to see me, Agent..." she breathes. BREATHES!!! All Marilyn Monroe like. Wes looks... concerned... Frightened. I decide to toss him a bone, though I'm not sure why.

"Actually, I did," I say, redirecting their attention to me. "I am the lead detective in this case."

"But he's FBI..." she pouts.

"I don't give two craps if he's the Pope, this is still my case," I say firmly. "Now, please have a seat. I have a few questions for you."

"Fine," she snaps as she lifts her chin and folds her arms over her chest.

I see the wicked sparkle in her eye but Wes does not. *Uh-oh.* She then moves and sits right next to him on the tiny little sofa. I almost want to laugh at how uncomfortable he looks, but he deserves this awkwardness for his behavior at the neighbor's house. A maniacal glee takes over me.

"I'm Detective Claire Goodnite, as I said before, I'm the lead investigator on your brother's disappearance," I tell her. "What can you tell me about the day he went missing?"

"We came home from school like always . . . and then you know . . . he wasn't there," she says and I sit there for a minute thinking, that's it? That's all she has to say about her baby brother's disappearance?

"It's really awful!" she screams suddenly and hurls herself at Wes, sobbing into his chest.

He pats her on the back once, twice, before dislodging the hormonal teen back to her side of the sofa. Mrs. Ascher just sits there like this is all totally normal, dabbing a hanky under her eyes. I, on the other hand, think that this is really fucking weird.

"Did anyone come over that day?" I ask.

"No," she sniffles as she rubs herself all over Wes. He's blatantly trying to remove her, but all of a sudden she's like an octopus of teenage girl proportions.

"So, no one rang the bell?"

"No."

"Did you see any suspicious vehicles in the neighborhood?" I ask.

She sighs, "I mean I guess. There was a weird white van for a while, but it left."

"Did it leave before or after you noticed your brother missing?"

"I don't know, maybe after," she barks. "Wait a minute, are you trying to pin this on me?"

"We're not doing anything," I say. "I'm just trying to piece together what happened that day so that I can find your brother."

"Maybe he just doesn't want to be found," she says cryptically.

"He's six years old," Mrs. Ascher says. "Don't be silly, he loves it here, why would he leave?" Kasey doesn't answer. I continue to question her.

"And you didn't have any friends come over?" I ask watching both Mrs. Ascher and Kasey for their reactions.

"No," she bites out as her spine stiffens. "Why are you being so mean to me?" she wails as she throws her arms around Wes's neck and throws her face into the crook between his neck and shoulder and nuzzles.

"We're not being mean," Wes wades in while peeling her off of his person.

For a minute I was thinking she was going to straddle his lap in front of her mother and me. And speaking of Mrs. Ascher, she just sits there looking extremely bored. Wes stands up and walks around behind the club chair that I'm sitting in. He places his hand on my shoulder in an effort to make it look like we're *together* together, and that he's not in the market for committing a misdemeanor. Now I understand his use of the royal we. I look up at him and smile sweetly, his eyes narrow, knowing that what I really mean is retribution.

"We're trying to explain to you both really, how important the first forty-eight hours of a disappearance are, and they've already come and gone," he admonishes.

"What we're trying to say," I wade in, "is the time to stop playing games is now. So, sit back and answer the questions."

"Fine." This kid is a brat. I hate to think badly of people, but I want out of this house.

"Alright then," I say as I uncross and recross my legs. It does not go unnoticed that Wes follows the movement. Kasey does not look impressed by my actions. Apparently, I've inadvertently issued a challenge. "Did you have a boyfriend over?"

"Which one?" she smiles coyly, looking up at Wes through her lashes. "I have many." This appears to have finally pushed her mother to some kind of action. Anger flashes through her eyes.

"Do you really have to be so crude, Kasey?"

"Don't be jealous," she coos to her mother. Mrs. Ascher clenches and unclenches her fists at her sides.

"I would never be jealous of a child."

"I wouldn't be so sure about that," Kasey says as she buffs her black painted fingernails on her torn t-shirt, a malicious smile twisting her lips.

"Did you see any suspicious people in the area that day?" Wes asks.

"Yes," she purrs. "I saw a very sketchy looking man."

"What did he look like?" I get excited.

"Well," she smiles seductively as she taps the tip of her index finger against her painted red lips. "He was very tall, with big, sexy muscles, and dark eyes. He had lush dark hair I just wanted to pull when he kissed me. He looked like a very, very bad man . . . I bet you're a very bad man, aren't you Agent?"

Well, that's the ballgame, folks. I stand up and pull Wes along with me. "Call me when you're ready to help us find your son, Mrs. Ascher."

They both follow us to the door. Mrs. Ascher pulls it open for us, but says nothing. Kasey on the other hand has sided up to Wes who is looking particularly uncomfortable. She runs a fingernail down his chest before speaking.

"Call me when you're ready to ditch the old chick," she purrs. "I promise you, I'm better." And then she kisses him square on the mouth.

"I seriously doubt that," I say to myself.

Wes and I walk down the block before climbing back into my waiting SUV. He climbs into the passenger seat, not even arguing with me about who's driving. Which is good because I'd hate to have to fill out the paperwork because I shot him.

"So, I take it you're mad . . ." he hedges.

"Do not talk," I growl before putting the car in drive and peeling out.

I drive around the neighborhood for awhile, taking turns down side streets here and there, but staying close to the street that the Ascher's live on. I take another turn and then back. I feel the hairs on the back of my neck tingle.

"Are you going to talk to me?" He sighs.

"No."

"Are you going to at least tell me where we're going?" he asks.

"No," I say taking another turn. "Actually yes. Could you at least try to be less appealing?" I snap.

"What?" The bastard laughs.

"You know as well as I do, flirting with the neighbor in front of me was fucked up and unprofessional," I growl. "But the daughter, that was messed up."

"Did you not see me pleading for help the whole time we were in that Goddamned house?" he shouts. "I couldn't get away from Lolita fast enough. I have never been more uncomfortable and you just sat there."

"You're being ridiculous!"

"Really?" he questions. "Did you ever think I flirted with the neighbor because I want something from you? Anything really. Just give me something!" he thunders, but I've found what I'm looking for. A strip mall with a Subway, an electronics repair shop, a Starbucks, and other businesses comes into view.

"Bingo," I thump the steering wheel as I turn into the parking lot.

I pull my keys from the ignition and jump down from my truck. I head into the Starbucks first because coffee. Enough said. Wes is storming in behind me. I walk up to the counter and order the sweetest most disgusting coffee on their menu and a cookie.

"Add a large coffee," Wes says from behind me.

"Did you just crawl out from under a rock? They don't do larges here," I snap. The jerk just shrugs.

"I just want a coffee. Are you sharing your cookie?" he asks.

"No," I snap but he just laughs as he peels a couple of bills out of his wallet and hands them over to the barista that is sufficiently stunned by his smile. Stupid gorgeous life ruining bastard. He scoops up the bag with my cookie in it and his coffee then heads over to a table while I wait for my coffee and make small talk.

"Is your manager here?" I ask, snapping the star stuck barista out of her fog.

"Umm, yeah," she hedges. "Am I in trouble?"

"No, I need to ask her some questions about another matter altogether. You're fine," I add for good measure.

"I'm good," she sighs, eyeing my badge and gun on my hip. "I was worried. I swear, I didn't know there was pot in those brownies."

I sigh.

She keeps rambling on and on to me about her drug use.

"Look, you seem like a nice kid, but I'm going to have to ask you to stop talking right now before you accidentally confess to a serious crime. I'm searching for a missing person, so I'm a little busy to be busting you for recreational marijuana use, okay?"

"Okay," she takes a huge breath. "That's my boss over there." She points to the man walking from the back hallway.

"Great!" I smile brightly and make my over to the slightly chubby, middle-aged man with the florid face and pants situation happening.

"Oh shit," I hear Wes mumble as he jumps up and follows me towards the manager.

"Hello," I say as I approach him, smiling fully. He has beady little eyes and I don't trust him. "I'm Detective Claire Goodnite with GWTPD and I'm investigating the possible kidnapping of a child," I say as I show him my badge.

"I didn't do it," he flusters.

"I didn't say that you did," I say sweetly. "But I was wondering if you had security cameras pointing away from the shop?"

"Yes," he whispers.

"Can I see them?"

He just nods before leading us back down the little hallway where he just came from. I take note of bathrooms, a break room, a storage closet, and lastly, the doorway to a tiny office just before the emergency exit out back.

He pushes open the door allowing Wes and I to follow him inside. He rounds an awful aluminum desk much like my own at the station and logs into an ancient computer before pulling up the security feed.

"You wouldn't have a flash drive, would you?" he asks, but I just smile and pull a purple flash drive from my pocket, handing it to him.

"Of course," he sighs. I swear I hear Wes snicker, but he keeps it tamped down.

"Thank you," I say as we take my flash drive and our coffees and head out the door.

"Where to now?" Wes asks as we pile into my SUV. "More of the same?"

"Of course," I look over at him as I sip my coffee.

I drive us over to the bridal shop and pull into the parking lot. I shudder as I step down from my truck and look at the offending building. It's like an invisible wall is built up between me and the building, not letting me pass. It's like I'm froze or I'm stepping in gum, or super glue. I can do this. I can do this.

I force myself to take a small step forward, and then another and another. I stop to take a deep breath, totally forgetting that Wes is there until he speaks his deep, sexy voice in my ear making me shiver.

"Not a big fan of weddings?"

"No," I choke out, shaking my head.

Wes runs his fingertips down the slope of the side of my neck and over my shoulder. "That's sad, I bet you'll make a beautiful bride."

"I'm not ever going to be a bride," I whisper.

"What would your mother say about that?" he asks. It's like he's got me hypnotized and I can't help but answer him. I'm stuck in his vortex until he releases me.

"She'd say I should find a nice man and settle down."

"Maybe you have found a nice man . . ." I snort because the idea of one of the guys I have hooked up within the last year being a nice man is funny. They might have been nice, just not when they were doing decidedly not nice things to my body.

"Probably not. Although, I don't usually stick around to find out." I sigh.

"That's over now," Wes growls, my spine goes straight.

"What?"

"I'm not talking about the little pricks you play around with, I'm talking about me, Claire."

"What?"

"You're done toying with them and you know it," his voice rumbles in my ear.

"I know no such thing," I snap coming unglued from the parking lot floor. "Let's go get their tapes."

"Sure, we can walk into that bridal shop, and we can go get those tapes, but you do it with the knowledge that I'm done fucking around. So, pick a date, a dress and some fucking flowers, I'll be there."

"Fuck off, Wes!" I shout as I pull out of his grip and stomp into the bridal shop to retrieve their security footage, if they'll give it to me. Something tells me that Wes is going to be the one to walk away from this one as the winner of the footage. And I don't know how to feel about it.

The bell over the door tinkles as we pass through. I'm still scowling, but Wes has a big ass fucking grin on his face looking at all the tulle, lace, bullshit and lies filling up this den of horrors.

"How can I help you?" A pretty young thing in an awful sweater twinset and loafers asks.

"My fiancé is not finding the dress of her dreams," he purrs. "And there is nothing too good for my pudykins."

"Awe, that is so sweet," she coos. I try to control my gagging. "Well, what are you looking for?"

"Big!" the bastard booms. "The poufier the better, and lots and lots of lace . . . and buttons!"

"I know just the thing!" she cries with excitement for all things bridal. I'm pretty sure she has an apartment full of cats, bridal magazines, and toe nail clippings.

She pulls me to a dressing room, pulling the curtain back and shoves me.

I'm ordered to strip down to my panties and she tosses me a fancy corset type bra. With one look I see she guessed my size exactly. I give her a questioning look and she just winks at me. Cat lady is good.

By the time I've wiggled into the crazy contraption that I must admit, makes my ass and boobs look amazing, she's back, breezing in with what has to be over two hundred pounds of tulle and lace and glitter.

She pulls back the curtain and says, "I think we'll try this one first. It's exactly what your fiancé described."

She quickly helps me into a white strapless ball gown that laces up the back and has a huge skirt of layers upon layers of rhinestone adorned tulle. I learned two things: No one in the bridal industry uses or appreciates the word rhinestone, and second, Cat Lady can lace up a dress to rival Scarlett O'Hara's hand maid.

"Let's just step outside and onto the block and take a look," she says. Since I'm basically here to do nothing while Wes does who knows what in the back with the manager, I decided to go along with it.

She pulls back the curtain and I step up onto the carpet covered block. As soon as I look into the mirror, I laugh. I look like the Abominable Snowman. Cat Lady makes a face and then busts up laughing too.

"Okay, maybe not this one."

She leads me back into the dressing room and has me out of the poufy monstrosity in seconds. She slides a plain white, no frills dress with a sweetheart neckline over my head. She does up the hidden zipper and the ties a wide pink ribbon belt with fake flowers around my waist.

Again, we step outside of the dressing room and when I look in the mirror, I don't laugh. I don't look silly, I look sweet and demure. Like a lady. Like a girly lady. I think that if things had gone differently, I could have been the girl who would wear this dress and walk down the aisle to guy like Wes, but I'm not. That girl is dead. And Wes had a hand in erasing her from the universe.

"I'm sorry, I didn't mean to make you sad," she says softly. "Let's try one more."

"Okay," I say.

She leads me back and pulls off the beautiful pink and cream dress and pulls an ivory satin dress with cap sleeves and a V-neck. This dress is different. It has a delicate lace overlay with bits of gold beads woven in. The skirt is not full at all, in fact it skims my waist and hips and thighs like it was made for me. The back has soft satin covered buttons that go from the back of my shoulders to the underside of my ass where the skirt is gathered and opens up into a tasteful train.

She walks me outside, and for the first time, I wish it were real. This is a dress I could wear and feel beautiful, but still feel like . . . *me*. She holds my hands as I step up onto the box again.

"Forgive me," she says and I don't know what she means until she laughs, "Okay, just don't shoot me," she says as she pulls the rubber band from my messy bun letting my jet-black curls fall almost artfully around my shoulders and breasts. Then she sticks a comb in my hair at the crown of my head hold a long, sweeping train of the same ivory color.

We both stand there, for however long, looking at me. I'm stunned to see a beautiful woman. Someone who could be loved and cherished, not thrown away and so casually discarded. It's only until I hear a masculine throat clearing, that I realize, I could be loved and cherished, if I let him.

At least, if the look in Wes's eyes is anything to go by. He's stopped at the mouth of the manager's office. Whether he got the tapes or not, you couldn't tell by his expression. The only thing there is reverence, a sparking sexual tension, and maybe . . . love.

I shake away those thoughts. This man whom I once loved deeply, discarded me like old toilet paper without a backwards glance for me or my feelings. He flirted his way through witnesses this morning to get to me and kissed me silly outside my brother's office. There is nothing professional or even safe about the way Wesley O'Connell is handling me and the only thing I know for sure is it's time to put a stop to it.

I step down from the pedestal and am about to tell Cat Lady, whom I've grown rather fond of until this moment that the dress isn't what I'm looking for. Playtime is over, there is no room for make believe or could haves and would haves, but Wes beats me to it, "We'll take it."

chapter 8

just peachy

THE DRIVE BACK TO the station is relatively uneventful. I think we're both too busy mulling over what happened in the bridal shop. Wes wants things to change, and me, I just want him out of my life, right?

As I pull into the station I firm up my resolve to keep Wes at arm's length until he moves on to his next conquest. Which he will. He always does. But this time, I'm determined to keep the pieces of my heart intact long after he's gone. Wishful thinking? Maybe.

"Tell me you have something," Liam hollers from his office.

"It's uncanny, really," Wes says. "How does he do it?"

"I think he has surveillance cameras set up all over the station, my car, my apartment, and our parents' house. It's the only explanation that I'm willing to accept. Otherwise, he isn't human," I nod.

"Well," Liam says as he rounds the corner.

"We have hours and hours of storefront surveillance to go over looking for a white panel van that may or may not be there," I sigh.

"What else? Wes?"

"Wes is still recovering from man whoring his way through witness testimony," I say petulantly.

"I don't need to recover."

"Okay, I do."

"What's going to with you two?" Liam narrows his eyes on us speculatively.

"Nothing." we both say at the same time, maybe just a little too quickly.

I sigh when he won't let up on his death stare, "Something is off with the Ascher's."

"Like what?" he asks.

"Like the mom is in a fog and doesn't seem to care that her son is missing," Wes explains to Liam. I nod.

"And?"

"And the sixteen-year-old sister was seriously hot to trot for your old buddy, Wes, here," I laugh. "Seriously, it was uncomfortable."

"It was," he shudders. "I think I'm scarred for life." I just laugh.

"She's a cold-hearted woman," Liam commiserates.

"Don't I know it," he nods.

"Alright, Casanova, let's start watching security feeds. You take your boon, I'll take mine," I tell him before I head out of Liam's office and make tracks for the galley to grab a cup of coffee.

I settle down at my desk and set my coffee mug on top after taking a long hit of my favorite jet fuel. I insert the flash drive into the side of my geriatric computer and hope for the best.

The little black window pops up and I groan, it's nothing but static. Fuck. My. Life. Wes can't do better than me. That would suck big time.

"Yippee!" I clap when the screen flickers and then images start to tick by on the screen.

"You alright, over there?" Wes smirks.

"Just peachy. You look for the van on your side, I'll look for it on mine."

"And we meet in the middle?" Wes asks.

"Not ever."

I go back to watching the tape tick by and see not one panel van. I sip my coffee and peel my eyes open. I scan the scenes as they play out in black and white and hope for the stupid van to make an appearance.

At three hours I have to get up and stretch my legs. I hit pause on the tape and stand up. My brain was getting fuzzy and I still haven't seen a panel van. Wes did his walk about an hour ago.

"Want more coffee?" I ask. "I'm headed for a refill."

"Yes, please."

I pace the back-hall way for awhile and then make my way to the galley for more coffee. I fill up our cups and head back to my desk. Wes isn't anywhere to be found so I set his mug on his desk and walk around to my side.

I twist side to side until my back cracks, then I sit down at my desk and fire the video back up. I see mothers with babies in strollers, businessmen grabbing another cup of coffee, minivans, SUVs, sedans, no white panel van. I sigh to myself.

I look at the clock in the corner of my computer screen and realize that I haven't seen Wes in over an hour. I look around. His desk is empty. His computer is shut down and his keys aren't in the top drawer. That fucker left me.

I head down the hall to Liam's office because if Wes is still in the building, he's with Liam. There's a nervous pit in my stomach and I don't like it. I have a great gut. It's kept me from getting shot, only ever got me stabbed the once, and it's currently telling me that there is something about Wes and Liam together, that can't be trusted.

The walk down the hall to the Captain's office is blaringly quiet. There's no one milling about in the hall which is weird on its own. When I get to Liam's office I see that the door is slightly ajar and I can hear voices inside. Voices of the two men in my life who keep telling me at every turn that they love me and want what's best for me. Those same men, it appears, also enjoy stabbing me in the back at every turn.

"Pull her off the case, Liam. Now," Wes barks.

"I'm not sure I have enough reasoning to."

"I found the van myself, she was off getting coffee, that's plenty of reason to pull her and you know it."

"You know that it's not. I'm also legally required to offer all of my officers a bathroom break and the option to eat."

"Ok, how about that I got this security tape all by myself while she was dicking around trying on fucking wedding dresses," he says as he throws me under the bus. Beep, *mother fucking beep*, here comes Wes the dirty dealer.

My gasp draws their attention to me standing in the doorway to Liam's office, obviously eavesdropping. Liam bites out a *"Goddamn it,"* but otherwise they glare at me like it's my fault that their conspiring to ruin my career.

"This is a private meeting," Wes growls.

"Oh, I got that," I say to Wes, feeling the tears burn in my eyes. I won't give them the satisfaction of seeing them fall. They don't get that from me. Plus, it would probably be the final nail in my law enforcement career coffin. Obviously, the girls are too emotional to be cops bullshit.

"You don't belong here, Claire," he says softly, reaching out to me, but I jerk away.

"You don't get to decide that. I know where you stand now. I'll do my end, you do yours. Stay the fuck away from me."

"Claire," Liam pleads. "I don't want you doing this."

"Oh, I got that," I snap. "But listen to me, that is not what happened today. You and Wes both know it. Apparently tanking my career is more important to you than finding a little boy. This is your final warning. If I find you two colluding to sabotage my career and reputation again, I'm going to IA."

"You wouldn't!" Liam yells. "You know how hard I've worked for this."

"And you know how hard I worked for this, but apparently it doesn't matter. I know that Wes is a cheating, double crossing prick, but you, you're my brother, or at least I thought you were. Right now? I'm not so sure. Have fun looking for your van, I'm off the clock."

I walk straight out of Liam's office and don't look back. I don't care. This time, no one follows me. I guess I know how they both really feel. I don't care about that either. I walk right through the station and can feel the stares of fellow officers but I don't make eye contact, not out of shame, but pride. They all heard, they had to but I won't let any of them see how much Wes and Liam hurt me. So, I keep my head held high. I am not the one in the wrong here.

I beep the locks on my Tahoe and jump in. I lock my badge and sidearm into the special safe in my glove box. I sniffle, I feel it coming. I cover my eyes with my hands as a sob tears free from my chest. I feel so betrayed. I lean forward, with my eyes still covered and lean my forehead on the steering wheel.

I sit there and cry. For how long I don't know, but until I feel eyes on me. I look up and lock eyes on Wes. The smug, angry look on his face is replaced with one of anguish. Liam is with him. I let them see. Let them look at what they did to me. This is on them, not me.

Wes makes a move to step forward and I quickly dash away the tears from my cheeks and start the engine. I buckle my belt and look over my shoulder as I back out of my space.

The drive home is boring as usual, except for all of the thoughts pinging around in my brain like rogue bullets. My phone has been ringing constantly with calls from both Wes and Liam, but I don't answer. I'm off the clock, if something changes, dispatch will call me, not those two assholes.

I climb the steps to my apartment and unlock the door. It's the same disarray that I left it in this morning. I lock up my sidearm and badge over the fridge and the strip off my clothes on the way into my little bathroom where I take as hot a shower as I can stand.

By the time I get out I feel moderately better, but also restless. I need to take the edge off. I decide to do what I'd usually do. Wes doesn't spare my feelings so why should I spare his.

I toss my long hair up into a messy bun and pin it in place. I throw on a silky gray tank top with lace trim, jeans and my tall boots. The look does great things for my boobs. Nice. Then I pad back into my bathroom and slap a little man-eating makeup on my face. Mascara, a rosy blush, and a deep raspberry lipstick. It's the kind that's meant to stay on forever and doesn't come off on a cheek or a wine glass. It's the very color a man can't stop thinking about wrapped around his dick. And it doesn't smear. Double win.

I toss a dark peacoat over my shoulders and pocket my money and cellphone. I see that I've missed a bunch more calls from the guilty group but shrug it off. I unlock my sidearm and badge. Then check the magazine before pocketing them both.

I lock the door behind me and head down the stairs to my truck. I beep the locks and hop in, locking up my badge and gun. I don't need them on me at all times when I'm off duty, but I do need them near just in case. But I have found that it's a bit of a dick wilter to have a man stripping me down, only to stop in his tracks when he sees that my gun is bigger than his.

I fire up my truck and head towards my favorite bar. It's two towns over and a bit of a drive, but it keeps me from shitting in my own front yard. It's a bummer when your hookup turns out to be a detective from a neighboring station. That's totally not awkward when your paths cross professionally or anything. But I wouldn't know, as that's totally never happened to me.

When I pull into the parking lot, the dim lights are spilling out into the lot, as is the loud music. This is just what I need tonight. I feel my shoulders physically lower as I slowly relax and gain back some of my control. What I do not feel, is the presence behind me that's followed me here all the way from my apartment in George Washington Township. No, I don't notice it at all, I just lock my doors and pocket my keys, walking into my favorite bar and heading straight for disaster.

chapter 9
major mistake

"THE USUAL?" JOE, MY favorite bartender asks as I walk in.

"Yeah," I smile and take a seat at the end of the bar where I can watch the people who move around the establishment and pick my next victim.

Joe slides the seven and seven on a cocktail napkin in front of me. I smile my thanks as I pick up my drink to take a sip. I swivel around on my barstool and watch the crowd absentmindedly. There's a couple of cute guys, but nobody peaks my interest.

I feel someone sit down next to me and I look up. He's about five eleven or six foot with a mop a sandy blonde hair and brown eyes. He has an easy smile and he immediately turns it my way. I look back at Joe who winks and shakes his head. He knows my drill.

He looks at me and smiles, "I'll have what she's having," he says to Joe and I think he might do. But I'm just not that into it. I'll see how it goes.

Joe slides the drink in front of him and he happily sips it while waiting for me to say something. I finally decide to help him out.

"Well, what do you think?" I ask.

"I think it's not bad. Is it your signature drink?"

"I don't have a signature . . ." But I'm stopped by Joe.

"She does and it is."

"I'm Mark," he smiles at me and holds out his hand for me to shake. As I take his hand in mine and notice a firm grip on a smooth hand with no calluses and clean trimmed fingernails. The callous on my index finger grazes his knuckles and he bites his lip.

"I'm Claire," I say smiling.

"So, Claire, do you live around here?" he asks. "Wow, was that as bad as it sounded?" I laugh.

I feel eyes on me and I start to scan the room. I come up short when I see Wes scowling from a table in the corner. A waitress with a trim waist and balloons for boobs grazes his elbow with her rock-hard nipples as she delivers his drink, a cold beer in the bottle, but his gaze stays locked on me. I roll my eyes and turn back to Mark.

"No, it wasn't that bad," I lie.

"So, what do you do Claire?" Mark asks.

Joe groans.

I bite my lip and shake my head no. I'm not going to tell him. It will end all the fun. There's no way Mr. Businessman or Mr. Lawyer wants to go home with a police detective. I look over at his polo shirt and jeans and think he's cute in a very country club sort of way.

"Oh, you want me to guess do you?"

I smile wider because he'll never guess while nodding my head. I sip my drink and wait for him to guess. This could be fun. And I need fun. The missing boy, Anthony, and Wes and our fucked up past have my emotions too close to the surface.

"A dental hygienist."

"Ew, gross. I would never stick my hands in people's mouths." I laugh. Although I have stuck them in a dead body. I'm not sure what that says about me.

"A librarian."

"Do I look like a librarian to you?" I laugh.

"Only in my dreams," he laughs. "That was cheesy too, right?"

"Yeah, kind of. What about you? What do you do?" I ask. I feel eyes on me again and I look over my shoulder. The waitress with the flotation devices and huge hair is sitting in his lap, with his ear caught between her teeth. Her crooked teeth, I notice uncharitably. I'll drop an extra twenty in the offerings tray on Sunday and ask for forgiveness. It was worth it.

"You know that guy?" Mark asks.

I look back at him and see him looking at Wes and the hooker. "No," I say as I look at him. He's handsome and nice. I should choose a guy like him. I toss the remainder of my drink back and ask, "You want to get out of here?"

"Hell, yes."

"Your place, I'll follow you out," I tell him as I stand. Mark throws some money on the bar top for Joe and I see him tip his imaginary hat at me behind Mark's back as thanks for the huge tip. Or maybe it's my ability to leave with a guy in less than an hour. I mentally shrug, who knows.

As I found out following his nondescript sedan home, Mark lives around the corner from my local bar. That's going to be awkward later. I pull into the visitor spot closest to where he parked his car. He waits for me by the door like a gentleman and then leads me up the stairs to his second-floor apartment.

Mark holds the door open for me but as soon as it closes behind me I grab him by the shirt and pull him against my body, breast to chest, and kiss him deeply. Not bad. Not great, but not bad. Mr. Country Club is not an aggressive lover.

He breaks away from my body to push my jacket over my shoulders. I pull his polo over his head and toss it to the ground. Mark sees to it that my t-shirt and bra go the same way. He smiles his coy smile at me again before taking my hand and leading me to his bedroom where I make my second major mistake of the night.

chapter 10

rough

"COME SIT IN DADDY'S lap," the man coos. I don't want to, I know that I don't want to. He holds out his hand for me and I shake my head no. I don't want to sit in his lap. He's not my daddy. His face turns mean and I'm scared.

"If I have to come get you it'll hurt worse. I promise."

"I don't want to hurt at all," I whisper.

"That's not a choice for you to make, pet," he says through gritted teeth.

I turn on my heels and run, but I'm so small that I don't get far. He snatches me back by my arm and I scream out it hurts so bad. He drags me back to the dirty sofa where he sits back down and stands me in front of him. I don't look at him. I'm scared.

He pulls my pants and panties down my legs. I shake, I'm so scared but I can't stop. I know he'll be mad that I'm not holding still, but I can't stop. He tips me over his lap and I cry out.

"This hurts me more than it hurts you," he sighs.

I never get the chance to believe him as his hand hits me on my bottom again and again. He spanks me over and over. I'm sobbing. The words coming out of my mouth don't even make sense but he keeps hitting me harder and harder. The mean man who is not my daddy hits me twelve times, two for every year that I lived. Part of me hopes I don't live much longer. I don't like spankings.

Hot tears roll down my cheeks and I can't stop them even if I want to.

Then it's over. Except it's not. I go to stand back up, but his hand pushes my shoulders down and he touches me. Mama always told me not to let anyone touch me there, but I don't have a choice. He won't give me a choice.

He won't stop no matter how much I cry or yell or try to get away. He just won't stop.

"See? Daddy knows what his kitten likes," he says before he finally stops hurting me.

He places me on my feet right in front of him. My clothing is long gone and I'm embarrassed to be standing there in nothing but my t-shirt. I try to pull the bottom of it down so the he can't see my private place but he slaps my hands away.

"Now you give to daddy," he says as he opens his pants.

He touches himself and he slides his hands up and down, up and down. He squeezes it tight and I don't want to watch. I try and look away but he yells at me, tells me to watch.

"Look at me, Claire! Look at what you do to me, what you make me do."

I just stand there and stare, hoping for it to be over. I hurt in a bunch of places and I just want to go lie down. No, I want to go home, but he hurt me when I tried to run away. So, I have to just stand here.

I stand here and watch as his hand that does mean things holds himself tightly. I watch as he looks at me as he slides in and out of his fist. He's making funny noises now. I want to cover my ears because I hear my name in there every so often and I don't like it. I know that he would be mad if I blocked out his sounds so in my head I'm practicing my math facts.

I'm doing everything that I can to not make this last any longer than it has to. He's getting faster now. Up and Down, up and down. His sounds are louder and louder. Will someone hear him? Will they come to rescue me? Somehow, I don't think so and that thought makes me sad. He moves his hand faster and faster. Then he shouts my name as he sprays my favorite t-shirt with something yucky.

He smiles at me, happy with himself. But soon that smile turns mean again. He zips up his pants and grabs me by the arm, shoving me back towards the closet he keeps me in. He shoves me inside and I fall to the floor.

I look up at him, but his face changes from the mean man to Wes's beautiful face when he says, "You were a very bad girl today, Claire. I'm so disappointed in you."

• • •

I wake with a start. Well, that's a new twist to the dream. That's the worst part, that I dream. Lately, it's every fucking night. It would have been a mercy if God took all of my memory, but no, I got to keep just enough snippets to slowly drive me crazy. The psychologists all said that it was a sign of my strong mental strength. That it was a sign that my mind was protecting itself. It was a sign of something. But that's not what woke me up either.

A shrill ring woke me up from a restless sleep. And I had had the dream again. My phone bounces around on the unfamiliar night stand that I must have left it on last night. I wipe the errant tears leftover from my dream from my face with the palm of my hand and answer my phone.

"Goodnite," I rasp, my voice heavy with sleep.

"Detective, this is dispatch," the disembodied voice from my phone informs me. *"We were told to notify you that the body of a male child has been recovered at the rocks near the bottom of the falls. Possible match for your missing person."*

"I'm on my way."

That's all I need to know, and I am throwing the blankets back that are tangled around my body—my naked body. I pull my jeans on without panties and then my boots. I quietly search for my bra, hopefully not waking . . . NOT waking . . . I look over at the bed where a man with warm blond hair and a stubbled jaw sleeps on the bed that I just vacated. Nope, not ringing any bells. At least he's good looking.

I should be embarrassed. Letting some random pick me up at a bar in the next town over. But I'm not. This case has been . . . *rough* . . . and I needed to blow off some steam. *Will I call him again?* Uhh, no. *Will he call me?* He'd have to find me first. *Did he have a good time?* You betcha.

I see my bra hanging from a lamp shade and grab it, tucking it into my back pocket. I pull my tank top on and then my t-shirt, having found both rumpled on the floor. I reach into the front pocket of my jeans and find a—*thank God*—a hair tie and toss my long hair on top of my head in a messy bun. I pull on my coat that was dropped by the front door.

I palm my phone and pull my keys out of the same pocket the hair tie came out of. I step out into the New Jersey cold without ever looking back at . . . *Mike?* No, that's not it. I shrug to myself, oh, well.

I unlock my car and climb in. I unlock the glove box and I pull out my badge and sidearm, placing both on the dash. I fire up my nondescript Tahoe and head towards tragedy.

chapter 11
it burns

THE GRAVEL CRUNCHES UNDER my boots as I hike down to the bottom of the falls. The crisp breeze cuts through my coat and clothes making me wish I had a warm hat and gloves on. But this isn't about me.

As I approach the cluster of officers I can already tell that it's bad; whatever it is that dragged me out of bed this early in the morning. Jones looks up and drops his chin to his chest once, silently telling me what I already knew.

I pull the picture the Ascher's gave me of Anthony Donovan out of the inside breast pocket of my coat and look down at the tiny bundle under the yellow tarp. One of the other uniformed officers pulls back the sheet so I can see the boy's face. It's bloated from being in the river for so long, but even through all the distortion from the elements, I can tell that this is our boy.

My heart sinks. I know in my head, that not all kidnapping victims end up back at home, warm and safe. I know that the chances of survival are slim. But I always hope. Later tonight, I'll feel the guilt associated with being one of the rare survivors. A kid who managed to escape. And I moved on to the best of my ability. But tonight, when I'm home by myself, with bad take out and whiskey to keep me company, I'll wish it was Anthony who was able to escape and not me.

"What do you have for me?" I ask as I roll back my shoulders.

"The body of a juvenile male was seen by teenagers partying on the footpath to the falls. They called their parents who showed up and then called it in at 0114 hours," Jones reads from his notes. "The teens were released into the care of their parents, but I have a list of names of those who were present and contact info for their parents."

"What else?"

"Juvenile male, appears to be between the ages of four and eight years old, and approximately forty to forty-two inches tall. Will know more following positive identification."

"Characteristics appear to match description provided by the victim's mother and stepfather. They also appear to match the picture provided by the mother. Will know more pending positive fingerprint and dental identification," I respond tucking the photo back into my coat pocket.

I pull out a pair of latex gloves and snap them on my hands. All around me officers are combing the area looking for clues as to what happened to this little boy. I crouch down next to him. His clothes are water logged. I pull his pockets out, there's nothing in them.

I don't see any obvious signs of cause of death and trust me, I'm looking. I look up at the footbridge, it is possible that he fell, but what was he doing here. If this is Anthony, and I'm pretty damn sure that it is, how the hell did he get to the falls. This part of town is nowhere near where he lives—where either of his parents live.

I look back down at the little boy, "What happened to you, Anthony? Tell me your secrets," I say hoping to find some clue as to what happened. Anything really.

Out of my peripheral, I notice movement, but there's always a lot of movement at an active crime scene so I quickly dismiss it. It's not until a pair of wingtips step into my view that I groan. Damn it.

"Get out of my crime scene, suit," I snap barely offering him a glance. Damn he looks good. Fucking the slutty cocktail waitress clearly agrees with him.

"If I was a lesser man, I'd have my feelings hurt that you didn't invite me to the party," he chuckles. I'm not laughing. He cuts his humor short when he sees the look on my face.

"I didn't want to bother you and the big boobed waitress."

"Tut tut tut, jealousy doesn't become you." He smiles.

"I am not jealous, I'm working," I growl.

"This site is out of your jurisdiction," he says softly. "It's time to hand it over, Claire."

"The hell it is," I snap, standing up and ripping off my gloves.

I stomp all the way over to Wes and shove him hard. He backs up a step and then I shove him again. I'm angry—not just angry—livid. Red colors everything I see. How dare he come here in the eleventh hour and try to steal my case. Again.

"This case started in my jurisdiction so it is mine," I growl as I push him again.

"Stop," he commands as he grabs my wrists in his, turning me as he pulls me into the warmth of his body. "This is crazy."

"No, what's crazy is you telling me time and time again that I should trust you and here you are, again, trying to steal my case. *My case, Wes.*"

"You know you shouldn't be on this case, Claire," he whispers into my ear as he holds me tight to him, my back to his front. To anyone else, it would look like he's comforting me, but we both know there's no comfort here, only restraint and deceit.

"Let me go," I plead.

"Your emotions are too close to the surface, Claire. You're heading for a crash and we can all see it."

"I don't see it. I only see you taking one more thing from me, Wes. Tell me, when will you have had enough?"

He rears back as if I have slapped him. And then the shutters slam down behind his eyes. Gone is the boy who went off to the Navy that I once knew and loved. Here is the SAIC hell bent on ruining my career and my life.

"Okay," he sighs running his hand over his face. For a split second he looks tired. "I thought you'd be reasonable . . ."

"Ha!" I interrupt.

"But if you can't then I will arrest you for interfering in my investigation."

"You wouldn't dare," I growl.

"Try me," he snaps standing nose to nose with me.

We're both breathing hard. Huffing and puffing like the big bad wolves we are. Either one of us could come out on top but I won't give Wes the satisfaction of arresting me in front of my officers. With one false move I could not only lose my case to this asshole, but hand him the ammunition he and Liam need to end my career once and for all.

I see the ME loading up the body into their van. Emma winks at me. We women have to stick together in this sausage fest of a profession. I have always wondered if she and Liam had a thing but that's neither here nor there right now.

Emma is silently telling me she'll hold the evidence for me to see first. That will go a long way toward my keeping the case where it belongs—with me. I take a deep breath and a big step back. I roll my shoulders back and throw down the gauntlet.

"Well, I guess we'll just see about that." I smile sweetly.

"I guess we will," he smiles back.

"No one touch a damned thing until you hear from me, do you understand me? Not one damned thing!" I shout before I head to my SUV and jump in.

The drive back to the station is not a fun one. I spend the entire time working up a plan to protect myself and keep my hold on the case, and my job. Both are not looking so good. Worst of all, I know that Wes is somewhere behind me actively tearing apart my life.

I pull into the parking lot and head inside. I take a deep breath, I'm not going to go off halfcocked and act like an asshole. I will not give Liam any ammunition. I will not lose my job. I say those things over and over again in my head like a mantra as I walk down the hallway and knock on Liam's door.

"Enter," he hollers.

I push his office door open and cautiously walk inside. "Can I talk to you for a minute?"

He sighs, "What is it now, Claire?"

"I need you to call off your dogs, Captain," I say as I take a seat in the chair facing his desk.

"I don't have time for your stupid fight with Wes, Claire," he grumbles. "Maybe you guys should just fuck it out and be done with it."

"That's not what I'm talking about. Your special friend threatened to arrest me at a crime scene this morning."

"I can't imagine what you did to warrant the FBI's interest," he says blandly.

"What makes you think it was something I did?" I can't believe he would side with Wes over me. Actually I can. Bastards. "I didn't do anything wrong. I was working my crime scene and Wes showed up late and tried to pull rank."

"He does out rank you," Liam adds.

"That has nothing to do with it!"

"It could. What case was he trying to take over?"

I sit silently with my hands folded in my lap while I wait for Liam to catch up. I see his eyes widen slightly with a sparkle to them that I do not like one bit as the lightbulb goes off over his head.

"You don't say?" he mumbles.

"Don't even think it, Liam," I bark.

"You know that I'm right," Wes says quietly from behind me. I close my eyes. I feel the weight of defeat on my shoulders, but I'm stubborn enough not to give up until I'm dead. You know what they say about pride and the fall . . .

"It's still my case. I'm getting closer."

"You're no closer than you were two days ago. The only difference is now the boy is dead," Wes says. I feel the guilt already. It's thick and suffocating.

"He's dead?" Liam asks.

I just nod.

"Turn it over to me," Wes pleads.

"No," I whisper.

"You're too close to it, you know that."

"No."

"When were you going to tell me that the Donovan boy is dead?" Liam thunders.

"When we had a positive ID," I answer. "He's with Emma now."

"It's time to pull in the FBI, Claire, officially," Liam says calmly.

"Over my dead body!"

"It might be if you don't give on something," he shouts back. "Look at you. Are you eating? Sleeping? Because you don't look like it."

"Gee thanks, asshole."

"The dreams are back, aren't they?" Wes asks, outing me at the same time.

"What dreams?" Liam asks.

I just stay silent.

"Claire . . ." Wes calls softly. Quietly ordering me to lay all my secrets out into the light.

"No."

"No, they're not back or no?" he betrays.

"What dreams?" Liam thunders.

"She has nightmares about her abduction," he says softly to Liam. "She always has."

"I didn't know," Liam pains. "Why didn't you tell me?"

"It wasn't my story to tell."

"Bullshit!" My brother roars. "Claire?"

I don't answer, I just sit there staring at the wall just over my brother's shoulder, unable to look at him or Wes as my world unravels. My vision swims and I feel the hot tear as it burns down my cheek.

"Claire! Answer me!"

"No!" I scream as the thin thread of my control snaps. "You don't get to know all the little bits of my life so that you can use them against me."

"Is that what you think?" He looks stricken.

"Can you honestly tell me that you're not thinking about how you can use the information to pull me from the case?"

"What about a task force?" Liam changes tack.

"No," Wes and I both stay at the same time.

"She's off the case and the FBI is taking over," he demands.

"I'll work it alone if I have to."

"I'll ban you from the case if I have to," Wes threatens.

"Over my dead body," I snap.

"I'd prefer to be over your naked body."

"How can you say that?" I snap. "Like I would take the flotation device's sloppy seconds."

"Jealous much?"

"Not at all," I say sweetly. "One of these days that nasty dick is going to rot right off."

Wes just smiles. The fucker knows that he's gotten to me. I'm too tired, too emotional to not be jealous of the idiot that spent the night in his bed with him. How sick is that? And he ruined my favorite bar. I can never go back there after seeing that.

"You're too close to the case, Wes is right," Liam interjects.

"And Wes isn't?"

"It's not the same and you know it," he barks.

"How is it not? We were all there."

"You were taken for six days, baby," Wes says softly from behind me. "You're right, I live with that. It burns to know that I played a part in it, but I wasn't the one who had to escape hell," he says as he brushes hair back from my face.

"I did escape hell, so let me use that to do my job."

"It's going to take you down if you don't start taking care of yourself, Claire, and you know it." He's right. The job takes down too many who can't leave their cases at the station. Whether it's stress and bad diet or the bottle and a bullet, we don't have longevity on our sides.

"I won't give up my jurisdiction for a dick."

"But it used to be your favorite dick," Wes circles back to his favorite topic.

"It was never my favorite dick, it's short and crooked," I lie.

Wes just laughs. "Liar," he winks.

"Well, what I do in the back of vans these days has nothing to do with you or your dick," I shout. There goes my temper again.

"That's not fucking funny, Claire." Liam jumps to his feet.

I shrug. "And you two threatening my job at every corner is?"

"That's not what we're doing."

"Isn't it though? If you loved me, you'd let me do my job," I implore.

"Liam don't cave to her," Wes barks.

"You don't get to control me either, Wes."

"The hell I don't. I'll take you over my knee if I have to once and for all," he barks.

"You don't have it in you. You don't have the balls."

Wes pulls his handcuffs from his back pocket and swings them around his index finger, smiling away like a loon all the while. Liam just laughs.

"I gotta go," I shout as I race out the door.

I barely make it out the door when Wes nabs me around the waist and pins me against the wall in the hallway. He brushes the loose strands of my hair out of my face with the tips of his fingers.

"So beautiful," he says absent mindedly. "That's all I could think of the morning after we slept together. That you were so beautiful and your life was almost over before you got a chance to live it."

"Wes . . ."

"I made love to you and then you screamed in your sleep about that man touching you. Years after he took you, he was still taking from you, from me, from us. *I couldn't stand it.*"

"Wes . . . stop." I shake my head, I can't hear anymore.

"So, I pushed you away," he whispers, his lips hovering just over mine. "I can't stay away."

"So . . . don't," I whisper just before his mouth crashes down on mine.

Wes kisses me like his life depends on it. His hands crushing my body into him. I open my mouth under him and he plunders. Gone is the gentle young man who made love to me twelve years ago and in his place is a man tired of waiting.

I dig my fingers into his shoulders and kiss him back with all that I am. I rake my nails down his back hard enough to leave marks through his clothes. He groans into my mouth. And pulls back.

Wes tips his forehead to mine. We're both breathing heavy. I squeeze my eyes tight. Again, he brushes my hair back from my face before trailing his hand down the side of my face and running the pad of his thumb over my swollen bottom lip.

"Claire," he calls softly. "Don't make me lose you again."

"That would imply that you already have me," I whisper back.

"Don't I though?"

"No, I'm not anyone's to have," I say softly. "That girl died a long time ago when she had her heart broken by the only boy she ever loved."

I can't let the hurt look on Wes's face stop me. History shows he won't stick around. I need to make sure my job is protected for when he leaves. And really, everything I said to him is true. We all have to live with the mistakes we make. He's paying for his now.

"Claire, don't do this," he pleads.

"I have a murder to solve," I say as I duck under his arms and walk away.

I hear a fist hit the wall and his deep voice cry out my name, but I just keep walking. I'm already gone and like I said, I have a murder to solve.

chapter 12
nightmare

I WALK INTO THE station earlier than usual the next morning. Last night I left the station and Liam and Wes behind, or so I thought. I went home and when I walked through my front door, the first things I did were lock up both my sidearm and my drop gun in the safe. Then hid the key from myself. The last thing I need is to do something I couldn't take back—in the permanent sense—when the demons creep in. Just like I knew they would.

I kicked off my boots and dragged myself into the kitchen where I climbed on top of a kitchen chair to acquire my emergency bottle of whiskey. And it was an emergency. I poured myself two fingers and shot it back, cringing at the delicious heat that burns its way down my throat and through my chest.

I added ice to my glass and poured myself two more fingers. And then I ordered more fried rice from my favorite place around the corner. Bobby is the kid who delivers for them and he knows the drill on nights like this: bring the food, take the money, and leave ask no questions. He follows directions to a tee.

After Bobby leaves, I placed my bounty of little foldy take out containers on the old battered coffee table. My mom is dying to pick out new furniture for this place, but honestly, why bother, I'm barely ever here. I strip out of my jeans leaving me in my t-shirt and panties. I still don't know where my bra is and I don't care.

I carry the bottle with me back to the living room where I turned on the tv. That was a mistake. Not my first mistake of the evening and definitely *not* my last. I sit down on the couch and watch the news.

"And the top story tonight, what is believed to be the body of a missing local child was found at the falls late last night by a group of high school students celebrating last night's win against Ben Franklin High School . . .

"This is believed to be the body of six-year-old Anthony Donovan who disappeared from his George Washington Township home three days ago. It is our understanding that no ransom was ever recovered."

"That's correct, June. And here comes the late statement from the local police precinct and the FBI . . ."

"Good evening everyone, my name is Captain Liam Goodnite with the George Washington Township Police Department. I'm here with Special Agent in Charge Wesley O'Connell of the FBI and we will be answering your questions to the best of our abilities without compromising an ongoing investigation."

I set down my Chinese and pick up the bottle of whiskey. Maybe I shouldn't have hid the key to my gun after all . . .

"Is it true that the body of Anthony Donovan was found late last night?"

"We cannot confirm or deny that the body found belongs to Anthony Donovan as it is currently pending identification," Liam says clearly.

"When will you know for sure?"

"We hope to have a clear identification or rule out that it is Anthony via fingerprints and dental records as early as tomorrow afternoon."

"Is it true that your sister, Claire Goodnite, is the lead detective on the case, Captain?"

"I will not confirm the activity of any of my detectives or officers, not now or ever, as it compromises the safety of the officer and the integrity of the investigation," Liam says. His eyes narrowing just slightly in his frustration.

Someone leaked the discovery of Anthony's body to the local news. I'd be more pissed, but he was found by a bunch of scared teens who were already up to some mischief last night. I'm sure someone sold the story for some quick cash. I can only hope is that it pays for college and not crack.

"Is it true that she is the same Claire Goodnite that famously escaped captivity by a deranged child molester and murderer?"

"We are not here to comment on ancient history, only the facts as they pertain to the discovery of a body at 12:42 this morning," Wes comments.

"So, it is the same Claire Goodnite! Would she be willing to do a follow up interview on her case? I would love to do a 'Where is she now?' story and tie it in with her investigation of the missing boy," a reporter in the crowd chirps enthusiastically.

"Ma'am, this is an open FBI investigation, there will be no interviews of any sort until the case is closed. Thank you for your time," he smiles a feral baring of his teeth before walking back into the station with Liam on his heels.

As much as I hate him right now, he's still handsome. I still want him even though I know that I shouldn't. Those assholes took my case away from me and publicly threw me to the wolves. It's all out there now. My past, my involvement with the case, all of it. And then they took it all away.

"We can confirm that Detective Claire Goodnite of the George Washington Township Police Department is in fact the daughter of retired Police Captain Callum Goodnite and sister to current Captain Liam Goodnite.

"As you remember, Claire was kidnapped on June 8, 1997. She was six years old at the time. Her family, with the help of the police and the FBI searched for six days before she was found dirty and malnourished in the woods mere miles from her family home.

"It is believed she was held by an unidentified man in a shack in the woods for the duration of that time. While the family and law enforcement have remained tight lipped for decades, it is believed that she suffered sexual and physical abuse at the hands of an unknown assailant who was never identified or subsequently tried for her kidnapping . . ."

I close my eyes tight. I can't hear any more so I switch off the tv. My dinner sits cold and untouched on the coffee table. I don't have the stomach for it now. Even my whiskey earned a certain ambivalence from me. Part of me wants to drink it all and let the darkness come for me, and the other half knows that I shouldn't.

There's a knock on the door while I sit debating whether or not to finish off my drink. I pick it up and knock it back with a shaky hand when I hear his voice call through the door, "Claire, let me in. Please . . ."

On unsteady legs, I stand and make my way to the door, the locks tumble and I pull open the door. Wes stands there with weary eyes and stubble overgrown on his cheeks. He looks hesitant . . . and then he reaches for me.

The culmination of the last few days, this case, the kidnapping, the ghosts of the past, it all comes rushing out as I pull Wes in the door and slam it closed. He's on me before I can say boo. His mouth greedily claiming mine and I lay my own claim to him right back.

Twelve years ago, Wes took everything I had to give and then walked away leaving me broken hearted. Now, I'm a big girl and I know exactly what I'm getting. And I'm going to give it just as good right back. For twelve years, every man after Wes left me aching and wanting, not completely fulfilled so I'm taking this one night for myself. Tomorrow, I'll go back to my life the way that it was . . . or at least I'll do my best picking up the pieces.

I rip at his shirt, the buttons popping everywhere as I nip and kiss and bite at his mouth. There's an aggression here that wasn't there twelve years ago. Wes slips his hand down the front of my panties and into my core. I let out a hiss as his fingers stretch me, the burn both beautiful and tortuous.

I tip my head back against the door and hold on to the open sides of his shirt as I ride his hand, taking everything he offers me and more. It feels so good and I'm so close. Just a little bit more, I'm almost there.

"Give it to me, Claire, it's mine and you know it," Wes growls in my ear as he adds his thumb to my clit. Swirling around and around. The delicious pressure is exactly what I need and I come on his hand with a keening cry I don't recognize as my own as I rock harder and faster against him. "Yes, take it!" he shouts as I cling to him as my heart races and my climax barrels through me.

I hear his belt buckle hit the floor and the rasp of his zipper and that is the only tell that Wes is about to give me his cock. My heart still blasting from my orgasm as his rips my panties down the center.

Wes grips my thigh in his strong hand and pushes it up against my side. The stretch and burn of my overtaxed muscles is welcome. And then he enters me in one full thrust.

Wes buries his face in my neck and groans as he begins to move. Harder and faster than I think either me or my front door can take. It rattles on the hinges as he pumps into me. His cock thick and hard.

I'm going to come again. It's upon me before I can even brace for it. I'm not sure I'll survive an orgasm of this magnitude. By the way the muscles and tendons are corded on Wes's neck I think he feels the same way.

His thrusts grow wild and erratic as we both race towards the edge. Harder and harder, faster and faster he powers his hips into mine. I bite my lip until it bleeds in my mouth. When he sees the red drops, he sucks my lip into his own and groans at the coppery tang we both taste.

I tip my head back and he buries his face in my neck again. I scream and Wes calls out my name as we both barrel over the edge at lightning speed. And then I can't breathe.

I open my eyes and it's not Wes I see, but the monster who took me when I was six years old. He has his hands wrapped around my neck and his knuckles turn white as he tightens them around my neck, cutting off my air.

I close my eyes again and when I reopen them, I realize I'm standing at my front door. I'm paralyzed by what lies on the other side. There's a pounding that shakes the door on its hinges.

"Claire!" Wes screams from the other side of the door.

This was all a daydream. There was no moment of passion. There is no scent of sweat and sex lingering in the air. This was all a daydream.

"Claire! Let me in, God damn it," he pains. "I'll knock it down if I have to."

"Just go, Wes," I say as I place my palm flat on the door. I know he knows that I'm here. "I'm fine."

"You're not fine, baby. I heard you scream."

"I'm fine, Wes, just go home."

"No, I won't leave you like this. Don't make me leave you like this."

"Why not? You have before," I say. I know it's a low blow, but it has to be said. I need him to leave me alone with my demons.

"I was a boy then, I wasn't ready." He slaps the door again. "I won't leave. You won't let me in, that's fine, but I won't leave either."

I hear him lower his body to the floor and lean back against my door. It appears that Wes is settling in for the night.

I was wrong, it wasn't a day dream, this is a nightmare, a living nightmare.

I, too, lower myself to the floor and fall into a fitful sleep in the entryway to my apartment. I know that I cry out for him in my sleep throughout the night. He cries back, begging me to let him in, to let him protect me, to hold me, but I can't. I can't let myself want something that I know will be ripped away from me in the near future when the next shiny toy with big boobs and spread legs comes along.

So here I am, dragging my ass into the station in the early hours of the morning. Wes must have gone home when he heard me turn on my shower. And that's about all I was able to muster enough energy for this morning, shower, coffee, jeans and a sweater.

He's waiting for me at our shared desks when I walk in. A cup of coffee in his hand and another one from the shop I love waiting for me on my desk. He's beautiful even with bloodshot eyes with dark circles under them and more stubble on his cheeks than one of those guys that lives in the wild on those tv shows. A little wild, a lot sexy, and if he keeps this up, I'll fall again, I know it. Fuck, maybe I already am.

"Thank you," I say to the spot just over his shoulder.

Wes just nods.

In my head, nothing has changed. I figure if they're gunning for my job, I might as well hand it to them on a silver platter with my own head. So, I sit down at my desk and unlock my file drawer and sign into my geriatric computer.

I flip through my notes again and again. At this point, I'm starting to bug myself, but there's that little niggling in the back of my mind. I'm missing something, I know it.

"I know that look," Wes says rounding the desk to stand behind me. "What do you see?"

"Nothing," I snap. "I see nothing. But, I know that something's there. I just can't figure out what. You know?"

He nods, "Something's off."

"Yes! That's it exactly. And I'm going to find out what it is," I say as I stand up and lock my desk and grab my coffee and keys.

"Then let's go."

"Oh no," I growl. "I'm not going anywhere with you, Benedict Arnold."

"You either go with me or I tail you. Don't you think the great state of New Jersey and the US government would like to save on fuel costs and emissions?"

"Oh my God, I hate you. Get in the fucking truck. But. Not. One. Word."

Wes mimes zipping his lips and then follows me out into the cold with a ridiculously smug smile on his stupid, beautiful face. We climb in and head off to figure out what the fuck is going on here. I can't bring back Anthony, but I can get some fucking answers. And that's exactly what I plan to do.

chapter 13
a choice

I PULL OVER TWO houses down from the Ascher's house. For some reason, I feel like I'll find answers here. The ride here was silent, both of us lost in our own thoughts. Wes and I both step down from the car and our faces go blank. It's game time.

We step up to the porch and I ring the bell. *Nothing*. I lean back and look at the driveway. Mrs. Ascher's car is there. Mr. Ascher's vehicle is not present, but it's nine in the morning on a work day. I would assume he's at the office. Well, I assume he'd be with his wife since she was notified this morning that the body found is her six-year-old son, but what do I know?

"Oh, hello Agent O'Connell, Detective," Mrs. Ascher answers the door coolly. "What brings you here today?"

"We have a few more questions for you and Kasey, is she around?" I ask.

"I heard you're not on my son's case anymore, Detective, so I guess it doesn't matter if she home or isn't."

Well this is a new Elizabeth Ascher. *Interesting*.

"Detective Goodnite is still on the case," Wes lies smoothly. He's trying to earn points with me and I hate to say it but it's working. It's never glamorous to find out you have a price.

"Hmm," she says noncommittally as she holds open the door for us.

"Thank you," I say kindly. "We won't take up much of your time."

"Kasey," she screams. "The police are here to talk to you!"

Well, there goes the "we're just checking in" vibe I was hoping for. I chance a glance at Wes and see he finds the shift in the family dynamic here interesting as well. His dark brows are drawn over his eyes.

Kasey ambles down the stairs like the sullen teen that she is. She's not happy that we're here. I wonder why. Or she's not happy with her mother, which is probably more likely. Teenage girls aren't supposed to like their mothers.

I always loved mine, but I avoided her when she looked like she saw too much during my teenage crush days over Wes. In hindsight, I wish she would have told me what an asshole he'd turn out to be and save me some heartache. But she wouldn't have said that any ways. Mom always did have a gigantic soft spot for the big jerk.

"What do you want, mom?"

"The police are here to ask you some questions," she says giving her daughter the stare down.

By the twinkle in her daughter's eyes, I would say a challenge has been issued and accepted. *Oh shit*. I see her turn her creepy Lolita charm on when she notices Wes and her mom ever so subtly twitches. So, the teen flirt vibe doesn't sit well with mom? Interesting.

"Oh, hello Agent," she purrs. "I didn't see you over there."

I roll my eyes. Wes visibly tenses. He knows that I won't bail him out this time. Good.

"Hello," he nervously clears his throat. "Detective Goodnite wants to ask you some questions."

Thanks for throwing me under the bus, buddy.

"I'd rather you ask them," she says petulantly.

"Well Detective Goodnite is asking them."

"Over coffee. Wouldn't that be nice?" She coos as she runs her fingertips up over his bicep.

"No, I don't think so."

"Or dinner. I'd love it if you asked me out to dinner," she breathes her underage siren call. What the actual fuck is this?

"No."

"For fuck's sake, Kasey, stop acting like a little slut," Mrs. Ascher snaps.

"Don't be jealous, Mother, it ages you."

Oh shit. Are they fighting? Over Wes?

"You're a child!" her mother screams. "A man wouldn't find that attractive."

"That's not what he said last night . . ."

"Excuse me?" I ask.

"I swear, it's not me," Wes pleads.

"I know that." I cut my eyes to him. "I know where you were last night."

"Thank God."

"We're getting nowhere here. Let's go," I tell him.

"Thank God."

We leave them fighting in the middle of the living room. I don't know what to make of that. Of any of it. None of the Aschers seem like they're grieving. At all. I guess everyone handles grief differently.

Kasey's Lolita act is creepy as fuck. I wonder if I was that obvious when I was sixteen. I already knew that I was in love with Wes back then. I wonder if that's how he saw me. Like a little kid that made him uncomfortable. It still doesn't explain why he slept with me that night. Maybe I'll never know.

I beep the locks on the truck but Wes pins me to the side before I have a chance to climb in. He runs his thumb down my cheek, stopping at my chin. He tips my head back so I'm forced to look him in the eye.

"What's bothering you?"

"Mostly I was hoping that I was never as desperately obvious as Kasey when I was sixteen," I blurt out, cringing as soon as the words are out into the universe. I wish that I could pull the words back into my mouth but I can't. His eyes immediately soften.

"You were beautiful even then," he says softly. "But with a wild innocence I kept desperately hoping would be gone every time Liam and I came home."

"Why?" I can't help but ask.

"Because I knew when you offered it to me, I wouldn't be able to walk away."

"And yet you did." I smile sadly.

"And it was the worst mistake of my life. But I knew that with my workup and deployment schedule, I would never be able to offer you the kind of support and help that you needed to recover. That was abundantly clear when you had your nightmare," he says sadly. "Will you ever forgive me?"

"Probably." I sigh, disgusted with myself and my easy capitulation. "I really don't want to, but when you say things like that you just make sense and I have nothing to say to it."

I really don't want to. But maybe, I don't have a choice where Wes is concerned. Maybe I never had a choice at all.

"What are you thinking?"

"Mostly that I can't think when you're around. I'm going to need you to give me some space," I say gently to soften the blow.

"Nope."

"What?" Maybe I misheard him.

"I said 'no' as in no space," he says calmly. "If I give you an inch, you'll bolt again."

"I'm not going to bolt," I put my hands on my hips and square off.

Wes just raises an eyebrow.

"Okay, I might," I rally. "But you don't know that for sure!"

"Babe," he sighs.

"I just need you to give me the space that I need to do my job, Wes."

"No."

"Wes!" I snap.

"Baby, I can't," he visibly shudders. "I can't let anything else happen to you," he says, his voice gruff with emotion.

"You can't protect me for forever, Wes," I say softly.

"I have to try."

"At what expense, Wes?" My frustration leaking into my voice. "We'll never work like this and you know it . . . Plus, we'll both get fired and then we won't have money to eat or pay rent and I can't move back in with my mom and dad."

That makes him crack a smile.

"Well, it wouldn't win me any points with your mom if she found me in your bed," he smirks.

"Are we talking about the same woman?" I joke. "She'd have china patterns and baby names picked out by dinner time," he laughs.

"It's my dad and Liam you have to worry about."

"I wouldn't be so sure about that," he says cryptically. Whatever that means.

"So, are we going to be okay?"

"Yeah, baby. We'll be okay."

"And you'll let me do my job?" I need to be sure or Wes might as well take his toys and go home. But I can't help but feel like things are changing.

Wes growls. "I won't stand in the way of your career, babe. I'm more man than that," he rumbles. "But I won't stand back and watch you get killed either," he barks just before he crashes his mouth to mine.

His kiss is like a tsunami, all-consuming as it rolls in. He's fierce and dominating as he plunders my mouth. Our teeth clash as we both kiss and bite, lick and soothe the wounds we keep inflicting on each other. It won't be long before I let his storms consume me, I only hope this time I'm a strong enough swimmer to survive.

"I can't go back," I whisper against his mouth.

"I'm not that boy anymore," he says one more time.

"Oh no, now you're all man." I swallow as I feel his erection press against my belly, his hold on me still firm.

"I'm glad that you noticed," he smirks before regaining his composure. "I swear to you that I'm the man you need me to be. I won't run or let you scare me off."

I'm about to tell Wes that I might be ready for him to prove it, prove to me that what he says is true, but our heart to heart is cut off by a blood curdling scream emanating from the Ascher's house. We both take off running.

chapter 14

fucking run

"**YOU STUPID BITCH!**" Mrs. Ascher can be heard from the street. The neighbors are all coming out of their houses. Screams and fights in the late morning hours are not part of the everyday norm for this sleepy suburban town. Missing children aren't either for that matter.

"You better hurry," the next-door neighbor hollers from her front porch. "Something isn't right over there. I just can't put my finger on it."

You and me both, I think but don't say out loud.

Wes and I race down the street and back up the walk of the Ascher's house. My hand moves to the handle of my sidearm as the screams get louder and louder. I hear glass break.

"I hate you!" Kasey screams, then grunts as if something hits her.

"Police! Open up!" I shout as Wes pounds on the door.

We both stand off to the sides of the door just in case. He pounds his fist again. Nothing. You can still hear the furniture toppling over and the screams as Mrs. Ascher and her daughter beat the shit out of each other.

I look at Wes and nod. It's time to kick the door in. I take a step back to make room for him. His hand still on his service weapon in its holster. He leans back, puts his pretty shiny shoe to the door and kicks it in off the hinges. Both women scream as we move through the door.

"FBI!"

"Police!"

"Hands where I can see them," Wes says his voice ringing with authority.

The women jump and walk away with their noses turned up. They sit on opposite couches as if nothing had happened. What the fuck is going on here? I eye Wes and he raises his eyebrows. My guess is as good as his.

"What brings you back, detective?" Mrs. Ascher asks casually. Big words seeing as how the lower floor of this house is in shambles.

"Funny you mention it," I start. "We were about to go interview some more of your neighbors, but heard a commotion in this house and came right back."

"I have no idea what you're talking about," she says indignantly.

"Really?" I roll my eyes.

"We don't have time for this shit!" Wes booms from behind me. For a minute, I had forgotten that he was there.

"She started it!" Kasey snaps petulantly.

"Kasey!"

Wes shoots Mrs. Ascher a withering look. I feel bad for her.

"What did your mother start, Kasey?" he asks gently.

"She's jealous, that's all."

"That's enough, Kasey!"

Kasey shoots a mean glare at her mother. Her eyes are cold. The neighbor was right, there's definitely something wrong going on here. And I think it's about to blow up in our faces.

"What is she jealous of, Kasey?" Wes asks, giving her his full attention.

"Me, of course," she preens. Mrs. Ascher pales.

"How is she jealous of you?" I ask.

"Isn't it obvious?" She snarks. "I'm young, beautiful, and know how to keep a man happy. She's old and doesn't." She shrugs her narrow shoulders.

"You're both young and beautiful," I say to her and she relaxes a bit. "What makes you think your mom can't keep a man happy?"

"Well daddy left, duh." She rolls her eyes.

"And you know how to keep a man happy," I say repeating back the words that she chose to use. They taste funny, foul even in my mouth and I don't want them there anymore. Wes stays quiet but watches.

"I do . . . I do all the things men like that older women can't or won't," she says looking straight at Wes.

He scowls, his dark eyebrows drawn. It doesn't take a rocket scientist to tell that she's implying her sexual prowess over mine. I have a sinking suspicion that they weren't fighting over a teenage boy.

"Shut up, Kasey!" Mrs. Ascher screams.

"You're just jealous that Jonathan comes to me every night and not you!" She volleys back at her mother.

Oh fuck.

I had a feeling this is where their fight was headed. Now that it has flopped in my lap, I can't help but wonder what the fuck. I'm glad I don't live in the suburbs.

"You bitch!" Her mother screams before launching at Kasey again. "You slept with my husband!"

I notice Mrs. Ascher isn't furious that her husband has been molesting her sixteen-year-old daughter, but is instead more concerned that her daughter seduced her husband. I kind of want to throw up.

"I did. And I'll do it again," she screeches. "Did you know that his throat makes this little catching sound in the back right before he . . ."

"Don't you finish that statement!"

"And that he loves this thing that I do with my mouth . . ."

Mrs. Ascher unleashes a battle cry worthy of an ancient warrior but I grab her from behind before she can renew her assault on her daughter.

"Enough!" Wes shouts.

"Kasey," I whisper, but she just takes a haughty tone with me.

"I could take him from you too," she snaps. "They all want me. All the while, their wives and girlfriends don't know that he's giving it to me every Tuesday, Thursday, Friday . . . On my back, on my knees, any way they like it."

"Yeah, no, Kasey, a real man doesn't have sexual relations with girls," Wes snaps.

Just then the door opens and Mr. Ascher walks in. He takes one look at his living room, his wife being restrained by the police, and the disgusting smile on his teenage stepdaughter, and the smile on his own face slides right off.

"Mr. Ascher, you're under arrest on allegations of child molestation, statutory rape, and . . ." Wes starts but doesn't get to finish because Jonathan Ascher turns on his heels and runs. "God damn it, why do they always run?" Wes shouts as he bolts after our suspect.

I pull my phone out of my pocket and call in for dispatch, "This is Detective Goodnite, SAIC O'Connell and I responded to a domestic at 1312 Orange Drive, I have two I need brought in for questioning. SAIC O'Connell is pursuing a suspect northbound on foot. Requesting backup."

"Request for backup acknowledged, officers are in route."

"Thank you." I hang up.

It's not long before we can hear the sirens and Mrs. Ascher groans. Yep, this will be a fun filled little reunion down at the station.

Jones and his partner walk in through the broken front door. The blue and red lights of their cars flash through the opening. The sirens are silenced. They take Mrs. Ascher and Kasey out through the open entry way and into the waiting police cars.

I follow them out onto the lawn and see Wes half a block down hot on the heels of Mr. Ascher, whose fatal mistake was pausing to look over his shoulder. It gave Wes the opportunity to jump and take his runaway to the ground.

"When I say, 'stop running,' stop fucking running!" Wes shouts as he handcuffs Jonathan Ascher.

He looks up and sees me. I bite my lip to stop the laughter inside but I'm losing the battle.

"They always fucking run," he shouts.

I lose it. I bend over, clutching my knees as I laugh. Wes tries his best to wipe the grass off of his fancy ass suit and I laugh even harder.

"I didn't see you running," he pouts.

"Why should I when you were doing just fine." Another laugh bubbles up from my chest.

Wes just groans as Jones reads Mr. Ascher his *Miranda Rights* and then loads him into the back of the second police car. Wes and I stand there and watch as they pull away from the curb and head towards the station.

chapter 15

doomed

"WELL, THAT WAS FUN," I sigh, wiping a stray tear from my eye. Wes just grunts.

He holds out his hands for my car keys. I know what he's asking—demanding really—but I refuse to cave that easily. That's not me and we both know it. I raise an eyebrow.

"Give me this one thing, Claire," he growls.

"What would that be, Wes?"

"Claire."

"Oh fine, you big bully. You can drive." I cave.

I pull the keys from the front pocket of my jeans and hold them up in front of us. Before I can blink, Wes snatches them from my fingers and turns on his heels, marching back down the street towards my department SUV. I can't help it, I let out a little snicker.

"I heard that!" He shouts over his shoulder.

I follow Wes down the drive and climb into the passenger side of my truck. The ride back to the station is quiet. Not just quiet but silent. A lesser woman would be bothered by it, but I'm not a lesser woman.

We both quietly climb from my car and head up the walkway towards the front door of the station. Wes gets there and pulls the door open for me and that is exactly where the silence dies.

A brutal keening can be heard throughout the building right before Mr. Donovan, who I had forgotten was supposed to come into the station this evening for an update on his son's case, rushes Mr. Ascher taking him to the ground where he proceeds to beat the shit out of him.

"You hurt my baby," he screams. As he hits him again and again. Mr. Ascher's face is swelling and covered in blood. "You raped my daughter!"

There are a lot of brothers and fathers that work out of this station. Lots of women are loved by the men who work in this building. I can see them all sit there and watch Mr. Donovan get just enough licks in before they separate them. It may not be the right thing to do, but it's also not wrong.

Mrs. Ascher comes running around the corner, "You beat up my husband, you animal. I'll kill you for this!"

"I slipped once, Elizabeth. Once," he growls, shaking out his hands. "You have been punishing me for one stupid mistake for two years now. You split up our family. You kept the kids from me, and all for what? Our son is dead and your husband has been raping our daughter. Are you happy now?"

"You don't know what you're talking about," she looks away.

"Oh, I think I know plenty, Elizabeth. You'll be hearing from my attorneys. It'll be a cold day in hell before you see your daughter again."

"Do you think I want to?" She screeches. "She tried to steal my husband!"

"Do you even hear how disgusting you sound?" He shakes his head. "I can't even stand to look at you right now."

I chance a glance at Kasey. She's standing in the corner, away from everyone else. She looks like a lost little girl as she watches her mom and dad duke it out. Her bottom lip quivers.

"Come on, Kasey, let's go," he says to his daughter.

She hesitates a moment and looks back at her mother.

"Go, why would I want you," Mrs. Ascher says, not even bothering to look her daughter in the eye.

Something passes through Kasey's gaze but it's gone in a blink of an eye. And then she follows her dad out of the station. She's got a long road ahead of her, my only hope is she gets the therapy I know she's going to need.

Jones leads Mrs. Ascher to an interview room. A few uniformed officers haul Mr. Ascher to booking. They're both going to get to sit for awhile. There's nothing else we can do here.

"What's next, Detective?" Wes whispers in my ear. His voice tickles the shell as he brushes a strand of hair back from my face.

"Now we let them implode all on their own and hope they tell us who killed Anthony."

"Sounds like a great time to get a bite to eat," I can hear the smile in his voice.

"I'm not hungry," I say just in time for my belly to growl.

"Want to try that again, maybe with the truth this time?" He smiles as he catches me in a white lie.

"I could eat," I shrug. Wes just laughs.

"Great, let's go to *Mama's*," he says as he leads me out to his own car. I love *Mama's*. It's the best Italian place in the area, maybe even the state. My belly growls again at the thought.

When we walk into the restaurant there are the same potted ferns hanging from the ceiling and the same white taper candles in the chianti bottles in the middle of the tables, that provide most of the light in the room, that there has been for the last fifty years, or so I'm told.

"Wesley!" Mama coos when we walk through the door.

Figures he's loved here. Everyone loves Wes. He and Liam were the darlings of the area. They took our football team to state, they got scholarships to college, joined the Navy, became war heroes, and came home to follow in their father's footsteps. Me, on the other hand, no one really knows what to do with me.

"Hello, Mama," he smiles that heart melting smile. *Bastard.*

"And who have you brought with you tonight?" She asks before getting a good look at me. "Oh, it's you," she deadpans. Wes just laughs.

"You remember Claire," he says politely.

"Yes," she clips. "You know, you don't have to scrape the bottom of the barrel, my granddaughter, Gianna, is still single."

"That's kind of you to think of me, but I'm spoken for these days," he semi-lies. At least he better freaking be talking about me or he's a dead man.

"Oh, who is the lucky lady?"

"Claire."

"Really?"

"Pretty sure."

"I'm right here, guys."

"Just think of Gianna," she pleads.

"I hear Liam is single these days," he slips in coolly.

"He always was my favorite," I snicker.

"Abby will see you to your table," she says no longer involved in the conversation.

We're lead to a quiet table in the back. Candles flicker from the table top. Music plays softly through the room. It's romantic as hell even if I did have to hear Mama try and steal Wes away for her crazy granddaughter.

Wes pulls my seat out for me. Such a gentleman. I thank him as he pushes the seat in for me. Who is this man and what has he done with the Wes that I know? Wes shoves my chair in a little harder. Whoops, that part might have been out loud and I smile sweetly at him.

He takes his seat next to me, not across from me and Abby hands us our menus. Nothing at *Mama's* has changed in fifty years so locals already know what they want. She scurries away and hurries back with water glasses and a basket of breadsticks.

"Are you ready to order?" Abby asks softly. I look at her, she's maybe all of eighteen and seems to have a little bit of a crush on good old Wes. Spoiler alert, me too, Abby. Me too.

"We are, we'd both like to start with the house salad, followed by the linguini in clams and a bottle of the pinot grigio please," he says politely.

"I'll have that out right away, Sir."

I would normally be mad that he ordered for me, but the big bastard ordered my all-time favorite meal and wine. I lean back in my chair and fold my arms over my chest. I raise one eyebrow. Well played, Wes, well played.

Wes just smiles at me, his eyes twinkling with mirth. Abby brings out our salads as the bartender follows with our bottle of wine—denoting Abby's young age—before uncorking it and pouring us each a glass of the cool, crisp wine.

"Thank you for joining me for dinner," Wes says with so much meaning that I set my fork aside and look up at him.

"Of course," I say honestly.

He's looking at me with so much emotion in his eyes that I want to look away. Wes is usually so cool and collected. Totally unflappable. It's unnerving to see him laid bare for me like this. It makes me . . . want things. Things that I swore were better left alone twelve years ago.

As our meal is served, Wes reaches for the salt and pepper, accidentally brushing the side of my breast. My skin heats at the contact. My face burns with the knowledge that he still affects me. Out of the corner of my eye, I see him smile, he knows it too, *fantastic*.

My main dish is a perfect mix of garlic, cheese, and pasta. I love it. I pop a bite in my mouth and moan as the flavors burst on my tongue. I chance a glance at Wes as he squirms a bit in his seat. It looks like I'm not the only one affected by our heat. Perfect.

I'm sipping my wine as Wes pats his mouth with his napkin and then drops it on the floor. He bends over to grab it but slides his finger up the outside of my thigh on his way back up. I choke on my wine, his bold hands surprising me. His husky laugh fills my ears and my nipples pucker against my t-shirt. Wes slaps me on the back a couple of times before I stop coughing.

I look to Wes and smile. I notice he has a tiny bit of sauce on the corner of his mouth. I lean in almost like I'm about to kiss him, but I stop inches away and use the pad of my thumb to wipe the missed sauce away.

I suck the tip of my thumb into my mouth and hold his gaze with mine as I lick all the sauce away. I scrape the last bit with the tip of my teeth and smile at poor, sweet, *doomed* Wes and the look on his face. Two can play this game. Wes wants to play with me, that's okay, I'll play right back.

"Check, please."

chapter 16
everything to him

I HAVE MY BODY wrapped around Wes as we walk up the steps to his house. My cheek is pressed to his chest sweetly as he unlocks the front door. I'm sliding my hand up and down the bulge in his pants, making the task of opening the door as difficult as possible.

But he succeeds. We go flying through the front door and as soon as it's closed with the lock clicked into place, Wes pins me to the door, my back to the wood, his mouth punishing mine. He licks and bites and soothes as he goes. His hands gripping the sides of my face.

His hardness presses into my belly and I do my best to rub against it. I need some kind of friction. My body heats to unnatural levels. Whether it was the wine and the candles or just Wes, I don't know and I don't care. I have never wanted anyone the way that I want Wes, then or now, the thought is unnerving, but I don't let it get to me.

I pull on the knot of his tie. I need him naked. *Now*. I push his suit coat off of his shoulders and let it drop to the floor. He toes off his shoes and I do the same with my boots as I press my lips to his. I open to him and let him lick in. I suck his tongue into my own mouth and he groans.

Wes unbuttons my jeans and the sounds of the zipper sliding down echo through the entryway of his home. He puts his palm flat against my belly, his fingertips pointing down, and then he slides it down into my panties and straight to the promised land.

I tip my head back and close my eyes as he slides a finger through my wetness. Back and forth, before swirling it around my clit.

"Is this for me?" He asks, his voice rough.

I nod.

"Tell me," he purrs as he slides a finger in deep before pulling it back out and swirling it again around my clit.

"Yes," I gasp. He slides two fingers back in and I try to wiggle, to gain . . . *something*. Anything. "It's for you, it's all for you," I get out before he crushes his mouth back down on mine.

Wes swallows my cries for more as he pumps his fingers in and out of my pussy, his thumb circling my clit. No one knows how to play my body like Wes, no one. Others have tried, most have failed, but Wes has always known how to make me come. I should hate him for it, but right now I can't.

I feel my skin flush again, heat rising and pooling all over, I'm close, so, so close. He knows it too as he increases pressure on my clit. I grind my hips down, riding his hand and he growls against my mouth. I clutch at his shirt, my fingernails digging in and then I'm spiraling down, down, down.

I close my eyes again and lean against the door as Wes pulls his hands free. He gently pushes my jeans and panties down my legs and I step out of them when he taps my ankles one at time. And then he's lifting me up into his arms. Wes carries me to his bedroom like I weigh nothing, but as though I'm everything to him.

He stands me in front of his bed while he pulls the covers back. Then he gently pulls my t-shirt over my head and drops it to the floor. With hooded eyes, he watches me as I unsnap my bra and slide the straps down my arms before tossing it down on top of my shirt.

"Get on the bed, Claire," he growls low and a shiver racks over my body as I crawl into his bed.

When I'm on my hands and knees moving towards the center of the bed, I look over my shoulder at Wes. His hands are frozen on the buttons of his dress shirt as he watches my naked body move across his bed.

I roll over and lay back in the middle of the pillows. Wes snaps out of it and pulls his shirt from his body. His eyes are locked on me as he unbuckles his belt and lets it fall to the floor with a clank.

I decide to see how far I can push Wes as he unbuttons his slacks. I run my hands up my sides and feel the weight my heavy breasts in my hands. I hear his breath catch in his throat as he stops to undo the zipper and push his pants to the floor.

He pushes his boxer briefs to the floor and has to squeeze the base of his cock in his hand when I pinch my nipples. But it's when I trail a hand down over my belly that he comes unglued as I part my knees and swirl a fingertip in my own wetness.

Wes dives for me on the bed. I scream a little in surprise and then laugh. But my laughter dies in my throat when he buries his face between my legs and devours me. Taking as much of me in his mouth as he can and rolling his tongue over my clit. My orgasm hits me like a freight train and I scream as I come.

In a single breath, Wes is over me and driving in deep. I clench around his cock as I continue to pulse and the movement seems to drive Wes wild. He pumps harder and harder, faster and faster, his movements are wild with little to no finesse, but I don't need it. I dig my nails into his back and arch my back as I continue to climax, or maybe I come again. I don't know and I don't care.

Wes drives his cock into me once, twice more before burying his face in my neck and groaning as he follows me over the edge. He rolls us to the side so that I'm no longer taking all of his weight, but I'm still wrapped in his arms, his body still joined with mine as we drift off to sleep.

• • •

I wake before the dream can fully grip me. I'm not sure how I did it, but the department shrink would probably call it a break through.

I look around and realize that I'm not in my bed, but Wes's. He's asleep beside me, his face looks younger when relaxed by sleep. I wonder what would life have been like if he had never witnessed my night terror and ran. But then I remember, I can't get used to this. I have hoped for this life before and it always leads to devastation. Not to mention, hope is a real bitch and this isn't my real life, so I quietly slip from his bed and dress in the hall gathering my clothes as I go.

When I'm done, I call a cab and wait outside. The older man eyes my disheveled appearance but wisely says nothing as he drives me back to my apartment across town.

When he pulls up, I quickly toss him the last of the cash in my pocket and race up the steps to my apartment. I head straight for my bathroom, strip off of my clothes, and crank up the heat in my little shower.

I step in and let the steam surround me. I tip my head under the spray and shampoo my hair, rinsing it until the water runs clear. Then I tip my head under the spray so it falls over the back of my neck and shoulders, bracing my hands against the smooth surface in front of me.

I gasp when steel bands wrap around my body and a very long, very hard cock presses into the small of my back. He smells like sweat and frustration, like sex and my Wes.

"Don't. Run," he growls.

I open my mouth to respond but he quickly covers it with his hand. Feeling him shaking his head no over my shoulder so I hold still. His cock is behind me reminding me of what I missed by not staying in his bed, so I squirm and wiggle my ass back against it. He groans and drops his head to the spot where my neck meets my shoulder. And bites.

I widen my stance and tip my hips back. His cock slips between my legs and I rock back and forth sliding him through my wetness. My fingers turn white with the pressure as I grip the shower wall.

"You want me," he says as he nuzzles my neck while I ride his cock.

"Yes," I gasp.

Wes has my upper body pinned with an arm firmly wrapped around me, holding my back to his chest. He glides his other palm down my belly and straight to my center where he cups me before pushing my hips further back.

"I think I should teach you a lesson on why you should always stay with me," he whispers in my ear as he slowly feeds his cock into my body.

"Yes," I moan.

I'm so full. From this angle, he's so tight, I can feel every inch as he slowly pushes in to the hilt and then pulls back out. Wes slides back in and we both groan. He's going so, so slow, it's torturing us both.

His fingers find my clit and he is not gentle. I'm so sensitive from fucking him last night. His touch borders on painful. But it's so good. I want it. In this moment, I want all of it.

Wes takes a step back and slides me back with him, but my hands remain on the shower wall. The movement bends me forward and deepens his reach inside me. He pushes me forward with a hand between my shoulder blades. He slowly pulls out and the thrust back in.

"Are you going to run from me again, Claire?" He growls as he painstakingly pulls back out and then pumps in again.

"No!" I shout, his torture almost unbearable.

"Promise," he growls as his fingers dig into my hips.

"I promise."

"Tell me you're mine," he slides back out.

"I swear it!" I scream as he thrust back in.

"You are mine, Claire," he chants as he pumps into my body.

He's so hard and stretching my body. The punishing rhythm he sets is about to be my undoing. I can't keep up. It burns. I burn. I'm burning up as Wes thrusts harder and faster. And then through all the hurt and the anger, we come, together.

I lose my grip on the shower wall and we both fall to the shower floor. Wes surrounds me with his body trying to take the brunt of my fall. As our breathing slows back down he holds me in his arms tenderly, reverently and I hope against hope that I'm not falling in love with Wes, but like I said, hope is a real bitch.

chapter 17
fix me

"WE'RE GOING TO HAVE to talk tonight," he says as he touches his mouth to mine and lets his cock slide from my body.

"I have no idea what you're talking about, Wes," I say as I stand and start to wash my body.

Wes stares at me for a moment. He blinks once, twice, before he begins to shower himself. We turn off the water and towel off side by side. Wes handed me a towel before grabbing one for himself. Sometimes he's so damn considerate, tender even, that I forget that I want my life just the way that it is and start playing the what if game. But that game has never lead to anywhere good before.

One look at Wes's face tells me he is not pushing the conversation issue right now, but that he's definitely going to push it later. *Yay me.* I am not going to be available for this conversation about who knows what.

"Claire," he says softly.

I'm lost watching him dress. I stand there for who knows how long, watching him pull one of his tailored fed suits from my closet. He does up the buttons on his white collared shirt and my skin flushes at the memory of my removing a similar shirt from his body last night.

One night. It was supposed to be one night with Wes to tide me over for the rest of my life, and now he has a suit hanging in my closet. What the hell is happening here.

"Claire," he calls again.

"Did you have a suit hanging in my closet?" I ask and instantly regret it.

His smile goes lazy. "Yeah, baby, I brought it with me this morning."

"Why?"

His smile turns predatory. "Because you seem determined to be here and I'm determined to be with you. So, I brought some things . . ." He trails off.

"By 'some things' what do you mean exactly?" I ask still standing in nothing but a bath towel and Wes is fully dressed for a full day as a federal agent. This revelation is annoying.

"Just that. I brought some things to keep here. Later, I'm taking some of your stuff to my place," he tells me coolly as I start to throw things around in my closet.

As I toss on a light green lace bra and panty set and I notice Wes's eyes grow dark. He takes a step towards me, but we don't have time for anymore shenanigans so I quickly skirt him, snagging jeans and a wine colored long sleeved t-shirt. His eyes twinkle with humor at my expense so I pointedly ignore him and his sexy twinkle while I pull on socks and my tall brown boots.

I feel the heat of his eyes track me as I walk through the apartment to brush my teeth and put on a little makeup. I tag my badge to my belt and holster my sidearm next to it before looking back at Wes. He leans against the door jamb, his long body stretched out and his feet wide as he watches me.

"You ready to go?" I snap.

"Yeah," he breathes as he straightens his body to full height. "I'm ready for anything you want to throw my way." That doesn't sound good.

"Oh, okay . . ."

"Today or any other day. You want to avoid me for twelve years, I'll wait for you. You want to run head first into a sketchy situation, I'm at your back. You want to run the first chance you get after I have my dick so deep in you that we both forget our own names, I'll chase you down. But if you think you're going to run and hide and avoid me when we have so much shit to talk about after the first time I get in there in over a decade? You. Are. Wrong. You can't shake me babe, so get used to it."

I don't know what to say to that other than *well, fuck*, so I just nod my head once and turn on my heels to walk away, but I don't get the chance because I'm tagged around the waist and hauled back up against Wes's hard body.

"One more thing, baby," he says and I can hear the laughter in his voice.

"What?" I snap.

"Kiss me," he rumbles next to my ear. I turn to look at him over my shoulder and freeze. His eyes are hooded and crinkle at the corners. Before I can get my wits about me, he drops his head close and kisses me in a way that scrambles my brain for the foreseeable future.

"Okay," I whisper when he leans back to look at me.

"Great!" He says cheerfully. "Glad we got that all cleared up. Let's get coffee on the way to work. I'll drive."

With that he walked out the door of my apartment, holding it open for me. What else was I supposed to do but follow? So I do.

• • •

"Goodnite. O'Connell, my office. Now," Liam shouts through his open office door the minute my boots are through the front doors of the station.

I hang my head and sigh, "How does he do that?" I ask my shoes.

Wes just laughs. Asshole.

We make our way back to through the station. Everyone is watching. There are virtually no secrets in a room full of detectives. We're paid observers, so I know that everyone in this room sees exactly what there is to be seen. Wes has a stupid grin on his face as he swaggers through the station behind me. I roll my eyes. I see others smile at their paperwork or bite their lips to quell their laughter and look away.

I could fucking kill Wes. Although fucking Wes seems to be the problem. I hope these assholes don't think I'm available now. I'm not dating anyone. *Ever*. Well . . . I might have accidentally started dating Wes. God damn it! He has me so jumbled in my head.

"You wanted to see us, boss," I ask as we walk through the door of Liam's office.

Liam's gaze seems to burn as he takes us both in. His lip twitches as he avoids a smile that he knows will piss me right the hell off. "I see you've worked out some of your differences."

My spine straightens and my eyes harden. Wes hooks me from behind for the second time that morning and hauls me back against his body.

"I would go easy on her, Lee." Wes laughs. "She'll be out for blood by lunch time."

"Is it that obvious?" I snap.

"Let's just say I have an overwhelming urge to punch Wes in the face and then pat him on the back and welcome him to the family."

I throw my hands up in the air. "You've got to be kidding me!"

"Nope," he says as he leans back in his stupid fucking chair and crossing his arms over his broad chest, smiling like the dumbass that he is before turning to Wes. "Like I said, welcome to the family, brother."

With his arm still binding me to him, Wes laughs. So, I do what any woman in my shoes would do. I deliver a slight open palmed slap to his nuts, effectively cutting off his laughter as it turns to choking.

Liam starts laughing so hard, he falls out of his rolly office chair. He's hysterically rolling around on the floor and cackling like a loon as he clutches his stomach. Since Wes dropped his hold on me when he bent over to check his junk, I round Liam's desk and see him still rolling around, so I do what any younger sister would do in my shoes, I land a soft, swift kick to his nads. His laughter turns into howling.

My work here is done, so I turn on my heels and walk towards the door. One of us might as well get some work done while the two of them are horsing around like little boys.

"God damn it, Claire!" Liam thunders from his position on the floor.

"Don't be a dick and you won't get kicked," I snicker.

"You are such a bitch," he growls.

"You can't call me that!" I yell, whirling around to face him head on. "You take that back or I'm telling mom."

"You're such a baby, Claire," he rolls his eyes and groans.

"You know what, fuck you both. I don't need either of you guys in my life," I snap

"Thanks ever so much for your help, buddy," Wes quips from his spot on the floor.

But I don't care. I step out the door and slam it to. Fuck both of them. Fuck everyone in this room. I. don't. Care. I'm just going to do my job and go home. Actually, I can do my job from home. I go to my desk and unlock the flash drive with the video footage and head home.

I make it to the parking lot in time to remember that Wes drove this morning. I sigh and feel my shoulders sink in defeat. I could go back inside and wait for him to forgive me and get to work. Or I could wait for another officer or detective that I know to head out and see if they can drop me on the way. Or I could call an uber. *Or* . . .

Or I could tap into the skills of my misspent youth and hotwire a federal vehicle. Yes. Yes, I think I will.

I look over my shoulder and make sure no one is watching or milling about the parking lot not minding their own fucking business. Then I march over to his stupid nondescript town car. If there was ever a vehicle that said *Federal Agent*, it's this one.

I reach down the neck of my shirt. There's a little tear in the corner of this bra. I had forgotten about it when I put it on this morning, but it's been bugging me since we left for the station. I use my fingernail to widen the tear just enough to pull the underwire out. Those little mistresses of torture are such a pain in the tit. Not for the first time, I wish I had smaller boobs. One, they get in the way on the range, and two, underwires are a real bitch.

I insert the long strip of plastic in between the seal of the driver's side window and the pane of glass like a slim jim. Sometimes spending so much time with criminal types has its perks. The lock pops and I pull open the door.

I feel eyes on me and turn to search out the interloper as I slide into the driver's seat. Nothing. I see no one. I shake off the weird feeling that making the hair on my arms stand on end like a static charge.

I need to get this show on the road.

I pull off the plastic panel underneath the steering column and pull out the wiring harness connector. I reach into my right front pocket to pull out my swiss army knife. It's pink and sparkly. Mom bought it for me as a present when I graduated from the academy. Though I'm not sure this is how she intended it to be used.

I pull free the battery, starter, and ignition wires that are bundled together neatly. Thank you, Ford manufacturing plant, for making this so freaking easy.

I strip about an inch of the rubber coating off the ignition and battery cables with the blade of my pocket knife and then twist them together. The dash lights up. Yes! I'm almost there.

I let those two dangle while I strip part of the starter wire. This is where things can get a little dicey. If I remember this shit wrong, I'll electrocute myself.

I put my foot on the brake and hold the bundled wires in one hand and the stripped starter wire in the other. I hear someone shout my name just as I tap the exposed wires together.

"Claire!"

Shit!

I look up towards the front of the station. Liam and Wes are running out of the door and are headed straight to me. Shit! I don't want to get caught stealing a federal vehicle. I mean I am caught because those two clowns are watching me do it, but if they reach me before I have a chance to get away they'll never let me live my life the way that I want to. Plus I'm pretty sure that's jail time. Normally, I wouldn't think my brother would turn me in, but he's not real happy with me right now. And he doesn't want me on my chosen career path.

I tap the wires again. I get a little bitty spark but the engine doesn't turn over. God damn it! I see them stalking towards me like big feral cats. Fuck. *Tap, tap, tap.* Jesus Christ, I'm sweating.

"Come here, Claire," Wes calls out. I shake my head and tap the wires together again. I get a little bit more. But still nothing.

"God damn it, this isn't funny, Claire," Liam barks.

I tap the wires together one last time, they're about fifteen feet away now, and the starter catches, the engine turns over. *Fuck yes!*

I feel a maniacal smile stretches over my lips as I put the car in reverse and back out of the space. They're running towards me, but they won't catch me, we all know it.

I throw the car in drive and peel out of the parking lot. I roll the windows down and crank up the radio to *Born to Run* as I hold my middle finger up out of the window. Childish, yes, but it feels oh so good.

I let the wind float through my hair as my favorite station plays some choice cuts. I feel free. It's nice to best them every once in awhile knowing that they think I'm not capable.

I pull into one of the visitor spots at my apartment complex and kill the engine. I neatly tape up the wires and roll them back up into the column. I replace the panel and use my pocket knife to tighten the screws that hold it in place. I open the glove box and pop the trunk before stepping out of the vehicle.

I run upstairs and unlock my apartment. That big bastard should feel a little of the humiliation that they've made me feel. This is why I don't date. Anyone. I don't want the other officers to know my business. It's bad enough that the local news put it all out there for the world to see and Liam basically confirmed it all at his weasley little press conference.

I march straight to my closet and scoop up all of Wes's clothes and shit. As much as I can in one go, then hustle back down stairs and dump it all into his open truck. I have to repeat the process once more. I slam the trunk closed and march back upstairs, throwing all the locks closed. Including the chain. Good riddance, fucker.

The weather has cooled down a bit so I strip out of my jeans and boots and into a comfy pair of fleece leggings and thick, cable knit socks. I sit down on the couch and open my laptop. My home screen opens when I put in my password. I insert the flash drive and wait for the grainy black and white footage to load.

I wait for what feels like hours, when my stomach grumbles. I look at my watch, it's noon. I don't want to stop watching the footage and I don't want to risk running into Liam, Wes, or any other agency that might currently be looking for me. So, I pause the video and pick up my phone.

Oh whoops, I have thirty-six missed phone calls. Two are from my mother, the rest are pretty equally divided between Wes and Liam—the *traitors*. I ignore all of the voicemails and text messages and call my favorite Chinese place for an order of Mu Shu chicken and some eggrolls.

I resume the video and see a white van. Holy fuck there was a white van! It has no markings on it and I can't see a full license plate. Fuck. I finally catch a break and I have nothing to go on with it. I write down on a sticky note the two letters in the middle that I can make out. No matter what I try I can only get two freaking letters, not that I have superior computer skills, because I don't. And those two freaking letters are in the middle so I'll never be able to figure it out.

The doorbell rings. I sigh and pause the video and close my laptop. I'm breaking enough rules working from home, I don't need to let the Chinese delivery kid see what I'm looking for.

I look through the peephole, Bobby stands there with the bill of his ball cap pulled low over his face, but I can tell by his jaw that it's him. He's holding a white paper sack.

I reach down and tag my jeans from the floor and pull out a twenty-dollar bill before opening the door. He smiles at me when he sees my face.

"Here's your usual, detective," he says as he hands me my lunch. Apparently, I'm a creature of habit.

"Thanks, Bobby," I smile back. "What's new with you?"

"Oh, nothing much," he smiles a smile that I'm not completely comfortable with. I'm kind of hoping Bobby hasn't developed a little bit of a crush on me, I'd hate to have to change Chinese places. I'm also aware that this makes me sound completely shallow.

"Oh good, well, I better get back to work. Thanks for this," I say holding up the bag as I hand him the twenty. "Keep the change."

"Thanks." He waves as he turns and walks back down the stairs to a white delivery van. I shrug. I guess they're more common than I thought.

I settle back in on the couch and open my bounty on the coffee table. I crack open a can of coke and shove an eggroll in my mouth before opening my laptop again. I eat as I watch the various surveillance videos until my belly is full and my eyes burn. I can barely keep them open.

And then I can't.

• • •

There's a ringing in my ear. Why is there a ringing in my ear? I slap around by my head to silence the disturbance when I realize it's my phone. I swipe my finger across the screen before putting it to my ear. I never open my eyes.

"Hello?"

"God damn it, Claire, you're late for dinner!" My mother shouts.

I sit straight up on my couch. My back and neck are killing me from falling asleep here.

"Dinner?" I ask knowing that I'm screwed. No one is ever late for dinner at my mother's house.

"Yes, dinner," she snaps. "I left you two messages about it."

"I'm not really feeling up to it, mama," I whisper. I can feel her softening towards me, giving in, but at the last minute she shores up her reserves and shuts me down.

"You're fine. Be here in ten," she barks as she hangs up.

"Shit!" I jump up and start running around.

I have no time to change or make myself presentable, so I grab my black Ugg boots and exchange my socks for them. I throw my coat on over my burgundy t-shirt form this morning. I'm almost to the door when I taste something awful in my mouth. It's bad Chinese.

I wonder if there was something wrong with my mu shu. I shrug. I'm still breathing so it couldn't be that bad. I run to my bathroom and swish some Listerine really fast before spitting it back into the sink. I grab my keys and head out the door.

I climb into my SUV and notice that Wes's crappy fed car is gone. I shrug. There's a small pain searing through my chest at the thought of his walking away so easily after all of his bluster. I brush it aside as I put my car in gear and head for my parent's house.

The drive is not long. Liam and I both live relatively close to the house we grew up in. The woods surrounding the historic neighborhood welcome me home. I'm sure a lot of people would find them creepy, but I'm not a lot of people. I'm running so late, knowing how mad my mom must be I don't even notice the other cars parked at the curb of our family home as I rush inside.

I pull open my mama's front door and hang my coat up in the entryway closet. I smell her lasagna and I can't wait. It's my favorite dinner. Actually, it's everyone's favorite dinner I think as I round the corner. Dad, Liam, me and even Wes love mama's lasagna.

"I smell a rat!" I shout as I take in the sight of the aforementioned rat. Wes stands in front of me with a small smirk playing on his full lips. Liam, on the other hand is out and out grinning.

"Don't be rude, Claire Ann," Mama chastises. Liam's grin turns into a maniacal smile.

Shit!

"Well, say hello to our guests," Mama chastises.

"Hello, Wes," I growl. It's then that it dawns on me, she said, "guests" as in plural, more than one.

I turn around and there sitting on the sofa are Wes's parents. They look anything but thrilled to be here looking at me. Oh. Shit. *Double shit.* Wes's mom is my mom's best friend. And she has never liked me. I mean never. Mostly because she could see how much I was in love with Wes and felt I wasn't good enough. That I would never be good enough.

"Hello, Claire," she says softly with mean eyes.

"Hello, Mrs. O'Connell."

I freeze. I'm frozen with my eyes wide, unbelieving my personal misfortune. I'm stuck in her old lady powers. It's like I'm twelve again and she's telling me why riding my bike in the mud isn't befitting of a lady. How I'll never be a lady. How I would never be good enough to be an O'Connell was definitely implied.

"Hey, babe," Wes whispers in my ear as he puts his arm around my shoulders and draws me in close.

I cringe. That was the wrong fucking move, Wes. Wrong. Fucking. Move.

"So, it is true," she huffs.

"No," I shake my head vehemently. "Nope. No. No, ma'am."

"Then why does my son have his arm around you?"

"He's just joking. Always the joker this one," I jerk a thumb over my shoulder. Shit. I'm panicking. I always babble when I panic.

"Really? Because I've never know my son to be a practical joker," Judge O'Connell says softly. Shit!

"It's not a joke, mom," he says and I choke loudly. "I have feelings for Claire and I want her in my life." I cringe.

I have feelings for him too but not all of them are nice. My head is swimming. My forehead is sweating and my pits are gross. I bet everyone can smell me. Smell my panic. My fear. Mrs. O'Connell hones in like a rabid dog. Perspiration dots my upper lip and my knees shake.

"Are you okay, Claire," Wes asks, but he's at the end of a tunnel. A long tunnel. Underwater. The Holland Tunnel.

"Claire?" Mom leans in and tips her head to the side looking at me.

"I-I'm not feeling so well," I whisper.

"Sis?" Liam says from somewhere, but I don't see him because the lights are dimming. Everything goes dark.

• • •

"I can't believe you impregnated that girl!" I hear Mrs. O'Connell shriek.

"The fuck?" My dad barks.

"Dude, you knocked up my sister! I have to beat the shit out of you now. It's a rule," Liam growls.

"What rule?" Wes asks. "This afternoon you were all welcome to the family."

"I said that I wanted to welcome you to the family after I punched you in the face, but before Claire punched us in the dicks. At least now I know why."

"That's my girl," dad cheers and I can hear the pride shining in his voice.

"Your father is a sitting Judge, Wesley. How could you do this?" His mother wails.

"Melanie, it'll be alright," Mr. O'Connell comforts. "I always kind of wanted to be a grandad."

"Me too," my dad sniffs.

"My baby's having a baby," my mom sniffs.

The feeling is starting to return to my limbs and I'm able to flutter my lashes a bit but not quite open them.

"I think she's coming around," I hear Wes say softly.

And not a moment too soon. What's with all the baby talk?

"Baby? Are you there?"

"Of course I'm here, dipshit. Where the fuck else would I be? The moon?" I growl with my eyes still closed.

He crushes me tight to his body. "You had me worried there for a minute, you okay?"

"Yeah," I gasp unable to breathe his hold on me is so tight. "No, I can't breathe . . . I think the Chinese food I had this afternoon gave me food poisoning."

"Babe, the shit in your fridge is disgusting," he admonishes.

"No, Bobby brought me fresh."

His body goes taut, "Who the fuck is Bobby?"

"Language, Wesley!" His mother barks. I just roll my eyes.

"He's the sixteen-year-old kid who delivers for Szechuan Gardens." His arms loosen around me. Wes looks at me, his eyes soft and full of care and concern.

"Food poisoning is bad for the baby, Claire," my mom says softly, the concern weighing heavy in her voice.

"There is no baby, mom. We've had sex like twice," I shrug.

"Like four times if you count twelve years ago," Wes adds unhelpfully.

"You had sex twelve years ago!" His mom screams.

"She was like seventeen," my dad growls.

"She was eighteen," Wes defends.

"Barely," I add. Take that fucker.

"Not helping, babe," he whispers in my ear.

"It's like you want me to beat the shit out of you, buddy," Liam wades into the fray.

"But why is there no baby?" Mom shouts obviously grasping onto the idea of a grandbaby in the future. Danger! Danger! DANGER!

"Because I'm on like nine kinds of birth control, Mom," I say softly. "It's not like we're getting married."

The room goes quiet and the air takes on a weird charge.

"Why wouldn't we?" Wes asks. Uh oh.

"Because we have way too much going on. What with a murder to solve to even go on a date. We've never been on a date," I grasp onto that idea and run with it. "So, we can't get married."

"I took you to dinner last night, then to my place and made love to you all night."

"There was that . . ."

"Gross, dude, that's my sister," Liam moans. "Now I think I'm going to be sick.

"Shut up, Liam!" We both shout.

"So why can't you guys get married?" My mom asks. Shit.

"Mom," I whisper looking into her eyes and hoping she sees what I'm trying to show her. I can't get married. Ever. I can't saddle someone to the baggage that I have been carrying since I was six years old.

Mom sees and she gets it. She bites her bottom lip and then looks away. Tears are glittering in her eyes. As a mother, it hurts her that her child is stuck in this weigh station in life. Unable to move on, unwilling to go back. She nods once but doesn't look back at me.

Wes's whole body is tight. He sees the byplay between my mom and I and he knows. Wes knows that I can't marry him or anyone. And it kills him. He wants a life that I can't give him. Even if I did, one day, he wouldn't be able to take it anymore. One day he would look at me the way that he did twelve years ago. One day, Wes would know that he cannot help me and he will never be able too. And if we were too far down the line he would not only take himself from my life, but the home that we would have built together, the babies we would have had. I can survive a lot, I already have, but that one we both know, would kill me dead.

"No," he growls pushing up from beside me. "No! I refuse to accept your bullshit reasonings to push me away. So that you can run and hide because you're scared."

"You know that it's not bullshit, Wes," I say softly.

"It is!"

"It's not," I take a deep breath. "You think right now that you care for me enough to fix me, but there's nothing to be fixed, Wes. So, say we keep on the way that we are, we get married, and we have a ton of babies. Then one day you can't stand the night terrors . . ."

"What night terrors?" My mom asks but I keep on.

"And you can't stand the screaming in my sleep . . ."

"What's happening? What is she talking about?" Judge O'Connell asks.

"And you can't stand to look at me anymore because you know that I'm broken and you can't fix it. What then, Wes? Do you take everything away from me?"

"Why wouldn't he be able to look at you?" Mom asks.

"Because he can't. He thinks he can now, but in the long run, he'll see that I'm not the same girl that he thinks he married. He'll walk away."

"I would never—" he starts.

"You already did."

He drops his eyes to the floor because he knows that it's true. Every last bit of it is true.

"What are you talking about, Claire?" My dad asks.

"I'll tell you later, Pops," Liam says quietly.

"I should go," I say not looking anyone in the eyes. It's tough to be such a Debbie Downer but the truth would come out sometime. "I'm sorry I ruined your dinner party, mama. I told you I wasn't feeling well."

She takes me into a fierce hug and kisses my cheek. When she lets me go I stand on shaky legs and head to the front door. When I get there, I turn back and see Wes is still looking at the floor. Liam, my dad, and Judge O'Connell are all looking at him with scowls on their handsome faces.

I feel bad for him. I'm not sure when that happened or why. Maybe because I have loved him my whole life. Maybe because I've known for just as long that he was never meant to be mine. He hurts and we all know that he deserves some of it because what he did twelve years ago was not nice, but the other part of me doesn't want Wes to hurt at all, ever again.

I grab my coat and wrap it around my body. I pull my keys out of the pocket and pull the door open. The biting wind stings my cheeks as I step out onto the stoop.

Just before I close the door, I hear voices. One of them sounds like my dad's and I swear I heard him say, "Now it's my turn to beat the shit out of you."

But that can't be right. My dad is a great guy. A big teddy bear. He wouldn't hurt a fly. Liam and I get our tempers from our mother.

I close the door behind me and jump in my car to head home. The drive is quick and quiet, but I don't like the voice in my head telling me that I was too cold, too brutal back there. I hurt too, damn it. But there's nothing I can do about it.

When I get into my apartment, I take as hot a shower as I can stand, but part of me thinks I will never be warm again. I dress in sweats and climb under all of the covers and wrap them tight around my head and hope that as sleep claims me I will feel better in the morning. But I know not to count on that either.

chapter 18
any other way

"COME OUT OF THE closet, baby."

"No," I whisper, tears hot on my face and snot stuffing up my nose. Liam and Wes were right, I'm just a baby. A big kid wouldn't be crying in the dark corner of a closet hoping it'll all go away if you just wish hard enough. I bet Wes never cries. I know Lee doesn't.

"Come out now, Claire. Playtime is over."

"No," I cry louder. "Please don't make me."

"Now!" He growls as the closet door rattles. I gasp.

"Leave me alone!"

"Get out of the fucking closet, Claire!" He roars.

"Please no," I cry harder, my body shaking with each sob.

"When," he kicks his hard boots against the closet door and it shudders.

"Please."

"Are you," he kicks it again.

The doors are the kind with the slats that fold sideways. We have them at home and mama says I always pinch my fingers in the accordion. Whatever that is.

"I just wanna go home," I whisper.

"Gonna," he kicks again.

"I just want my mommy," I sob. "Please. I just want my mommy."

"Fucking," the boards snaps and I scream.

"I just wanna go home, please." I beg.

"Learn!" he shouts as he kicks the broken boards out of the way. He leans down and grabs me by my upper arms.

"Please," I wheeze but my words are cut short when he slaps my face hard. So hard I taste blood in my mouth and it's so yucky I feel sick. I'm going to throw up from the yucky taste. I try as hard as I can not to. I know that if I do, he'll punish me again. I don't want that. Anything but that.

"You are home, baby." he coos right before he slaps me again. I cry out again, falling to the floor with his last hit. It's so strong he knocks me down with it. "And I thought I told you to call me daddy," he says as he lands a hard kick to my back.

"You're not my daddy, you'll never be my daddy," I whisper. "My daddy is a nice man. He would never hurt me. You'll never be my daddy," I say again but the bad man can't hear me, he already walked away. I have nowhere to go, but one thing is for sure, I have to escape.

• • •

I sit straight up in my bed, gasping for air. My heart is beating a million times per second. That can't be good for my health. The *beep... beep... beep* of my alarm is pounding through the room in tandem with my close to explosive heart.

I press my hand to my chest willing my heart to slow. I try to hold my breath, forcing my heart to slow down when it won't. Sweat has the old academy t-shirt I wore to bed plastered against the skin of my shoulders, back and chest. My hair is also matted with sweat.

I have to use the breathing they taught us at the academy to slow my breathing, my heart. I take a deep breath in, not letting it out, then another in, still not letting it out, then one more, a third breath, but this time, I slowly let them all out. Like a light switch that someone flipped, my focus snaps into place. My eyes no longer blink wildly around. My heart no longer feels like it will blow out of my chest at any minute. It hurts, it will for awhile, but I'll live. It's a sign of my mortality. The blood that pumps through my heart keeps me living, grounded to the earth. My lungs sear with the oxygen I can finally absorb.

I hug my knees to my chest and drop my head to them. I have to gather my thoughts. My sanity. The dreams never fully leave me, but they also never happen this often. It scares me. I'm running towards a precipice, a cliff, I can feel it coming. But I can't stop it. I only hope someone will be there to catch me when I fall. Maybe Liam was right after all, but I can't go back now, I have come way too far for that.

I pick up my phone from the nightstand next to my bed. The metal and glass, cool from the night air, stings my overheated palm. I stare at it for a moment before coming to the same conclusion that I always do. I wish I was stronger. I would give anything to be less weak, but I am weak. I can't stop the nightmares no matter what I do. They seem to be getting worse and worse, building to something, but I don't know what. I wish I didn't need this so badly, but I do. I won't ever be right if I don't. That much I know is true. That much I can admit to myself.

I stare at the little black lifeline in my hand and swipe the screen bringing it to life and dial the one number I know better than my own.

"Hello," she answers on the first ring. A sign that she sleeps as little or less than I do. No wonder we're friends.

"Hi, Anna," I whisper.

"Is everything alright, Claire?" She asks in her shrink tone. I have come to know this one well over the last couple of years.

Imagine my surprise when Liam demanded that I see a department shrink before I could sit for the Detective's exam. And that bastard would not budge one freaking inch. So off I trotted to the department shrinkey dink. Turns out she was a pretty cool chick and we both find Liam exhausting, so we joined forces. It's not often you find another woman in our field. Double points if she's not a raging bitch trying to prove she's tougher than everyone. News flash, we all have to prove we're as tough as the boys. You don't have to take out the rest of the women on your road to the top. As it turns out, Emma, Anna, and I are the cool kids. And just maybe the troublemakers too.

"No, doll," I answer her. "No. I'm not." With Anna and I, there is no bullshit, no prevarication. Which is probably really fucking stupid on my part since she could end my career with a snap of her fingers if she ever decides I'm more broken than I claimed to be.

I listen to her breathe into the phone while she processes my words. Too often, I tell her that I'm fine. It was no big deal. I'm great. I love my job, my life, the string of men I don't tell my name to. Whatever lies I happen to be telling everyone including myself that week. This is the first time I have ever told the truth. And that is, I am not okay.

"You had another nightmare," she wisely surmises.

"Yeah," I answer as I pull my knees to my chest and tuck my face into the sheets that cover my legs. I wish I could hide from it all.

"You're remembering." I have maintained that I don't remember anything for twenty-four years, but Anna and Wes have always believed the dreams were memories. And they are. But I will never admit that. Not even to Anna, my closest friend. Too bad she's so damn annoying when she's right. I sigh.

"We don't know that."

"Are you sure about that, Claire?" She asks zeroing in on my lies.

"Absolutely."

"What happened this time?" She asks after a long pause.

"I begged to go home, he beat me, told me I was home. Lather, rinse, repeat." I shrug into the darkness. Into the nothing.

"You know you don't always have to be so indifferent, Claire," she whispers. I can hear the hurt in her voice. She wants me to be more honest, more open with her, and I am. But not completely and she knows it.

"This is who I am, Anna. I can't be any other way, honey," I say softly into the phone hoping she understands I don't mean to hurt her. I just can't.

"I disagree," she says firmly.

The doctor is back *in situ*. I sigh.

"Do you think they're right?" I ask, my voice small and I hate that. It fucking kills me. But there's a part of me that wonders if they're right. I'm not cut out for this job. I'm too weak.

I'm always too weak.

"Liam and Wes?" She asks, obviously surprised by my question.

"Yeah," I whisper.

"No," she says firmly, so much it scares me a little. "Not at all. I think you're hurting. I think the case is bringing up old ghosts you should have laid to rest years ago. And I do mean years! But I do not think they are right. This is where you were meant to be, Claire. Besides if you quit, who are Emma and I going to torture those moronic apes with?" She laughs.

"This is true," I murmur. And it is. I'm the best at taking the Neanderthals down a peg or two.

"You know it is." She laughs. I can hear her voice relax. I know that I do that to her.

"Alright." I sigh. "I think I'm okay."

"I think you're getting there," she says going back to business. "But I would like to see you in the office this week. I have heard great things about a new hypnotherapy that I think can really help you regain those memories," she says excitedly.

Whoops. Time to go.

"Well, look at the time, I really must be going now . . ."

"Don't you dare hang up on me, Claire!" She shouts. "I know where you live!"

"What's that *kussshhhhhh* . . . you're breaking up . . . *kkkuuuusshhhhh* . . . I think I'm losing the connection," I lie just before I hang up.

I peel the sweat soaked covers back and toss them in the washer in the hall closet. I peel my sweatpants and t-shirt off of my body and step into the shower. I stand there for a minute just letting the hot water wash away the dreams, the memories, I'm not sure which they really are anymore. The water eases my sore muscles.

I soap up my body and shampoo my hair. It's not lost on me that twenty-four hours ago, I was in this shower with Wes. His hot, hard body here with mine. He worshiped my body, me even, time and time again, I threw it back in his face. One day, Wes will realize that I'm not a sweet kitten but a mean rattlesnake. I ruin everything I touch. Today, I'm here alone and it's no one's fault but my own.

I turn the water off and squeeze the residual moisture out of my hair. I grab the towel that Wes dried my body with yesterday, sensuously wiping all the moisture from my skin while creating heat—a burn—in other places. Today, I dry myself with a brutal economy.

I walk to my closet and pull on plain cotton panties and a jog bra. I do not feel sexy or worthy of worship—by Wes or anyone. Today, I am just a broken toy, long forgotten. I grab jeans and socks, pulling my favorite brown boots on after. I pull a sage green, long sleeved henley over a white tank top and add a brown leather belt to the loops of my jeans. That's all she wrote.

I walk back into the bathroom, most of the steam has dissipated from the mirror over the sink. I take a black hair band and a handful of bobby pins, pinning my hair up into a messy bun on top of my head. I brush my teeth feeling loads better than I did the night before. Well, my stomach does, my heart, not so much.

I slap a bare minimum of makeup on my face. Just because my life has taken an epic shit doesn't mean I have to look like it's taken an epic shit. So, I slap a little light pink blush on my cheeks and black mascara to my lashes. My lips are dry and cracked from a night of being ill so they get a swipe of my lip balm. Glamorous, I know.

I head down the short hall to my kitchen. I see all of the Chinese takeout containers on my coffee table that were abandoned in my mad rush to get to my mother's house for dinner. Then forgotten in the throws of my food poisoning and heartache. My stomach rolls at the thought. I grab a garbage bag and quickly scoop them all up to take them out.

I holster my sidearm and drop gun to my hip and ankle. I pin my badge to the front of my jeans. My cell phone goes in my pocket. I grab my coat and wrap it around my body before pulling open the front door and locking it behind me.

I drop the trash bag into the dumpster and wipe the imaginary bad food germs on my jeans before brushing my hands together before a shiver wracks up my spine.

"Someone must have stepped on my grave," I mutter to myself. At least that's what my grandmother would have said.

I take a quick look around. The hair at the back of my neck standing on end. But my scan of the parking lot comes up empty. I shrug. This case can't close soon enough. I'm starting to jump at everything. And I refuse to live my life like that damn it!

A crow caws and flaps its wings somewhere. I hear a piece of gravel roll on the blacktop, but I could have sworn there was nothing here to have knocked it loose. It's official, I'm losing my mind.

I beep the locks on my SUV and climb in. I start the engine and I could swear, that someone's watching me. I hit the button on the door for the auto locks and then casually check my mirrors for any sign of someone somewhere that they shouldn't be. To the casual observer, it would simply look like I'm a careful driver, when in reality, I'm anything but. Really, I'm looking for something . . . anything, but there's nothing to be found.

I pull into my spot in the parking lot of the station. I grip the steering wheel tight in my hand and drop my head for a minute, shoring up my courage before I kill the engine and step from the car.

I pull open the big glass front door and buzz myself into the back with my ID. Wes is standing in front of my desk. His sexy ass rests against the edge of the table. His strong arms are closed over his powerful chest and he holds a paper coffee cup in his hand. His brows are pulled low over his eyes.

I notice a similar paper coffee cup on my desk waiting for me. Taunting me. I take my jacket off and hang it over the back of my desk chair. We stand there, silently staring at each other for what seems like years when Wes finally raises his dark eyes to mine. I gasp at the look on his face, not to mention the black eye that makes him look a little bit like a panda bear. It's so clear and open, Wes, who is normally closed off completely, which happens when you go to work for agencies with letters, is open for me to see everything.

"Bad news," he says.

chapter 19

here you go

"I'M NOT SURE I can handle any more bad news, Wes."

"Couple of things," he says as he straightens. "Last night did not go great."

"You think?" I snap.

"But I will not be deterred by you, your past or anyone else."

I sigh, "Wes."

"Now for the bad news," I suck in a breath. If dinner with our families wasn't the bad news, then we are completely and totally fucked. "Jonathan Ascher was found dead in his cell early this morning."

"What?" I bark.

"They think he was poisoned sometime last night."

"How? He was locked up in a jail!" I'm shouting.

"Sit down and lower your voice," he quietly demands. "I don't know if this is an inside job or not. Don't give us away yet," he whispers against my ear. His hands hold me tight by my hips. To anyone else, it would look like a couple of lovers having an early morning chat before work picked up. We are and we're not.

"Okay." I whisper. "Tell me."

"Last night, he was complaining about a stomach ache after dinner. He said his head hurt, he was tired and sweating profusely. When asked about it, he said it was probably just a bug and he needed to sleep it off. So, the deputies at county left him alone instead of taking him to medical."

"Shit."

"Yep," he agrees.

"What now?"

"Now he goes to the M. E. for an autopsy because it seems a little fishy to me."

"Obviously," I snap.

"I don't think you're understanding me, baby," he says softly in my ear, still holding me.

"What's to get? Someone killed him because of his affair with the daughter. The list isn't long, Wes. If she was my daughter, I would have probably killed him too."

He sighs, "Don't you think it's just a little bit odd that Jonathan Ascher exhibited the exact same symptoms that you did last night at dinner? Right before he died?" I feel my eyes widen.

"But I had food poisoning . . ." I justify.

"Maybe," he says nodding his head. "Then again, maybe not."

"Shit."

"My thoughts exactly."

"Shit!" I shout.

"Babe, we covered that already."

"No, I threw out the containers this morning because just the sight of them made me want to yak all over again," I shout. "We have to go find them. The lab can tell us if there's something other than botulism in them."

"You need to go to the hospital, Claire."

"No," I say adamant that I keep up on this case. The pieces are swirling in my brain and I know that I won't settle until they all find their places where they fit.

"I can't let anything happen to you, baby."

"I'm fine," I reassure him. "Take me to the lab."

"Okay. Get in the car, I'll drive."

I roll my eyes. I would argue with him about his being a big bossy bastard this early in the morning but we don't have fucking time. So, I race out of the station, hot on his heels. We jump in his Federal issued sedan and take off.

It should be said that Wes can drive when he wants to. And how sick is it of me that we are on our way to grab evidence that I was poisoned last night, along with a suspect in a high-profile murder case, and I'm sitting here thinking about how sexy he is when he drives like he means it. I groan.

"What is it, babe, still feeling bad?" I feel my eyes widen a bit in panic.

"Yeah, that's what it is. Exactly that."

We pull into the parking lot of my apartment complex and Wes heads towards my actual unit. He's smart to figure that I would throw away my garbage close to where my unit is so that I wouldn't have to schlep it all over. He knows for a fact that I park close as well.

"That one, over there!" I shout pointing at the big dumpster in the far corner just feet away from the stairs to my apartment.

Wes barely has the car in park before we are unbuckling our seat belts and throwing open our doors. Energized by the possibility of a lead, I race towards the fence that surrounds the dumpsters. I hear Wes's feet beat the pavement behind me.

I already know that they keep the dumpster gate locked to keep animals and vagrants out so I don't even try it. Without breaking my stride, I push off of the ground with my back foot and land my front foot on the wall pushing upward. I follow the upward momentum and grab the top of the fence with my hands and pull myself up and over to drop down on the other side. Sometimes it's good to know I still got it.

I immediately start sifting through the bags looking for the one from my apartment. I use a specialty trash bag because I hate germs. And spills and the disasters that come from garbage bag tears. So, the ones from my place are a light robin's egg blue, like the color of hospital scrubs.

I climb over garbage bags and the other detritus of human life, tossing bags back and forth. It's not here. Shit. I climb over more shit, some literally. Mrs. Fratelli's dog is possibly the most disgusting dog in life. Adorable, don't get me wrong, but the shit that comes out of that dog is truly disgusting.

"Shit!" I shout one more time for good measure. "It's not here."

"I figured that out," Wes calls. I look up and he's standing there swinging the evidence bag holding the remains of the broken padlock in his gloved hand so that I can see it.

"Broken or cut?" I ask.

"Definitely cut," he says. "I'm calling it in." I just nod.

I climb back out of the dumpster and this time walk through the gate with the broken lock. Wes and I stand together waiting for the Crime Scene Unit to come and collect evidence. I wish I had gone back to my apartment to shower and change clothes, but I didn't and I will regret that for all time.

The CSU van pulls up and a bubbly blonde with personality traits which can only be described as sorority girl or Chihuahua on crack hops out and bounds. Yes, bounds like a goddamn Labrador, up to Wes.

"Hey, Wes," she breathes. Oh yes, *breathes*.

He does his best not to cringe but it's there and I see it, so yeah, that's fantastic too. I try to remind myself that this is what I wanted, what I always knew would happen. Wes would move on. Although by the way she was slithering all over Wes, I'd say he had moved this particular direction before we were ever on and she's not so thrilled to be put aside.

"Hey, Sarah," he responds with a tight-lipped smile. "We need fingerprints from the gate, the lock, and anything else you can find to tell me who broke in here this morning after Detective Goodnite left for work."

It's at this moment that she looks to me and gives me the up and down. Maybe it was department gossip. Maybe it was how close to me Wes is standing. I don't know, but whatever it was it made her give me an assessing once over and by the look on her face she finds me sorely lacking. Or maybe it was the banana peel on my shoulder. Who knows.

"Oh God, what is that smell?" She asks with a twinkle in her eye.

I smirk. It's cute she thinks she can embarrass me. She obviously doesn't know who I am. Or that I don't care. Ever.

"What were you guys looking for?" A man asks as he steps around the van towards us.

"A blue green trash bag," Wes looks to him.

"Gross, why would you do that, babe?" She tries to draw herself back into the conversation. I roll my eyes. The other man snickers and we have a moment. It looks like he doesn't like her either.

"It's evidence in an ongoing investigation."

"That little boy, right?" She asks as she lays her hand on his chest. He looks down at where her hand is pressing into his suit. "That's so sad. I'm glad the FBI finally got the case. Too bad you couldn't get it before that poor boy died," she adds helpfully. *Bitch*.

"De we have access to a control sample of the bag?" The other man asks.

"Yeah, I can run and grab you one," I answer.

"Thank God, you're disgusting. Not to mention in the way." She turns her sharp gaze to me. "I mean can you do anything right?"

I have to bite my bottom lip hard and hold my breath to keep from strangling the bitch. I get that she wants him and she thinks I'm in the way, but damn, does she have to be so awful. I mean power of the sisterhood and all. I take in a deep breath and turn to the other guy and smile.

"I'll go run and grab that for you," I wink at him to let him know there's no hard feelings toward him. "Do you have gloves and an evidence bag?" I ask.

"Sure do," he answers before handing me clean gloves and a bag.

I take both with a quick, "Thanks," and then jog across the lot to my building.

I do not stop and look back even though everything in my belly is telling me that I should. I just can't bare to see them together at work. Being without Wes will hurt, but I know that it's better for us both.

• • •

"What a bitch," I mumble as I step through my front door.

First things first, should I take a quick shower and change my clothes? Or do I stay in the garbage stink and show Mr. $800 Suit how different we really are? Part of me wants to show Bubbles that I am easily as pretty as she is, but that would be defeating the purpose of trying to shake Wes off my tail.

I stand with my hands on my hips in the entryway to my apartment while I debate the merits of showering or staying in the stink of garbage filth. I'm not going to let Bubbles get to me. No, I think with a maniacal glee, I'm going to make them suffer. I mentally brush my hands off. Well, that's that.

I walk into the kitchen and pull open the drawer where I keep the trash and sandwich bags. I pull on the latex gloves and shake open the evidence bag. Then I drop one of my funky green trash bags inside and seal her up.

I point my nose in the air and sniff. I have to admit, it's not great. I see some of those strings that come from bananas stuck in my hair and shrug. Oh well. I can't help the smile that spreads across my face as I walk back to the front door and pull it open with my free hand, making sure to turn the lock before it closes behind me.

I take my sweet, sweet time as I walk down the stairs and head back across the lot to the dumpster. I wouldn't want either Bubbles or Wes to think they run my show. No, that job is for me and me alone.

"Any day now," she snaps at me from her spot cozied up to Wes. I smile brighter.

"Sorry it took so long, I had to remember where I stuck the rubber gloves you gave me," I wink at Bubble's partner. He smirks.

"For God's sakes you put them in your pants pocket! Even I noticed."

"Awe, isn't that sweet," I croon. The other man snickers at my game. Wes pulls his eyebrows down low in a deep scowl.

"Here you go," I smile as I hand over the bag.

"Jesus, I was hoping you were showering with how long you took," she spits. "It would have done us all a favor." I just smile.

"It's not like we have all day, you know. Parker, Wes and I are very busy people." Oh so Wes is busy but I'm not. I see how it's going to be. I mean I knew, but still.

"No, I had no idea," I smile. "I do apologize. I was busy running a murder investigation."

She bristles at my comment. I'd like to stay and appreciate pushing her every last button and all that it entails, but Wes grabs me by my upper arm and hauls me away. My feet are dragging and running at the same time to keep up with his long, angry strides.

"Hey!" I call out. "I was working."

"No, Sarah and Parker were working, you were doing your best to be you," he growls. My spine turns to steel and I pull my arm from his grasp.

"Excuse me?"

"You heard me, you just can't help yourself can you?" He shouts at me as he grabs me again and resumes dragging me back to my apartment. I'm sure Bubbles is just loving this.

"Let me go!"

"No."

"I'm not a child!" I shout trying to pull free again.

"Then stop acting like one."

"You just did not!" I shout back.

"I did!" He barks back as he reaches into my pocket and deftly pulls my keys out, opening my front door and then giving me a good shove into my humble abode.

"You just had to push, didn't you?" He asks as he shoves me gently back.

"Stop shoving me," I snap, but Wes keeps pushing me back, further and further until I'm in my bathroom.

Wes crowds me into the small room and reaches around me, switching on the light. Then he keeps crowding me back and back, more and more, until my shoulder blades hit the wall. He reaches in and turns the water on. His dark eyes look me up and down. I shiver. It feels like his gaze burrows under my skin and see right through to my soul. Every last thought and feeling laid bare to him.

"Strip," he commands.

"What?"

"I said, strip," he barks out. "You can do it now or I'll do it for you."

"No." I cross my arms over my chest as I dig my heels in.

Wes does not answer me. Instead, he slides his suit coat down his arms and folds it neatly before placing it onto the bathroom counter. He unknots his tie and then, again, neatly folds it, placing it on top of his coat. Slowly, oh so slowly.

"Wh-what are you doing?" I rasp.

"I already told you, you could strip, or I would do it for you," he looks me dead in the eye. There's a coldness behind his that I haven't seen before. I shiver.

"And I said no."

Wes watches me huff out another protest but doesn't say another word. Slowly, methodically, he unbuttons the cuffs of his shirt and rolls them up his forearms. Can forearms be sexy? If so then Wes's are. They are strong and muscular with veins that pop out travelling up the inside to his elbows.

When he's done he takes a step towards me. I put my hands up to block his chest. I expect him to grab my arms again, but he reaches for my belt. Before I realize what he's doing, Wes has divested me of my badge and holster. Because that's not embarrassing. He sets them on the bathroom counter.

My t-shirt is whisked over my head and my button and zipper are undone by his quick, efficient movements. He nods towards my feet. I sigh loudly and toe off my boots. Wes surprises me by dropping to his knees in front of me. He glides his hands down the outsides of my thighs on his way down before putting the sole of my right foot on his strong thigh and pushing up my pant leg. He removes my ankle holster with little fanfare.

Wes uses his hands to push my jeans and panties down my legs. He picks up one foot at time, freeing my legs from my clothing. He then stands on his powerful legs and it's the first time I see him for the predator that he is. How did I forget about the SEAL? I couldn't look past the suit and now I'm about to pay for my mistakes.

"Get in the shower, Claire," his voice rumbles.

I look up at his beautiful face and see the seriousness in his eyes. I could push him, but I wouldn't like the outcome, that much is obvious. It's clear now that Wes has been keeping his temper on a tight leash. And Crime Scene Sarah was a trigger. Who knew?

I always knew Wes had a past. I never once doubted that it was littered with women of all shapes, sizes, and occupations with the only common denominator being that they were beautiful. Hell, I never even thought he would be interested in me again. I never planned for any of this.

Wes pursued me. He chased me down. As early as this morning he told me that he wouldn't give up on me, on us, that he wouldn't let me chase him away. Turns out he didn't need me to chase him away, he just needed Bubbles to wave her magic twat around in the air. I guess I wasn't that important after all.

I'm angry. I'm really, really angry. But most of all, I'm hurt. It hurts to know that I'm so replaceable. That Wes could fuck me and then bail on me. Twice! He is the king of the hit it and quit it.

I don't want him to see my cry. The tears are burning up the back of my throat. I look at him one more time and bite my lip to stop the quiver. God damn it! I am tougher than this. So he broke my heart? So what? I never should have let him get close enough to do it again, this one's on me.

I nod once and then open the door to the shower stall and step in. I close the door behind me and turn to face the steam. The heat and mist envelope me as the water beats down on me. I drop my head so that the stream hits my shoulder blades.

His phone rings and he answers it with a clipped, "Yeah," he sighs. "Alright, I'll tell her."

And I no longer care. I don't care if he's still standing there. Nor do I care if he hears me cry or if it bothers him. The sob bubbles up from my chest and tears free. I press my palms to the tile wall in front of me and let the tears run free, unchecked.

The shower door bangs open and his heat wraps around me instantly. Wes turns me into his body and tucks my face into the crook of his neck. He strokes my hair gently and coos in my ear.

"It's okay, baby," he soothes. "I'm sorry. I'm so very sorry." But for the life of me, I can't figure out what for.

Then it dawns on me, he must be apologizing for his feelings for Crime Scene Sarah. I sigh and try and pull from his embrace. His arms tighten around me.

"Not yet, baby, I need this too."

"It's okay," I whimper. "I'm sure you'll be very happy together."

"What?" He stiffens.

"You and Bubbles. You'll make a lovely couple," I choke back another sob. "I didn't mean to make you that angry."

"Bubbles?"

"Crime Scene Sarah," I clarify.

"Babe," he sighs again. On further thought, Wes seems to sigh a lot around me.

"What?"

"There's nothing going on there?" I ask narrowing my eyes.

"No."

"So, you've never slept with her?"

"I didn't say that," he says softly. I pull from his arms.

"Claire," he warns. "I told you not to pull away from me."

"Why don't you go pull out of Sarah instead," I snap instantly regretting my words. Wes smiles a smile and it isn't nice.

"Yes, I slept with her. So has half the department. So has your brother," he growls.

"Oh,"

"Yeah, oh."

"Gross," I shudder.

Wes sighs and pulls me back into his arms. He brushes my wet hair back from my face and plucks out a few banana strings, shaking them off of his fingers.

"It's you that I want, Claire."

I just nod because I don't really know what else to do. We seem to be on this carousel and there doesn't seem to be any stopping it. We just go around and around as one or both of us get our hearts broken along the way.

"I don't know what to say to that," I whisper.

"Don't say anything, just be," he shakes me a little as he emphasizes his words. "Just be."

"I don't know if I can."

"We're a swirling storm, baby. You can either ride it out and hope something good comes from it, or we can let it drown us. From the little taste of us that I've had, I can already tell that we're headed towards something special."

I stand there and stare at him. How I wanted those words or ones like them twelve years ago. I would have given anything for him to want me then like he says he does now. Is he right? I feel the attraction between us, there's no denying it. I'm just not sure he won't drown me when this is all over.

"I can't make you any promises," he says softly. "But I will take care of you. I have a right to be mad when I find out you've been poisoned by a suspect and I don't even know which fucking one!" He thunders, the rumble of his voice in his chest shaking me where my head rests against him.

"Oh."

"Now, let me wash you up because you positively stink," he says and I can hear the smile in his voice.

Wes gently washes my hair, massaging my scalp as he goes. He pours body wash into his hands and then rubs it into my body, taking a few liberties along the way. When he's satisfied that I'm all clean and banana garbage free, Wes shuts off the water and opens the shower door.

He grabs a towel from the rack and wipes the water droplets from my body before wrapping it tightly around me. He snags the other towel and quickly dries off. He takes his towel and wraps my hair up in it, squeezing all the water out.

Then Wes scoops me up into his arms like a princess, like I'm everything and carries me to my closet. He pulls a bra and panties out of my drawer and quietly dresses me. He snags a pair of jeans and holds them out for me to step in. I let the towel fall to the floor and do just that as I watch his eyes darken as he takes in my body. Then he grabs a red, long sleeved vee neck t-shirt and pulls it over my head.

Satisfied with my dressed form, he moves to put his clothes back on quickly and I mourn the loss of view if his hard ass and long cock. Even if we're not meant to be forever, I can still appreciate his form whenever possible.

Wes walks back towards me with long, even strides and stops in front of me. He holds his hand out to me, palm up and in it are my badge and holster. The gesture means everything to me and I show him. I let Wes see the emotions that I would usually keep locked away play across my face. His own face softens as he looks at me. The view is even better than his perfect ass and you could bounce a quarter off that for sure.

I grab my ankle holster, clean socks and boots. Then we're ready to go. Wes holds his hand out to me and I take it. Without thinking, I take his hand and his partnership on this assignment. And I take a little more of what he's offering. I don't know if it's forever. I don't even know if it'll last longer than the week. But for this minute, right now, today, I'm taking it.

chapter 20

for all to see

"WHAT I WANT TO know is, why you?" Wes asks as we power down the highway back towards the station.

"What do you mean, why me?"

"Why poison you?" He rephrases his initial question. "You know something. You have to. We just don't know what that is yet."

"We have to go back."

"We have to go back," Wes parrots my words back to me.

I can't help but think he doesn't mean Orange Drive where the Donovan-Ascher's live. I can't go back. I won't. Whatever Wes has up his sleeve, I will avoid it at all costs. I'm hanging on by a thread as it is. I will solve this case without trudging up the past. Even if it kills me.

Wes takes the next highway exit and angles us towards George Washington Township Savings and Loan, where Jonathan Ascher was a Vice President until this morning when he bought the farm. There is something . . . *off*. I just can't put my finger on it.

Wes pulls into the parking lot of the bank. I unbuckle my belt and step from the vehicle. Wes is by my side as we walk through the shiny glass front doors. Badges in hand we walk up to a pretty young thing sitting at the front information desk. She takes one look at Wes and I swear the top button on her collared shirt pops open revealing even *more* cleavage.

I roll my eyes.

Wes clears his throat and I stop my eyes mid motion. There's a sexy smirk playing about his stupid face and I find it incredibly irritating. I hate that he sees me so clearly. I hate that he knows I get jealous and I really freaking hate how much he seems to be enjoying it.

I clear my throat, "I'm Detective Goodnite, George Washington Township PD, and we have a few questions regarding Jonathan Ascher."

"And you are?" She preens to Wes. If she was a bird in the wild she would be ruffling her glossy feathers. Fuck my life.

"Special Agent O'Connell, FBI," he smirks again. She's reeled in and he knows it. This makes me irrationally angry.

"I've never met an FBI agent before," she says all breathily like when Marilyn Monroe sang "Happy Birthday" to JFK.

"Here we go." I mutter under my breath.

"Well, here I am and I sure would like to ask you some questions about Mr. Ascher," he shoots her his panty dropping smile.

"Oh brother."

"I'd do anything for the FBI," she says as she places her hands on her desk and leans forward, her breasts hitting the desk with a plop. "I mean anything," she says as she looks up from under her lashes.

I sigh. *Heavily*. It's five o'clock somewhere, right? I am going to need a bottle of whiskey to get me through this witness interview.

"I was wondering if you could tell me a little bit about Mr. Ascher and what it's like to work for him," Wes says calmly,

"He's a great man," she says and it dawns on me that they don't yet know that he's dead. "He's always been really nice to me," she blushes.

Uh oh.

"I bet he was," Wes says softly. "How nice was he?"

"He always buys me coffee when I run out to get him his. He takes me to lunch sometimes or buys me dinner if we have to work late."

"How often do you and Mr. Ascher work late into the evening?"

"Oh, about once a week," she blinks into Wes's eyes.

"Did anything inappropriate ever happen during those times?" She visibly bristles at the question.

"Did you ever have a relationship with Mr. Ascher?" I ask softly. She blinks before turning her gaze to me. "I know what it's like to love someone that you shouldn't," I whisper as I touch a fingertip to the top of her hand.

"Yes," she whispers. Bingo.

"Does it bother you that he's married?" I ask softly.

"No," she says a little stronger as she looks around to make sure no one is listening. "I don't think he ever really loved her. Elizabeth is so . . . old and stuffy."

"Then why do you think he married her?" Wes asks.

"I don't actually know. He never wanted children. Everyone knew that. Then one day, he's married with two step kids living in his house. It was weird."

"Do you think anything is off in that home? What is their family dynamic like?"

"I don't think there really was much of one, you know? A family dynamic." She takes a deep breath and then continues, "I think there was the family of Elizabeth and her kids, and then I think there was the couple of Elizabeth and Jonathan, and I think there was an image of what they wanted everyone to see."

"What do you mean?"

"I don't think he had anything to really do with the kids. He and Elizabeth go out all the time and the kids are never with them."

"Where are the kids when they go out?"

"I assume with a sitter if Elizabeth's teenage daughter isn't watching the little boy. I know they preferred her to babysit as much as possible."

Interesting. So, the perfect family was all an act. I already knew that they were a disaster but hearing someone else say it only adds to my theory.

"I just don't get it, you know?" She babbles.

"What don't you get?" Wes asks.

"What did he see in her? Before they got married, he dated women a lot younger . . . and prettier. Sexier maybe," she adds.

I'm not touching that one with a ten-foot pole. I'm sure they'll all find out soon enough what Jonathan Ascher was up to. And it wasn't nice. I only hope Kasey can get the help that she needs to move on from this sad time in her life.

"I think we have all we need," Wes says. "Thank you for your time."

We turn together and head for the door. Wes puts his hand on the small of my back and it burns my skin through my clothes. He's protecting me, claiming me for all to see, but at the same time, respecting me to do what I need to do to run my life and my career. The promise of this particular side of Wes is almost too good to pass up. But I'm still not sure. *Only time will tell.*

chapter 21

trust

"WHAT'S GOING ON HERE?" Wes asks when we climb in the car and shut the doors behind us.

"I have absolutely no fucking idea but I'm going to find out," I say as I buckle my seatbelt.

"I couldn't agree more, babe."

Wes puts the car in gear and we head out, once again. Hopefully find something, anything, to piece this puzzle all together again. I know that I won't be able to rest until I figure out what happened to Anthony and by the look on Wes's face and the set to his shoulders, he won't either.

The phone clipped to Wes's hip rings and he answers it with one hand while driving. Men. I roll my eyes as he talks to whomever is on the phone.

"O'Connell," he answers. "I see ... We'll get right on it ... Thanks, Jones," he says before hanging up.

"You can't have Jones, he's mine," I snap.

Wes just raises one dark eyebrow before ignoring my outburst completely.

"It seems you and Jonathan Ascher had something in common," he starts. I just raise my hands out, indicating that he should continue. "You both had shit Chinese for dinner."

"What?" I whisper.

This can't be a coincidence. It just can't. But why would someone want us both dead? Thoughts are swirling through my head as Wes pulls a u-turn and heads back towards my neighborhood. I'd ask him where we are going, but I already know. And I may never be able to eat Mu Shu Chicken again. God damn it. I love Mu Shu Chicken. I don't want to live in a world where Chinese takeout is dangerous to anything other than the size of my ass.

Wes exits the highway and traverses the old, narrow streets of our home town. He pulls into the parking lot of my favorite place, *Szechuan Gardens*. Chinese and Italian places are a dime a dozen in George Washington Township, but this one has been my favorite for as long as I can remember. It appears Wes remembers too.

I look at him, his strong profile in view. His angular jaw covered with dark stubble. He bites his full bottom lip between his teeth but doesn't look at me. Is he afraid of what I will say? I have to say, I'm a little surprised he bothered to pay that much attention to me over the years. I always figured he saw me as little more than a nuisance. It seems there is more to Wes than meets the eye.

He turns the car off and pockets the keys before stepping out. I scramble to catch up to him, but he just stands there waiting for me. Whatever this might be between us, he won't sacrifice my safety over his pride. That is probably the most surprising part of him yet.

Wes pulls the door open for me and the smells of hot and sour soup and fried dumplings fill my nose. I take a deep breath and my belly rumbles loudly. Wes turns to look at me and raises an eyebrow.

"Really, Claire?"

I glare back.

"What? I love Chinese food," I shrug.

Wes just shakes his head like he can't believe that I would go back to eat at a place that should have killed me. Like that is the craziest thing I have ever done in my life. I snicker to myself. Poor Wes. He should really know better. He thinks he wants all of this, well he should figure out sooner rather than later that all off me is a veritable shit show.

Bobby is loading up take out containers in paper sacks as we walk up. I smile brightly at him and wave. If I had to put a name to the emotion that just blew across his face for a split second, I would say it was surprise. To see me? That's weird. I eat here all the time. Well, I order delivery from here all the time. I almost never eat in the restaurant.

"Hey, Bobby!"

"Hey, Claire. What's up?" He asks. "Back for more Mu Shu Chicken so soon?"

I cringe at the mention of my favorite dish, the dish that almost killed me the other night. Although, I should really be thankful because it saved me an evening of torture with Wes's parents. If anything, Judge and Mrs. O'Connell are the biggest reasons that I shouldn't be with Wes. As much as I loved him as a kid, and how hot he is in the sack, they're still major assholes. Wow, it feels good to get that off my chest.

"No," I shudder outwardly. "Not yet."

"I'm Special Agent in Charge Wes O'Connell and I'd like to ask you some questions," Wes starts with his whole title like an idiot. Although, if I had a ridiculous title I'd probably throw it about all over the place too.

"I was just on my way to make a delivery," Bobby says holding up a brown paper sack.

"It won't take too long. I promise," Wes narrows his eyes and probably lies. Somehow, someone here slipped both me and Jonathan Ascher deadly dinners.

"Oh," he hedges, shifting from foot to foot. "I guess that would be ok." Clearly Bobby is uncomfortable, but why?

"Is there somewhere we can go to talk more privately?" I ask.

Bobby turns to look at me full on and really study me. I take the opportunity to do the same. Bobby is about eighteen or nineteen years old and tall. Not as tall as Wes, but Wes was always built like a mack truck. He took after his dad in that way even though his mother is tiny. Bobby, also like Wes, has some bulk on him. His face has the hard planes of a man and the round cheeks of youth. His brown hair, gone just a little too long between trims hangs over his forehead shading kind brown eyes. Bobby is on the cusp of manhood, stuck between a child and an adult. He's a man cub and my friend who delivers me delicious Chinese food.

Bobby leads us to a booth in the back corner of the restaurant. Wes and I sit on one side, Bobby on the other. I slide in first towards the wall and Wes slides in after me. His large, muscular thigh is pressed up against mine and the heat of his body, a body I have come to know every inch of over the last few nights, sears through his pants and my jeans, burning me, branding me as his. My body knows who owns it and there is not one thing I can do about it, for better or worse. But I can't think about that now.

Water glasses sit on the table in front of us and I pick up mine and sip it, letting Bobby know through my actions that this is a casual question and answer.

I want to show him that he has nothing to worry about. Bobby and Wes follow suit. We sit silent, not talking as we drink fucking water. Part of me wants to get the show on the road. That's the part with no patience. And the other part of me wants to be as gentle as possible with this sweet kid.

Finally, Wes clears his throat.

"Can you tell me where you were last night?" Wes asks.

"I was working," he stammers. "Here. Why?" He asks but Wes sallies forth.

"On a regular work night, do you ever handle the food?"

"Sure, everyone does," he answers and I hold my breath. "What's this all about?"

"Did you deliver a meal to Detective Goodnite last night?"

"Yeah," he says before looking to me. "Claire, what's this about?" He asks but Wes redirects his attention back to him.

"Did you help prepare the meal that you delivered to Detective Goodnite?"

"I didn't cook it but I boxed it up," he snaps. "What's this all about?"

"Did you deliver a meal to the George Washington Township Police precinct last night?" Wes asks.

"Yeah, why?" He asks. "Tell me what's going on."

"And who did you deliver that meal to?" Wes pushes on.

"A woman," he says. "I can't remember the name. I can look at last night's tickets though. Why?"

"You don't remember the name of the woman?"

"No, why?" Bobby asks.

"You don't remember what she looked like?"

"She was stuffy. Wore one of those button up sweaters with the matching sweater shirt underneath like grandmas wear."

I want to laugh at his description, but I know that he's describing Elizabeth Ascher so I hold my breath. I sit tight and clench my hands into fists on top of my thighs under the table while Wes continues to question Bobby.

"Did she say anything to you at all?"

"No. Yes. Maybe?" He questions. "I don't know. I didn't know I should be paying attention. What's going on, Claire?"

"Did anyone else handle the food that you delivered last night to Detective Goodnite or the meal you brought to the precinct?"

"I don't know. Everyone in the building could have touched it. What's going on?" He asks one last time before losing his cool. "Damn it! Tell me what's going on?"

"Last night, the meals that you delivered to Detective Goodnite and a woman whose husband was in custody contained enough poison to drop an elephant."

"What?" Bobby asks. "It wasn't me! You have to believe me."

I want so badly to tell him that I do. That I don't believe he would ever do anything like that, and I don't, but I need to let Wes handle the questioning. As much as it pains me, I am no longer impartial. But make no mistake, I will nail the bastard to the wall.

"Have you ever seen this child before?" Wes asks as he slides a picture of Anthony Donovan across the table. Bobby looks at it for a second.

"Is this the kid from the news?" He asks.

"This is Anthony Donovan. Have you ever seen him before, other than on the news?"

"No."

"Have you ever seen this man before?" Wes asks sliding Jonathan Ascher's driver's license photo across the table. Bobby again looks at it before sliding it back.

"No."
"Are you sure?" Wes prods.
"Yes."
Again, a one word answer.
"And this woman?"
"That's the woman who ordered the take out last night," he says. "What's this all about?"
"You don't recognize the woman?" Wes asks. "You've never seen her before last night?"
"No, why?"
"You mentioned seeing the child on the local news?"
"Yeah, so?"
"But you've never seen his mother and stepfather before last night?"
"So?" Bobby asks clearly agitated. "What are you getting at?"
"Nothing," Wes says. "Stay available."
"What does that mean?" Bobby snaps.
"Don't leave town."

Wes unfolds out of the booth like a cheetah stretches. The big cat knows he is the top predator here and has nothing to worry about. I find the movements equal parts annoying and sexy. Annoying because I'm a predator to damnit. But my lady bits are all tingly and can't wait to see his muscles up close and uncovered again. Fuck.

I scrape my hands down my face. This is why I don't fuck coworkers. It's never a good idea to shit where you eat. And now I can't get my head in the game. The realization has me feeling dejected. I should call Anna but I'm afraid one day she'll decide that I'm so fucked in the head that she has to report me to Liam. That would suck, so . . .

I push up out of the booth and follow Wes to the glass doors at the front of the restaurant. He pauses at the entryway and holds the door open for me. I mock curtsey, holding my imaginary dress out wide in my hands. He rolls his eyes at me. I toss my head back and laugh before walking through the door.

"So, what now?" I sigh after we climb into the car and close our doors behind us. I'm feeling down and it shows.
"What's got you down, babe?"
"I don't know," I shrug. "I mean it takes a lot out of a girl getting poisoned and all."
"How about we go to dinner?"
I shrug again, "I don't think I feel up to it."
"How about we go back to my house and order take out?" He asks me.
I raise my eyebrow. "You really think offering take out to a gal who was just poisoned by delivery is a good idea?"
Wes shrugs, "I did not think about that until right this second." I sigh. "How about pizza instead of Chinese?"
"I don't know." I do know. I love pizza and Wes knows it the dirty rat.
"I'll show you my murder board . . ."
"You have a murder board?" I shout.
"Uh huh."
"And you never told me!"
"Nope."
"I don't think I can trust a man who doesn't share his murder board with me," I say petulantly as I fold my arms across my chest.

Wes, the bastard, just throws his head back and laughs. And then drives us towards his house. He better have a fucking murder board. Oh shit. I bet he doesn't!

"You better have a murder board," I glare at him out of the corner of my eye.

"I do," he laughs. "Don't you want to see it?"

"Of course I want to see it!" I snap. "But it better be an actual murder board and not your 'etchings' that you want to show me. Read: your penis."

I didn't think Wes would laugh any harder, but I was wrong. He can. And he did. The bastard. Wes laughs his sexy ass off all the way back to his house. He better show me his murder board. And after that, maybe I'll be interested in seeing his penis again.

chapter 22
don't move

BY THE TIME WES pulls into his driveway the sun is setting and I'm nervous. I don't know how I keep ending up here. With Wes. I keep saying I'm done, that I'm not coming back, but here I am again. This is embarrassing, not just for me, but for women everywhere. I'm being ridiculous and I know it but that doesn't mean I'm about to stop.

"You sure you're alright, Claire?"

"Of course. Why wouldn't I be?"

Wes knows that he can't say because this case is too close. This isn't the first time someone has slipped me a substance that shouldn't have been put into my body and we both know it. I should have died last night, but I didn't. I'm actually alright. But Jonathan Ascher is not.

"Come on," he says as he steps out into the cool evening air. "Let's go figure this out before you think yourself to death."

I roll my eyes and follow him up the front walk to his house. I am careful to keep my distance as he unlocks the door. I need space to keep my head clear until I can't. Wes keeps me confused, my thoughts fuzzy and unfocused. More than anything I want to solve this case. Even more than I want Wes. And I do want him.

He opens the heavy wooden front door and I follow him in. Wes shuts the door behind me and the lock clicks loudly. I have to steel myself not to jump when I realize that he's right behind me.

"Should we order a pie?" He asks, his lips right next to my ear.

"Yes," I whisper as I leap away from him, desperate for distance.

We both know that I am going to fall back into his bed tonight. It's inevitable, but at the same time, I need this moment. To be able to work beside him and get our jobs done before anything else happens. And I think on a deeper level, Wes understands that as much or more than I do.

Wes takes a deep breath and then pulls his cellphone out of his pocket and calls in my favorite pie. First, he knows my favorite Chinese place. Then how I take my coffee and where I get it from. Now he knows my favorite pizza. I'm not sure I can handle how observant Wes has been where I am concerned after all these years.

I wonder if Liam or my dad know. And how they would feel to find out that Wes has been watching—*closely*—maybe even a little too closely. Although it's probably all water under the bridge now. Liam and dad have all but physically given me to Wes and I'm not sure how I feel about that. Hell, Liam even welcomed him to the family.

"Well, shall we go see my murder board while we wait?" Wes asks me as he pockets his phone and turns to me.

"Yes, we shall. And this still better not be code for your penis." I link my arm through his elbow which he holds out for me like a gentleman. The action makes me think of the ungentlemanly things he has done to my body over the last few days and my nipples harden. "Well, we better go see this murder board."

He laughs and then walks me down the hall. At the end we could go left towards his bedroom or right towards another set of rooms. Wes turns right. He pushes open the door and there are rows and rows of full bookshelves. In front of that sits a massive, old, oak desk. It must have been his father's from their old home. To the right is a large stone fireplace. Wes tosses in a match with a well practiced hand and the logs ignite. And to the left is a giant whiteboard. The kind that you can roll around and stands on its own. I gasp when I see it.

"I've never seen anything so beautiful." I fake cry as I wipe away an imaginary tear with my fingers.

"You are such a pain in my ass, beautiful," he shakes his head. "You're lucky I know what else you can do with that mouth besides drive me to drink."

"Ugh," I groan. "You just ruined it."

"You want to see it or not?"

"Are we still talking about your murder board or have we switched to your penis?" I ask sweetly. "Because yes to the murder board, maybe but leaning towards probably not for your penis. You're being annoying and I'm over it."

"Over it?" He laughs as he tackles me from the side. We land on a tufted leather sofa that I didn't realize was hiding behind the door.

I let out an embarrassing squeak when Wes grabs me. Some tough chick I am. I land with my back to the sofa and Wes on top of me, his lip crushing down on mine. I can't help it. I kiss him back. My mouth moving under his.

"Why do you fight it?" Wes asks when he tears his lips from mine. "Why do you fight me?"

"I can't," I say as I pull him back down to me. "I can't fight anymore." I kiss him again. I press my body to his. "I can't."

Wes presses his hips into mine. He groans when I buck against his hardness. His body provides the friction that I need in all the right places. I gasp when his cock rubs against me one more time and Wes uses that to his advantage, moving his mouth down to nip at my earlobe. He then drags his lips and scrapes his teeth down my neck where he bites, then soothes my skin with his lips and his tongue.

I pull at the buttons of his dress shirt. Wes sits back on his heels and undoes the rest of the buttons. I laugh when he pulls his white dress shirt free from his body only to realize that his blue tie is still tied around his neck.

"You think that's funny, do you?" He asks with a sexy smirk playing on his lips.

"Uh huh." I nod. "I do. I really do." I laugh only to moan when he rocks his hips again and his hard length hits me in all the right places.

"Still think it's funny?" He growls.

"Yes," I rasp.

Wes reaches forward and pinches my nipple through my t-shirt and my bra. I arch my back pushing my breast into his palm. The movement presses my core against his cock and we both hiss at the contact.

"Still funny?" He asks as undoes the button on my jeans and pulls down the zipper. I hold my breath as he flattens his palm against my belly and slides his hands into my wet panties against my heat. "Well?"

"Yes," I pant as I rock against him.

Wes slides two fingers deep inside me and I toss my head backwards and arch my spine. He curls his fingers in a come here motion and I am about to come undone. I'm about to come. Wes plays my body like he owns it and I'm beginning to think that he actually does.

"Is it still funny, Claire?" he asks one more time.

"Yes," I buck against his hand. It's not actually funny but all I can say is yes to Wes as my body shows me truths it has always known. It was always Wes. It will always *be* Wes.

"See, I don't think it's funny when you play games with me Claire," he says his voice rough as he continues to fuck me with his hand. My heat pours between his fingers betraying how much I want him and how much control he actually has. "Do you think it's fun to play games with me, Claire?"

"Yes," I cry out but the words are wrong. He pulls his fingers out just enough that he's not hitting the good spots anymore, but his other hand, flat against my belly, holds me still so I can't use him to find my own completion. "No!" I wail.

"What is it, Claire?" He asks as he swirls his thumb gently against my clit. It's just firm enough to make me moan, but not enough to get me anywhere.

"I'm not playing games!" I cry out, desperate to have him, his fingers, his mouth, his cock, any which way I can have him again.

"When are you going to learn that you can't lie to me, Claire?" He asks as he thrusts his fingers back in, curling them as he goes, but he immediately pulls them back out. "Your body knows the truth. Feel how wet you are for me?" He asks as he wipes his fingers against my inner thighs.

"Please," I beg.

"Please, what?" He commands. "Are you ready to stop fighting me, Claire?" He gives another gentle swirl to my clit.

"Yes!" I scream as he thrusts his fingers back in, this time adding his thumb to my clit.

I grab the tie that still hangs around his neck and pull it. It anchors me and is something I can hold onto while my world spins wildly out of control.

"That's right, baby. Take it. Take what's mine to give you."

"Fuck! Wes—" He pumps his fingers again and again and then I arch my back and squeeze my eyes tight as I come.

Before my world starts to right itself and I can flutter my eyes, Wes grabs me by my hips and stands me at the arm of the sofa. My legs are still Jell-O and I flop around like April the giraffe's baby. Wes quickly puts a hand to my back between my shoulder blades and arches me over the arm. My hands cushion my fall.

He uses his foot to spread my feet wide and I hear the telltale clink of his belt buckle and the grind of the teeth of his zipper. He still has his hand on my back and it burns my skin. Wes uses his fingers to circle my core. I look back over my shoulder at him and I see the proof of my climax glisten on his fingers. Wes sees me watching and circles my pussy again before holding his fingers up to the light.

"Do you see this?" He asks, his voice rough.

"Y-yes," I stammer. I have to clear my throat before I can answer him clearly. "Yes."

"This is mine, Claire," he says. "This is for me and no one else. Not some asshole from the bar or one of the guys from the station. This is mine and mine alone. Do you understand?" He circles me again. He shoves his finger in deep when I hesitate and I groan.

"Yes," I buck against his hand but he pulls his fingers free and swats my ass. Hard. "Yes! I understand," I cry out when he slips his fingers in one last time.

I look over my shoulder again as Wes locks eyes with me. He swirls his fingers one last time before slipping them from my body. I watch with rapt attention as he raises his hand to his mouth and licks his fingers clean. His eyes roll back in his head and he moans. I could come from watching his face alone.

And then he opens his eyes.

"I always knew there was sweetness hidden in you somewhere, baby. I should have known it was in your tight pussy."

I narrow my eyes and open my mouth to bite back because really, he deserves it but he takes the opportunity to thrust his cock home. We both groan as he circles his hips. This angle makes me take him deep. Wes could go deep before, but Wes like this is a beautiful thing. So beautiful that I forget my earlier irritation.

He circles his hips again and I feel my ass press up against his lower stomach. Wes runs his hands up and down my sides before they come to rest on my ass. He squeezes a cheek in each strong hand before pulling his cock out to the tip and slowly driving it back in.

His fingers bite into my ass as he pulls back out only to slowly slide back in. He does it again and again. It's so slow it's painful. I'm so turned on I need him to fuck me, hard and fast but he won't. I grip the couch cushions in my hands as he glides out again and slowly drives back in.

Wes's grip on my ass tightens as he pushes my cheeks up and separates them. He holds them there, tight. I look back again and watch him as he watches his cock slowly sink into my body over and over again. The look on his face of pure pleasure and passion has me completely undone. And now I need to undo Wes.

Wes pulls back again, but this time I'm ready, with my hips pressed as tight against the sofa as possible. When he moves to glide his cock back in, I use my hands on the cushions to leverage my weight back and impale myself on his hard cock.

Wes's eyes darken and he growls. I lean forward and then thrust back onto his cock again. I repeat my move once more before his grip on my hips tightens and he meets me thrust for thrust.

"Is this how you want it?" He demands.

"Yes," I moan as he pumps hard into my body.

"You want it hard, all you have to do is ask, baby," he croons as he thrust into my body. "And I might see fit to give it to you that way."

"Wes," I plead as he stops to circle his hips.

"But if I want to take my time and watch my cock sink into your sweet pussy, I'm going to," he says as he thrusts home, hard. I whimper and arch my back tipping my hips up, hoping that he'll give in and give me what we both want. "And if I want to fuck you hard, that's what I'm going to do," he says as he pushes all the way in in one quick move.

"Yes," I call. "Wes!"

"Hold on, baby."

"Yes!" I scream as he pumps harder and harder, his cock hitting all the right spots over and over again. I push my hips back against his cock.

"Yeah, baby," he groans and he picks up his pace pumping faster and faster. My climax is barreling at me full speed ahead. I clench around his cock. "Fuck yes, take it! Take my cock," he shouts as he moves faster and faster.

My feet are slipping against the carpet on the floor as the sofa moves just a little bit more with each of Wes's powerful strokes. But I don't care.

"Wes," I plead. It's so strong I don't think that I can take it. I need him. I need Wes. I need his body. I need his strength. And with overwhelming clarity, I know that I need his heart. "Please."

"Come for me, baby," he chants as he pumps faster and faster. "Let go." And I do.

"Wes," I cry as I find my release. Wes thrusts once more before planting his cock deep and following me over the edge, calling out my name as he does.

Sweat rolls down my naked back. Wes's hard, chiseled chest is flush against my back and his cock is still mostly hard and deep within my core. His face is buried in the crook of my neck and he groans as I clench around his cock once more as the aftershocks still wrack my body. There is so much to say and I don't know how to say it.

"Wes," I whisper.

And then the doorbell rings.

"Saved by the pizza guy," he laughs as he pulls out of my body, pausing to look at my nude frame slumped over the arm of his sofa. "Don't move," he says the smile evident in his voice as he does up his slacks. I realize now he never even bothered to take them off. Something about that is very sexy. "Definitely don't move."

I roll my eyes.

I definitely do not stay with my bare ass on display. As I stand and stretch out my overtaxed muscles, I watch the muscles play in Wes's bare back as he walks down the hall towards the front door.

Once he passes through the room, I scoop up his shirt from the floor and do up a few of the buttons. I leave the cuffs open and loose. I'm just plucking my panties up off of the floor when I hear a throat clear behind me. I peer around my legs as Wes walks in and catches me. He has a large pizza box tucked under his arm and a ridiculous grin on his face.

"I like this look, babe," he says as he sets the pie down on the desk and runs his calloused palm up the back of my thigh and over my bare ass cheek. "I'll be taking these though," he laughs as he snatches the underpants out of my hand.

"Hey!"

"What?" He laughs. "You won't be needing these."

I sigh and walk on over to the pizza box. I pull the lid open and inhale the scent of tomato and basil. My favorite. I pull off a piece and take a huge bite. The hot, melty cheese pulls free and a string catches on my chin.

"Classy," Wes laughs.

I growl and chomp another big bite off to Wes's raucous laughter. He grabs his own piece and a napkin before plopping down onto the sofa. The very same one we just used. I raise my eyebrow but Wes just snuggles in deeper into the cushions.

"This might just be my favorite couch ever," he sighs.

I roll my eyes.

chapter 23

stop

"I JUST DON'T GET it," I say as I crumple my napkin into a ball and toss it into the wastebasket next to Wes's desk. I miss and have to walk over to scoop it up.

"Well, let's figure it out," Wes says as he slams the lid down on the now empty pizza box. He crumples his own napkin and tosses it in the basket . . . and makes it.

I glare.

Wes just laughs.

"Sometimes I really hate you."

"Let's start at the beginning," Wes says seriously, ignoring my competitive outburst.

I roll my eyes again and walk over to where he stares at the murder board. I have to admit, I'm a little jealous. I want my own murder board for my apartment. Why didn't my mom get me one as a housewarming? Why didn't my dad or Liam for that matter? Oh, that's right, because they don't want me in this field. I sigh to myself. I should have been a teacher or a waitress. They probably would have been pleased as punch if I went out for New York Fire, but I didn't. Tale as old as time . . .

"Alright," I sigh. "Let's start at the beginning."

"On Thursday, Anthony Donovan left Adams Elementary School with his older sister, Kasey Donovan, and returned to the residence at 1312 Orange Drive that they shared with their biological mother, Elizabeth Ascher and her new husband, Jonathan Ascher, now deceased," he recites.

"Kasey Donovan, sixteen years of age, is the oldest child of Elizabeth Donovan Ascher and Anthony Donovan, Senior. Older sister to Anthony Donovan, Junior, age six years old."

"By all appearances, Kasey is the perfect teenager. Babysits her younger brother regularly. Gets good grades in school. She's picture perfect," he adds.

"Yeah, right," I snort.

"I said picture perfect, not that she is!"

"Yeah, Lolita is definitely not perfect," I say snidely, but the minute I think of her stepfather abusing her I sober. All my earlier humor lost.

"You didn't know, Claire," Wes says softly.

"I know, but I do now. Moving on."

"Kasey Donovan is perfect at face value, but behind closed doors, she's engaging in an inappropriate relationship with her stepfather, Jonathan Ascher."

"And let's not forget illegal. Speaking of Jonathan Ascher, forty-two years old, works for GWP Savings and Loan. He was newly married to Elizabeth Donovan Ascher after her divorce from Anthony Donovan."

"And even more newly dead," I add helpfully.

Wes rolls his eyes but the smile on his face is indulgent, loving even, and softens the blow of his annoyance.

"Married to Elizabeth Donovan Ascher," Wes talks over me, obviously ready to move on now.

I sigh, picking up where he left off. "Elizabeth Ascher, forty years old. Previously married to Anthony Donovan, Senior. Mother to Kasey and Anthony Donovan. Previously worked for GWP Savings and Loan," I add.

"By all evidence, looked the other way while her husband was molesting her teenage daughter," Wes snaps. Obviously angered by how awful her mother actually is.

"Showed signs of jealousy over her husband's relationship with her daughter."

"We witnessed an altercation between mother and daughter over the stepfather," Wes adds.

"We also witnessed an altercation between the father and stepfather over the illicit relationship Jonathan Ascher was engaging in with Kasey Donovan," I said using finger quotes over the word altercation.

"Wouldn't you be pissed if she was your daughter?"

"Oh yeah, I would have kicked Ascher's ass WWE style," I laugh.

"That brings us to Anthony Donovan, Senior, forty-six years of age. Previously married to Elizabeth Donovan Ascher. Is an executive for Kline Mini Blinds. Biological father of Kasey and Anthony Donovan."

"Was visibly distraught over the disappearance and murder of his son," I chime in.

"The rest of the immediate family was oddly . . . *not*." Wes runs a hand over the stubble on his jaw as he turns over the information in his mind.

"Mrs. Ascher said Kasey was too upset to be interviewed the day that Anthony disappeared."

"But then you were poisoned."

"And Jonathan Ascher got dead," I add. "Kasey wouldn't do that. She claims to love him," I shudder.

"Elizabeth Ascher claims to be in love with him as well," Wes comments. "So, I doubt she would poison him either. But I think she would poison you."

"Thanks ever so much, dearest," I narrow my eyes on him when he laughs. "Anthony Donovan would kill Jonathan Ascher."

"But he is still in lock up," Wes shoots down my easy answer. "And the kid at the Chinese place identified Elizabeth Ascher is who he delivered the take-out dinner to."

"Bobby," I remind him.

"Who?"

"Bobby, the boy who delivers for the Chinese place by my apartment," I say and shudder. God damnit, I love Mu Shu Chicken! And I can never eat it again.

"You close with him?" Wes barks taking me by surprise.

"What?" I ask back. "No. Of course not. Well, kind of. I mean he delivers me take-out Chinese like twice a week. Maybe more."

"He did know your preferences. Should I be worried?"

"Don't be ridiculous," I roll my eyes. "So, he knows what I like," I shrug my shoulder in a so what effect.

"I know what you like," Wes says in a super douchey come on and I laugh. I laugh until he tackles me to the floor in front of the fireplace.

I let out an eep as we fall to the floor. Wes moves his body to take the brunt of the fall. I land on my back with Wes on top of me, he keeps his weight on his knees so that he doesn't squish me. His hips are between my thighs which instinctively open for him.

I laugh. Playful Wes is one I could use more of. He is so serious most of the time that it's nice to see him be able to cut loose once in awhile. Especially in the middle of a tough case.

"I think it's time I take possession back of my property that was wrongfully acquired," he says seriously as he begins to unbutton the buttons on his shirt. Wes pushes the two sides open, parting them, and grazes the outer sides of my breasts with his fingertips. "So beautiful," he whispers, almost to himself.

"Wes," I whisper as I take notice of the adoration in his face. For so long as a girl, I wanted Wes to notice me, to look at me this way, it's almost too much to hope. I think he has finally worn me down. "W—," I start but I don't get the words out because he presses his lips to mine.

This kiss is different. This time feels different. As Wes gently touches his mouth to mine, I can't help but feel like everything is changing. Is it possible to get everything you once hoped for?

I can't help but open my mouth to him under his lips and Wes gently licks in, his tongue tangling with mine. He moves his hands over my collarbone and down to my breasts where he holds them, weighs them in his hands. Wes skates his thumbs over my nipples and they harden under his touch.

He sits up on his heels in between my parted legs and softly tugs on one of the sleeves of the shirt I'm wearing until my arm slips free. Then he repeats the process with the other side before tossing the shirt aside. I fight the urge to cover myself as he sits and silently stares at my naked body.

I finally give in and wrap my arm over my breasts. I turn my head slightly to one side and avert my gaze, but it's when I try and close my legs that Wes finally stops me, pulling my arm back to uncover my breasts before placing his palms to my thighs and gently opening my legs for his inspection. My face heats at his attentions.

"Don't hide from me, Claire," he whispers. "Not ever."

"Wes," I say feeling the weight of the moment.

"I could look at you forever."

I open my mouth to say something but Wes moves like a big cat, all graceful sudden movements. He folds his body over mine and silences my words with his mouth. And what a mouth it is so I leave those words unsaid. For now.

As it always is with Wes, my body heats and is primed with just a few kisses. He knows this too so when he runs his fingers through my wetness he is not surprised and just groans against my mouth. One hand holds his body up, hovering over mine, while the other opens the fly on his slacks. His mouth touched to mine with his eyes open and trained on mine the whole time.

Wes slides his hard cock through my arousal before plunging all the way in. I lift my legs high on his hips and wrap them around his waist. He slides out of my body all the way to the tip and I wrap my arms around his neck pulling him close to me. This time I need close. I think Wes needs it too.

Wes glides effortlessly in and out of my center as I cling to him. I need to be as close to him as possible. The base of his cock rubs against my clit as I wiggle against him, making me try to force Wes to go faster but he continues to keep his pace slow. I growl and he smiles against my mouth. Wes doesn't pick up the pace, but instead swivels his hips so he grinds against my clit as he hits all the right spots.

And then it builds. The burning starts in the pit of my belly. A fire lit when I wasn't even paying attention. But Wes knew. He always knows me. He has always known me. What I wanted. What I needed.

"Wes," I gasp as it washes over me like gentle waves in a bay.

"I'm right here, baby," he says as his own climax washes over him. "I'm always here."

And he is.

We lay here on the plush rug in front of the fireplace. The sweat cooling on our skin. The look in his eyes as he brushes the hair back from my face is one I want to remember for the rest of my life. I want to hold onto this moment and whatever may come, no matter when or where, no matter how hard times may be, I can pull out the memory of this tender moment with Wes. And I know that I will.

"It's time, baby," he says softly his voice rough.

"What time?" I ask smiling up into his handsome face.

"We have to talk about it."

And I know he doesn't mean the Donovan case. Wes wants to talk about my case. My own disappearance and kidnapping. And I know that I cannot. I will not. My body goes tight. Wes's does too and I know that he has registered the change in me.

"I don't know what you're talking about."

"You do," he tells me. When I don't answer he pushes on. "You were six years old when you were kidnapped."

"Wes," I plead.

"Liam and I were both sixteen and didn't want to be saddled with a little kid so we pushed you away, told you to leave us alone so that we could talk about girls like Kira McIntire and her early developments."

"If by that you mean her bra stuffed full of Kleenex," I snap. "Then, yes."

"So, you do remember?" He asks me with a raised eyebrow.

"I don't want to talk about it."

Wes strokes my cheek with his fingertips before speaking. "A man in a white van took you, drugged you."

"Stop."

"He abused you," Wes chokes out.

"Wes, stop." But he doesn't.

"We looked for you. For days, Liam and I got all of our friends to help search the woods for you. For so many nights I thought, 'Will tomorrow be the day that we find her body in the woods?'" His breath catches in his throat.

"Wes."

"I thought, 'it's all my fault. If we had just let her follow us around one more day. If we'd of just been a little less selfish, none of this would have happened.' But it *did* happen. And I carry that guilt every day, Claire."

"Well, you shouldn't," I snap.

"Don't you have any feelings you want to share with me about that time, baby?" He pleads. Wes is begging me to open up to him and I want to, but I just . . . *can't*. So, I lie.

"I don't honestly remember anything from that time Wes. So, put your guilt aside. I'm fine," I lie through my teeth. The look on his face says he doesn't believe me for one second, so I switch tactics and change the subject. "Besides, I'm hungry," I say as I roll over, gently nudging Wes over to his back.

I take his rising cock in my hand and gently run my fist over it. He begins to fill and harden in my hand. I squeeze him in my fist and his breath catches. I pump him in my fist a little faster.

"Claire, babe, we-we-we're not done here."

"I know, baby, we're not done here, not by a long shot," I say as I lean down, brushing my hair to the side over my shoulder, as I take him into my mouth.

Wes groans as I swirl the tip in my mouth before sliding down as far as I can take him before I choke. That is never attractive. I come back up and swirl the tip again, this time, pumping him in my fist as I go before sliding down again.

I rub my legs together like a cricket as I suck on his cock, turning myself on as I go, so I slide my free hand in between my legs. I moan around his length as my fingers find my clit.

"Claire," Wes growls when he sees me start to get myself off. "You better not make yourself come."

Wes pulls my hand out from between my legs, pulling me up, up, up, until he can suck my fingers into his mouth licking away my wetness. But he pulled me so far, I had to let go of his cock which is now throbbing against my center as I straddle his waist.

"I could probably meet all of your demands, Agent." I smirk as I rise up on my knees and sink down on his cock.

Wes's hips buck underneath me and I lean back, reveling in the fullness of him. I lift my head and look in his dark blue eyes. Then I rise up and slam back down. His fingertips dig into the fleshy part of my thighs. I rise up and slam back down again and again and again. Neither of us will last long this way and that's fine by me. I want—no, I *need*—Wes so lost to his lust that he forgets all about the questions he wants answered. Questions I will do anything to avoid, obviously. By the look in his eyes as we fuck on the floor, Wes knows it too. He always did see me just a little too clearly.

Sweat rolls down my spine as I rise up on my knees and slam back down over his cock. Wes watches where his body meets mine, letting me have this moment. His hips come up to meet mine thrust for thrust as I ride his cock.

"Claire," he says through gritted teeth. "I'm almost there."

"I know," I say as I move faster and faster chasing my own climax and his. I'm almost there. Almost. One more time, I rise up and slam back down. I rake my nails down his chest.

"Baby, I'm . . . I'm," he says as I rise up one last time and slam back down over his cock, taking us both over the edge, together.

I lay sprawled over his body, his cock still inside me, the mixture of our sweat making our skin stick together. Our breathing evens out and then sleep takes me. My last conscious thought is this is bliss.

• • •

It's dark. So dark. At night my mommy leaves a nightlight on for me and my favorite piggy stuffed animal that I've had for ages to help me sleep. I hate the dark. Monsters only lurk in the dark. I want my mommy but I can't cry. If I cry, the bad man will come and he will hurt me again. He always hurts me. Even though I don't want him to, I know, he always comes, but this time I will be ready.

I was digging in the closet when I knew that he was asleep. I found a pile of old junk. He must have been too lazy to clean out the closet that has been my prison for I don't know how long. But his laziness is my win. In the corner under the pile of old stuff, I found a baseball and then a glove, and in the very bottom of the pile, I found an old metal bat. Just like the kind Liam and Wes used when they were my age.

Sometimes it pays to be the little sister. My whole life I've been following Wes and Liam around hoping that they would play with me. I even told Wes that one day he would marry me. He just laughed and said, "I'm not so sure about that, squirt." That's what he calls me. Squirt.

So, all the times, I followed them around when they played ball or walked in the woods finally is going to pay off even if Wes never wants to marry me because I learned how to swing a baseball bat watching them. I learned to run through the woods following them. I am going to run away from the bad man because of all that I watched them do.

So, I wait. And I wait and I wait and I wait. I almost fall asleep. Almost. I feel my eyelids getting heavy but then I hear footsteps and I know that he's coming. He always comes.

I sit quietly and try not to make any noise. I hurry to my feet and grab my bat. I crouch in the corner with the bat over my shoulder just like Liam showed me how to do. When I hear the lock that he keeps on the closet door open I know that it's time.

My hands sweat and I feel shaky all over.

"Wake up, Claire, it's time," he says as he pulls open the closet door. "What are you doing?" He asks when he sees me but I don't answer. I swing the bat as hard as I can, hitting him in his big belly.

When the bad man falls forward, I swing one more time, hitting the side of his head just like Liam and Wes taught me to hit a baseball when I finally got them to include me. And then I run.

I run out of the closet while the bad man screams my name. I run out of the ugly house that smells funny and then I run out into the woods.

I run and I run and I run.

I don't hear him, but he's a sneaky man, I have to be smart. I look all around me. The sun is just setting to my left. I close my eyes and hear water to my right. And then I know where I am. I turn a little to the right, towards the water, and I run as fast as I can.

But I'm slow. Slower than I can usually run. I'm so tired. I haven't slept since I woke up on the dirty blanket in his stinky living room. My belly hurts, he doesn't give me much to eat either. But I have to run. I have to get home to mommy and daddy and Liam and Wes. Even if they're mad at me, I have to get home. Away from the bad man.

My feet don't feel like they can go much farther, but I see the clearing up ahead. I know my house is just beyond those trees! So I push my legs and run faster and faster.

"What's that, Wes?" I hear Liam ask.

It's me! But I can't shout. I'm breathing too hard from running. I just break through the trees and I think I see Wes, but it's blurry, my eyes are blurry.

"Lee, it's Claire!" He shouts. "It's Claire! I got her, Lee. I got her!" He shouts.

I can hear his feet running on the grass and the dirt the twigs crunching under his feet as they eat up the ground to me. But when he sees me. He sees my swollen face and dirty t-shirt and panties his face looks awful. So awful I want to cry. I don't ever want to see Wes look at me that way again. But it turns out I don't have to because as he shouts my name, everything goes black.

• • •

"Claire!" Wes shouts and he shakes me. "Claire!"

Someone is screaming. It's me. I'm screaming. I can't let the bad man get to me again. He can't get to me again. He can't find me. I have to run home. I have to find my family.

"Claire!" someone shouts. "Claire wake up, you're dreaming," he shouts shaking me again.

It's Wes. I'm safe, I'm finally safe. I open my eyes, see a grown-up Wes, and remember where I am. Naked on the floor tangled up with Wes. I smile until I see the look on his face. It's the same horrified look he had worn the day I made it home. Wes doesn't know that I remember, but I remember everything. But I especially remember that horrified look I have seen on him twice before, three times including now.

The first time was the day I made it home, the second was the morning I woke up with him after bequeathing him my virginity at the ripe old age of eighteen, and the third time is now. Now when I finally realized how badly I wanted him, a life with him, how close within my reach it was, only for him to discover that I am just as broken as he always knew I was. The funny thing is I knew we would eventually get here, and yet, I was helpless to stop it.

"Claire," he whispers but I can't bare to look at him.

I jump up and grab his shirt pulling it on swiftly and wrapping it tight around my body. I start grabbing my clothes off of the floor of his study. I race around the room plucking them up as I go.

"Don't do this, Claire," he pleads as he jumps up and gets in my space, crowding me in.

"No!" I shout as I duck under his arms and race around him.

I run down the hall with my clothes balled up in my arms. I find a downstairs powder room and rush inside, slamming the door shut and locking it just as Wes reaches the door. He pounds on it with his fists so hard that the door shakes. He is pounding so hard I'm afraid that he will knock it off of the hinges.

"Don't do this, Claire," he shouts. "Let me in."

I turn on the water in the sink so I can't hear him. I splash some water on my face to cool my overheated skin down, but I know it's the combination humiliation and the lasting effects of the dream that still have me in its clutches.

I leave the water running and pull on my jeans and t-shirt. Once again going without my bra and panties. God, I'm such a tramp. My mother will need to light thirty candles and I'll need to say two hundred hail Mary's just for this month alone. It's moments like this, I halfway wish the poison killed me.

"God damn it, Claire! Open the fucking door!" He roars.

I'm running out of time. I need to figure out what I'm going to do. I know that I can't go back out there and face him like this. I just can't. I know that I won't survive it.

"Lee, I need you," I hear him bark into his phone. *"Something's happened . . . It's Claire."*

I need to get out of here, but how? I turn around looking everywhere. Over my shoulder and take stock of the room. A mirrored medicine cabinet, commode, towel rack, sink basin and cabinet . . . and then I see it. There is a small window at the top of the wall perpendicular to the toilet. It's small, but I'll fit. I climb up onto the toilet seat and unlatch the window. The glass panel tips out smoothly. Hooray for Wes and his anal-retentive home repair schedule!

"Please, Claire," he pleads as he pounds on the door again. "Fuck! Let me in or else I'll break this door down and I'm rather fond of this fucking door."

I grab onto the window ledge and start to pull. Fuck I'm out of shape. No more beer and onion rings for awhile. Oh shit. I might have to start running. Actually, that sounds like a great idea. I think I'll take up running right now, just like the chickenshit that I am.

"One . . ."

I get my head and shoulders through the window. The only way I'll fit is head first. Fuck, sometimes I hate my life. My need for self-preservation is warring with my need for survival.

"Two..."

Self-preservation wins out as I dive head first into the bushes. Executing my best tuck and roll as I go. I'm barefoot and running down the street when I hear Wes one last time.

"Three!" He shouts and then I hear him clip out, *"Fuck!"* when he realizes that I'm gone but I keep running and running.

The icy cold sidewalk is burning the soles of my feet but I can't stop. Like that god damned fish in the movie, I just keep swimming. I just keep running a path of streets and turns until I'm sure that he can't find me. I'm not ready for him to find me even though I know that he eventually will.

I pause in an alleyway when I realize my jeans still have my badge and sidearm clipped to the hips. I have just been fucked hair, running makeup, and no shoes on my feet. My boots are back on the floor of Wes's study with my drop gun and it's ankle holster. In other words, I look like a crazy person.

That's when I realize that my cellphone is still in the back pocket of my jeans. I whip it out and dial the one number that I know by heart. The one person that I know I can turn to even though I know that I shouldn't. That one day, I will call this number one too many times and it will cost me everything.

They pick up on the first ring just like I knew they would and before they can answer I say, "Anna, I need you."

chapter 24

low blow

"GET IN, LOSER. WE'RE going shopping," she shouts when the wheels of her white Mercedes screech to a stop.

I sigh and open the door. "Really, Anna?" I question her.

"What?" She shrugs. "I love that movie." But the wide smile slides right off of her face when she sees me.

"Sometimes it's hard to picture you as a world renowned shrink," I say as I climb in her car and the door quietly closes behind me.

"Psychiatrist, I'm not a shrink," she sighs.

I pull my belt across my chest and then sit staring at my hands in my lap. I scrub at the dirt on my palms that only I can see. Anna interrupts my Lady Macbeth routine.

"What happened, Claire?" She asks. "You're scaring me," she says when I don't answer.

"It's all falling apart?" I whimper.

"What is?" She asks.

I look over my shoulder. "My case, my life . . . *me*."

"Claire, look at me," she softly commands.

"Can we get out of here?" I ask, still looking over my shoulder. I'm not ready to be found.

"Okay, babe. Let's get you out of here."

She drives us back through the quiet streets of New Jersey. The interior of the car is dark but the streetlights we pass give short glimpses of illumination. I would like to find some symbolism in that, but I know in my heart of hearts, there is none to be found. In my world, there can only be darkness.

Anna pulls into the driveway of her suburban home, an old Victorian. Not huge, not small, with one bathroom. Otherwise, it's perfect and very Anna. She shuts of the engine and steps out of the car. I follow her into the house when she unlocks the door.

Anna sets her keys and purse on the table in the entryway before moving through the house straight to the kitchen. I follow her in my dirty, bare feet. She pulls an old, well used kettle off of the stove and moves it to the sink to fill it with water. I watch as she sets it back on the burner while switching on the knob. She pulls mugs out of the cupboard above the coffeemaker and then a box of tea out of the pantry and sets them both on the island countertop that separates her from me.

Anna stops to take a hard look at me. I feel laid bare, like she sees everything I wish to keep to myself. The things I most need to keep hidden. Finally, she looks away, having taken the pulse of me and the situation, before she moves back to the small pantry and pulls down a bottle of bourbon from a top shelf, and slams it down onto the counter with the tea and the mugs just as the whistle blows.

"Well," she sighs. "How are we taking our tea tonight?" She asks as she pours hot water into the mugs before depositing tea bags in the steaming liquid.

I look her dead in the eyes. "With bourbon."

She sighs as she uncorks the bottle and pours with a hand so heavy that it reminds me why we're friends. Finally, she passes me a mug across the large marble countertop before grabbing her own.

"Let's go sit down and get the shit part over with," she sighs before heading into a comfortable living room.

It's a large yet cozy room with big windows and tan walls. There are big, squishy corduroy couches that could swallow you whole. A large glass topped coffee table sits in the middle of a multicolored rug over dark hardwood floors. I love this room.

Anna sits in the corner of one of the huge sofas and I sit as far away as possible on the other one. She sighs. Anna knows that this can't possibly be good if I need distance from her, but she never lets the hurt my actions cause show on her face.

I take a long sip of my tea and let out a huge breath. Anna is visibly frustrated.

"Are you going to tell me what the fuck is going on or what?" She finally snaps.

"How very therapeutic of you," I joke. "Is this a new method?"

"Not funny, Claire, and you know it."

"I do, I'm sorry," I whisper tears stinging my eyes. "I-I just . . . I'm just so overwhelmed and I don't know what to do."

"I do," she sighs. "You start at the beginning and tell me everything. As your friend, not your shrink."

"Okay," I say and then I do. I tell Anna all about the nightmares which really are horrible memories.

I tell her about little Anthony Donovan and how I can't tell up from down with his case and the guilt that I feel that I escaped, that I survived and so many kids don't. I tell her how I'm beginning to fear that Wes and Liam are right and that I have no place in law enforcement and how much that hurts because I love it more than anything. I love following in my dad and my brother's footsteps. I tell her all about Wes and how much I'm afraid to love him. I tell her about all of the amazing sex and how sure he's been that we were meant to be together right up until I had another nightmare when I was with him and it transported me right back to twelve years ago when he broke my heart. I tell her about the look on his face. How he pities me and how he now knows that I was right all along, that we could never really be together. And then I told her how I bolted in a panic.

Anna sits there wide-eyed staring at me for what feels like forever. Finally, she slowly blinks once, twice, and then slams back all of her bourbon doctored tea and slams the mug on the coffee table before looking back up at me.

She blinks. "Other than that Mrs. Lincoln, how did you enjoy the play?"

I slow blink.

I stare at her like an idiot for who know how long. Was she not listening? Does she not understand what a shit show my life has turned into? I continue to sit there and stare at her, not saying a word. My mug is cooling in my hands but the residual warmth keeps me grounded.

"Say something," she implores. "You're scaring me."

I shot the last of my mostly bourbon tea back and slam my mug down on the coffee table in front of me. I narrow my eyes on her. She throws her arms up in the over her head in a "well?" motion.

"Are you listening to me at all?" I shout.

"Yeah, so?"

"So? So? So my life is fucking falling apart!" I shout standing up.

"No it's not!" She stands, screaming in my face right back.

"How so?"

"Okay, I'll tell you," she shouts. "One, you are not broken. Two, you are the toughest woman I know. Three, you are a survivor. You survived everything that you have for a reason. Hear me out," she says when I open my mouth to correct her. "You couldn't save this boy. I know that that hurts, but maybe he wasn't saveable."

"What?" I ask as she turns my brain around in a different direction than the one my thoughts were originally going in.

"You said it yourself the other day, there was never a ransom," she reminds me.

There's something niggling at the back of my mind, but before I can give it a chance to break free, Anna is back in my face throwing old shit at me. If I didn't love her so much, I would wonder why we're friends.

"And there is definitely something there with Wes."

I growl.

"Don't argue with me," she snaps. "I'm right and you know it. And it's more than just the past. That was then, this is now," she finishes triumphantly, pointing her index finger aggressively towards the carpet. Anna would make a great politician. Or third world dictator.

I sigh. "It's both. It's then and now," I say look at the ground, my hands still on my hips. "I don't want to want him. But I do," I whisper as my eyes fill with tears.

"I know, honey," she says as she moves towards me and wraps her arms around me.

I put my head on Anna's shoulder and cry. For the first time in a long time I don't feel so alone. I have a friend. In my heart I know that I'm not alone, but my head does funny things with the information. The truth is, I have a loving family and great friends in Emma and Anna, in my life if I let them.

"Thank you," say through a watery smile.

"For what?" She asks.

"For not making fun of me when I became such a whiny girl. I swear it was just for a moment," I laugh.

"Anytime," she laughs too. "Now, what are we going to do about this man?" She asks.

I sigh, "I have no fucking idea."

"I have one," she says softly, a knowing smirk playing on her mouth. I also know I don't want to hear what she has to say.

"I already told you, Anna, you're good looking but I'm not interested, I like a huuuugggeee . . ."

"Ha!" She scoffs. "Like you could get me into bed."

"Don't be jealous because you don't do it for me," I tease.

"I bet Wes does it for you," she says just under her breath.

"What?" I shout. "Low blow!"

"And I bet he's got that huge . . ."

"Low. Fucking. Blow. Anna!" I shout at the top of my lungs. She just laughs, the bitch.

"I'm just saying," she laughs. "Maybe you already found what you've been looking for," She shrugs.

"And what about you?" I ask.

"Maybe I already found it too but it slipped right through my fingers."

I look at Anna more closely than I have over the last year. Maybe there's more to her than I realized. Or maybe I'm a really shitty friend and I just never bothered to ask. Why is she even friends with me?

"Do you want to talk about it?" I ask.

"Not even a little bit," She looks over her shoulder.

"Well hello, Pot. It's nice to meet you, my name is Kettle," I say as I try to lighten the mood. When she rolls her eyes, I know that it worked.

She sighs heavily. "He decided undercover work was more important than me. Thought he could drop me like a bad habit for two years and I would be happily waiting for him when he surfaced. I don't even know if he's still alive." She shrugs. "I'm just saying, it's old news," she says before she visibly brightens and her eyes twinkle with wicked glee. Well, fuck. "Wes on the other hand, is breaking news."

"Ugh, don't remind me," I say as I cover my face with my hands.

"I take it you have seen the coverage your case is getting?"

"Speaking of old news . . ." I sigh. "And yeah, I did. I wish they would forget about it. I wish everyone would just freaking forget about it."

"Everyone else will move on when you have," Anna says softly.

"What makes you think I haven't?"

"Do I look like I'm new here?" She asks as she rolls her eyes.

"No," I concede.

"You'll get there," Anna assures me.

"I'm not so sure that I will," I say. "Too many things are bubbling just under the surface. I feel like I'm drowning and I can't pull myself out of it."

"Maybe you just need to reach for one of the hands that's been waiting to pull you out," she says softly. "We've all been waiting, Claire. All you have to do is reach out."

"I know. Maybe one day I will."

"You will," she smiles confidently.

"Can you take me to my car?"

"Yay! I love walks of shame!" She claps her hands with glee.

"Why do I keep you?"

"Because you love me best," she smiles brilliantly.

"That I do."

"Now say please and thank you and I will not only take you to your car, but I will give you my spare set of keys to said car and your apartment."

"Please and thank you!" I jump up excited. I had forgotten about my keys which are probably somewhere in Wes's house. "You're the bestest ever!"

"Thank you! What have I been trying to tell you all this time?"

chapter 25

how long

"NO BRA? CHECK," ANNA ticks off on her fingers as she pulls into a spot in front of the station.

"Anna."

"No shoes? Check."

"Anna."

"No wallet or purse? Check check."

"This is unnecessary."

"Do you want my spare keys or not?" She asks triumphantly.

"You know I could just shoot you, right?"

"You won't," she shrugs. I'm getting more and more frustrated by the minute as she dangles them just out of reach.

"Anna."

"Hair that says you've definitely just been fucked and well fucked at that? Check!"

"This is beneath you," I add.

"Your brother and Wes staring at you from the front door of the station?" She prattles on.

"What?" I look over to where she's looking and sure enough there they are. They look both worried and pissed.

". . . Check!"

"God damn it, Anna. Give me the fucking keys!" I shout.

"Don't do anything I wouldn't do!" She cheers as she tosses me the keyring.

I snatch the keys out of the air and take off running barefoot towards my SUV. Wes and Liam see me and hot foot it in the same direction but they'll never reach me in time. I am significantly closer to the car than they are. And I'm faster.

"Don't do it, Claire!" Liam shouts.

"Claire!" Wes calls for me, but I can't look at him. Not right now. Maybe not ever.

"Not now," I shout as I beep the locks.

"Please! We have to talk," he pleads.

The minute my hand hits the door handle, my foot is on the running board and I'm jumping into the car. I hit the door locks as soon as the driver door closes. My hands are shaking so bad, it takes me three tries to get the key in the ignition. It causes me to lose precious time that I could be using to escape.

Wes pulls on the handle of the passenger door as he pounds on the window. I get the engine to turn over and put the car in reverse.

"Claire," he shouts as he pounds on the window. "Let me in, baby."

I shake my head no, looking straight ahead.

"Please, baby. You have to talk to me. We have to talk about this."

"No," I say quietly but I know he hears me by the way his pounding on my passenger window becomes more frantic.

"This is fucking crazy, Claire!" He roars. "Let me the fuck in. Now!"

"No," I say as I start to back out of my spot.

"Claire," Liam shouts from behind Wes. "This is ridiculous. Get out of the fucking car."

"No."

"Claire, baby, get out of the car," Wes goes back to pleading.

"Claire, I will fucking fire you if you don't get out of that car and talk to Wes and I right the fuck now," Liam barks.

I shake my head. I can't. I can't look at them and have them see me as weak and broken. They know that I am and so do I, but I just can't face it. I can't watch Wes shut me out again because of it.

I tap the gas again.

"Stop, Claire!"

"No," I say. "I can't."

I keep backing up. I'm almost out of the parking spot when Wes hits the window so hard I think he might break the glass.

"God damnit, Claire. I fucking love you!" He thunders, but it's too late.

"I'm sorry," I say as I drive away. "I told you you shouldn't," I whisper to no one.

It was always too late for us. It was too late when that man took me and it was too late for us when I stumbled into his arms when I escaped. It was too late when I gave Wes my virginity and he threw it all back in my face. And it sure as hell was too late now when he blew into my life like a hurricane and he'll blow back out leaving the same wake of destruction.

We were simply never meant to be.

• • •

The drive back to my apartment is not a silent one.

My phone rings over and over again from the cup holder next to me. It rings again. I pick it up and look at the screen . . . *Wes*. Again. I silence it and keep driving.

It rings again and I sigh, frustrated. I stop at another red light. I pick up my phone again and look . . . *Liam*. Fuck. I silence it and hit the gas when the light turns green.

I know that they will both be looking for me. They want to convince me, sway me around to their way of thinking. As I sit in my car, I realize that they always do. Liam plays the protective big brother who recruits our father when he needs to for his cause. Dad is ever so helpful when it comes to thwarting my plans.

And don't even get me started on Wes. Wes does not dote on me in an effort to force me into compliance. Oh, no. Wes fights with me and fucks me into his way of thinking. And he's good at it.

It is no secret that I was in love with Wes from the time I was a little girl. A harmless crush, that's what my mother had said. But over time it has blossomed into something more. I had thought that he would always be the one.

In my youthful naivete I thought that Wes would come home from the Navy to me. And in a way, he did. I was a newly minted eighteen-year-old when Wes and Liam came home on leave and for the first time, Wes had looked at me the way that I had always hoped for—the way I yearned for—and so I gave him everything I had. I gave him my body and my heart. Simply put, I had given Wes *me*.

And at the first hurdle, he turned his back on me.

But now he's back. This week, Wes returned to my life like an unruly storm over the sea and I was helpless to stop him. If I was being honest with myself—which I am *definitely* not—I would admit that I have never stopped loving Wes and he knew it. He seized upon it and made me feel like I had something to hold onto, something to believe in. Again.

Wes gave me his body, his magnificent body, which has only gotten better with time. He is no longer the lean twenty something, but a man bulky with muscle and lines around his beautiful eyes that show he both scowls and laughs and does both of them often, but in the sexiest of ways. And when he turned those eyes on me, I was hopeless. Oh, I fought, I did, but looking back now, I can see that I always knew I would fall to him, I would fall for him. Again. I probably always will. I can't say that this makes me feel good things for my future.

I pull into the parking lot of my apartment building and realize I can't park in my usual spot. Wes and Liam will see me at first glance and know that I'm back in my space. I drive right past my usual section and pull around back of the building and park there. I will have to walk a bit to and from my vehicle but it should give me at least one extra day before I have to deal with the two cave men. And possibly a third of slightly advanced age.

I step out of my department SUV and look back at it after I get a few steps away. I can't help but wonder if today will be the day that Liam manages to take it from me. To take everything away from me. It's not just the car, it's my job, my livelihood, my way of life, but all my hopes and dreams too. Why can't I be the one to catch the bad guy? Why does it get to be them? Because they have the dicks, obviously. Or they are dicks.

I sigh and beep the locks before heading around to the front of the building. The metal steps leading to my front door are so cold and icy that they burn my bare feet. But I can't rush them. There is a weariness that has settled in my bones and I can't seem to make my body move any faster. In my head I know that this is just the adrenaline let down after my last great escape, but in my heart I can't help but feel like everything is coming to a head and I just might not come out on the winning side.

I let myself into my apartment, quickly shutting and locking the door behind me. Not that it will stop Wes and Liam. I'm sure they could con my spare key from mom and dad in a heartbeat if they played the situation right. I'm pretty sure they could con the panties off of a nun with the intentions of a three way if they played the situation right, but that's neither here nor there.

My phone starts ringing again. This time I don't even stop to look at it. I just toss it onto the sofa after silencing it and keep walking towards my little bathroom, shutting that door behind me too. I turn the water to as hot as it will go which isn't much in this old building, but at this point, I'll take what I can get.

I strip off all of the clothes that I could manage to find over the floors and furniture of Wes's house, which is most definitely not a full set, onto the floor of my bathroom unceremoniously. I kind of want to dump them straight into the garbage, but those are my favorite jeans and I already lost my favorite boots this week.

Speaking of garbage, I can't help but turn my thoughts to the garbage bags that were stolen from the dumpster of my place. Who would want to cover their tracks badly enough to steal my kitchen trash? And for that matter, who would poison me? Besides Wes's mom, that is. I'm sure she wouldn't shed any tears if

I left this world a little earlier than originally scheduled.

The scalding hot water sluices over my back and shoulders. The heat stings with a delicious bite, one that I need to keep me grounded in the here and now. Now, when I feel like I am on such unsure footing. My ground is shaking and the world is spinning. If I can't right myself, who will? The answer is no one. I can't rely on anyone to take care of me but me.

I soap up my loofa and scrape it over every inch of my skin. I need the sting and the burn. I need it to distract me from the ache in my heart. I suppose that I should be thankful Wes showed me his true colors sooner rather than later, but part of me can't let go of the anger that I shouldn't have had to. I knew all along that this was how it would play out, but Wes pushed and pushed. And now look where we are.

I scrub my skin harder at that thought, but the sting doesn't seem to take away the hurt in my heart, the sourness swirling in my belly, or the guilt that I feel over Anthony Donovan. At the thought of the little boy that I couldn't save, I realize I have failed.

Suddenly, my loofa feels like a coiled snake in my hands. I drop it to the shower floor and rinse the soap from my hands. I hear my phone ringing through the bathroom door, but I know longer care. I shut the water off and step out.

I pull on clothes and pin my hair up on top of my head still wet. I don't care that it's cold and icy outside. I don't care about anything except finding Anthony's killer. And I will, damn it. I will find them.

I sigh as my phone rings again.

I pull on soft, thick socks and my second favorite pair of boots. My drop gun, the small .38 that I like to keep in my boot for backup, is lost to Wes. I hope he treats it well. It was one of my favorites but I have absolutely no intention of seeing him again to get it back any time soon. Maybe in like five years . . . maybe eighty. Give or take.

I clip my badge and my sidearm to my belt. Until the day I die, I will never know how I managed to have foresight enough to grab those on my way out the bathroom window. But I'm thankful I did. The department frowns on losing either of those and I feel like *left them in a random man's house* is not a suitable excuse. But then again, Wes isn't just some random man and that's what makes this all the worse.

My phone rings again. I think for a minute that I should change my ringtone to something like a fire alarm or the dive horn from a submarine. Nothing says your angry ex-lover and pissed off big brother are blowing up your phone quite like a klaxon. *Ahh-ooohhhh-Gah!*

I exit my bathroom, walking towards the front of my apartment with nothing but coffee on my brain and then I stop in my tracks because sitting there on my battered sofa is my dad. His eyes, that same haunting shade of violet as Liam's, as my own, shoot lasers at me. I am clearly in trouble.

"Hey, Pop," I wave my hand lamely. The smile on my face falters because we both know that it's bullshit.

"Sit down, Claire." He gestures towards the other end of the couch.

"I was actually just leaving," I whisper. "I'm really in kind of a hurry."

"I said sit down." I sit down.

"How long, Claire?" He barks.

I just stare at him. I'm not sure if he's asking how long I have been having the nightmares or how long I have been fucking my brothers best friend. At this juncture I feel it behooves me not to answer.

"I'll make it easier for you. How long have you been having nightmares?" He asks answering my unspoken questions.

I look down at my hands in my lap. I feel the tears pool in my eyes and sting my nose. I don't want to answer this. I'll tell him anything—anything at all—but this.

His rough fingers tip my jaw up to look in him the eye. "Answer me."

"Always," I let out on a sob.

He immediately pulls me into his strong arms, holding me close and stroking my hair like he did when I was little and upset because the boys wouldn't let me follow them around.

"I'm so sorry, my sweet girl," he hums, his voice gruff with emotion. "I'm so, so very sorry."

I let him rock me for a minute while I cry. It feels good to let someone else carry my burdens for awhile. But I know in the end, I will take them back because they are mine alone to carry. I don't want my dad or anyone else to hold onto the guilt anymore.

"It's okay," I sniffle. "I'm okay," I say as I wipe my face and pull back to look at my dad.

"It's not okay, babydoll," he says as he looks me in the eyes. "You're not okay, but you will be," he finishes with a twinkle in his eye. Uh-oh.

"Dad," I hedge.

"So now, let's talk about Wesley."

"Dad."

"He's a nice boy."

"Dad."

"Your brother was a little miffed but they worked it out."

"You mean Liam got in a good hit?" I roll my eyes.

"Of course," he laughs. "That's how they've always handled their misunderstandings. Even when they were little boys. And I'm here to tell you that it'll only get worse as they become old men like me."

I sigh.

"He loves you."

"He doesn't. He just thinks he does."

"He does, babydoll."

"You don't see the way he looks at me when I have a nightmare. I disgust him."

"And you don't see the way he has always looked at you when you're not looking."

"I deserve to have someone who will fight for me, not with me," I tell him.

"That you do, my angel. That you do," he smiles at me with that twinkle in his purple eyes.

I look at my dad, really look at him and can see love and hope in his eyes, not fear or disgust. But he's my dad, he is always going to want the very best for me. No matter what.

"I'm broken, dad," I whisper, looking just over his left shoulder.

"You're not," his voice rings out, adamant. There is no swaying his mind.

"Dad—"

"You're a little scuffed and dinged up, but you're not broken, babydoll. I see too much fire in you. You get that from your grandmother," he laughs. "God help us."

"She's a pistol, for sure." I smile back.

"That she is."

"I need to get going," I say softly. "I've got bad guys to catch."

"I mean it, Claire," he implores. "You're not broken."

I can't answer so I just nod as I stand up. My dad stands too and pulls me into his arms one more time for a dad hug. I don't know how he does it, but he always makes me feel a little better. Maybe not one hundred percent, but enough to feel like I can handle what life seems to be throwing my way.

My phone rings again as I walk to the kitchen to grab my borrowed keys from the counter. I look out at the sofa where it sits on the cushions face down. I could guess who it is or at least whom it might be, so I grab my keys and keep walking on by.

"You're going to have to answer them one day," he shakes his head.

"Yeah, but that day is not today, Pop," I toss over my shoulder.

He just laughs, "Just like your grandmother. Fuck us all."

I take a quick look through the peephole to make sure no one is lurking around my front door. With keys in hand, I exit the building keeping a watchful eye of my surroundings. Every time to exhibit this maneuver, I feel like an extra in *Charlie's Angels*.

The coast is clear so I carefully make my way back to the rear parking lot. I hold my breath hoping that neither Wes or Liam are waiting for me. I let it out in huge gust of air when it looks like I am alone. *For now.*

chapter 26
a small reprieve

MY DRIVE TO THE station is fraught with anxiety over seeing Wes. I hate that I ran. I hate that he makes me run. It's so unlike me. I'm a stand my ground, don't shoot until you see the whites of their eyes kind of gal, but Wes makes me feel weak and powerless. And I fucking hate that.

I feel the tension creep up my neck. I check my mirrors once more time before I circle around the station to park in the back, passing up my lucky spot out front. Later I would find out that I needed all the luck that I could get.

I climb out of my truck and head to the back door of the station. It puts me right outside of the Captain's office, but I'm hoping to use the opportunity to find out if the burrs in my bonnet are in situ before I reach the bull pen. As it turns out, they are not.

I do not stop to get coffee or visit with the other detectives and officers. They read my mood, or more than likely, Liam and Wes have already blown through here and told the tale of my break with sanity to all who would listen. This is more likely since my own father showed up to give me shit—loving shit, but shit nonetheless—this morning.

Either way, they are leaving me alone. That's a good thing. I need my space to figure everything out. But I see the side eyes that my fellow officers are giving me. They know. Everyone knows it all. By the pointed looks that they're throwing each other and the looks they are not throwing me, I know. They think I sold out. And really, I did. I slept with a Fed and then I lost my shit. That's about as low as a cop can get. I know now without a doubt that I can't stay here. My mission is clear: get in, get what I need, and get the fuck out.

I sit down at my desk, unlock the drawers and retrieve my flash drives. I pick the locks to retrieve the ones Wes stored in my partner's desk as well. I know without a doubt that I cannot stay at the station. Not today. So, I quickly stuff them in my pockets and relock my desk.

I hear a commotion and mix of voices at the front desk so I make quick time of leaving through the back, my desk chair still spinning in my wake when I hear familiar voices and realize I was right to leave.

"Lee, look," I hear Wes say.

"Where is she?" He barks. "Dammit, Jones. Fucking answer me!"

I creep down the hallway towards the rear exit. I need to leave. Now.

"You just missed her." I hear him say as I push open the door and run for my car.

I jump in my car at record speed and peel out of the parking lot just as Wes and Liam bust out of the door. I can see them standing there with their hands on their hips watching me leave again in my rearview mirror.

I see Wes pull his phone out of his pocket and dial what I assume is my number, but I don't hear my phone ring. I didn't notice it's absence until now. I probably would have answered it if it was here. Wes has a way of wearing me down. But it's not with me so I get a small reprieve.

•••

My drive from the station is filled with anxiety. Again. I can't help but wonder if I'm making the right choice. Should I be running from Wes, or should I be running to him? But I know that I can't. What I told my dad rings true to me. I need someone to fight for me, only then will I know that that man is worth it to me. Wes has only ever fought me. Over my career, my life, my abduction. He can't control those situations and therefore, he can't control me. But I'm not meant to be controlled. I have always been a free bird, at thirty years old, nothing has changed.

My belly rumbles loudly and I remember that I skipped breakfast during my jailbreak this morning. I would normally get delivery from the comfort of my apartment but I don't want to go back there. I'll be restless until I can figure this case out. I can't sit still. I can't go home because I need to stay away from Wes. Wes clouds my head. I can't think clearly when I'm around him and that is a dangerous position to be in. Without a clear mind, someone could get hurt, or worse . . . *killed*.

My stomach growls again and I decide to stop for lunch. I briefly consider Chinese when I see the characters on the sign of my favorite place. My former favorite place. But the thought of being poisoned has my stomach turning sour and I decide against it. I will drive another block to a sandwich place.

I turn at the light and drive around to the parking lot where I pull into the first available space. The wind is cold and biting as I step from my SUV reminding me that winter is almost upon us. I pull my coat tight around me as the wind whips.

The hair on the back of my neck stands on end and I'm overwhelmed with the feeling of being watched. I stop and look over my shoulder but there is no one there other than the normal everyday lunch crowd. Still, I can't stop the feeling that something is not right. Someone out there is not the everyday lunch goer, someone is operating on malice and ill will. Could it be the bad man? Has he finally come back for me?

My face has been all over the news in conjunction with the Donovan case. Could that be what finally led the bad man back to me? The worst part is, of all I can remember, everything that I dream of, I cannot for the life of me, remember his face. The smell of his breath and the feel of his hand as it slapped my face? Every bit of it. But his face is veiled in shadows. Anna thinks my brain won't let me remember, that it's locked the information away to protect me from the horrors I experienced at his hands.

I look back over my shoulder one more time hoping to see something . . . someone. I don't know what. But there is nothing, not one thing, that stands out to me. But the feeling remains. Something is wrong. I pick up my pace as the rain and sleet start pouring down and I dive through the door to the deli with my hair soaking wet and chilled to the bone. The bell rings as I push the door open and the kids that work the deli counter look up at me and wince.

"It must really be coming down out there," the teenage girl says as I walk up to the order counter.

"It just started while I was walking across the lot," I say as I push my wet hair back from my face.

"Well come on in and get something good to eat," she smiles a white smile splitting her mocha face in half. "What can we get you?"

"A bowl of chicken noodle, with a huge hunk of crusty bread, and hot, hot coffee. As hot as you can make it, please," I smile back.

"Coming right up!" She says as she rings up my lunch.

I give her my money and take my number and my coffee mug over to the drink counter. Steam rises from my mug as the coffee pours from the big carafe and I can't help but sigh. I doctor it up just the way that I like it and find myself a table.

A shiver runs up my spine. My grandmother would say someone stepped on my grave. I can't help but hope that that is later rather than sooner. I scan the deli but don't see anything out of place. I'm lost in my thoughts when the young girl from the counter drops off my soup with an extra huge hunk of bread. I jump a little at the intrusion but she smiles sheepishly so I wink at her and offer up my thanks before digging into my meal.

As I eat and warm up I stare out the window, watching the ice and rain fall. I lose myself in my thoughts of Wes. If I'm being truthful with myself, I have feelings for him. But whether or not we have a future? I don't know.

What I need to do is lose myself in thoughts of this case. I can't help but be frustrated that it's taking me this long to figure it out. Although my focus has been lacking, the heart of the matter is a lost little boy who will never come home. Poor Anthony Donovan had to have trusted someone that he shouldn't have. I know from firsthand experience how dangerous that can be.

His family will never see him happy and alive again. I feel a twinge of guilt in my belly again at the idea that I survived and he did not. It's almost as if there can only be so many kids recovered and my taking a spot took one of them away for all of the lost kids to come. I know that it's an irrational thought, but when faced with the idea that a family lost their child, it's very real in my mind. But could one of his own be responsible for his death? As awful as it seems, it happens more than I care to admit.

Jonathan Ascher is out, mostly because he's dead. And whoever delivered him to the pearly gates tried to send me along for the ride. I'm trying not to cheer them on because he was molesting his stepdaughter.

Elizabeth Ascher is an odd duck. She was so upset when she found out that Anthony was missing and now that he's dead, she is fully removed. She would not let us interview her daughter, Kasey, and then turned on her when she found out she was sleeping with her husband. I can't figure her out. What's right and what's wrong? What's the truth and what is the lie?

Anthony Donovan, Senior was inconsolable when he found out that his son was missing and livid when he found out that his ex-wife's new husband was violating his daughter, rightfully so. But poison doesn't seem like his style. Especially given the way he laid Jonathan Ascher out in the police station.

Kasey Donovan is also a contradiction. On one hand she flirts with Wes in the most inappropriate ways. She was carrying on what she thought to be a romantic affair with her stepfather when she was only sixteen years old. But on the other hand, she was too emotional for us to interview her when little Anthony went missing, which makes sense since it was on her watch that he was taken.

My spoon scrapes the bottom of my bowl before coming up empty and sadly, I am no closer to solving this case than I was before. My only prize is that I am warmer and fueled up. What I need is to be on the street. I stand up and throw back the last of my coffee. I wave to the nice kids behind the counter and head back out into the ice and rain, but I don't care.

This ends today.

chapter 27
drive

I PUSH OPEN THE door to the deli, the tinkling bells are drowned out by the pouring rain. I beep the lock on my SUV and make a run for it but I'm soaked through again by the time I jump in.

I buckle my seatbelt and start the car as the rain pelts down all around me. As I pull out of the parking lot I'm lost in my thoughts. I drive down a small side street and get stopped at a light. There is something that I'm missing when it comes to the key players of this case. There has to be.

A white panel van at the cross-street drives through the intersection in front of me as lightning crashes and I am instantly lost to another time. Taken back to the last time I was truly lost and helpless.

• • •

I'm stomping through the woods behind out house. I don't need those gross boys to have some fun. And those boys are gross! They smell weird and put on too much spray stuff when they think I'm not looking.

I just make it to the street on the other side of the trees from our house when a white van pulls up next to me. I hear my mom in my head telling me not to talk to strangers. I feel my eyes going wide as he steps out of the van.

"Claire!" He says and I wonder how he knows my name. "There you are. I need your help!"

"What do you need help with?" I ask.

"I'm so glad you asked, Claire," he says my name again like he says it all the time. It's weird but I don't think too much about it. "My puppy, Millie, got out. She's missing. Can you help me find her?" He asks.

"I don't know. I should probably go back home . . ." I say.

"No!" He shouts and it startles me. His eyes widen when he notices my reaction. "I need you to look for her while I drive around. I'll give you this candy bar if you help me . . ." He offers, holding up my most favorite kind. I instantly grab for it, but he pulls it back.

"Okay, what does she look like?" I ask.

He smiles a creepy smile, but I open the front door and get in the van. He hands me the candy bar and I realize that I don't even know what his name is.

"She's little and fluffy and white . . ." He trails off as I dig into the sweets my mom never lets me eat before dinner. Ever!

• • •

A horn beeps behind me pulling me out of my daydream. But it's not dream, it's a memory that won't let me be.

My palms and my hairline are sweaty but I'm chilled to the bone. I step on the gas and pull through the intersection. The light had turned green and I missed it because I was lost in my own head. I raise my hand to wave my apology to the driver behind me but my hand is shaking so I put it back on the steering wheel and grip it tight.

My head is pounding and the soup in my belly is threatening to make a reappearance. What happened? Am I finally losing it? I have never had a dream in the middle of the day—while I was awake. I have always had them while I was sleeping. Always. I'm scared. I don't know how to process this new development.

I pull into the parking lot of a strip mall. I need to get my bearings. Right now, I'm freaking out. My heart is beating wildly in my chest and I can't catch my breath. I throw my SUV in park and set the brake. My hands shake the whole time.

I need Anna. Anna is the only one who can talk me down from something like this. It feels like the walls of the car are closing in on me and sucking up all the air. I need Anna. I reach for my phone in the cupholder where I always stick it when I'm driving and realize I left it in my apartment when I was so mad at Wes for blowing up my phone and Liam for calling my dad in as back up in their war to get me off the job and barefoot and pregnant. Not. Happening. But I still need my phone. I need to talk to Anna. Shit!

Wait. I can do this. I can. I'm stronger than this I know it. I hold onto the steering wheel to keep me grounded in the here and now. I breathe in long and deep once, twice and a third time without letting any out, and then I slowly let it all out. I repeat the exercise they taught us in marksmanship training at the academy. It works to slow your heart rate and narrow in your focus.

When I open my eyes again, I feel calmer. The panic driving my erratic breathing and anxiety has lessened, but not left me fully. I take one more deep breath. I pop the brake and put my car in drive. I can and I will do this.

I like to drive to clear my thoughts. I always have. When something was bothering me as a kid, my dad would put me in the car and we would just drive around. While he drove us, we talked about anything and everything. By the time we got home, usually after a stop for the world's best ice cream, I felt better. Not one hundred percent, but enough to know that I could tackle anything.

To this day, I still love to drive when I need to work out a problem in my brain. There is no bigger problem that I can't work through than the disappearance and murder of Anthony Donovan. There are too many twists and turns, too many snarls along the way for me to be able to see clearly what happened. And truth be told, I have no ideas.

I drive for what feels like ages with no specific destination in mind. I drive through the neighborhood where Anthony lived with his parents, but the street is barren. No one is home, no kids are out playing and it looks like a ghost town.

It's such a pretty little neighborhood with tall brick houses and others covered with pristine white siding. The lawns are all carefully manicured, not one blade out of regulation length. The flowerbeds are perfectly tended with delicate rose bushes lined up like neat little soldiers. But it's the secrets that hide inside those houses that make this beautiful street ugly. Those secrets are sharper than the thorns on those rose bushes and can do way more damage than one little prick. It's my job to find out what they are and expose them.

I straighten my shoulders and firm up my resolve. I can do this. I exit the neighborhood and keep driving, thinking about secrets. What do those secrets have in common with Chinese food? Who would want to keep those secrets hidden so badly that they would poison both me and Jonathan Ascher with the same take out? That's what keeps getting me. The why and the who.

Elizabeth Ascher does not want me to expose her secrets, but by all accounts, she loved her husband and didn't want him to die. She sided with him instead of her daughter. But according to the teller at the bank, Mr. Ascher was just Elizabeth's meal ticket. That there was no love lost. No one even knew that they were seeing each other until they turned up married.

Anthony Donovan, Senior definitely wanted Jonathan Ascher dead. But I can't see him being so sneaky or underhanded about it. I see Mr. Donovan as more of a beat someone to death or give them a bullet to the brain kind of guy. Poison is so sneaky. And where does that leave me? What beef would he have with me that was large enough for him to want to poison me? I can't find one reason why he would want me dead.

Wes's mom, on the other hand, I could totally see poisoning me to keep me away from her precious baby boy, but even I have to admit that she wouldn't poison Jonathan Ascher. They didn't even know each other and besides, she's not the kind of woman to get her hands dirty.

Wes.

My mind will always go back to where it doesn't belong. I let myself imagine a life with Wes while I drive around. One where we both go to work in the morning, fighting crime like superheroes. Well, I'm the super hero, he wears wingtips for crying out loud. But I digress.

We would come home to each other every night. Wes and I would share meals and laughter. In my perfect world, he would hold me when I was sad or scared, but let me live my life like the independent woman I am and not like some china doll meant to be put up on a shelf where life passes her by. He wouldn't look at me like I was crazy, he would look at me like I was powerful and important.

Maybe one day, there would be a little boy with Wes's brown hair and my violet eyes and a little girl with black hair and green eyes chasing after him. Without a doubt, Wes's children will be beautiful. So smart and vivacious. I can see them wanting to know every little thing and bouncing around with excitement as they figure something new out, as they find other things in this world waiting to be discovered. And I find myself very much wanting those children to be mine. But it's wasted time dreaming of things that can never be.

I continue to drive around George Washington Township hoping that something, anything will jog my brain, but I stay locked in my thoughts about Wes and my past, unable to put those demons to rest until the radio breaks me out of my fog.

". . . This just in . . . We have it on good authority that the infamous Detective Claire Goodnite of the GWTPD has been released from duty, effective immediately. A statement was released from the office of Captain Goodnite also of the GWTPD. Whatever happened can't be good if your own brother fires you,"

"That's right, Marsha. As always, we will be following up on this story and all other news as it comes in. Now, what's new in sports . . ."

Fuck! I slam my palm against the steering wheel. Fired by my own brother. Not that I didn't see that coming a mile away, but still, it stings. I can't believe Liam had the balls to do it. I'm not going to be able to speak to him for a month of Sundays. God damnit! My job was everything to me. And I need this case. He knows it. He knows how much I need to solve this case.

And he didn't even call me. But then again, I left my phone at home with dad, so he could have tried, who knows. But still. A press release. He couldn't wait to fire me to my face.

I drive and drive until I find myself just a block away from the falls. The last place Anthony Donovan was possibly ever alive. Or maybe not. All we know so far is that his body was found on the rocks at the bottom of the falls.

It's then that I notice someone standing at the fence overlooking the falls. The silhouette is familiar. And suddenly, all the pieces of the puzzle start falling into place.

Oh. Fuck.

chapter 28
demons

Wes

I FUCKED UP.

I fucked up so bad I don't know if I can ever fix it. But I have to fucking try, or die fighting. Because this is everything. *She* is everything.

Twelve years ago, I was barely a man. I was infatuated with the idea of Claire finally becoming a woman. A woman that I could have, that I could touch. I was taken with her beauty, her hair the color of midnight and eyes so purple they belong to a witch. A beautiful witch who commanded my every thought. And with curves like hers, they were naughty thoughts. I thought of nothing but commanding her body, my mouth on her skin and my cock so deep in her pussy we lost where I ended and she began.

But I was unprepared for reality when I took her. I took her love and her body in ways I would dream about for years to come. I made love to Claire like I never have to any other woman because in my heart, I knew it was always her.

The hard truth was Claire was haunted by demons from her past and I was still tied to an enlistment in the United States Navy. I had planned to marry her as soon as I could and take her back to Coronado with me. However, I knew I couldn't take her away from her home and her family and move her all the way across the country only to leave her at a moment's notice when I was called up.

The life of a SEAL is never easy, but the lives of their wives is even harder. Your husband could leave in the middle of the day or the dead of night depending on the time of the call. Then you hope and you pray that your sailor comes home from that mission in the worst possible places all while knowing there is always a chance that they won't.

When I woke up the morning after spending the best night of my life with Claire, the girl of my dreams, I realized she was being held hostage in the tight in the clutches of a nightmare. When she screamed out, my heart broke because I realized there was no saving her. Claire had to find a way to save herself. I also knew that there was no way she was coming with me to California like this. And I knew without a doubt that my sweet, loving Claire would fight me if I told her the truth, so when she woke up, I broke her heart too. All while vowing that I would finish out my enlistment and come back home to New Jersey to start a career in law enforcement. Then, only then, would I claim my girl for once and for all.

And I did that. I did all of it, never realizing how badly I had hurt Claire. Never knowing that her heart was irrevocably broken and she would never trust me or any other man again. I had no idea how deep her pain ran. I also had no idea that she was still living within the nightmare she endured twenty-four years ago.

So, while I was forcing my way into her life and strong arming my way into her heart and her bed, never letting up, never giving her a moment to catch her breath, I didn't realize that she was suffering. I didn't realize that the nightmares gripped her so deeply. That is until last night when she woke up screaming in my arms again. But this time, I didn't force her back to her family for help. Help I now realize she never got because she hid her trauma so well, like a wounded big cat, never letting you see their weakness or vulnerability. No, this time, she ran. My girl was so afraid that I would break her all over again, that she ran. From me. And that stings.

I realize now that I should have hid the emotions rolling across my face when we woke up. But I was tired. Claire and I have been working the Donovan case for days with no breaks and her being poisoned scared the ever-loving shit out of me. Not to mention that instead of sleeping, I have been fucking Claire at every available moment. So, I was tired. Coupled with the fact that I want her as my partner in life and in my bed, *forever*, I did not think to mask my feelings. And that was when I fucked up.

I should have hidden my emotions because if I had known last night what I know now, I would see that showing her my sorrow for her suffering would only make her think I was disgusted with her, that I thought she was broken and unworthy of my love and affections. That couldn't be further from the truth. If anything, I don't deserve her. Sure, I'll give her shit and I will own her body, but in reality, we're equals, we're partners.

When she locked herself in the bathroom, I realized she was freaking out so I called Lee. Not only is he her brother, but he's my best friend. I needed his help. I knew he wanted her out of the field and behind a desk or at home in some man's kitchen, but I didn't realize how deep their feud over the matter ran. So by calling him, I fucked up again. Hindsight is always twenty-twenty and all that bullshit, but even I can see the pattern of my own stupidity where Claire Goodnite is concerned. Claire didn't see it as me reaching out to our family for help. Oh no, she saw it as me calling her brother to come riding in with the men with the big butterfly nets, elephant tranquilizers, and funny jackets to cart her off to the funny farm. Fuck!

Never in my wildest dreams would I have imagined the girl of my dreams, the woman I have been rapidly falling in a forever kind of love with, jumping out my guest bathroom window. That's the kind of moment that can traumatize a guy for life.

So, I chased her ass down the street. But Claire is one of the best fucking cops I have ever met. Even without her spare gun, boots, and underwear, she managed to escape me. For now.

Lee and I tracked her. From the moment I realized I had lost her, I back tracked to my house. I threw on jeans, a sweatshirt, my favorite running shoes. I also grabbed my jacket, badge, and gun on the way out before locking up my house.

Liam had shown up by then, a little irritated to have been forced out of some woman's bed but unlike usual, he wouldn't tell me who. I don't have time to question his SOP. I was so distracted that I missed the right hook that landed on my left eye when I opened my front door to him.

"Don't even ask what that was for," he shouted.

"I think I can draw my own conclusions."

"I told you not to hurt my sister," he growls.

"I didn't mean to, it was a misunderstanding, but now I have to find her," I pleaded like a big fucking baby. Thankfully, being my pathetic sad self seemed to pull Lee to my side.

"I'll help you, but let's not make a habit of this."

He then seemed to shake off his anger and was back to being my lifelong best friend. Here to help me get my girl.

I tracked Claire's whereabouts while Lee called in his dad who was none too pleased to hear I had taken up with his daughter before talking to him or Lee about it. Once he found out that Lee hit me when I opened the door, he roared with laughter and said he had an idea of where she might be. We just had to hang tight, but until then, I was going to trace all of the places I thought she might be.

By the time we hit the station I thought I had her, but once again, she slipped through my fingers. Lee chose to stay behind and keep me posted. His dad said he thought he had gotten through to her, but only time will tell. All I know is that I need to make things right with her, I need to stitch up the wounds that I didn't know I had cut into her so deep. Claire is mine, she's my everything and I need her to know that. I want to protect her, but I also want to stand by her side in all things. This case has shown me how great we work together both in and out of my bed.

So here I am, what feels like just a few steps behind her still, when I trace the different crime scenes of our case. I just left the suburb where the Donovan children lived with the Ascher's. Claire was right, we're missing something. I just can't figure out what.

I take the highway a few miles and exit at the falls. I make my way towards the falls, an iconic spot here in New Jersey, long before poor Anthony Donovan's remains were found on the rocks.

I'm maybe less than a block away when something tells me not to drive in so I pull into a lot and park. I lock up my vehicle and pocket my keys. I pull out my phone and send a quick text to Lee.

Me: I'm at the falls, something doesn't feel right. No sign of Claire.

Lee: I'll send a black and white by. Hang tight.

Me: Willco

My last message to Lee was willco, or I *will comply*, but it was a lie. I know in my gut that something is off. And my gut is never wrong. It saved both Lee and I on many an op so I know in the end he will understand that when it comes to his sister, I'm not waiting.

I take off on foot, careful to go unnoticed by those on the streets. At this point in the case, I'm not sure who I can and can't trust and that is not a good thing. It's damned dangerous. So far, the good guys are me, Lee, and Claire.

I turn the corner and I am across the street from the fenced in area overlooking the falls. I take one step across the street, and then another. I'm almost there when the world explodes around me. Or you could say, my world explodes as someone I do not recognize at first raises their arm towards Claire, with a gun in their hand, right before Claire goes over the edge of the falls.

I don't even think before I act, the movements ingrained in my brain and my body hardened by years as a SEAL and then with the FBI. I pull my own sidearm from my belt and fire before screaming.

"No!" Is torn from my lungs. And just like that, I have lost her again. My Claire, the only girl I will ever love.

chapter 29
in for a penny, in for a pound

Claire

"KASEY?" I ASK AS I step out from the shadows. Anger and malice flash across her face before she drops down her mask of faux innocence.

All of a sudden the last tumbler rolls into place. And it all makes sense. I'm not looking at a lost little girl, I am looking at a cold-hearted killer.

"Is everything alright, Kasey?" I ask choosing not to show my hand too early.

"Of course, Detective, why wouldn't it be?"

"We haven't found your brother's killer yet," I say softly. "That has to bother you."

"You're not going to," she laughs a mean laugh. "I heard your own brother booted you off the case."

"I admit that stings a little," I nod. "But it doesn't mean I will stop before I find the responsible party."

"So, you're here alone?" She asks. "No one knows where you are," she surmises.

"Of course they do," I lie. "Captain Goodnite and Agent O'Connell know every move I make. In fact, I just got off the phone with them."

She chuckles again. This can't be good. And fuck if I'm not out here in the cold with no back up just like she said. Shit, shit, shit!

"You know what I think?" She asks.

"No, Kasey, what do you think?"

"I think no one knows you're here," she smiles a Cheshire Cat grin. "I think you figured it all out, didn't you?"

"Why did you do it, Kasey?" In for a penny, in for a pound.

She lets out a menacing laugh. "Why do you think?" she snarls. "They always left me to take care of him. I was tired of it."

"But Anthony was your brother, Kasey."

"Do you think I care about that?"

"Tell me what do you care about, Kasey?"

"I just wanted my own life, you know?"

"I do," I tell her. "My own family is very overbearing. Tell me about it?"

"I just wanted to go on a date with a boy," she whispers sounding all of the sixteen years old that she is.

"And what boy was that?" I ask softly.

"That's not important," she snaps.

"Okay," I hold my hands up, palms out, placating her. "Tell me what is important."

"They wouldn't let me go!"

"Who wouldn't let you go?" I ask all while knowing.

"My mom and Jonathan. He said he didn't want me dating boys but it was so he could keep playing his games with me while my mom was gone or asleep."

I knew it. That sick fuck was keeping his step daughter isolated so that he could keep molesting her for as long as possible. He kept her unsullied by teenage boys so that he could have her himself behind his wife's back. No wonder the kid snapped.

"I couldn't keep doing it, you know?" She asks, breaking the silence that surrounds us.

"I do, honey."

"But none of that matters now."

"Why is that?"

"Because I'm leaving Jersey,"

"How do you figure?" I ask. "You're sixteen years old. You need a car, a job, and parents."

"Parents?" She laughs again. "That's rich. Haven't you met my parents? My dad left me to my mom who doesn't give not one shit about me." I had to agree that her mom is kind of a huge bitch.

"And my mom left me to that monster who hurt me, like all the time!" She screams. "And then when he wanted to parade my mom around I had to watch the baby! How unfair is that?"

"It's very unfair," I whisper. "Did you ever try to talk to your mom about the abuse?"

"Why bother?" She asks.

"Because she's your mother and could have stopped it." That little nugget of wisdom only makes her laugh harder.

"My mom married Jonathan so he could get to me," she looks at me with her cold, dead eyes. "He gave her and Anthony a lavish life in exchange for me. My own mother sold me." Oh fuck. I hadn't figured on that.

"So, you poisoned him in the jail."

"Of course," she looks at her fingernails with obvious teenage boredom. "He had to die."

"But what about me?" I ask. "Why poison me?"

"You ask too many questions," she sighs. "And Wesley is dreamy." Oh fuck. That's awkward.

"But why not your mom?"

"Oh, she's next. Just as soon as I get rid of you," she says. "Come over here . . . About how good of a swimmer would you say you are?"

Shit, shit, shit! I look around me for anyone who might have heard her. Someone who might have seen us talking at the falls. All I see is a drug deal going down about half a block away. A big, burly white biker guy and a couple of teenage thugs. What the hell?

I only have one real choice to make, so I take a deep breath and pull my gun from my hip. "I'm afraid I'm going to have to stop you right there," I tell her.

Unfortunately, during my survey of the land and various drug dealers, I did not hear the approach of a new comer. That is, until I heard the click of a gun being cocked behind my head. Well, damn.

Kasey's smile grows wide.

"I'd like you to meet my boyfriend, Detective. I think you know each other," she laughs again.

I turn around and come face to face with the last person I ever thought would pull a gun on me. "Bobby?"

"The one in the same," he smiles at me. "Drop the gun," he says as he points to my hand and I do because I'm out of options.

"You poisoned me?"

"Of course," he answers.

"And Jonathan Ascher?" I ask.

"I couldn't let him hurt her anymore," his eyes narrow and he gets visibly angry.

"But why Anthony?" I ask.

"He was in the way," Bobby shrugs. "And she asked me to."

"It's that simple?" I ask incredulously. "She asks and you carry out?"

"Yes," he says simply. "I would do anything for her. No one is ever going to hurt my Kasey ever again."

"You won't get away with it," I say lamely. They both laugh.

"We already have," Kasey says. "Look around you. No one is coming to save you."

I do as she asks. It's just us here and the drug dealers in the twilight haze of early night. She's right. No one here is going to save me. Well hell, if I'm going to die, I might as well go down swinging.

Kasey is in between me and the fence to the falls behind us. Bobby is in front of me. He raises his arm holding the gun. I back up a few steps, getting some distance between us.

Bobby just laughs.

"Just shoot her already!" Kasey snaps.

"You have nowhere to run," Bobby laughs, obviously enjoying his cat and mouse game.

"Just watch me," I say as I turn around and run.

I hit Kasey in the middle of the chest with my arms, driving both her and I through the fence and over the edge of the falls. Her screams echo all around us but I still hear the two gunshots that rent the air.

We hit the ground with a thud, Kasey on the bottom of our pile after we hit every rock and sharp edge on the way down, her more than me. Not that I'm going to let myself feel sorry for her. I hit my head on one of the last rock outcroppings right before we land at the bottom.

I open my eyes and look straight into the blank, unseeing eyes of the dead. I try to push myself up off of her but my wrist snaps all the way through when I lean on it. My head swims and my stomach rolls. And then everything goes black.

epilogue
tell me a story

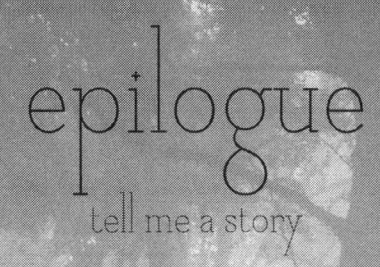

Claire
Four days later...

MY HEAD FEELS FUNNY and my ears feel full of cotton like last summer when I got an infection from swimming too much. I open my mouth to tell him something is wrong, but my words don't work. They won't come out! I turn my head to look at him, a scream stuck in my broken mouth. He just smiles his big, creepy smile and everything goes black . . .

When I wake up I'm on an old, yucky blanket on the floor of a dark, smelly house. It's not my house. I know that. I rub the side of my head, it hurts so much. When I look up, the strange man is leaning back in an old torn chair, his feet spread wide and there's a strange bump in the front of his pants that he keeps rubbing his hands on. He smiles when he notices that I'm awake and for the first time ever, I'm scared.

"Hello, Claire, I'm glad that you're awake," he says to me in a scary voice. I just sit there staring with my eyes big. "You may call me daddy."

• • •

A scream rents the air. My head is foggy, heavy even. My eyelids feel like they're full of lead but I have to open them. I have to get out of here. I have to help whoever is screaming. But then I realize . . . *it's me*.

"Claire!" I hear Liam shout. Someone shakes me. "Claire! It's me, Lee. Wake up. You're having a nightmare."

"It's no use, she won't wake up," I hear Wes say, he sounds broken. "I can't sit here, man. I can't sit by and watch her suffer like this. I have to do something."

"She's going to come out of it, Wes, you know it."

"At this point I don't know anything."

"You gotta have a little faith, brother," Liam says softly.

"Without her, Lee, I don't have any faith . . . I have nothing."

And then the darkness sucks me back in.

• • •

"It's time to come back to me, baby," I hear Wes's gruff voice say. I try to open my eyes but . . . *nothing*.

"She will, son," my dad says. "Now we just have to be strong."

"No, we thought we'd be weak," my mother snaps.

"Yeah, seems like a great day to pull her plug," my granny snaps. I can hear her roll her eyes out loud.

Pull my plug? What the fuck.

"You take all the time you need, my sweet girl," my dad whispers.

"That's right. We'll be here waiting, my lovely," Mom says. I feel someone's lips brush my hair and a strong hand squeeze mine.

And then the tide pulls me under. Again

• • •

"It's time to wake up, sis," Liam says.

He squeezes my hand.

"I need you to wake up, Claire. I thought we lost you once, I can't do it again. I barely survived it," he takes a deep breath. "Why do you think I try so hard to keep you out of the field? It's not because you're a girl. And it's definitely not because you can't do it. You're one of the best cops I know. But I can't live in a world without my baby sister."

I need to open my eyes. I need to reach out. I need to comfort my brother and tell him how much I love him. That I'm okay. That everything is going to be okay. I try and fight the waves that pull me under with everything I have. I feel a tingle zing down my arms and through my fingers. The warm current runs through my belly and down my legs and through my toes. Which I wiggle under my itchy blanket.

"If not for me, do it for Wes," he whispers.

"I would do anything for you," I rasp, my throat parched. I cough.

"Shit. Shit. Fuck! You're awake," my usually cool calm and collected brother flits around the room like a chicken with his head cut off. I never really understood that saying until right now, huh. I continue to cough. "Shit, let me get you some water. Fuck, let me get the nurse!"

"Water," I cough again.

Liam reaches for the cup on the bedside with the straw and puts it in my mouth and take several greedy sips and then cough again.

"Oh shit!" Liam barks again. "A nurse, we need the nurse!" He shouts as he bounces out of the room.

Does my brother, the Police Captain, calmly stand and walk out the door, or even pick up the call button and call the nurse on duty? No, he again runs all over and knocks a tray of medical tools over before shouting more curses and then running out the door. But only after he got tangled in curtain in front of the door to the room.

"Welcome back!" The nurse chirps as she walks swiftly in the room.

She checks my eyes, my throat and my blood pressure, all seem to check out, so she smiles sweetly at me.

"Your throat may be sore from being intubated. So liquid diet for the time being. I'll bring you some beef broth when you're up to it." I must have made a face because she throws her head back and laughs on the way out the door. I notice Liam watches her ass as she leaves.

I sigh.

"What?" he asks.

"You'll never change."

He laughs, "What? There is no handsome Fed waiting to sweep me off my feet. I just have to make due until then," he winks.

I sigh again.

"You need to talk to him," he says softly.

"I know."

"He's been beside himself. He helped pull you up from the falls. He chased you down when you went in with no backup and no phone or radio like a moron. You're suspended, by the way."

"I'm not fired?"

"No," he sighs.

"But on the radio . . ."

"Wes and I were hoping to flush the real killer out while taking the heat off of your back."

I nod, that makes sense. It was a great play, really.

"It was Kasey," I say softly.

"I know, honey."

"She killed her baby brother," I say.

"I know."

"She said it was because she was tired of babysitting, but Mrs. Ascher had said something about her missing pets. I missed so much."

"You can't beat yourself up over it. She was sick."

"Was?"

"You killed her with the weight of your fat ass."

"Not funny." Why do I have a brother again? Right now I'm not so sure. "And Bobby?" I ask.

"Wes shot him. It was a clean shoot. No suspension." After letting out a heavy breath he says, "I'm sorry, sis. I never wanted you to get hurt."

"It's not your fault, Liam," I say as I take his hand back in mine.

"I know. It's yours because you didn't let us help you."

"How long is it going to take for you to let that one go?"

"A long time. Longer than your suspension." I sigh. "Now about Wes . . ."

"I know."

"Just go easy on him, you put him through the ringer."

"Okay."

"He's out in the hall waiting."

"Send him in," I say. When Liam stands up and heads for the door. "I love you, fart breath," I say as I repeat the words of our childhood.

"And I you, dipshit."

I turn my head and look out the window. I don't know what to say to Wes. I don't know what he will have to say to me. I still have nightmares. I still don't know who took me, who hurt me all those years ago. I don't know if he can live with that. I only know that I have to for the time being.

A throat clears behind me. I turn to look at where the sound came from and there is Wes standing just inside the door leaning against the wall with his arms folded across his chest, his face blank but guarded. His hair is rumpled and he looks like hell. But still gorgeous. So much so, it's hard to stare at him knowing that he could hurt me so much. But Liam said to go easy on him.

"Hi," I say with an awkward little finger wave.

"Hi, beautiful," he rumbles from deep in his chest. But he doesn't move from his spot.

"Would you like to come in?"

"Yeah, baby."

"Okay."

Wes walks over and sits in the chair next to my bed that Liam had just vacated. I keep my hands carefully open but still on top of the blanket on either side of my legs. Still, but open. Wes looks at me and then down at my hands, then back at my face again before sighing heavily and taking my hand in his. A golden glow fills my heart and warms my body. I want to smile but it's too soon. He could still dump me.

"I see you're going to make me do all the work this time," he sighs again.

"No," I whisper.

"It's okay," he says. "I fucked up, baby," he says the words coming out of his mouth shocking the shit right out of me.

"What?"

"I pushed you too hard. I backed you into a corner and I made you feel like you couldn't talk to me about your dreams. Your memories of when you were taken and that is not the case."

"But . . . but you said you couldn't do it. You said I was too much drama twelve years ago."

"I lied."

"What?" I shout but I can't really shout because my voice is still raw.

"I knew that I was tied to the Navy for the rest of my contract, honey," he continues to rock my world. "And so was Liam. When you woke up screaming, I knew that I couldn't move you across the country away from your family. So . . . I lied."

I sit there with my mouth hanging open for who knows how long until he touches my chin with his calloused fingertips and closes my mouth for me. I look into his eyes and for the first time feel . . . *hope*. It's all going to be okay.

". . . so I was thinking we could try dating . . ." I must have missed something important. How embarrassing that I was so lost in his eyes that I missed what Wes was saying to me. By the smirk on his face, that big bastard knows it too.

"What?"

"I was saying that I won't push you too hard this time. We can take as long as you need before we settle down."

"How magnanimous of you," I grumble.

"But then you looked at my mouth like that and I remembered how much I like to eat you . . ."

"Wes." I look at him with a wariness in my eyes.

"I know," he sighs. "Slow. But I'll be ready when you are."

"Okay," I say smiling easy for the first time in a long time.

"Okay?" He asks. "We can date?"

"Yes."

"But no one else."

"Wes—"

"What?"

I sigh.

"Okay fine. But now I'm going to kiss you."

"What happened to slow?"

"I didn't say I was going to fuck you."

"Wes!"

"What? You don't have to sound so put out about it," he laughs.

"Just shut up and kiss me already."

"Yes, ma'am," he smiles and then he does, kiss me, enough to make my toes curl and just how I like it.

"You guys are so gross!" Liam shouts from the other side of the door.

"Go home already, Lee!" Wes shouts.

I just laugh. Yes, everything is going to be alright. It's a leap of faith for sure, but with my family and Wes, I'm ready to take it. I'm going to take it all because my life is waiting for me to live it. So I will.

the end . . . for now

VOLUME 2 OF THE claire goodnite SERIES

tuck me in tight

in loving memory . . .

Charlotte Jameson Atienza

November 14, 2017—November 17, 2017

For three days we held and angel in our arms and those were three of the best days of our lives. On her third day on earth, she went to sleep and never woke up. Charlotte was truly too beautiful for earth and born with a purpose far greater than we will ever comprehend.

While we will never truly understand the how or the why of infant loss our hearts go out to the families who have walked the same path. We miss her every day and know that we will hold her in our arms again one day.

As it always is with loss so deep, one day the dark sky will break into a beautiful dawn until then . . .

If our story has moved you please consider making a donation in honor of Charlotte to one of the following organizations so that we may one day see an end to infant death.

The March of Dimes (marchofdimes.org)
The American SIDS Institute (sids.org)

"Like a comet pulled from orbit
As it passes a sun
Like a stream that meets a boulder
Halfway through the wood
Who can say if I've been changed for the better?
Because I knew you
I have been changed for good . . ."
-*For Good* (Idina Menzel and Kristin Chenoweth)

dedication

To the last boy who ever broke my heart,
It hurt and at the time, I didn't know that the hurt would ever stop, but it was a blessing because it freed my heart to find Sean and he is my everything. He has given me a life of beauty. Our children are my world and I find a reason to smile and laugh every day. You were right to walk away when you did. Thank you.
Also, thank you for not becoming a serial killer.

prologue

THIS IS HOW MY heart breaks
What. The. Fuck.

I had sat down at my desk and opened a manila envelope that was left on top of my stack of mail. It had seemed harmless enough.

But it wasn't.

I blink my eyes over and over trying to make my brain process what it's seeing—but I can't. I can't unsee the images in the stack of pictures in my hand. Giant glossy eight by tens from different angles so there is absolutely no doubt that my heart is breaking.

And it is broken. It's not just broken, it's *shattered*.

"It's not what it looks like," I hear from behind me as he looks over my shoulder and I have to grit my teeth to keep from screaming.

I shuffle the pictures sliding the top one to the back of the stack so that I can see the next one. This one is zoomed in. His head is tipped back and his face is distorted with both lust and passion as she straddles his lap. Her hands hold his to her breasts and I can see the play of tendons flexing through them as he grips them tight. It was only two nights ago that his hands were on my own breasts in much the same way as I rode his cock on the sofa.

"Claire, did you hear me?" he asks but I shuffle the stack again.

In this picture, he has his arms wrapped around her back and he's pulling her close, her breasts mashed up against his strong chest. Her hands with long, red painted talons press in on either side of his face and as they kiss hungrily, their mouths open as their tongues tangle.

"Goddamnit, Claire! Did you hear me?" My spine turns to steel.

"I did. I'm just choosing to ignore you," I respond coolly.

"Don't do this, baby," he pleads.

"I'm not the one who did anything," I snap.

"I can explain." But I'm not interested in listening to him plead a case when he is more than guilty.

"I'm going to need you to leave, Wes."

"No."

"This changes everything," I say so softly even I struggle to hear the words that are coming out of my mouth.

"This changes nothing! Fuck that, Claire," he yells. "You want to run away. You have *always* wanted to run away. And here is your fucking reason to served up on a goddamn silver platter." Everyone around us in the bullpen is doing everything they can to make it appear that they are not listening, not studying the tragic demise of Claire and Wes with rapt attention. But we all know that they are.

"No," I shout back as I throw the stack of glossy betrayal down on top of my desk. I push my rolly chair back and stand. It slams into the desk behind mine. "You do not get to come in here, where I work, and tell me that I am to blame for your bullshit."

"Okay," he says quickly as he holds his hands up in surrender. "You're right. I'm sorry. I can see you need time."

"I need a lot of things. One of them is definitely distance."

"I don't know if I can give you that. I can't lose you, baby." His words burn hot behind my eyes and the last thing I want is for the guys in the bullpen to see me cry.

"You should have thought about that before you fooled around with that stripper."

"Claire—" he starts but I don't let him finish.

"You need to go now," I say softly.

I stand with my feet apart, my hands on my hips, and my head bowed as if I'm waiting for a blow. But I see him clearly even if only in my peripheral. He looks at me and opens his mouth as if he's going to try to explain again. Something in my stance must have told him it was a losing battle because he snaps his mouth closed before moving towards the exit.

Wes pauses just before opening the door to turn and look back at me, I see him in my peripheral, but I'm looking at his lies and deceit spread across my desk for all to see. He pulls open the door and slams it on his way out. I'm Detective Claire Goodnite and this is how my heart breaks.

chapter 1
bad girl

48 hours earlier...

"FUCK," HE GROANS AS I unzip his jeans and reach in, pulling out his hard cock.

It doesn't take much to have Wes hard and wanting—needing me and I love it. I had just finished dressing for the evening as he had let himself into my apartment. Wes had said that he wanted to see me before he went off to Jones's bachelor party and I went to dinner with Emma and Anna.

I'm wearing a tight black dress and matching four-inch heels. Anna wanted to check out some new swanky place in the city and despite spending her days being elbows deep in dead people, Emma can really turn herself out. She loves a good stiletto and I would hate to be the ugly friend in the group.

I'm standing over my bathroom counter slicking my lips a deep, sexy pink. I feel him standing there, my body always knows when Wes is near and it always has in one way or another. Deep in my heart I wonder if Wes and I were always meant to be.

I feel myself cracking, caving in, to love him. I fought it so hard but as it turns out, I never had a choice in the matter.

I cap the pink color and set it down just as he clears his throat. Then uncap the clear gloss that goes on top. I turn my head to look at him and the mood in the room goes electric. His gaze scorches my face as he looks me over. My face, my mouth, down to my breasts where they press up and out of the top of my dress, down my waist and hips to where the hem falls just shy of showing anything important and down, down my legs, before snapping back up to meet my eyes. By the sizeable bulge in jeans—he likes what he sees.

I smirk as I turn back to the mirror and slick my lips with the gloss. A feral growl rips from deep within his chest as he grips my hips in his hands and pulls me into him, his hard length cradled between my thighs as I lean over the counter. I drop my gloss to the vanity top.

Wes slides one palm down my belly and then down, down, down to press against my sex over my dress. He presses the fingertips of his other hand to my jaw to turn my head before crushing his mouth to mine in a hungry kiss.

When he pulls back I'm out of breath and wet.

"You're so fucking sexy," he pants. "Tonight, all I'll be thinking about is what might be underneath this dress and what those shiny pink lips look like wrapped around my cock."

"Then maybe you should find out." My voice is husky with my arousal.

"First things first," he says as his hand at the apex of my thighs slides a little lower. He hooks his fingers under the hem of my skirt and inches it higher and higher as he nibbles at the spot behind my ear that does things to me.

I open my eyes and look in the mirror. I gasp at what I see. The couple in front of me burns in the heat of passion. Her purple eyes are bright with excitement. Her skirt is rucked up around her waist exposing a tiny, lace thong with pencil thin strings.

The man stands not only behind her, but all around her—lost to her and his need. He not only worships her body as he kisses and caresses but possesses it as well. I'm lost in the vision of Wes and me. His dark smoky eyes open and meet my bright ones in the mirror making me burn for him from the inside out.

"So, you want to watch?" he asks.

I bite my lip and just nod. I'm unable to find the words to tell him what I want, what I need, but then again, Wes always knows before I do. He hooks his fingers in my panties and slides them to the side, sliding his fingers through my opening but not pressing deep enough.

"My bad girl is so wet for me."

"Yes," I pant as he swirls his index finger around my clit. I want to buck my hips to ride his fingers, but Wes has me pressed between his hard body and the counter. I'm unable to move anywhere.

"I love it when you burn for me," he says as he slips his other hand down the front of my dress and pinches my nipple—hard—as he applies pressure to my clit.

I gasp. "Wes—"

"I know, baby," he nips at my ear overloading my senses. "Just a little bit more."

Wes pushes two fingers into my pussy and hits just the spot as his thumb takes over circling my clit. I pant as my fingers lose their grip on the counter and I reach for Wes to keep me grounded. I grip one of his forearms in each hand—up at my breast and down at my center—as he pushes me closer and closer to the edge of bliss.

I tip my head back against his chest and moan as my nails score his tanned skin.

"I've got you, baby. Just. Let. Go," he says as he rolls my nipple between his thumb and index finger as his other hand pumps hard and fast. His thumb flicks my clit faster and faster. "Let go," he commands as he pinches my nipple and I do with my head thrown back on his shoulder as I scream his name.

Wes lightly kisses my neck while his fingers slowly slip in and out of my heat until I can't take it anymore. My heart rate slows and my breathing is less choppy. I open my eyes and meet his in the mirror.

"You're the sexiest woman on the planet, Claire," he says and I can feel his hard length press into my ass as he rocks his hips just a bit. "What are you doing to me?" I smirk.

"Well, I could tell you what I'm about to do to you … but I'd rather show you," I reply to him as I turn in his arms.

Wes crushes his mouth to mine in more than a kiss, it's a meeting of lips and teeth and tongues. It's hard and hot. I push his worn leather jacket from his shoulders and let it fall to the bathroom floor. His belt buckle clanks as I unhook it and pull his zipper down before pushing him backwards so that his shoulders collide with the wall.

"Fuck," he groans as I reach in and pull out his hard cock.

I push his jeans and boxer briefs down his hips together so that his hard length can spring free before dropping to my knees in front of him, my skirt still hiked up over my hips. Wes watches me on my knees before him like a hungry predator. His eyes lock to mine as he licks the fingers that were just in my most secret places. It renews my lust and I have to squeeze my thighs together on an aftershock of my own.

"I want that pink smeared on my dick while I'm at the club. I want your mark on my body," he commands but I have a surprise for him as I wrap my fist around him and pump his cock once ... twice before licking the tip.

I let my eyes meet his with the tip of his cock just brushing my stained lips. "It's the kind that doesn't smear."

"Oh fuck. That's hot."

"I know," I say before taking the tip into my mouth and swirling it around.

Wes groans deep and loud before tangling his fingers in my curls and pulling just to the point that it stings. He rocks his hips and I let his cock slide in and out of my mouth, deeper and deeper. I pump his base in my fist as he pumps in and out of my mouth.

"So good, baby. Suck me harder." And I do. I know he's close because his movements are becoming a little frantic. "Fuck, fuck, fuck. Jesus Christ it's so good."

I squeeze him tighter in my fist and move my hand faster and faster. He pulls at my hair with his hands and groans.

"Yes, oh fuck yes. Baby, I'm going to come." Above all else, I love that I am the only one that takes him there. "Claire," he shouts as his whole body tightens and he pours himself into my mouth. I swallow every last drop.

Wes pulls me to my feet and wraps his arms around me tight, crushing his mouth to mine. His tongue licks in and I'm lost to his kiss. When he pulls back, there's an emotion playing behind his eyes but I'm not ready to put a name to it.

"What?" I ask.

"That mouth," he growls. "Will be the death of me."

I shrug. "I just felt compelled to remind you of what you're leaving behind while you're in that strip club."

"Do you not want me to go?" he asks suddenly concerned.

"No, not at all," I smile. "I'm going out to the city with Emma and Anna."

"Or we could both not go out," he growls. "And I could fuck you on the bathmat."

"As tempting as that is," I say patting his chest while he groans at my rebuff. "We're going out."

"Not if we have a better offer," he says as he backs me up into the counter and hikes one leg around his waist. His still hard cock rubs against my pussy and I whimper at the connection. "You're still wet for me. Still so hot for me. I could make you feel better, baby. . . End that suffering," he says as his cock glides through my wetness.

I arch my back and rock my hips against his hard length getting closer and closer to the knife's edge of bliss but I know that if I come on his cock, Wes will fuck me on the bath mat just like he promised. While a night of carnal pursuits with Wes is amazing, we need to get out and if all that starts we never will. So I kiss him one more time before gently pushing against his chest. He groans again when he realizes I'm telling him no.

"Just think," I tell him. "In a few hours we can drunk fuck. It will be fun."

"With you, it always is, baby."

We straighten our clothes and there is not one damn thing I can do about the sex hair, but it's kind of hot so I go with it. Wes just laughs and swats my ass as we walk out the door to meet our friends. He's going to drop me off with Anna before heading across town to meet the guys at the club.

I look up at his handsome face and smile. We've never been so close. Wes has burrowed so deep into my life and my heart. If only I had known that in a few short hours that foundation would be rocked—that everything would change. Maybe I would have stayed home after all. Then again, *maybe not*.

chapter 2
nothing bad

SHE'S MINE.
   I have to have her. I need the bad girl. I watched as she danced for a man that shouldn't want her. I watched as she rubbed her body all over his with lust in her eyes. She wants him too. And the hard-on in my pants shows how much I want her. It's a conundrum of sorts.

   When she kisses him, thrusting her pink tongue into his mouth I have to look away and shift my body to ease the burn in my balls.

   She finishes her dance and takes the bills he offers her but nothing more. His loss is my gain. She stands from his lap and walks through the club. I follow her down the hall. My companions don't miss me, they think I'm making a phone call out front.

   "Hey," she says jumping when I startle her. "I didn't see you there."

   "My apologies, I didn't mean to frighten you."

   "You didn't," she's quick to add.

   "You smoke?" I ask holding up a pack that I always carry with me for just this purpose.

   "Now you're speaking my language," she laughs as she pushes through the exit door at the end of the hallway. "Join me?"

   "Of course."

   I tap a cigarette out of the pack and point it at her, my fingers never touching the actual cigarette. She doesn't seem to notice as she only has eyes for the slim white stick and the lighter in my other hand. She turns away from me to light it, not wanting to be rude and blow smoke in my face. This is my opportunity and it's perfect, just like I planned.

   She never noticed me slipping on a pair of latex gloves. Her lack of cognizance will be her downfall.

   She doesn't even make a noise when the needle slips into her neck. Her body goes rigid as she falls, but her eyes are wide. She sees everything.

   I stamp out her cigarette on the asphalt under my boot and drag her behind the dumpster. We don't have much time, something I will lament later, hopefully much later.

   I lay her down on the ground behind the dumpster and strip off her G-string. That's it, that's all there is. She didn't even bother to cover up before she came out here with me to smoke.

   Her eyes flash with her unspoken why.

"I wish I could tell you," I whisper to her as I straddle her hips, my erection pressing into her mound through my pants. *"I won't apologize to you though, I need this more than you could ever understand."*

My belt buckle clanks in the silence as I undo my pants. I slip a condom down my hard length and I wrap my hands around her slim neck. Her lovely purple eyes go wide.

"So lovely," I say as I poise my tip at her entrance. I don't bother to spread her legs, she'll be tighter this way. I apply the perfect amount of pressure as I slide in. I revel in the blood vessels popping in her eyes as I steal the breath from her lungs. *"Yes, absolutely lovely."*

• • •

"Stop!" I laugh clutching my belly. There's a real fear that my Macallan 18 is about to come out my nose. That would really burn.

"I'm serious!" Emma shouts just a little drunk on her martini. "You would have grabbed your panties and left too."

"I think that seems a little cruel," Anna shares, obviously feeling bad for the man with the tiny dick.

"I'm just saying, 'ain't nobody got time for that!'"

"I mean I know it's not eight inches, but … it can't be that small," Anna rallies.

"Oh, it was. It was smaller than my thumb." Emma laments.

"So, you just left?" I ask.

"Of course. I stood up, grabbed my panties, said, 'Don't call me,' and left," she answers.

"Have you heard from him?" Anna asks obviously feeling bad for the poor guy.

"Ugh, don't get me started."

"No, let's." I clap my hands with glee like a circus monkey. Emma's dating woes are some of my most favorite bedtime stories.

"Asshole," she coughs.

"Please," I beg holding my hands up in prayer fashion.

"Ugh. Okay, fine, but don't say I didn't warn you," she clarifies before continuing her dating tale of woe. "Not only has he spent all week calling and leaving me voicemail messages about how much he loves me and misses me…"

"Homeboy loves you?" I ask, cutting her off.

"Apparently," Emma drolls.

"How long did you guys go out?" Anna asks.

"One."

"One month? One Week? One Year?" I ask. "Help us out here, Em."

"One. Fucking. Date. He's a God damned stage five clinger."

"That's not very nice talk for a doctor," I remind her laughing.

"Fuck off," she laughs as she flips me the bird.

"So not only is he a clinger… but what?" I ask.

"His *girlfriend* sent me a Facebook message telling me to back off her man."

"No!" Anna and I both say at the same time.

"Tiny dick has a regular girlfriend?" I ask.

"Oh yeah, the prick—pun intended."

"Shut up," Anna chokes out through her laughter.

"Go ahead, yuck it up you little shits," she sighs as she takes another big sip of her martini. "Is it so much to ask for eight inches of hard cock on a built alpha guy with a good job that worships me?"

"Yes!" Anna and I both say simultaneously.

"You shut your damn mouth. She points a drunken finger at me and closes one eye to better focus on me.

"Clearly, she's ingested more gin than steak," Anna whispers to me.

"I heard that!" Emma snaps. "But I was talking to you."

"Me? What did I do?"

"You have eight inches of hard cock on an alpha god waiting for you."

"He's not perfect," I tell her. "And neither am I."

"Say that to my face when you don't have sex hair," she laughs.

"I do not!" I shout as I comb my hair with my fingers.

"You totally do," Anna laughs.

"Ugh fine. So, Wes is pretty great. So, what?"

"Nothing bad," Emma says. "It's just proof that it's out there and we shouldn't settle for less."

"Like little dicks?" Anna asks.

"Exactly," Emma answers. "We won't settle for little dicks. The real deal is out there."

I open my mouth to shoot her a sassy reply about all of the tiny, and not so tiny, dicks she has encountered in her search to find the perfect cock when my phone rings. It's Liam's ring. I sigh.

"What's wrong?" Anna asks me.

"Nothing. That's Liam's ring. Wes must be super drunk and needing a ride home."

I pull my phone from my purse. I missed the call but it immediately starts ringing again. "Hello?" I answer.

"Claire, it's Lee. I need you. There's been a homicide."

chapter 3

step on it

"*SO, WHAT HAPPENED WAS...*"

"Let me stop you right there," I say as I clench my fists in an effort not to scream. I am so freaking mad right now.

There I was, having a great girls' night out with Emma and Anna, when my phone rang. Never before in my life have I been so scared as when I answered the phone. I will never forget the sound of my brother, Liam, telling me that he needed my help.

Emma, Anna, and I threw down copious amounts of cash to get us out of the swanky NYC restaurant we had been dining in while Lee and Wes were at a bachelor party. Anna threw her scotch back like a boss and we headed out in the night air. We all knew that it would take us awhile to get back to New Jersey and time was of the essence.

We grabbed our purses and wraps and beat feet out the door. Our feet—in ridiculous heels by the way—ate up the sidewalk as we made our way to the coffee cart that sits on a corner about a block away from *Filet de Boeuf*, the fancy assed restaurant that Anna insisted we splurge on.

After dropping five dollars on three black coffees, Emma stepped her long ass legs just off the curb, her skirt hiking up just enough as she raised one hand over head. The fingers of her other hand were in her mouth letting out a whistle that would make any New York baseball fan proud.

A yellow cab comes screeching to a halt in front of us—thank God not over us— and Anna pulls the front passenger door open and drops in offering the cabbie her dazzling smile. Her real mission is to distract him so that Emma and I can haul ass into the back seat and shut the door behind us.

"Where to, gorgeous?" he asks.

"George Washington Township, New Jersey." She smiles brightly at him knowing full well what he's about to say in his heavily accented voice. We all do. Emma and I smirk at eat other in the back seat.

"No! No New Jersey! Get out of my cab."

"We can't do that," Anna pouts.

"Why not?" he shouts. "You get out now or I call cops."

"Lucky for you, we are cops." I smile at him as Emma and I hold up our various badges.

"Cop!" he yells as he pulls on his thinning hair. I hope he doesn't pull too hard, he doesn't have much left to lose. "Freaking cops."

"Yes, Sir. And could you please step on it."

"Ugh," he lets out a strangled sound before pulling away from the curb at breakneck speed. When he enters the highway breaking the land speed record, I think I've found my soulmate. I see him taking the first exit for George Washington Township when he shouts, "Where to, crazy lady cops?"

"Technically, I'm the Medical Examiner," Emma says after clearing her throat.

"And I'm the department shrink," Anna admits through her laughter on a delicate shoulder shrug.

"You tricked me!" he wails. "You're not even real cops!"

"Well, I am a real cop," I sigh at my two best friends and their ridiculousness. "And we need to go to the Pink Kitty Lounge."

"That place is disgusting!" He spits. "Why do you want to go there? Are you whores?"

"No!" we all shout at the same time.

"Only girls there are tricks and dancers," he says adamantly.

"We have a case there," I explain.

"That's not much better. You should be home with your babies," he says with all seriousness.

"He must be in the same bridge group as my mother," Emma growls. I just throw my head back and laugh. We all get the same crap from our families *When are you going to meet a nice man? When are you going to get married? When are you going to have babies?* Too bad we're all busy fighting crime and taking down the bad guys. But that's alright by us. We wouldn't have it any other way.

Before I know it, we're pulling into the front lot of the Pink Kitty Lounge. Police cars are everywhere, the sirens off but the blue and red lights swirling on top. The cab comes to a stop and we all pile out of the yellow car as I hand a credit card to the cabbie—who gives me the side eye for not having two hundred and seventy-eight dollars and fifty-two cents in cash. How dare I?

I roll my eyes as he hands back my card and I slip it into my little clutch. I will be filing an expense report in the morning, thank you very much!

"Where have you been?" Liam yells as he comes into my line of sight.

"Well, hello to you too, brother dearest." I bow. Man, I was hoping he wasn't going to be a pompous windbag but I guess I spoke too soon.

"This is serious, Claire," he says as he grabs my arm to pull me close before he lowers his voice so that only I can hear him. "A woman is dead."

"So, you said." I roll my eyes. "And why, exactly, did you drag me all the way out here from my nice fancy dinner in the city to show me a dead stripper? Why aren't you investigating it?"

"Because I can't," he mumbles.

"What is that?" I ask with a huge, shit eating smile spreading across my face.

"Because I can't," he says louder through gritted teeth.

"And Wes?" I ask mildly.

"He can't either."

"And that would be because?" I hum.

"She was dancing for our party right before she died."

"Care to run that one by me again?" I ask.

"She was giving private dances to Jones's bachelor party right before she took a break that she never came back from," he explains. I close my eyes and pinch the bridge of my nose.

"Please tell me that you weren't the last lap dance she gave before she bought it tonight, Lee." I need him to tell me that he's not going to be a suspect. I cannot handle having to arrest my brother.

"No. She didn't dance for me. The other girl did," he says answering my question. I take my first deep breath of the night before he soldiers on. "But Wes was."

"Excuse me?" I ask over the ringing in my ears but all I can think is what a waste of a perfectly good blowjob.

The rest, as they say, is history.

chapter 4
it's personal

THIS IS GOING TO be a long ass night.

"Show me the body." I sigh.

"It's right over here behind this dumpster."

I follow Liam over to the alleyway behind the club and sure enough, there's a dead girl back there. But that's not what's surprising.

The victim, who I would place at early to mid-thirties has blonde hair. Her eyes are closed and she's laying on her left side on the asphalt. While all that may seem fairly normal for your everyday homicide, that's where the "normal" ends.

Her eyes are closed and her hands are folded up in prayer under her cheek. At first glance you would think that she's just sleeping and her clothing choice is . . . *odd*.

"Is that what she was wearing earlier?" I ask wondering what kind of freaky kink these assholes I work with are into. When no one answers I look up from the young woman next to the dumpster and at the men standing around me. "Well?"

"No," Liam says after clearing his throat. "She dances here. Danced."

"I'm going to need all of you to head inside the club. No one leaves," I say after I sigh. Sometimes my job really sucks a monkey's testicle.

"Claire . . ."

"Nope." I say firmly. "I'll be inside in just a second." They all turn and tuck tail before heading back into the strip club like little boys who got a slap on the wrist from the school principal.

"Well it can't be said you guys don't know how to show a lady a good time," Emma says as she snaps on a pair of latex gloves that one of the crime scene techs handed to her. Liam looks back at her over his shoulder and blanches. I just stare at her.

"Really, Em?"

"What? Too soon?" She shrugs.

"Of course it's too soon!" I shout to the heavens as if Jesus and all the baby angels could help me. I start counting backwards from ten. I love Emma, but she's a little bit of a loose cannon.

"I meant us, loser!" she shouts. "Like, you, me, and Anna. Not the dead stripper."

"I could have a field day with all the shit you guys are slinging around tonight," Anna chimes in. "I'm going to schedule you all for in depth appointments this coming week. We need to log some serious couch time."

"Now will you look what you did?" I shout at Emma. She just shrugs in a so what fashion.

I sigh and roll my shoulders back. "What do you have for me, Emma?"

"Well, she looks to be about mid-thirties, blonde hair, could be bleached but it doesn't look like it based on her roots. Victim appears to have been posed post-mortem," Emma shares.

"No immediate evidence on scene that suggests the victim was murdered here," one of the crime scene techs chimes in.

"I agree," Emma says. "There is bruising present at the back of the victim's shoulders that suggests the blood stopped pumping as she laid on her back, not her side. I won't know cause of death until I get her on my table, but there is also evidence of bruising on her neck."

"Strangulation?" I ask.

"On first look? Most likely," Emma agrees.

"That's messy," I mumble.

"Not messy," she corrects. "It's personal."

I stand there watching Emma as the crime scene techs comb the area for any evidence to the crime. Why was this woman murdered? Who would want to strangle her? I watch as Emma gently pulls the victim's lower lid down.

"Now that's interesting," she says softly.

"What?"

"She has violet eyes."

"And?" I ask.

"There's no contact lenses in her eyes. The color is natural."

"Okay," I hedge not sure what she's trying to say. I hope she just spits it out already. "What's so interesting about a woman with natural eye color?"

"It's not that she chooses to showcase her natural eye color that's interesting so much as the color itself," Emma explains. "I have never seen that natural color on anyone other than your dad, Liam . . . and *you*."

chapter 5
that's angel

"DON'T BE RIDICULOUS." I roll my eyes.
"I'm not being ridiculous," Emma replies. "I'm serious. I have never seen purple eyes on anyone outside of your family."

"Well, now you have. She's not related to me, I can tell you that much!"

"I didn't say that she was related to you." She sighs. "I'm just saying, it's rare."

"Can we move along to the actual important facts of this case, please?" I'm tired and more than a little frustrated and it's beginning to show. I just wanted one freaking night off.

"Yes," she says.

"Fantastic." I'm letting my sarcasm show. It's not becoming but it's too late at night for me to care.

"The dress is interesting to say the least," Anna adds.

"It is," I say. "I'm not even sure I want to know why the killer would dress her up like a prairie person."

"It's almost like a doll," Emma muses as she takes in the floral dress with poufy sleeves and pin-tucked skirt underneath the white pinafore.

"It's almost like those people on the *Big Love* show we used to watch when we drank too much wine and were lonely—like now," Anna adds. I roll my eyes.

"I miss that show. It was a good one," I agree.

"I think I had an American Girl doll with the exact same outfit as a kid. Holy fuck, that's creepy," Emma shares.

"No kidding," I say.

"This case is definitely . . . interesting," Anna shares. "You're going to need a profiler on this case. What if it's a serial killer?"

"Shut your damn mouth and do not repeat those words until we have more than one body like this. This is creepy enough that the press will eat this shit up. I don't need any of those vultures hearing you say that shit right now," I bark out.

"Sorry," Anna says as she mimes locking her lips with a pretend key and throwing it away over her shoulder.

"Thank you." I nod.

"Anytime." She winks at me. God, I love my friends. They're crazy as hell, but I love them.

"I'm going to head on inside and interview the suspects." I say to the laughter of my friends.

"Oh, Liam will just love that," Anna says.

"Don't you know it." I laugh.

"Go easy on him." Anna bites down on her bottom lip like she wants to tell me more but doesn't.

"Never." I wink and Anna sighs.

"Give 'em hell, babe." Emma laughs.

I toss a wave over my head as I walk across the parking lot towards the back of the club where I pull open the back door. I hear the whispers from other dancers coming from the dressing rooms at the back of the building but as I pass, all talk stops. I know they are nervous about talking to the cops, but also scared because one of their own is dead.

There is a uniformed officer at the mouth of the hallway just after I pass the doors to the restrooms. I flag her down.

"Are these empty?" I ask pointing to the bathrooms.

"Yes, Detective. We cleared them."

"Good work. Thank you," I tell her. "I'm going to need a quiet booth or office to question the witnesses in."

"I'll get right on that, boss," she tells me as she moves to do just that. I think I like her.

I start to make my way into the main room when a large man, with sweat stains on the underarms of his white dress shirt and sweat beading all over his florid face, approaches me. Interesting. He could be in poor health or he could be nervous. But what about? That's the question. Could be he whacked her in the lot and he's a total mental case with the dresses and shit, but more than likely he's afraid the little stripper that bought it in his parking lot will hurt his bottom line. *Douchebag.*

"Excuse me, officer—" he starts before I stop to correct him. "Detective."

"Detective," he says as he rolls his eyes. Awesome. My favorite kind of witness. "What's going on here?"

"Who are you?" I ask as I tip my head to the side slightly in order to study him.

"I'm the manager of this club and you can't just shut me down for no reason," he demands.

"You're right, I can't." I nod my head casually.

"So, you're leaving," he tells me, not asks.

"No." I sigh. This is going to be a long fucking night. Lee so owes me. Wes too. I'm thinking cake cases from Liam and sexual favors from Wes. Yep, that sounds good.

"But, you just said!" he shouts sending little drops of spittle flying towards my face. Gross.

"I said," I say as I wipe a hand down my face. "That I can't shut you down for no reason. I can shut you down to investigate a homicide." I stop letting that little nugget of information sink in for a minute.

"What?" he shouts getting louder with each response. "Who? Why?"

"That's what I'm going to find out," I say.

"No," he shouts as he reaches for my arm. "This is my club. No bitch is going to come in here and shut me down without telling me what the hell is going on!" Just magical, this one is. I sigh gearing up to let him know that just because I have boobs doesn't mean I am any less of a detective. In fact, I'm the best, when Wes beats me to the proverbial punch.

Well, hell.

"Don't," Wes growls from behind him. "You let the nice detective go." I mean, it is kind of hot when he lets everyone know that I'm the boss.

The big, fat man releases my arm. "I meant no harm," he stammers.

"Sure, buddy. Just let her do her job so we can all go home." Wes winks at me.

"Yeah, that's a good idea," the club owner says. "I'll just be over . . . over there . . . *somewhere*," he trails off. I barely hold in my snicker at his hasty departure.

I walk back to the uniformed officer that was at the door and see her in a heated debate with a large man with the clear coil of an ear piece curling down from his left ear. He could be the bouncer, but I'm not sure. He's not secret service because there's no ugly ass black suit. He's in jeans and a gray t-shirt with muscles peeking out of every porthole.

"Hello again," I breeze through on a smile.

"Hello, Detective Goodnite," the officer says to me.

"Detective?" the bulky man asks on a raised eyebrow. *Asshole.*

You know, one day, it would be just peachy if everyone would just assume that I'm a lead detective and not, say, a cocktail waitress because I have a nice rack. Or someone's secretary because I have a vagina. I let out a quick breath before answering.

"Yes? Can I help you with something?"

"Yes, ma'am," he smiles a bright white smile as he holds out his hand. "I'm Chad Perry, the head of security here at the club."

"Fantastic," I say. "Why don't you come sit with me over here? You can give me the lay of the land."

I motion to the secluded booth that the officer and I had chosen for me to conduct my initial interviews. I turn and wink at her over my shoulder as I lead him away. She just rolls her eyes and laughs silently. Men! What will we ever do with them?

Chad slides into the booth with his back to the wall like he's Wild Fucking Bill Hickock and I kind of want to gag. Apparently, Wild Bill here thinks he's running this show. Well, that's just fine by me. He'll give me all the answers I need if he thinks he's helping out the little woman in the big scary job.

I slide into the booth beside him barely keeping my rolling eyeballs in check. The struggle is real, that's for sure. Chad snaps his fingers in the air and a woman in a string bikini and six-inch stilettos hustles on over. Just. Freaking. Charming.

"Sparkling water, Bubbles. Two," he barks before she turns and runs back towards the bar. When she returns just shy of two minutes later, I'm both impressed at her bar skills and sad for her. Bubbles sets two tall glasses of ice and sparkling water with lime wedges on the side of the glasses on the table.

"Thank you." I smile gently at her before she hustles away out of the eyesight of Wild Bill . . . I mean Chad.

"So, what do you have?" he demands as he takes a sip from his glass.

"A homicide," I say a little more cheerfully. He just looks at me and blinks once, twice . . .

"Is this your first one?" he asks not at all aware that his line of questioning is mildly offensive. Then again, I did see it coming a mile away.

"Come again?"

"Is this your first murder? Did you just pass the Detective's exam?" I sigh. What is he new here? It was only a few months ago that I made headline news—*national news*—as I investigated the kidnapping of a young boy. It also brought up a lot of unanswered questions in regard to my own kidnapping from years ago. But that's neither here nor there.

"No," I answer. "It's not my first homicide. I've been doing this for awhile now."

"That's hard to believe," he says thoughtfully as he studies my face. "You seem so . . . *young*. You're beautiful." Awe, fuck. I hope he doesn't hit on me.

"Well, thank you. What can you tell me about this club?" I ask hoping to change the subject to my questions.

"I almost went to the PD, you know, but decided the private sector was more suited for me. I'm a lone wolf," he says not taking my hints to stay on topic. And God damnit. He is hitting on me.

"You don't say," I mumble before moving on. "What can you tell me about the club?"

"It's a strip club," he tells me like I'm slow. Fuck this is going to be a long night.

"I meant about the operations," I pause to take a breath. Clearly, praying for strength to keep me from strangling this moron. "Who owns the club?"

"Bob Byrd," he says like that explains everything. I quirk one eyebrow in question. "Bob, the big guy running around being kind of a dick to everyone. He's the owner of the club." I had guessed as much, but Wild Bill and I had to start somewhere.

"And the dancers?" I asked.

"What about them?" Clearly, he's a prince among men.

"Do they like working here?" I ask.

"I don't know." He shrugs his overly muscle-bound shoulder. "I mean, who cares? Am I right?" He laughs. Uhh, no dude, you are, in fact, wrong. I barely keep myself from sharing those thoughts out loud.

"What do you mean by 'you don't know'? You work here as the head of security. Don't you know if the dancers are happy?"

"No," he shrugs his shoulders. "It's not my job to know if they're happy or to keep them that way."

"Did you ever date any of the dancers?" I ask changing tack.

"Define 'date'?" he smirks. Ugh, gross. I swallow the bile back down my throat. "I might sample the wares, but I don't stick around to see if they're happy in the long term—only in the short term." Yep, a real prince.

"Did the dancers ever complain about men that took too many liberties?"

"What do you mean?" he snaps. *Shit.* Me thinks the douchebag doth protest too much.

"I mean were there ever complaints about men that may have scared them?"

"There are always creeps in a strip club," he shrugs. Yeah, buddy, I'm looking at one of them right now.

I sigh. "Any issues with the parking lot?"

"We've had a light out for a week but nothing serious."

"Have you ever seen this woman before?" I ask as I pass him my phone with the picture I took of the victim's face.

"That's Angel," he says quietly.

"Angel?" I ask.

"She's—she was one of the dancers," he says. "She was on shift tonight for the bachelor party. She's one of the club's top performers so they bring her out to squeeze all of the money from the groom-to-be and his drunken buddies."

"Is Angel her real name?" I ask quietly trying to be gentle. There's something about Chad's mannerisms that tells me her death has struck him hard.

"Of course not. Don't be dumb." And he's back. "Her name is—*was*—Bonnie Bradley." And I have a name to match the face of a beautiful woman struck down before her time.

"Did she have an ex?"

"Don't they all?" He shrugs. Clearly, I'm not going to get anything else out of him. It's time to move on.

"Thank you for your time, Mr. Perry," I say as I stand from the booth.

"Wait," he says standing quickly. "I'd like to call you sometime, take you out and show you a good time." He winks.

"Thanks, but I'm seeing someone," I say politely.
"Your loss, babe."
"I'm sure," I say as I head to the back of the building towards the dressing rooms.

The crowds thin out as I move to the mouth of the hallway. The officer stands her ground and tips her chin to me ever so slightly. She and I see each other—the real woman there or at least as much of her as we might let others see—and tip our hats to the women we are and the women we have to pretend to be.

I pass by her and knock on the plain oak door that blocks the entrance to the dancers' dressing room. After a beat, the door opens a crack and a woman peeks out enough that I can see just one pale, blue eye.

"Who are you?" she whispers.

"I'm Detective Claire Goodnite." I smile genuinely at her.

"I-I-I've seen you on the news," she says before pushing the door open just a little bit more. "C-c-c-come on in."

Once I pass through the door she pushes it shut and then throws the lock. I look around. There are at least a dozen women in this room in various stages of dress—or I should say, *undress*. Most are wearing robes of some kind.

"I'd like to ask you all a few questions, if that would be alright," I say softly as I pass by each woman, looking each one in the eye to silently show them that I will find out what happened to their friend. That I will protect their confidences and I will do my best to keep them safe. "Would that be alright? I can ask the female officer outside to step in if that would make you all feel better."

"Yeah, do that," the one who opened the door said.

I stick my head back out the door after she unlocks it for me. "Officer Alexander, could you please come here. Officer Bostwick, would you please take her post at the door. Thank you."

"You wanted to see me, boss?" Officer Alexander says as she steps around the crappy wooden door into the dressing room.

"Yes." I smile kindly at her and the other women in the room. "We all think it would be best if you were in here while I interview the witnesses." I stress the word witnesses because I'm not really sure what to call them and I don't want to offend them in any way.

"Sounds like a plan," Officer Alexander states.

"Ladies, this is Officer Alexander," I say out loud for the whole room to hear.

"You can call me Jasmine," she says.

"Jasmine," the gatekeeper woman by the door tests out. "I'm Hoots. That's Serenity and Bubbles."

"Nice to meet you, ladies," I say politely.

"Glad to know you," Jasmine shares to the chorus of same here's around the women in the room.

"Now, what can you all tell me about Angel?" I ask after I settle in, leaning back against a makeup vanity with big lights.

"She was nice enough," Bubbles shares.

"Did you know her well?"

"She helped me with my Algebra homework before the club opened."

"How old are you?" I ask Bubbles.

"Eighteen," she says as she looks at the floor. "Said I was the same age as her daughter."

"So, she had a daughter. Did she have any other children?"

"A son. He's nineteen and in the Army," Hoots informs from the door.

"And another one who's ten," Serenity says softly from the corner.

"And a husband?" I ask.

"Ha!" she cackles. "The sack of shit that knocked her up never married her."

"Would he ever harm her in anyway?" I ask.

"No, he was a little weasel who liked the dog track just a little too much and couldn't be bothered with things like regular work enough to pay child support or even hold down a job. But he wasn't mean."

"And she loved him," Serenity says.

"Serenity is still young enough to believe in that line of bullshit," Hoots shares causing both Jasmine and I to bite our lips to keep from laughing.

"Am not!" Serenity yells.

"Was there anyone Angel was afraid of?" I ask after the ladies who are obvious friends settle down.

"No," Hoots shares.

"I can't think of anyone," Bubbles adds.

"Were there any customers that gave her—*or you*, for that matter—the creeps?"

"Honey, they're all creeps in one way or another," Hoots shares from the door and I can't help but think about the fact that tonight's resident creeps were my colleagues, my boyfriend, and my brother. *Lucky me!*

"No one that bothers you?" I ask.

"Well, Bob is a jerk who only cares about the talent in terms of the bottom line. He likes his paychecks too much to care about anything else."

"Yeah. He's a jerk, but he's harmless," Bubbles says.

"Now, Chad is a little shit but he's good with his cock so we've all seen the ceiling of the backseat of his car a time or two, but nothing past that," Hoots says candidly.

"You'll find who did this to our Angel?" Serenity asks me in a child-like voice.

"I'm going to do my very best," I promise her.

"Should we be worried?" Hoots asks when I push off the table top to make my way to the door.

"You should always be cautious," I hedge. "I can't divulge any pertinent facts of the case at this time," I say as the words *serial killer* flash in neon lights across my brain. So far, I only have one body on my hands, but God damn Anna for suggesting otherwise. Now it's all I freaking see.

"Remember, ladies," Jasmine says in a confident voice. "It's that dipshit Chad's job to see to your safety. Make him walk you to your cars at night—*every night*. Don't go out those back doors alone. Be aware of your surroundings. And take my self-defense class at the community center on Wednesday nights." I quirk a brow in her direction. She just shrugs her shoulder in a so what motion.

"Thank you, Officer," I say once we've cleared the dressing room. She just tips her head in a nod before resuming her post outside their door. I think I like her.

I make my way back to my booth and stop halfway across the room at a table where most of my male colleagues are sitting. I sigh. What a bunch of beautiful morons. Only these guys would be at a strip club for a bachelor party where one of the dancers got killed.

"One at a time, come on over to that table and give me your statements gentlemen," I say as I point towards my booth.

"Linda is going to fucking kill me," Jones whines. He's drunk as a skunk and crying with his face in his hands like a big baby—not like the two-hundred-eighty-pound Mack truck of a police officer we all know and love.

"Linda isn't going to kill you," I reassure him. But honestly, if I was Linda,

I would so kill him.

"I'm going to fucking kill you if you don't quit God damned crying right this minute," Liam grumbles under his breath. There's that family resemblance we know so well. The thought sobers me as I remember the bright purple eyes that Lee and I also share—along with our victim.

"I'm just going to be right over there," I say as I motion to my table.

I walk across the room and sit down. Bubbles brings me an unopened bottle of water before moving along without saying a word. I think she likes me. Look at me making friends and shit.

Liam slides into the booth across from me.

"Tell me everything you've got," he demands.

"I'm not sure that's what should happen here, Lee."

"Don't feed me that line of bullshit, Goodnite. I'm your Captain and you'd do well to remember it," he threatens me. Always with the threats, this one. I sigh.

"How can I forget it!" I snap. "You remind me every day, including when we're at Mom and Dad's!"

"This is a homicide, Claire," he says as he softens his tone of voice towards me.

"I know that," I respond after taking a deep breath. "But you're a witness here. Why don't you start at the beginning and tell me everything that happened tonight?"

He sighs. I know that he sees the truth in what I'm saying. The last thing we need is questionable police work on this case after what happened with the Donovan case. Five months ago, I caught a missing persons case. A six-year-old boy, Anthony Donovan, was reported missing from his modest suburban home where he lived with his mom, sister, and step-dad. The case should have been easy, but it was anything but.

He sighs, running his hand through his hair before answering. "We went out to dinner at the Bullpen before walking over here."

"So, you guys went to the nastiest sports bar in town for beer and wings before coming over here for more booze and naked ladies?" I ask, my eyes narrowed.

He looks nervously back over his shoulder at the table of guys before looking back at me. Well, that's not a good sign. I wonder just how much looking at the pretty, naked ladies my boyfriend did.

"It's not like that," my brother says pointedly homing in on my weak moments. Wes and I are so new, I can't help but wonder when the love bubble will burst. There's that ugly word again.

"Okay," I say thoughtfully.

"I mean it, Claire," he says, his voice low and full of meaning.

I sigh. "I know. Tell me what happened."

"We came back here and had a few drinks. We bought Jones a few lap dances to send him off into marital bliss with."

"I will never understand why men think having another naked woman rub all over them before settling down is a good idea."

"Claire." Lee stares me down.

"What?" I ask holding my arms out.

"That's it, Claire," he sighs again. I wear on his patience, I know that already. "We just sat there, drank, talked, and watched some pretty girls."

"And when you found the girl?" I questioned.

"We had gone out to smoke, she was laying by the dumpster. I checked her pulse, but I already knew that I wouldn't find one. Wes called it in. Then I called you. The rest, as we say, is history."

"Okay," I say. "If you think of anything else, let me know."

"I will," he tells me. "Once you clear us, I'd appreciate being caught up to speed."

"You got it," I tell him before he stands up and walks away.

I crack the seal on the cap of the water bottle that Bubbles had brought me and looked down at it. I can feel the frown pulling at my brows. She brought me a bottle—a *sealed* bottle—not a glass like Chad had ordered for me. I can't help but wonder if it's for safety or protection. Protection from who? Chad? Bob? And then I wonder how many times the girls here had to watch out for things like that.

"Hey, Cruz." I smile at the man as he sits down across from me. He smiles brightly back at me.

Abraham Cruz is the newest detective to arrive at our station. He's from somewhere in the Midwest. I can't remember where. He replaced Hudson, a seasoned detective who broke cover and took a bullet for me a few months ago. Last I heard, Hudson was chasing a redheaded Game Warden with big boobs and brass balls all over East Texas. And if rumors were true, he married her one night in Vegas after one too many drinks. Good for him.

"Hey, Claire," Cruz says. "Fancy meeting you here."

"I know, right?" I laugh. "I should be eight martinis deep with Anna and Emma."

"That sounds like fun," he says quietly but his words have my brain turning. I tip my head to the side to study him. I wonder if he has a thing for Emma or Anna. That has to be it.

"They're both single, you know," I whisper. His smile dims a bit. "Emma and Anna, I mean."

"Yeah. I know." He smiles at me again.

"So, what can you tell me about tonight?" I ask.

"We started at the Bullpen. Jones got drunk. We came here. Jones got more drunk. O'Connell and the Captain went out to smoke and found the dancer with the purple eyes," he explains. But all I see is red. I can't believe both of those assholes told me that they had quit smoking when they, in fact, did not quit smoking! "Come to think of it, they're a lot like yours."

"If you think of anything else, call me?" I ask him, even though he already knows to.

"Of course," he says as he shoots me a crooked grin. God the guys in this unit love to mess with me. I should kick all their asses.

He stands from the booth and touches the tip of his index finger to the back of my hand where it rests on top of the table and heads back over to the guys. What the fuck was that? But I don't have time to contemplate it as Wes walks up to the booth and sits down.

"What the fuck was that all about?" he quietly roars.

"Umm, excuse me?" I retort.

"What the fuck is going on with you and Cruz?"

"Nothing," I say as I narrow my eyes on him. "Why are you being this way?"

"Because you're mine, Claire," he growls. "Learn it, live it, love it, baby, because it ain't changing."

"God, you're such an asshole." I roll my eyes at him.

"And you love every bit of it." He winks at me. There's that word again.

"Not currently," I sigh. "Look, I need to know what happened tonight so I can go out and catch a killer. Whatever drunken jealousy this is," I say as I motion back and forth between us with my hand, "I don't have time for it."

"I'm not drunk," he says. "I know what I saw."

"Okay," I say in an effort to redirect. "What happened tonight?"

"We went to the Bullpen and ate too many chicken wings, Jones drank too much beer and told everyone who would listen 'What an angel his Linda is' and then we came here. He got more drunk. There were dancers. Lee and I went out to smoke which I already know you're pissed about but we like to smoke when we drink," he shrugs his impressive shoulders. "It's a Navy thing. Then we saw the girl. Lee checked her and she was for sure dead. So, I called it in and he called you. Now here we are."

"That's it?" I ask frustrated that not one professional can give me anything to go on.

"That's it," he confirms.

"Alright. Thanks, Wes."

"Come see me before you leave," he demands as he stands from the table. "I love you, Claire."

I sigh. "I know."

Wes walks his tall body back to the table with all of the guys. I'm not ashamed to admit that I watch him go and enjoy the view. He's kind of an asshole sometimes, but he's my asshole so there's that.

"Well?" Bob, the club owner snaps drawing me out of my Wes induced fantasy.

"Well, what?" I ask.

"Did one of those guys do it?" he asks as he points to the table of cops.

"Uhh, no," I say looking at him like he's lost his damn mind.

"Yes, one of them did," he tells me.

"You do know that that is a table of seasoned cops, right? They're ultimate professionals."

"And one of them killed my dancer. Find out who. He's costing me money." It's official, Bob Byrd has a major fucking screw loose.

"I'll do my best," I say before he turns on his heels and storms away.

Jones drags his heels, sniveling as he comes right up to the booth I'm sitting in. I motion for him to take a seat across from me but instead he slides in next to me and rests his big, bald head on my shoulder as he cries his heart out, wiping his nose on my shoulder. It just goes to show that the bigger they are on the outside, the bigger babies they actually are on the inside.

"Linda is going to be so fucking mad . . ." he wails.

Oh, fuck me running. I am not equipped to handle this shit.

I look up wide eyed to the table of cops and they all stare at me with merriment and mischief twinkling in their eyes. Those fucking bastards. They knew that Jones was way too drunk to give a statement.

"Linda will never forgive me! What do I do?" Jones asks as he wipes his nose on the back of his hand before nuzzling into my shoulder.

"I'm sure it'll all work out, Jones."

"You're so nice and sweet and smart and pretty. No wonder O'Connell likes to give you the business."

"Jones—" I say but am cut off by the raucous laughter of the morons I work with.

"And oh man, was the Captain pissed when he found out you had banged the Fed. I mean *pissed* pissed." Jones drunkenly rambled on.

"I got it, Jones," I say hoping to move this train right the hell along.

"But I'm glad to see it all worked out." He nods.

"Me too."

"I'm sleepy, Goodnite. Do you think I can just sleep he—" but he doesn't finish the sentence before a snore rips from his face. Boy am I glad I'm not him. Jones is going to wish he was dead in the morning.

I crook my index finger at the table of my friends and colleagues in a come here motion and they all shake their heads and mouth, "Nu-uh." But I don't care.

"Come here right now or I will have you all arrested and thrown in the drunk tank tonight! I hear Big Betsy was picked up tonight for solicitation. Last I remembered she had a thing for Wes and Lee. Isn't that right, Jasmine?"

"Absolutely," she smiles knowing that we can have some fun with them too.

"Coming!" they all shout as the rush over to grab Jones off of my person.

"Don't leave town, boys. You'll be hearing from me," I say. With that I push up from the booth and walk back outside.

Emma is finishing up clearing the scene.

"How's it going out here, ladies?" I ask them.

"Oh, you know, it's going," Anna says thoughtfully. "How's it going in there?"

"They are all a bunch of idiots," I mumble under my breath.

"That good, huh?" Emma asks gleefully. Apparently, it wasn't that much of a mumble.

"The guys are morons. Wes and Lee are smoking again claiming 'it's a Navy thing,' so there's that. The owner and the bouncer are both the creepiest of creeps and the dancers are worried about something but won't tell me what."

"Well," Emma says as she closes the back of the Medical Examiner van. "I'd say their fear has something to do with the fact that one of their friends bought it behind the shitty strip club where they work and was laid out to look like she was sleeping dressed like a fucking prairie person."

"As always," Anna drawls. "Emma is direct and to the point."

"Thanks, babe." Emma smiles brightly and I'm reminded that with her blonde hair and blue eyes, she could easily be a movie star. "I'm uhh . . . just going to take our girl back to the morgue," she says looking at something over my shoulder.

"Yeah, sure, babe. I'll talk to you later," I say distractedly.

"I'll call you when I know more," she says before climbing into the passenger seat of the van. I turn and see Liam watching her every move.

"We're going to have to talk about this," Wes says quietly from behind me.

"Actually, we're not," I say not even turning to look at him.

"Claire—" he starts.

"No," I stop him as I turn around. "This is my job. And I'm not arguing with you or Liam about it. Again."

"We need to talk about this," he says again.

"Not until you're clear. We're not talking about anything. By the book, Wes."

"You can't possibly think I did this!" he snaps.

"And you can't possibly think that my job isn't on the line after the Donovan case," I snap back. "I can't risk this case by playing favorites, Wes."

"I'm not asking you to play favorites, honey. I just need you to know that I love you. I'm here for you. I need to know that you trust me enough to know that I didn't kill a stripper—that I just met by the way." He calmly explains.

"I know," I say as he pulls me into his arms. It's highly unprofessional but I'm tired and I needed the comfort of him for just a minute. But once there in his embrace, I realize he smells like sweat, bourbon, and someone else's perfume. Suddenly Wes's hold isn't so comforting.

"Don't be mad, baby," he says when I pull out of his arms.

"I'm not. I just need to do my job and wrap this case up. There's something about it that's bothering me."

"Honey, the whole thing should bother you. The way she was laid out—" He shudders. "It was bad."

"It is bad," I say and then I open and close my mouth trying to decide if the words that are choking me should be the words that come out of my mouth. "I just—"

"*Don't*," his voice sounds harshly in the dark. "Don't you dare use a bad case as an excuse to run. You have been looking for a reason to for months and I hate it." He tears at his hair with his hands.

"Well, it's true." When will Wes see that, while we . . . care for each other, there is no possible way that this relationship can go anywhere but to a terrible and tragic end.

"The fuck it is!" he shouts.

"You know it's true, Wes. It shouldn't be this—"

"No." He cuts me off.

"Complicated." I finish.

"No, it's not, baby," he pleads. "It's really fucking easy. It's you and it's me. That's all it needs to be."

"Look," I say as I pull from his hold. "I have to go. I'll see you later." And then I leave him there, behind a shitty strip club as I walk to Anna. I climb into the cab that she has procured for us to get home. I let the door shut behind me with a resounding click and hope against all hope that it wasn't the final straw in the Claire and Wes story. No matter what I may have told him only moments before, I'm not ready for it to end.

chapter 6
cold-blooded killer

"ARE YOU ALRIGHT?" ANNA asks.

It's a simple question but the answer is complicated. The fact of the matter is, I just don't know. What started out as a night of fun ended in one of the creepiest murder scenes I have ever seen—and my last case was a doozy.

"Claire?" she asks again as our cab flies down the road. "Are you okay?"

"I don't know."

The cab pulls to a stop in front of my apartment building and I shove open the door like I'm jumping from a sinking ship. I know that Anna is going to want to talk about the case and how it makes me feel. That scene with Wes and how that makes me feel. *All the freaking bullshit and how it makes me feel.* But tonight, I just need to process everything and she can shrink my head tomorrow. But as for right now, I'm not even sure how that makes me feel.

But I also know that she won't wait that long. Anna can hold her own with Emma and I. Even with Liam and Wes. She won't let my bullshit slide and we both know it.

"I'll call and check in when I get home," she says quietly.

"I wouldn't expect anything less."

"Count on it." She smirks.

"I always do," I say suddenly feeling tired. Defeated.

"You know that I love you Claire, right?" she asks me.

"I love you too, Anna. I'll be okay. I promise. Go home and find some poor asshole to torture on your internet dating sites."

"Hey! Mr. Right is out there," she says thoughtfully before adding. "He's probably just being held hostage in some war-torn nation." At that I smile.

"Goodnight," I say as I shut the door.

"Goodnight, Goodnite!" she shouts out the window as the cab rolls out into the night making me laugh.

I climb the steps to my second story apartment and unlock the row of locks down the door. After the last case, my dad insisted on adding some unnecessary hardware to my door. I love him, so I humor him and lock every last one of them.

I repeat the process as soon as I enter my apartment with a sigh. I look at the worn couch and know that if I sit down, I won't be getting back up until morning. I'm so exhausted. So, I walk straight through to my bathroom, brush my teeth, and scrub off my makeup.

It takes longer than usual because I caked it on like a fancy hooker for girls' night out.

I twist my long hair up into a messy bun with a rubber band before padding my way down the hall to my bedroom. I could put on pajamas, but I could also just lay down and sleep in my clothes. Then I remember the crime scene that pulled me away from a fun night of dinner and drinks with my friends and I feel dirty—*unclean*. So, I strip out of my clothes and toss them in a pile by the door. Once I'm naked, I crawl under the sheets ready to drift off to sleep, but my phone has other plans.

Or I should say, my meddling best friend on the other end of the line has alternate plans.

"Hello?" I answer.

"Hello, Claire," she says. "I'm home."

"I'm in bed," I inform her.

"Will you be okay?" she asks. "I can head back over."

"No, I'm fine. I just need some sleep and to hit the trail again tomorrow," I reassure her.

"And Wes?" she asks casually but I can tell her question is anything but.

"I don't know," I say thoughtfully. "What I told him is true. We feel too complicated. Like it should be easier and it's not."

"Do you love him?" she asks, saying that little four-letter word again.

"Yes," I answer with the truth in my heart without hesitation.

"Then it will either work out or it won't," she says sagely.

"Thank you so much for your expert opinion, Dr. Spock." I laugh.

"Dr. Spock was a baby doctor you moron. Shut up and go to sleep." She laughs.

"You too," I respond softly.

"Goodnight, Goodnite."

"Goodnight, dumbass. I love you." And then I hang up, placing my phone on the nightstand before I drift off to sleep.

• • •

Wes and Liam are so mean! I can't believe they won't let me hangout with them. I bet they're just afraid that I'll tell mom and Mrs. O'Connell about the magazines they're hiding with the girls in bikinis in them.

I'm stomping through the woods behind our house. I don't need those gross boys to have some fun. And those boys are gross! They smell weird and put on too much stinky spray stuff when they think I'm not looking.

I just make it to the street on the other side of the trees from our house when a white van pulls up next to me. I hear my mom in my head telling me not to talk to strangers. I feel my eyes going wide as he steps out of the van.

"Claire!" he says and I wonder how he knows my name. "There you are. I need your help!"

"What do you need help with?" I ask.

"I'm so glad you asked, Claire," he says my name again like he says it all the time. It's weird but I don't think too much about it. "My puppy, Millie, got out. She's missing. Can you help me find her?"

"I don't know. I should probably go back home . . ." I say.

"No!" he shouts and it startles me and I jump a little. His eyes widen when he notices my reaction. "I need you to look for her while I drive around. I'll give you this candy bar if you help me . . ." he offers, holding up my most favorite kind. I instantly grab for it, but he pulls it back.

"Okay, what does she look like?" I ask.

He smiles a creepy smile showing all of his teeth, but I open the front door and get in the van. He hands me the candy bar and I realize that I don't even know what his name is . . .

"She's little and fluffy and white . . ." he trails off as I dig into the sweets my mom never lets me eat before dinner. Ever!

All of a sudden, my head feels funny and my ears feel full of cotton like last summer when I got an infection from swimming too much. I open my mouth to tell him something is wrong, but my words don't work. They won't come out! I turn my head to look at him, a scream stuck in my broken mouth. He just smiles his big, creepy smile and everything goes black . . .

When I wake up, I look down, I'm wearing a funny old timey dress just like the one Angel was wearing and I know that it's my turn to die.

• • •

A scream rents the air. It's my scream but I can't seem to stop. I can't make myself leave this dream. And the worst part is knowing that I am alone and I have no one to blame but myself.

"Claire." I hear the voice I most want to hear say my name as my dream takes on a cruel twist. I whimper but I don't open my eyes. Someone shakes me. "Claire," he says louder as he pulls me free from the dream.

"Wes," I sigh.

"I'm here, baby. I told you I would always be here." He pulls me into his arms and I realize that he's laying in my bed. Wes came home. Well, to my home, but right now I don't care. I wrap my arms around his neck and crush my mouth to his.

"Wes," I plead when I pull back to look in his eyes.

"I'm here, baby."

"I need you." And I do. I need Wes.

He rolls me to my back before using his knees to slide my legs apart. I instantly pull my own knees up high and wide as he settles in between my thighs.

"Wes, I need you," I plead.

"I need you too, baby. I need you so much." And then he touches his forehead to mine and slides in to the hilt.

Wes braces his weight on his forearms as he slowly pumps his cock into my waiting body. He frames my face with his rough palms and I love it. I love getting lost in the feel of his hard body, the coarse hair on his chest, as he moves against me—*with me*.

This is everything that I need.

The way Wes makes love to me in the middle of the night, chasing away the bogeyman, is all that I need—that it's all that I'll *ever* need—I can't help but feeling like maybe he was right after all. Maybe it's not complicated at all, maybe it's real fucking simple.

I arch my back against Wes, my arms and legs grip around his body as my pussy grips his cock tight. I let out his name on a gasp as I climax and he follows me right over the edge into bliss.

"I love you, Claire," he says just as the gray of sleep takes me under, my body still wrapped around his. I can't help but think the words that most need to be said but I know that it'll wait until morning.

I love you too.

Too bad that it really wouldn't wait.

chapter 7
that stings

*B*EEP... BEEP... BEEP.
My alarm blares from beside my bed. I reach over to silence it on the nightstand when the bulky arms that are wrapped around my body squeeze the breath right out of me.

"I meant what I said last night." His already deep voice is burred by sleep. The sound of it next to my ear makes a shiver wrack up my spine.

"I know," I whisper.

"Good," is his only response as he coasts one palm up my belly to cup my breast where he casually circles his thumb around my nipple.

I bite my lip to hold in a moan as I arch back against his hard body.

Wes drives his other hand down my belly to between my legs where he finds me wet and wanting. I grip his hand between my thighs.

"Claire," he rumbles next to my ear as he circles my clit with his fingers but I don't want to talk this morning. There are too many things that need to be said and I'm not ready to say them. So, I tip my hips back against his groin.

"Shut up and fuck me, Wes," I demand.

"Yes, ma'am," he says before he slides his cock into my waiting body.

"Yes," I purr.

Our bodies move as one as we rock together. Our coupling is as loving as it is frenzied and urgent. I'm glad that I can't see his face. I know what I would see there and we both know that I'm not ready. I have been barely hanging on to this relationship business since I was shoved over the falls by a deranged murderer five months ago.

And we both know that Wes wants more. He has been silently guiding me towards holy matrimony the same way one would try to tame a skittish colt.

He circles his fingers faster as he picks up pace. Thank God. The coarse hair on his thighs abrading my legs as I rock my hips against him, meeting him thrust for thrust before finally throwing my head back to rest on his shoulder as I claw at the sheets and the pillows in front of me with my free hand. The other is hanging on to Wes's at my center like a lifeline. My body tightens from head to my toes and I come. Wes rocks into my body one more time before planting himself there and following me over the edge, growling out his release.

"Claire," he groans with his face to the side of my neck.

"I love you too," I whisper hoping he doesn't hear it but by the stiffening of his body as every muscle contracts, I know that he does.

We lay there, neither one of us wanting to break the spell by moving—for what seems like an eternity when the alarm on Wes's phone blares bursting our love bubble.

"Claire—" he starts.

"You need to go," I tell him.

"I don't want to go."

I sigh. "Let's just get this day over with. We can talk later."

"Claire—" he starts.

"Not yet, Wes," I plead. "I'm not ready yet."

He sighs in frustration over my lack of enthusiasm regarding our relationship as he slides his softening cock from my hold before throwing the sheets back and prowling off to the bathroom.

Our love bubble is officially toast.

I hear the water kick on in the shower and I wonder if it's too cowardly of me if I hide under the covers until he leaves my apartment. Deciding that sounds like a fantastic idea I grab the blankets he tossed away and am just starting to pull them back up the bed when a firm hand clasps my ankle and tugs me down the bed.

And I scream like a little girl. Some badass I am.

Wes tosses me over his shoulder like a fireman and I meet the glorious vision of his firm backside. I think I might be drooling just a bit and my eyes glaze over at the sight of all that sculpted muscle. He might be approaching advanced age at his thirty-eight years, but Wes still has a banging body.

I'm distracted by my thoughts when his large hand smacks my ass as it hangs in the air. I let out and embarrassing *Eep!*

"God damnit, Wes!" I shout.

"You are not going to chase me away every time you're a chicken shit," he says as he swats me again.

"Damnit! That stings."

"You get to be scared," he says as he swats me again and the soothes the sting with his palm. "I'm scared too. But you will not run from me."

"I'll do what I want, you big bossy bastard!" I shout as I try and protect my ass which—if I'm honest—doesn't actually hurt.

"I love you and your colorful use of alliteration," he says softly as he steps into the shower and the frigid water slices over my skin.

"Holy fuck this is freezing!"

"I know," he tells me with a smirk after he lets my naked body slide down his. "I can't go into work with a raging hard-on. They'll never let me live it down."

"That doesn't sound like my problem," I pout.

"It's not. But when you're around, I'm always hard. Fuck, I can be sitting at my desk and remember something funny you said or how beautiful you looked the night before and bam! I'm hard."

"I think that might be a compliment wrapped in vulgarity," I pout.

"It is. I love all of you, baby. The good and the bad," he says smoothly.

"Bad?" I purr. "How bad?" I ask as I wrap my hand around his cock and stroke him with my fist. The cold water doesn't seem to be helping his . . . *problem.*

I let him go to fill my hands with shampoo and start washing my hair. Wes swats my hands aside and gently tends to my long mane. I love how tender he can be when it's just us. It's one of the many different facets of Wes that I seem to be falling more in love with each one every day.

We take our time washing each other in the cold spray, using our hands and our mouths to say the things that I know that I'm not ready for—at the same time Wes is eager to shove us over the cliff.

And the truth in the moment is clear—we want the same thing—to love each other.

Wes shuts the taps off when the soap is gone and the water runs clear. We dry off and silently dress for our day. We stop on the landing outside my front door as I pull it tight and turn the key in my many locks.

"I have to come into the station to sign a statement for Liam," he says before curling his body around mine and landing the mother of all kisses on my lips. "Don't run."

"Okay," I whisper against his lips.

"Okay." His voice vibrates against my mouth. "I'll see you later." And then he kisses me one more time before letting me go.

We walk down the stairs to the parking lot and turn in separate directions for our vehicles. I'm in a hurry so I don't stop and look back. Later, I would wish that I had because if I had seen the look of love and longing on his face my response when tested later would be different. *Maybe.*

chapter 8
blink of an eye

FUCK I NEED COFFEE.
All I could think about the whole drive to the station was how bad I wanted coffee. I didn't drink a ton last night because over indulging in booze scares the hell out of me. I have seen way too many good cops go down dark paths because they couldn't handle the really shitty parts of the job so they chose to cope with liquor and sex. We're all capable of it. Add in my own tale of woe—the mystery surrounding my own kidnapping twenty-four years ago—and the potential is there for me to go off the rails for sure.

So, I had a few mixed drinks with the girls over dinner, but it never went past that. I was sober by the time our cab made it back to New Jersey. A good thing since I came face to face with one of the creepiest cases I've ever seen as soon as my feet touched the asphalt of the parking lot.

But now I need coffee. I don't just want it, *I need it*. It's my life's blood and it might actually be what flows through my veins.

I pull into the parking lot of the station and take a deep breath as I pull the glass door open. I love it here. In fact, I grew up here. My dad was the Captain at this very station when Liam and I were growing up. No one was surprised when Lee followed in his footsteps, yet everyone acted like I had said that I like to kill baskets of puppies on the weekends when I chose to do the same.

Life can be a real bitch sometimes.

I walk straight past my desk, dutifully ignoring the massive stack of inter-office messages and mail and head straight for the kitchenette in the back where the magical coffee maker lives. I pull a cup from the stack and pour myself a cup of the good stuff. I guzzle it down like a hooker on her knees and give not one fuck that it's steaming hot.

I set my cup down and let out a deep sigh. "Thank God."

"You alright there, Claire?" I hear from in front of me. I didn't notice any-one follow me into the kitchen because I had a one-track mind and that track was on coffee, glorious, magical coffee.

"Just peachy," I sigh again before opening my eyes and taking in Abraham Cruz. His blue eyes twinkle as he takes me in. I pretend like I don't notice his eyes track down my body before slowing on all the places a bathing suit might cover.

"Understandable," he says as he nods to the coffee cup that I am refilling. "It was a pretty rough night."

"That it was," I agree. "Coffee?" I hold up the coffee carafe in my hand offering him a warm up.

"If that's all you're offering," he mumbles. *Interesting*. And unwelcome.

"That it is," I say on a tight smile.

"Then, yes, coffee." He holds out his cup and I fill it up for him. "Thank you."

"Anytime." I smile at him from behind my cup. He's a nice guy although nobody really knows him very well yet. We will. We don't let detectives go rogue. Around here, there are no lone wolves.

"I have to say, Detective, I like the jeans and t-shirts you wear here—but that dress you wore last night was amazing." He winks.

"An LBD is hardly crime fighting gear," I say in a mock stern tone.

"I don't know what a LBD is, but hard-ons are the only thing anyone was fighting."

His comments are crude and inappropriate, but they make me laugh. I've been one of the guys for ages. I avoid flirtations like this because I wouldn't want to give anyone the wrong idea. But now that I'm with Wes, *really with Wes*, and everyone knows that I'm taken, I can engage in ridiculous flirting which is harmless and fun.

"An LBD is a little black dress and you're an idiot." I laugh.

"You wound me, Goodnite," he says as he clutches his chest in an overly dramatic attempt to show me that he's heart broken.

"Somehow I think that you'll survive."

He opens his mouth to respond but Liam bellowing from within his office interrupts him.

"Goodnite! My office. Now!"

I sigh. "Duty calls."

"Good luck with that one, Goodnite."

I make my way down the hall to Lee's office and knock on the door.

"Get your ass in here," he shouts just before I push the heavy door open. I'm barely through when I'm grabbed by my arm—ambushed really—and shoved against the wall. A large, hulking mass of angry man crowds me in and stares me down.

"What the fuck was that?" Wes snaps.

"What the fuck was what?" I ask. What the hell is he so mad about? I just left him like an hour ago. He's barely had time to check in at his field office before heading to this station house. So, I'm not sure what the hell he could be so mad about now.

"You know what," he seethes.

I blink. "No, actually, I have no idea what you're talking about." And I don't. Truly.

He seems to weigh my words for a minute before asking me, point blank, "Are you interested in Detective Cruz?"

"What?" I ask shocked. I'm truly shocked. "Why would you even think that?"

"Because I saw you with him on my way in. You had that look on your face you get right after you come," Wes says pointing right at my face.

"Too much information about my sister in my office, asshole. Thanks," Liam grumbles from his seat at his desk. I watch him over Wes's shoulder as he shoots Wes's back the bird. *Nice.*

"Answer me," Wes demands softly as he uses a fingertip to push me back to face him by my chin.

"Nothing happened," I explain.

"And the face?" he questions.

"Jesus Christ," Liam gripes from across the room.

"I was drinking coffee. It was my first cup of the morning after a long night. I would have had one—or eight—at home but someone distracted me." I give him a pointed, you-know-what-I'm-talking-about look that obviously speaks volumes.

"Just shoot me," Liam groans.

"Gladly," I say over Wes's shoulder.

"And Cruz? It looked like you were flirting."

"I was, kind of. Better?" I ask.

"How is that better?" he gripes.

"Because it was nothing. A little harmless flirting as a joke because everyone knows that I'm with you. All hope of getting into my panties is lost for the foreseeable future." I nod with my eyes wide in all seriousness.

"For the foreseeable future?" He asks, his tone deadly.

"Yes," I reassure him.

"That is ridiculous!" Wes shouts picking his mad back up to speed. "None of this shit would happen if you would just marry me!"

"Marry you? Are you insane?" I shout.

"No. I need something to go on. You say everyone knows that you're taken, but *I* don't even know that you're taken. You have to give me something."

"Are you saying that you're not taken? Are you seeing other people?" I ask feeling like my heart is about to shatter.

"No! I *am* taken, but it feels like I belong to a woman with one foot out the door." That is an alarmingly accurate depiction. "Marry me. Be mine."

"Actually," Lee wades in. "This is good. This would solve a lot of my problems."

"How does my marrying your lunatic best friend solve any of your problems?"

"Easy." He shrugs. "You become Wes's problem, not mine."

"Ugh," I groan as I roll my eyes so hard my head hurts. "You're both morons."

"So that's a no?" Liam asks for Wes.

"Yes!"

"She said yes!" Lee shouts.

"I said yes, I'm saying no, you assholes."

"You're saying no?" Wes asks, his voice low and angry.

"I'm saying this is ridiculous. I am not marrying you because you're a jealous Neanderthal. Ask me again some other time when you actually mean it and I *might* say yes."

"She's going to kill me," Wes muses to Liam. "I'm surprised my hair isn't a shock of white by now or that I haven't keeled over from a massive coronary yet."

"The day is still young, asshole," I cheer.

"Welcome to my world, brother," Liam commiserates.

"Har-de-har-har, assholes." They both look at me expectantly. "What?"

"Nothing."

"No reason."

"Well was there an actual reason why you called me in here or was it just to be a bunch of crazies?"

"I want an update on the Angel case," Liam commands. His posture is rigid showing his full power and importance in this office. This is Captain Goodnite.

"She's dead," I say.

"No shit, Sherlock," he grumbles. "Tell me more."

"That's it," I tell him. "I just fucking got here."

"Well, what did you find out last night?" Liam asks as an odd look crosses over Wes's face briefly. It's gone in the blink of an eye.

"That you guys are a bunch of assholes who drank too much and acted like a bunch of morons. Oh, and Jones is in love with his soon-to-be-wife. He is included in the drunken morons category."

"You have nothing," he states.

"Bupkis," I agree.

"Better get back to the salt mines then."

"Gladly." I slip out from behind Wes and bow towards Liam. "Always a pleasure, douche canoe." I take a step towards the door when Wes stops me with a hand on my upper arm.

"Wait," he says.

"What is it?" I ask.

"Are you mad?" He looks concerned. He acted like an idiot but I'm kind of used to it by now.

"No," I answer and he visibly relaxes.

"Have dinner with me tonight?" He smiles that panty melting smile that I can't say no to.

"Okay." I smile warmly at him knowing that we're okay even though I said no to his ridiculous proposal.

"Good. Pack a bag," he says before crushing his mouth to mine.

"I'm going blind!" Liam shouts causing both Wes and I to laugh.

chapter 9
nothing

IT'S ALWAYS WEIRD TO me how things can look more sinister in the daylight.

As kids, we're told that the bogeyman only comes out at night. That monsters hide under the bed or in the closet—but you'll never see one during the daytime.

In my profession, we see the bogeyman at all hours and monsters can be dressed as anyone.

Standing in the alleyway behind the strip club where a woman was murdered last night should be less scary today in the daylight, but right now, I feel anything but calm. There is no blood on the sidewalk, no torn clothes or bullet casings. To any other person, this would seem like any ordinary back alley, not a murder scene.

But I know differently.

I'm frozen staring at the dumpster, the backdrop of where she was found, but that's not what scares me. I feel someone watching me. I know that sounds crazy, but in my gut, someone is near and it has the hairs on my arms standing on end.

I turn and look over my shoulder but no one is there.

I look back to the dumpster where "Angel" also known as Bonnie Bradley was left—posed to be sleeping, really—as a gift. But for who? I vow to find the killer of this woman cut down in her prime—but also the reason why. There has to be a reason why someone would do something so evil.

Through my swirling thoughts and the facts of this case, all I can hear is Emma's voice saying, *"I have never seen that color on anyone other than your dad, Liam . . . and you."*

Surely, we're not the only ones in the entire tri state area with violet eyes. Bonnie is just a few years older than Liam, who was a honeymoon baby for our parents. I know it's possible that my mom and dad had lives before us, before each other, but I seriously doubt my dad would have a daughter that he didn't tell us about. My dad is all about family.

I'm so lost in my thoughts staring at this damned dumpster that I don't hear anyone approach. I barely cover the jolt that the voice behind me sends through my body. So, there is one thing to be proud of.

"No one's supposed to be back here. This is a business not a circus side show!" I turn around at his booming voice. "Oh, it's you, Detective."

"Hello, Mr. Byrd."

"Please, call me Bob," he purrs as his eyes make a slow pass down my body and the back up again, seeming to get stuck on my breasts and unable to move back up to meet my face.

I clear my throat. "Do you need something, Mr. Byrd?" The sound of my voice seems to snap him out of his fog.

"No, no," he says. "I'll just let you get to it."

"Thanks," I say as I turn back to the dumpster. I need to give this alleyway my full attention. I'm missing something but I just don't know what.

"Actually . . ." he hedges.

"Yes?" I ask.

"Do you dance?"

"What?" What in the hell is he asking me? I'm trying to find a killer and Bob Byrd is asking me if I dance. Is he asking me out? Oh hell no.

"Well, I couldn't help but notice that you have a beautiful body . . ." he trails off.

"Umm . . ." I'm not really sure how to respond here. This isn't something they cover at the Academy.

"And as of last night, I'm short a dancer. I think you would make a wonderful addition to the weekend lineup—"

"Let me stop you right there." I hold up a hand silencing him. "While I appreciate the offer, I am very busy as a police detective trying to solve the murder of the woman who had previously danced in your establishment. So, if you don't mind, I'd like to get back to that."

"Sure, sure." I again turn back to the alleyway, already having moved on from the conversation when he interrupts my thoughts again. "I was wondering if you're free for dinner tonight."

"I'm seeing someone," I say without turning back to look at him.

"Is it serious?"

"As a heart attack," I answer gravely.

"Okay, carry on." He waves his hand out magnanimously and I want to rip his arm off and beat him with that hand. I could never be a politician. Or a politician's wife. Just reason number four hundred sixty-seven why Wes's parents hate me. Oh well. Can't win them all.

"Thank you." I don't bother to turn back to him that last time either.

After a beat, I hear the back door open and close. It seems that Mr. Byrd is done waiting for me to answer him. Good. I run through the facts in my head.

Last night, after performing for a bachelor party, Bonnie Bradley was murdered and then dressed in odd clothing—old fashioned floral prints with lace collar and cuffs. Looked to be homemade. She was then laid out as if she was sleeping, as if she was a doll, but why?

Her eyes.

Something tells me that the key to why is in her eyes. I just don't know why. I walk around to the back of the dumpster. Last night, Crime Scene found scuff marks from the back door of the club to behind the dumpster. All signs leading to Bonnie being dragged back her before she was killed.

A condom wrapper was also recovered behind the dumpster. Emma will be able to tell me after she performs the autopsy if Bonnie had consensual sex with a lover before she died or if she was raped. Or maybe neither. Maybe someone had a little too much fun in the club and decided to carry it out here. What did the cab driver say? Only tricks and dancers in the club. Someone could have paid for the extra special treatment out back. Only time will tell. Until then, I have more rocks to peek under in this investigation.

There is nothing left for me here. At least not right this second, so I turn on my heel and head to my department SUV at the end of the alley. I unlock the doors with the key fob and climb in heading back towards the station.

I need to see it all laid out before me. Sometimes that helps me see the bigger picture and connect all of the dots.

I don't turn on the radio in the car, instead, I opt for silence and the company of my own thoughts, which is never good. By all accounts Bonnie Bradley was a nice woman who lived a quiet life other than when she was taking her clothes off for money. And yet, somebody wanted her dead. But who?

I pull into my usual parking spot at the station, shut the car off, and grab my folder full of notes and pictures. I let my frustration over the lack of evidence or really anything in this case show by slamming the door a little harder than I should.

I walk straight through the station and do not stop at my desk. I do not stop at the kitchenette for some coffee. I do not pass go and collect two hundred dollars. I keep walking until I reach the door to the conference room.

I slam my file down on the table and start piecing together the timeline, laid out for me to see across the table. I take each piece of evidence, each picture, each slip of paper, one by one and pin them to the bulletin board in the conference room. Hoping beyond all hope that something will click into place. Something will lead me to the who or the why or the how.

And nothing. Nothing makes sense. I beginning to think that the worst is yet to come. That after forbidding everyone to say what we were all thinking last night, that there is no refuting the fact that this case is different. That if more women turn up having been left the same way, that we have a serial killer on our hands.

I stand there with my hands on my hips staring at the board for who knows how long. It could have been minutes but my guess is it was hours. I hear a throat clear behind me and I know who it is. I'm not ready to give up and yet, I know that I need to. I need to go home and rest. I need to recharge my batteries so that I can hit the trail again tomorrow and pray to all that's holy that we don't have a psycho on our hands when I'm really afraid that we do.

"It's time to go, honey."

chapter 10

it's not that

TIME TO GO.
    I feel my spine straighten at Wes's softly spoken words. I look to the clock on the wall, it's a quarter past seven, the regular shift is long gone and only the night shift would be here by now.
    "Lee's gone." he says as he slowly saunters my way. "You want to grab some dinner?"
    "Yeah." I don't really, but I don't want to tell Wes that either. He's slowly earning his place with me. I feel guilty for having put him through his paces, but I want to believe he won't let me down.
    "Let's go."
    Wes helps me collect my notes and stack them in a nice, neat pile in my folder. I slide my arms into my jacket and we head out of the station. The bullpen is barren. The lights are dimmed and the chairs are tucked into their matching desks. The geriatric computers have all been put to sleep for the evening. Everyone has gone home for the night.
    It feels a little like that kid book, *Goodnight Moon*. Good night papers, goodnight folders, good night battered desks and broken chairs, good night crime is everywhere.
    Wes holds the glass doors in the front open for me as we both wave goodbye to the night desk sergeant, before walking silently through the parking lot with his hand on the small of my back. When we reach his car, he pulls the passenger door open for me and I climb in. We don't say a word to each other, both lost in our thoughts as he drives us towards the familiar building of comfort and family—well, not for me. Mama still holds out hope that Wes will choose her granddaughter instead of me. I find comfort in the food and the wine—and she loves Wes so much she lets me eat there, but only with him.
    "Ready?" He asks me breaking into my thoughts.
    I turn in my seat and look at Wes unsure of how to answer his question or the true meaning behind it. Does he mean am I ready to eat? Am I ready to find a possibly unhinged killer? Or ready to get married? Hopefully, not that one. So, I answer him the only possible way I can as I unbuckle my seatbelt and move to open my door.
    "I was born ready."
    We climb out of the car and head inside out of the spring chill. Mama's face immediately brightens when she sees Wes.
    "Wesley! You've come to see Mama!" But then she catches a look at me holding Wes's hand and her face dims. "Oh, it's you."
    She grabs menus and leads us to a table in the back. Wes—the total shit that he is—is chuckling under his breath. I'm glad he finds this so hilarious. I

mumble asshole under my breath. I know that he hears it because he only laughs louder and squeezes my hand tighter.

Wes pulls my chair out for me and Mama grumbles something about a waste before dropping menus in our laps.

"You know, I'm not sure the food is worth it," I muse as I look over the menu even though I already know what I'm getting.

"It is."

"Your opinion is invalid!" I snap and Wes just laughs.

"No, it's not."

"It is. This is all your fault anyways," I gripe.

"How is it my fault?" he asks his eyes dancing with amusement.

"She doesn't like me because she wants you to marry her granddaughter," I explain.

"So?"

"So? So, if you could get on that it would be great. Then I could eat in peace." Although the idea of Wes marrying Mama's granddaughter turns my stomach sour.

"There's only one crazy woman I want to marry and you know it. Have you thought anymore about my proposal?"

"Shh!" I panic and hide behind my menu. "Don't let anyone hear you say that!"

"Why not?" he asks.

"Because the crazy old bat with the delicious food will throw us out without said delicious food and I'm starving!"

"I have something else in mind that I wouldn't mind eating," he says his voice husky.

"Oh no you don't!" I shout. "I'm getting linguini and you're not stopping me."

"Whatever you want, dear." Wes imitates the perfect nineteen-fifties husband. I roll my eyes as his dance with merriment.

"I like the sound of your capitulation."

"Not as much as I like the sound of yours," he says pointedly, eyes locked on mine.

"Lame. Not happening." I cross my arms over my chest.

"You know it does. Especially when you want my cock so bad that your pussy weeps and you beg me to fuck you."

"Stop. I'm losing my appetite." I say as Wes just chuckles under his breath.

After we order, I sit sipping a glass of white wine and enjoying the banter I have with Wes. I have to admit—the man gives good banter. He's sexy as hell and as we talk, laugh, and push each other's buttons, the stress of the day, of this case—of the messiness of this crime—starts to melt away. And on top of it all, Wes takes care of me too.

Our meals come and Wes and I eat in companionable silence. We're comfortable enough with each other—even after everything that's happened—that we don't need to fill the space with mindless chatter. I can't help but feel like that means something pretty significant, but I'm not ready to admit my true thoughts to myself or anyone else again.

Wes pays the check and leads me out to the car. The short drive to my apartment is quiet but the butterflies in my stomach are loud. Usually, Wes takes me back to his home instead of my small, arguably a piece of shit apartment. He hates it here. Maybe he's finally tired of me and my shit.

He parks the car and kills the engine before unbuckling his seatbelt and turning to me. I keep my eyes cast down towards my own buckle and busy my hands with that to avoid looking at Wes as he gives me the brush off. All while wondering why it was okay for me to try and scrape him off—but it hurts so bad when I know he's about to do it himself.

He gently touches his palm to my cheek and presses his fingertips into my jaw to lift my face to meet his.

"I know what you're thinking. I can see the hamster on the wheel in there, but it's not that," he says softly.

"Okay."

"I would take you to my house, like I always do, but it's shit waking up alone after spending a great fucking night with you. Talking to you. Fucking you. Falling asleep with you in my arms. Only to then waking up to cold sheets and an empty bed." He takes a breath before continuing. "I just like being with you baby. So, since you always run here and I'm tired of chasing after you in the wee hours of the morning we're staying here tonight. Even though it's a shit hole. So, wipe the sad look off of your face. It's not that."

"Okay." I can't help the wave of relief that courses through me.

"So now let's get inside so I can get inside you." He winks—the cheeky bastard.

"Okay," I say feeling my lips twitch before climbing out of the car.

Wes rounds the hood and places his hand just above my ass on the small of my back silently letting me know that for now, he's not going anywhere. I'll take it. We walk up the steps and I let us in.

Wes softly closes the door behind us with a soft click before turning all of my locks one by one. He turns to me and I stand there watching him. Watching his surprisingly graceful movements for someone so big—so larger than life—and wondering how he decided he wanted me.

He uses the rough pads of his fingers to brush the hair that's fallen around my face back behind my ears.

"Christ, you're so beautiful," he says softly. "I could look at you forever."

"Wes—" I start but I don't get to finish my thought because his mouth crashes down on mine.

"No. No talking," he says when he lets me catch my breath. "Not tonight." Then he takes my hand and walks me back to my bedroom at the back of my apartment.

The second the door click closed behind us, Wes frames my face with his hands before touching his mouth to mine. His kiss is deep and wet and so much more. He tips his head forward when he breaks the kiss to catch his breath and his forehead touches mine. When he opens his eyes, I can tell that everything is changing between us and I'm powerless to stop it.

He skates his hands down my sides before reaching the hem of my shirt and pulling it up until it slides over my head. He reaches for the button on my jeans and pops it open before sliding the zipper down. I brush his hands away and pull his tie from around his neck. Then meticulously unbutton each button down the front of his super Fed dress shirt and then his cuffs. I slide my hands over each and every muscle on his chest and shoulders as if it's the first time I have ever touched him before letting his opened shirt slip to the floor. His belt buckle clanks as I unhook it and unzip his slacks letting them fall around his feet before pressing my palm to the prize I was searching for.

I only get to squeeze his hard length once before Wes is throwing me over his shoulder as he steps out of his shoes and pants before carrying me to the bed. Where he drops me down.

Wes slides the zipper down the side of my first boot, pulling the folded knife free and setting it on the nightstand before dropping the boot to the floor. He unzips the second boot and I get an eyebrow raised as he notices my drop gun in its holster but I just shrug. Hey, I like to be prepared for anything. He places the gun and holster on the nightstand before letting the second boot follow the first to the floor.

"Any other surprises I should know about?"

"It's always been there, I'm not sure how you've missed it." I smirk.

"We'll I guess I'll just have to frisk you then—to be sure and all," he says as he skates his hands down over my legs, gripping my ass tight in his palms before moving on and cupping my center.

"Do what you have to."

With my boots out of the way, Wes pulls my pants down with my panties stuck inside. The look on his face is soft and his eyes blaze as he stares at me. "So fucking beautiful," he says stealing the breath from my lungs.

"Wes—"

"I'm in love with you, Claire." My eyes go wide and my mouth pops open. "I've always been in love with you. I was in love with you when you were a tiny baby in a pink blanket with bright purple eyes. It was different then. I was in love with you when you were ten years old and riding your bike to the library. I loved you before Lee and I left for the Navy. It was still different then, but still special. I was in love with you—totally gone for you—when I came home and you gave me all that was you at eighteen and it killed me to walk away. But I have always been in love with you. Now so much more than ever, baby."

"Wes—"

"You don't have to say anything now. You don't have to say it back again or as often as I do," he says wearing nothing but his underwear as he kneels between my open thighs and lays his heart at my feet. And he won't let me tell him that I love him too. He is so annoying like that.

"Wes—"

"Serious. I just needed you to know. You're so beautiful laying there, spread out like that for me. Only me."

"God damnit! Shut up." I bark and his spine goes straight. "I love you, you idiot! I have always loved you. Loved you so much it scares the shit out of me. Love you more every day. Although less right now because you were being so sweet and so romantic. I've never had that before and now you're being obnoxious not letting me get a word in." I huff out a breath.

"Are you done now?" he asks.

"Maybe. I haven't decided yet," I answer honestly.

"You're done," he says.

"You don't just get to decide that I'm done being irritated with you," I snap.

"Baby, I waited almost thirty years for you. We've been through so much. I thought I lost you twice—not in good ways—once in a really bad way. So now that I have you—in my life and in my bed—and I just told you that I have always been gone for you and you tell me that you love me but you're irritated with me. I'm going to tell you that you're over it now because my girl just gave me her heart while she's pissy. Pissy, but laying naked and fucking sexy in her bed. So I'm going to eat her and then I'm going to fuck her. Then I'm going to fuck her slow and sweet before falling asleep with her in my arms. Only to wake up with her tomorrow morning and fuck her all over again. So, you're done so I can commence that plan, okay?"

"Okay," I say stunned and definitely turned on. "You can commence your plan."

"Babe," he says as he hovers his bulky body over mine. He kisses me hard and wet and warm.

I gasp when he lets go of my mouth and trails his lips down the column of my neck, down over my collarbone, and then down to swirl around my nipple before pulling it deep into his mouth. I arch my back to give him more access as he sucks my nipple hard and then let out a whimper as he bites down on it before letting it go with a pop.

"Wes," I pant as he skims his mouth down my belly.

Wes nips my bare mound as he goes but it's not hard or mean—it's playful and tender. Before he dives in, spearing my core with his tongue as he sucks my clit into his mouth. A tingle starts at the base of my spine and I grip the sheets with my toes. I plunge my fingers into his dark hair and pull hard as he fucks me with his mouth.

I rock my pussy against his face as he shoves me over the edge into the climax that was barreling down on me full speed ahead. And I come.

Fireworks are still blasting off behind my eyes and I'm still in throws of the most magnificent climax ever to notice Wes slide his hard body up mine—divesting himself of his shorts somewhere along the way—and my pussy is still spasming when he slides his cock in deep.

My first orgasm steam rolled right into my second one as he pumps deep and hard. Faster and faster. I rake my nails down his shoulders as he chases my climax with his own, shoving his face into the crook of my neck, his lips against my skin rumbling with his groan as he comes.

When he raises his head to look at me there's a cocky smirk on his face and a twinkle in his eye. He softly touches his mouth to mine before sliding his still hard length from my body and rolling us together to his back with me laying across his chest on my belly.

Wes pulls the covers over us and tucks us in tight with my head against his chest. I hear his heart beating its steady rhythm and it pulls me into an almost deep sleep. *Almost.* But it's his words that rock me the rest of the way to dreamland.

"I've loved you your whole life and I'll love you the rest of mine." My eyes were closed and I was halfway asleep, but in the days to come I would wish that I had seen his face as he heard my returning words.

"It was only ever you, Wes. It'll only ever be you."

Then he rolled me to my back again taking my hands in each of his and holding them up by my head. I wrap my legs around his waist and hold on tight as Wes commenced the rest of his plan. Making love to me slow and sweet until a climax so bright washes over both of us that we drifted off to sleep clinging to each other.

chapter 11
someone watching

"*COME OUT OF THE closet, baby.*"
    "*No,*" I whisper, tears hot on my face and snot stuffing up my nose. Liam and Wes were right, I'm just a baby. A big kid wouldn't be crying in the dark corner of a closet hoping it'll all go away if you just wish hard enough. I bet Wes never cries. I know Lee doesn't.
    "*Come out now, Claire. Playtime is over.*"
    "*No,*" I cry louder. "*Please don't make me.*"
    "*Now!*" He growls as the closet door rattles. I gasp.
    "*Leave me alone!*"
    "*Get out of the fucking closet, Claire!*" He roars.
    "*Please no,*" I cry harder, my body shaking with each sob.
    "*When,*" he kicks his hard boots against the closet door and it shudders.
    "*Please.*"
    "*Are you,*" he kicks it again.
The doors are the kind with the slats that fold sideways. We have them at home and mama says I always pinch my fingers in the accordion. Whatever that is.
    "*I just wanna go home,*" I whisper.
    "*Gonna,*" he kicks again.
    "*I just want my mommy,*" I sob. "*Please, I just want my mommy.*"
    "*Fucking,*" the boards snaps and I scream.
    "*I just wanna go home, please,*" I beg.
    "*Learn!*" he shouts as he kicks the broken boards out of the way. He leans down and grabs me by my upper arms.
    "*Please,*" I wheeze but my words are cut short when he slaps my face hard. So hard I taste blood in my mouth and it's so yucky I feel sick. I'm going to throw up from the yucky taste. I try as hard as I can not to. I know that if I do, he'll punish me again. I don't want that. Anything but that.
    "*You are home, baby,*" he coos right before he slaps me again. I cry out again, falling to the floor with his last hit. It's so strong he knocks me down with it. "*And I thought I told you to call me daddy,*" he says as he lands a hard kick to my back.
    "*You're not my daddy, you'll never be my daddy,*" I whisper. "*My daddy is a nice man. He would never hurt me. You'll never be my daddy,*" I say again but the bad man can't hear me, he already walked away. I have nowhere to go, but one thing is for sure, I have to escape.

• • •

I have that creepy feeling you get when you know that someone is watching.

It's a feeling that has saved my life a handful of times so I snap my eyes open and see Wes is laying on his side. He's propped up on his elbow, with his head resting on his hand and his warm eyes on me.

"Hey," I rasp hoping he didn't realize that I was gripped in another nightmare.

"Morning, baby." I swallow to try and clear the sleep from my throat and open my mouth to speak but Wes beats me to it by dropping his mouth to mine. I open mine underneath his when he licks at the seam of my lips and he deepens the kiss as he rolls over my body.

"We have to get up."

"Not yet," he hums against my mouth as he slides his knees between my thighs spreading them open to his invasion of the very best kind.

"We have to go to work."

"Not yet," he murmurs as he trails his fingers down my hip and over my mound and down further. "Always so wet." He swirls his index finger around my clit making me whimper into his mouth.

"Wes—"

"Not yet," he says as he removes his finger from my clit, only to guide the tip of his cock into my wetness. I arch my back to try and take him deeper. "Not yet."

"Please, Wes." And that was all he needed to slide all the way to the root.

Wes takes my hands in his and intertwines our fingers in an intimate move that I both love and hate. I love it because it makes us so close—nose to nose—and other more fun parts. And I hate it because it's so intimate—that scares the hell out of me.

He places our joined hands up on either side of my head and as he looks into my eyes, his nose brushing mine. Wes rocks his hips softly into mine. There is no restlessness, no rush this time. Wes is not a man in a hurry, but he is a man with a desire to make love to his woman. You can see it in his eyes as he slowly puts his mouth on mine and takes us both over the edge.

When our breathing slows and the sweat on our bodies begins to cool, Wes finally looks at me and says, "Now we have to get up and get ready for work." I just roll my eyes and he laughs.

Wes pulls me up and out of bed and leads me down the hall to my small bathroom where he lifts me up by the waist and sets me on the small, soapstone countertop. He pulls the glass door open and cranks the water up. I live in a piece of shit apartment so even though the apartment is small, it takes awhile to heat up the water. So, Wes saunters back to me gloriously naked and then pushes his hips between my legs as I sit on the counter and kisses me. He doesn't just kiss me, no, Wes lazily makes out with me in his arms while we wait for the shower to heat up.

Then he plucks me from the countertop and walks straight into the shower with me in his arms. I turn into the water to wash my hair. I tip my head back under the spray to rinse the suds from my hair. Before I have a chance to stand back up I'm hauled out of the water and up against a very hard Wes.

"Do you know what you do to me, baby?" he asks. I have an idea because it is also very hard and pressed against my belly.

"I'm starting to figure it out." I grip his hard length in my fist and pump him once, twice, before I find my front pressed against the shower wall.

"Be careful, baby. You're playing with fire." He presses in close against my back and I feel the heat of him against my ass.

"Maybe I like the risk."

He growls low in his throat before tipping my hips back and thrusting his cock deep. Wes keeps me pinned to the shower wall with his chest pressed to my back. The cool material of the shower wall at my breasts and the heat of his body at my back does things to me.

Wes sets a fast tempo of push and pull that won't keep us going long. My cheek is against the wall and I whimper. I'm so close and I want it, but Wes is even closer.

"Touch yourself, baby. Get there." Wes takes my hand from the wall in his and slides it down the wall to between my legs where his uses my finger to circle my clit and push me closer. He skates our hands deeper to where his cock moves hard and fast in and out of my body. "Feel that. This is us when you end and I begin and this is only ever going to be us. No one else." He pumps faster and faster.

"Wes—"

"Get there," he says as he moves our hands back up to circle my clit. I whimper and cry out because I'm there. He lets go of my hand and I take over as he grips my hips and thrusts harder. "Yes. you're there." And I am. I press my cheek harder to the shower wall as my finger circles my clit. Wes pushes into my body and pulls back one out, once, twice more, and then I come. Wes follows me over the edge calling out my name as he does.

As he comes back down to earth, he slowly glides his cock in and out before kissing my shoulder gently and then slipping free from my body. I lean all of my weight against the shower wall. I think I'm dead. I must have died just now but what a way to go.

I hear Wes swallow down a chuckle from behind me and then his soapy hands roam all over my body. He rains kisses down all over my shoulders and the back of my neck as he soaps up my body and his before rinsing us clean.

He shuts off the water and towels me dry before drying himself. Then we both dress for work—including my stuffing my drop gun and holster back in my boot. All while Wes watches with a twinkle of amusement in his eyes.

chapter 12
this changes everything

"BABE, YOU NEED COFFEE."

"That is no lie," I share as Wes diverts from his path to the station to our favorite coffee shop. It's my favorite because the coffee is to die for. It's Wes's favorite because there is a twenty-year-old barista who fawns all over him but in an adorable—totally shy—way, so I can't even be mad at her.

Wes pulls into the parking lot as a front space magically opens. As is the way for all things where Wes is concerned. He's always been the golden boy that great things just happen to. Liam as well. Honestly, it's exhausting.

I hop out of the car intent on a caffeine infusion with Wes hot on my heels. He wraps his arm around my waist and I stiffen. I'm not used to anyone holding me while I'm wearing my duty rig. I force my muscles to relax one by one. This love and couple business is hard.

Wes pulls open the door to the coffee shop for me and the bell over it chimes. We walk in and are greeted by Tammy the ever shy, ever adorable barista. She smiles at me like she smiles at everyone because she's just that sweet. But when she sees Wes she positively glows. Her crush is still in full swing and I love it. It's adorable in its harmless young girl to woman way. She's growing into herself and she's got a good eye, Wes is a catch. He's just my catch.

"Hello, Detective, the usual?"

"Yes, please!" I smile as she writes my name on the paper cup and hands it to the other kid to make my fancy ass coffee.

"And the usual, Sir?" she asks Wes. "A large black coffee." She knows his order by heart. It's not a hard one, but still . . .

"Yeah, Tammy. Thanks." She physically brightens at the use of her name which we both know because we come here so often. Not to mention it's on a name tag on the front of her apron.

"Coming right up. It'll be nine dollars and eighty-five cents." He glares at me as he hands her a twenty.

"Hey, these fancy coffees aren't cheap but they make me so happy." I smile sweetly at Wes.

"Keep the change," Wes adds when Tammy tries to hand him back his change.

"Oh, thank you, Sir." She breathes. I barely keep from rolling my eyes. That's a new one, the Sir bit. I wonder if she's been watching those Fifty Shades movies. She's not going to find her dom in my overly dominate guy, that's for sure. He's mine. Well, it seems a couple rounds of ridiculously good sex make me down right possessive. Who knew?

We collect our coffees and head out the door. Both climbing into the car when Wes beeps the locks with the key fob.

"Not one word," he rumbles.
"I wasn't going to say anything."
"Lord love a liar."
"I have no idea what you're talking about. Drive me to the station, Jeeves!" I laugh, then I sit back and drink my fancy ass coffee with a smile on my face as Wes drives me to the station.

He pulls into the lot and parks the car, finding another ridiculously good space. I do roll my eyes at that and catch the flash of white teeth as he smiles. We climb out of the car and walk towards the station. This time Wes does not hold me close because he knows how important it is to me to be treated with respect here—respect that I have earned with hard work and determination.

He does open the door for me and I walk through it with him on my heels.

"Goody, Emma called and the autopsy on the dancer is done," another detective calls out when I enter the bullpen.

"Thanks." I'll head down to the basement after I check in at my desk.

"I'm going to go check in with Lee. If I don't see you before I head to my office I'll see you tonight."

"Okay," I say distracted my mind already turning to what Emma has for me. Wes just shakes his head with a smile and heads down the hall towards Liam's office.

I walk straight to my desk and sit down, placing my paper coffee cup on the desk in order to boot up my geriatric computer. Once that task is done I notice a huge pile of mail on my desk and sigh. It's only seven in the morning, how can I possibly have so much mail?

The biggest is on top. It's a giant manila envelope with no postage or address on it. Just my name typed out on the front. Someone must have dropped this off in person. I flick back the little metal clip that holds it closed and pull out the stack of papers neatly tucked inside. On top is a typed note.

Do you know what your boyfriend is doing when you're not looking?

That's all that the note said. That's all that was typed on one white sheet of printer paper. The hair on the back of my neck stands on end. It's an omen of things to come—and not a good one. I flip the note over, face down next to the stack and am greeting with a series of glossy eight by tens. Enough to burst the happy love bubble that I was in with Wes and leave nothing but shrapnel and carnage.

What. The. Fuck.

When I had sat down at my desk and opened the manila envelope that was left on top of my stack of mail. It had seemed harmless enough.

But it wasn't.

I blink my eyes over and over trying to make my brain process what it's seeing but I can't. I can't unsee the images from the stack of pictures in my hand. Giant glossy eight by tens from different angles. So there is absolutely no doubt that my heart is breaking.

And it is broken. It's not just broken it's *shattered.*

"It's not what it looks like," I hear from over my shoulder and I have to grit my teeth to keep from screaming.

I shuffle the pictures sliding the top one to the back of the stack so that I can see the next in line. This one is zoomed in. His head is tipped back and his face is distorted with both lust and passion as she straddles his lap. Her hands hold his to her breasts and I can see the play of tendons flex through them as he grips them tight. It was only two nights ago that his hands were on my own breasts much the same way as I rode his cock on the sofa.

"Claire, did you hear me?" he asks but I shuffle the stack again. In this picture, he has his arms wrapped around her back and he's pulling her close—her breasts mashed up against his strong chest. Her hands with long, red painted talons press in on either side of his face and as they kiss hungrily, their mouths open as their tongues tangle. "God damnit, Claire! Did you hear me?" My spine turns to steel.

"I did. I'm just choosing to ignore you."

"Don't do this, baby," he growls.

"I'm not the one who did anything."

"I can explain." But I'm not interested in listening to him plead a case when he is more than guilty.

"I'm going to need you to leave, Wes."

"No."

"This changes everything."

"This changes nothing! Fuck that, Claire," he yells. "You want to run away. You have *always* wanted to run away. And here is your fucking reason to served up on a goddamn silver platter."

"No," I shout back as I throw the stack of glossy betrayal down on top of my desk as I push my rolly chair back and stand. It slams into the desk behind mine. "You do not get to come in here, where I work, and tell me that I am to blame for your bullshit."

"Okay," he says as he holds his hands up in surrender. "You're right. I'm sorry. I can see you need time."

"I need a lot of things. One of them is definitely distance."

"I don't know if I can give you that. I can't lose you, baby." His words burn hot behind my eyes and the last thing I want is for the other guys in the bullpen to see me cry.

"You should have thought about that before you fooled around with that stripper."

"Claire—" he starts but I don't let him finish.

"You need to go now," I say softly.

I stand with my feet apart, my hands on my hips, and my head bowed as if I'm waiting for a blow. He looks at me and opens his mouth as if he's going to try to explain again. Something in my stance must have told him it was a losing battle because he snaps his mouth closed before moving towards the exit.

Wes pauses just before opening the door to turn and look back at me. I see him in my peripheral, but I'm looking at his lies and deceit spread across my desk for all to see. He pulls open the door and then slams it on his way out. This is definitely how my heart breaks.

"You okay?" I hear from over my shoulder. I'm not in the mood to deal with anyone right now. I need to be alone to sort my feelings. I need to be alone to sort this fucking case.

"Yeah, I just need to get down to the morgue." I shrug. "Duty calls."

"You sure about?" I look up at Cruz and his face is so open and honest—something I have not had a lot of in my life—that I feel compelled to answer him when he asks again. "Are you going to be alright?"

"I'm not sure I even know the answer to that."

"Then he didn't deserve you to begin with." I'm not sure how to respond to that. At all. "I'm here if you need me."

"Duty calls," I say again and head to the elevator that will take me to the basement. The doors open and I step inside. Just as they're about to close Cruz is there with a hand to the door.

"Just think about what I said." And then he lets go of the door and the elevator takes me to Emma's lair in the basement.

chapter 13
windows to the soul

"STEP RIGHT UP, LADIES and gentlemen. We have a winner! Whaaaa," Emma shouts in her best game show host voice as I step off the elevator.

"And they think I'm the one who needs the department shrink." I shrug.

"That's because you do." She winks at me to lessen the sting of what we both know to be the truth.

"Thank you." I roll my eyes.

"Because you're a lunatic. Totally batty. Mad. Bonkers," Emma says in her best impression of the Mad Hatter.

"Takes one to know one." I stick out my tongue which only makes Emma cackle. I'm really mature, I know.

"'Only the best people are,'" she says finishing the *Alice in Wonderland* quote.

"Am I down here in your evil lair for a reason?" I change the subject.

"You are!" she cheers brightly.

"And that would be?" I'm a little shorter than I usually am with her and it makes her tip her head to the side to study me.

"Is everything okay, Claire?" She asks.

I sigh. "Just peachy."

"Claire," she whispers. "No."

"It's fine . . . I'll be fine."

"Is Liam okay?" Now it's my turn to study her.

"Why wouldn't he be?"

"No reason," she hedges.

"Is it Anna?" she asks.

"No."

"Wes?" she asks with her hand to her chest.

"Cheated. He's a filthy fucking liar."

"You don't know that for sure," she says after a pregnant pause.

"I have a stack of pictures on my desk that say otherwise, doll," I say softly.

"Oh no."

"Yeah." I sigh again. There's a band around my chest that keeps getting tighter and tighter and there's nothing I can do to ease the tension. Maybe I'm having a heart attack.

"Do you want me to call Anna?" she asks. That's my Emma, always ready to rally the troops in an emergency. But Wes isn't going to be an emergency. He was the slow-motion car crash I saw coming from miles away.

"No." I take a deep breath. "So, what do you have for me?"

"Maybe we shouldn't do this now."

"Why not?" I ask.

"I had to let Liam know I needed him for this. Maybe you don't want to see him right now."

"What?" I jump. "Why would you call Lee?"

"Why wouldn't she?" he barks from behind me. "I'm the fucking Captain, *Detective*," he says reminding me of my place here at the station while dressing me down at the same time.

"Because you were there the night the homicide took place."

"We don't know that it's a homicide yet," he snaps making me wonder if mom dropped him on his head as a baby.

"Don't be dumb, Liam."

"I'm just saying . . ." He holds his hands up at his sides in a *so what* gesture.

"Actually, we do know that she was murdered." Emma interjects.

"What do you have?" I ask.

"She had enough benzene in her bloodstream to immobilize her pretty quickly."

"How quick?" Lee asks.

"Maybe a minute or two."

"What's benzene?" I ask.

"It's a chemical—man made—that can be found in everything from dry-cleaners to gasoline."

"So, our guy is a dry cleaner?" Lee asks.

"Your guy can be anything, *El Capitan*," Emma snaps at him obviously losing her patience. "You can Prime that shit and have it delivered to your doorstep in two days."

"Fuck." Lee bites out.

"How did he give it to her?" I ask.

"Here." Emma peels back the sheet showing us the victim from the shoulders up pointing to a tiny little dot in between her neck and shoulder that I never would have noticed. "He injected it here."

"So, the killer poisoned her."

"No," Emma tells Liam and I like were the slow class. "He *immobilized* her first. Then the other stuff."

"Start at the beginning," Lee barks.

"My guess would be he lured her out back or found her there. Once the benzene was in her body, she would have dropped quickly. She would be like an over cooked noodle. He could have undressed her then—"

"She was already naked," Liam says quietly. "She was the dancer at Jones's party."

"Then she was raped," Emma says filling in the gaps.

"DNA?" I ask getting excited for a lead.

"No. Vaginal tearing and condom lubricant were all that was present."

"God damnit!" Lee bites out.

"Then how did she die?" I ask.

"He strangled her." She takes a deep breath before continuing. "She would have had to be dressed and posed quickly before rigor set in."

"Jesus." He rubs a heavy palm down his face.

"Okay," I say hesitantly. "This case is weird. But why did you need Lee here?"

She looks at me hard. "Are you sure you want to do this right now?"

"Emma," I warn.

"What am I missing?" Liam asks.

"She caught Wes cheating," Emma says bluntly.

"What?" Lee shouts. "I'll kill him. But when? With who?"

"With whom, you mean," Emma corrects.

"With her." I point to the dead stripper. Liam starts laughing. "What's so funny?" I snap.

"Nothing. Nothing at all. But Wes didn't cheat." Liam says, still laughing.

"I have a stack of pictures on my desk that say otherwise."

"I was with him all night. She danced for most of us, Claire."

"Even lap dances?" Now he looks at me like I'm the stupid one.

"Yeah, sis, it was a bachelor party. Either her or her friend rubbed their body glitter off on everyone in the group."

"Even kissing?" He laughs harder. "Stop that!"

"Honey, that's part of their thing," he explains gently.

"You made out with her the other night?" Emma asks from the corner sounding a mix of disgusted and disappointed.

"No." He shrugs. "Her friend. Actually, I was going to get a little more from her, but your boy needed a smoke and there this one was."

"He didn't cheat?" I ask. Lee's face softens and his laughter cuts off.

"No, honey. He loves you," my brother says softly, reverently as if I somehow stumbled onto the holy grail.

"Fuck!" I shout.

"What?" Lee asks.

"Fuck, fuck, fuck!"

"What?" Lee repeats his earlier question.

"She broke up with him," Emma drolls.

"I didn't break up with him . . . *per se*. I said I needed time and distance. But the note made it sound like he's been cheating all along."

"What note?" they both shout in unison.

"The note that came with the pictures."

"I think you were set up, sis. I need to see that package." We turn to head towards the elevator to get to the bottom of this whole Wes cheater drama when Emma stops us in our tracks.

"Wait!"

"What?" we say together.

"You haven't heard it all. Why Lee needed to be her too. It's not because it's your case," she says before pulling the rug out from under Lee and me. "It's because it's personal."

"How is it personal?" I ask. "Lee didn't kiss her and Wes didn't cheat."

"Remember I said her eyes were unusual? Windows to the soul they are," Emma explains.

"Yeah . . ." I reply hesitantly.

"That I had only ever seen eyes like that on you, Lee, and your dad," she continues.

"Yes." I enunciate the word.

"That color is rare. You don't see it often. And I was right, she doesn't wear contacts. So I tested her DNA . . ."

"And?" Lee snaps.

"She was your sister."

chapter 14
bad at love

I STEP INTO THE coffee shop. It's familiar but not because I get my coffee here. It's familiar because she works here.

Her black hair is driving me mad. I have to have it. It's dark and shiny but not glossy like a raven's wing and that makes me angry. Because this she is not the one that I want—the one that I need. No, she won't fucking notice me. I showed her how awful he is, how he doesn't deserve her, but does she choose me? No!

This one wants him too. I can see it the way she smiles at him when he comes here for coffee. She's practically begging him to want her. I feel the same way for the other one. The one I want but I won't beg her to love me. She will. I'll make sure of it.

But until then . . .

"Can you help me?" I ask sneaking up on this one as she stocks some shelves in the back all alone.

"Oh! I'm sorry, you startled me."

"You're lovely," I say to her.

"What?" she asks surprised as the tip of my needle slides into her pale skin of her neck.

"I said 'you're absolutely lovely.'" I tell her as I drop her to the storeroom floor and reach back to lock the door. "Almost perfect."

She looks at me with judgement in her eyes.

"This isn't for you to judge or decide," I seethe. "This is for me. I need her."

I look at her clear blue eyes and they're all wrong. Her eyes aren't purple. All. Wrong. Allwrongallwrongallwrongalwrong.

I strip her of her hideous clothes—she'll be perfect when I'm done with her. Like a little porcelain doll.

I might have given her too much of the benzene. Even her eyelids don't move.

Well, better get to it.

The condom wrapper crinkling is the only sound around. I roll the rubber down my length thinking of hair as glossy as a raven's wing and then I pull gloves onto my hands before wrapping them around her slim neck which is not as graceful as a dancer's, not like hers. And then I squeeze.

"Absolutely lovely," I lie.

• • •

"What?" Liam asks softly.

"I compared her DNA with Claire's sample from her file. Bonnie Bradley, age forty-three, is your sister—well, half-sister."

"That doesn't make any sense," I say. "That means—"

"Dad had another life before mom," Lee adds. "Don't you remember, I was their honeymoon surprise? They weren't even married a year when I was born and I'm thirty-eight."

"Okay," I sigh as the truth sinks in. "Dad didn't—"

"No," he says. "But it does mean we just lost a sister we didn't know we had."

"Now, I'm super glad she's not the one you kissed," Emma adds. "But it does make it weird that your boyfriend kissed your sister." She points at me. This is very true. My life is not a fun place to be right now.

"This is also true," Lee says looking at Emma like he's seeing her for the first time. Oh hell, this is going to blow up in our faces. Wes and I are bad at love, but Lee and either of my two friends that have feelings for him—or both, can anyone say *love triangle*—is a bad fucking idea.

"Lee—" I start but I'm interrupted by the ringing of my phone.

"Goodnite," I answer.

"Detective Goodnite, this is dispatch."

"Go ahead, Dispatch."

"We have officers responded to a homicide at a coffee shop. Case details are . . . similar to yours. They advised we notify you."

"Send me the address, I'm on my way," I say before ending the call.

"What's up?" Liam asks, suddenly alert.

"Got a fresh one."

"Another body?" He asks.

"Yep."

"Oooh, ooh, ooh. Pick me!" Emma jumps up and down.

"Yes, Em?" I ask.

"Is it as creepy as the last one?" She just can't help herself. We all know that these are real people who have been victimized, some even murdered. But in our line of work if we don't find some kind of levity in all of the seediness and evil, we'll crack.

"I don't know yet as I am not there—I am here. So, I gotta go." I look at my phone, the address of the restaurant when my body is. "Oh, fuck."

"What?" they both shout again.

"It's our coffeeshop," I explain.

"What?"

"The one that Wes and I always go to that costs a ton but I love it. So, we go and there is an adorable college girl that is over the moon for Wes. It's fucking adorable and she's so sweet." I make a strangled noise before bolting for the door to the stairs. There's no time for the elevator.

"Claire!" Lee screams.

"Fuck! Lee, she was on shift this morning. I have to go."

"I'm right behind you!" he shouts following me out.

• • •

If someone had asked me, I wouldn't be able to tell them how I got here. I ran up the stairs and out of the morgue. I know that I must have jumped in my department truck, but that's it. Between the phone call from dispatch and now—looking at Tammy's body laid out like a God damned doll—I couldn't tell you how I got from there to here.

Tammy Campbell, a nineteen-year-old college coed who this morning had the whole world laid out before her, now lays on her side in a dress that looks like it belongs in a production of *Our Town*. Her black hair is fanned out around her and her eyes are closed. Her hands are up in prayer, forever dreaming under her cheek—like a *fucking doll*.

I can already see the purple bruises coming up on her neck.

"Claire," Wes says from behind me, his voice pained. But of course, it would be. This is Tammy. *Our Tammy*. The girl we always buy coffee from. The girl who harmlessly flirts with Wes every single time.

But maybe it wasn't so harmless.

"This is an active crime scene, Agent O'Connell," I clip.

"Claire?" he asks. He sounds confused. "Lee called and said I needed to come here. He said you needed me."

"I need to solve this case and to do that I need you not here." I take a deep breath.

"You don't mean that," he pleads.

"I do, Wes. I have to figure this out before more people die."

"Claire—" he starts but I don't let him finish.

"You have to go. Someone else you were near died and I have to find out why."

"That's not fucking fair!" he yells, his hips and his feet wide.

"But it's true."

"You can't possibly think I did this." His tone is incredulous. Wes is mad, maybe a little hurt, I don't know. All I know is that I have to figure this shit out before it gets any worse.

"I don't know what to think anymore, Wes. But the signs are pointing to this being about you and you know it. Angel danced for you, kissed you. She's dead. The whole world knew Tammy had a mammoth sized crush on you and now she's dead too. Who's next, Wes?" I ask. It's an unfair question and we both know it but I ask it anyways.

"Low blow, Goodnite," he clips out. Wes's entire body is perfectly still as a statue but his eyes, his eyes are wild.

"Someone has to ask the question. Now if you'll excuse me, I'll get back to doing just that."

"You have to talk to me, Claire. We have to talk about this."

"Don't leave town," I say as I move around another officer and make my way away from Wes.

chapter 15
old news

I STAND IN THE hallway of the small coffee shop that I will never be a patron of again and watch the hustle a bustle of the Crime Scene Unit. Cameras flash and bootied feet shuffle as people poke and prod Tammy Campbell in the last place she was ever vibrant and alive.

I stand as a silent sentry guarding her in her last moments before she heads to Emma's lair in the morgue, giving her these last vestiges of dignity and privacy. With my hands on my hips and my feet shoulder width apart, I watch as the team loaded her onto a gurney and then rolled out the back doors into the alley to load her into the back of the Medical Examiner's body mover van. And through it all I can't help but think that her hair is black just like mine.

When the heavy metal doors slam closed behind her I turn on my heels and get back to work. I notice Liam and Wes are standing there—eyes locked on my every move like heat seeking missiles. That's fine. They won't bother me. I'm in my zone, this is my world and they just get to play in it. I will find out what happened to Tammy and Bonnie no matter the cost—even if the high price is my affair with Wes.

I walk back inside the shop and another girl is hysterical. She's sobbing so hard she can't catch her breath. She's sitting at a table with a woman of middle age with some slight silvering to her hair. She's the manager. I've met her before.

"Can I sit down and talk to you guys for a bit?" I ask.

The older woman looks to the younger one in her arms. The young barista nods. So, does the manager.

"Thank you," I say softly. "Were you both working this morning?"

"I was," the manager tells me.

"No." The girl sniffles.

"Who found her?" I ask.

"I did," the young woman says before biting her lip to hold in a wail. "I had just clocked in and Maggie told me to find out what Tammy was up to."

"Where were you?" I asked the manager.

"I was in the office doing payroll. I hate math. I do it when the store is slow between rush hour and lunch."

"That's understandable." I smile sweetly.

"Thank you."

"Were either of you close with Tammy?"

"Of course," the manager says. "My girls are like daughters to me."

"That's true," the younger woman agrees. "Tammy is . . . *was* my best friend," she chokes out.

"Would you say you knew her well?" I ask.

"Yes," she answers immediately.

"Was she seeing anyone?"

"Sh-she was umm," she clears her throat. Her eyes are searching wildly around the room, she's looking anywhere but at me.

"Whatever you have to say is okay. You're not in any trouble," I reassure her. I can see that she's afraid to hit me with some old news.

"She was in love with your boyfriend. She was hoping he would take notice of her one day. Tammy said she had a plan to make that happen." Apparently, Tammy wasn't as cute and sweet as I had originally thought. And instantly I feel bad for thinking ill of the dead.

"So, she wasn't seeing anyone?"

"No," she whispers. It appears that I'm not the only one who was in love with Wes. This is really getting old.

chapter 16

crash and cry

IT'S BEEN A LONG fucking day.
When I finish up with the manager and the barista it's late into the afternoon and I know that I can't take anymore. I need booze and food. I need to cry and to crash. In that order.

So, I head out. I toss a hand up in a wave to the officers left at the scene that I recognize and head out to my truck and fire her up. It's days like these that I wish my favorite Chinese restaurant that delivered wasn't ruined for me—for all time—by an idiotic asshole who was lead around by his dick by a murderous psychopath. I mentally shrug off that negativity as I remember I found a new place that's decent.

I could really go for some Chinese right now. But the thought of fried rice or even my favorite mu-shu chicken has my stomach turning sour. That could also be because the last time I ate there the murderous psycho duet tried to poison me so that's out.

I'll just get a pie. Pizza is always good.

I pick my phone up out of the cup holder where I always put it while I'm driving to call my favorite place for delivery so that it gets there the same time I do when my phone rings.

"Hello?" I answer.

"I heard you had a rough day, Claire. Do you need to talk?" Anna asks.

"Hey, Anna. I'm alright."

"Are you sure?"

"Yes." I sigh. "Maybe."

"Are you going home to binge on pizza, bourbon, and old episodes of the Real Housewives?"

"Are you spying on me?" I ask. "It's like you're in my brain."

She laughs. *"No, silly. That's the girl solution to heartbreak and a bad case rolled into one."*

"You sound like you're acutely familiar with this particular brand of medicine . . ." I bait.

"Nah, I'm a tough chick. The dating prospects are just worse than usual this month," she says after a long pause.

"This is a really shitty case," I say, my mood taking a turn for the worse.

"They do seem to be pretty personal lately," she agrees.

"Yeah. That they do."

"Okay, so, girls' night?" she asks. *"Pedis, facials, and enough Ben & Jerry's and Wild Turkey to kill a herd of elephants. And of course, Emma and I."*

"I appreciate it, I do. But I just don't think I'm up to it tonight," I explain as I pull into my usual spot at my apartment complex and my thoughts shifting to last night in Wes's arms as he told me that he loved me.

"*Which is exactly why we should do it tonight.*" She rallies as I climb the steps to my front door.

"Look, I just got home," I tell her. "I promise not to drink a whole bottle of Wild Turkey and then drown myself in the bathtub over a lousy man." I let myself into my apartment. There's a box that looks like it's flowers on the kitchen counter. Wes was here.

"*One, that's not funny and two, you don't have a bathtub,*" Anna chastises me.

"See? Exactly! I'm safe to order a pizza and just be. Look I have to deal with Wes's lame attempt to garner my forgiveness and find something to put in my belly to soak up all the booze I'm planning to drink." Truth be told, I just need to be alone in the quiet with my thoughts.

"*Ooooh, what did he do now?*" she asks.

"It looks like he dropped off flowers as an apology," I explain. "I gotta go."

"*Okay, but keep me posted!*" she says before she rings off.

I set my phone down on the kitchen counter and reach for the big red bow on the box to untie it. I can't help myself, I have to see what Wes sent even though I know that I should just throw it into the garbage. I pull the white cardboard top off of the long, rectangular box and see what has to be at least two or three dozen—maybe even four dozen—of the most gorgeous blood red, long-stemmed roses.

I dig my fingers through the stems careful of the thorns but find no card. Weird. But then again, why would Wes send a card? I know it's him. I just thought that maybe he would, I don't know, explain, or tell me how much he loves me, apologize even. But then again, men are stupid. I should be the bigger person and call him to thank him for the flowers.

I pick up my phone off the counter and turn my back to the box of flowers on the kitchen counter while I listen to his phone ring and ring. I'm just about to give up when he answers.

"*Claire.*"

"Hey, yeah . . . umm . . . it's me," I say feeling as awkward as I sound. Maybe even worse.

"*I know who you are, baby,*" his deep voice rumbles over the line.

"Okay, yeah, well. I just wanted to say thank you for the flowers." But I'm met with silence on the other end. "Wes?"

"*Honey,*" he says hesitantly. "*I didn't send you any flowers.*"

"No, the ones you left in my kitchen on the counter. Don't play games, Wes. Who else would leave flowers in my apartment for me."

"*Claire,*" he says and there is something in his tone that makes my back go ramrod straight and stop everything. "*I didn't leave you any flowers either. Get out of there.*"

"What?" I say as I turn around to face the box of flowers on my countertops. I see something flash.

"*Claire—*"

"There's something in the box."

"*Claire, get out of there—*" but I don't hear the rest of what he was saying because like a flash of lightning something jumped out and struck my forearm.

I let out a blood curdling scream worthy of any dumb chick in a scary movie.

"*Claire! What's happening?*" Wes shouts.

"R-r-r-rattlesnake," I say as I hear the *ch-ch-chhh* of its warning rattle *after* it strikes. And then everything goes black.

I watch her as she races home to find my gift and it's even better than I could have anticipated. She has absolutely no idea!

When I saw the flowers in the florist's window, I knew she had to have them. Everyone knows that red roses signify admiration or devotion but that a deep red rose, can mean regret and sorrow. These were absolutely perfect for the message that I wanted to send her. How much I long for her, how much I want her, how devoted I am to her. But the regret and sorrow for killing. I shouldn't have to kill the imperfect, I should be with her. Yes, the blood red roses were the perfect message to send.

And so was the snake.

I am angry with her. How hard should I have to work to show her that she belongs to me? I am her everything and she can't even see it! She needs to learn her lessons. To take what is being offered to her and leave the Fed in the dust or else there will be consequences. Grave consequences.

I hear her scream as she finds her other present and the sound has me rock hard. I unzip my jeans and pull out my cock. I stroke myself thinking of hair the color of a raven's wing and eyes like bright amethysts, but it's the sound of her scream repeating in my head that has me coming in my fist.

chapter 17

awake

"WES?"

"I'm right here, honey." I hear a beeping and look around. I'm in a hospital room. The scratchy sheets and blankets abrade my legs.

"Wh-what happened?" I ask. My voice sounds timid and weak. Young. I sound so young and helpless and I hate it.

"You were bit by a rattlesnake." I tip my head to the side to look at him. Is he joking? "There was no poison in your body so it was either a baby and you got fucking lucky or it had had its venom removed which is creepy as hell. But also makes you lucky and also makes you not lucky because you've caught the attention of a lunatic. I have to tell you I do not have good feelings about that."

"A rattlesnake?" I ask.

"Yes."

"Where would I have found a rattlesnake . . ." I trail off before the memories come crashing back into my head. "The roses."

"Yeah, honey," Wes says and his voice is grim.

"You didn't send them." It's not a question that I have asked. We both know something nefarious is happening here.

"No, baby."

"Someone sent me flowers with a rattlesnake."

"Yes."

"Someone put flowers with a rattlesnake in my apartment," I say and my panic is audible.

"Yes—" he starts. I can tell that Wes is going to try and placate me.

"Someone was in my house."

"Yes—"

"Someone was in my house!" I shriek.

"Claire."

"Someone was in my house!" I scurry back in the hospital bed afraid and I hate that. I hate that some monster in the dark has made me afraid and that makes me fucking angry.

"Claire, baby."

"Someone was in my fucking house!" "I need help in here!" he shouts as he jumps up from his chair and is rounding my hospital bed but I continue to scoot back. I can't trust anyone. I don't even know if I can trust Wes. And that is the scariest part of the whole shit sandwich that has become my life.

"Don't come any closer." He freezes.

"Claire, honey. You can't mean that," Wes says. His voice is full of hurt and regret.

"Someone went into my apartment and left me a box of gorgeous roses that contained a rattlesnake, Wes. I mean everything." I pant. I can't seem to take a deep enough breath. I'm losing my cool. I'm panicking. I feel like the walls are closing in and the room is spinning. I can't catch my breath. I can't breathe as spots dance before my eyes.

"Claire, baby. You're scaring me." And then someone turns out the lights. "Claire?" he calls out but it sounds like he's far away. Like he's at the far end of a tunnel or under water. Maybe I'm the one who is underwater because it feels like I'm sinking down, down, down, so very deep down. Why is Wes so very far away?

Just as the world goes black I hear, "I need some help! She's crashing!"

• • •

I love him.

I love Wes. He's so handsome and so grown up. He's got dark hair with just a little wave to it and light brown eyes. But best of all he's nice to me.

Today Wes and Liam promised mama that they would be here for supper. I love when we all hang out together. The boys don't stay here very often anymore. They say they're going into the Navy, whatever that means, and I won't see them anymore. I don't like that.

The doorbell rings before it opens. That's weird, Wes never rings the bell. He's family. Always has been, daddy says. Wes walks through the door with two girls. This is terrible. Two grownup girls with makeup and boobies.

Liam meets them in the entryway and kisses the one with dark hair. Wes has his arm wrapped around the one with yellow hair and I hate her.

Tears start rolling down my cheeks and I wipe them away with my hands. I hate crying. Liam and daddy always told me to be tough so I don't cry much. I turn on my heels and run to my room and climb under my blankets.

I don't know how long I lay there deep in my blankets, all I know is that I finally stopped crying when there's a knock at my door.

"Go away," I say just loud enough.

"Can't do that squirt," Wes says as he peers around my door. "My girl isn't at dinner and I miss her." His words hurt in my chest and I want to cry all over. I'm not his girl. I won't ever be his girl. The ugly girl with the yellow hair downstairs is. I just know it. It's so unfair.

"I don't want dinner," I tell him.

"But your mom made your favorite chicken with the tomatoes and the cheese on top."

"Go eat it then," I gripe.

"Or . . . you could stop being a brat and tell me what's wrong," he snaps making me mad right back.

"You! You're what's wrong. Happy now?" I shout.

"What did I do, squirt? I'm always nice to you." He sounds so surprised. Like, can't he tell that he's breaking my heart?

"That's the problem!" I roll my eyes. Why is he so dumb? Are all boys this dumb?

"Why is my being nice to you a problem?" He laughs.

"Because you're nice to me and you have great hair and I love you and you brought a girl!" I shout my eyes widen and I slap a hand over my mouth when I realize all that I just said before diving back under my covers. But Wes won't let me.

"Oh squirt," he sighs.

"Don't call me that," I whisper. "Please just go."

"No."

"Please," I beg.

"Sweet girl, you're ten years old and I'm eighteen. I can't love you back the way you want me to because that's wrong. I'm too old for you. I'm always going to be too old for you. But I can love you like a friend or a little sister. But that's it." *I don't want to be Wes's little sister or his friend. This is terrible.*

"Do you love her?" *I ask knowing that I shouldn't.*

"No."

"Good. She's not good enough for you." *But all I could hear in my head was that Wes would never love me. That is was always going to be wrong for him to love me.*

• • •

Beep . . . beep . . . beep . . .

"I can't lose her," I hear my dad cry.

"You're not going to lose her. She's sedated. That's all," I hear Wes reassure him. *I want to open my eyes and tell them that I'm fine. I want to open my mouth but I can't. Wes said that I'm sedated but I don't know why.*

"I can't lose another daughter this week," Dad sobs.

"You didn't know," Wes says, his voice grave.

"I didn't know. *I didn't know!*"

What is dad talking about? Another daughter? All I know is that I'm so, so tired. I need to sleep like I need to breathe. It's like I fell into the Hudson River and I'm being sucked down into the inky, black water. It's like when a murderer I was hunting this year shoved me over the bridge and down to the falls. I can't make my muscles move, I can't shout for help. I just sink down into the river until the blackness takes over.

• • •

This is it.

I won't take no for an answer. Wes and Liam are home on leave and I am not a little girl anymore. I am a newly minted, full-fledged woman of eighteen and have been for three whole weeks. Wes's argument that I am a little girl is invalid.

He's staying at his parents' place but they're in France this Christmas. It's the perfect opportunity to make Wes mine—guerilla warfare style.

I walk up the step and ring the bell. Wes answers the door wearing only jeans. His chest and feet are bare.

"Claire?" he asks when he opens the door but I jump through the opening and wrap my arms around his neck. I'm tall but he's taller so I have to pull him down to press my mouth to his in the kiss that I have been waiting my whole life for. And I have to do it quickly for two reasons: one, he will reject me if I give him a chance, and two, I might chicken out.

"Don't say no." I press my fingers to his lips to keep him from talking before moving them out of the way to kiss him again. "Just don't say no."

Wes pauses for a minute, just standing there looking at me with my arms around his neck and my fingers twined in his hair. And then he moves. Wes pulls me into his arms and crushes his mouth down on mine before yanking me into the house and slamming the door shut behind me.

"I won't stop," he says when he pulls back to let me get a breath in. "Unless you need me to."

"I need you to not stop," I tell him.

"Then I won't."

• • •

I'm thirsty.

My mouth is so dry that it feels like it is full of cotton balls. It feels like I haven't had any water to drink in ages—lifetimes even. My eyelids feel like sandbags are holding them down. I'm sinking in quicksand and there is no way out but I have to fight it.

And I do.

I wiggle my fingers and arch my feet until a large hand clamps down over mine. I slowly blink my eyes once, twice, and the fingers grip mine again. Then I shake free the last of the weighted fog that held me down for however long and open my eyes.

"Dad," my brother says from next to me. "I think she's coming around."

"Claire," my dad says, his voice rough and pained.

"Dad? Lee? What happened?" I ask.

"You panicked," Liam says before clearing his throat. "But you're okay now. You're alright."

"I'm alright," I repeat my brother's words like a parrot.

"Yeah, honey," my dad says blinking back tears.

"Wes was here," I say tasting the words like I'm not sure they're quite right.

"I'm right here, honey," the man in question says before pushing off the wall to walk up to me.

Wes brushes the hair back from my face. The way he's looking at me is so soft and so tender. It makes me want to believe that the feelings he spoke of were genuine. I know Lee said everyone kissed the strippers, but still. This gives me . . . *hope*.

"You're off this case," Lee says from beside me, ruining all of my warm and fuzzy feelings. I feel my mad growing stronger and stronger.

Wes sighs.

"What?" Liam asks.

"You couldn't give it like, say ten minutes before you start in on this shit?" We snaps.

"What are you talking about?" Liam shouts at Wes. "You were right here with me the last few days. You were just as upset as the rest of us."

"Because I love her too," Wes says, his deep voice rumbling.

"You want her off the case. You want her off the force just as much as I do." I hold my breath because he does—as much as Lee does—if not more.

Wes sighs again. He seems to do that a lot around me. "I want her to be safe, but I also want her to be happy. She's happy being a cop, I can keep her safe."

"You don't know that you can keep that promise," Lee grounds out.

"I will or I'll die trying," Wes promises.

"You better, brother," Liam says coldly and I startle at the tone in his voice towards his lifelong friend. "Or there will be consequences. Big ones. Lifelong friendship ending consequences."

We sit in tense silence for who knows how long. I feel nervous—edgy. So much so that I don't even want to move or speak let alone breathe or blink. There's a knock at the door just before it opens.

"Well, look who decided to join us today," an older doctor says as he walks in with a pretty nurse who winks at Liam and smiles sweetly at Wes.

"I guess that's me." I shrug.

They check me over up and down, top to bottom before declaring me fit for public . . . or well, resting outside of this hospital.

"We'll get some paperwork going and then you're free to go, Detective."

"Thank you." I practically bounce in my seat because hospitals have always given me the willies. I'm ready to get out of here.

"But you need to rest. No running around chasing bad guys just yet. Give it at least a few days."

"Sure," I say but we all know my fingers are crossed in my head.

It's not much but I'll take it . . . that is until I realize I have to go back to my apartment.

"Babe?" Wes asks.

"D-d-did they get it?" I ask hoping that he understands what I'm asking.

"Did they get what?" Liam asks and the room goes wired.

"The snake," I whisper.

"He's gone, honey," Wes reassures me.

"Okay," I say, my voice small and pathetic.

"You're not going home either." Wes shares with us all and the room goes ultra-wired.

"Come again?" I ask tipping my head slightly to the side.

"You're coming home with me."

chapter 18

home again, home again, jiggity jig

"WHAT?" I ASK, I KNOW I couldn't have heard Wes correctly.
"You're. Coming home. With me," he declares and my brother looks a little maniacal with glee.

"No."

"And your attack is now under the investigation of the FBI," he states crossing his arms over his chest and challenging me with a stare down not to argue with him. So that's exactly what I do.

"I'll repeat, no." Hell has frozen over if Wes thinks I'm just going to let him take over.

"It's as good as done, Claire."

"You can't," I stumble over my words. I must have been out harder than I thought. "You can't just takeover this case."

"I can and I did."

"The original case is being handled by the GWTPD," I challenge.

"It was. It's not anymore." Wes sighs before looking over his shoulder and then back at me before he speaks again. "Do you need help getting dressed?"

"No," I say petulantly crossing my arms over my chest. Wes lets out a frustrated breath.

"Everyone out." I look around—Lee, my mom and dad, my granny—they all stand around my hospital room or sitting in chairs, all with unhappy looks on their faces.

"Now, Son—" my dad starts but Wes cuts him off.

"No. Out *now*. Claire and I need to get a few things straight."

"I don't know that she's up to it," Liam adds softly. His eyes never leaving my face. I have to admit that it's nice to know that my brother has my back.

Wes rolls his eyes while I try and look my most pitiful. "She'll be fine."

Liam sighs before capitulating to his best buddy and leaving me alone. Benedict Arnold. "It'll be okay, Dad. And we'll be right outside if it's not."

"You're sure?" Dad asks Lee as he eyes Wes a little wary.

"Yes," Wes says emphatically.

"Yeah, Dad. I trust Wes and if he's wrong it's his funeral," he says casting me a sideways glance. At least I'm not losing my touch.

"Well . . . if you're sure," Dad hesitates.

"I am." And then they all shuffle to their feet and file out the door. Wes follows them shutting it firmly behind them and locking me in this room that's shrinking by the second—with one supremely pissed off FBI agent.

"Wes—"

"Oh no." He holds his hand up to me. "You do not get to lead me on a wild goose chase only to end up in the hospital and then tell me to take a hike. *Again*," he thunders. "I told you before, Claire. I am done fucking around. Done."

"Wes—"

"I've been living in hell since you wouldn't listen to me at the station. That was three days ago, Claire." Three days? I've been unconscious for three days? Holy shit.

"Umm . . ." I hedge.

"I didn't do anything wrong, Claire."

"I might have jumped to some wrong conclusions . . ." I admit.

"You think?" he thunders.

"Well—" I cringe.

"So, here's how it's going to be. You're going to come home with me." He ticks off on his fingers. "I am going to head up the investigation on an attack on a GWTPD Detective—that's you."

"Hey now!" I try to defend myself but clearly Wes is just getting started.

"No. I am doing this. I have to do this, Claire." I don't really know what to say to that, but by the sadness in his eyes and the pain that's written all over his face, I know that if I really love him—and I do—that I need to give him this.

"Okay," I say calmly.

"Okay?"

"Okay." I repeat.

"Third," he ticks off. "You and I will continue your investigation into the baby doll murders, together."

"The what?" I ask.

"While you've been in here the press did a big expose on the murders. They're calling them 'the baby doll murders.'"

"Shit."

"You got that right. They've been all over the GWTPD and the FBI. It's a nightmare. You're attack only added fuel to the fire." Shit. The last thing I want is to make the news again. When they talk about my cases and my police work, they love to make the jump to my disappearance. That was so long ago. Those vultures are incapable of letting sleeping dogs lie.

"Claire," Wes says as he steps forward. There is so much meaning and emotion packed behind his words that the air seizes in my lungs. He's just about to reach for me and I know that when he does, everything will change.

But then there's a knock at the door.

chapter 19

takin' it easy

"**Y**OU READY TO GO, Detective?" the nurse asks as she walks into the room oblivious to the tension swirling in the air.

"Yeah."

"Fantastic. Now if you could just sign here acknowledging that we are releasing you from the hospital and if you have any of the following symptoms you will come back to the ER." The nurse instructs.

After I signed my life away, the nurse scoops up the papers and hands Wes a plastic bag with the hospital's logo on the side that contains all of my clothes and a shudder rolls up my spine. I hate the thought of that snake touching my clothes and I know in that moment that I never want to see them again. I wonder if it would be weird if I asked to wear the hospital gown home . . .

"Anna went and bought you some things to take to my house and to wear home until your apartment has been cleared by the crime scene unit. Which should be soon—but you don't have to go there anytime soon. Or I could just move your shit to my house and you never have to go there again." Wes says as if reading my thoughts.

"Umm . . ." I mumble.

"I see that might be too much too soon."

This time it was my turn to snap. "You think?"

"Anyway, here's an outfit. Let's get you dressed." he says effectively changing the subject by handing me two Target bags. I love Target!

Wes lifts the glossy white bags with red targets painted all over them from the chair in the corner. He pulls out a pair of panties and a jog bra, before pulling back the covers and slipping the blue gown down my shoulders.

Wes pulls the bra over my head and I slip my arms through. I don't see this caring side of Wes very often. I'm not sure if it's because I don't need it, or just that he doesn't like to show it. He hands me my underwear and I shimmy them up my legs while I sit on the bed. Then he pulls a pair of black yoga leggings out of the bag and rolls each leg up so that I can slip my feet in. He lifts me to the ground and crouches down so that he can pull my pants up. The gesture is so intimate and I don't know what to do about it.

Wes pulls a tank top and a zip up sweatshirt from the bag and slips the top over my head before holding the sweatshirt out for me to slip my arms into it. It's oversized on me and says NAVY across the chest. It was Wes's from back in the day and he knows how much I love it. When I was a kid I would make up any excuse to need to borrow it. I had always planned on stealing it one day. I love that he thought to bring it here to comfort me. He gently slides the zipper up the front of my sweatshirt to close out the cool spring air when we leave here.

Wes motions for me to sit back on the bed as he slides my favorite Converse sneakers onto my feet. The last two items were from Wes's house and I realize how intertwined our lives have become as he takes care of me in such a deep way.

Wes holds out a hand for me and helps me stand up. "Ready?" he asks.

"Sure."

"Claire—" he starts but I don't let him finish.

"I want out of here, Wes. I'm just not sure how I feel about my apartment or going home with you. It's been a rough year. You have to understand that." I explain.

"I do, baby. But you have to let me make it up to you. I need to take care of you." There's something in the way that he looks at me. I know—I would follow him anywhere. Wes will probably keep breaking my heart until the end of time, but I love him so much that I can't help but keep coming back for more. Whether I should or not.

"Then let's get to it."

Wes gently pulls me to my feet as if I'm the most precious and irreplaceable thing in the world, as if I'm made of spun glass. Even at my height he makes me feel soft and delicate. I love that. He brushes the hair back from my face before turning me around to face away from him. I want to ask him what he's doing but then his fingers sift through my hair separating it into three chunks before braiding it down my back. And then I'm hit with a memory.

When I was little I broke my arm when I fell off of my bicycle. I remember how frustrated I was that I couldn't get my wild hair out of my face. I was so upset that I couldn't get it up and out of the way so that I could continue to do whatever it was that I wanted to do to terrorize the neighborhood. Hot tears burned down my face with my frustration and my cheeks burned with embarrassment when Wes and Liam had found me sulking on the side of the house.

Wes had pulled me into his arms and hugged me. He had called me Squirt again like he always did and told me that I was too stubborn for my own good—and well, I always have been—before turning me around to face Lee who had pulled me into his arms with a soft smile on his face for his favorite sister while Wes began braiding my hair. Wes has always handled me with so much care and tenderness.

"Claire?" he asks breaking me free from my trip down memory lane. "Are you okay?" It's the first time in a long time that my memories haven't taken me down a dark and desolate path.

I let a smile break free on my face as I turn around and face him to say, "Yeah, I think I am."

"Okay," he says as he looks me over and I think for the first time in a long time that I really am alright and by the look on Wes's face he thinks so too.

"Let's go home."

Wes looks at me before looking at the plastic bag of the clothes I wore when the snake bit me and I see him notice me shudder. He tosses the clothes in a trashcan before turning to me.

"Now we can go." I knew I loved him for a reason.

"Thank you. But—" I start.

"Don't worry, I have your guns locked up in my safe at home." I nod to him before he motions to the door.

My family is all waiting in the hall but they don't say anything as we start to leave. I narrow my eyes on the nurse who brings a wheelchair around for me. Her eyes widen when she sees the expression on my face and then turns right back around.

Wes and Liam chuckle.

"Yeah, she'll be alright," my dad says.

Wes wraps his arm around me and pulls me into his side before leading me to the elevator. We ride down to the parking lot and Wes pulls open the door to his car for me to climb in. He buckles my belt and I'm not sure how I feel about this overly attentive side of Wes. I equal parts love it and hope it doesn't last long. Wes is already too overprotective. I need him to let me be me and love me at the same time.

The drive back to Wes's modest house is silent but he holds my hand in his on his muscular thigh the entire time. He parks in the driveway and then leads me inside. He closes the door behind us and turns the lock with a resounding click. It's the first time since we left the hospital that I realized I'm alone with Wes in his house. I have no car, no clothes, no gun. I'm at his mercy. And I'm not sure if I can forgive or forget yet. Or at all.

"Dinner or a bath?" he asks.

"A bath."

Wes takes my hand in his again and leads me slowly up the stairs and down the hall to where I know his bedroom waits. He doesn't flick on the light, but instead passes through the darkening room in its afternoon glow to the bathroom. Here he drops my hand in order to turn the taps in the bathtub to let the water begin to fill it up.

My mouth dries to dust when he slowly raises his hands to the plaque of buttons down the front of his shirt and one by one slides each button through the hole. I'm attracted to him, but then again, I always am. This isn't where our problems lie. But I'm also not sure that the answers can be found here either.

"What are you doing?" I ask when he peels the white fed shirt from his body and tosses it in the hamper by the door.

"Helping you with your bath." He doesn't make a move to take off the rest of his clothes. I breathe a little easier but I'm still not fully relaxed.

"I've been bathing myself since I was six years old," I inform him.

"This isn't that kind of bath," he says as he prowls towards me.

When Wes reaches me, he slowly slides the zipper of my sweatshirt down before sliding it down my arms and to the floor. He skims his hands down my sides to the hem of my tank top before gathering it in his hands and pulling it up and over my head.

"Wes," I whisper as he slides his fingers into my leggings and panties to shove them to the floor. Once I step out of them he sweeps me up into his arms like a bride and carries me across the bathroom when he gently sets me in the tub.

I settle back into the hot water and begin to relax as it seeps into my muscles. I crack one eye opened and watch Wes as he toes off his dress shoes and socks before padding back over to the tub where he kneels down beside me. He dips his hands into the water before grabbing a washcloth from the basket next to the tub and soaking it. Wes raises the washcloth up over my breasts and neck and squeezes out the water watching as it trickles down my body.

He does it again and again and I feel my body tingle as I watch the heat in his whiskey eyes blaze bright. I rub my thighs together like a cricket to ease some of the burn his gaze ignites. The water bobs around my breasts.

Wes drops the washcloth into the tub before trailing his wet fingers up my side while he leans against the tub. He cups the weight of my breast in his hand and I arch my back into him.

"Wes," I whisper. "What is this?"

"This is you takin' it easy."

"Hmm." Just when I think I can't take anymore and he'll give me what I want, what I need, Wes scoops the washcloths up from the bottom of the tub and squeezes some soap into it from the bottle on the edge of the bathtub. He gently washes my body like you would a child—definitely not taking the liberties with me that I have come to expect from him.

"Lean back," he says as I scoot down into the tub to dip my hair back to wet it. Wes scoops up water in his cupped palm and pours it over my hair before lathering shampoo between his hands and massaging it into my scalp. I close my eyes as the tension begins to leave my body.

"Hmm, that feels nice." I sigh as he leans me back into the tub to rinse the lather from my hair. When the water runs clear again Wes pulls the plug from the tub to let the water drain before lifting me out. He wraps me up in a big fluffy towel and I realize that, at least in this moment, maybe more, Wes is everything that I need.

"Hungry?" He asks me.

"No, you?"

"No, baby," he says as he brushes the wet mass of curls back from my face. I must look like a mess.

I grab my favorite t-shirt of Wes's out of his closet and put it on before hanging up the towel. I pull open his bathroom drawer and grab his comb to try and tackle the bird's nest that is currently my hair. Our eyes meet in the bathroom mirror and he smiles at me for no reason at all from where he casually leans against the wall watching me.

"What?" I ask.

"I like seeing you at home here, Claire," he says as he pads across the room to me. Wes takes the comb out of my hand and begins to work on my hair.

"Wes—" I start.

"I know you're scared, baby, but if you thought about it for more than a second, you would realize that you belong here with me." He takes a deep breath before pressing, on all while gently combing the knots from my hair as if I was more precious than a porcelain doll. "I'm not perfect and I've made a ton of mistakes with you. But I love you, Claire. You're it for me." My heart stutters and skips a beat over his words.

"What?" I ask. Wes drops the comb in the sink before turning me to face him.

"I love you. I have never loved anyone but you, Claire."

"I love you too, Wes." He closes his eyes and seems to savor my words before opening them again. He presses his mouth to mine in a hard but quick kiss.

"Good. Let's go to bed." I start to get excited. These kinds of proclamations come with sex, right? And right now, sex with Wes seems like a great idea especially after the lusty way he touched me in the tub before he just . . . stopped.

"Excellent idea," I purr.

"Good." He shuts off the lights and turns down the blankets before dropping his slacks and climbing in in his black boxer briefs that do something to me. "Goodnight, Goodnite." And then he grabs me and wraps me in his arms before closing his eyes. Umm . . . what?

"Wes?"

"Yeah, honey?"

"What are you doing?" I question him.

"Going to sleep." "Why?" I ask.

"Because you need your rest."

"Not that much." I narrow my eyes.

"Claire—" he starts but my name on his lips turns into a choking sound when I press my palm over his hardening cock.

I turn in his arms to face him pressing my mouth to his. This time I slide my hands down the front of his shorts and grip him tight in my fist before stroking him once.

"I'm fine, Wes." I stroke him again.

"You're sure?"

"Yes." I nod. "Now are you going to fuck me or what?"

"Yes, ma'am," he says before rolling me to my back and looming over me. He braces himself on his forearm by my head while he glides his other hand up my thigh and under his shirt where he finds me wet and wanting.

"Wes," I pant as he plunges a finger inside me. I stroke him harder and faster with my hand wanting him to lose just a little bit of the control he holds over himself but it's me who is quickly losing control.

"Is this what you need, baby?" He asks as he circles my clit with his thumb.

"Yes!" I cry out as I rock my hips into his hand but this isn't what I wanted. I want Wes and I want all of him. "No! I want you."

"Then you'll have me," he says as he slides his finger from my center and pushes the shirt higher on my chest where it's gathered just above my breasts.

I push his shorts down with my hands and he reaches between us to help me get rid of them before he tosses the fabric to the floor. Wes leans back down over me and I cradle his hips between mine. The tip of his cock parts me, dipping inside and we both groan.

Wes covers my body completely with his, framing my face with his hands. He looks in my eyes with so much love, so much emotion that my heart hurts to look at him in the very best of ways. I gasp when he slides deep inside me. Then, only then, does Wes make love to me. He does not fuck me like I asked, instead he slowly slides his body against mine as we ride wave after wave, whispering sweet love words to each other long into the night before drifting off to sleep held tight in each other's arms, twisted up tight in each other's hearts.

chapter 20
back at it

*I*T'S DARK. SO DARK. At night my mommy leaves a nightlight on for me and my favorite piggy stuffed animal that I've had for ages to help me sleep. I hate the dark. Monsters only lurk in the dark. I want my mommy but I can't cry. If I cry, the bad man will come and he will hurt me again. He always hurts me. Even though I don't want him to, I know, he always comes, but this time I will be ready.

I was digging in the closet when I knew that he was asleep. I found a pile of old junk. He must have been too lazy to clean out the closet that has been my prison for I don't know how long. But his laziness is my win. In the corner under the pile of old stuff, I found a baseball and then a glove, and in the very bottom of the pile, I found an old metal bat. Just like the kind Liam and Wes used when they were my age.

Sometimes it pays to be the little sister. My whole life I've been following Wes and Liam around hoping that they would play with me. I even told Wes that one day he would marry me. He just laughed and said, "I'm not so sure about that, Squirt." That's what he calls me. Squirt.

So, all the times, I followed them around when they played ball or walked in the woods is finally going to pay off even if Wes never wants to marry me. Because I learned how to swing a baseball bat watching them. I learned to run through the woods following them. I am going to run away from the bad man because of all that I watched them do.

So, I wait. And I wait and I wait and I wait. I almost fall asleep. Almost. I feel my eye lids getting heavy but then I hear footsteps and I know that he's coming. He always comes.

I sit quietly and try not to make any noise. Then hurry to my feet and grab my bat. I crouch in the corner with the bat over my shoulder just like Liam showed me how to do. When I hear the lock that he keeps on the closet door open I know that it's time.

My hands sweat and I feel shaky all over.

"Wake up, Claire, it's time," he says as he pulls open the closet door. "What are you doing?" He asks when he sees me but I don't answer. I swing the bat as hard as I can, hitting him in his big belly.

When the bad man falls forward, I swing one more time, hitting the side of his head just like Liam and Wes taught me to hit a baseball when I finally got them to include me. And then I run.

I run out of the closet while the bad man screams my name. I run out of the ugly house that smells funny and then I run out into the woods.

I run and I run and I run. But I know he's going to catch me. A mean hand *grabs me by my arm from behind and I scream . . .*

• • •

The alarm on Wes's phone blares from the night stand beside me but I'm already awake. The dreams are changing and I'm not sure what that means. Maybe my fear is mixing with reality.

"Sleep, baby," he whispers in my ear before kissing me lightly just below.

"Umm . . . no," I say when he starts to rise from the bed.

"Honey, I have to go to work."

"I know," I say honestly, because I do. I totally understand and I don't want him to feel guilty, but I also need him to know that so do I. "I do too, Wes."

"No. It's too soon, Claire." He narrows his eyes on me.

"It's not and you know it. I'm fine, but I have to find out what's going on."

"The snake incident is under FBI investigation." I flinch as he intended for me to do at the mention of my gift. "That's what I thought, you're not ready."

"I am ready," I explain. "But I am never going to like snakes again."

"Not even this one?" he asks trying to distract me by pressing his hard length into my hip. I've decided to let him do just that for another thirty minutes or so.

"It's alright." I shrug.

"Alright? Just alright?"

"Yeah."

"I'll show you 'alright,'" he says as he smacks my ass flipping me to my hands and knees on the bed. I can't help the giggle that escapes my lips when I look back at him. "You naughty witch. Is this what you wanted?" he asks as he rises up on his knees behind me with his hard cock in his hand.

"Yes," I pant.

He runs his tip up and down against me and I arch into him trying to take what I want from him. He swats my ass again.

"Unh-uh."

"Wes."

"Say please."

"Please." Then he slams inside me so hard that the bed thumps against the wall. He plunges in hard again and again.

"You're so tight and wet, baby. And I love knowing that it's mine. It's all for me," he growls as he pounds into me.

"Yes," I pant. "It's all for you."

"Say it again."

"It's all for you."

I lay my cheek on top of my hands as they grip the sheets tight in my fingers. He sinks his cock into my center over and over with an urgency that took both of us over. My lips part on a gasp when he pinches my clit between his fingers. I moan out loud when he lets go and the blood rushes back all while he continues to pump hard and fast into my body.

"I want it, Claire. It's mine. Give it to me," he demands as he rubs my clit with his fingers. The sensations are overwhelming. I'm close but not there.

"Oh God, don't stop," I plead.

"Never."

"Don't stop."

"Never," he growls again. "I'll always give you what you need."

"I need it."

"I know." He pumps harder and harder as the bed bangs against the wall.

"I need to come."

"I know and I'm going to get you there." He pinches my clit again and I arch my back to take his cock and scream.

Wes pinches me again and I come. He roars my name before biting my shoulder where it meets my necks as he plants his cock deep inside me as he climaxes.

We're laying flat on the bed, me on my belly and Wes on top of me. My head is turned to the side so that I can breathe and my eyes are closed as I revel in the feel of Wes's hard heavy body on top of mine. He kisses the spot that he bit softly.

"Shouldn't have taken you so rough." I hear the sadness in his voice because he lost control and I won't have it. It was exactly what I wanted and more.

"Maybe it was exactly what I wanted," I tell him. "What I needed." He studies me before coming to some conclusion, I only hope it's the right one.

"You mean that."

"I do," I reassure him.

"I love you."

"I love you too." I smile at him. "Now, I need a shower before we can head out and so do you." He gives me a hard stare down.

"You'll stay with me?"

"Yes."

"You promise," he asks. He's not even trying to hide the fact that he doesn't believe me. That's annoying as hell but I don't want to miss my chance to get back out there. I need to get back on the horse and Wes and Liam need to see me do it too. If I don't do it now, it'll never happen so I weigh my words carefully.

"Of course." I reply as Wes narrows his eyes on me.

"Really?"

"Oh, for fuck's sake, yes! Yes, I swear I'll stick to your side like freaking herpes. Are you happy now?"

"Yes." The big bastard laughs. "To the showers!" he shouts as he swats my ass and takes off for the bathroom.

• • •

The surprise of the day goes to the tires on my department SUV for being slashed. I'll give it to Wes though. We walked out the front door of his house and there she sat in the driveway all flat and deflated.

"Well, there's that," he said before pulling out his cell phone and calling a tow truck to come and change all four tires.

"Mother fucker!" I shouted.

"Time to go to work," he declared as he herded me into is Fed-mobile and drove me to the station.

• • •

The ride to the station is eerily silent as Wes and I both mull over the facts in our minds. I can only think that I was getting close and that's why the killer left me the gift. I refuse to think of it as the creepy reptilian that it was. Or the fact that it was in my apartment.

Truth be told, I'm not sure which was a bigger violation.

Wes pulls into the parking lot of the station and cuts the engine. I can feel his eyes on the side of my face as I stare straight ahead—through the windshield to the glass doors and windows that cover the front of the building. I can tell that he's having regrets about bringing me along but I can't allow that so I unbuckle my seat belt. He lays his hand over mine to stay my movements.

"You're sure that you're ready?"

I nod once. "Yes."

He lets out a heavy sigh. "Okay." And then he moves his hand to unbuckle his own seat belt before climbing out of his unmarked sedan. I follow his lead and climb out too.

He pushes the door open and I duck under his arm to walk inside. Almost all conversation comes to a halt when everyone notices us. Officers I have known for years tip their chins in my direction as I head down the hall to the conference room that I had commandeered for my murder board almost a week ago before I was attacked.

I hate the word *attacked*. It makes me sound weak and helpless. I'm not a victim. I'm not. I protect the weak and the innocent. I fight for them and against the injustices they have been served. I am not weak. I am not a victim. But I was attacked. So now we have to find a way to link it all together to solve the case.

Wes pulls the glass door of the conference room open for me. It's a sweet gesture but in the moment, I'm not paying much attention to it. I'm focused on my murder board that's covered with photos, notes, and anything else that might be remotely relevant to the case.

I don't stop moving until my feet carry me to directly in front of the board. I place my palm to it and quietly pray for some kind of sign, some divine intervention, anything. I feel the weight of Wes's hand hit my shoulder pulling me back into the present.

"We're going to figure this out," Wes assures me.

"I have to, Wes. You don't understand."

"I do, honey. We're going to stop him." I nod my head in acceptance. I have to believe him. I can't constantly be looking over my shoulder and wondering where the bastard is, if he's still watching. This has to end. Soon. "Now, let's go over it again. From the top."

"Okay," I say moving to the start of information as it came it from the left side of the board. "Our first victim is Bonnie Bradley, age forty-one. Blonde hair, violet eyes. Divorced."

"The ex?"

"Not in the picture," I answer. "That's why she was dancing according to the other girls."

"The bouncer is a piece of work."

"Nah, he just wants to be one of us." I wink.

"No, he wants his dick to be one with your pussy and that's mine," he growls.

"Wes!" I scold.

"What? No one can hear us and you know that I'm right. He's into you."

"How should I know? I wasn't looking. May we continue?"

"Fine," he grumbles. He's so cute when he pouts.

"Thank you." I roll my eyes before continuing. "Second victim is Tammy Campbell. Twenty years old. Black hair, blue eyes. Works at the local coffee shop."

"Both victims dressed and posed in the same manner."

"Autopsy shows Bonnie was injected with Benzene to subdue her."

"That's not creepy at all," Wes says.

"Nope."

"Autopsy number two?" He sighs.

"Results should be in tomorrow. Emma is pretty reliable on time frame."

"Until then . . . what else do we have?" he asks.

"Let me show you."

• • •

Wes and I work long into the evening never stopping to eat or even leave the conference room. Wes and I go over every piece of evidence, every person of interest, with a fine-tooth comb. When the grit is so thick in our eyes that we can't stand it anymore Wes leads me out to the car waving to the night desk sergeant on our way out.

I can barely keep my eyes open in the car on the way home. In fact, I'm pretty sure I nod off from time to time. Thankfully, Wes doesn't live that far from my station so I haven't slept long when he pulls into the driveway and cuts the engine.

With slower than usual movements, we unbuckle our seat belts and climb out of the car. Barely noticing my newly fixed SUV sitting tall and proud on the other side of the driveway. Wes really did take care of me. Our limbs weighed down with a combination of exhaustion and frustration, side by side, Wes and I make our way up the walkway to the front door. I may already be half asleep again but as Wes stays my movement with a hand to my belly I am instantly awake.

"Stay here," he commands but all I can see is the gold and black movement on the front porch. The purr of its rattle has me immediately on alert.

Without thinking I pull my side arm from the holster at my hip and unload the clip—all sixteen rounds—into the swirling body of one big mother of a rattlesnake on Wes's front porch. It's body dances like the gunfighters in the old western movies finally coming to rest as the last bullet is spent from my chamber.

My gun is still raised as if that monster could come back from hell and wake up to torture me some more. I have to force the air into my lungs as I take a deep breath and the push it back out again. Wes slowly walks up to me and wraps his hand over the top of the gun, slowly pushing it down. It forces me to make all the muscles in my upper body relax.

"Well, I think it's safe to say that it's dead now," Wes deadpans from behind me I want to laugh but it's not funny. Tonight, I lost my cool and if Liam finds out he could take my badge for it once and for all. "Why don't you go back to the car and I'll call it in to dispatch."

"Okay," I say embarrassment burning my cheeks.

chapter 21
freaking out

WES DOESN'T HAVE TO ask me twice. After releasing my gun into his waiting hands, I turn to go back down the driveway but decide at the last minute to go wait in the house. I don't want to be standing out here like a lost little puppy when the cavalry arrives to see how far I have fallen. I follow my path around to the side of the house. I punch the code into the keypad on the door and let myself in. Wes gave it to me months ago. Yet, I have had few reasons to use it. We're always together.

At the time, I had told him he gives out a passcode so he can change it when he's done with the girl he was seeing. I teased him and said it was less messy than hunting down keys from women unwilling to part with them. Wes didn't correct me then and it's funny to me now that that is what is running through my head while I'm obviously being used as a play toy for a mad man. It also isn't lost on me that I don't currently have a key to Wes's house in my possession. I haven't been offered one either.

Love is a fickle bitch.

I walk through the house by memory, not stopping to turn on any lights. Instead, I make my way straight to the back windows in the kitchen that overlook the woods—woods that have haunted me almost my entire life—even now.

I know that Wes has to call in the incident. Not only did I fire my gun but the snake was obviously left by someone *for me*. Any minute this place will be crawling with Police Officers and FBI agents, but I need a quiet moment to collect my thoughts. Thoughts that are currently so jumbled that they are swirling around my brain so fast I can't seem to grasp onto any one of them at all.

Why?

The overall question I keep asking myself is why. Why is any of this happening? Why me? Or is it Wes? As far as I can see Wes is the only thing both Bonnie and Tammy have in common although only time will tell.

I don't know how long I stand there staring past my reflection in the dark glass. I must have missed the red and blue lights as they swirled up the hill—their sirens silenced as they made their way to Wes's beautiful home to ask the big questions. All of which include why.

I startle when Wes wraps his arms around me from behind. I close my eyes and hold my breath when he tightens his arms around me and gently places his mouth in the curve of my shoulder. I exhale when he tips his head up and rests his chin on my shoulder. I open my eyes to meet Wes's in the glass. I know what he's going to say even before the words leave his mouth.

"They're here, honey," he says softly.

"I know."

"Lee's here too," he informs me in a gentle voice.

"Okay," I say out towards the dark night behind the glass.

"So is your dad." I don't say anything just nod. I should have known that this would happen. I can't keep the secrets no matter how hard I try and the truth is I'm freaking out. "He's worried. So am I." "I know." I feel the tears burning behind my eyes and I would do anything right now to keep them from falling.

"Do you want to talk about it?" he asks me, his tone laced with the worry I see mirrored in his eyes.

"No, I just want to answer their questions. That's going to take long enough. Then I want to go home and go to bed." He stiffens at my mention of going home.

"You are home, Claire. For the night at least..." The timbre of his voice leaves no mystery to his purpose. Wes is gearing up for a fight. He's digging in his heels.

"Wes—"

"Like you said, this is going to take all night so let's go answer their questions."

"Sure," I say for lack of anything better. "Let's go."

Wes unwraps himself from around me and holds his hand out. I know I shouldn't, but I can't help myself, I pause looking at his hand. He deserves so much better than the broken half person I am. And before I have a chance to take it, Wes sighs with deep frustration before turning to walk out the door.

At this juncture, I have no choice but to follow.

We walk back through the house—which is now lit up like the Christmas tree in Rockefeller Center—back to the dining room. I'm not sure how often Wes has ever entertained in this room, but here it is with his huge oak table that seats over twenty people and his matching upholstered, high back chairs. My dad sits in one of the chairs. He's staring at his hands that rest on top of the table. Liam is pacing around the room like a caged tiger. I already know what his response will be.

I'm about to get canned.

"Sit down, Claire," Liam says to me when he notices me enter the room.

"I'm good where I am, Lee. Just spit it out," I say as I fold my arms across my chest. He stares at me from across the dining room. Lee's stance is mirroring mine as he studies me as I study him.

"Oh, for fuck's sake I'm not firing you! Just sit the fuck down!" he yells.

"You're not?" I ask. I'm as shocked as I sound right now.

"No!" he snaps. "Am I worried about you? Yes. Am I going to let some sicko grab you? Fuck no. So, sit down and let's get to the bottom of this."

"Okay," I say as I start to sit down.

"Wait!" He yells and I freeze with my ass only partially lowered to the chair as Lee makes his way through the room to me. He pulls me up out of the chair and hugs me to his chest. "I love you, Claire Bear." Tears spring up in my eyes at his use of my childhood nickname. I hug Lee back tight before shoving him away and roll my eyes.

"You're so stupid," I say shooting him a weak smile before sitting down. Wes stands guard behind me. His presence reminds me that I'm not alone—at least not right now. Right now I have him in my corner and it feels really good. Even if I don't deserve it, I'm going to take it.

I take a deep breath and look around the room. Cruz is talking with Jones. They look absolutely pissed that this is happening. We take care of our own in our department and they're both very protective of me. There are a bunch of suits looking nervous—one man and one woman, Agent Procter and Agent Webber—probably because someone planted a snake at their boss's house for him and his girlfriend to find. And lastly, Anna and Emma are speaking in hushed tones in the front of the house.

"Can you tell us what happened?"

"We left the station and drove ho-here." I catch myself just before I refer to Wes's house as home. I see the smirk on Lee's face as he catches my blunder—the bastard.

"We were going to make something quick or order a pizza," Wes chimes in. "This case has been brutal. We spent all day at the station catching up on it, going over the details again."

"And then what?" Liam questions.

"As we were walking up to the front door we noticed the snake."

"And then what happened?"

"I-I-I . . ." I can't get the words out. They're frozen in my mouth which is locked down tighter than Riker's Island. I can't tell this room full of people—my peers, people that I *love*—that I panicked. I choked. I freaked out.

"It's okay, Claire. You can say it," my dad tells me as he lays his hand on top of mine.

"It scared me and I lost it," I admit.

"What scared you, Claire?" Anna asks as she and Emma move closer into the dining room. I hate that she's asking me on record about what startled me. But she is and this is where we are now.

"The snake."

"And then what happened?" my dad asks.

"Wes called to me to stop but I wasn't paying attention. And then when I got to the porch, I saw it."

"And what did you do when you saw the snake?" Liam asks.

"I shot it."

"How many times did you shoot the snake, Claire?" Liam questions.

"I emptied my gun," I whisper ashamed that a stupid non-poisonous snake would startle me.

"It's gone now, honey," Wes says softly placing his warm hand on my shoulder and giving me a squeeze. He's infusing me with some of his warmth whether he knows it or not.

"I mean it's so silly that it would rattle me so much. Get it? Rattle me . . . because it was another de-venomed rattlesnake." Emma and Anna look to each other and then to Liam and Wes. And then back to each other. Emma shakes her head no.

I'm missing something here.

"Wait. The snake wasn't poisonous, was it?" I shudder thinking of the snake that bite me in my apartment and how this one could have done the same.

"Claire," Liam says softly.

"After she shot the snake, I told Claire to go into the house through the side door using my personal passcode to disable the lock and alarm while I phoned it in. That was where she was when I came in to tell her that the troops had arrived," Wes adds trying to change the subject but I can't let him do that. I can't let them baby me. It might be coming from good intentions or it might not. With Wes and Liam, I don't know, but this is my life and I will always fight for control of it.

"No," I demand. "Someone tell me what's going on here. Anna? Emma?"

"It was poisonous," Emma says point blank. Crime Scene said the glands were intact and the specimen had not been milked recently either."

"What?" I shake my head at her science geek speak. "Stop. Just say it so it makes sense."

"The snake was poisonous. Very poisonous," she adds at the last second. The room is silent as we all take in just how serious this is getting.

"I think that's all we need for now," Lee says closing a notebook before he stands from his seat at the large table. "I think I speak for everyone from both agencies when I say if you two want to take a day off tomorrow, everyone will understand."

"No!" I shout. "I'll be there. This monster has scared me from two homes. I won't let him take work from me too."

"Okay," Lee says as he pulls me into his arms again. "I love you, kid."

"I love you too, fart breath," I say into his chest.

"Take care of her," he says to Wes as he reaches out to shake his hand.

"Always."

Lee looks anywhere but at Emma and Anna standing just inside the dining room which is super awkward since he has to pass by them *closely* to leave. I'm assuming he's going to manage the pack up and move out of the crime scene techs, the detectives, and the feds.

"Asshole," Emma whispers loud enough for everyone to hear while Anna looks sick to her stomach. *Interesting.* And unfortunate.

My dad stands up to follow him out, only stopping to hug me and Wes.

"She's my little girl, Wesley. Protect her."

"With my life." Dad nods once and then follows Liam out the door. The detectives follow closely on his heels.

"I'll be okay," I say when I see Emma and Anna move closer to me. "Everything looks better after a good night's sleep."

"Claire—" Anna starts but I interrupt her.

"No, it's fine. I didn't survive everything that I did so that this asshole can take me down. I'll be vigilant, I swear." Anna opens her mouth to argue with me but Emma stops her with her hand to Anna's arm.

"That's all we can ask." Anna pauses before seeming to agree with Emma. They both hug me and then follow my welcome home party outside.

When the last person had left, Wes shuts the door behind them and lets the locks tumble into place. He turns around, leaning his back against the front door and watches me. Whatever he seems to see, I'm not sure that I want to know. Tonight, I was forced to let it all hang out and that's not very becoming. Let's face it, I'm a mess.

"You hungry?" he asks me.

"Not even a little bit."

"Good. Me either," he says. "Let's go to bed." Wes walks towards me and holds out his hand. I gladly take it.

"Okay, honey," I say softly, my eyes on his and he smiles at the outward show of trust that I'm handing him on a silver platter.

"A wise woman once said that everything will look better after a good night's sleep." He winks.

"Oh, I have a regular wise guy on my hands, huh? Cracking jokes . . ."

"Definitely." He smiles. "Besides, it's always a good night when I get to fall asleep with you in my arms."

"Okay, Romeo. Let's go to bed."

"Now, you're talking."

And we do just that. Wes and I do not make love. We do not kiss or touch as we ready ourselves for sleep. We do not talk about our day or our feelings as we pull the sheets and blankets back on the bed and climb in. It is obvious that there is a slew of emotions riding both of us hard right now and we do not share any of them. Instead we lay down in the huge bed, me on my side facing the window that looks out over the back of the house. Wes is behind me. He snuggles in close, his knees nestled behind mine. Wes drapes his arm around my waist and slides his other arm under the pillow beneath my head after pulling the blankets back up over us.

"I love you, Claire," he says before I feel his body slowly slip into sleep.

I do not respond.

I continue to stare out the window into the dark night. What monsters lurk out in the trees and moonlight? I wish I knew because then I could stop them. But also, I don't because I'm so afraid of what those monsters might look like in the daylight. Everything is scarier in the daylight.

Right now, I have nothing but questions with no answers. I force myself to relax each muscle in my body one by one and close my eyes before finally allowing myself to sink into the nothingness of sleep.

Here's hoping tomorrow will be brighter. Too bad that it won't. I just wouldn't realize it until later, much later. Some monsters only come out in the day time.

chapter 22
why you

BEEP... BEEP... BEEP...
Wes reaches over to shut off the alarm clock on his side of the bed and I'm beginning to feel like I'm trapped in that movie, *Groundhog's Day*. I want to pull the pillow over my head and hide under the blankets, I want to wait until all of this is over to come out from hiding, but part of me knows that this isn't going to end without me being an active participant. For some reason, everything seems to be circling around Wes. I just can't wrap my mind around why.

This morning is different from the last.

There is no laughter, no light banter. And definitely no wild morning sex. But also, no nightmares. I guess I should be thankful for small favors. Instead we both peel back the covers feeling every bit of the exhaustion we have accrued over the last few days. Without speaking a word to each other, we dress for work, me in jeans and a sweater that I top off with boots and my backup weapon—seeing how my service weapon was surrendered last night pending the investigation of my shooting the rattlesnake on Wes's front porch. Wes dresses like every inch of the fed that he is in another one of his gray suits—striped tie and all.

We don't stop to make coffee or eat breakfast. We both know that there is no use arguing over it. I need to get to the station. I need to do more interviews. Go over the evidence again. Something is missing and I won't be able to rest until we figure out what it is. We both won't be able to rest until we figure out what it is. That's the nature of our occupations, but also, it's just the nature of us, of Wes and Claire. We have always needed to find the answers that weren't always visible. We always asked the questions others wouldn't dare to.

So, we climb back into Wes's fed car, the one that drove us home last night. And there's that word again. *Home*. That's not the first time I caught myself referring to Wes's house as home. It was awkward as hell when it almost slipped out while giving my statements to the police and the feds. Everyone heard me stop myself. I know it. I could see the acknowledgement on their faces, the recognition that I'm in too deep and realizing it. Especially with everything constantly coming back to Wes at every turn.

So now I'm questioning everything else. Including Wes.

I'm itching to run as he pulls the car into a parking spot in the lot at the station. I'm damn near desperate to put a little real estate between us. Basically, I need some space to sort out this case and my head. But I also know that is the last thing Wes will grant me. It's really starting to suck that I know him so well.

"I'll understand if you need to head to your office for a bit," I hedge. Wes narrows his eyes on me.

"In a hurry to get rid of me, are you?"

"No!" I answer just a little too quickly.

"You're not going to run from me again, Claire. I thought I made that perfectly clear the last time you tried it." This time I narrow my eyes on Wes.

"You don't own me, Wes," I growl. "I am my own person. For fuck's sake, I'm a respected and decorated police detective!"

"I know all that," he rumbles low in warning like a wolf I've just pissed off. "But I do own you, baby. I own every part of you from that long, dark hair I love to wrap my fist around, to your heart you keep so heavily guarded, down to your sweet as fuck pussy and all the fucking way down to your toes that you love to keep painted pink. I own every bit of you just as you own every bit of me and I always have. So get fucking used to it." With that he gets out of the car and slams the door closed—which only moves to piss me off. I'm sure Anna would tell me that I'm avoiding the highly romantic declaration Wes just made by being pissed the fuck off. So, I step out of the car and slam my door too.

"And I'm a fucking grown up!" I yell.

"Then fucking act like one!" he shouts back as he pulls open the glass door to the station for me.

"Well aren't you just a merry fucking ray of God damned sunshine this morning!" I holler as I step into the lobby of the station for all to hear.

"Yeah!" he shouts right back at me after the door slams closed behind us. "I'm having a great fucking day! I get to follow my girl around. Again! While she chases a killer all while hoping the woman I'm in fucking love with doesn't get fucking killed before I have a chance to ask her to fucking marry me! So yeah, it's gonna be a great fucking day!"

The bullpen is so quiet at Wes's outburst that you could hear a pin drop.

"What?" I ask. I had no idea he was serious about me. About us. That he was considering marriage. Holy fuck.

"Hey!" Liam shouts from his office. "Ralph and Alice, mind getting your fucking asses into my Goddamned office before you knock each other to the moon!"

"Fuck!" Wes bites out.

"Wes—" I start.

"Not. Now." I just nod, not sure what else to do. I'm so lost.

We make our way down the hallway and Liam is standing there holding the door to his office open for us. Like naughty children on their way into the Principal's office we drag our feet in single file, one after the other, with our heads hanging in shame. Well, Wes's probably is. I have no shame and we all know it.

Liam follows us in and slams the door shut.

"Nice *Honeymooners* impression kids," he says holding up his thumb and index finger about an inch apart. "I am this close to pulling you from this case, Claire. I could suspend you for this shit, *without pay*."

"Now, hold on, Liam—" Wes starts but doesn't let us finish.

"Don't even start with me, Wes." Lee shakes his head. "Do you get that I can have your agency banned from this station for the shit you two are pulling? That your behavior is fucking embarrassing?"

"I'm sorry," I say sadly. "It's my fault. All of it. Don't blame Wes."

"You guys are so annoying with your ups and downs and at each other's throats and then defending each other. It's exhausting!" Liam whines. I roll my eyes. "Just get your shit together when you're here. That's all I ask."

"Okay," I say. "I'll lose my shit at home."

"I love it when you call my place home, baby."

"God damnit, I didn't!" I back pedal. "I was talking about my apartment."

"You should really consider moving in with me this weekend," Wes says and Liam nods. "It would make everything better."

"How would our not having our own space make anything better when we're already at each other's throats?" I ask.

"Because then you can fuck me whenever you want," Wes says on a wicked smile.

"Gross, dude, that's my sister," Liam says looking a little green around the gills.

"The idea does have some merits," I play up to annoy my dickhead of a brother.

"Gross. Are you done yet?" Liam rolls his eyes.

"And think about all the times I could eat you on the kitchen table," Wes adds helpfully.

"I've eaten at that table, fucker! I think I'm going to be sick," Lee complains. I can't help but laugh.

"Seriously, Claire. Think about it?" Wes pleads.

"Oh fine! I'll think about it. But only because you are so pathetic." I throw my hands up in exasperation.

"I am. Thank you." Wes smiles at me.

"Good now that that's all settled do either of you have anything to add?" Lee asks and then quickly speaks again before either Wes or I can say something else to gross him out. "I mean about the case!"

Just then the phone on his desk rings.

"Goodnite," Lee says as he answers the phone. "Yeah, they're both here . . . Okay, I'll let them know." He lowers his voice so that Wes and I can't hear what he's saying but after a lifetime of being his little sister, that only makes me listen harder. "Then we need to talk about this . . . but it did happen . . . I don't care . . . we will talk about this!"

Liam holds the phone out in front of his face as is he can't understand what just happened. The dial tone sounds through the small room and it's evident that whoever it was hung up on him. He closes his eyes and shakes his head to clear it before hanging up the phone. I look to Wes and his face is carefully blank. Whatever just happened, he knows more than me and that is totally unacceptable. The Bro Code is bullshit.

"That was Emma, she has your autopsy results ready and said she's free to go over them now if you guys want to head on down to the basement." I arch an eyebrow at him. So that was Emma he was talking to in angry hushed tones. Interesting.

"Yeah, I'll get right on that." I smirk at my brother on my way to the door. I need to do some serious investigating over this shit. Too bad I have to catch a killer first.

"I could still suspend you, Goodnite," he shouts from his desk.

"You could try! But I'd tell mom on you," I call out as I leave his office.

"God damnit," he grumbles. Wes just laughs as he follows me out the door.

• • •

This one is special.

This one is different from all the rest. This one has actually fucked him. I could tell by the way she watches him. The way she watches him with her.

There's a sadness in her eyes.

He doesn't deserve her or this one. But this one has to die.

She's almost perfect. But not. She has eyes the color of violets and hair like a raven's wing. But her face is wrong. Her nose turns down instead of up. There are no freckles across the bridge of it. Her body has more bulky muscle—not much—but enough that it's noticeable that she is not the one that I want.

But she fucked him when he wanted her. They lie to her every day about what happened and she has no idea. Yet, she still chooses him! How could she be so stupid? I have given her everything and still she goes to him every fucking time.

Last night I left her a snake as a punishment. How I hoped it would strike her the way I want to. It's fangs slipping into her skin the way I will slip in the needle. Soon. It'll be soon, Claire.

But not yet.

This one approaches as she walks back through the restaurant where she stopped for lunch. She still goes to the same restaurant every day that she dined with him in while they were together. Hoping he'll come back for her. But he doesn't. He never will.

She steps outside and I'm waiting over by where she's parked.

"Oh hey, it's you," she says when she recognizes me.

"Hey, it's you too." I smile at her. "Hey, I've been thinking about something . . . do you mind if I ask you a question?" I say as I step closer to her, just inside her personal space.

"Sure. Ask me anything," she says nervously. Her pupils dilate. Her instincts are telling her that something is off, that something is wrong. And they are correct.

"Why couldn't you keep him?" I ask as I jab the needle into the side of her neck and push down the plunger.

The effect of the benzene is almost immediate. Her body goes limp and her eyes go wide in panic. She can't even open her mouth to scream for help. I smile at her.

"You?" she whispers. I just smile indulgently at her.

"Don't worry, this will be over quickly."

I drag her towards the back of the lot. It's terribly unsafe here. No cameras, it's dark and dingy. You would think it would be safer with so many FBI agents around, but tragically it's not. I sigh. The world can be so cruel.

Tears slip free from the corners of her eyes as I strip her of her ugly suit and gun. I lick them from her cheeks. I need to taste her fear, her helplessness, and the realization that loving a man that she couldn't have is what ultimately cost her life.

"If only you had kept him," I say sweetly. "We wouldn't be here."

I unbuckle my belt and unzip my slacks. My cock is hard and just free from my pants. It's because she's almost perfect. This one might be the last one before we claim her. The thought makes the tip seep with pleasure and I can't help but close my eyes and stroke myself with my fist before.

"You should be pleased," I say as I dress her in the brown floral dress I made for her myself. She's beautiful in it. She'll be just like a doll. "You're almost perfect."

I straddle her and rub my cock against her pussy. A groan slips free. She feels so good. I brace my hands on her shoulders and drive into her, impaling her on my dick. I can't stop myself as drive myself closer and closer to climax.

I wrap my hands around her neck and she closes her eyes. This one knows that the end is near. I drive in one more time as my cum fills her body and I squeeze the life from her.

I pull out and stand while zipping up my pants. I'm disappointed that she distracted me so much I forgot to use a condom but I don't let it frustrate me too much. By the time the police figure out who I am, I'll have already taken her and I will be long gone. Again. Just like last time and the time before that.

I turn this one onto her side and place her hands up under her cheek in prayer position. I don't have to close her eyes for her and that's kind of a fun *change. Although, I prefer to watch their eyes when they realize they are dying.*

I stop to take one last look at her. She looks perfect. Almost. And then I turn and walk away.

• • •

My belly is full of butterflies as we ride in the steel box down to Emma's lair. Our arrival is sounded by a ding as the doors swing opened.

"Where the hell have you two been?" she shouts from her desk. "I called. Like a ton."

"We were in a meeting with Liam," I say casually.

"I know," she says, her frustration clear in her voice. "That's where I found you."

"So, you found us . . . What were you and Liam talking about on the phone?"

"I have no idea what you're talking about," she snaps before looking around nervously. Uh-huh, sure. I'll believe that. It was nothing. "Besides, I have your autopsy results."

"Okay, show me."

"Victim: female, age nineteen identified through fingerprints as Tammy Campbell. Brown eyes, black hair. The color is natural, no dyes."

Interesting. I'm not sure how I feel about that. She can't be my long-lost sister too, that would be ridiculous. Too coincidental.

"Her stomach contents contain a bagel and coffee which is consistent with her employment at a coffee shop. There was vaginal tearing and condom lubricant found during exam."

"Cause of death?" I ask.

"Good old strangulation. But wait! There's more." Emma says in her game show host voice.

"Such as?"

"Your victim was subdued with an injection of benzene. Needle marks found in the shoulder area."

"Just like Bonnie Bradley," Wes adds from his spot next to me.

"Exactly!" Emma claps.

"But who? Who is doing this shit?" I ask. I hate that I can't figure it out. I hate that there's a serial killer in my fucking town killing women that look kind of like me. That shit is creepy as hell.

My frustrating thoughts are interrupted but Wes's ringing phone.

"Agent O'Connell," he answers. "Say again? . . . You've got to be shitting me." Wes turns with his back to Emma and I. He has one hand holding his phone to his ear and the other is clenched in a fist at his hip. His feet are braced apart and his hold body radiates tension. His anger ripples across his broad back.

"Wes," I whisper but he's too busy yelling at the person on the other end of the phone.

"Nobody touches anything until I get there. Especially not the PD!" he shouts before hanging up his phone and stuffing it back into his pocket.

"Wes?" I ask again.

"I have to go. *Do not* leave this station," he barks out before jabbing the button for the elevator. The doors open immediately and he walks through the steel doors without ever looking back. I can't help but feel like everything just went to shit.

I'll find out later that it really just did.

chapter 23

just like you

LOOK BACK. LOOK BACK. God damnit, look back!
I'm damn near shaking as I plead with Wes to look back at me, to give me anything at all, but he doesn't he just walks away. No, Wes stormed away after issuing me an order not to leave the station. He didn't even kiss me goodbye.

I know I shouldn't care, that I shouldn't need his reassurances, but something happened and God dammit I do! I do need them. I have no idea how long I stood there staring at the elevator doors with tears burning the backs of my eyes before Emma voices my exact thoughts.

"What the fuck just happened?"

"I-I have no idea," I whisper.

"It'll be okay, honey", she says as she rounds her desk and puts her arms around me. Emma is as tall as I am and her arms are strong—so she hugs the breath right out of me. In our little unlikely trio, Anna is the shorty. She calls us, "Two talls and a small."

"I just don't know."

The phone on her desk rings and she squeezes me one more time before walking back around to answer it. Our department isn't exactly loaded so we have old fashioned black phones on our desks that look like they're straight out of *Get Smart*. Sometimes that's exactly how it feels. Like we're stuck in a slapstick comedy routine, I just haven't found the punchline yet.

"Parker," she answers before listening. "Where? . . . Awe isn't that sweet, you're calling me in. You know who I work for . . . If you think I'm neutral territory you're a bigger moron than I had originally thought." With that she slams her phone back down in the cradle and looks to me with wide, unsure eyes. Before I have a chance to ask her what happened my cell phone is ringing in my jeans pocket.

"Goodnite," I answer.

"Goody, this is Cruz. We've got another body."

"Where?" I ask.

"Down at the Greek Cafe over on third."

"I'm on my way. Make sure the crime scene is secure," I bark out as I head for the elevator and jab the button with my finger.

"About that," he hedges.

"Yeah?"

"We got a problem." The pause after he speaks is pregnant with all of the department bullshit.

"That's not something I want to hear, Cruz," I tell him after a moment.

"The Feds tagged this one."

"Nope, not possible. This is our case. This is *my case*," I growl.

"*She's one of them*," he says softly so only I can hear it.

"Who?" I ask, the pit of dread in my stomach taking up more and more room.

"*Agent Webber*." The female agent that was at the house last night looking worried and very uncomfortable to be in Wes's house. Damn it!

"Shit," I bite out.

"*Yeah*."

"I'm on my way," I say and hang up as the elevator doors ding opened.

Then I realize that I don't have my fucking car here because I've been riding with Wes. *Wes*. That asshole who took off after declaring that whatever happened did not go to the PD—*my fucking department*—and then demanded that I not leave this station. He is un-freaking-believable.

The elevator doors have just closed when I push the button to open them again. When they swing opened Emma is standing there looking at me with a smirk on her pretty face.

"I need a cab," I shout.

"You going my way, pretty police lady?" she asks on an evil cackle. Emma is definitely one to bust your balls but in the nicest of ways.

"Yes," I say emphatically. "I'll even put out."

"Fantastic!" she cheers. "Get in the van."

Damn. I hate the van. It's the Medical Examiner's body mover van and it gives me the willies. I make the sign of the cross over my body before following her out of her morgue and into the back-parking garage where they keep it.

"Pussy!" she snickers.

"Fuck you." I laugh.

The drive over to the Greek Cafe would have me a nervous wreck under normal circumstances. I hate it when we lose one of our own regardless of department or agency. At the end of the day it all boils down to we're just different kinds of cops.

However, Emma likes to shake the newly dead with classic rock at the highest decibel she can tolerate. Today is AC/DC. She did a nice segue from *Hell's Bells* to *You Shook Me All Night Long*. Classy as fuck if you ask Emma. But what it does do is help me maintain a certain level of calm.

Well, as calm as one can be while in an ME's body mover van while said ME is driving like a nineteen-year-old lunatic who was just handed the keys to daddy's Porsche. Hand to God, I swear she took the last turn on two wheels and then pulled into the parking lot of the Greek Cafe with screeching tires.

As soon as the car stopped, I jumped out and almost hit the grass on my knees praying for the safety of all around her and screaming "Land!" But I decided that was probably a bit much. Instead, I pulled my badge from my hip and held it up to any Fed that might think they can boot me from this scene.

I see my officers huddled over by a tree, standing in various poses of pissed off, one with his arms folded across his chest, another with hands on his hips and feet spread. All with scowls on their faces. I'm making my way to them when I'm stopped by a hand on my arm.

"I wouldn't do that if I were you," I seethe.

"This isn't your crime scene, Goody," the male agent from last night says. Agent Procter, I believe.

"That's not what I heard."

"The boss won't want you here," he snarls at me and I find that very interesting. Up until now, we've been mostly together investigating this case.

"And why is that?" I ask.

"Because he and Tawnya had a thing." It's like a fist to my gut and I know he sees it, he delivered the blow with unfailing accuracy. I just can't understand why. Either way, it knocked the wind out of me.

"Excuse me?"

"You heard me," he says, his voice low. "He needs time to grieve. If you ever cared for him at all, give him that."

Obviously, he doesn't know me because I think not.

"Take your hand off me, Agent Procter."

"Don't say I didn't warn you," he sneers.

I make my way over to the officers and detectives that I know. I see that they caught my . . . *disagreement* with the Fed. Well, that can't be helped now and it looks like we'll have to move quickly to take control of this crime scene. I so love a good pissing contest with the stuffed suits.

"Alright, guys," I say taking a deep breath before pressing on. "Tell me what we got."

"We have the body of a female, mid-thirties, dressed in an old timey dress and posed to be sleeping. Victim has been positively identified as Federal Agent Tawnya Webber," Jones recites from his notes.

"At which time the feds gave us the boot," Cruz adds.

"Not for long boys," I say with confidence I am not currently sure is real or not, but right now I'm going to go with it. I put my fingers to my mouth and let out a shrill whistle. "Listen up! We at the George Washington Township Police Department would like to thank you finely dress suits for showing up and pissing all over my crime scene, but you are dismissed. Effective immediately! Emma, your team doesn't touch shit until my guys get a good look."

"You got it, girl!" she cheers like a looney tune.

"Now see here," Agent Procter who dropped the little Wes and Tawnya sitting in a tree with naked genitals bomb shouts. "This is Federal jurisdiction."

"Since when?" I shout back. "I have two bodies that match this one. This is mine. So, get your shit and get out."

"And clearly, you're doing a right fine job with them," he sneers. The fucker. My guys visibly bristle and start to move towards the jerk to pound his face in. I would love nothing more myself, but it won't win us the battle at hand so I put a hand out to stop Jones and smile my brightest smile.

"I'm sure glad you think so. You know we've just been working so hard on this case while you've been shining your wingtips so you can go right on ahead and get back to that now. Okay, thanks, bye!" I wave.

"Handle this, O'Connell!" he shouts.

"Ooooh, nice one!" I snap my fingers. Before motioning to my officers. "Move in guys. I want everything. I want to know what she ate last, her mother's maiden name, and who she fucks at night." I add that last one just to see if I can get a reaction out of anyone and I definitely do when Wes cringes. *Awesome.*

"Yes, ma'am." The all file out.

"Claire," Wes growls as he stalks towards me.

"Speak of the Devil. Say his name and he shall appear," I say under my breath.

"I thought I told you to stay put at the station," he growls.

"Yeah, about that, I didn't." I shrug.

"I can see that. But why?" he bites out.

"Because I have an active crime scene to go over," I answer honestly.

"This is my crime scene, Claire. Back off," he warns.

"No can do, Buckeroo." I shrug. "One, this matches two of my crime scenes and you know that. Two—" he cuts me off.

"She's one of my agents. This case is now mine," he thunders.

"She's also your lover, this case is not yours and if you push me, I will go to Lee and see that he backs my claim."

"You'd play your brother against me?" he seethes

"I'm sure he knows all about your history with Agent Webber. It's the right thing to do and you know it. For one reason or another, this case is all about you."

"It's not what you think, Claire," Wes pleads, changing tack.

"I don't care about what I think. I care about facts and finding the killer before he kills anyone else," I say with a calm I do not feel.

"Claire, you have to listen to me," Wes pleads.

"No," I stop him. "Don't say anything. I expect you in the station by five this evening for questioning."

"Don't do this, Claire."

"You can either surrender yourself for questioning or I can have an officer bring you in." I take a breath before leaning in to whisper. "Please do not make me do that."

He whispers back, "It was before you."

"Then let me do my job. I promise we'll take good care of her." He closes his eyes and nods at my words before turning and walking away.

I make my way to the body where Emma and her team are taking pictures and marking evidence.

"What do we have, Emma?"

"We have a female victim, mid-thirties, black hair and violet eyes." I had a feeling. For whatever reason, this killer is targeting Wes but the physical similarities are staggering.

"Natural?" I ask.

"Hair yes, eyes are contacts, but . . ." Emma answers but then lets her voice trail off.

"But what?" I ask suddenly feeling incredibly tired.

"I have to say . . ." I know what's coming. I steel myself for it even as I make my spine go straight, standing taller with my shoulders back, I hold my breath and look her in the eyes. But no matter how much I brace for it, I know that I'm not ready to take that blow too. "She looks just like you."

chapter 24

before you

IT'S A SLAP TO the face.
No, it's not. Hearing that this woman who I know Wes was intimate with—and even though I don't know the nature of their relationship, did he love her? Did she think of marriage? Was it just a cold, hard fuck? I don't know, but I do know, without a doubt that they *were* intimate—looks a lot like me is not a slap to the face. It is not a shock. It's a knife to the gut. A wound so deep that I know it will kill me. *Slowly.* I'm hemorrhaging here in the parking lot of the Greek Cafe next to my boyfriend's former lover in front of everyone and no one can be bothered to see that I'm bleeding out one obliterating heartbeat at a time.

It's dirty, it's messy, and it's so incredibly *painful.*

It's not an injury that I will never be able to recover from.

"Claire—" someone calls but I'm too deep in my thoughts to recognize who is speaking to me. I don't even acknowledge them until they grab me by the upper arms and shake me.

"Hey!" I shout, to no one and everyone, all the same.

"Hands off, buddy!" Emma snaps at the same time. And I look up into the kind face of Detective Cruz. He's a handsome guy, has an alpha side from what I can tell, strong jaw and stronger... *muscles.* But he's a man and a cop and I'm finding as of late those don't make for great romantic partners. I never should have shit where I ate. But then again, I always hoped that Wes would be different, even though I knew all along that he really wasn't.

And to top it all off, he's not *just* Wes.

I never should have let myself fall in love with him, but I just couldn't stop it. Wes has held my heart in the palm of his hand my whole life.

Something darker than concern flashes across his eyes as he looks to Emma. "I just wanted to make sure she was okay," he snaps.

"Of course, I'm okay," I say softly trying to diffuse the situation. "Why wouldn't I be?"

"Because that jackass hurt you *again!*" he roars.

"I'm fine," I say for everyone to hear. "I'm sad that another life was lost this one being one of our own. We will solve this together."

"That's it?" he asks incredulous.

"That's what?" I say feeling my frustration ramp up.

"You're just going to run right back to him after all that he's done," Cruz sneers.

"Excuse me?" How dare a fellow detective question my personal life. I'm so done with this bullshit. They all do it. Every last one of the men in my station think that they have free reign to put their nose in my business and judge me. Or worse tattle on me to my brother like we're back on the kindergarten playground.

"Detectives?" Liam says as he approaches us. Speak of the devil himself. My day is either about to get better or it's about to go straight to hell. Lee's appearance at an active crime scene where I had to remove my boyfriend—a.k.a. his best buddy—as a suspect tells me that and more.

"Nothing," Cruz says before walking away. "Not a damn thing."

"What was that all about?" Lee asks quietly enough that only I can hear him.

"I'm not entirely sure." I shrug. "It'll all work itself out." He studies me as only a brother can. I do my best not to flinch or squirm, keeping my eyes locked on his like I used to do when I was little and I had challenged him to a staring contest.

"You okay?" he questions softly for only me to hear. "It's alright if you're not. A lot has happened."

"You, know what? I'm not. But I owe it to Tawnya to keep my shit together. For now."

"Okay," he says before turning to the crowd of officers, agents, and crime scene people. His eyes linger on Emma until her cheeks burn bright red and she looks away. Then he calls out, "Listen up people. This is one of our own. Not GWTPD, but FBI, but you and I know that we're all blue on the inside. The blood in our veins all runs the same." He pauses to take a moment to make eye contact with every officer and agent on the scene. "I want this scene spotless. I want you all to be so far above par that the investigation is perfect. Because Agent Webber deserves that. And she deserves nothing less than that. I want this fucker caught *now*!"

A cheer goes up among all of the police officers and agents. I have to admit, Liam gives a good speech. He's a great Captain—when he's not terrorizing me and my career choices, *that is*.

When the dust settles again, everyone goes back to what they were doing. Crime scene is still taking pictures and samples. Emma is instructing her people on how to prep the body for transport to her lab. The officers and agents are questioning everyone in the cafe if they saw anything out of the ordinary.

"Emma," I call out.

"Yeah?" she asks as she runs up to me effectively angling her body so that she has her back turned to Liam.

"I want that autopsy first thing in the morning," I tell her.

"You got it, boss." She mock salutes.

"But I'm the boss," Liam corrects.

"Sure, you are buddy. Sure, you are." She winks as she pats him on the chest before walking by. Lee's jaw tenses as he clenches his teeth. It appears my girl really knows how to push his buttons.

"It's nothing," he grounds out.

"Sure, sure," I say to appease my brother who is also my boss. "I didn't see anything."

"If I say it's nothing, it's nothing!" he barks.

"Okay," I say as I hold my hands out in front of me in surrender.

• • •

Five hours and no answers later, everyone is frustrated and angry.

"I can't believe no one saw a Goddamned thing!" Tawnya's partner shouts. "Are you *officers* good for anything?"

"I get that you're upset. We all are," I say keeping my voice low and my warning private. "But you cannot speak to me or my officers that way again."

"Oh yeah," he sneers leaning in, nose to nose with me. "Watch me."

"You wouldn't be threatening one of my detectives would you, Agent Procter?" Liam asks casually as he saunters up. Knowing Lee, he is anything but casual. He's about as casual as a tiger ready to strike.

The Agent laughs meanly. "Of course, you would have her back. Big brother's always do, don't they? Even though we both know that she should have been sacked years ago."

He doesn't get to say anymore because Liam punches him in the mouth.

"Did you see that?" the Agent shouts. "Look at what your Captain is so willing to do."

Liam just stands there with his arms folded across his chest and his mouth closed while he glares at the Agent.

"You just assaulted a Federal Agent, asshole. I have witnesses."

"Oh yeah?" I ask. "Who?"

"Well," he splutters before pointing to me. "You!"

"I didn't see anything."

"And those guys over there." Agent Procter points to Jones and a couple of other officers but they quickly turn away. His eyes widen with panic now that he knows that he's on a sinking ship. He's trying. I'll give him that.

"We didn't see anything," they call out.

"Yes, you did!" he shouts. "This is police corruption!"

"You clearly have an ax to grind where me and my officers are involved," Liam says. His arms are folded across his broad chest and his feet are spread wide. The look on his face is filled with a menacing challenge as he draws his brows down to stare at the angry agent. "I think you need to leave."

"Are you shitting me right now?" he seethes.

"No, I'm dead serious," Liam says, his tone eerily calm. "I think you need to leave. Now."

"Do you know who I am?" Agent Procter demands.

"Do I look like I care? Right now, I have a fresh body in the morgue that needs answers and a murder to investigate. You, Sir, are impeding both so unless you'd like to be brought in on charges of interference of a peace officer in the performance of their duties, please continue."

"You wouldn't dare."

"Try me," Liam leans in, his sharp, white teeth gleaming in the sun as he dances his dance with the angry agent one last time. The agent seems to ponder his options for a moment realizing that Lee will not back down on this instance. He's lost this round and he knows it.

"This isn't over," he snaps as he turns to walk away.

"You could have fooled me," Liam says to his back. The agent's back goes ramrod straight and he pauses in his tracks. I'm sure he's wondering if he can get away with beating Lee to a pulp. But Lee was a SEAL just as Wes was, not much has slowed him down in his advanced age of thirty-eight and it shows, so the man wisely keeps walking. But I have a feeling this won't be the last we hear from him.

Lee's phone rings, breaking the silence.

"Goodnite," he answers. "Roger that . . . I'll see if I can get to her before the desk sergeant does."

My ringing phone interrupts his conversation with the mystery caller.

"Goodnite," I answer.

"This is the desk sergeant, I have Special Agent Wesley O'Connell here in an interview room with his attorney, Detective."

"I'm sure there is a detective available to take his statement," I say coolly.

"He's asking for you."

"I'm not sure that that is appropriate," I say keeping my voice low. I'm hoping to not draw too much attention to myself as I answer the Sergeant. I place my fist of my free hand on my hip and lean forward, staring at my boots as if they will suddenly give me the answers I need, the secrets of the universe. But I feel their eyes on me anyway. I sigh and start walking in any direction to keep my thoughts private. I hope.

"*Let me rephrase, he says he will only speak to you.*" That stops me right in my tracks. I'd like to say that Wes's cool maneuvering blindsided me, but it doesn't. This is straight out of the Wesley O'Connell playbook.

"Fuck!" I bite out to no one in particular. "I'll be right there." I hang up and start to make my way back to my car when I hear a phone ring.

Liam answers it, "Goodnite." I don't pay much attention to him or anyone else as I make my way to the street where we parked until I realize that I don't have a car here because I rode here with Emma so I turn around and start stomping back to where she stands.

"Things aren't looking so good, brother. I think she knows now . . . willco," he says before he hangs up.

"Sooo . . ." he starts.

"Do. Not." I hold my hand out to him. "I need wheels." In the blink of an eye, Liam maneuvers me so that he is next to me and my arm is linked through his elbow as if he was a true, old fashioned gentleman. Which we all know that he is not—*Emma*, it seems, in particularly at this moment in time.

"It would be my honor to escort you back to the station, sister dear," he snickers.

"Ugh. Fine." I surrender just this once. It's so out of character for me that the words taste like ash in my mouth.

I see Liam start to open his mouth to say something to me as we make our way to the street where all of the department vehicles are parked side by side. I hold my hand up, palm out and stop him before he ever gets a chance.

"I said not one word, Lee." He snaps his jaw closed. "I need that right now. We'll see where we go from here once I wrap this case up. And listen here and listen good. I *will* wrap this case up."

Liam doesn't turn to look at me as he nods once to show me his understanding. He beeps the locks on his department vehicle and we climb in. My brother does not try to talk to me during the entire drive across town to the station. I take the time to think over what awaits me when we get there.

I can't help but think that Wes only wants to talk to me in order to prove his motivations where Agent Webber was concerned. And while part of me hates that he was intimate with her—my stomach is rolling at the thought—but it is my job to find out what happened to her and stop whoever did it. One thing I know for sure, the killer isn't Wes. I need to clear him and move on as quickly as possible.

Whether or not Wes is proving to be a good boyfriend is yet to be determined.

Lee pulls into his spot in the parking lot at the station. He turns towards me. I feel his stare heat the side of my face. He's not my brother now, he's my boss, and that's exactly what I need him to be. My Captain needs to know that I can do what needs to be done or else he'll pull me from the case. My brother, however, would punch Wes in the face and ask questions later. I don't look at him, instead I keep my gaze trained forward through the windshield until I can't take it anymore.

I close my eyes tight and take a deep breath.

"Not now, Lee," I say before taking another breath in an effort to slow my rapidly increasing heart rate. "Let's just get this done and move on."

"But what if it hurts?" he asks me in the quiet of the car.

"Then I'll let it and then move on. Just like always," I say before pushing open my door and climbing out.

Liam follows me through the front doors of the station. It seems as if all conversations drift off into the ether, it's as if all movement comes to a complete stop in the lobby of the station. The desk sergeant motions to me raising his left hand. I look to him and nod my head.

"He's in interview three. His lawyer too."

"Thanks." I wave to the desk sergeant as I make my way to interview room three with Liam hot on my heels.

His heavy palm lands on my shoulder stopping me just as my hand lands on the handle of the door, stopping me from pulling the heavy steel panel opened.

"You don't have to do this, Claire," he says, his voice low and heavy with meaning. This here, is my brother, the man who cleaned up my skinned knees and patched my bicycle tires when we were kids. Now as adults, he still wants to protect me from all of the hurts of the world, but this time, we both know he can't. "You could just go sit in the observation room and watch. I'll take his statement. It'll be fine."

"You know that's not true, Lee." I sigh. "He said he won't talk to anyone but me. *Not even you.* So, we're going to talk. I'll get his statement and we'll move on from there."

"What if it's not the information you want?" he asks me.

"But what if it's the information that I need? For Agent Webber? Or for me?"

"What if you find out something and there's no turning back?" he presses.

"Then I put one foot in front of the other and keep moving forward. Just like the kid in that Disney movie says," I say to which Liam sighs.

"Sis."

"What?" I ask.

"We were having a moment and you just ruined it." I roll my eyes. "Are we good?"

"Yeah, Lee. We're good."

"Okay. Let's do this."

"Let's? As in us? Together?" I ask.

"Of course. He might only talk to you but this is still very much my house and you're still my sister, he knows that. So, let's do this, but we do it by the book. Everything is on the level because between you and me, IA are a bunch of dickless weasels and they would just love it if this turned into a three-ring shit show." I can't help the laugh that bubbles up from my chest.

"Okay, let's do this so the dickless weasels can't win the day!" I cheer.

I pull open the door to the interview room and the wave of pain and helplessness that spreads out from Wes's face slides the smile right off of my own. He does not say anything, just sits there with his palms flat on the steel table and watches me, studies me—my heart breaks for him and the desperation, the hopelessness that seeps from his pores.

Liam steps into the room behind me letting the door click softly closed behind him. The tension radiates out from everyone within these steel walls.

I clear my throat. "From here on out this conversation is being both monitored and recorded," I say as I flip the switch on the table to start the recording. We all know that the gallery is full of lookey loos wanting all the gossip on me and Wes.

"Wes," Lee says softly. "I have to do it."

"I know," Wes says, nodding his head in acceptance.

"You have the right to remain silent. Anything you say can and will be used against you in a court of law. You have the right to an attorney. If you cannot afford one, one will be provided for you. Do you understand these rights as they have been described to you?"

"Yes," Wes says clearly.

"Present are myself, Detective Claire Goodnite, Captain Liam Goodnite, and Agent O'Connell's counsel," I say for the sake of the recoding. "Please state your name."

"Special Agent in Charge Wesley O'Connell, FBI." His voice rings strong and true.

"And do you have counsel present with you, Agent O'Connell?"

"Yes," Wes answers at the same time an older man in a suit similar to the ones Rex Harrison wore in *My Fair Lady*, vest and all, answers as well.

"Present."

"And for the record you are, Sir?"

"Anthony Garrison of *Garrison, Garrison, Parker, & Stroop*, Counsel for Agent O'Connell."

"Thank you. Let's get started," I say looking at Wes. He looks determined yet sad. "Agent O'Connell, did you know Agent Tawnya Webber?"

"Yes."

"What was the nature of your relationship?" Wes opens his mouth to speak but his attorney interrupts his answer.

"Define the term relationship, Detective."

"Sure thing." I shrug. "How did you know Agent Webber?"

"We both work for the FBI. I am her senior agent in charge," he answers.

"Is that the extent of your knowledge of Tawnya Webber?" I ask.

"As of late." Wes calmly responds.

"And before then?" I press. He swallows.

"I knew her."

"How so?" I further press, not sure if I want the answer.

"We engaged in an after-hours affair for three months but it was years ago." Wes admits.

"How many years ago?" I need the specifics.

"Five years ago."

"Does the FBI allow relationships as such?" I press on.

"It's not encouraged, but it is allowed," Wes answers honestly.

"Did it affect your job?"

"Never." He states.

"Did the affair end amicably?"

"As much as they ever can?" He shrugs.

"Did you not want to part ways with her?"

"I did, she didn't."

"Did the breakup affect your working relationship?"

"No."

"Why did you end your affair?" I ask.

Wes looks me dead in the eyes as he answers, "She wasn't you."

"Inappropriate and not pertaining to the case, Wes," Lee interjects while I try and catch my breath.

"It's true. We—Lee and I," he says for my benefit before turning back to Liam. "Came home and built our careers. By the time I was ready for something serious with your sister she was ignoring me and avoiding me as if it was her job. It was clear that I wasn't going to make any headway any time soon so, ashamed as I am, I didn't give up my extracurricular activities. I realize now that I should have.

"One night we had wrapped up a pretty rough case—a kidnapping, but not like the Donovan's. Like hers—I was keeping it together, but I was in a bad way. Webber offered to take me to a local bar and get me drunk and I agreed. Once I was good and hammered, she offered to take me home and make me forget. I also agreed. But not to forget. As sick as it sounds, she looked just like . . .

"For a night I just wanted to pretend. I let it go on for three months. When she started voicing feelings for me, I knew that what I had done was wrong. I had to let her go. So, I did."

We all let his words weigh heavy in the room. The tale of Wes and Claire is not overly a happy one. And sad to say, it's future isn't looking so bright either. We've both done so many things we shouldn't have. So many wrong turns have been taken.

But this isn't about us. This right now is about catching a killer. I square my shoulders and straighten my spine. Everyone else follows my lead and knows that we are about to get back to the business at hand here.

"Agent O'Connell, did you murder Agent Tawnya Webber?"

"Don't answer that," his attorney chimes in.

"No," Wes answers anyway.

"Where were you at twelve o'clock this afternoon?"

"I was with you and Emma Parker in the morgue going over the autopsy reports of Tammy Campbell."

"Does the Greek Cafe or it's parking lot hold any meaning to you?" Wes looks me in the eye and clenches his mouth closed. I know he's holding back on me know. Whether for the case or his former affair I have yet to find out. "You might as well tell me."

"You don't have to answer," his attorney shares.

"Tawnya and I used to have lunch there." I tilt my head to the side because to my knowledge I've never eaten there. And then the embarrassment sears across my face. He doesn't mean me, he means her. "Once or twice, we fucked in the parking lot."

"Where were you during the time of Tammy Campbell's murder?"

"You have to know it didn't mean anything," he pleads. "Not to me. It didn't mean anything to me."

"Where were you during the time of Tammy Campbell's murder?" I repeat.

"Claire, please. It was only ever you. It was only you. I never loved anyone else."

"I'm going to ask you one more time before I conclude this interview. Where were you during the murder of Tammy Campbell?"

"I was with you, here at this station."

"Did you murder Tammy Campbell?"

"Don't answer!" Wes's attorney shouts.

"No." Wes states firmly.

"Where were you during the time of the murder of Bonnie Bradley?" I ask.

"At the club with your brother and a half dozen other officers."

"Did you know that she was a direct relative to me or to Captain Goodnite?"

"No."

"Did you murder Bonnie Bradley?"

"Don't answer!" The attorney shrieks. "Captain get your detective under control."

"Agent O'Connell was informed of his Miranda Rights, he is free to answer or not answer," Liam shares.

"No, I did not."

"Did you think that she looked like me before her death?" I ask.

"No, it never crossed my mind."

"No further questions," I say as I click off the recorder. "Don't leave town, Agent O'Connell. We'll be in touch."

"Claire, I love you! It was a long time ago. You have to believe me," he shouts as he rises up from the table and moves to follow me to the door. His attorney grabs him by the back of his arm and whispers something in Wes's ear. He looks pissed but Wes just keeps yelling. "You have to believe me."

My eyes flood and my nose stings as I look at Wes.

"The sad thing is I do. But we'll deal with that later," I say softly, hopefully for his ears only.

"No!" he shouts. "Fuck. Claire! I need you. You have to come back, Claire."

"Just let her go, man," I hear Lee say softly.

"No. I can't. You can't ask that of me."

"For now," Lee pleads. "Just let her go. For now."

I let the steel door close behind me but not before I hear Wes sob and call out my name one more time. I put one foot in front of the other and walk out of the station. Despite what it looks like, this time, I'm not running.

But I do have to clear my head. It's been a long day and I'm starving. I'm exhausted—both physically and emotionally and tomorrow I need to be at the top of my game. Tomorrow, I'm going to find a killer. I'm going to catch the piece of shit responsible for ending the lives of a stripper, a barista, and the former lover of my boyfriend because they deserve justice. Only then I can figure out what to do with me.

chapter 25
tribal drums

MY PULSE IS POUNDING in my ears like a tribal drum as I walk down the hall.

I pull in a deep breath through my nose and slowly force it out of my mouth. I do it again. And again, until the edges of my focus snap into place. Instead of waving all over like a flag in the breeze, I see a tunnel in front of me as I pass through the hall and down to the door.

I choose to push out of the side entrance instead of the front door where I know a ton of lookey loos are waiting to see the aftermath of my interview with Wes. I'm sure they're all waiting with baited breath to see an explosion or a meltdown. What will happen next? Well, stay tuned because I have no idea.

I need to get home and go over the case. It's been a long couple of days. I need to step back and look at everything from a different perspective. Why Wes? Why is Wes the central focus?

I push out the side door and the purple sky tells me that my showdown with Wes took longer than I thought. Not to mention we were at the crime scene all afternoon. My stomach growls loudly as I palm my cell phone. I'm hungry and need a burrito, or like twenty tacos. It takes a lot of junk to fuel all of this magnificence.

I swipe the screen on my phone and dial the one number I know that I always can. The one person that will never judge me and will always try to guide me towards the right path. Or the one who will go down swinging with me if I do. It's also the number of the one person who will always pick me up when I need a lift.

"Hello?" they answer.

"I need a ride," I explain.

"I thought as much. I'll be there in five."

"Meet me at the cafe on first. I need a cup of coffee and to not be loitering here at the station."

"So I heard. See you then." And then they hang up. I put my phone in my pocket and start walking towards the little coffee shop on first. It's not the one that Tammy worked at, the one that Wes and I usually go to together.

This is the place I go when I need to be alone and off the radar.

I walk the last two blocks and pull open the door to a place where nobody knows my name. Where they see cops of all ranks and uniforms come through the doors because of its close proximity to the station. Here the coffee is poured, cash is accepted, and no questions are asked.

I stand in the back of the line behind the tired and weary. It's clearly been a fantastic day all around. Although whisperings of a serial killer around town is enough to put anyone in the dumps. Or excite them. Some people are weird.

I shuffle forward inch by inch as each person before me orders and then grabs their paper cups with little brown coffee collars on them before shuffling off into the ether. Finally, I step up to the counter where a young woman—probably seventeen to nineteen years old—greets me with a smile that makes my stomach clench when I think of Tammy and her adorably harmless infatuation with Wes.

Wes.

How could one word, three little letters, make my heart ache so badly? The answer is easy. Behind those three little letters is eleven years of my loving him. No, that's the lie I tell myself. That I stopped loving him for awhile when his misguided attempt to protect me and provide for me what he thought that I needed was leaving me at eighteen—shortly after I had given him my heart and my innocence on a silver platter. The cold hard truth is, I have been in love with Wesley O'Connell my entire life. That is twenty-nine, almost thirty years, on this earth. And for that entire time, all t*wo hundred sixty-two thousand, nine hundred eighty* hours, *fifteen million, seven hundred seventy-eight thousand, eight hundred* minutes, and *nine hundred forty-eight million, seven hundred twenty-eight thousand* seconds of it I have been in his orbit.

The look on my face must have forced her—Emmy, her name tag says Emmy—to take a step back with wide eyes. Her smile turning just a little bit brittle around the corners of her mouth. I turn up the wattage on my own smile thinking that clearly my resting bitch face got the best of us both. *Oopsie Whoopsies.*

"Hi there. What can I get for you?"

"Just a coffee. Black," I answer before noticing the tightening of the corners of her mouth. She's clearly not impressed with my two-dollar coffee order and I can't help but find her assessment of me startling. So, I scramble to add more to my order. "Umm . . . with room for cream. Lots of room. And one of those big oatmeal raisin cookies."

"Sure thing," she says softly as she reaches over to bag my cookie. "That'll be six dollars and seventy-eight cents please."

I pull a ten-dollar bill out of my pocket and hand it to Emmy. "Thanks," I say as I take my cup and paper bag filled with a cookie that will probably taste like ash in my mouth due to all the stress I'm under.

She gives me a reproachful glare and I drop all of the change she just handed me into the tip jar. Her face instantly morphs into a look of pure delight as her new financial boon registers.

"Thank you! Come again. Anytime!"

I back away slowly and head towards the cream and sugar counter. I take the lid off my paper cup and pour a shit ton of creamer in. I chance a look over my shoulder and see Emmy watching me with an arched brow so I pour a little more in before replacing the lid and pushing out through the glass doors.

The bells chime and the sun is bright as it's setting behind the trees. I take a deep breath and shake off the mental shackles that Emmy and her teenage judgement put me in, instantly feeling silly for feeling that way. Just then Anna rolls up on what feels like two wheels in her Merc.

"Get in, loser. We're going shopping." Always with the *Mean Girls* references. For as level headed and rational that Anna is, *Mean Girls* is her Achilles Heel. The thought makes me smile.

I pull open the door and hop inside.

"Thanks for the lift, A."

"So why aren't we with the man friend?" she asks.

"What?" I volley back. "I can't call my dearest friend?"

"Save it." She shoots me a side eyed glare. "Emma called me. I know what went down at the crime scene earlier."

I sigh. "Then what are you asking me for? Clearly, you already know everything."

"She also told me that he said he would only speak to you to give his statement." She widens her eyes expressively.

"Your face is going to freeze like that." It's petty and childish I know, but currently I can't seem to help myself.

"I'm assuming that did not go well and that is why you needed me to help you execute an escape plan."

"Maybe we shouldn't bandie about the word *execute* right now."

"Stop prevaricating," she challenges.

"I don't know what you're talking about," I say folding my arms across my chest.

"Don't be petty, it doesn't become you."

"Yes, it does."

"Okay it does but stop it because I don't like it."

"Fine," I pout.

"Besides," she starts with a Cheshire Cat grin that I know for a fact means trouble. "Emma is meeting us at your place so we can both pin you down and torture all the details out of you."

I sigh. I'm well and truly fucked now.

chapter 26

grownup

THE DRIVE FROM THE little coffee shop to my apartment is silent. Anna isn't one to fill the void with useless chatter and I can already tell that she's saving up her lecture for when she has backup. If Anna is anything, she is a planner. Anna is calm, cool, and collected. *Rational*.

Emma, on the other hand, flies by the seat of her pants. Emma operates solely on emotion and instinct. She acts first and thinks later. If she were in this car with me she would be all over me like a cheap suit. Thankfully she's not.

This gives me a moment to think up an excuse for why I cannot tell them all the gory details of my romantic life as they seem to be intersecting with my case right now. And as my dad would say, what a cluster fuck. That's actually one of my most favorite phrases as it just seems to sum things up so well. Although I never seem to have an actual reason to apply it. But with this case already running me ragged, with murder victims dressed like creepy little dolls coming out of my ears and snakes popping up at inopportune moments—I shudder at the thought—even I couldn't dream up a scenario where one of the victims had a romantic history with Wes.

It can't really be as bad as it seems. I want to tell myself that everything will work out the way that it is supposed to. That I can clear Wes's name and find the killer. And if Lady Luck is really on my side, I can repair the relationship that I wasn't even sure that I wanted until recently. All while avoiding Emma and Anna's inquisition like a long-tailed cat in a house full of *River Dancers*. Who am I kidding? I am well and truly screwed. I might as well just tell them what they want to know.

She pulls the Merc into a spot just in front of the stairs as if it had been waiting for her to drive up all along. Ugh. I groan. How does she have all the luck? In all the years that I have lived here I have never been lucky enough to nab this space.

Anna turns to look at me when that terrible noise crawled up from my throat and rolls her eyes. I'm assuming that she mistakes my groan for not wanting to be ambushed and tortured by my two closest friends instead of envy of her ridiculous parking karma.

"Come on," she says softly. "Let's just get this over with."

"Okay."

She turns, unbuckling her seatbelt and pushing her door open. Anna climbs from her Merc with the grace of a ballet dancer. She works so closely with the department sometimes that I forget that she isn't really one of us, the rougher crowd that can seamlessly mingle with the city's underbelly to root out the answers we need. Anna, is a trust fund baby who went to an Ivy League school—Princeton! It's moments like this when she lets the mask slip for a second, she's pushing her door open and climbing the stairs to my place with a look of sadness in her eyes that she doesn't usually show to the world. I wonder what a weight this life is on her, what toll does it really take from her, when I see her like this.

"Christ, Claire, hurry up," she shouts at me. "Christmas is coming!"

And then, when she turns back to me, I see that that look, is gone. So, I brush off those feelings, the maudlin thoughts that can weigh any of us down from time to time, and I follow her up the stairs. Emma throws open my front door when Anna and I reach the landing.

"Fucking hell! It took you long enough. I'm dying here. Literally. Dying."

Anna rolls her eyes. "You're not literally dying or you would, in fact, be dying right now."

"Shut it, Fancy Pants. She knows what I mean."

"I'm just saying . . ." she grumbles. I can't help but laugh.

"And you!" Emma wheels on me. I hold my hands up in surrender.

"I'm starving," I say quickly changing the subject. Sort of. "I need sustenance before you interrogate me."

"Ugh. Fine," Emma shouts, throwing her hands up over her head as she makes her way over to my refrigerator. She pulls open the door and stops in her tracks. "You have got to be kidding me."

"What?" I ask feeling a little offended at her reaction to the contents of my fridge.

"There's like an old container of eel sauce in here that smells like used cat litter and a quart of milk so curdled it's cottage cheese from hell. How do you live like this?"

"Like what?" I ask.

"Like . . . like a toddler or a frat boy."

"That's ridiculous," I complain.

"Is it really?" Anna chimes in.

"Yes!" I say.

"No!" Emma volleys back.

"Ugh!" I grumble throwing my hands up like ET over my head. "I am a grown up!"

"You could have fooled me," Emma mumbles.

"What was that?" I snap. I'm spoiling for a fight. At this point, I'll do anything to keep them from asking me the hard questions, even if that means a knock down drag out with one of my best friends.

"Look," Anna tries for diplomacy. "Let's just order delivery. What does everyone feel like?"

"Chinese," I answer immediately. Both Anna and Emma stare silently with their jaws hanging open. "What?" I ask after a moment of awkwardness.

"Ch-Chinese?" Anna asks after clearing her throat.

"Yeah, why?"

"Really?" Emma asks.

"Really." I nod.

"But you were poisoned with Chinese food!" Emma shouts.

"Oh!" I say realizing what they were talking about. "That was ages ago. I love Chinese food." Emma closes her eyes and shakes her head side to side rapidly, almost like she's trying to clear an Etch-a-sketch.

"Oh-kay . . ." Anna agrees.

"Great!" I cheer excitedly. Chinese food really perks me right up. "I have a menu right here." I pull open one of the kitchen drawers and start rooting through all of the take-out menus."

"Sweet Christ!" Emma barks. "There must be menus for every restaurant in the tri-city area." She does not seem nearly as impressed about that as I am.

"I know. It took me a long time to collect them all." I finally find the one that I want and hold it up like the monkey holds the baby lion in the beginning of *the Lion King*. Emahama emee momabah! "Got it!"

"What was that you were saying about being a grown up?" Anna drolls.

"Shut up!" I snap. "You want food or not?"

"Mu-shu chicken please." She bats her pretty blue eyes at me.

"You're lucky you're so pretty," I say as I slide my finger across the screen of my phone to unlock it. I press the number one speed dial setting to connect with my favorite Chinese place.

"I'm not even going to comment on the fact that you have a take-out place as the number one speed dial in your phone . . ." Emma rolls her eyes.

"Even before us?" Anna asks sounding just a little appalled as the phone rings.

I nod my head yes. "Don't worry your pretty little heads." I smile evilly. "It's also ahead of Wes and the station."

The line connects. "Hello and thank you for calling Szechuan Palace. How may we help you?"

"Hi, Mr. Yao," I answer.

"Claire! So good to hear from you. The usual?"

"Of course. And another order of Mu-Shu Chicken and an order of Beef with Broccoli please." I wink at Emma just to rile her up.

• • •

"So . . ." Anna says breaking the silence as we all poke at our take-out containers with chopsticks. "How about them, Yankees?"

"What the fuck are you talking about?" I ask.

"Wes." She nods. I groan.

"I mean, you did walk right into that one," Emma adds cheerfully. "I'm surprised the good head doctor didn't just come right out and say it."

"What's that supposed to mean?" Anna asks clearly a little offended at the head doctor comment.

"Don't get your panties in a wad, Fancy Pants. I just meant that you're usually more direct than this."

"Well . . ." she hedges. "I was just trying to be a little considerate of Claire's feelings."

"It's alright, Anna," I say softly. "You may proceed with your interrogation."

"Thank you," she says politely before rolling her shoulders back and carrying on with her intended mission. "Emma said that Wes knew the Agent that was killed today."

"Ha!" Emma snarks. "Knew her, he was banging her."

"Presently?" Anna asks.

"No," I answer, my voice still quiet.

"Are you sure?" Emma asks.

"He says so."

"Do you feel like you can trust the veracity of his claims?" Anna asks not at all unkindly, just . . . interested. She's evaluating the situation.

I sigh before standing up. "I was wrong. We're going to need my boyfriend for this conversation."

"Boyfriend?" Emma and Anna ask in unison.

"I believe you might know him as Gentleman Jack."

"Ahh." Anna nods.

I grab the bottle from the top shelf in my little kitchen. I unscrew the cap and take a heavy swig straight from the bottle.

"Classy as always." Emma winks before reaching for the bottle. She belts back a sip before handing it to Anna.

Anna takes her own swig before coughing. Emma pats her on the back hard. "God, that's truly terrible."

"Hush your mouth! You might hurt his feel bads." I laugh.

She rolls her eyes at me. "Quit evading the question."

I shrug. "I'm not evading, I just thought this conversation would be more bearable if we were shit faced." I take another swig from the bottle before passing it on and picking up my take-out container.

"That's such a hideous turn of phrase." Anna laughs before taking another hit from the bottle. "It does become more manageable the more you drink it."

Emma and I both snicker.

"Now answer the question Fancy Pants asked you." Emma urges.

I sigh. "I do trust him. Wes that is."

"Okay," Anna says taking a deep breath after another sip. "What happened at the scene?"

"Agent Webber's partner was upset and rubbed my nose in the affair that everyone knew about but me."

"And how did that make you feel?"

"Shitty," I answer. "How would you feel?"

"Not good," she says after a pause. I look to Emma to see if she knows what's up with our favorite shrink but her face is purposely blank.

"It was not good." I take a deep breath and prepare myself to spill it all to my two closest friends whether or not I want to. "Wes had to leave the scene because it's now a conflict of interest."

"How do you feel about that?" Anna questioned.

"It is a conflict of interest. I would rather Wes recuse himself to be cleared by a third party than have him muddy the waters by being a dumbass."

"Fair enough," Emma adds.

"Then Lee basically threw down with her partner," I add.

"What?" Anna asks, her back going straight. I barely had time to register how Emma bristled at the mention of my brother's name. Something is going on here.

"He kept bad mouthing me and the department in front of everyone working the scene. Lee sent him packing but it almost came to blows." I explain.

"That's terrible," she breathes.

"I'm sure Captain Goodnite can handle himself just fine." Emma snorts before she realizes what she said and her fair face turns beet red.

"What is going on between you and Lee?" I ask unfortunately before I see Anna's flinch. Oh shit. I thought she was over her crush.

Emma looks pointedly at Anna while answering my question. "Not one Goddamned thing."

"Fair enough," I say.

Anna rolls her shoulders back before pressing on. "What happened after Liam—*Captain Goodnite*—turned the agent away?" She quickly corrects herself.

"We worked the scene. It was the same old, same old, and then Emma hauled her away in her mondo body mover." I shrug.

"Not so fast there," Emma wades in. "Let's back up the old Sioux canoe here."

"I'm not sure I know what you mean . . ." I hedge.

"Of course, you do," Emma says looking me straight in the eyes and calling out my bold-faced lie before turning to Anna. "Agent Webber had an uncanny resemblance to our singing squaw over here," she says to Anna while tossing her thumb over her shoulder at me.

"I wouldn't say we look that similar . . ."

Emma shoots me a withering glare. "She could have been your sister."

"I mean . . . not really."

"Wasn't Bonnie Bradley actually your sister?" Anna asks quietly.

"Umm . . ." I mentally grapple for any answer that doesn't seem as bad as it is.

"That's what I thought." Emma sits back folding her arms across her chest.

"What are you thinking?" Anna asks.

I blow out a breath. "That it's kind of messed up that Wes was with someone for so long that looked like me. Just because she was available and happened to look like me."

"That doesn't sound good," Anna says before biting her lip, a sure sign that she is not sure of the situation.

"It's not." I shrug. "It is what it is. There's no putting the toothpaste back in the tube on this one. I guess what it really comes down to is how much do I love him?"

"And do you?" Anna asks. "Love him?"

I take another sip from the now almost empty bottle. "I do."

"Alright then. What happened next?" Anna presses on.

"The desk sergeant called and told me Wes was at the station to give his official statement."

"That's it?" she asks to which Emma snickers.

"Oh no, it's not." She giggles. Emma is clearly a little intoxicated. But then again, so am I.

"He said he would only talk to me," I spit the words out as fast as I can.

"Oh fuck," Anna says.

"You got that right," Emma agrees.

"Then what happened?"

"He told me all the dirty details of his affair with Agent Webber and promised that he didn't kill her."

"And then what?"

"I left the interview room."

"And Wes just let you go?" she asks confused and I can see why. From the moment Wes re-entered my life eight months ago he had made his intentions towards me crystal fucking clear. So, for him to just let me go seems a little anticlimactic.

"Not really . . ." I hesitate.

"Did you fight?" Emma asks.

"No." I sigh. "There was nothing more to talk about and I knew that everyone and their mother in that station was piled up high on the observation deck. So, I left to go recharge my batteries and regroup. That's when I called Anna."

"But he just let you go?" Emma asks.

"No. He was screaming my name. He was with Lee the last time I saw him. But I have to solve this case and to do that I have to clear him of any wrongdoing aside from the affair. I can't do that clean with him so closely connected to me. It has to be by the book."

"I can see where you're coming from . . ." Anna hedges.

"Maybe you should call him," Emma jumps in.

"I can't. I can't show any conflict of interest or manipulation of the case or the FBI will rip it right out from underneath me." I take the bottle from Emma and take a long sip. "I'm close. I know it. I'm so close to figuring it all out that

I can feel it."

"Well." Emma sighs. "There's nothing more we can do tonight. Especially while I'm this drunk. I will have the lab reports back on Agent Webber in the morning so let's just decompress tonight."

"Sounds like a plan," I agree. "Movie?"

"Yes!" Anna cheers. Clearly excited for a girls' night.

I push myself up off the couch and sway just a teensy tiny bit before walking down the hall to my bedroom. I change into a pair of pajama shorts and a tank before grabbing some clean pajamas out of the dresser drawer and heading back to the living room.

"Here you bitches go," I say as I toss the content towards their faces. I squint in an effort to make them fly in the direction I was hoping for.

I toss my hair up into a messy bun on top of my head and sit—and by sit, I mean flop unceremoniously—on the floor by the sofa and pick my take out back up. Emma and Anna take turns changing in my little bathroom before we all sit back down.

"Anyone want a microwave warm up?" I ask as Anna flips through the channels on the TV. There's a chick flick movie marathon on one of the local channels. Hooray. I don't think we could handle anything bloodier than a broken heart right now.

"Nah," Emma says. "I kind of prefer Chinese food cold."

"Amen to that!" Anna cheers. She's cute when she's tipsy. I just wish she wasn't headed towards a heartbreak from my dipshit brother. He can be such an asshole sometimes.

We settle in and relax. Emma was right, there's nothing we can do now. I only hope that Wes knows that while I can't contact him, he needs to trust me. It will all work out tomorrow.

"This just in . . ." the TV station cuts to the local news. *"We're here with breaking news as it appears a Serial Killer is on the loose in George Washington Township."*

"You have got to be kidding me," I growl as I turn up the volume on the set.

"This station received a tip from a credible law enforcement source who wishes to remain nameless . . ."

"I'll just fucking bet he does. I'll have his badge for this," I growl.

"That's if you can prove it," Emma says. "I bet that fucker covered his tracks."

"Our source claims that George Washington Township PD has been keeping valuable information away from the public. Information that could very well keep you safe at night. And those responsible for withholding the truth are none other than Captain Liam Goodnite and Detective Claire Goodnite . . .", I groan.

"You all will remember Detective Goodnite, who graced headlines during the high-profile kidnapping of a six-year-old boy, Anthony Donovan. This is the same detective who was abducted herself at six years old. That case is still unsolved."

"That's right, Cynthia. In fact, some George Washington residents wonder how fit she is to actually be a police officer in this district. In fact, some have said that she only holds the job because her brother is Captain Liam Goodnite. Not to mention their father is retired Chief of Police Adam Goodnite."

"I bet those are fun family dinners."

"I'm going to shoot them." I seethe.

"Now Claire, you can't threaten to shoot the public," Anna says softly whill giving me the side eye.

"Watch me."

"Not to mention Detective Goodnite has been linked romantically to Special Agent Wesley O'Connell. That's Judge O'Connell's son to you."

"That would be the same Agent O'Connell who our source tells us was being interrogated at the precinct this afternoon." I groan.

"No, I'm not going to shoot them. I'm going to shoot that fucking fed!" I yell.

"We have it on good authority that all three victims of this serial killer were dressed and posed like old fashioned dolls."

"That mother fucker is releasing closed details of this case!" I seethe.

"It's all rather disturbing. Am I right, Ted?"

"They won't go there, right?" Emma asks. Me? I'm not so sure.

"Surly not," Anna agrees. I'm still not holding my breath. I've been thrown under this bus before so I recognize the beep-beep as it heads my way.

"Absolutely. In fact, we're told that all of the victims have been linked to Agent O'Connell. So, the question remains, is Detective Goodnite too close to the case? Will these poor women ever find justice or will the GWTPD cover up for the true killer?"

"Omigod," Anna whispers.

"Fuck me, they went there." Emma agrees.

"I guess we'll just have to stay tuned . . ."

"I'm going to go to bed," I say quietly. Even to me, my voice sounds toneless, dead.

"Everything will look better in the morning, Claire," Anna tells me.

"She's right," Emma says.

"Sure," I agree. "I'll see you both in the morning. It'll all be better in the morning."

Too bad in the morning we'd all find out just how wrong we were.

chapter 27

results are in

*R*UN! *I'm running as fast as my little feet will take me through the woods behind my parents' house. I have to get away from the bad man. If he catches me now, I'll never get away. I have to be free.*

Run! I have to run faster.

I see the blue gray light as it spills through the trees. Mommy always told me this was her favorite part of the day—looking at the sun as it comes up in the morning. I ran away late in the night when the bad man was sleeping. It was my only chance. After he broke the lock on the closet door I knew that I had a chance to get out.

Free.

I'm free. That's the words in my head as the trees break and I see Wes standing at the edge of the backyard. I'm free. I'm finally free. Wes looks up and he sees me.

"I've got her!" he shouts to someone.

My heart is beating so hard in my chest and it hurts to breathe. I'm so tired but I have to keep running. I see Wes, his face, I know that he'll protect me. Wes always protects me. He will keep me safe. He will keep me free.

I push my feet just a little harder. I run just a little faster. I'm almost there. I'm almost free when a strong hand wraps around my arm so hard that it hurts, pulling me around to face him, not Wes, the bad man. Wes is gone and the only person near me is the man I would do anything to get away from.

"No!" I scream.

"You're mine, Claire. You'll never be free."

• • •

Beep . . . beep . . . beep . . .

My alarm blares on the table next to my bed. A bed which in the cold light of day seems unrealistically huge and cold without Wes's body in it next to mine. Somewhere along the way, I got used to his presence in my bed, in my life, and in my heart.

I squeeze my eyes closed. That bright morning light is like ice picks in my occipital sockets. Oh, a gentleman you were not, Jack. My head is pounding with the beat of my heart and it feels like my mouth is stuffed with cotton. I halfway think I might have died last night and no one told me yet.

Coffee. I need some fucking coffee.

I peel the covers back and gingerly push my body to sitting. I have to bury my face in my hands to stop the room from spinning. So far, not so good. I swallow back the bile that pools in my mouth and force myself to stand. I press my brain to try and see his face, a tattoo, a scar, anything, but just my luck, to me the bad man is still a blur.

I push myself to my feet and instantly regret it. The combination of the Jack and the nightmare have me running for the bathroom. I barely make it, dropping to my knees in front of the toilet before emptying my stomach of its contents. Sweat mats the baby hairs to the back of my neck and my forehead. I wipe my mouth with a piece of toilet paper before dropping it in and hitting the handle.

More slowly this time, I rise to my feet and rinse my mouth out at the sink. Now I really do need some coffee. I walk out into the kitchen and find Emma and Anna gone but a note on the counter.

C,

We look like shit and headed home. Jack is a real dick. I'm considering a breakup. Nah, who am I kidding? He'll be my hot date this weekend. I'll see you at the station don't forget, the results are in.

Oh, and we made coffee. You're fucking welcome.

Xo, Emma (Anna too but with less curse words)

The note makes me smile. Those two are ridiculous and I love them. Who would have thought my besties would be a chick who likes to put her hands in dead bodies and my shrink? Not me.

I move to the counter where blessedly—praise Jesus and all the baby angels—a fully loaded coffee pot is waiting for me. I pull a mug down and pour the steaming liquid into my cup. I don't even replace the carafe, I just hold it in one hand while the other hand raises my full mug to my lips and I gulp half of it down hot and black before refilling the cup. I drink the next cup with cold leftover Chinese food as a chaser. Perfect cure for a hangover.

I take my mug into the bathroom with me and turn the water on. I keep it icy instead of letting it heat up because my body still feels too hot and sticky. The coffee isn't helping matters either but it's a necessity at this juncture.

I strip off my clothes and step in letting out a hiss as the cool spray lands on my back. I make quick work of my shower because I have important shit to do today and standing here letting my nightmares take me back down isn't one of them. Somewhere halfway through my brisk scrubbing, I reach a hand out of the shower and grab my mug off of the counter. I drain it before setting it down on the shower floor—where I'll forget it as soon as it's there.

I turn off the water and grab my towel off of the rack. It's old and worn and rough to the skin. It's nothing like the fancy shit Wes keeps at his house. Maybe I'm not as much of a grown up as I had originally thought.

I follow my earlier path back into the bedroom and through to my closet where I pull on panties and a bra. My favorite jeans and t-shirt come next and then my boots. I grab my gun and holster from the bedside table and clip them on. My badge follows. I grab my drop gun and ankle holster from the safe and check the rounds before inserting them in my boot.

I grab my keys and cellphone before heading out the door only to find that my car is still in Wes's driveway. Today is really frustrating. I pull out my phone and open the find-a-friend app. I click all the buttons to see where Wes is and find that he's at Lee's house on the opposite end of town from his own home which sits in the same quiet neighborhood as our parents have always lived.

I close out that app and order an Uber to Wes's house. Just what I need to start my day, a walk of shame slink away from my boyfriend's house. What can I say? My life is magical.

A white dodge neon that's missing all of the paneling on one side pulls up and rolls down the window.

"You Claire?" he asks.

"Yeah."

"Get in." I do as I'm told and pull open the rear door, climbing in. The entire inside reeks of pot. Classy dude. He eyes me in the rearview mirror and sweat starts to bead on his forehead. "You a cop?"

"Yep." I pop the *p* in my response to let him sweat a little more.

"You making me drive myself to jail?"

"Nope."

"You making me drive you to another cop's house?"

"No." I smile my sweetest smile at him in the mirror. "A Fed's."

"What?"

"It's okay, I'm going to steal my car back, not bust you for a little Mary Jane."

He takes an audible breath. "Thanks, lady."

"No prob, Bob." And then he drove me to my boyfriend, the Fed in questions' house, so that I could steal my car back.

Once in the driveway, I step out of the car. "Thanks, bud—" I start to say but before I can close the door, let alone finish that sentence, he's peeling out. I shrug. He seemed like a nice kid. I snicker to myself at the thought.

And then I realize I'm loitering around a Fed's house in the early morning hours. A Fed I am not supposed to be hanging around. Plus, if he comes back and catches me, I'll have to explain myself and then we'll all be in a pickle because I won't be on the case anymore. That will probably really piss me off.

This is when I enact my very best *Charlie's Angels* maneuvers. I creep around the building to the driveway on the far side of the house. I press the unlock button on the key fob and jump a mile when the locks beep. Jesus Christ it's like I forgot all of my training.

I sigh to myself and then jump into the driver's seat. I crank the ignition as fast as I can and put the pedal to the metal and head for the station. I need to go over all of the case details again. I wasn't kidding when I told my friends that I could feel how close I was. I know that the killer is out there. And I know that he's close. I just have to figure it out before anyone else gets killed or Wes gets thrown in the old hoosegow. That would really be a bummer.

chapter 28
find out

LIKE A DOG WITH a bone. That's what my dad always said about me when I had to find out the answers to whatever questions were plaguing my mind. He would also tell you that's what makes me a decent detective.

Liam would tell you that it just makes me a pain in the ass. Wes, I'm not so sure. I just hope he can hang tight a little longer. Just a tiny bit longer.

I pull into the parking lot and take the first available space I see regardless of whether or not it's in the back of the lot. I don't care. I grab my keys from the ignition and jump down from my Tahoe, slamming the door closed behind me. I'm running as soon as my boots touch the ground.

Running. Just like in my dream, I'm running.

I slow my pace just in time to avoid hitting the glass doors as they pushed open and Detective Cruz walks out.

"Good morning, Claire," he says to me with a sweet smile.

"Hey," I say. I'm trying my best to avoid talking to anyone. Not because I'm that anti-social, well, I am, but I need to get down to the basement and talk to Emma. She promised me results and I want them.

"Where's the fire?" He asks.

"I have to get to the morgue," I explain as I move past him. "Emma promised me results."

"Gotcha. Feel like grabbing a pizza later?" His harmless question stops me in my tracks and I turn to look back at him. I tip my head to the side and study him a bit before answering.

"I can't," I say softly hoping against hope that I haven't hurt his feelings. We do have to work together for all time.

"Sure," he says but his tone is weird. Maybe this is the last time he'll ask me out. Maybe I'll regret it later if—or when—Wes and I explode into a fiery blaze of not glory but until then, I'm a little relieved. It's hard being a nice person, all considerate of people's feelings and shit. I should just go back to being a bitch.

I push through the doors without ever looking back and hot foot it to the elevator. I jab the call button again and again hoping it will make the elevator come faster. A couple of detectives walk over to where I'm standing in the elevator bay and look as if they are about to push the call button. I shoot them a dark glare and they immediately change directions and head for the stairs.

Good fucking choice, assholes.

The elevator announces its arrival with a ding. Finally! I hop in and stab the button for the basement morgue with my finger. Thankfully, the steel cart deposits me in the basement without stops.

"Fucking finally!" Emma shots and then winces. Clearly, she's feeling about as spectacular as I am this morning.

She stalks over to her desk in the corner like a hungry lioness and rips open the drawer. Emma pulls out a massive bottle of ibuprofen and shakes out what has to be an unhealthy amount of little white tablets into her hand before tossing them all into her mouth. I cringe when I hear her crunching them between her teeth before she swallows down a cup of coffee on her desk like a hooker on a first date.

"Want some?" She shakes the bottle at me. We both jolt at the rattling sound the pills make in the bottle.

"No, thanks. I'm good."

She shrugs. "Suit yourself."

"So, what do you have?" I ask.

"Well, the results are in."

"And?" I can barely stand it. Something is about to give way. I just know it.

"Agent Webber's death is exactly the same as the others right down to the handmade old timey dress and the creepy sleeping pose."

"Tox screen?"

"Benzene injected right between the neck and shoulder. Would have rendered her totally paralyzed within minutes."

"Did you do a rape kit?" I ask feeling my excitement build.

"What? Are you new here?" Emma snaps. Someone is not a happy camper this early in the morning after a night out with Gentleman Jack.

"No, I'm not new here, asshole. But I do need all the details and quick."

"She was raped. But wait for it, no condom lubricant was found in the vaginal cavity. No DNA was found on her body. Semen was present and accounted for."

"You're kidding me. He left DNA?" I ask.

"DNA that is currently being run through CODIS," she tells me. I blow out a breath of frustration. The hardest part of this job is being patient when you want action. Liam always described his time in the military as *hurry up and wait* and that's exactly what case work feels like.

"This is the mistake I was waiting for him to make." I state.

"This is the mistake, you were waiting for him to make," Emma repeats.

"Cause of death?" I ask but I already know.

"Strangulation."

"Overall, it's creepy as hell," I add.

"It really is." She nods and then closes her eyes. Clearly the fist full of pills didn't completely take away her hangover.

"Where is the benzene coming from? It can't be that easy to get."

"Actually, it really is," she answers. "Benzene is a man-made chemical used in a lot of different businesses. It's used in rubbers, plastics, pesticides, detergents, drugs, explosives. You can even buy it online from one of those websites where they ship it to you in two days in a little brown box."

"Ugh. This is so frustrating!" I shout as I pull at my hair which I left loose this morning because the thought of pulling it up had my still pounding head screaming.

"We'll figure it out," she says softly from behind me. "I emailed you the report."

"Thanks, Em." I sigh. "I'm going to go upstairs to the conference room and go over all of the case details."

"Let's grab some disgusting cheeseburgers or greasy pizza around noon to break this hangover."

"Sounds good to me," I say as I toss a wave over my head as I head back to the elevator. But as sick as I feel, I still have too much pent up energy over this case so I bypass the elevator and push open the door to the stairwell. I take the stairs two at a time.

I make my way to my desk where I boot up and log into my geriatric computer from the stone age. The department resources are stretched ever so thin. I kind of want to call up those news anchors from last night and be like see this computer that is older than me? Clearly, I am getting all the favors being the Captain's little sister. I roll my eyes but the action rattles something loose in my brain.

I log into the department server and pull the reports that Emma had sent me. She's pretty meticulous about her autopsy reports and making sure all of her i's are dotted and her t's are crossed. It makes it easy for us to pull the pertinent information from her doctor speak.

I send the files I need to the printer at the back of the bullpen. I could go stand over another one of the dinosaurs in this office while it takes four hundred years to print or I could go grab another cup of coffee from the kitchenette. I choose the coffee.

I bump into Jones who is also pouring himself a cup in the kitchen area.

"Hey there, Detective." He smiles at me.

"Hey, Jones. How's the wedding planning going?" I ask.

"Great. My girl says she bought her dress so we're all locked and loaded."

"That is great," I agree.

"Will we see you and O'Connell there?" he asks me before squeezing his eyes tight and biting his lip in obvious regret for asking the question. I shoot him my most genuine smile. "I'm sorry. That was insensitive."

"It's okay," I reassure him. "I'm sure everything will blow over by the big event."

"You're probably right, Detective." Jones takes his cup of coffee before heading back out.

I step up to the coffee maker and pour myself another cup. Station coffee is usually so thick it's a caffeinated pudding you can eat with a spoon. So, I doctor it with as much cream and sugar as I can find before heading out to the massive dinosaur printer which is wheezing like a ninety-eight-year-old lady with emphysema. It probably does have emphysema. It sounds like it could keel over and go tits up at any moment.

I stand there and watch it spit out the last of my reports as I sip my cup of coffee. When the last pages struggle to slip free, I grab them all up in my arms and head for the conference room that has become my battle station ever since this case turned from one creepy murder to a serial killer that has me trapped in an epic game of cat and mouse. I only hope he knows that I'm not the mouse. I'm a fucking lioness.

I spread out the reports in front of me: Bonnie, Tammy, and Tawnya. I match up all of the same details. I make notes of what links the three of them all together. But still, all arrows point to Wes and I know that it has to be a false lead. I just know it.

• • •

At noon, Emma comes to get me and as promised, we head to a burger joint around the corner. We each order giant burgers on buttery buns with fries and vanilla milkshakes. We bypass the vegetable station after we pick them up, opting for the nacho cheese dispenser. Grease is not only the word, but also the ultimate hangover cure. And who knows? Maybe it will shake something loose that's been lodged in my brain and everything will make sense.

"What's got you so down?" She asks me.

"I just can't find the real lead that I need. By all accounts, every detail points to Wes."

"How so?" she asks me.

"Well, Agent Webber, obviously. But also, Tammy had a huge crush on him. We went to that coffee shop almost every morning on our way to work."

"Okay, but what about the first victim?" Emma asks before taking a huge bite of the cheese covered burger. "What's the connection there?"

"He was at Jones's bachelor party at the strip club."

"Those connections are week, babe," she says after taking a sip of her drink. I bite into my burger and mull over her words. "There were tons of people at the strip club that night, not just Wes. And he wouldn't have sent you pictures with the intent to incriminate himself."

"That's true," I agree.

"In fact, half of our station was at the strip club that night for Jones's party," she says calmly. "And only about a billion people go to that coffee shop because it's more personable than the other one near the station. You know, the one you had Anna pick your bum ass up from yesterday after you made your grand exit—stage left."

"Shut up," I grumble as I dip a fry in a big blob of orange cheese goo in my basket and swirl it around before popping it into my mouth.

"So really, it could be a number of people including someone who works at or near the station."

"There's no way an officer in our station would do those things," I say with a confidence in my voice that I'm not quite sure that I feel. But could she be right? Could it really be as easy as all that?

"Sure," she says but as I look up I realize maybe Emma doesn't really feel very sure of that statement either.

Emma and I walked back to the station in silence after we finished our lunches. I couldn't help but think about all that she had said over lunch. Maybe I'm missing something simple. As I go to push open the glass door at the front of the station, Emma stops me by placing her hand on my arm.

"It'll all be okay," she says softly and it startles me. Emma is bold and brash. Soft isn't necessarily a word that I would use to describe her. But in this moment, it does. There's something going on with Emma and I can't quite figure out what it is.

"Sure," I say back just as softly.

"I mean it, Claire. It has to . . . it has to work out for you and Wes. It just does," she says before pushing open the front door and heading straight to the elevator. Something is definitely off with Emma. When this case is over, I'm going to have to get to the bottom of it.

• • •

Emma's words tumble over and over in my brain and I can't seem to shake them. I just can't make heads or tails of this investigation.

I spend the rest of the afternoon not pouring over the details of the case, but the lists if officers, detectives, and federal agents who were present at each crime scene. The fact of the matter is that the same names keep popping up over and over again. What if what Emma said is right?

Holy shit it's someone from this department.

I stand before I even realize that I'm doing it. I gather up as many of the papers as I can. Suddenly I need to be anywhere but in this station house. I need to go home and be alone. I need to wrap my mind around the idea that someone I know, that someone I work with every day could, in fact, be a serial killer.

Who could be the wolf in sheep's clothing?

I scoop up my messy stack of papers in my arms and hustle out the door. I practically run through the bullpen and then out the front door of the station—not even bothering to wave hello or goodbye to the desk sergeant on my way out even though he called out my name.

Instead I beep the locks on my department Tahoe and climb in like my hair is on fire. I start up the engine on the only piece of department equipment in my possession that isn't four hundred years old—even my service weapon is probably from the first world war—and race for my apartment like my life depends on it because if I'm right, it does.

• • •

They think they're so smart.

Everyone thinks they are so smart but I'm about to show them how brilliant I really am. They think they know, they don't know. I can't help but laugh at the thought that the world think's that stupid Fed is behind all the murders.

Part of me wishes I could take credit for all of my work. Part of me yearns for the world to know how much planning and hard work goes into my master pieces. That I had sewn each of those dresses late at night and first thing in the morning before heading to work. That I wanted to make those women perfect, just like her. But they'll never be perfect.

She's going to be my final piece here—my last hurrah before I move on—and I always move on. A new name in a new town and a new project. Let's be real, a new . . . obsession. I have obsessed over her for months and still she doesn't see my devotion! I had thought she would be the one to stop the compulsion to kill. That her perfection would curb the desire but in the end, she isn't as perfect as I thought and now she has to die.

The feel of the weight of the syringe in my pocket gives me a sense of closure, of completion. I feel my cock start to harden at the thought of her in the dress I made just for her that is currently all rolled up in a paper sack in my other hand.

Mother always told me that there was no such thing as a perfect woman but I can't believe that. She has to be out there, somewhere and until then . . . well, I'll just keep looking, keep creating perfection where none can be found.

• • •

The minute the door to my apartment shuts behind me I tumble all of the locks on the door and then lean back against the wood and breathe my first sigh of relief in over an hour.

Could it really be a cop killing these women? And if so, who? The thought of it being police officer has me shaking. Sweat beads at my hairline and rolls down my back between my shoulder blades.

I walk into the kitchen and pull a glass down from the cupboards. I fill it with water from the tap and then drink heavily as if it will clear all of the anxiety pooling deep in my gut like a poison. When my glass is empty I fill it again and drink until I need to put the glass down to catch my breath.

I close my eyes and take a deep breath before reassuring myself that I'm safe here. And I am safe. No one can get to me in my own home. Although there is a little voice in the back of my head reminding me of the snake that was left for me in a bouquet of roses. And how the killer did already get to me here.

It makes me want to jump in my car and head to Wes's house. Maybe I was wrong and there is safety in numbers. Maybe Wes and I should have stuck together all along. Was I wrong in thinking I could go it alone?

I pick up my phone to call him and realize that it's dead. I must have never plugged it in last night. Which, of course, is the first thought of anyone who drank too much Jack before going to bed. I roll my eyes at myself. What an idiot I am.

I walk into my bedroom and plug it into the charger by my bedside table before walking back into the kitchen and pulling a Chinese take-out carton from the fridge. I swear, the longer it sits in the fridge the better it is. One time, Lee's dog ate some old sushi that he threw away and puked it all up all over himself and Lee while he was sleeping on the couch next to my brother while he watched a ballgame. I was kind of pissed Liam threw it away even though it was four days old. I still would have eaten it. I did want to eat it. Shit. I'm really not a grownup after all.

I'm lost in my own thoughts of grownups and how one should probably not eat leftover sushi after, say, day three and the benefits of a well-stocked fridge and pantry that the knock at the door surprises me.

I nervously look through the peephole and relax when I see my friend. I smile as I open the door to greet them.

"Hey. What are you doing here?" I ask.

"I found something."

"What is it?" I ask eager to find out what they found. It's not until I feel the pinch in my shoulder that I realize it too late.

chapter 29
too fucking late

Wes

I NEED HER.

I need to find Claire. I hate this. I hate this fucking silent treatment. I hated watching my girl walk out of that interview room yesterday. It killed me to watch her walk away but I vowed then and there that it would be the last time she ever did it. If it's the last thing I do, I will show that woman how special she is to me, how much I love her. How much I have always loved her.

I'm not going to lie, when she walked out of that room I lost my shit. I screamed her name and begged her to come back. I did not give one fuck how many officers and detectives I knew were crammed into that observation deck, I just wanted Claire back.

Thank God for Lee.

Liam has been my best friend ever since we were born. Our families have always been close. Not too long ago I was worried how he would take the feelings I had building for his baby sister but he took it like a champ. After he TKO'd me—*total knock out*—like Muhammad Ali it was fairly smooth sailing. So, when I lost it yesterday in the interview room he dragged my ass back to his house and deposited me onto his sofa. Lee bought me a pizza and handed me a brand-new bottle of Jack that he claimed he had been saving for this very occasion. I'm still not sure how I feel about that.

This morning I woke up feeling like hammered horse shit. Most of a bottle of Jack will do that to a man. I drank a pot of coffee in Lee's kitchen before puking my guts up in the flower beds in front of his house on the way out to his car.

"Real classy, asshole," he'd grumbled before laughing as he climbed into his Tahoe and drove me back to my house so I could shower and change. When he pulled up in my driveway, the first thing we both noticed was the glaring absence of Claire's department vehicle.

"Well there's that," I had said.

"It's probably not what you think," Lee had tried to comfort me. Which, truth be told, was a little fucking awkward.

"I don't care what I think or what it looks like," I'd said. "I'm going to find her and I'm going to make it right."

"And what if she makes it difficult. What then?"

"Then I'm going to marry her ass."

After that Lee had laughed his ass off and mumbled something that sounded suspiciously like "Poor bastard."

After that I had let us into my house where Lee made more coffee and toast in my kitchen while I showered and tried to make myself somewhat human again. I pulled on jeans and a t-shirt with my boots instead of my usual suit but

I wasn't going to the office today. Today I was tracking down one wayward woman so that I could profess my love. My palms sweat and I kind of want more Jack. I'm never nervous but today I am.

At the last minute, I tuck a pancake holster into the back of my jeans—pulling my shirt out to cover it and clip my badge to my wallet and stuff both into my right back pocket just because. Lee and I were Cub Scouts way back when. I guess that *always be prepared* shit just sticks with you. I pull on my boots and grab my cell phone. I try and call Claire on my way back down the stairs to the kitchen but it just goes straight to voicemail.

"Here you go, Princess," Lee said when he handed me two pieces of toast and another cup of coffee, both of which I fell on like a starving man.

"Thank you, Cupcake," I had said before kissing his cheek. Lee swats me away and tells me to stop being an idiot before we lock up my house and climb in the car.

Now we're headed back to the station and I can't help but feel like something is wrong.

"Have you tried calling her?" I ask.

"Yeah, but it went straight to voicemail," Lee says and his brows scrunch in worry. I want to tell him that it's probably nothing but in my heart, I know that that's not true.

"Huh."

"I'm sure it's nothing," he tries to reassure me but it doesn't feel like nothing.

I was in such poor shape this morning, it's taken me almost all day just to get my shit together. The mid-afternoon sun is shining bright as we pull into the station parking lot. I look around desperately hoping to find her or spot her SUV but there's no sign of it here.

As we walk in the front door to the station, someone bumps into me in that dick way that says they did it on purpose and harder than necessary.

"Watch where you're going, asshole," someone barks. Unfortunately, I am in no mood to let it slide. Between missing Claire and the bottle of Jack I am in poor shape and spoiling for a fight.

"You got a fucking problem?" I snap.

"Yeah, you're my problem." I look up and see one of the detectives staring me down. I can't remember what his name is right now, but I'm not surprised he jumped my shit when the opportunity presented itself given the way he pants after Claire.

I smile at him letting him know that I know he has no chance in hell with Claire. "You're wasting your breath, buddy."

"We'll just see about that," he says before walking away.

"What was that all about?" Lee asks apparently having missed the whole exchange because he was conversing with the desk sergeant.

Claire's friend, Emma the ME, breezes through and Lee goes wired. Interesting. I wonder what that's all about.

"Hey Emma," I call her attention, stopping her, as she heads for the door. "Got a minute?"

"Sure, Wes. What's up?" she asks me pointedly ignoring Liam.

"I was wondering if you've seen Claire."

"Not since lunch. I'm actually bummed she didn't tell me she was leaving. I was kind of hoping we could get dinner together. But when I looked in the conference room she was gone and half of the pages she was looking over left with her."

"Did she seem alright at lunch?" I can't help but ask.

"Yeah. She's struggling to solve this case. She wants to solve it, clear you, and do it all by the book to boot." I can't help but feel a warm glow unfurl in my chest at the thought that Claire's goals include clearing my name. She believes me.

"What was she looking over?" I ask.

"Oh, just the autopsy reports and personal lists from the crimes scenes."

"Why?" Lee asks.

"Because if it's not Wes connected to all three murders then it had to be someone and the best bet would be someone from this station," she explains.

"That's crazy!" Liam shouts clearly angry that she would point a finger at one of his officers, but I can't help feeling like there's a frisson of truth in there somewhere.

I take off for the conference room and see that papers are scattered all over the table haphazardly and the chair that she was obviously sitting in has been swung back quickly—then not tucked back into the table as if she left in a hurry.

The hairs on the back of my neck stand on end.

I pick up several of the papers from the table and study them. Emma was right, it's a hodgepodge of the autopsy reports on all three victims with Claire's notes made in the margins. Then there it is, sitting right in the middle of the table. A list of names with check marks next to them. Claire was doing just as Emma said she had been. She was looking to see who was at each and every crime scene.

Suddenly looking at the list one name stands out and it's like a punch to the gut. I need to get to Claire. *Now*. My only hope is that I'm not too fucking late.

I race back through to the lobby where Liam is quietly arguing with Emma but there is no doubt in my mind that they are arguing. I snap my fingers in front of his face.

"We gotta go, man."

"Give me a minute," he says. "I'm in the middle of something."

"No time. We gotta go now." He must hear something in my voice because all of a sudden he's barking commands at me as we race back out the door.

"What's going on?" he clips out as we run for his truck.

"We have to get to Claire," I shout. "There's no time. I know who it is."

As we race back through town towards Claire's apartment, I have never been more glad that Lee drives like a bat out of hell. He pulls into the parking lot and I jump out of the SUV before he's even come to a complete stop. In my gut I know that there is no time.

I race up the steps to her door, pushing myself to go faster and faster. I knock on the door and call out her name.

"Claire, it's Wes. Are you home, honey?"

But no one answers. It's complete and total silence until I hear her scream. I reach behind me for my gun as I place my boot to the door and kick it open. I hear Lee climbing the stairs behind me but when the door swings fully open and I see her lying there in that creepy fucking dress with that asshole's hands wrapped around her neck and the blank look on her face—I realize I was too fucking late.

So, I do the only thing my brain will let me. I raise my gun and pull the trigger.

chapter 30
fade to black

Claire

I DON'T WAKE UP with a start, but in stages. Ironic for all the times I have been cast into consciousness with a quickness after a night terror only to wake up and realize I am safe and fine. Now, my brain finally lets me ease into being awake and I find myself in a real-life nightmare.

I feel my body pitch back and forth like a ship tossed about on the sea. One time, when I was nine, I was sure that I could man the two-man sailboat that Lee and Wes were racing that summer before they left for boot camp. *Anything you can do, I can do better and all that.*

But there were life lessons to be had here—like beware of snakes and slashed tires and men who come on too strong but I wasn't listening. I never listen.

We'd had a summer storm come up suddenly. Having never actually been taught how to sail, I had no idea that I needed to check the weather before I took a boat out. And by take a boat out, I mean, I stole their boat.

One would think that by now I would have learned my lesson, but no, I'm hard headed like that.

Back then I was minding my own business toodleing around when a huge gust of wind caught my sail and pitched my little boat to one side, spinning it around, and then back to the other side again. I was flopped around like a shopping bag caught in a breeze. Where you run and run after it, feeling guilty that you'll never catch it, but no matter how hard you try because no one likes a litterer, you can't catch it. That's exactly what it was like. And that's exactly how my body feels right now as my body is pulled and twisted and flopped about rather unceremoniously.

I test my toes—wiggling them as if my life depends on it, because it likely does—and nada, bupkis. Shit, shit, shit! I try my hands, my fingers, something anything. The only thing I seem to be able to move is my right eyelid, my left is paralyzed like the rest of my body.

Paralyzed.

Panic seized me and robs me of the breath from my lungs as I realize I have absolutely no way to protect myself. Just like Bonnie, Tammy, and Tawnya, I'm going to die.

My body is rolled backwards and I am flopped on my back. I feel my one moveable eye go wide as I recognize the man looming over me is none other than Detective Abraham Cruz. The man who has been cognizant of my feelings for weeks and acted as if he was truly protective of me, worried about me. He asked me out several times pretending to be interested in me when all along he was ruthlessly planning my murder.

He smiles a blinding white smile at me that crinkles the corners of his eyes. I can't believe I thought him handsome. I can't believe that in the midst of my relationship turmoil with Wes, I thought I might regret turning down this kind, handsome man who was clearly interested in me. The thought makes my stomach roil.

"I'm glad you're awake," he says as he straddles my thighs, pinning them down. "Do you like your dress? I made this one special for you."

I begin to blink my one eye furiously. It feels like it rolls around in my head like a marble but I'm still able to take stock of my dress—a word I would never like to hear again if I survive this, which likely, I won't.

The dress is made of light pink fabric with tiny, little rosebuds all over it in a slightly darker shade of pink. There are delicate lace cuffs at my wrists and a Peter Pan collar at my collar bone made of the same material.

My first thought is that I look like I escaped from the Juniper Creek compound on *Big Love*, my second is that I am surely going to die.

"I knew you'd like it," Cruz says as he pushes the voluminous skirt ever so slowly up my legs.

His eyes glitter at me with lust and I know to him that this is a seduction. Not too long ago, Wes looked at me the same way before he crawled over my body in his big bed and made love to me. I let my eye close on the sweet memory. I want that to be the last thing I see before I die.

"Why?" I ask but my lack of muscle control makes it come out more of a *Unghiiiiigh*. Fortunately for me he's feeling like talking.

"I thought you were perfect." He sighs as if the world weighs heavy on his shoulders. "But you were such a disappointment. At least, we'll be able to enjoy each other this one time before I move on."

I watch with a weird sense of detachment as his hands caress my newly exposed thighs.

"No!" I scream but it comes out *Nurrr* through my closed lips.

"Don't worry," he reassures me. "I'll find my perfection in a new town. I'm truly sorry it wasn't you."

There's a knock at the door. Cruz puts his hand over my mouth to silence me.

"Claire, it's Wes. Are you home, honey?" Wes calls through the thin slab of fake wood. Cruz holds a finger up to his lips to emphasize his orders to be quiet.

But fuck that.

After a moment of silence passes, he reaches for his belt buckle and I know this is it. I'm beginning to really panic. It can't end like this. It can't all be for nothing. I scream at the top of my lungs, pushing the noise as hard and as fast as I can out of my body and hoping it reaches Wes before it's too late and he leaves.

"I was hoping we could enjoy each other first," Cruz growls at me. "But it appears you'll have to die first. Don't worry at all, my pet. I'll still enjoy you after."

Acid burns in my stomach at the thought of him touching me after I'm dead. He wraps his hands around my neck and begins to squeeze. He applies light pressure at first. He's testing the waters—enjoying his kill.

Then gradually, he squeezes my neck a little harder. It becomes increasingly harder to breathe. Black spots dance in front of my eyes and I realize it's too late. Wes didn't hear me after all. It's all over now, or it will be in another minute or two. And a calmness, a sense of peace washes over me.

I love you, Wes.

The words dance around in my mind as if I can send them out into the universe and somehow, when I'm gone, he'll know that I have always loved him. Maybe he can find a peace in that too.

And then the door explodes, splintering everywhere as Wes kicks the door in and my brother, Liam follows him in. He raises his sig. I always thought it was kind of funny that Wes was so set in his ways that after years of trotting around the globe doing God knows what, God knows where as a SEAL with a Sig Sauer P226 he still fancies them. Old habits never die and all that.

And then he pulls the trigger.

I wish I could stick around and enjoy the show. Wes's face is fierce with fire and determination. He's a warrior through and through and it's a sight to behold. But then everything fades to black.

epilogue
perfect

Three weeks later...

THIS MORNING I RECEIVED three dozen daisies and a note.
*Meet me at the house at 4 PM. Come around the back to the patio.
I love you always,
Wes*

My heart had thumped in my chest and I bit my lip and smiled at my flower delivery men. After the rattlesnake in the roses, flowers had lost their appeal. I wouldn't have trusted just anyone to bring me flowers and Wes knew that so these were delivered by my dad. My Wes has an eye for detail. He's also cognizant of my needs and wants—of which there have been more than usual after my attack.

"He's a good man, baby," he had said to me.

"I know," I had whispered back.

"Be happy," Dad said softly.

"I am."

After my dad left my apartment, I climbed in the shower. My body is still sore from being tossed around like a rag doll by Cruz so I let the hot water beat down on my body for a bit before I scrub every inch.

I turn off the taps and dry off with a towel before heading into my closet where I pull on panties and a matching bra. Wes and I haven't been intimate since my attack but I'm hoping to change that tonight so I choose a delicate lavender silk pair with care. I don't want to look like I'm trying too hard and I'm still battered and bruised so I cover my lace with black leggings and a vee-neck t-shirt.

I twist my towel dried hair up into a messy bun on top of my head and slide my favorite chucks onto my feet. I pull on a denim jacket and slip my car keys and phone into the pockets.

I walk out of my apartment, locking the door behind me and head down the stairs to my car. I have no idea what Wes has planned for tonight and I don't care. I just want to be with him.

A happy calm, a contentment rolls over me as I drive across town to the neighborhood we all grew up in. The one that Wes still lives in to this day. I park my car in the driveway and follow his instructions to come around back—bypassing the front door for the old wooden gate with lattice trim at the top.

I pull the string to pop the latch and walk right into a secret garden fitting of one of my favorite childhood novels. Mom and I read that book over and over again. We both loved it and couldn't get enough. I used to vow one day I would live in a house with a secret garden and Wes would be my husband.

Silly childhood thoughts bounce around in my brain as I take in the yards and yards of twinkle fairy lights that sparkle in the trees and dozens of brightly colored paper lanterns that hang from the wood and lattice pergola that covers the patio. Tons of candles glow and flicker in the cool spring breeze on the black iron and glass table in the center while music plays softly.

And there are daisies and violets everywhere. And not one rose.

I look to Wes who stands in the middle of it all in jeans and a blue button-down shirt tucked in at his trim waist with a worn, brown leather belt with a silver buckle. He has the sleeves rolled up to show his corded forearms and his feet are bare.

I suddenly feel self-conscious looking at all of the beauty that is Wes standing before me. I feel my face heat with a blush that I'm sure is covering more than my cheeks. I duck my head as I brush loose tendrils of hair back behind my ear.

"Look at me, Claire," he says, his voice sure and true. I look up at him and what I see there catches my breath in my chest. "You're perfect."

"Wh-what," I have to stop and clear my throat. My voice is unsteady or shaky at best after being strangled. "What's all this?"

"Dance with me?" he asks and the tentative smile that plays on his mouth makes him look more like the boy that I knew and less like a thirty-eight-year-old man. I can't help but accept.

"Okay," I rasp. I kick off my shoes as he makes his way down the steps from the deck to me and meet him in the middle of the lawn.

"May I take your jacket?" he asks me and I bite my lip and nod as he slides the denim down my shoulders and places it on an iron bench near where we're standing.

Wes returns to me and wraps his arm around me and I place my hand at the back of his neck. Wes smiles down at me before he takes my hand in his and holds it out to our sides as he slowly begins to sway and circle us to the music. It suddenly dawns on me that I have never danced with Wes before. And he's really good at it.

I can't help but sigh and it's frustrated at best.

"What is it, baby?" he asks me, his voice gruff with emotion.

"When will you ever stop saving me, Wes?"

"Never, honey. I'll always catch you when you fall."

I hate that my voice sounds small and unsure when the word slips out from my lips but it does. "Forever?"

"Until the day I die." Wes's voice rings true and strong.

I look over his shoulder as we continue to move to the music. We silently dance to the quiet music for awhile, until Wes breaks that silence by rocking my world.

"You have to know, Claire."

"Know what?" I ask.

"That I am hopelessly and irrevocably in love with you," he says as he stops our swaying. My throat catches and his hands rise up slowly to cup my cheeks. He holds my face tenderly in his hands as he looks into my eyes with so much love and light that I just want to sink into it. "Marry me, Claire."

"Do you think it's too soon?" I ask feeling a little unsure, not of us or of Wes but of me. "We've only been together for a little while."

"I have loved you forever, Claire."

"You can't mean—" I start but he interrupts me gently.

"You have been mine for forever, Claire, and I have been yours. No matter what's happened or what will happen. None of it matters because I have loved you one way or another since the day you were born. It's grown and it's changed over the years and I know that it will continue to grow because we will tend it and nurture it for the rest of our lives."

"But—" I start and he interrupts me again.

"Whatever it is we'll get through it, Claire. It's not you against me or me against you anymore. I promise you that it is us together and we can take on anything." I feel tears prick my eyes. For the first time in a long time they're happy ones. "Say it," he says softly.

"Yes."

"You're going to marry me?" he asks.

"Yes, Wes," I say through the huge smile that splits my face and the sweet tears rolling down my face. "I'll marry you."

His mouth crushes down on mine hard and fast before he scoops me up into his arms and twirls me around. I throw my head back and laugh.

Wes places me back on my feet before letting me go. He reaches into his pants pocket and produces a small velvet box before dropping down on one knee.

"Give me your hand, baby." And probably for the first time ever in history, I do what he asks me to and hold out my hand.

He opens the box and the biggest diamond I have ever seen glitters on the satin pillow. Wes plucks it up and tosses the box over his shoulder to the grass before sliding the ring up past my knuckle.

A perfect fit. Just like Wes and me.

I sit down on his knee and wrap my arms around his neck. I touch my lips to his before smiling. "Could you have found a bigger ring?" I laugh.

"Nope," he says against my mouth. "I want it to be seen from space. I told you I was done fucking around, baby. You're mine now." His whiskey eyes burn bright into mine.

"Now and forever."

"Abso-fucking-lutely," he says.

We tumble down into the grass all hands and mouths and bodies. It's soft and sweet and a little wild, just like Wes. And then he makes love to me as the sun sets in the middle of our own little secret garden. I guess some childhood dreams really do come true.

And it was perfect.

the end . . . for now

VOLUME 3 OF THE claire goodnite SERIES

say a sweet prayer

dedication

For Sean Always:

*"I'm hard to love, hard to love,
Oh I don't make it easy,
I couldn't do it if I stood where you stood
I'm hard to love, hard to love,
You say that you need me,
I don't deserve it but I love that you love me good."*

-Lee Brice

"For sin shall no longer be your master, because you are not under the law, but under grace."

-*Romans 6:14*

prologue

raw

*P*AIN. What a stupid little word to describe what I am feeling right now—*just four fucking letters*—such a mundane word to explain the white-hot lightning rips through my torso near where my heart used to be. It sears so acutely that my breath catches in my throat.

"No!" someone screams. I think it was me. It might have been me, but I don't know.

Hands grab me from behind to stop me from closing the gap between me and the bloody body on the altar steps of my family's church. These slabs of muscle and bone and joint and tendons restrain me, holding me back from the jarring loss. But the cold truth of what has come to pass is front and center for all to see.

Anguish.

This is anguish. This severe pain. A wound licked so raw that I know it will never heal. This is a wound that will only fester and turn putrid.

"Let me go!" I wail. My voice is harsh and raw. The words are ripped from my chest leaving a raw wound in its wake.

"No," someone says. I don't know who. I don't care either. I can't stop staring at the broken remains of someone I had loved above all else. Someone who managed to do the unthinkable, to break down my walls and invade my heart.

Before I had looked at victims and wondered why couldn't I save them? Or it should have been me. But looking at the shell of what had been as it's splayed on the plush carpet of the altar steps I know without a doubt that I would trade places in a heartbeat. If only it was my blood that was spilled and not theirs.

Grief.

If this is what grief feels like I don't want it. I want to go back to this morning when my life was normal. I had had the world at my feet, and my family was whole. I feel raw . . . *exposed* . . . I'm a wound that's been flayed open down to the bone. But it cannot be stitched or cauterized.

Maybe this is shock. I don't know. All I do know is that the world is a darker place tonight. This is not a loss that I or anyone else will get over. Not now, not ever. My name is Detective Claire Goodnite, and everything has changed.

I guess it's best we say our prayers . . .

chapter 1
beautiful

"DANCE WITH ME?" Wes's husky voice sounds from behind me, echoing the words he said not too long ago on the night he asked me to marry him.

I'm standing with several of our guests, a cool glass of wine in my hand when he approaches me. Other than at dinner, we have been separated from each other this evening. After the dinner service was over, we had been pulled in different directions. And all evening, I've watched that ass prowl around the room filled with our closest friends and family who have all gathered to celebrate our engagement.

Wes was wearing a custom-tailored suit in a rich, dark gray. A far cry from his usual Fed Special, but he said for this special night he was pulling out all the stops. I guess it pays to be the only son of a prominent judge. Somewhere along the way he ditched the coat and tie and rolled up the sleeves of his aqua shirt. Between the play of muscle under his corded arms, his firm ass in those fitted slacks, and the free-flowing wine, I'm having some wayward thoughts about my husband-to-be. Judging by the smirk on his face as I turn to look back at him, he knows it too.

"So?" he asks. "What'll it be, baby?"

"Yes," I whisper feeling a little breathless.

Wes extends his hand out to me and without hesitation I take it, letting him lead me out on to the makeshift dance floor.

"You are so beautiful," he says as he wraps me in his arms and slowly sways me to the music. I can't help but feel that with this man, in this moment, everything is finally right.

"Wes." I whisper. "That's just the wine talking." I duck my head down and feel a blush steal across my cheeks. I'm still a little uncomfortable with his softer side and more romantic undertones. Ever since a fellow detective tried to murder me a few weeks ago, Wes has been extra loving and attentive.

"It's true, baby," he says softly as he trails his fingertips down my jaw and gently pushes upward so that I'm coaxed into meeting his gaze. "It's not the wine, I'm the luckiest man alive because in just a few short months, I'm going to be your husband."

"Months?" I ask putting on my best faux appalled expression. "I'm going to need a minimum of two years to plan the perfect society wedding for your parents and their crowd."

"What?" he chokes out as he stops our swaying to the music.

"These things take time." I nod seriously.

"Years?" he asks on a smile.

"Years," I confirm. Wes looks me in the eye and I can't help but throw my head back and laugh.

Wes rolls his bottom lip in between his teeth and bites down as he studies me. I want to squirm under his gaze, my laugh caught in my throat as he no longer looks at me to evaluate the truth of my bold statement—which is a lie—but he now watches me with a hunger in his bright amber eyes. There's a certain . . . *carnality* to the way that he's looking at me in the middle of a room full to the brim of our closest friends and family.

I can't help but wonder if it's suddenly a little warm in here and fight back the urge to fan myself. Wes sees my discomfort and an incredibly sexy smirk plays on his mouth.

"Wicked minx," he says as his eyes twinkle with mischief. "I don't believe you."

"Why wouldn't you believe me," I play coy, nodding my head with my eyes wide. "I'm very trust worthy. I'm a police officer."

Wes pulls me in tight to his chest, his arms tight bands around my body. I let out a yip as he swats my ass in front of everyone in the middle of the polished wood of the club's dance floor.

"I don't know about that," he growls. "I think you like to play games with me, Claire. But you underestimated just how much I like to play games too. I think you'll find that I rise to the challenge." And then he crashes his lips down on mine. Wes kisses me hot and hungry, and I can't help but open my mouth under his.

I lose myself in Wes and his kiss. The world falls away as we hold on to each other. This year has been hard. Hell, the last twenty-five years can't even be called hard—that's the understatement of the year—and after all of it was said and done, Wes and I finally found our way back to each other. I knew when he said he was done fucking around that he was done. But most of all, I know that he loves me above all else, Wes was willing to fight me, and everyone else, until we made it here to this place that we are in right now.

Right now, it's just us, Wes and me. We walked through fire to get here and we made it.

As Wes mouth moves over mine there is a roaring in my ears. He's always had a strong pull over me but even this is too much. Or at least I think it is until Wes pulls back and smiles against my mouth. The roaring is still there. I feel my face heat when I realize that the noise is actually a room full of wine infused former Navy SEALs cheering and stomping their feet at the show that Wes and I were so happy to give them.

"*Hooyah!*" goes up all around the room.

I chance a look across the room at Wes's parents—who do not look happy—before Wes distracts me and the thought slips from my mind.

"Who invited this band of rebels, ruffians, and miscreants?" he asks me with a twinkle in his eye. I can't help but smile at him.

"You did, silly. I have it on good authority that the SEALs came with you," I inform my better half with wide eyes.

"So they did, good lady. So, they did," he says as he bows over my hand like an old-fashioned gentleman. I can't help but throw my head back and laugh.

"'Good lady'?" I question.

"Okay, that didn't work." He laughs as he twirls me around the room.

"Not so much."

"But it was worth a try." He shrugs his shoulder. "For you I would try anything." And I know that what he says is true. I duck my head in an uncharacteristic show of shyness as my face heats again and I let Wes tow and twirl me around the room.

"You know, I thought a bunch of cops were bad but . . ."

"Us SEALs put the term 'bad' to good use, baby." He shoots me a lascivious wink.

The music changes to something soft, slow, and decidedly more sensual. Wes pulls me in close and we sway for a little while. My body heating with each soft brush of his body against mine. Wes stops our movement but doesn't let go of me.

"So, what do you say, gorgeous? You wanna get out of here?"

And I answer him the only way I can. Ignoring the room full of people, the music, and the wine. The world around us disappears once more when I look into his beautiful whiskey eyes and give him the truth.

"Yes."

chapter 2

go all the way

Six weeks earlier . . .

"WELL," MRS. O'CONNELL SAYS just a hair shorter than necessary. Her tone definitely doesn't say *I'm so happy to be here with my favorite son and his lovely girlfriend*. "Are you going to tell us why we all needed to be here?"

Here being *The Farmer's Market*, the best brunch place this side of the Hudson.

"Yes," my mom says with a twinkle in her eyes. She knows what's up. "Tell us what was so important." She winks.

Wes turns to me and smiles that panty melting smile, the one that always gets to me. The one that when I was a little girl always told me that everything was going to be alright. In his way—the way of us, Wes and Claire—he's telling me that everything will be okay. And it will . . . in the end.

I only hope there's minimal bloodshed. That's a bitch to get out in the wash.

Wes turns back to address the occupants of the massive table in the back of the restaurant that includes: my parents, Wes's parents, Lee, Emma, Anna, and my grandparents. "I asked Claire to marry me."

"*You what?*" both his parents shriek at the exact same time. I can't help but wonder if they rehearsed their reaction.

I look across the table to Emma and Anna. Anna had the grace to wince. Emma rolled her eyes before pretending to scratch her eyebrow in their direction with her middle finger. Liam, I notice, is biting his lip to keep from laughing as he watches Emma's less than patient display.

"I said, I asked Claire to marry me," he repeats as if they didn't hear him in the first place all while squeezing my thigh under the table. I wonder if he's afraid I'm going to run away. Well, I figure if I've come this far, I might as well go all the way.

"And she said . . ." Mrs. O'Connell hedges. What the hell does she think I said? Clearly, we brought everyone out to brunch to tell them that I said no. I turned him down so we're politely telling our families that we're going our separate ways like those celebrities who *consciously uncouple*. I snort as I crack the joke in my head and realize everyone is looking at me waiting for my answer. Whoops.

"Oh," I mumble a little embarrassed to be caught in front of the class not paying attention. "I guess I said yes."

"You guess, dear?" Wes's mom presses.

"No, I said yes. Wes and I are getting married," I tell her. My smile faltering to an awkward grimace.

"Are you sure that's wise, son?" Judge O'Connell asks. Even though I knew it was coming, I won't pretend that didn't sting. Although, I always knew Wes's parents did not approve of me. They were always honest about that one.

"Yes," Wes says calmly. "I do."

"I love hearing you say those words about my baby girl, son," my mom says to Wes with happy tears in her eyes.

"Welcome to the family, asshole." Lee laughs.

"Thanks, brother," he says tossing a roll at Lee.

"No, your father is right, Wesley," Mrs. O'Connell weighs in again. "We need to talk about this."

"No, we don't," Wes says, his voice low like a wolf's growl.

"Now, there's no need to get your back up. No one is saying you can't continue your relationship with Claire . . . privately," Mrs. O'Connell condescends.

"Don't," he bites out.

"Think about your father's political career." Mrs. O'Connell continues.

"No, I'm going to think about Claire and I and any children we might have."

"Children!" his father booms. "That's ridiculous. She will make a terrible mother."

"Thank you for your vote of confidence," I snap under my breath. I'm barely able to hold back my epic eye roll.

"You need to marry someone your own age who will add to this political family," Judge O'Connell orders.

"No, I don't. I will not be trotted out on your political campaigns anymore and neither will my wife."

"Of course, I will. I will do anything I damn well please and don't you forget it," Judge O'Connell seethes. This is a side of him I've never seen before. "Fuck her in private if you have to but for God sakes, don't throw both of our careers away over a piece of ass. Call me when you find a real wife who can benefit us all," he says before tossing his napkin on the table and pushing his seat back to stand.

"Don't bother contacting me," Wes says his voice low enough that only our table can hear. "I care about Claire and I always have. If you try and make me choose between her and you, I promise you won't like the consequences."

"Wesley—" his mother pleads.

"I mean it," he responds, his voice is low and calm, but also firm and unyielding.

His dad shakes his head before looking disappointed and then storms out of the restaurant. His mother pauses at our table to plead her case one more time but it falls on deaf ears.

"Look what you've done, Wesley. I hope you're happy," Mrs. O'Connell dresses down her grown son in front of a table full of people.

"I am. I only wish you could be happy for me."

"Mark my words, she'll ruin us all," my future mother-in-law tries one last time before giving up—for now—and following her husband's footsteps.

"Oh look!" my Nana shouts clapping her hands, she draws all of our attention. "Champagne! I love champagne!"

"Don't let those stuffed shirts bother you, baby doll," my dad whispers in my ear from my other side. "Wes always fit in better with us than with them and it always rankled them a bit. They'll come around."

"That's what I'm afraid of, dad."

"Oh shit—I mean shoot—we need to book the church ASAP before some other Joe Schmo books it for their kid," my mom shouts as the thought obviously jumps into her head. "Do you kiddos have a date in mind?"

"Mom—" I start before she and my Grandma cut me off again.

"Goodness! There's just so much to do!"

"I don't know if we're going to get married in a church . . ." I add quietly.

"Of course, you'll get married in the church!" my grandma laughs as if I'm joking. I would correct her but truthfully, we're all a little afraid of her.

"See," my dad whispers in my ear. I can hear the laughter in his voice and I'm sorely tempted to stomp on his foot under the table. "There's nothing to worry about."

All around the table my mom and grandma, not to mention Emma and Anna, are planning our wedding. I can't help but sit back feeling a little shell shocked. I hear my dad finally lose his battle with the chuckle that's clearly been choking him to make its way out when I say to him, unable to break my gaze away from my life spinning wildly out of control, "I'm not so sure I agree with you, Dad."

He throws his head back and his soft chuckle gives way to a full booming laugh. I'm so glad he finds all of this so funny. Just wait until he gets the bill.

chapter 3
get there

Present day...

"SO, WHAT DO YOU say gorgeous? You wanna get out of here?" Wes smiles at me as the music changes again but I know that we won't segue into another dance at our engagement party. I place my hand in his outstretched one and answer him from my heart.

"Yes."

Wes leans in and kisses me hard and fast before walking me through the room, the skirt of my pretty black cocktail dress swishing around my thighs. As we make our way to the door, someone shouts, "Looks like this party just became a private one."

We push through the side door of the country club with a quiet clank as it shuts behind us. Wes and I, hand in hand, turn our heads to look at each other and laugh.

"That's my favorite sound," he whispers into the night.

"What?" I ask feeling a little confused and a lot of expensive wine.

"When you laugh."

"Wes—" I start but I'm cut off by his shrill whistle as he hails a cab to take us home.

"Let's go home," he says softly as he pulls the yellow door open for me and I bunch up my skirt to slide all the way across the cracked vinyl seat to make room for the only guy to ever hold my heart. He slides in beside me and pulls the door closed.

"827 Adolphia, and step on it," he says to the driver.

"If my wife looked like her, I'd be in a hurry too," he mumbles before pulling out into traffic. I smile at my lap while pulling my skirt flat nervously and my cheeks heat.

Wes leans into me and slides his nose down the skin behind my ear, whispering, "I love you."

"And I love you."

Through break neck twists and turns and a couple very yellow lights, Wes holds me tight in his arms. He skates his hands over all very appropriate places. But still, when we finally pull up to the front of his house in the suburb we grew up in, I'm still a little drunk and more than a little on fire.

Wes tosses some bills and a heavy tip to the driver before flinging open the door and pulling me out with him. He slams the door to the tune of the cabbie's laughter ringing in my ears and as I look at Wes, I can't help but let the smile grow wider across my face.

There is a twinkle in his eyes that I know now, after all that we have been through, is so much more than wine and lust. This is a lifetime of love. This is everything.

I have to practically run to keep up with Wes as his long, muscular legs eat up the ground of the walkway to the front of his—soon to be our—house. He stops in front of the door and punches in the code on the dead bolt before swinging the heavy piece of wood and steel open and pulling us through.

Wes has gone a little crazy with home security ever since my near miss a few months ago.

But I don't have time to think of that now as the door slams closed and the lock tumbles over. Wes leans back against the door and slides his whiskey gaze over my body as I stand in the entryway. The laugh that threatens to burst free from me dies on my lips as my body heats like a fever rolling over my skin. I bite down on my bottom lip to quell the shudder that rolls through my body but there's no stopping it.

"You're so damn beautiful," Wes says, his voice rough.

"Wes—" I start but I barely get the words out. Wes stalks towards me with sure, even steps. When he reaches me, he pulls my body to his, crashing his lips down on mine.

"I love you, Claire," he whispers against my mouth. He tangles his fingers in my long hair. "So fucking much."

"And I love you." My words light him up from the inside out. His tongue swipes into my mouth and he groans at the taste.

"You're mine, Claire," Wes rumbles as he lifts me up so that his lips don't have to leave mine as he stalks down the hallway and up the stairs toward the master bedroom. I wrap my legs around his waist and we both groan as his hard length comes in contact with my center.

"Always."

"Damn-fucking-right," he growls as he slides my body down his, lowering my feet to the floor. "Turn around."

I do as he says, slowly turning around so that my back is to his front. I hear his rumble of approval and I let my eyelids drift lower as a happy glow settles over me. Wes uses his free hand to brush the heavy length of my hair over my shoulder to hang over my right breast.

I hold my breath as his unhurried hands lower the zipper on my little black dress. When the sides of the dark fabric slip apart, Wes slides his hands underneath the edges, his rough palms electrifying the skin of my back and shoulders as he guides my dress off my body, letting it pool around my heels on the floor.

I release a heavy breath just before he lets a fingertip trail down my spine, stopping at the clasp of my black lace bra, unhooking it in the process. It floats to the floor, joining my dress. We reaches around me and holds a heavy breast in each hand. His thumbs graze my nipples ever so slightly and I arch against his hard body behind me. Wes lowers his lips to my shoulder placing the softest of kisses there before straightening and ordering me in a rough voice, "Take off your panties."

Keeping my legs straight, I hook my fingers into the black lace of my panties and bending at the waist lower them to the floor. As I do, my uncovered flesh slides against Wes's hard cock behind the wool and zipper of his slacks. My breath catches in my throat when I feel his heat and strength exactly where I need him. There's something to be said about being naked, vulnerable, and bent over in front of a fully clothed man. I give this to Wes freely, not because he demands it, but because he deserves it.

"Go lay down on the bed," he rumbles after I stand back up, kicking my discarded clothing aside and stepping free from the bulk of it.

Wearing nothing but my tall, strappy heels, I make my way over to the big bed and pull the bedding back before lowering myself down to the cool sheets.

I turn to my back, propping myself up against the mountain of pillows.

Wes stands there fully clothed, radiating suppressed energy. Slowly, oh so slowly, he pops open the buttons on his collared shirt before parting the soft material and slowly sliding it down his body. The buckle of his belt clanks as he pulls it free from his slacks, letting it drop to the floor before toeing out of his shoes and pulling his socks from his feet. And I lay there in rapt attention as each piece of skin is uncovered.

I hold my breath as he reaches for the clasp on his slacks. I breathe again when he lowers the zipper and pushes his pants and underwear wear down his strong legs as one. His hard length springs free and I watch—fascinated as he grips it in his fist. He lets his head tip back on his shoulders

"Spread your legs," he rumbles as he slides his fist up and down his length. "Show me what's mine because this is all yours, baby."

Wes watches me through narrowed lids as I let my knees drop to the sides. My body burns from the inside out as I watch him watch me put myself on display for him. Only for him. My body burns hot from the wine and from Wes. He has always had this effect on me.

Slowly Wes stalks towards me before lowering himself to sit on the edge of the bed beside me. I lay perfectly still, holding my breath, waiting to see what his first move will be. Tonight, Wes will lead. Luckily for me, I don't have to wait long.

Wes watches the movements of his hand as he caresses my cheek with the back of his fingers before placing his palm flat between my breasts. He leans down and softly places his mouth on mine, soft and sweet to start before sliding his tongue into my mouth and taking it deeper. There is no hurry to his movements or frantic pace. To Wes, it seems as if he has all the time in the world, and we're getting married so he does, but I'm a little drunk and I want more. I want so much more.

I press my body to his as I nip at his bottom lip before soothing the hurt with my tongue. Wes smiles against my mouth and I know that he can see right through me. But then again, he's known me since forever.

"I want slow," he rumbles against my mouth.

"Uh-unh," I mumble as I wrap a leg around his hips trying to entice him to my way of thinking.

"But slow can be so . . . *rewarding*," he says as he circles my nipple with his fingertips before finally scraping his nail over the tip making me arch into him.

"I want fast while the champagne bubbles are still in my head," I say as I dig a heel into the mattress and roll taking Wes with me. We land with him on his back, diagonally across the middle of the bed and me gracelessly sprawled across his body. He grips my hips tight in his hands.

"Is this what you had in mind?" he asks as he smiles up at me.

"Yes." I smile triumphantly as I wiggle my hips to straddle Wes as he lies beneath me.

I lean forward to kiss him. I open my mouth to him, letting him control the kiss. I lose my head as I rock my body against his. When I break my mouth away to catch my breath, I push back, impaling myself on his hard length. We both let out a groan as we hold eat other tight, adjusting to the way that we fit together.

I smooth my palms over Wes's chest and scrape my nails down his abs before slowly rising up and then sliding back down his cock. He lets a hiss out between his teeth as I rise up on my knees and slowly slide back down again and again.

I brace myself on my hands, my palms pressing against Wes's tight abs as

I slide up and down his length, faster and faster. There is a heat that spreads out over my body as I get closer and closer. I drop my head back letting my hair brush over his strong thighs. Wes arches his back to meet me.

He pushes his hands to glide up my sides from my hips before gripping one of my breasts in each hand. I place my own over his, encouraging him to squeeze me tighter, to pinch and pull my nipples as I ride him.

I bow backwards and feel the muscles of his legs tense behind me. My movements become more frantic as I try and get closer and closer before bending back forward and bracing myself against his chest again.

"Get there, baby," Wes says through gritted teeth.

"I-I'm trying," I cry out in almost a whine, but I can't care. I'm so close and yet . . . not. I keep pushing harder and harder but I'm not getting any closer to the edge and it's making me panicky.

"You gotta get there, baby," he growls as his hips rise up to meet me as I sink back down over him.

"I can't!" I cry out.

Before I know it, Wes is gripping me by the hips and pulling me up and up and up off his cock. He lifts me up and over, so that my upper body is hanging off the side of the bed, my fingertips barely brushing the carpet, and my most secret places right over his face.

Wes pulls me down to meet his mouth and presses his tongue over my clit hard and fast, not letting up for even a moment. I grip the edge of the comforter in my left-hand and the nails of my right-hand rake over the carpet. Panting, I'm not sure if I'm trying to get away from his sexual onslaught or if I'm trying to get even closer. I roll my hips and receive a masculine groan and a nip to my clit for my reward, sending me spiraling out of control as I come.

Wes knifes upward, taking me with him in one fluid move. I land on my back with Wes moving over me, sliding in deep. He hooks my left leg over his right arm lifting it higher, taking him deeper, while I wrap my right leg around his hip as he plunges hard and deep.

Before I know it, my body is heating up again. I rake my nails down Wes's back and he rolls his hips causing me to clench tight around him. I'm building again.

"Yes," he growls as he powers into my heat over and over again. "Give it to me. Again."

I'm helpless to stop it so I do, and Wes follows me over the edge, roaring out my name as he does. He tucks his face into the crook of my neck as our breathing slows and he lowers my leg.

"You're right," he rumbles in my ear after a minute or two of silence. "Fast was fun."

"I told you so," I purr as I stretch like a cat underneath him.

"We'll do slow next," he tells me seriously.

"Okay," I whisper and then we do just that, we go slow before drifting off to sleep in each other's arms with the world at our fingertips . . . or so it had seemed at the time. If only we had known we were on the cusp of losing everything, we might have played things a little differently.

chapter 4
light in the dark

*I*T'S DARK. SO, SO dark. And scary.

At night my mommy leaves a nightlight on for me and my favorite piggy stuffed animal that I've had for ages to help me sleep. I hate the dark. Monsters only lurk in the dark. I want my mommy but I can't cry. If I cry, the bad man will come and he will hurt me again. He always hurts me. Even though I don't want him to, I know, he always comes, but this time I will be ready.

I was digging in the closet when I knew that he was asleep. I found a pile of old junk. He must have been too lazy to clean out the closet that has been my prison for I don't know how long. But his laziness is my win. In the corner under the pile of old stuff, I found a baseball and then a glove, and in the very bottom of the pile, I found an old metal bat. Just like the kind Liam and Wes used when they were my age.

Sometimes it pays to be the little sister. My whole life I've been following Wes and Liam around hoping that they would play with me. I even told Wes that one day he would marry me. He just laughed and said, "I'm not so sure about that, squirt." That's what he calls me. Squirt.

So, all the times I followed them around when they played ball or walked in the woods finally is going to pay off even if Wes never wants to marry me because I learned how to swing a baseball bat watching them. I learned to run through the woods following them. I am going to run away from the bad man because of all that I watched them do.

So, I wait. And I wait and I wait and I wait. I almost fall asleep. Almost. I feel my eyelids getting heavy but then I hear footsteps and I know that he's coming. He always comes.

So, I sit quietly and try not to make any noise. I hurry to my feet and grab my bat. I crouch in the corner with the bat over my shoulder just like Liam showed me how to do. When I hear the lock that he keeps on the closet door open I know that it's time.

My hands sweat and I feel shaky all over.

"Wake up, Claire, it's time," he says as he pulls open the closet door. "What are you doing?" He asks when he sees me but I don't answer. I swing the bat as hard as I can, hitting him in his big belly.

When the bad man falls forward, I swing one more time, hitting the side of his head just like Liam and Wes taught me to hit a baseball when I finally got them to include me. And then I run.

I run out of the closet while the bad man screams my name. I run out of the ugly house that smells funny and then I run out into the woods.

I run and I run and I run. But I know he's going to catch me. A mean hand grabs me by my arm from behind and I scream . . .

• • •

I gasp, feeling the band tighten around my chest as the nightmare leaves me in its wake. Fuck, it's still happening. A small part of me had hoped that with my life finally becoming normal that the dreams would go away. But you know what they say about hope being a fickle bitch and all that . . .

My body is covered in a sheen of sweat, my head is pounding with the drums of the old Salvation Army band, and my stomach is roiling. I jump up and run to the bathroom, dropping down to my knees just in time to lose my very expensive celebratory dinner and champagne.

My body stiffens when I feel a hand brush my hair back from my face.

"Too much champagne?" he asks with a note of humor in his voice. The miserable bastard would just love for me to be hung over.

"Yeah," I whisper.

"Claire?" he asks. I hate the worry in his voice. I hate that I put it there. I thought I had escaped—that I was *finally* free—but I'm not free, I'll never be free. I've brought Wes straight into hell with me and I hate that most of all.

"Just let it go, Wes." My voice is rough in desperation, for him to leave it alone, to leave me to my own devices, I don't know which.

"No," he grounds out his voice firm. I hang my head unwilling to look at him yet. I can't stand that this is how he sees me, at my lowest, covered in sweat with the scent of vomit in the air.

"Wes—" I begin to plead but he stops me before I can even get the words out.

"No!" he shouts. "No, I won't let it go and no, I won't go away. I want in there, Claire. You have to let me in, baby." He's pleading, and I can't stand the desperation in his voice or the knowledge that I am solely responsible for it.

"It's too dark, Wes," I whisper. "I can't drag you further into hell with me."

Wes drops down onto his knees behind me, wrapping his arms around me as if he can block the world from seeping on to my shoulders. In this moment, Wes is my shield, my protector, my big, bad warrior and I know in my heart that with him I can do anything, be anything, but without him, I don't even want to try.

"I've already been to hell, honey," he says softly, his chin resting on my shoulder, reminding me that he has been to hell and knows its demons on a first name basis. "Let me walk in there with you. Let me be your light in the dark."

"It's not that easy."

"But what if it is?" He asks softly. "What if together we can beat it back?"

"I just don't know," I say softly, my voice harsh. "I'm so scared."

"I know, baby." His arms grip tighter around me, easing the invisible band around my chest. "Let me be your light."

"You already are."

And in this moment, I realize the veracity of my words. The power they hold rings true for both of us. No longer have I craved the bite of my own bullet and while I struggle with the nightmares, the trauma that still lives inside me, twisting me up, I no longer feel alone, because I'm not. Maybe, just maybe, we can beat back the darkness, together. Wes is right, it's time to let him in. If we're really lucky, I won't drag him into hell with me, but he might just be able to help me pull myself out once and for all.

"Then let's go back to bed," he whispers.

"Okay."

chapter 5
easy

*R*UNNING. I'M RUNNING AS fast as I can.
 The tree branches sting my face as the slap at me and grab at me as I run past. The briars cut into my feet but I can't stop. I can never stop.
 I trip over a tree root but don't fall. I have to keep running, running, running, I can't let the bad man get to me. I can never let him get to me.
 I'm running as fast as my little feet will take me through the woods behind my parents' house. I have to get away from the bad man. If he catches me now, I'll never get away. I have to be free.
 Run! I have to run faster.
 I see the blue gray light as it spills through the trees. Mommy always told me this was her favorite part of the day—looking at the sun as it comes up in the morning. I ran away late in the night when the bad man was sleeping. It was my only chance. After he broke the lock on the closet door I knew that I had a chance to get out.
 Free.
 I'm free. Those are the words in my head as the trees break and I see Wes standing at the edge of the backyard. I'm free. I'm finally free. Wes looks up and he sees me.
 "I've got her!" he shouts to someone.
 My heart is beating so hard in my chest and it hurts to breathe. I'm so tired but I have to keep running. I see Wes, his face, and I know that he'll protect me. Wes always protects me. He will keep me safe. He will keep me free.
 I push my feet just a little harder, I run just a little faster. I'm almost there. My feet are covered in blood and dirt, all of me is really. Wes is running towards me. No. Wes! The bad man is coming! I want to shout but when I open my mouth, no words come out.
 Wes reaches for me, his arms out ready to grab me. This is good. I'm so tired. I just need to close my eyes for a second. I blink a few times to wake up again. Rest, I just need a little rest. Mommy will be happy, she's always trying to get me to nap.
 "I've got you!" he says to me. "I've got you."
 "Don't let me go," I say.
 "Never! I'll never let you go," Wes declares in his strong voice and I know that he is telling me the truth. Wes is so strong and so brave. Mama says that he's going to go to the Navy with Lee and they only take the very bravest there is. So, I know that I'm safe here with him. I'm finally safe.

• • •

"I've got you," Wes rumbles from behind me. His strong arms close around me.

"Don't let me go," I plead as I cling to him. "Don't ever let me go."

"Never, baby," he says squeezing me tighter. "How many times do I have to tell you. I'll never let you go."

"Good."

"Just be free and easy," he rumbles softly next to my ear and I feel the muscles in my body release their tension one by one, knowing that Wes is on duty and he's watching my back I drift back to sleep. This time it's a totally dreamless—*peaceful*—sleep.

• • •

Beep . . . beep . . . beep . . .

I groan as Wes reaches for his phone to silence his morning alarm. Saying it was a long night last night is the understatement of the century. We shouldn't have to wake up early the day after our engagement party. Come to think of it, we don't have to.

I scowl at Wes who is smiling bright. There is a wickedness twinkling in his eyes that I don't quite trust.

"What's that face all about, Mister?" I ask as I swirl my finger around in the air roughly circling Wes's face. The look in his eyes softens and his breath catches in the back of his throat before narrowing his eyes.

"Don't be cute," Wes reprimands me playfully. "I don't have time to properly fuck you."

"Who's being cute?" I ask seriously wondering. No one has ever accused me of being cute before and for sure not before I've had a cup of coffee in the morning.

"Shit," he groans before tackling me to the bed. "Now I have to fuck you."

"Wes!" I screech as I land flat on my back with Wes looming over me, his hard length rubbing against my pussy creating a delicious friction under my panties.

"Don't worry," he says against my mouth. "I'll be quick."

"When are you ever 'quick'?" I laugh.

"Okay." He nods his head sitting back on his heels before sliding my panties down my legs. "I won't be quick, I'll be thorough. But we're going to have to get breakfast on the way."

"Deal," I say because Wes is circling his fingers around my entrance and there is no possible way that I can hold a decent conversation at this juncture in my life let alone a single thought in my head.

I grip the sheets in my hands and arch my back. I grind onto Wes's hand before he pulls it back shoving his shorts down and growling, "You're ready," before plunging inside me.

I wrap my arms and legs around him and cling tight as he thrusts deep and then slides back out over and over again electrifying me from the inside out. I rake my nails down his back and Wes tips his head back and groans.

Every slip and slide of his cock sends me closer and closer to the edge. I tip my hips to meet his every time needing that just a bit more to take me there. My body clenches around Wes and he knows how close I really am and picks up his pace.

He plunges in once, twice, and then three times before proclaiming, "You're there."

And I am.

"Wes—" I gasp out as he thrusts home one more time and then I am flying right over the edge.

"Claire," Wes growls as he plants himself deep within me and follows me over.

We lay together for what seems like ages and at the same time, never long enough, while our hearts slow and the sweat cools, clinging to each other. This has become one of my favorite moments with Wes. There is no pressure to be anything, to do anything, we simply just are. And we are together. There is a peace that I can only find inside of Wes's arms and I will do anything to keep it.

He slides the tip of his nose down the side of mine before kissing me quickly on the mouth. "It's never been like that with anyone before," he rumbles in his sex deep voice that I love so much.

"Wes." My breath catches in my throat.

"It's only every been you, Claire."

"Wes?" I ask.

"Yeah, baby?"

"Shut up," I say softly, smiling so he knows that I'm not being mean.

"I can't, baby. We've got places to go, people to see," he says before slipping free from my body and knifing out of the bed.

"And what would those places be?" I ask. "Who are these people?"

"Didn't I say before?" he asks playfully. I love this side of Wes that doesn't get to come out very often.

"No, dear, I'm pretty sure that you didn't."

"Oh," he says as if he's thinking seriously on the subject but we both know that he's not. "I guess I didn't," he says before scooping me up and throwing me over his shoulder, laughing as he goes.

"Wes!" I shout.

"I told you, we don't have time." Wes swats my ass hard and laughs as I growl. He swats me again. "We definitely don't have time for me to make you come in the shower so quit your wiggling. It does things to me."

"Would you quit doing that?" I snap.

"No." He shakes his head. "Probably not. You all fired up does things to me too."

"Seriously, Wes? Not everything can turn you on."

"Wanna take a bet?" he asks as he slowly lowers me down his body, his hard cock brushing against me as Wes lowers me to the ground. My feet touch the soft cotton of the bath mat.

"I stand corrected. Apparently, it doesn't take more than a stiff breeze."

"Not even that with you around," he says before grabbing me as he opens the shower door and hurdles us inside under the freezing cold water.

"Are you kidding me!" I screech.

"It should heat up soon." He shrugs.

"Soon?" I snap.

"Okay," he laughs. "I'll heat you up. I'll be quick this time. I promise." And then he does heat me up against the shower wall before soaping me up and tossing me out, drying me off with a towel as we go.

I need to talk to Anna about the dreams that seem to be coming on with more and more regularity. I don't understand what it all means. But for now, this morning, I have to find out what kind of surprise my guy has in store for me.

chapter 6
no fucking way

"**Y**OU'VE GOT TO be fucking kidding me?"

"Now why would I kid about this?" Wes's laugh rumbles in his chest behind his words.

I clap my hands over my eyes. There is no possible way I saw what I think I saw. Wes loves me, he wouldn't try to kill me . . . at least, I'm pretty sure. Almost positive. I mean he went to all that trouble to save me a couple weeks ago. So, he wouldn't just off me now . . . I think.

"Babe, what are you doing?"

"I'm hoping that when I uncover my eyes there isn't a deathtrap standing in front of me," I answer him honestly before uncovering my eyes. "Nope, it's still there."

I cover them again as quickly as I can.

"I'm pretty sure your lady just offended me, O'Connell," someone says.

"She sure did, Palmer," Wes says with a smile in his voice. "And if you don't shut your mouth I'll tell her how you got that name."

"You mean Palmer isn't your last name?" I ask as everyone either snickers or groans.

"It's really a funny story . . ." Wes starts.

"Don't you fucking dare, or I'll push you out myself without a god damned shute," Palmer threatens. "I need at least a halfway decent chance with the cute bridesmaid."

"And which bridesmaid would that be?" I ask hoping to change the subject away from my impending doom.

"The cute little brunette. You know, the fancy one. I just want to dirty her up a bit."

"No, I want the hot blonde with the long legs and the smart mouth," someone else shouts. How many guys are here anyways?

"Good luck with that," I say. "You have my blessing. She could use a good dirtying."

"Thanks." He winks.

"Hey," I say after thinking better on just giving away my closest friend. "You're not a serial killer or anything? I've had my fill of those lately."

"Babe." Wes says with a little light censure in his tone.

"What?" I ask. "Too soon?"

"Yeah, honey. Too soon."

"Okay," I shrug.

"So are we going to do this or what, ladies?" Palmer asks.

"No," I say with my hands still firmly locked over my eyes. "I'm not doing anything."

"Claire," Wes says.

"No," I say shaking my head in the negative. Definitely not, he's asking too much.

"Would I ever do anything to hurt you?" he asks honestly.

"Well," I start ticking off his offenses on my fingers. "You took my virginity when I was eighteen and broke up with me the next morning causing me to never commit to another relationship again. Then there were the many times you tried to get my brother to fire me. Or there was the time you tried to steal my case from me. Actually, come to think of it, you did that a couple of times too. Then—"

"Alright!" he shouts. "We get it, I'm an asshole."

"Sounds like I should punch your nose again, brother," Lee says from somewhere near. Of course, I can't see him because my eyes are closed firmly in denial.

"Oh hey, Lee," I greet my brother casually.

"Hey there, Claire Bear."

"Come to rescue me from impending doom?" I ask but Wes's growl drones out all other conversation.

"You both should know damn well by now that I wouldn't do anything to physically hurt Claire or put her safety at risk." He sighs heavily like he usually does when he runs his hand through his hair. Usually after I have done or said something to drive him up a wall. "Now I have a dick so I'm going to fuck up from time to time."

"Sounds like you fuck up on the regular, O'Connell," someone chimes in.

"Here, here," I shout.

"Really?" Wes grumbles. I have to bite my lip to keep from laughing out loud at poor Wes's outrage. He's really been a good sport about our ribbing him. I sigh heavily. I guess I'm going to have to let him try to kill me. I just won't make it very easy.

"Oh, very well," I say.

"You're going to do it?" Wes ask me.

"Yes," I answer. "I'm going to let you try and kill me."

"Hey!" Palmer shouts.

"Palmer really is a damned good pilot," Lee assures me. "If he says the bird is good to go, it is. Even if it looks like a steaming pile of shit that's about to fall out of the sky any minute."

"Thanks, man, that was really touching," Palmer says with mock sincerity.

"Anytime, buddy. Anytime." Lee laughs.

"Can we move along now, ladies," Wes taunts.

"Hey, Cupcake, what's the rush?" I begin to panic all over again.

"We only have the air space for so long today and we already took up some valuable time this morning because you didn't want me to rush," he whispers in my ear. Even though the others couldn't have heard his words my face still burns beet red.

"Oh, yeah. Right," I say softly. "Well, then, carry on."

"Thank you." He wraps his arms around me from behind. "But first you have to uncover your eyes. I promise you won't regret it."

"Fine," I say before slowly lowering my arms. Maybe it's not as bad as I originally thought it was. I slowly pry open my eyelids and . . . nope, it's still pretty fucking bad. "Okay. I'm ready."

Slowly he lowers himself to squatting behind me. Wes taps my legs to lift them. "Step into your harness, honey."

"Are you sure you're not having some weird bondage fantasies?" I snark.

"No, I have tons of fantasies and trussing you up like a Thanksgiving turkey is definitely one of them. This is just for fun."

"And a little kink isn't fun?" I ask. Wes turns and looks at me curiously.

"Trust me, baby, when we cut loose, fun isn't going to be any word near your mind in the moment. Maybe intense, or wild. You might beg me to let you come, but fun won't be part of it." At the end of his little monologue I'm breathing a little heavy and I'm trussed up like a turkey, just like Wes had said. Shit! How did that happen?

I look around and all of the other guys are in flight suits and jump gear. Even freaking Palmer!

"Hey! Why does the freaking pilot have a parachute?" I shout. "That's not right!"

"Your lady's concern for my welfare is endearing," Palmer says without looking up from his clipboard.

"It's Standard Operating Procedure, babe. Everyone on board needs one. Kind of a just in case thing." Wes shrugs.

"Just in case?" I shout, my voice is getting louder and louder.

"It's fine," he reassures me. "Everyone has one."

"I don't have one!" I shout.

"That's because I am your parachute. Nothing will happen to you with me there." He sighs giving me huge puppy dog eyes. "Would you rather jump with Lee? We'd have to change some things around, but he can take you if you'd feel more comfortable."

He had to go and break my heart and make me feel like a grade A asshole all at once.

"No, Wes. I want you," I tell him honestly.

"Damn right, you do." He nods his approval.

"Okay." I clap. "Let's go die!"

"Not funny!" a bunch of the guys chime in.

"It was a little funny," I say as I follow them all onto the plane.

Palmer is standing at the opening between the interior of the plane and the cockpit, if you could call it that, with another man I vaguely remember meeting last night. Everyone has whispered about his belonging to an agency with initials and clandestine operations. The rest of us are sitting on rickety benches that line the sides of the plane with no seatbelts.

"There's no seatbelts," I harshly whisper. The other guys around me bite back smiles.

"Babe, we're not supposed to be in the plane when it lands," Wes explains.

"Oh, right." I look around wondering if anyone heard my blunder. I feel my face heat when I see a lot of smiling eyes looking at me.

"Alright, ladies. Listen up!" Palmer shouts. "Surfer will be your Jumpmaster today."

"Surfer?" I ask. "He looks so . . . *serious*."

"He is. He's also from San Diego. That's all it takes for a call sign," Wes explains to me. "Later I'll tell you all about how Palmer got his."

"There is no static line today as we have spare parts with us so free jumps it is," Palmer continues. "And no, you will not!"

"Hooyah!" They all shout in unison.

"I'll meet you all back at the hangar."

"Hooyah!"

"That's a little unnerving," I say as Palmer climbs into his seat and starts flipping switches to start the plane.

The plane bounces and rambles down the pothole lined runway before suddenly leaping into the air. It seems a little too ambitious of the little plane that couldn't. I hold my breath but before I know it we're climbing higher and higher until suddenly, Palmer shouts, "We've reached jump elevation."

"Oh fuck," I pant as I start to panic.

"Later," Wes say before placing a kiss on the corner of my mouth. "We'll do that later."

"Stand up!" Surfer shouts.

"Aye, aye!" they all shout in unison.

"Tandem, hook up," he says looking to Wes who starts clipping my harness to the front of his.

"I feel like there should be more here hooking us together like steel bars or a roll cage," I mumble.

"You'll be fine," Surfer says to me before winking. "Enjoy your walk in the clouds, Eyes." And then Wes pushes me out of a perfectly good airplane. Well, I guess it wasn't a *perfectly good* airplane, but still, it was an airplane and it was in the fucking sky.

"Open your eyes," he shouts to me and I do.

It's the most amazing thing I have ever seen. The sky is so bright, and the clouds feel so close that you could reach out and touch one. In fact, I do and Wes chuckles behind me. We soar over the tree tops and all too soon a field is coming into view.

And when Wes touches his boots to the ground in the most perfectly executed landing and keeps me from falling flat on my ass I think I'm glad I put my faith in him once again.

I guess I'm not going to die today after all.

• • •

"So, are you going to hook me up with the hot blonde bridesmaid or what?" I hear one of the guys ask Lee while we're all sitting around tables clustered together at some dive bar near the airport.

"No fucking way," Lee growls and I sigh to myself.

"You have to let them figure it out for themselves," Wes whispers into my ear and I realize my sigh wasn't to myself at all.

"I know." I don't know but I'm going along with Wes's sage advice . . . for now. No guarantees when it blows up in all our faces, but hey, what do I know?

"Sorry, man. I didn't know I was poaching."

"You're not." Lee sighs before looking directly at me for help, or to reassure me, I don't know what. "It's not poaching. She's just off limits."

"But the brunette isn't?" someone asks.

"No, she isn't," Lee answers. I can't help my flinch at his words and the sadness that crosses his eyes, so I look away as quickly as I can just like the coward that I am.

"Sounds like there's a story there," someone says.

"With a woman there always is," Surfer says. "I think I need another beer." Then heads to the bar at the back of the building.

"Maybe some other time," Lee says.

"Yeah, some other time."

"I never figured you for a chicken?" Wes rumbles in my ear.

"Shut up," I snap, and Wes tosses his head back and laughs. The conversation quickly turns to what the guys have been up to over the years and how glad they are to be back together again. Surfer stays notably absent during the conversation.

Overall, it's been a great day.

• • •

Now, we're here in our bed, still snuggled together and it's the perfect ending to a beautiful day. Lying in bed with my head on Wes's chest, the blankets pulled up around me even though we're both still naked underneath them, skin to skin as the sweat cools down after he brought me back home after eating too many hot wings and drinking too much beer. All me not Wes. Then he made good on his promise to fuck me later and it was fabulous.

"Did you have a good day, baby?" Wes asks me, his voice soft and a little unsure.

"The very best of days," I whisper back. "Thank you."

"Anytime, Claire. I would do anything to make you happy," he says as he twists a lock of my hair around his index finger studying the way the curl clings to his finger.

"I know that, Wes, and . . . thank you. But you have to know—"

"What is it, honey?" he asks with sincere interest both in his tone of voice and written on his face. I blink and take a deep breath before answering with the truth in my heart.

"That all of my best days have been with you."

"Mine too." Then we curled into each other as if we were born to do so and drifted off to sleep. If I dreamed at all, I was too tired to be bothered by it. I slept through the night and I did it in Wes's arms, right where I was meant to be, and I slept soundly . . . that is until I didn't sleep at all.

• • •

"Come out of the closet, baby."

"No," I whisper, tears hot on my face and snot stuffing up my nose.

Liam and Wes were right, I'm just a baby. A big kid wouldn't be crying in the dark corner of a closet hoping it'll all go away if you just wish hard enough. I bet Wes never cries. I know Lee doesn't.

"Come out now, Claire. Playtime is over."

"No," I cry louder. "Please don't make me."

"Now!" He growls as the closet door rattles. I gasp.

"Leave me alone!"

"Get out of the fucking closet, Claire!" He roars.

"Please no," I cry harder, my body shaking with each sob.

"When," he kicks his hard boots against the closet door and it shudders.

"Please."

"Are you," he kicks it again.

The doors are the kind with the slats that fold sideways. We have them at home and mama says I always pinch my fingers in the accordion. Whatever that is.

"I just wanna go home," I whisper.

"Gonna," he kicks again.

"I just want my mommy," I sob. "Please. I just want my mommy."

"Fucking," the boards snaps and I scream.

"I just wanna go home, please," I beg.

"Learn!" he shouts as he kicks the broken boards out of the way. He leans down and grabs me by my upper arms.

"Please," I wheeze but my words are cut short when he slaps my face hard. So hard I taste blood in my mouth and it's so yucky I feel sick. I'm going to throw up from the yucky taste. I try as hard as I can not to. I know that if I do,

he'll punish me again. I don't want that. Anything but that.

"You are home, baby," he coos right before he slaps me again. I cry out again, falling to the floor with his last hit. It's so strong he knocks me down with it. "And I thought I told you to call me daddy," he says as he lands a hard kick to my back.

"You're not my daddy, you'll never be my daddy," I whisper. "My daddy is a nice man. He would never hurt me. You'll never be my daddy," I say again but the bad man can't hear me, he already walked away. I have nowhere to go, but one thing is for sure, I have to escape.

• • •

I gasp and come awake all at once. I look over at Wes asleep in our bed with a happy look of contentment playing on his face and thankful for once that my personal nightmares didn't wake him.

I carefully slide out of bed and grab my phone off my nightstand before tip toeing my way out of our bedroom, carefully closing the door behind me. I tread softly through the hallway and down the stairs all the way through to the living room in the front of the house. As far away from the bedroom as possible because I do not want Wes to wake up and find me making this call in the middle of the night.

And it is a call I have to make, but one I am not sure that he would understand the necessity of.

I slide my finger across the cool glass surface to unlock my phone and dial the number that I know I can always call.

"Hello?" she answers in her sleepy voice.

"Hey, it's me," I say.

"Claire, is everything alright?" she asks.

"Yes," I start. "No. I don't know." I sigh.

"You had another nightmare," she says not asking a question. She doesn't need to. With me, Anna just knows.

"Yes."

"Do you want to tell me about it?" she asks me.

"No, but I need to," I tell her.

"Go on," she directs me to start.

"I keep dreaming about the events leading up to my escape."

"You're remembering more," she surmises.

"I don't know because the dreams are the same, but they are also always changing. It's the endings or the little details. I don't know what's up and what's down anymore and it's scaring me."

"The subconscious is a complex creature," she answers calmly. "It will take time for your brain to weed out fact from fiction, but I think that is exactly what you are doing. Let's not worry about the details right now as you're obviously trying to sift through those while you're sleeping. Those will come with time. I'm sure of it."

"Okay," I say.

"For now, let's work on some exercises to help you combat the panic when you do have a nightmare. What are you doing now when you have one?"

"I call you?" I ask, and she laughs.

"You are always welcome to call me, but what does Wes think about that?" After a pregnant pause she says, "Wes doesn't know you're calling me, does he?"

"No," I admit.

"Where are you hiding?" she asks.

"I'm not hiding, I'm in the living room," I blurt out and she laughs again. I sigh and then admit, "He wants me to let him in. To share my dreams and nightmares with him."

"And what did you say?" she asks me.

"I told him that I can't blindly lead him into hell with me."

"I can understand your feeling that way," she says. "I do, but I think Wes is a pretty tough guy. If he didn't want to be there or thought that he couldn't handle it, he wouldn't be there in the first place."

"Yeah," I agree. "That's pretty much what he said."

"What did he say exactly?" she asks.

"That he wants me to let him be my light in the dark."

"Well there you go," she says softly.

"Yeah," I agree.

"You think you can go back to sleep now?" she asks.

"Yeah," I answer. "I do."

"Okay then," she says softly. "I'll call you tomorrow and check in."

"Sounds good, Anna, and thanks."

"For what?" she asks.

"For everything."

"Anytime, honey," she says honestly. "Get some sleep."

"You too." She hangs up and I pad back up the stairs, down the hall and, quietly click open the door to our room before climbing back in bed with Wes. In his sleep he pulls me back into his arms and I let myself go, drifting off into sleep.

chapter 7
someone else's ass

I'M WARM AND SAFE cocooned in the fluffy comforter on Wes's bed—our bed. The room is gently bright in a soft light that I can see through my eyelids.

This is the most fabulous dream. It's about time I had a good dream, one where I am wrapped up in all the goodness that is Wes. The place where I am finally safe and whole again.

He places soft kisses at the joint between my neck and shoulder, moving his mouth slowly over one of my most sensitive places. It always drives me a little wild and heats me up when Wes does it. Speaking of heat, I'm warm, warmer than I had originally thought but too hot to be under this blanket.

I'm on fire but not in a bad way.

"Come back to me, baby," Wes rumbles against my shoulder. His morning bristles scrape my skin. "It's time to wake up." I growl in response.

Wake up? Why would I want to wake up? This is an amazing dream. He's lighting me up from the inside out.

"Come back to me," he rasps next to my ear.

My eyes flutter open and I realize that it wasn't a dream and I'm not trapped under the blankets, I am wrapped up in the safety and warmth of Wes's arms—his heat and strength and weight. Wes is placing soft, open mouthed kisses on my neck and shoulder, but the heat might just be coming from the way that I am rocking my hips and sliding my center along his hard cock that I have trapped between my thighs. *Whoops.*

"Wes," I breathe.

He lowers his hands from my waist, sliding them down around my hips to press firmly against my belly as he tips his hips back and slides all the way in to the hilt. The way that he presses his hand against my belly makes me feel so full and achy. I clench around him.

"Wes," I gasp as he gently rocks our bodies, gliding in and out, in and out. His movements are slow and steady as he softly rocks his body into mine. This coupling isn't a hurried fuck but a tender coming together.

"Yeah, baby," he rumbles as his other arm wraps tightly around me holding me securely to him.

"Yes." I tip my head back, resting it on his shoulder as he slides his cock into the heat of my waiting pussy at a maddeningly slow pace but still I can't stop the climax that's building within me like a low wave cresting in the ocean.

"That's it, baby," Wes encourages as he rocks his body into mine again and again.

"Yes," I say for lack of anything else. He has my mind totally wiped of all thought.

"You're almost there." And I am. I so am.

"Yes," I pant in agreement.

Wes slides in and out once, twice, and I cling to his arms that hold me tight, desperate for something to ground me. He pumps his hips one more time and I arch back against him, screaming, "Wes!"

"Claire, Claire, Claire . . ." Wes chants my name over and over again until he finds his own bliss.

We lay there in silence, wrapped up in each other, the walls we had erected so many years ago are finally in taters all around. There is nothing left between Wes and I anymore and if we work hard enough at it, there never will be again.

My heart is finally cracked open wide in Wes's hands and I couldn't be happier.

Our quiet peace is interrupted by the *beep . . . beep . . . beep . . .* of Wes's alarm clock signaling that it's time to wake up and begin the day. When Wes reaches over to silence it, I still his arm placing my hand on him and touching my mouth softly to his.

"What was that for?" he asks.

"Because I love you is all."

• • •

"Goodnite!" my brother shouts from within his office as soon as I walk through the front door of the station and pass into the bullpen. "Get in here. Now!"

"You know, I have always wondered how he does that?" I hear Wes muse from beside me. He claimed this morning that there was something he wanted to see Lee about before heading to his own office for the day, so he had followed me into the station instead of continuing to his own office. "It's uncanny really."

"I'm pretty sure he has me bugged somewhere, I just haven't found it yet," I say as I turn the pockets of my jeans inside out. Wes notices my actions and laughs as he pushes open the door to Lee's office.

"Maybe it's lojack?" he says on a laugh.

I sigh. I wouldn't put it past my brother to have some kind of GPS tracker or RFID key somewhere on my body. I start to wonder if maybe I have an implant somewhere like a dog when we push open Lee's office door.

"What's up, Lee?" I ask.

"I got a missing person for you," he barks.

"Well, good morning to you too, asshole," I grumble under my breath.

"God dammit, Claire!" he shouts.

"Who is it?" I ask.

"Kerrigan Adams," Lee answers.

"Why does that names sound familiar?"

"Because she went to school with Lee and I," Wes tells me.

"Oh, right. I remember her! She had huge . . . *you know*." I hold my hands way out in front of me to explain the attributes that a teenage Lee had found most appealing. "Lee had the hots for her and she wouldn't give him the time of day."

"Would you cut me some slack? Today of all days?" Lee gripes.

"Uhh . . . sure." I'm not really sure at all what has Lee so spun up but I guess he'll tell me when he's ready. Until then we're all just along for the ride.

"What's going on, Lee?" Wes asks.

"Isn't it fucking obvious?" he snaps. "My life is a fucking wreck." So many f-bombs, my goodness. I really want to point that out, but it would probably just make it worse.

"You're right," I snark. "It must be so hard being the big, bad Police Captain who loves to lord his rank over his lowly detective sister."

"Really, Claire?" Lee raises one eyebrow.

"I'm pretty sure he's talking about Emma, honey," Wes stage whispers.

"Ohhh, right. How's that going for you?" I ask Lee.

"Not fucking great. Also, thanks for the sympathy. I'm so glad my broken heart brings you, sister dear, joy."

"Your heartache doesn't bring me joy," I sigh. "I just don't know how to sympathize with you because you're breaking the hearts of both of my friends. I kind of want to kick your ass for messing with them in the first place, Lee."

"I know, I know," he holds his hands up in mock surrender. "I was wrong to fuck and run the way that I was, and I never should have touched either Anna or Emma, but now? Now I can't go back. I'm in love with her, Claire."

"And Anna is in love with you," I say sadly.

"Yeah," he agrees dejectedly. "So, what do I do?"

"Nothing," I tell him. "You're fucked."

"What the hell, Claire!" Lee shouts.

"What?" I ask. "You made this bed and I don't have any answers other than stop messing with my friends and fucking lay in it. They both look like their puppies have been kicked lately and I fucking hate it."

"I don't know," he says before injecting some steel in his spine. "Now get the fuck out of my office."

"Not so fast," Wes says. "I have something I need to talk to you about."

"I'm pretty sure I don't want to hear about you banging my sister so . . ." Lee laughs when I pull face.

"Go chew someone else's ass, douche canoe. We didn't fuck up your life, you did that all on your own," I snap.

"You're right," he says. "I'm sorry. Go on."

"I wanted to ask you to be my best man," Wes says looking at little green at all the displays of emotion lately. Lee looks pretty choked up too as he rises from behind his desk and hurries around to wrap Wes in a big bear hug.

"I'd be honored, brother," he says clapping him on the back the way that men do. It's so weird, you know what women don't do? Beat on each other to show our affection.

"Awe, that's precious," I snicker.

"I'd watch it, baby sister," Lee warns. "I wouldn't want the guys in the bullpen to hear about how you screamed like a little girl during your jump yesterday."

"I did not!" I protest.

"You kind of did, babe." Wes laughs.

"Well, even if I did, you can't prove it," I snap.

"You're right it would be your word against mine . . ." Lee says baiting me.

"That's what I thought—" I start.

"If I didn't have a video," he finishes.

"What video?" I jump. He wouldn't? He couldn't possible have a video, could he?

"The one I took of the jump," Lee says triumphantly. "I was behind you with a GoPro." Well fuck me running.

"I hate you," I tell my brother.

"No, you don't. You love me."

"I think I have a missing person to look for," I say as I snatch up the folder from Lee's desk and storm out of his office with their raucous laughter chasing me on my heels. "Don't forget we have a family dinner at Mom and Dad's tonight, assholes. Attendance is fucking mandatory according to Gran," I toss over my shoulder on my way out.

chapter 8

gone

WHAT A SHIT SHOW those two are. Sometimes I wonder if I'm the third wheel in this scenario.
Oh God, what if I'm the Yoko in this equation?
I shake off those negative thoughts and drop down into my rickety desk chair with its five out of six functioning wheels and drop the file down on top of my desk flipping it open as I go. Kerrigan Adams is thirty-eight years old and a graduate of George Washington High School, class of 1998, along with Wes and Lee just like they had said. She is unmarried and without children. According to her office she never showed for work Friday morning and they became concerned. They contacted her parents, Mike and Molly Adams, who called it in.

I scoop up my keys and head over to Mr. and Mrs. Adams's house. They live over in the old neighborhood not too far from where Wes and I live now—or I will as soon as I finish dragging my shit over from my apartment. Part of me wants to just leave it and buy new shit because packing sucks.

I jump in my department Tahoe, which stays at the station more and more lately as Wes likes to ride to work together. After being apart for twelve years, then my almost being killed a couple of times, Wes has become a little clingy. At least he stopped trying to get me to quit my job.

The drive to the Adams's home is a silent one. I don't often listen to music or podcasts or whatever while working because I like to be lost in my own thoughts. I like to take every moment to go over what I know about the case whenever I have a free moment. You never know when something might click into place and send you on the right path.

I pull over and park next to the curb across the street from the Adams's family home. I see the curtains flutter and am not surprised. I would be nervous too if my daughter was missing. No matter how old she might be.

I will probably be the kind of mom that hovers after everything I have seen as a police officer and because of my own experiences that still haunt me almost every night. The thought of having Wes's daughter crosses my mind and for the first time in my life, I am excited at the prospect of having a baby.

I pull my keys from the ignition and step down from my truck. I walk across the street and up the front walk with a purpose. I don't like to leave people waiting or feeling like I'm not taking their case seriously. The truth is, I take every case more seriously than I should and ever missing persons case comes home with me and snuggles in my bed, unwilling to let me go from its grip late at night. These cases haunt me as much as the mystery of my own does.

I am not surprised when the front door opens before I have a chance to ring the bell. A woman in her early sixties with graying dark hair stands before me worrying a tissue in her hands. Her eyes are red rimmed. She's dressed in navy blue slacks with a crease pressed down the front of the legs and a light blue, short-sleeved sweater.

"Mrs. Adams?" I ask. When she nods I continue. "I'm Detective Goodnite with the George Washington Township PD. I'm here about your daughter, Kerrigan. May I ask you a few questions?"

"Yes," she says sounds like she's trying to catch her breath. I hear the sniffle behind her voice. "Please come in."

"Thank you," I say politely before following her into a family room in the back of the house.

"May I get you some coffee or tea?" she asks me.

"No, thank you, ma'am," I decline.

She nods before shouting over her shoulder, "Mike, the police are here about Kerrigan!" She turns to me as she sits down across from me. "My husband will be right down. He'll want to be here, so we don't miss anything. He's just beside himself. He and Kerrigan are very close."

"I understand." I smile softly. "I'm sorry that you're going through this but we're going to do everything we can."

"Thank you," she whispers.

A large man in his sixties dressed in a pair of khakis and a short-sleeved button-down shirt lumbers into the room stopping by Mrs. Adams's side. "I'm Mike Adams," he tells me as he holds out his hand for me to shake. I stand and take his hand. "My Molly says you're with the police department."

"Yes, Sir. My name is Detective Claire Goodnight with the George Washington Township PD. I'm here to ask you a few questions about your daughter, Kerrigan." He visibly suffers hearing her name, shuddering before nodding his head.

"Yes, ma'am. We'll do anything to find our girl." And I can hear the veracity of his statement. The hard truth is that these sweet, loving people would do anything to bring their daughter home safely and chances are that's not going to happen. Hopefully, she's shacked up in Atlantic City with a secret lover.

"What can you tell me about Kerrigan?" I ask as I pull a small notebook and pen from my pocket.

"She's a good girl," her mother informs me. "She goes to church and works an honest job. She is home every Sunday night for dinner." I smile at her. I too spend a lot of time with my own family. We're not that different from the Adams.

"And where does she work?"

"She works for Smith and Redmond Financial as a tax accountant."

"She the best damned accountant they've ever had," her dad says obviously taking great pride in his only daughter.

"And about how long has she been working there?" I ask.

"Ever since she interned there in college. She was hired on right away," Mrs. Adams tells me. "Where could my baby have gone?" she sobs obviously losing her composure. "She's just . . . *gone*."

"I don't know, Mrs. Adams, but I'm going to do my best to find out."

"Please do."

"Was she seeing anyone in particular?" I ask after giving them a moment to regain their composure.

"No," Mr. Adams answers. "She and her college boyfriend broke up about a year ago. They never married or had kids. And her high school boyfriend is a priest now." Ouch. That had to sting. Nothing like knowing that after you your boyfriend chose celibacy and God.

After spending some more time with the Adams, answering their questions to the best of my abilities and asking a few more of my own, I bid them farewell.

"I'll be in contact," I promise. "As soon as I can."

"Thank you," Mrs. Adams says before shutting the front door behind me.

I climb in my Tahoe and start the engine, wondering to myself, where could Kerrigan have gone? By all appearances, she's the perfect woman, but somehow, some way, she got lost and I need to find her.

My phone rings in the cup holder where I had placed it when I climbed in. I answer and hit the speaker button so that I can drive.

"Goodnite," I answer.

"Hey, chick-a-boo, feel like breaking for lunch?" Emma asks me. I look at the clock on the dash and see that it's about noon. By the time I get back to the part of town where the station is located it will be almost one.

"I can meet you in about forty minutes," I answer. "I was out on a call."

"Sounds good," she says. "Meet Anna and I at Luca's Deli at a quarter till."

"I'll be there," I tell her before ending the call. I head back to the station.

chapter 9

let go

"SO, WHAT'S KICKING, LADIES?" I ask as I plop into the booth after ordering a turkey and cheese sandwich and a lemonade.

"We were just commiserating, that's all," Emma sighs.

"Yeah, nothing you would be interested in." Anna winks at me. "Besides, what's new with you?"

"Well tonight is a mandatory family dinner at mom and dad's, all hands-on deck. Something about wedding prep." I shrug. "I don't know."

"I'm in," Anna says. "I've got a vested interest to not wear anything hideous or polyester."

"Me too," Emma adds. "And I've got nowhere to be."

"That's a recipe for disaster but I'll tell mom you guys are coming." I laugh. "And back to the original topic, I'm interested in everything you two do. What are we commiserating about?"

"Bad dates," The say simultaneously.

"Oh man, I've had some doozies. Buckle your seatbelts, girls." I laugh. "Did I ever tell you about the guy that talked non-stop about his iPhone. It was ridiculous. He had all these extras and a special backpack that connected to his Bluetooth! I couldn't take it. After we paid the check I left and ignored his calls for four days before he finally gave up calling."

"That's nothing!" Emma laughs. The last date I went on asked me if he could suck on my toes. Before the wine was even served!"

"Maybe you'd like it." I shrug.

"Maybe I want a decent, stand-up guy with a monster dick in his pants." Emma says with her usual candor. "One who isn't so free with sharing said monster."

"That is basically asking for the Chupacabra and Bigfoot to have a unicorn baby and name him squishy," Anna laments.

"Besides, Claire," Emma smiles at me to soften the blow. "Your opinion on this subject is now no longer valid."

"What?" I laugh. "My opinion is always valid. And right too."

"No way." Anna winks. "You got your happily ever after."

"Right?" Emma agrees. "That's the Holy Grail." I open my mouth to disagree with them to make them feel better, but I stop myself before the words can come it. It feels like if I lessen the importance of what Wes and I have, even to make my friends feel a little better, that it's a betrayal to Wes. I just can't do that.

We're treading into dangerous territory here, I want to dodge and evade as much as possible. If we tread onto Lee territory at least one of my friends, if not both will end up hurt and broken. My brother is a great guy and I love him with all my heart, but he's a grade A asshole with women and he always has been.

I'm pretty sure I was up front about that with both of my friends and they both jumped on his magic stick hoping for the best.

"Holy shit!" I laugh. The kid delivering our baskets of sandwiches and chips looks a little shell shocked obviously having caught part of our conversation. He drops those baskets and beat feet out of there. "Feet? But is that as bad as the guy I hooked up with from the station and two days later he'd had a case of guilty conscience and told his girlfriend *in Maryland* about it. She kept messaging me on social media to tell me what a whore I was. But I didn't even know he had a girlfriend! If anyone was a whore, it was him and not me. At least he transferred to a Maryland department shortly after."

"I'm pretty sure he didn't make that choice on his own," Emma says vaguely.

"Oh, I know. Liam told him he should strongly consider moving closer to his girlfriend for his own personal safety. I hear they're married, have roughly seventy-five children, and he fucks anything that breathes." I shrug. "Not my problem and it never was. He was a one off."

"I never got how you could be so cavalier about relations," Anna chimes in.

"I never wanted to get attached. Men do it all the time, why should I have been any different just because I have boobs and a vagina?" Too late, I realized my mistake. There was no way I could back pedal and not look like an asshole so Emma and I just stay silent while we watch Anna's face crumple.

Why couldn't I have just kept my fucking mouth shut?

"I'm sorry," I say.

"It's so stupid," she says, wiping her eyes with her fingertips. "It was one night, I knew he was only ever going to give me one night, I had just hoped . . ."

"Anna—"

"Like I said, stupid."

"The fuck it is!" Emma thunders. "He is such an asshole."

"No, he's not and you know it. He's a great guy." Anna takes a deep breath before pressing on. "I just need to let go, and I know it. But it's so hard and I want him so bad. You know what they say?"

"What's that?" I ask.

"You can't always get what you want," Anna answers.

"Or maybe we want the things that are bad for us," I say softly to Anna but really, to both of them. I love my brother and shouldn't speak ill of him, but he is toxic for both of them and they can do so much better.

"Anna, he's a jerk really," Emma pleads. "You don't know what he's done—"

"I do," she says quietly. "And it's okay. I love him enough that I want him to be happy. I want you to be happy too."

"I am happy," Emma denies.

"Are you?" she asks in her quack voice. Man, I hate when she turns those questions on me. It feels pretty good to see her point them at someone else for a change. I know that if I could see my face I would see a gleefully smug smile on my face. It's a little evil of me and I'm pretty okay with that.

"I'm happier without him than I would ever be with him. If he was so great he wouldn't be doing this—*to either of us*. He would just ride off into the sunset with you and live happily ever after," Emma explains her and I have to say, her logic is pretty sound.

"Only in my dreams." Anna sighs. "I just wished that I was enough, you know?"

"You *are* enough," I tell her.

"If anything," Emma snaps. "He's not good enough for you."

Anna shoots Emma a watery smile. "It's sweet of you to say. And I do appreciate it, but we all know that it's true. Sometimes, I just don't feel like I belong, you know? With you guys and Wes and Lee. Everyone is this badass with a gun, not afraid to get down and dirty with crime and I'm just . . . *me*."

"What?" Now I'm shouting. "Of course, you belong!"

"I know, and I do, but I also don't. I'm not a tough police officer. I drive a Mercedes. I'm just . . . different from you guys."

"Don't let that dick make you feel like you don't fit in because you do," Emma practically shouts. I can hear the tension in her voice, the strain of this love triangle is really getting to her.

"It's okay, really," Anna says, her voice is small, and I hate it. "I'm different and I know it. Anyways, I should go."

"You don't have to," I say but I know we all have to get back on the clock soon. She shoots me a watery smile before standing up and clearing her basket on the way out the door.

"Emma—" I start.

"Don't say it." She doesn't want to hear the truth, the real problem with her predicament. If Lee was just fooling around with them it would be one thing, but feelings are involved in a perfect storm of disaster and heartbreak.

"He loves you," I finish quietly.

"I love her more and he's tearing her apart."

"And what about you?" I ask. "Is this tearing you apart too?"

"None of that matters, and . . . well . . . he's an asshole. Plus, you know what they say? You can't always get what you want," she says sadly before following Anna out the door.

chapter 10

harmless little crush

MY HEART IS HEAVY.
My concern for both of my closest friends and my only brother is growing not by leaps and bounds but by mountains and valleys. There is no way the three of them can come out of this twisted love triangle unscathed.

But I have a missing person to find—yet, another woman from Liam's sorted past—so I toss my trash in the receptacle and place my basket on top of it before heading out to my Tahoe. I need to head over to Smith and Redmond Financial to poke around a bit.

The accounting office is on this side of town, so it doesn't take too long to get there. It's a small brown building next to a pizzeria and behind an old school diner, one of the ones shaped like a gigantic tin Twinkie. My stomach growls. I could literally eat all day long. It's kind of a situation.

I pull into the small parking lot behind the building and park my car. Then walk through the small alleyway that lets out on the main street a couple of doors down from Smith and Redmond, dodging the cracks in the sidewalk as I go.

I pull open the glass front door and a little bell overhead tinkles. A young brunette with thick glasses smiles at me from a small desk.

"May I help you?" she asks me.

"Yes, I'm Detective Goodnite with the George Washington Township PD and I'd like to speak to the owner if I may," I answer with a gentle smile on my face as I point to my badge on my hip to keep her from panicking. You never know who will panic when they see the cops.

"Mr. Redmond is in," she says. "I'll just go get him really quick."

"Thank you." I smile politely at her.

I look up at the sounds of footsteps on cheap office carpet and see the brunette leading a slim man with salt and pepper hair towards me. I catch him giving me a carnal appraisal with a crooked grin on his face. Over a year ago, I would have given him a chance but that was before Wes stormed back into my life and turned it all upside down. What a difference a year makes.

"Mr. Redmond, I presume," I greet him holding out my hand to shake his.

"I am. What can I do for you officer?" I feel my smile turn a little brittle at his honest question. I do my best not to roll my eyes. I mean, it's not his fault that he's kind of a sexist asshole. I guess that's not a very fair judgment but why can't they just assume the chick with the badge is a detective?

"I'm Detective Goodnite with the George Washington Township PD. I'm here to ask you a few questions about Kerrigan Adams."

Concern flashes across his face raising my own value of him. "Is everything alright?"

"Miss Adams has been reported as missing."

"I had hoped that wasn't the case." He sighs looking a little world weary. "Please, step into my office. We'll have more privacy there."

I follow him down the hallway of gray, nondescript office cubicles to his own office with several short glass windows peering out over the sea of cubes and middle management. I can't help but think that there is no way in hell that I could ever work here. I would slowly wither and die if trapped in this colorless world of numbers and boredom.

"Please, have a seat." He gestures to the crappy, uncomfortable looking chairs in front of his desk. Instead of sitting behind his desk he lowers himself to the chair next to mine. The chair that is *very* close to mine. It's both a little awkward and inappropriate. Not wanting to show that he is making me uncomfortable or off balance I force myself to stay rooted in my seat, taking out my little notebook and pen.

"What can you tell me Kerrigan Adams?" I ask.

"She's a great employee. Smart, beautiful, the whole package."

"The police report states that you called her parents when she was a no show here?"

"Yes," he answers.

"Is that normal for her?" I ask.

"Not at all," he answers. "Kerrigan is very responsible. Dependable. She's a diligent worker."

"Is Kerrigan involved with anyone here in the office?" I ask. His brow creases in thought over my question. Interesting because it should be an easy one—yes or no.

"My partner, Ken Smith, has had feelings for her for a while, but Kerrigan is unaware of how he feels."

"Would Mr. Smith be likely to stalk or abduct Miss Adams?" I ask.

"Not at all," he says sounding surprised by my question. "He's harmless. And more than that, he's heartbroken that she's missing."

"Were his feelings for her more than a crush?" I ask needing to know.

"No."

"Would you consider him obsessed with her or the idea of being with her?"

"No. Not at all."

"Is he in the office today?" I ask him.

"No, his mother had a heart attack early yesterday evening. He's been at the hospital with her ever since," he says sadly.

"Did anyone else here have a history with Kerrigan?"

Mr. Redmond pauses, he's obviously trying to weigh his words. "She and I had a . . . dalliance about two years ago. It was a onetime thing and before I knew how Ken felt about her. We never saw each other in that way again," he answers. I appreciate his candor. There was a lot there I wouldn't want to share if I was in his shoes.

"Thank you."

"It was just a way to scratch an itch, you know?" He shrugs looking a little concerned.

"Thank you for your candor."

"This might not be totally appropriate, but . . . are you seeing anyone?" he asks.

I opt not to inform him how inappropriate it is to ask me and simply just answer the later part of his question. "I am. I'll let you know if I have any more questions. Thank you for your time, Mr. Redmond."

I stand and see my way out, walking around the corner and back through the little alleyway wondering just where Kerrigan Adams has gone. By all accounts she lives a quiet life of accounting, church, and family dinners with her older parents.

I jump in my Tahoe and start the engine. I head back to the station thinking I need to look into Mr. Ken Smith. Maybe, just maybe, his infatuation is more than just a harmless little crush.

My phone rings. "Goodnite," I answer after hitting the speaker button.

"Hey, baby," Wes answers and I can hear the smile in his voice. "How's your day going?"

"Pretty good," I answer. "I have relatively no leads on a missing persons."

"Let me know if you need any help," he offers genuinely.

"Stay out of my case, Suit." I hit my turn signal and turn left on Main Street. The station isn't too far from here but it's rush hour traffic at its finest in New Jersey.

"It's a genuine offer, Claire," he says softly. I must have hurt his feelings with my less than smart quip. I need to remember that it wasn't too long ago that Wes and I were head to head over a case and it was fairly ugly. I need to get this conversation back on track and quick.

"I know, I know," I gripe. "How goes it in Fed-Landia?" I ask.

"Not too shabby." He laughs. "Hey, I'm calling because I was wondering about mandatory family dinner night?"

"You mean you're not calling just to hear the sounds of my glorious voice?" I ask with faux shock. "I'm hurt, Wesley, truly."

"Very funny, kid." I grumble at his long worn out reference to my being too young. He's joking but it still strikes a nerve.

"What do you want to know?" I sigh.

"Do you want to meet me at your parents' house or do you want me to pick you up at the station?"

"I'm heading back to the station now, come and get me, big guy. I feel like at this juncture we should present a united front." Wes laughs.

"Sure thing, honey." His throaty chuckle flows over the phone lines reminding me again how much I enjoy his company. "I'll see you in ten."

chapter 11
united front

EVERYTHING'S GOING TO BE FINE.
There is nothing to worry about going to dinner at my parents' house and other lies I tell myself with a regular frequency. I love my family, I'm not a monster after all, but they can be a lot to handle on a good day. And today is not a good day.

I mean it is, but Wes and I have handed them an impending wedding on a silver platter. We might as well have given them a golden goose with its ass stuffed full of diamonds and tickets to every World Series, Stanley Cup, and Super Bowl combined for the next forty years.

To sum it up, I'm nervous. What the hell were we thinking? Wes and I should have just run off to Vegas—an idea which I'm growing more and more fond of by the second—without telling anyone and sending them a postcard later.

By the time I pull into the parking lot behind the station where I lock up my Tahoe at night when I don't take it home I have worked myself up into a frenzy. There's not enough anxiety medication and booze in the world to talk me down off this ledge.

I turn the key in the ignition while doing some deep breathing and I look over. Wes is leaning casually against his Fed car with a *Rebel Without a Cause* cool. His suit coat is off, probably somewhere in the backseat of his car along with his tie. The top three buttons of his crisp, white shirt are popped open exposing his golden throat. His eyes are hidden behind a pair of dark black wayfarers, but I know that he's had a lock on me before I ever pulled into this lot. The thought has me warming from the inside out and my toes curling in my favorite boots.

Is it getting hot in here? I mentally fan myself, step down from the Tahoe, and make my way toward Wes. Awkwardly, I tuck a stray lock of my dark hair behind my ear.

"Hey, baby, you wanna get out of here?" he asks like all of my teenage fantasies of him rolled up into one memorable moment.

"Yeah." I smile at him. I'm genuinely happy to see him. He is a bright spot in my days.

"Then let's go," he says rounding the hood of his car and opening the passenger door for me. I drop down into the seat and tuck my long legs in.

"Thanks."

"Anytime." He gently closes the door behind me before walking back around the car and climbing in the driver's seat.

The drive back to the old neighborhood is longer than usual with rush hour traffic but still no more than twenty or thirty minutes. I continue to worry the entire time. As Wes drives down the turnpike with his eyes never leaving the road, I can tell that he sees all of my secrets. He knows I'm getting more and more nervous. Wes places his heavy palm on my thigh without saying a word. He just slowly slides his pinky finger up and down the inseam of my jeans on my inner thigh, effectively distracting me from our impending doom.

"It's going to be fine, baby," his deep voice rumbles over the sounds of the highway as we slow through traffic.

"Sure," I mumble.

"I mean it, Claire," Wes warns. I have learned that he doesn't appreciate my anxiety when it comes to our families and this wedding.

"Uh huh," I neither agree or disagree.

"Claire," he growls to get my attention.

"What?"

"Don't. Run."

"I'm not—" I start.

"I mean it," he takes a deep breath to calm himself. I like that he takes a moment to speak calmly when we both know that we're prone to short fuses and hot-blooded moments.

"I—" I start to deny it.

"Don't. Run," he enunciates. "Do not run from me. Do not run from us. I know that this is all scary for you but it's going to be okay. Don't run."

"Would you let me talk!" I snap.

"Yes."

"I'm not going to run." He quirks a brow in my direction. "I mean it! I know that I have run from you, from us, before but I have worked through that. I'm here now and I'm not going anywhere."

"You sure?" he asks. "You look like you have passports and plane tickets in mind."

"And I do." I shrug. "Sort of. I was thinking we should elope in Vegas and tell everyone afterwards. On a postcard." At that Wes throws his head back and laughs

"Let me get this straight," he rumbles. "You're not thinking of running from me, but you're planning on running away with me?"

"Yes." I nod.

"You don't have that deer-in-the-headlights look because of me but more because of your mom?"

"Yes," I answer. "Well, not as much Mom as Gran. She's scary." He chuckles at my response.

"What are you talking about? Your grandmother is a sweet old lady." I stare at him wide eyed. He can't be serious. Jesus Fucking Christ, he is.

"She just wants you to think that!" I'm practically shouting. "She's freaking crazy. And a little mean."

"You're kidding." Wes looks over at the serious expression on my face. "You're not kidding. You're really afraid of her. Holy shit, you're not afraid of anything to the point that you scare the shit out of me, and you're afraid of a ninety year old woman who can't even hit five feet tall on her tippy toes."

"You just wait," I warn him shaking my finger in his face. "Once you're officially family she'll be barking at you like she does the rest of us. You won't be off limits anymore because you're Lee's friend. You'll be digging ditches to hide the bodies like the rest of us."

"You don't really hide bodies, do you?" he asks. "Because I'm a federal agent and all that."

"Meh," I shrug. "Semantics."

"Uhh . . . no, it's not 'semantics' it's not something that's going to happen," he says before snapping his mouth shut. "You know what? You're stressed out and anxious about planning this wedding and I'm not going to let you scare me with a sweet, little old lady that I have known my entire life."

"Sure thing." I shrug. "Whatever you say."

Wes growls but before he can come back with something witty or extremely obnoxious we're turning onto the street that my parents have lived on for as long as I can remember. He has to park on the street because the driveway is filled with the vehicles owned by everyone we have ever known—Lee's Tahoe that's an upgrade from mine, it must be good to be the king, Anna's merc, and Emma's Mazda 3. Not to mention the Cadillac my grandmother has been driving since the 90's and the O'Connell's BMW. My nephew's vintage Charger rounds out the ensemble cast.

My late half-sister Bonnie's kids are the bright spot in all of our lives. We never would have known that any of them existed, our sister included, if she hadn't been murdered by a serial killer two months ago. Since her ex-husband had pulled a runner years earlier, her kids now live with my parents who had petitioned the court for custody and won recently.

Wes steps out of the car and comes around to open the door for me. He holds his hand out for me and I take it, letting him pull me from the car. He keeps hold of my hand in his as we walk across the street and up the walk to my parents' front door.

I can hear the noise, laughter and voices, an overall huge commotion. It's wild, it's love, it's joy and sometimes sadness and hardship, but it's all ours. I stop on the walk outside my family home and close my eyes, not because I'm overwhelmed don't know how to handle it, but because I know how all to fleeting these moments can be. I want to make certain that I soak them all in while I can.

When I open my eyes again, Wes looks worried until I smile at him, showing him that I am truly happy. We don't knock on the door. This is our family and our family home. Wes having grown up as Liam's best friend spent almost as much time here as Lee and I did.

When we first walk in all conversation stops. We all stand there looking at each other wide-eyed until my Gran breaks the silence.

"Good, now we can get started." She claps her hands making it so.

"Oh shit," Wes whispers.

"See?" I snap a little hysterical. "I freaking told you so!"

"I may have been a little naive before . . ." he admits, and I can't help but laugh.

"Quick, you two, get in here," my mom waves her arms trying to hurry us into the dining room with everyone else. "Before she starts throwing my dishes."

"She won't really throw the dishes, will she?" Wes asks. I just shoot him a withering glare. I hope he's happy now.

"Marta and Claire, come help me set the table," my grandmother demands. "You too, hussies!"

"Gran!" I shout at the same time my mother shouts too.

"Deirdre! You can't just call people hussies," my mom chastises my grandmother. The two have an interesting relationship. Both women married into the Goodnite family, but my Gran seems to forget that part and has spent the last thirty-nine years telling my mom that she doesn't belong. It's a little awkward and more than a little hostile.

"Yeah," Emma agrees. "Claire was a way bigger hussy than I ever was." My brother chokes on his beer while Wes looks down right murderous. I need to get this train back on track and fast!

"Let's not get ahead of ourselves here. We're all family. Let's get the food on the table," I say as I clap my hands in a fake cheer.

"Yeah, okay," my friends grumble but follow me into the kitchen.

"Shut it on the whore calling!" I demand under my breath.

We all pitch in and carry platters of food. My mom and my grandmother went all out for this meal. They must have been cooking all day by the looks of it. Each platter is piled high with mashed potatoes, pork chops, macaroni, green beans, a huge wooden bowl filled with a freshly made salad, and a large basket with hot rolls fills every available nook and cranny of the table.

We all take our places around the table, my dad at the head with my mom at the other end. Lee and I sit on either side usually, but with the house full of people and my parents now raising three more children, our places have changed. Lee sits on one side of dad and Eric, who is home on leave from the Army, sits on his other side. I sit next to my mom and Seth, who is the baby of the family at ten sits on her other side. Wes sits next to me and Gran on his other side, I snicker evilly at the prospect. Brooklyn, who is nineteen and studying social sciences at the local college sits next to Seth. The last to sit are Emma and Anna who are jockeying each other to *not* sit next to Lee whose face is turning a deeper and deeper shade of red as time goes by. While I enjoy watching him squirm, I can't let it go on too long.

"Oh shit," I say with obvious fake disappointment. "I forgot my wine in the kitchen."

I jump up and run into the kitchen before anyone can stop me. When I come back with it *and* the bottle in hand I snap my fingers like I had just remembered something important and set my bounty on the table in front of me, specifically, next to Lee. He is my brother after all . . . even if he is being a horse's ass right now.

"Lee, I need to update you on that missings case," I say sitting down in the seat next to Lee and shoving my friends out of the way with a just go with it smile on my face.

Everyone adjusts their seating accordingly. My dad looks at me approvingly. When I look over at Wes he smiles softly and shoots me a wink. These guys—my guys—they get me, and I love that. I love them, and I would do anything for them. Obviously.

Lee stretches his arm across the back of my chair before leaning in to whisper in my ear, "You're a good sister."

"Of course," I agree with a smile. "I love you, big brother."

"I love you too, kid," he says, and I know that he means it. Lee can be hard on me, especially at work, but it's not for a lack of love. He would do anything for me and just wants to protect me.

Our dad clears his throat. "I think it's only fitting that Eric says grace while he's home. Son, if you will . . ."

"Y-yes, Sir," he says as he clears his throat, his eyes swim deep with emotion on his stoic soldier's face. Eric was away, stationed across the country in the Army when his mom, the half-sister Lee and I never knew we had, was murdered. Now, with his brother and sister, we're all one big family. These kids are Goodnites in everything but name. Especially their looks, sharing our black hair and violet eyes.

I just wish our little family could have included his mom while she was alive.

"Grandad," my dad softly corrects.

"Yes, Grandad," Eric says before having us all bow our heads. "Dear Lord, thank you for the food before us and the blessings we have received, but also for this family which you have blessed us with. Thank you for watching over Lee,

Claire, and Wes so that they may do their duties—"

"And also, for watching out for our nephew, Eric," Lee adds softly.

"And for leading us home when we thought all was lost. Lastly, please watch over our mother as we know without a doubt she is in your house now. In Jesus name . . ."

"Amen," was said all around the table.

Everyone reaches for bowls and platters in front of them and then passing them to their left—as is the only way we do large family dinners. Everyone's plate is overflowing, forks are raised, and mouths are full, no doubt the way the old bird planned it. When she raises her glass and taps the tines of her fork to it, I narrow my eyes in her direction suspiciously. My grandmother just smiles an innocent smile that I know, without a doubt, is one hundred percent bullshit.

"I just wanted to let you all know that today while I was lighting a candle for your dearly departed grandfather and sister, I booked St. Michael's church for your wedding on October eighth," Gran says matter of factly. Everyone just sits there froze, staring on wide-eyed, no doubt the exact way she wanted it. "You're welcome. Now say 'thank you' like a good girl."

I might have growled. The noise was cut off when Lee kicked me under the table.

"I don't think Wes and I were planning on a church wedding, Gran," I say swallowing my nervousness. "But thank you for the offer. Also, October seems a little . . . fast."

"Well, I for one, think a church wedding is perfect," Mrs. O'Connell chimes in with a gleeful smile, obviously enjoying my being cornered and unhappy.

"Also," Gran wades in. "It's not too soon. If we give you too long, you'll run away again. You know, cold feet."

"Does everyone think I'm going to bolt?" I ask instantly regretting it when everyone looks at their plates awkwardly, except Wes, Wes just looks hurt.

"Claire—" my dad says my name.

"No!" I shout. "I think I'm done here." I push back from the table standing.

"Sit down, Claire," he orders and my inner twelve-year-old Claire has me do just that in true petulant fashion.

"I expected more from you all," I say softly. "I love you all and I thought you loved me."

"We do—" my mom starts but I don't let her finish.

"I love Wes and I'm not going anywhere, but I'm not real happy with any of you right now."

"I'm sorry, Sis," Lee says.

"Me too," Emma adds.

"Same," Anna says softly.

"Well, I don't really know you all that well, so you had my vote of confidence," Eric says from across the table. "Plus, you're a way better shot than the frog. Clearly, he's marrying up," he finishes shooting me and Lee a saucy wink. I love that kid so much and as I look at him, I realize that he's not a kid at all and we've missed all of it.

"Now that that's all out of the way," Gran adds and groans go up all around the table as everyone resumes eating dinner. "I also signed you up for marriage classes."

"What?" I shout. "I'm not going to more head shrinking!"

"Really?" Anna asks on a raised brow.

"You know what I mean!"

"I'm not sure that I do . . ." She shrugs.

"Anna . . . Emma . . . help me out here," I plead.

"Actually, I think it'll be good for both of you," Anna says. "Professionally speaking." I narrow my eyes at her.

"This isn't fair," I pout.

"Actually, I think it's great," Lee says on a wicked smile. "You're lucky to get to go to these classes," he says laying it on real thick.

"I'm glad you feel that way, Liam," Gran says, and I know this is going to be good. My smile splits my face and there is nothing I could do to stop it. "I signed you and the two trollups up for their singles group. Father Matthew has a great marriage success rate."

"Gran—" Lee warns.

"What?" she shrugs. "It's already done. Unless there's something else going on here I don't know about . . . You and the blonde would make beautiful babies."

"Nothing's going on," Emma barks looking irritated.

"Yeah, nothing to see here, Gran," Lee adds disappointed and poor Anna just looks so lost and sad. She's clearly losing her battle with her hope to let go.

"When do all of these classes start?" Lee asks on a sigh.

"Tomorrow at eight." She smiles triumphantly.

"I'm never getting married," Eric mumbles and my dad laughs.

"Yeah, me either," Seth agrees. "Girls are gross!"

"Well, that plan isn't working out so great for your uncle," Dad says to his plate. Lee just sighs again.

"I just love that new priest they have there," Mrs. O'Connell shares. "He's so young and insightful."

"I prefer Father Matthew," Gran says just to pick a fight. "He's been the priest at that church since my son was born."

"Well, maybe we need a change up for the wedding," Mrs. O'Connell says obviously feeling a need to come out the winner of this argument.

"We'll see," Gran says.

"I'm still not sure we agreed on a church wedding," I say to no one in particular.

"Didn't we, though?" Wes asks me with barely restrained laughter in his voice.

"So much for a united front," I grumble under my breath.

"I love these family dinners!" Wes says happily while Lee and I both plot his murder from across the table.

chapter 12
shit

"'*LET THERE BE NO SEXUAL immorality, impurity, or greed among you. Such sins have no place among God's people.' I had such high hopes for you and yet you were still a disappointment.*"

She blinks her eyes furiously and rolls her head side to side. The blow she took is clearly having an effect on her, but she won't suffer long. Our Lord is merciful tonight.

I pull the large hunting knife out of its sheath and trace it over her body. I let the blade skim her arms one by one. I offer up the gentlest caress of the tip along her pink cheek.

"P-p-please," she pleads with me. "D-d-d-don't d-d-do this."

"You, my dear, should have thought about that before you sinned."

"I-I-I didn't!" she cries.

"Fornication is a sin, Kerrigan. Didn't you listen to a word that I said?" I snap letting her big eyes get to me. I try and remind myself that she is a child of God and therefore imperfect, but she listened to Lucifer and his silver tongue.

"I didn't. I'm a good girl." She looks away because we both know that it's a lie. Just last week I had caught her letting a man paw at her like a common whore. She was better than that. At least I had thought so before then. But I have been wrong in the past.

"I really wish you were, Kerrigan. Trust me, this hurts me more than you."

She starts fighting the ropes binding her wrists in earnest now, but it doesn't matter. It's too late for her. It'll all be over in a minute or two.

I take the hilt of the knife in both hands and raise it up over my heads before driving it down in between her breasts. My blade hits bone and a gurgling sound falls from her lying lips. I slide the knife free from her body and raise it again. I thrust it into her body over and over again until I am sure that she is gone.

And then I slide the tip just below the surface of her skin just below her collarbone, marking her with the letter A—adultery is the ultimate sin after all and I am doing the Lord's work.

• • •

The rest of the evening was fairly uneventful if one considers being run over by a truck over and over again uneventful, but hey, who am I to judge?

After Emma, Anna, and I clear the table, I help Gran do the dishes. Emma slides in next to me at the sink with a dish towel and Anna armed with the same is on the other side.

"I guess I'll just go relax," Gran says with a huff before leaving the kitchen.

"She kind of scares me," Emma admits.

"Meh." I shrug. "She's a little mean but we love her."

"Awe, come on, she's not so bad," Anna laughs.

"Anna, she keeps calling us 'the trollops'. You can't tell me that you're okay with that," Emma challenges.

"She only has the power over me that I give her."

"Bullshit," Emma snaps.

"It's true," Anna tells us. "You're letting it get to you. Just ignore it."

"Don't you head shrink me!" Emma barks and Anna visibly shrinks back. As it turns out, Emma is one of the few who Anna gave that power to.

"I'm sorry," she says in a little voice that makes my stomach roll. I hate that this strong, confident woman has been reduced to feeling so very small and insignificant.

"Anna—" Emma starts.

"No, you're right. Let's just forget it," Anna says softly.

"Anna—" Emma starts again.

"I said I just want to forget it." Anna rolls her shoulder back mustering up the courage and I can't help but feel like when she said she didn't belong with us that that was only the tip of the iceberg. "So how ugly of a bridesmaid dress are you making us wear? What are our color options?"

"I'll literally wear anything but pink," Emma chimes in taking the hint and following the subject change no matter how abrupt.

"What?" Anna shrieks. "No! I love pink."

"Why am I not surprised?" Emma sighs.

"Pink it is!" I cheer enthusiastically. That's what Emma gets for being an ass to Anna. I'm the only one that gets to be an asshole to her. For years, Anna has been hounding me to fix my shit, first in an official capacity and now as one of my closest friends. She's been kicking my ass for years, but building me back up at the same time. So, I'm a little protective of her. If anyone is going to kick her ass it's going to be me and only in the nicest of ways.

We are just heading into the living room to settle in for coffee and cake when my phone rings. I pull it out of my back pocket wondering who would be calling me since everyone I know is currently under this roof. Shit, it's probably the station.

"Goodnite," I answer.

"Detective Goodnite, this is dispatch," they inform me. *"I have officers who have responded to a body in an alleyway."*

"I'm not the on-call Detective tonight, dispatch," I inform them of what they should already know. "I believe Juarez is tonight."

"I'm sorry, Detective, it's been a long day. The victim matches the description of your missing person. I should have led with that and I'm sorry."

"Next time," I say. "Where is this alley?"

"A body was found behind the Pig & Chicken on the corner of Fourth and Main."

"I'm on my way."

chapter 13

no fucking way

"**H**EY, BABY, YOU GOIN' my way?" Wes asks as he twirls his keys around his finger. I roll my eyes but smile anyways.

"Yeah," I say, my voice a little breathy. Plus, I don't have a car here.

"Then let's go," he offers while holding out his hand for me to take and like I always will, I do.

"Well, duty calls," I shout into the crowded room.

"I take it you gotta live one?" Dad asks.

"Nope, I got an *un*-live one," I laugh at my own joke. My dad just rolls his eyes at me.

"You got a body?" Lee asks.

"Yep." I nod my head looking him in the eyes, so he knows what I'm not saying out loud.

"The missing persons?" he asks me.

"Yeah, it's looking that way," I confirm.

"Damn." Lee shakes his head and with all that's going on with Lee, Emma, and Anna, I forget that a long time ago, Kerrigan meant something to him too so he will feel this one on a much deeper level.

"You said it," I sigh.

Wes and I stop to kiss everyone goodbye before heading out the door. He takes my hand in his and leads me across the street before pulling open my door for me. I climb in as he closes the door behind me before rounding the car and climbing in the driver's seat. Wes cranks the engine before leaning over and asking me, "Where to, Detective?"

"The Pig & Chicken on Fourth and Main," I tell him before adding, "And step on it."

Wes pulls away from the curb and heads towards the crime scene behind the Pig and Chicken. The bar isn't far from where my parents still live. George Washington Township is large in population but small in actual territory. Even though it should only take five minutes to get somewhere, with traffic and stop lights, it will probably take about twenty minutes on a good day.

"There's the ambulance," Wes says as he drives down Second Avenue. "Think we're in the right place."

"Shit," I mutter to myself. I always hope the call is wrong until I get there and see it for myself with my own two eyes. The ambulance behind the bar tells me that Kerrigan Adams is most likely dead, but then again, I always knew that she probably was.

Wes cuts the engine and we climb from the vehicle. Here I don't wait for Wes to open my door and he doesn't dote on me non-stop. Here we're a Federal Agent and a Detective, the fact that we go to the same house at the end of the night has nothing to do with the case and the facts.

I approach the crime scene tape and the officer guarding against civilian intruders and looky-loos. I pull my badge off my pocket and hold it up to view.

"Detective Goodnite, we've been waiting for you," the officer interrupts me.

"Show me what you got, Officer."

He lifts the bright yellow crime scene tape up for me to slip underneath, letting it drop back down into place after I pop up on the other side. Wes follows me through.

"Agent O'Connell, to what do we owe this visit?" the officer asks.

"I'm with her," Wes tosses a thumb over his shoulder towards me.

"I had heard something about that," the officer adds. "I can't believe the good Detective fell for your shit hook, line, and sinker."

"Yep," Wes adds with a ridiculous smile. "I finally wore her down."

"She seems too smart to get tangled up with the likes of someone like you," the officer laughs letting me know that Wes and this guy go way back, and I won't have to kick some ass tonight to defend my man's honor. And I would if I had to.

"Thanks for the vote of confidence, Rodriguez," Wes sighs.

"There's a crime scene, ladies," I roll my eyes at these two idiots. "Could we get back to that, please?"

"Oh, right. Sorry, Detective Goodnite," Officer Rodriguez says duly chastised.

"It's fine," I say.

"The victim appears to be mid to late thirties, brown hair and brown eyes," he rattles off the facts. This is what I need right now—just the facts—as he leads us around the corner to where the crime scene technicians are photographing the scene and taking samples. "The responding detective said you were looking into a missing persons this morning. Could it be her?"

"It's possible. Is CSU running fingerprints?" I ask.

"They are but it can take awhile. You know how it is." He shrugs his meaty shoulder.

"I do. Who found her?" I ask him.

"The bartender came out to toss some trash in the dumpster and there she was," he answers.

"Overdose? Slip and fall? How did she buy it? Do we know?" I ask.

"Uhh ... no," he says vaguely. "It's one of those things that you just have to see for yourself."

"Well, what happened?" I ask as I become frustrated with vague, half answers.

"She was stabbed to death," he says bluntly.

We round the corner just in time to get a quick glimpse of the crime scene and it was surprisingly clean of blood and gore for a stabbing. It's easy to assume that she was done somewhere else and moved here.

This isn't so bad. Maybe a mugging gone wrong ... I just start to think that this might be a fairly easy case when I realize all those sayings about counting chickens and eggs in baskets is sadly correct.

It's not until we get closer that I realize just how wrong my original assessment was. A dark-haired woman who I can't help but believe that the tests will come back as Kerrigan Adams, is sitting up against the wall just outside the back door to the Pig & Chicken. Her legs are stretched out in front of her and her ankles are crossed. Her head is slumped forward and red slashes crisscross all over her exposed skin and torn clothes.

But the most remarkable item that my brain seems to latch onto is the giant letter A carved into her exposed chest. It's not carved neatly enough to know for sure. Maybe it's just a bunch of randomly placed stab wounds. I don't know. Only time with Emma in her morgue will tell.

"No fucking way," Wes thunders from behind me. "Absolutely not."

"It's not your choice, Wes," I say firmly. "This is my job."

"The hell it isn't!" he thunders. "I have a say in your safety."

"This was my case from the beginning. I have to see it through," I explain.

"No, you do not. You've had this case for all of twelve hours. Let someone else take it."

"No," I tell him. "It's mine and I'm keeping it."

"I'll take it and pass it on to one of my agents," he explains with a self-satisfied gleam in his eyes.

"I don't think so!" I shout back. "This case is mine."

"I can't do this again, Claire," Wes pleads. "Please."

"Don't make me choose, Wes." It's not fair. Just when I think my life is finally becoming something good, something decent, someone or something is taken from me. Well, not anymore.

"Right back at you, babe," he snaps. It lands like a blow to my chest. "You think, for even one fucking second, that I want to sit back and watch you chase down some sicko again? You think I want to watch you die?"

"That's not going to happen," I try to say.

"Can you guarantee that?" he asks.

"No."

"I didn't think so," Wes snaps.

"Wes—" I start but he cuts me off.

"Don't. Don't even finish that sentence," he roars.

"Please," I plead, and I hate it. This isn't the place to be having an argument and yet, here we are, behaving about as unprofessional as you can get.

"I'm not going to ask you to pick me over this case, over your job, whatever you're working yourself up about in your head. I already know how that will play out and it's not good for anyone." He shakes his head sadly before looking me in the eyes again. "But I am asking you to think of me, *even just a little*, when you make your decision. Until then, I'll stay out of your way."

"Wes, don't do this," I plead softly.

"Let me know what you decide."

And then he turns on his heel and stalks off into the night. I let out a heavy sigh. Wes is right. I do need to consider his feelings, but Kerrigan also needs to find justice. He's right, I have a big decision to make. I should probably walk away from this case. Until then, we'll just have to wait to see what the morning brings . . .

chapter 14
no dice

SHIT! There's nothing I can do right now, and I hate that. Wes has gone home—to our home—the home we share together because three weeks ago I let my shitty apartment go once and for all. In reality, it's his home and always will be if he walks away from me.

Not a fucking chance.

For all the running that I did and the chasing Wes did, I am not letting him walk away without a fight. Too damn bad. No dice. We're engaged. I wear a ring the size of Rudolph's red nose—*his ring*—on my left hand. Our families are planning the most ostentatious wedding this side of the Hudson. He is not going to run from me.

I do, however, have to interview this bartender and follow up with the scene before turning it over to another detective. That means sticking around here until the wee hours of the morning and then crawling home to shower and hold onto Wes like my life depends on it.

That is going to prove more difficult that I had originally thought because I don't have a car. I do have house keys though, so I can still get in. Wes is mad, but he would never lock me out. The hurt and the fear that flashed in his whiskey eyes cut me to the quick. He's got his back up because he's scared, and not for himself, but for me.

No, Wes isn't ready to walk away, to throw in the towel on us, but he is asking me to pick him, and that is exactly what I'm going to do. When I think of all the things I have put Wes through over the last year, really the last thirty, he needs me to choose him. He has stuck by me through everything. Every little thing and not so little thing. It's time I stood by him too. I pull my phone out of my pocket and dial the one number I know I need to right now.

"Hey, Sis, what's up?" Lee answers after the first ring.

"I have a situation, think you can come down here and help a gal out?" I ask my big brother for a favor.

"Thank you, Jesus," he mumbles in the background. Clearly things haven't been all sunshine and roses at Casa Goodnite since Wes and I left for the homicide. "I'll be right there. Where are you?"

"I'm in the alleyway behind the *Pig & Chicken* on the corner of Fourth and Main."

"I know exactly where that is." Of course, he does. My trampy brother knows all the bars around town. Where else would he pick up all of his ladies of right now? The exact ones that got him in this predicament with my two best friends. *My only two friends*. I could just kill him sometimes.

"See you soon," I say before ending the call.

I walk back over to the door to the bar where the officer is waiting for me. He gives me a wary look after witnessing the entire embarrassing ordeal with Wes and then my calling my brother for help. I let out a heavy sigh before pressing forward. My street cred as a crazy badass is going to be sorely lacking after this.

"Let's go talk to the bartender," I say as he lifts the tape up for me one more time.

"Sure thing, Detective." He does not say another word. He does not comment on all that he's seen or voice his opinion. He will never know how much I truly appreciate that in this moment.

We push through the back door of the bar, careful not to disturb the crime scene. The bar is empty, having been shut down shortly after the body was discovered. Only low overhead lights are still on giving the room an eerie glow.

The officer leads me down a small hallway off of the back of the building towards an office. The bright fluorescent lights leak out of the partially closed doorway. I knock on the door jamb.

"Come in," a gruff voice says.

I push open the door and see a man about my age with a decent build, slumped over his desk with his face in his hands. I can't really blame him. Seeing a murder victim like that changes you and never for the good.

"I'm Detective Goodnite," I say introducing myself. "I'd like to ask you a few questions."

"Good," he says with his voice muffled by his arms. "I'd like to answer those questions and then fall deep down into a bottle of bourbon." And again, I can't blame him. Sometimes that's my own answer to the nightmares that plague me even if it's not completely healthy and Anna would cringe.

When he looks up and lets his eyes meet mine I see the shock in them. I am almost certain that this man had nothing to do with the appearance of Kerrigan Adams's body in the back alley behind his bar.

"Would you please tell me, in your own words, what happened tonight?"

"It was about eight and there was a lull in the crowd. It's never really busy on a Monday night anyways. Everyone is still recovering from the weekend. But I took the opportunity to take the trash out."

He pauses, taking a deep breath before continuing. I don't stop him. He obviously needs to regain a little bit of his composure.

"When I opened the door, I didn't see her." He runs his hand through his hair and I watch it shake. "The dumpster is straight out the door and I didn't see her. I had my back to her. But when I turned around, there she was, leaning up against the wall."

"What did you do then?" I ask.

"I touched my fingers to her throat looking for a pulse, but I knew. I looked in her opened eyes and just knew that I wouldn't find one. That was when I saw the . . . the marks on her torso and . . ."

"And what?" I ask.

"I threw up in the alley and then called 9-1-1." Most people do when they see a dead body for the first time and this one was particularly gruesome, so I don't blame him.

"Did you stay with her out there or did you go back inside?" I ask him.

"I went back inside to tell the assistant bartender to man the bar while I was waiting for the cops."

"And then what did you do?" I ask.

"I told them everything I just told you and showed them where she was when they showed up. When they told me to clear out the bar, I did. And when they told me to wait inside I came in here."

"Have you ever seen that woman here before?" I press on.

"No, but it's a busy bar. She could be in often and I wouldn't know if she's not someone I'm looking for, you know?"

"She's not your type," I surmise.

"She's not batting with the right equipment." He smiles cheekily before remembering what had happened to her behind his bar and letting his smile slip off his handsome face.

"Gotcha," I say. "Thank you for your time. If I need anything else, I'll let you know."

"Thanks," he says quietly.

"Enjoy the bourbon. Do you need someone to get you home safely?" I ask him.

"No, I think I'll take it to go," he says while looking me in the eyes and I believe him. I breathe a sigh of relief knowing that we won't be scraping him off of a tree or a guardrail later tonight because he couldn't deal with what he saw here and decided to combat that experience with booze before climbing behind the wheel of a vehicle.

"Good," I say before heading back out into the hallway.

I push back through to the door and out into the alleyway. The body has been moved, probably taken to the morgue where Emma will get to work on her in the morning. Tonight, her technicians will get me a positive fingerprint ID before moving on.

The most exciting find is that Lee is there and looking very relieved to be at a crime scene at ten in the evening.

"Well, if it isn't the prodigal son." I smirk.

"What do you have, Goodnite?" he asks. "I didn't come here to be harassed. For that I could have stayed at Mom and Dad's place."

"Things still rough with the ladies?" I ask.

"She hates me," he says on a sigh.

"She does," I agree.

"She took every opportunity after you left to call me an asshole in the most poignant ways."

"I'm not surprised, and you shouldn't be either. Honestly, what did you expect, Lee?" I ask letting my frustration seep into my voice.

"Not to fall in love with her," he says so quiet I almost didn't hear him.

"Excuse me, Detective," one of the officers interrupts. "We have a positive ID on the victim confirmed as Kerrigan Adams."

"Thank you," tell him.

"Has she been transported yet?" Lee asks the officer.

"Yes, Sir. The body mover just left with her," Officer Rodriguez informs us.

"Thank you," Lee also tells him. "Detective Goodnite and I will make the notification call to her next of kin."

"Yes, Sir," he says before leaving.

"Shall we?" Lee asks me.

"Yeah," I sigh.

We head down the alleyway to where his own SUV is waiting and climb in. Lee starts the engine and heads back towards our childhood home. He pulls over at the curb in front of the Adams's home.

"You ready?" he turns to ask me before we step out of the car.

"I never am."

"Me either," he sighs.

"Let's get it over with then," I say as the digital clock on the dash flips to midnight.

The walk up to their front door has my stomach turning in knots. Lee rings the doorbell and we stand there and wait. When the porch light flips on a calm rolls over me and a steel climbs up my spine. This is my job and I will do it well. This is my duty to them and their daughter and I will see it carried out.

The front door opens and Mr. Adams takes one look at me before calling up the stairs, "You better come on down, Molly."

He nods pushing open the front door but doesn't say anything to Lee or me. We follow him inside to the living room, Mrs. Adams is standing there in her robe and nightgown. When she sees me her face crumples and she begins to cry. Mr. Adams moves to her pulls her into his arms. Lee and I stand there giving them a moment before I give them the words we all hoped I never would.

"This is Captain Goodnite," I say pointing to Lee.

"I remember you," Mr. Adams says to him. "You had the biggest crush on our Kerry and she wouldn't give you the time of day, poor boy."

"That's true," Lee says with a soft smile playing about his mouth as he takes a walk down memory lane.

"I always liked you. Thought you treated her with kindness and respect even when she didn't deserve it," Mike Adams shares.

"I try," Lee says softly.

"She must be your sister," he says nodding towards me.

"She is," Lee confirms.

"Last I saw of her she was an itty-bitty thing. I didn't put two and two together when she was here earlier, but I see it now. You should be proud of her," he says to Lee.

"I am, Sir," Lee says, and I can hear the truth in his words. Despite the spike in blood pressure I cause him on a daily basis, Lee *is* proud of me.

"Thank you," I say softly.

"I'm ready now," he says looking me in the eyes. "Tell me what you can here to say."

"Mr. Adams, it is with our deepest sympathies that we have come here to inform you that the body of your daughter, Kerrigan Adams, has been recovered this evening," Lee says in his modest but commanding tone of voice.

"No!" Mrs. Adams cries but Mr. Adams looks on, I think he always knew this was the ending they would get. Stand up people like Kerrigan don't just run off one day.

"Was it an accident?" he asks.

"No, Sir," Lee answers.

"Can you tell me what happened?" he asks.

"Not at this time due to pending investigation but you need to know that your daughter was murdered," Lee says softly.

"What?" he cries. "Who would do this? My Kerry is a good girl!"

"I don't know," Lee says. "But we're going to find out."

Shit! I think. I never got around to telling him I need off this case. Fuck! How am I going to do that now? The web of my life is twisting tighter and tighter. Something tells me that before it's all said and done, I'll realize that I have made a terrible mistake.

• • •

It's after one in the morning by the time Lee pulls up in front of our home.

"You gonna be okay, kid?" Lee asks me just as I reach for my seatbelt to climb out of the SUV.

"Of course," I answer. "Why wouldn't I be?"

"I heard about the fight," he says, his voice low but it still resonates in the dark car.

"I don't know what you're talking about," I lie.

"You do," he presses on. "Wes freaked out when he saw the body and demanded that you choose between him and the case."

I pause hoping that the right response will pop into my head, but truthfully, I'm too freaking tired to come up with anything that will remotely sound plausible. When I open mouth with the intent to just let anything fall out, Lee stops me in my tracks.

"Don't even bother lying to me."

"Fine," I snap. "We fought. It was unpleasant. He left. End of story."

"You need off this case," he surmises. This might be my opening. I might be able to get Lee to let me off this case easy. But I need to tread lightly because it's Lee and because he can be an ass sometimes.

"I don't," I say denying the truth of it.

"You do," Lee presses.

"I do." I sigh.

"We're loaded down with cases department wide. I'll do my best, but I can't make any guarantees." Yes, I am getting off this case. Lee is going to help me out and I am so relieved.

"Just try," I plead.

"I will," my brother promises me.

"Thanks, Lee." I smile at him and I really appreciate his willingness to help me out of this tight spot. It makes me feel like everything is going to be just fine and I had nothing to worry about. Now, I need to get upstairs to be with my guy, *my forever guy*.

"Anything for you, kiddo."

"I hate when you call me that," I tell him making a smile tug at the corner of his lips. It makes him seem younger, softer, a little less rough around the edges even. I can see why both of my best friends are in love with him.

"I know." He laughs. That ass.

"And there you go, you just had to ruin the moment," I say as I push open the car door.

"I'll talk to him and try to explain things," Lee offers.

"He'll just think it's an excuse on my part to have my cake and eat it too." By the look on his face Lee knows that I'm right. It'll blow up in both of our faces and cost us both having Wes in our lives. That's not something I am willing to risk for either of us. Not now, not ever.

"Okay, your call. Just let me know," he says before I close the door and head up the front walk.

The house is totally dark. There is not light welcoming me home on the front porch, no lights left on in the front of the house, down the hall, or up the stairs. The sight is chilling. Above all I can't help but think that Wes didn't expect me to come home, he didn't expect me to choose him.

I climb the stairs in the dark, walk straight down the hall, and through our bedroom into the closet. I lock my sidearm and my drop gun into the small safe and pull of my boots letting them fall to the closet floor. I shimmy out of my jeans and do that bra pull through trick that junior high girls do to change in the locker room and drop my bra on the floor with everything else.

I pad my way back into the bedroom in nothing but panties, my t-shirt, and a pair of tall socks because Wes runs so hot the air conditioning is always set to arctic tundra. When I look at him, he's sound asleep. Wes doesn't even know that I'm home and I'm so afraid to tell him that I'm not officially off of the case that I don't want to wake him only to make up some lame excuses.

I pull the comforter and sheet back as gently as possible before climbing in. I roll over and wrap my arms around Wes, my front to his back with my forehead pressed to the center of his back. He does not move. With him safely asleep and oblivious to me I feel like I can finally pour my heart out, so I do.

"I love you Wes. With my whole heart, I love you. I talked to Lee tonight and he's going to do the best that he can to get me off of the Adams case. I know you won't believe me when you hear it, but it's true. This is me picking you. You told me to make up my own mind and it's you. I love you and this is me choosing you."

I thought I felt his body tighten under mine just a smidge but then it was gone. I close my eyes and hope to God that in the morning everything will be right again, that the sinking feeling in the pit of my stomach is nothing. But as I drift off into sleep I don't see that Wes wasn't asleep and not only didn't believe me, but that he was very, very disappointed in me. That maybe I should have realized that my gut is never wrong.

chapter 15
bad

"COME OUT OF THE closet, baby."

"No," I whisper, tears hot on my face and snot stuffing up my nose. Liam and Wes were right, I'm just a baby. A big kid wouldn't be crying in the dark corner of a closet hoping it'll all go away if you just wish hard enough. I bet Wes never cries. I know Lee doesn't.

"Come out now, Claire. Playtime is over."

"No," I cry louder. "Please don't make me."

"Now!" He growls as the closet door rattles. I gasp.

"Leave me alone!"

"Get out of the fucking closet, Claire!" he roars.

"Please no," I cry harder, my body shaking with each sob.

"When," he kicks his hard boots against the closet door and it shudders.

"Please."

"Are you." He kicks it again.

The doors are the kind with the slats that fold sideways. We have them at home and mama says I always pinch my fingers in the accordion. Whatever that is.

"I just wanna go home," I whisper.

"Gonna," he kicks again.

"I just want my mommy," I sob. "Please. I just want my mommy." I want my family. I want my mommy and daddy. I want my brother and Wes.

"Fucking," the boards snaps and I scream.

"I just wanna go home, please," I beg. Lee and Wes wouldn't kick at me like this. Why does the man hate me? Why is he being so mean? I just don't know. I don't know why.

"Learn!" he shouts as he kicks the broken boards out of the way. He leans down and grabs me by my upper arms.

"Please," I wheeze but my words are cut short when he slaps my face hard. So hard I taste blood in my mouth and it's so yucky I feel sick. I'm going to throw up from the yucky taste. I try as hard as I can not to. I know that if I do, he'll punish me again. I don't want that. Anything but that.

"You are home, baby," he coos right before he slaps me again. I cry out again, falling to the floor with his last hit. It's so strong he knocks me down with it. "And I thought I told you to call me daddy," he says as he lands a hard kick to my back.

"You're not my daddy, you'll never be my daddy," I whisper. "My daddy *is a nice man. He would never hurt me. You'll never be my daddy," I say again but the bad man can't hear me, he already walked away.*

I have nowhere to go except back into the closet, but one thing is for sure, no one will ever hit me or hurt me again. I'm going to make sure of it.

• • •

I wake with a resolve that I have never felt before.

For the first time in my life, my priorities are in order. Before I felt like I had nothing to keep me going but my job, which I love, but that wasn't entirely true. My job was all I had allowed in. But not anymore.

Now, I realize that the scope of my world is broader. I have my job and it's amazing, fulfilling, everything I could want, but I also have my family now without the barriers of my struggles between us. There are no more secrets. Because of that, Lee and I have a better relationship than ever. He no longer threatens to fire me every week and we work together well as part of a larger team.

I also have let in friends, for the first time in my adult life. When Anna started as my department shrink, I didn't trust her. I didn't believe that she had my best interests at heart, but now, I see that she has always had my best interests at heart. Even when that went against what Lee was paying her for. She has become my anchor in the fog of my broken memories, she's my voice of reason when I need it. And Emma, once just a colleague, is now my truth. She keeps me grounded but also pushes me when I need it. Emma with her brash tone and unvarnished opinions keeps life interesting. Both are totally opposite in every way and yet, I love them both equally. The sisters of my heart.

But with all this knowledge, with all of the people that my world includes, the center of that is and if I'm being honest with myself, has always been Wes. He has protected me and loved me, encouraged me and been by my side from the moment he realized this was our time. The only time we were ever going to get. We couldn't go backwards, but we can go forward.

It's time that I offer Wes the same unconditional love that he shows me.

I roll over to wrap him in my arms and tell him how much that I love him, to reassure him that everything is going to be alright, and to share with him the words I gave to him when he was asleep. But when I reach for him all I encounter is cold sheets and the stark realization that without a kiss goodbye or even a word, Wes is gone. Wes is gone from our bed, from our home, and I can't help the overwhelming feeling of being left behind.

This can be nothing but bad.

chapter 16
a scarlet letter

A DARK CLOUD HOVERS over me as I step into the shower—alone. It wasn't long after I had realized that Wes was gone that I had lost it. I completely lost it. When my hand encountered nothing but cold sheets, I clutched his pillow in my grasp and pulled it into my chest. The warm, woodsy scent that belongs exclusively to Wes still clung to the gray cotton and I buried my face in its pillowy softness and inhaled deeply.

And then I promptly burst into tears.

I let myself bawl for what felt like years, but in reality was only thirty minutes or so. Then I pushed myself up to sit on the edge of the bed, letting my feet hang over the side. I reached over to the bedside table and picked up my phone, dialing the one number who would never turn me away.

"Hello?" she answered. It's early still and I can hear the sleep still clinging to her smoky voice.

"Hey, Anna," I hurried to continue, not bothering to take a breath for fear that the words I need to say will choke me. That I will chicken out and refuse to say them. "It's me. I think I screwed up."

"Now why every would you think that?" she asked.

I wiped my eyes and sighed. "Because I did."

"How?" she said softly, ever the shrink our Anna is, always making me do all the talking while she only asks a question here and there.

"When we got to the crime scene last night," I explained. "It wasn't just a robbery gone bad . . . it was more."

"How so?" she asks me.

"A stabbing, a bad one," I answered.

"Well, that can't be out of the realm of possibility for a detective and a federal agent, can it?" she asks.

"Not normally, no . . ."

"But?" she asked. "Why do I feel like there is more?"

"Because there always is." I let out a weary sigh. "She was leaning up against the wall of the bar. Left there and there were these markings carved into her body. I couldn't see what," I described.

"I take it that she's your missing person?"

"Yes."

"Then what happened?" she asked.

"Wes took one look at her and the way she was dropped at the scene and freaked out," I explain. "I told him it wasn't his choice what I do with my career. While usually that would be correct, I can't help but feel like in this instance, I was wrong. But he just made me so mad!"

"Can you blame him?" she asked me.

"No," I groaned. "No, I can't. But we fought anyways."

"What did you fight about?" she asks me.

"He told me to drop the case," I say. "He told me he wasn't going to stick around and watch me die at the hands of another serial killer."

"Did you?" she asks. "Drop the case, I mean."

"Not at all . . . at least not at that moment. I was too mad at being ordered around at a scene," I admit embarrassed.

"Then what happened?" she questions.

"He got so mad, Anna," I whispered feeling the tears sting the back of my eyes again. "He told me—*in front of everyone*—that he knew I wouldn't choose him and then he left."

"And what did you do?" she had asked me.

"I called Lee for help. He showed up after I had talked to the bartender and we waited for a positive ID on the victim, which we now have. Lee and I went and informed the next of kin, which was awful. Then he drove me home."

"And how was Wes when you got home?" Anna asks.

"Asleep." By now the tears are streaming down my face unchecked. I sniffle. "He didn't leave on any welcoming lights, Anna."

"Welcoming lights?" she asked. "I'm not sure I understand you."

"He didn't leave on the porch light or the hall light or the one in the living room!" I shout panicking. "He didn't even leave on a bathroom light. Anna, Wes didn't think I was coming home to him, but I did. I had told Lee I couldn't work this case anymore. That I had to choose Wes."

"And what did Lee say?"

I sigh. "He said the department was stretched too thin right now and that he couldn't spare me but that he would try."

"I'm beginning to think he might be a bit of the ass Emma swears he is," she had mumbled but I just kept going, lost in my freak out.

"But when I climbed into bed, I had told him everything. I told him how much I love him and that I'm choosing him, that I will always choose him."

"And what did Wes say?"

"Nothing. He was asleep," I tell her.

"Claire—" Anna starts to warn me, but I cut her off.

"I know!" I bite my lip. "I told you I screwed up and I know it now. I thought I had time. But I didn't because when I woke up this morning, he was gone!"

"Maybe it's not as bad as you think . . ." she tries.

"He was gone, Anna, as in not in this fucking house!" I shout.

"Okay," she tried again. "Let's just take this one minute at a time. Okay?"

"Okay," I say taking a deep breath.

"Now, go get dressed. Go to work. Tell Lee to pull his head out of his ass. And call Wes and talk to him about it. All of it," Anna orders me about.

"Okay. I can do that," I say feeling much better for having a plan. Anna always knows how to calm me down when I'm freaking out.

"I know you can and honey?" she tells me and there's an encouraging kindness in her voice when she speaks to me like this that I treasure.

"Yeah?" I question.

"Everything will be fine."

And I mostly believed her as I showered and dressed for work in the early morning dark of the closet, but a dark cloud still hangs over me. I eat my bowl of cereal as quickly as I can before rinsing the bowl. It tastes like ash in my mouth. I pull my car keys off the hook by the door and realize I don't have a car because my department vehicle is once again at the station and I'm here.

"Fantastic," I mumble to myself as I pull my phone out of my pocket and order an Uber.

• • •

I push the glass front door of the station with a scowl on my face and my sunglasses covering my eyes. There is very little makeup on my face. I didn't even try to cover the bags from a late night at a crime scene and then an early morning crying. At the time I was getting dressed, I didn't even have it in me to try. Now that I'm walking in and looking at the faces of everyone I work with who by now have heard the latest chapter in the Claire and Wes tale of woe, I'm kind of wishing I had expended the effort. When I sit down everyone will take one look at my naked face and know without a doubt, that I chose wrong.

I walk straight to the kitchenette and pour myself the world's largest cup of coffee. As I stand there, I actually consider pouring the whole carafe into my mouth but I'm pretty sure that's not going to help me. So, I chug half of my mug letting it burn on the way down and reveling in that hurt. I need it. I embrace it. And then I tuck it away for later.

I top off my mug and head to my desk with my head held high, looking straight ahead. I refuse to cower or look anyone in the eye until I've had significantly more coffee than I have already consumed. I have just lowered my ass into my rickety office chair when the phone on my desk rings.

"Goodnite," I answer.

"Get your ass down here," Emma barks. *"You're going to want to see this."*

"Good morning to you too, Sunshine," I gripe.

"Har-de-har-har," she calls.

"I'm coming."

"That's what he said," she cackles into the phone before hanging up.

I groan as I push myself back up and out of this death trap on spiny wheels and snatch my cup of coffee up off of my desk, taking it with me. I stomp through the bullpen to the elevator and stab the call button with my index finger.

It dings its arrival cheerily and I feel anything but, my mood is sinking quicker than a New York football season. Still, I climb into the tin box and hope for the best even though I know that it's a wasted effort.

The doors pop open and spit me out into Emma's evil lair.

"Well, look what the cat dragged in," she says with a smile on her face that I just can't deal with right now.

"Yep, I'm here. Now tell me why," I demand.

"Well aren't we just a little merry ray of fucking sunshine this morning." Emma looks at me with a keen eye. I'm not really wanting to rehash everything but I'm also planning on sticking with my resolutions as of last night. That means not alienating one of the few people in my life who tolerate me well. Plus, I already told Anna, so I might as well even the score.

"I take it you haven't been to the water cooler yet to hear all of the juicy office gossip." I sigh.

"Oh, I have. I just wanted to see your face while you try and deny it," she says casually.

"It's true," I concede.

"How much of it?" she asks.

"Probably all of it. What did you hear?"

"In short?" she asks me.

"That will do."

"That Wes lost his shit at a crime scene last night and demanded you step down from the case, which you promptly told him to put in his pipe and smoke it. He then told you he didn't expect you to choose him and he wasn't going to stick around to watch you be gunned down by another sicko so he left."

"Is that all?" I deadpan.

"Well, you're down here, asking about the case, looking like hammered horse shit, so I'm assuming you chose wrong and are suffering the consequences." She takes a deep breath before pressing on. "I thought you were smarter than that!"

"Thank you," I sigh. "And I am but Lee won't let me off the case until we have someone to take it. So, I'm stuck."

"I always knew he was a miserable asshole," she mumbles.

"And besides, you called me." I shrug my shoulder and wink at her.

"So what if I did?" she asks looking down her nose at me.

"Well, then what the hell am I doing here?" I laugh at Emma's ridiculousness. There is this air of fun and a little crazy about her that balances perfectly with the utterly awful shit we see on this job. It makes me appreciate her more every day. I'm glad she's my friend.

"Oh, right," she says. "I wanted to show you what I found when we cleaned the body," she tells me.

"You mean the weird markings?"

"Yep."

"Well, what are they?" I ask losing my patience.

"Not markings, an initial."

"Like letters?" I ask. Shit I was right. I was hoping against hope that this case wasn't going to be weird, but it looks like today isn't my day to get the things that I want and I'd bet five dollars that my magic eight ball would show me that tomorrow's outlook isn't going to be so good either.

"Yes, well, a letter. To be specific the letter A," she says showing where she has cleaned the wounds and now you can see that the initial isn't as deep as the other stab wounds. I think it's safe to say that this was done on purpose. *Fantastic.*

Emma lifts up the sheet that was covering the body of Kerrigan Addams and folds it down to cover her breast. Sure enough, there over her clavicle, it the letter A carved into her skin.

"That's gruesome," I say thinking my thoughts allowed.

"It is. No wonder Wes lost his mind," she muses.

"Yeah, something like that," I agree.

"Are you going to cut him some slack?" she asks me. "Or are you going to kill this love story before it ever has a chance?"

"When did you become such a romantic?" I ask.

"I'm not and don't change the subject," Emma warns me. "But it's different for you. You have a chance at the holy grail, the full package with a decent package and I don't want to see you piss it away."

"I'll cut him some slack when he gives me a chance to explain," I answer.

"What do you mean?"

"Your knight in shining fed suit left before I had a chance to talk to him this morning. He's clearly nursing a grudge." I can't help the sigh that slips from my lips and there's a stinging behind my eyes every time I think about waking up alone and without Wes.

"Can you blame him?"

"Probably not," I say before changing the subject. "Can you email me some pictures of the carvings?"

"Sure thing," she says. "Maybe he'll show tonight."

I let out a groan. "Fuck! I forgot all about marriage counseling."

"I'm sure it'll be great." She laughs.

"Can you fail marriage counseling on the first night?" I ask half seriously.

"Well if anyone can it'll be you," she laughs again. "But I'm mostly sure that you'll be alright. Probably."

"On that depressing note, I'm going back to work," I tell her.

I climb into the elevator and ride it back upstairs. As soon as the door opens Lee bellows my name from within his sanctuary.

"Goodnite!" Lee shouts from his office.

"Seriously, how does he do that?" I grumble as I stalk over to his doorway.

"Yes?" I ask as I push open his door.

"Sit down," he orders.

"I don't wanna. I'll stand thanks," I say going out of my way to behave like a brat because I had a shitty night and a worse morning. I'm not willing to add Lee's shit to that long list of very unfortunate events.

"Can you cut me some slack, please?" he asks.

"Probably not, but I suppose I could try."

"How magnanimous of you, Your Highness." He rolls his eyes.

"Thank you," I bow and Lee laughs. "So, what's up?"

"Do you have autopsy results?" Lee asks me.

"I do. Kerrigan was stabbed to death, probably not behind the bar and the letter A was carved into her chest post mortem."

"That's gruesome," he says.

I sigh. "It is."

"A lover maybe?" he adds his theories into the pot.

"Her parents and coworkers say she wasn't seeing anyone," I answer.

"She could have been keeping it quiet—"

"Lee," I begin. That asshole is going to fuck me over. I can just feel it.

"Claire," he answers. "There's no proof."

"Lee," I start again. "You promised."

"There is no evidence that this is a serial killer, Detective Goodnite," he barks.

"You promised!" I shout at him.

"As your commanding officer I am telling you that this is the case that you were assigned. You will follow orders." Lee squares off with me and I have never been more hurt by his actions and angry with him before. Including all the times he tried to fire me and give my cases to Wes.

"You can't be serious . . . Lee?" I ask, hating all the while how small and scared my voice sounds.

"As a fucking heart attack," he growls at me.

"You miserable asshole," I bark leaning forward and placing my palms on his desk.

"Watch yourself, Detective," he warns, his voice low. "You are treading on very thin ice."

"You are miserable and alone in a bed of your own making and you can't stand to see Wes and I happy. I never thought the day would come when you would sabotage something so special to me. Something that I finally have that is so good and so real, because you've become such a fucking prick," I say standing and making my way to the door.

"You could always leave you gun and badge on my desk and see your way out of my department, Detective," Lee threatens.

"You would just love that, wouldn't you?"

"It won't break my heart." He shrugs his shoulder.

"Be careful what you wish for, Captain," I say before walking out the door. It only takes one quick look to realize that everyone heard. Everyone, even

Emma, is standing around all wearing sad expressions on their faces. Well, not Emma, she looks pissed? Maybe, disappointed? Definitely.

But I can't bother with that now. Now, I have work to do. But I'll regret that later too.

chapter 17
incompatible

I SPEND THE REST of the day going over case notes and tracking down witness statements all with the feeling of impending doom looming in front of me.

By the time five o'clock rolls around I am a nervous wreck. I grab my keys from my desk drawer after shutting down my geriatric computer and head out to the lot. I haven't seen or heard from Wes all day and now all I can think about is being stood up for marriage classes.

That would be my worst nightmare.

I push through the glass doors and out to where my Tahoe is waiting in the back of the lot. It's eerie out here and I can't help the shiver that wracks down my spine. My Gran would say someone just stepped on my grave. I certainly hope not.

I beep the locks with my key fob and climb in pulling the door firmly shut behind me and hitting the locks. I fire up the engine and head towards my family church. Or impending doom. Whichever comes first.

The drive isn't nearly long enough to get my head on straight, but it was just enough to allow me to work myself up even more. By the time I pull into the parking lot, I have convinced myself that Wes will be a no show.

I park in the first available space and climb out. I spot Lee on the steps of the church trying to talk to Emma who is ignoring him in favor of Anna. Oh Lee, how could you be so incredibly stupid? I hustle up the steps at ten minutes until the hour when all of our groups are meeting.

Anna takes one look at me and shakes her head in the negative. I let out a harsh sigh.

"He could still show . . ." Emma tries to make me feel better. My vision is floating again, and my nose is burning. Shit I don't want to cry in front of all of these people.

"Yeah," I say softly.

"Claire, I'm—" Lee starts but he's cut off by Wes running up the steps just as the priest opens the doors.

"Sorry I'm late," he says. "There was a pile up on the turnpike."

"Okay," I say softly as he places his hand on the small of my back guiding me into the sanctuary.

"We'll talk later," he says as he leans in, his lips to my ear for only me to hear. All of the hope I felt upon seeing him comes crashing down like a balloon with a hole in it. Maybe that's exactly what we are—a popped balloon.

"Okay," I say softly before I choke up.

"Who's ready for Tuesday Singles?" the young priest asks. "Well, come on inside!"

Anna and Emma follow directly behind the priest with Lee on their heels. There are a few more men lingering in the parking lot but I'm sure they'll make their way in soon. A gaggle of three women I have never met before—but their whole appearance screams man eater—follow Lee in like they just broke their Weight Watchers plan and he's a Krispy Kreme.

"I hope I get to sit next to him," one says.

"Don't worry about that," another chimes in. "He won't be single for long if I have anything to say about it."

"He looked pretty interested in the blonde," the third adds.

"Like I said, don't worry about it." And then they all follow him in cackling.

"Oh shit," I mumble more to myself than anyone.

"It's Lee's mistake to make, Claire," he warns. "You know that."

"I do," I agree. "But I don't have to like it.."

"Maybe it'll be good for him." Wes shrugs his shoulder. "Or maybe he'll fuck it up like we all think he will." I sigh.

"You're not helping," I whisper.

"I know." He sighs. Wes opens his mouth to say something else, but the older priest walks out of an office interrupting him.

"You must be Claire and Wesley."

"Yes, Father," we say in unison.

"Well, that's off to a good start," the priest jokes. If only he knew that it was all downhill from there. "Right this way."

We follow him back down a hall and into another office when he motions for us to sit down in a pair of chairs facing a third chair.

"Can I get either of you something to drink before we begin?" Father Matthew asks kindly.

"No, thank you," I say.

"No, I'm good. Thank you, Father," Wes adds.

The priest lowers himself into the chair across from us and opens a folder in his lap—a dossier really. I wonder how he can have that much information on Wes and me already but the answer is clear. Gran.

"Now," The priest begins. "Let's get to know each other a bit. It says here that you, Wesley, are an FBI agent."

"Yes, Sir," he answers.

"How exciting!"

"Not really," Wes laughs. "It's mostly paperwork."

"So, nothing like the movies?" Father Matthew asks.

"No," Wes says although we both know the last year has seemed like one thriller after another.

"And you, Claire," he turns to me.

"Yes?"

"You are a detective with the George Washington Township PD."

"Yes," I answer.

"Well, is that exciting?" he asks me.

"It can be," I hedge. Wes snorts pushing the worry I had spun up all afternoon out of the way and into a full blown mad. "It's mostly tedious."

"Sure, it is," Wes mumbles.

"And do you find it fulfilling?" he asks me.

"I do," I sigh.

"You don't anymore?"

"I do . . . at least I did. Today, I'm just tired." And I am. There is a world weariness on my shoulders knowing that Wes is so angry with me all because he doesn't understand. I feel frustrated—trapped really—in an outcome that's not only not of my choosing, but I also can't fix it.

"Ha!" Wes laughs sarcastically. "Claire will always find her job fulfilling."

"That's not true," I tell him.

"Isn't it, though?" Wes asks.

"No, it's not," I tell him. "If you had stopped for one minute today to listen to me, or even stuck around this morning, you would know that you are wrong right now."

"So, you're not on the Adams case anymore?" he asks. Wes leans back in his chair crossing his arms over his chest as if he hasn't a care in the world. It's a trap and we both know it. I narrow my eyes on him.

"Well . . ." I hedge.

"So, you are still on the case?" he questions me with that formidable look on his face and his whole-body language that he shows suspects that he does not believe and that kills.

"Yes," I admit to him feeling like I'm boxed into a corner and I can't find my way out. This is like an out of body experience. A nightmare.

"Do you not want Claire on this case?" Father Matthew asks.

"Claire knows how I feel," Wes says as he crosses his arms over his chest.

"And how does Wes feel, Claire?" Father Matthew asks me.

"He wants me off the case," I admit.

"But you're still on the case knowing how your partner feels about the situation?"

"Yes," I sigh. "But it's not what you think."

"Yeah, right," Wes barks.

"It's true!" I shout. "I talked to Lee last night. I asked him to take me off the Adams case."

"Then why are you still working it?" Wes asks, his voice deadly quiet. Wes might bellow and yell and make a lot of noise, but the truth is, he's most dangerous when he's quiet.

"Because the department is overwhelmed right now. Lee won't let me off the case," I explain knowing that after all we have been through, if I didn't know it was true, it would sound like bullshit to my own ears.

"Bullshit!" Wes thunders.

"It's true! He told me this morning that I could work the case and take my orders with a smile on my fucking face or I could turn in my badge." The pain in my voice at my brother's betrayal is there for anyone to hear if they are listening.

"Lee would want you off this case more than anyone. Even me."

"You would think that, but he doesn't, for whatever reason." I feel a scowl pull at my face. I know what the asshole formerly known as my brother is up to. He wants a link to Emma through me and if he can't have her, it won't bother him if my relationship falls to shit too.

"But you know why?" Wes asks me. I shrug. "Claire."

"I don't know for sure," I sigh. "But I think he wants a link to Emma through me."

"He wouldn't sink that low over a woman," Wes says. I just raise my brow in question. "Well, maybe for this one he would. But still . . ."

"Lee and Emma?" Father Matthew asks. "Two of our new singles members?"

"Yes, exactly," I answer.

"You're lying," Wes rallies. "Lee wouldn't sabotage my relationship because he's bitter."

I let out a heavy breath but so does the priest.

"I have to admit, your relationship is a little daunting," he starts.

"You're telling me," I gripe.

"At this juncture, I think you should go home and really evaluate what you want here." I look to the priest with wide eyes.

"What do you mean?" I ask starting to panic.

"I have to say, at least on paper, you two might be the most incompatible couple I have ever met." He sighs. "I'm sorry, but I'm not sure you should be getting married."

"Oh, okay," I say feeling dejected. I was wrong. Wes not showing up was bad but not the end of the world. Even a priest knows that we don't belong together. The only problem is, I don't want anyone else. Only Wes.

"Hold up," Wes says. "We're plenty compatible as long as she isn't lying to me."

"I'm not lying," I say feeling beyond exhausted, both physically and mentally all of a sudden.

"I'm going to stay in a hotel near the office tonight. Let me know when you decide to be honest," he says to me.

"Don't bother," I say as I stand up and head for the door to the office. "It's your house. Just give me an hour to get some stuff together." I don't have anything but some old shitty furniture there, but the apartment is still mine. I could go back there at any time. Part of me wonders if I haven't let it go yet because I always knew, even if only in the back of my mind, that this was going to happen all along.

"Claire, wait," Wes demands, but I don't. I'm so tired and disappointed and hurt. It really hurts that he's so quick to believe I lied to him to stay on the case.

I pull open the door with Wes on my heels. It takes only a second to realize that the entire singles group heard everything. Lee looks uncomfortable as he swallows hard.

"Lee? Brother, is it true?" Wes asks.

A disgusted look flashes across Emma's face while Anna just looks so very sad. I catch Lee's quick nod before pushing my out of the church and through the parking lot to my SUV. When I climb inside and start the engine my hands shake.

But it's not until I'm driving away that I let the tears fall.

chapter 18

so fucking sorry

I DON'T RUSH HOME or drive like a crazy person. I know what waits for me and that's okay. It's not okay, but I'm not going to die on the turnpike because I got my feelings hurt. But now I just want to get in there, get my shit and get gone before I lose it. I'm walking a knife's edge of emotions right now.

I pull into the driveway and put it in park before climbing out.

My whole body starts to shake, little by little, rolling over me like a wave cresting in the ocean, as I make my way up the front walk, as I unlock the front door and walk through the house. I stop in the kitchen and grab the bottle of bourbon that I keep for very special occasions as these. I don't open it, just carry it with me to stick in my bag. I'll drink it later when I'm back in my shit hole apartment.

I walk up the stairs and into the bedroom setting the bottle on top of the dresser. By the time I walk through the bedroom and see the bed where we had slept together for the last time with the sheets still rumpled.

I didn't have it in me to make the bed this morning after I woke up and knew that Wes was gone.

I have to cover my mouth with my hand to choke back a sob. The pain burns through my chest and a sweat breaks out all over my body. I feel sick to my stomach. I feel sick in my heart.

I take a deep, steadying breath. It doesn't help so I walk into the closet and grab my duffle bag off of a shelf. I toss it on the bed and open it before walking back into the closet. I let my tears flow freely, it's better to get them out than keep them in, but I only have an hour so I have to keep packing.

I grab a handful of t-shirts and underwear. I'll come back for a couple pairs of jeans and socks in a minute. I can only carry so much in my arms. I walk out of the closet and drop them in my bag.

"So that's it?" Wes asks from behind me making me jump because I didn't hear him come in. "You're just going to leave me?"

I turn to look at him, his face is a little bruised and his knuckles are bleeding. He's leaning against the dresser and drinking my bourbon straight from the bottle.

"You're the one who was going to sleep in a hotel," I answer. "This is your house. It always has been, and it always will be. I even always knew I would have to find a new place when you eventually moved on."

"And you think that's what I want?" he repeats my words back to me before taking another swig from the bottle. I can't read the look on his face to know what he's asking. "To move on?"

At this point I'm not even sure what he's asking. Wes was so angry that he wanted to sleep in a hotel instead of with me. That thought still burns. But now he's here and I'm not sure where we stand. I hate feeling like I am on uneven footing, like I might slip and fall at any moment.

"I'm not real sure of anything right now, Wes," I admit hearing my own voice thick with emotion.

"I'm sorry, Claire," Wes says as he sets down the bottle and moves closer to me. "I'm so fucking sorry."

"It's okay," I say softly as he pulls me into his arms. His lips are just inches away from mine, he smells like bourbon and Wes. It's a heady combination.

"It's not. Don't go," he pleads. "Don't go, baby. I never want you to go. I was just so mad . . . and scared."

"I know," I say lightly touching my fingertips to his bruised cheek. "What happened here?"

"I beat the shit out of your brother in a church." He lets out a heavy sigh.

"How did that come about?" I ask.

"I realized that he's being a dick because he put his life in the crapper and now he is taking it out on us," Wes sighs running a hand through his hair. "And I realized I should have believed you when I didn't. At the very least, I should have listened, and I got pissed when I looked at his face and realized the truth."

"Wow," I say for lack of anything better.

"I'm not one hundred percent sure we're going to be allowed back there. I'm also not one hundred percent sure I give a rat's ass either." I laugh, I can't help it. A lightness rolls over him slowly, like a dawn rising.

"He probably deserved it." I shrug.

"He did. Don't go, baby." He pulls me in tighter resting his forehead on mine.

"Okay," I say before his mouth crashes down on mine.

Wes does not conquer or plunder, he praises me with his mouth like a requiem before breaking away to sweep my bag and clothes onto the floor. The wildness of his actions takes my breath away. When he turns back to me and slowly peels my shirt from my body there's a tenderness in his eyes that I have never seen before. An unsure longing and a vulnerability brought out by the tension of the moment and the bourbon.

My bra goes next, Wes quickly unsnaps it and tosses it to the floor on top of my t-shirt. He cups my breasts in his hands tenderly before swiping his thumbs across my nipples and I arch my back into him. I have to hold onto his belt for balance. My fingertips sliding just underneath the waistband of his slacks to touch his hot skin where it lays hidden from view.

I slide my hands up underneath his shirt and rake my nails lightly down his abs before sliding them out and moving them to the placquet of buttons down the front. When each one is undone, I push the fabric from his shoulders and gasp at the deep purple bruise on his ribs. Tenderly, I touch the tip of my index finger to his still rapidly purpling bruise.

"Lee isn't one to take a beating lying down." He shrugs. "He got in a good punch or two. Now, where were we?" he asks as he grabs me by my ass and lifts me up, his hard length pressing against my center.

I have to grab hold of his shoulders to keep from falling when he bites down where my shoulder and neck meet, sucking the skin deeply. He soothes the hurt with his tongue and a tremor wracks my body. Wes is, after all, fantastic with his tongue.

And then I'm flying through the air, letting out an undignified squeak as I land in surprise. Not really flying, but falling quickly as Wes tossed me backwards onto the bed. I lay there and just watch without shame or trying to hide my interest at all as he undoes the buckle on his belt letting it hit the carpeted floor with a muted clank. He undoes the clasp and pulls down the zipper on his pants pushing them down with his boxer briefs. His hard cock springs free and I want it. I want him.

"I need you, Claire," he says as he pops the button on my jeans and pulls down the zipper.

"You have me, Wes," I breathe.

He pulls my jeans and panties down my legs before tossing them to the floor and he pushes my legs wide settling in between them, tracing a finger through my slit.

"Always so wet for me," he growls. "You're perfect."

"Wes," I beg. I can't help the needy sound to my voice as he circles his fingertip around my clit.

"I don't want to be too rough with you," he says as he replaces his finger with the tip of his cock. "I can't hurt you anymore.

"You can't hurt me even if you tried, Wes. I won't break. And besides, I like you wild," I say honestly.

"You really shouldn't have said that," he tells me as he plunges all the way in.

I moan and rock my hips into his as he pumps over and over. I scrape my nails down his back as he hits the spot deep inside me that drives me wild, scraping it over and over again.

"Don't ever leave me," he chants. "Don't ever leave."

"Never," I cry out as he thrusts harder and harder.

"You're mine, Claire," Wes growls as he moves faster and faster, more and more wild. "Say it."

"I'm yours," I say as I cling to him with my arms and legs wrapped tight around him as he moves faster and faster within my body.

"I need you, Claire," he pleads. "I need you so much."

"You have me," I say my voice high pitched and needy as he pumps his cock again and again. I'm so close that it won't take much to send me over the edge.

"I need you to get there," he says as my body clenches around him.

"Wes—" I pant, rocking against him to gain a little more friction. I just need a little . . . more.

"You're there." He thrusts hard.

"Yes," I tell Wes.

"And you'll never leave." He plunges in again.

"No, Never," I promise.

"You're mine." He moves faster and faster becoming more frantic as we get closer to the edge.

"Yes. Yes." I tuck my head into his shoulder needing as much of my skin touching his as possible.

"Only mine."

"Yes." And then I'm soaring, crying out his name, "Wes!" He plunges in one more time coming with me. We lay there, still clinging to each other. We've come too close to losing each other—what we have between us in one way or another—to not be moved by the moment. I feel the tears burn in my nose and behind my eyes.

"Why the tears?" he asks me softly as he wipes one away with the very tip of his index finger. "I hate to see you cry."

"I just love you so much," I whisper into the night.

I revel in the heavy feeling of his body pressing into me. And then he pulls out and rolls, taking me with him.

"I thought I had lost you tonight," he whispers into my hair.

"Me too," I tell him honestly. "It didn't feel very much like you wanted to have me."

"I'm so sorry," he says brushing my hair back from my face. "I'm so fucking sorry."

I lift his bruised and bloodied hand to my mouth and kiss just above his torn flesh. "Me too."

"I'm sorry I didn't believe you. It'll never happen again. I swear it on my life," he vows.

"Okay," I say softly not wanting to think about a time when he might have to cash in that vow. "I believe you."

"I believe you too," he says to me softly.

"I chose you, Wes," I tell him looking into his eyes so that he can see the truth lying there laid bare for all to see. "I'm going to always choose you from now on."

"I know," he says softly into the night. "And I'm going to do my best every day for the rest of my life to make sure that you never regret that."

"I know you will," I say with a mischievous twinkle in my eye.

"Oh yeah? How so?"

"You can start now," I say as I climb over him, straddling his hips. "I have a few ideas." And then I sink down over his hard cock.

Wes glides his hands up my sides, cupping a breast in each hand. I place my hands over his and squeeze showing him what I want as I start to move. I lean back letting his pull on my breast keep me balanced as I rise up and slide down his cock over and over again. His hips rise to meet mine each time making that slide down just a little bit sharper. Providing that little bit of bite that we both need.

"Wes," I pant. It's coming over me so fast that I'm helpless to stop it or slow it down.

"Yes," he growls as he thrusts his hips up again. "I want it, Claire."

"Yes, yes, yes," I chant as I rise up on my knees and drop down again and again. He moves his hands to my hips pulling me sharply down onto his cock harder and harder.

"Give it to me." And then I lean forward grabbing onto his shoulder for support as I come. Wes wraps his arms tight around me and shouts his release as he follows me over the edge.

And that is how I fell asleep, wrapped safely in Wes's arms, sprawled across his body. Sometime in the night he turned, curling his body around mine, protecting me from the storm, and it was the best night's sleep I ever had.

chapter 19

sorrier

I WAKE THE NEXT morning with the early morning sun streaming through the bedroom window curtains. I look over and see Wes, his face is softer in sleep, and I can't help but think that he might need a little TLC after the emotional run we took last night.

I slip below the blankets and slither down his body. I settle myself on my side, eye level with the neediest part of his body. I'm going to show him how I feel with my hands and mouth.

I take his firming cock in my hand and stroke him in my fist while I place soft kisses on Wes's upper thighs. He groans in his sleep when I swipe my tongue over the very tip of him making me smile.

He tips his hips towards what he wants, and I can't help but to give it to him. I take him deep into my mouth, slowly sliding down the length of him until I can't take anymore, before pulling back and swirling my tongue around the tip again. Letting the saliva pool in my mouth, I take him deep into my mouth again and again before a large, rough hand tangles in my hair.

"Claire—" he says, his voice rough with early mornings and steamy sex. "Baby, yeah—"

I grip his length in my fist and stroke while I swirl just the very tip of him in my mouth teasing him. Wes growls a warning but I'm enjoying playing with him. When he tightens his hands on the strands of my hair and pulls, holding my head still so that he can pump his hips ever so slightly.

I take pity on him and relax. I suck him hard as he thrusts in and out of my mouth ever so slightly. Wes flexes his fingers and I feel my core tighten and become slick. I slide my hand down my belly and trace my pussy with my fingers. I'm not close, but I am turned on.

I feel him swell in my mouth and I know that Wes is almost there. I glide my hand back up my body to scratch at his thighs while I pull him deep into my mouth, feeling the end of his cock hit the back of my throat. I swallow and feel Wes push deeper down my throat,

"Claire, baby—" he chants. "I'm-I'm . . ." And I know that he's there, so I push even farther towards the back of my throat and swallow him down. I hear Wes shouts as he floods my mouth and then I swallow down every last drop.

I let him slip from my mouth with a pop and Wes uses his grip on my hair to guide me back up his body so that we're pressed chest to breast. I get only a slight glimpse of the wild look in his hazel brown eyes before he crashes his mouth down on mine, which opens underneath his letting him lick inside.

After that, Wes throws back the covers and slaps me on the ass—hard—before jumping out of the bed and hauling me out with him. I let out a little *eek!*

Wes hauls me into the shower, naked as the day I was born and turns on the water. Cool water sprays all over us and he laughs when I jump before pinning me to the wall with his hands on either side of my head, pressing against the tile, and putting his mouth on me. I open my mouth to touch my tongue to his.

As the water heats up and the steam begins to rise, Wes kisses and licks his way down my body until his is kneeling before me. He raises my leg over his shoulder with a calloused palm before repeating the process with my other leg. My back is flat against the cool tile and I about come out of my skin the second his tongue touches my center. He spears my pussy with his tongue over and over before sucking my clit deeply and grab his hair in my hands, holding him to me.

I rock against his face, digging the heels of my feet into his back as he rolls his tongue over my clit and I scream out his name.

One by one, Wes pries my fingers from his hair and then places light kisses on each of them. He gazes into my eyes and the heat that simmers there has me wanting him all over again. Wes lowers my shaky legs to the ground before standing up. His hard cock raps its way up my body letting me know that he wants me too.

"Wes," I breathe before he touches his lips to mine. He doesn't remove them, but he does keep them just over mine, not quite touching, as he raises one leg to wrap around his hip.

I feel the tip of his cock line up with my center before Wes pushes deep inside. I have to hold on to Wes's shoulders when he really starts to move. I love the feel of the muscles in his back and shoulders as he works my body against the wall. I feel the flex and play of them in his ass under my leg. Wes's body is truly a work of art and I am more than willing to devote my life to the study if its beauty.

I stretch up, up, up onto my tip toes and arch my back against the tile trying to reach, to angle for Wes to hit the perfect spot, and he does. He leans forward and places little love bites all over my breast before taking my nipple into his mouth and sucking deep as he powers his hips into mine. When he scrapes his teeth over the pink tip I come. He lets my nipple go with a pop and pushes up, straightening his spine to tower over me as I cling to him. Wes pumps his hips once . . . twice . . . a third time and then he buries face in my neck and comes growling out my name.

And that in how Wes showed me just how *he* felt in the shower.

● ● ●

"'Heal me, O God, and I shall be healed; save me and I shall be saved: for you are my praise,' " I tell him. "I'm saving you."

"Don't do this."

"I have to do this," I tell him. "You have been poisoned by lust and adultery. I'm doing you a favor."

"Is this because I cheated on Amy?" he asks groggily as he pulls on his bindings. As if that could do anything.

"No, but I will add that you your list of transgressions when I pray for you," I reassure him. "This will be over quickly."

"But why?"

"Because you tasted of the flesh."

"What?" he asks but I am already raising the knife up above my head. I bring it down quickly, plunging it into his heart. A bloody cough rattles—the sound of death—but I slide the blade out and thrust it back into his flesh the way he slid his manhood into an impure woman, over and over again.

I'm sweating and winded by the time I pull my knife free one last time. But the sacrifice is worth it. I reassure myself that I am doing the Lord's work and then I slip the sharp tip just below his skin and carve an A just like before.

• • •

I spend the rest of the day chasing down dead ends and no leads on the Adams case. By all accounts and purposes, Kerrigan Adams was the perfect employee and daughter. She was even a regular church go-er. I can't find anything to link Kerrigan Adams to her killer.

And that scares me most of all because if she was chosen at random, that means Wes was right, there could be more.

When my cell phone rings at noon, I snatch it up off of my desk like a drowning man would a lifeline.

"Goodnite," I answer without looking to see who was calling.

"Hey, it's me," Anna answers. "Lunch?"

"Yes!" I shout a little too loudly and notice heads turn in my direction.

"Meet me at the new Chinese place in thirty. Emma is coming too."

"I'll see you then," I say before she disconnects.

The new Chinese place is halfway in between Anna's office and the station. We've been itching to try it but just haven't had the time. That and Chinese food, no matter how much you love it, loses its appeal once it has been used to poison you. But that was ages ago so I'm going to allow myself to be excited.

I log off my computer, leaving it open in a police station is a mistake you only make once, and stand up. I pull my keys out of my desk drawer and lock everything up before heading down the hallway to the door that leads to the back-parking lot.

I spare Lee's firmly closed office door a quick glance before shaking my head and pressing through the glass door. I climb in my SUV and head towards the main part of town. As I stop at a red light, I wonder if there will be a break in Kerrigan's case or if I am just chasing a ghost. I hate unsolved cases but after a while, I'm going to have to move on to the next case. I wish Lee wasn't being such a bonehead and would let me turn it over to someone else, someone with a fresh set of eyes who might see things more clearly than I do and connect the dots that I'm missing.

I pull into the parking lot and hop down from my vehicle. A bell on a red string tinkles overhead as I push the door open. I see Emma and Anna sitting in a booth towards the back of the restaurant when they wave to me and I slide in next to Anna.

"So . . ." Anna hedges.

"We ordered a round of egg drop soup and those crunchy things that are terrible for you but you love so much for the table," Emma blurts out clearly uncomfortable.

"Last night was intense," I say breaking the tension of the table.

"It was," Anna adds.

"What happened when Wes got home?" Anna asks me.

"We talked it out," I tell them.

"Is everything okay?" Emma asks.

"It's not perfect, but we're okay," I answer.

The waiter comes and we all order our lunches. We munch on soup and crunchy things for a while before I ask, "Did Wes really beat the shit out of Lee?"

"Oh yeah," Emma says as Anna says a decided, "yes," while biting her lip.

I wince. "Is he okay?"

"Yeah," Emma says nonchalantly as our meals are served, "I took Benedict Arnold home." At that it was Anna's turn to wince.

"So, wedding planning as scheduled?" Anna presses on.

"Yes."

"Are you going back to marriage classes?" she asks.

"I'm pretty sure we failed." I sigh. "Father Matthew said we were the most incompatible couple that he has ever met." At that Emma barks out a laugh.

"I'm sure it's not that bad," Anna says biting her lip again.

"It is," I reassure her on a smile. "I don't think I wanted to get married there anyway."

"I always thought I wanted to get married on the beach," Anna says in an uncharacteristically wistful way.

"That might be nice." I smile at her.

I can't help but feel like she is on a precipice, she's at a turning point in her life and I'm afraid of what she might do when everything is said and done with Lee. After we eat our lunch and pay our tab, Anna excuses herself to go back to her office. As we watch her walk away, Emma turns to me and I realize the dynamics of their little love triangle are even more dire than I had thought.

"Should I be worried?" I ask her.

"I've got it under control," she says shaking her head.

"Anything I need to know?"

"I slept with him," she admits to me. "Lee."

"I know."

"No, I slept with him again last night. I just can't seem to stay away even though I know that I should."

"Do you have feelings for him?" I ask softly.

"How could I hurt her like that? She's everything that's right and I'm everything that's wrong."

"I don't think Lee feels that way."

"When it started, I didn't know that she was in love with him," she explains.

"I know," I tell her softly.

"But now I love him too and I can't have him."

"Are you sure about that?" I ask.

"Yes," she says firmly.

"I'm sorry," I say, and I mean it. More than anything I want them to be able to be happy with whatever resolution comes about.

"Not any sorrier that I am." The ringing of my phone interrupts the line of conversation. "Saved by the bell," she mumbles.

"Goodnite," I answer.

"Detective Goodnite, this is dispatch."

"Go ahead dispatch," I respond.

"We have reports of a male body found, cause of death appears to be similar to the case you are currently working," he informs me.

"Fuck!" I bite out. "Where?"

"Behind the deli on Third and Third."

"I'm on my way."

"Everything alright?" Emma asks.

"Not even a little bit," I sigh running my hand over my forehead where no doubt a tension headache is forming. "Better come with me. There's another body and cause of death appears similar to Kerrigan Adams."

"Well, then let's go."

chapter 20

not sure

"OH SHIT," EMMA SAYS as we take in the scene. Emma who is usually unflappable—especially at a crime scene—seems a bit rattled.

"What's up?" I ask.

"I know him," she whispers under her breath.

"I'm so sorry," I tell her honestly. "Where do you know him from?"

"The church singles group," she says looking around. The concerned look on her face tells me she's hoping no one heard her until we figure out how to proceed from here.

"Shit," I mumble. I knew he looked familiar, but I didn't know him.

"Yeah," she says back.

"But you didn't really know him? Or know him from before—outside the group did you?" I ask feeling extra hopeful. I can't afford to lose Emma on this case. She's the best in the dead people business and if I have to work another serial killer case I'm going to need her.

"Can you handle this, or do we need to have someone else over see it?" I continue.

"I've got it," she reassures me.

"I need to call Wes," I tell her as I come up with a pretty decent plan on the fly. "If I can't turn it over to another detective, I'll pass it on to the feds."

"Lee is going to be so fucking pissed," she tells me.

"Then you'll just have to kiss his feel bads better." I wink to soften the blow of her addiction to her crappy hook-ups with my idiot brother.

"I am not your personal whore!" she shouts to me as she's walking over to the crime scene tech van causing everyone to turn and stare.

Emma is my wild card, no holds barred, crazy chick friend who will say whatever she feels like and unapologetically be herself. I love that. I also never know what's going to pop out of her mouth either. I am unapologetically who I am so I can relate—*sort of*—but Emma is bat shit crazy with a heart of gold. Why else would she be having such a tough time with this unfortunate love triangle? She can't stand the fact that she is part of what is hurting Anna and it's tearing her up.

"That's what you think!" I shout back to the music of her laughter.

I pull my phone out of my back pocket and dial a number that hasn't changed in twenty years. I spent plenty avoiding it, not calling the number, but when the rich voice sounds on the other end, I know I made the right choice.

"*Hey, baby,*" he says, and I can hear the smile in his voice. "*What's up?*"

"Oh . . . not much," I hedge.

"*Are you having a good day?*" he asks.

"I'm having a day," I say before pressing on. "Hey, are you busy right now?"

"I have fifty-six field agents to oversee and one hundred who work in the office, I'm always busy, baby, but for you I'll make time."

"Sure, we'll go with that," I say nervously. Shit, I hate being nervous. I am a fucking grown up. I am never nervous. I know exactly who I am and I own it. This is not a situation of my own making. I am just doing what I can to make the best of it.

"What's up?" he asks this time sounding more alert than before. So here goes nothing . . .

"I have another body," I tell him point blank.

"And?" I can hear in his voice that he doesn't understand what I'm saying. Wes isn't understanding *what kind of body* it is that I have on my hands.

"Second verse same as the first?" I crack.

"This isn't a joke, Claire."

"I know that," I snap.

"Then why are you calling me?" He sighs. It's that tone of voice Wes uses when he's more than frustrated. I can see him running his hands through his hair in my mind.

"I would like to formally hand this case over to the FBI." After a very pregnant pause I say, "I'm serious. If this is another repeater you take it. It's not worth risking us for it."

"Lee is going to have your ass for this," he tells me, but it's something I already know. I shrug even though he can't see it.

"Yeah well, he's all bark and no bite these days," I lie.

"Honey, he could take your badge for this," he says softly. Now it's my turn to sigh because Wes is right. Lee has been looking for years for a way to fire me or get me to quit and here I am, handing him one on a silver platter.

"Well, then maybe I'll just go out on my own and be the best PI New Jersey has ever seen, like those books Gran reads about that Stephanie girl. What's that author's name? Janet Something, I think."

"Claire—"

"Wes, honey, let's just cross that bridge when we get there," I say.

"Okay, baby," he says softly. *"Tell me where you are."*

"Behind the deli on Third and Third."

"I know the place. I'll be there in ten, hang tight."

"You know I will," I say just before he disconnects the call.

I make my way back to the scene and the officers who are monitoring the area and keeping looky-loos out. I take more than a cursory look this time. A man, probably early forties, with sandy brown hair and a lean build. He's leaning back against the exterior wall of the deli with his legs out in front of him and his ankles crossed casually. If it wasn't for the gruesome stab wounds all over his torso, I would think he was just resting.

"We need to talk," Emma says in a low voice when she reaches my side.

"We do," I confirm.

"There's an A," she says, her voice low, filled with worry and secrets.

"Shit. What else?"

"Like I said before," she says pausing to take a deep breath. "He was there last night. His name is Dennis and he's a dentist. I know because Anna and I kept calling him 'Dennis the Dentist' and now I feel like an asshole because he's dead."

"You didn't kill him, did you?" I ask looking at her sideways. "You know women with traumatic past relationships often go on to become serial killers."

"I hate you," she says as she slaps my shoulder.

"No, you don't." I wink.

"And Anna would say you're full of shit on the serial killers bit."

"Probably." I shrug.

"I'm not sure we're cut out for church groups," she says to me with mock seriousness.

"Me either." I sigh dramatically. We both take one look at each other and then laugh until we're interrupted by Lee's shouting.

"What the hell is going on here?" he barks.

"A murder investigation," I say as Emma and I turn to see not only is Lee standing behind us, but so is Wes. They both look like shit, but I get a modicum of joy out of the fact that Lee looks worse. He shouldn't have been such an asshole about this case. He could have sat us both down like adults—like the professionals we are—but he didn't and now he looks like his ass was handed to him last night, because it was.

"I see that, I mean him." He points to Wes.

"Special Agent in Charge O'Connell is here in a professional capacity," I answer Lee's question. What a fun turn of events after the last year of Lee trying to hand my cases to Wes, here he is now acting like a jerk because I am trying to do that very thing. Where's the popcorn?

"At whose request?" he snaps.

"Mine."

"You're fired!" he roars.

"Sure thing, boss." I shrug.

"You're just going to fire your sister?" Emma shouts snapping her fingers. "Just like that?"

"Yes," he says his tone neutral as he quotes her question. "'Just like that.'"

"Then you are a bigger idiot than I had originally thought," she says sadly as she walks away.

"You don't get to walk away from me, Dr. Parker," he shouts to her back.

"Watch me," Emma volleys back flipping him off over her shoulder, not ever bothering to turn around and look him in the eye. I watch the muscle in his cheek twitch and think *not my circus, not my monkeys*.

"Well, clearly you have this under control," I say patting Lee on the chest. "Since you don't need me, I'll just be heading out."

"I *might* have spoken too soon," Lee says.

"I'm sorry," I say holding up my hand to my ear. "I can't hear you due to your advancing age and all, what did you say?"

"I said I was wrong," he tells me. "And you're not fired."

"Thank you," I say softly. "So, let's turn this over to Wes and get back to normal."

"Not so fast," he says quickly.

"What?" Wes and I both look to Lee at the same time.

"I do not agree with handing this case over to the FBI," Lee says, this time more calmly than before.

"Dude, it's clearly going to be another messy one. That's not for me right now," I tell him the truth.

"So, you're not wanting to be a detective anymore?" Lee asks me.

"That's not what I'm saying," I say trying to defend my actions.

"Then what *are* you saying?" he snaps.

"That my voice is forever changed from being nearly strangled to death a few months ago," I say after taking a deep breath. "I'm saying I'll be fine, but my next case should not be another serial killer."

"Okay, I hear you," Lee concedes.

"Thank you."

"I'll agree to an FBI collaboration between you and Wes but that's it. This case stays within the department."

"You are such an ass," I mumble under my breath and Wes busts out a deep laugh. "Well, you can be my first witness interview."

"What?" Lee asks.

"I have been informed that the victim is Dennis Boyd of last night's Singles Group," I say feeling just a little smug about knocking Lee off-kilter for even just a little bit. I bite back a smirk.

"No shit?" he asks.

"No shit," I confirm.

"Why don't we all pitch in here for awhile," Wes wades in "And then we can all go to dinner and discuss what might have happened to Mr. Boyd?"

"Sounds good to me," Lee says.

"Me too," I agree.

"Good, you can talk to Emma and Anna," Wes says.

And that's exactly what we did. We closed up the scene together—Wes, Lee, Emma and me.

• • •

I regretted having dinner as a group from the moment we sat down.

What was Wes thinking? There is no way we should have Anna and Emma at dinner with Lee. We might as well pour gasoline all over this trendy restaurant with its mood lighting and its fusion cuisine and then play with matches.

That's exactly what being here is, playing with matches. Or a fucking bomb.

"So, tell me a little about Dennis," I ask.

"He flirted with Emma a little," Anna says. Lee narrows his eyes looking less than pleased but thankfully, he stays relatively silent. *For now.*

"But he left with that girl that was all over Lee, what was her name?" Emma asks.

"Sarah Holt," Lee says.

"That's right." She snaps her fingers as she remembers. "Slutty Sarah was all over Lee and then went off with Dennis the Dentist when class let out."

"I like this jealous side of you," Lee says low for Emma but we all hear it. And thanks to the round table we all see the pain that flashes across Anna's face before she buries it deep. And by deep, I mean *deep*. But it's a serious effort that she is making, and it's not lost on any of us, most of all Emma.

"I'm not jealous, I just like pointing out your many cases of syphilis." She smiles sweetly.

"What else do you know about Dennis?" I ask trying to get this train back on track.

"He's divorced," Anna quickly adds. "No kids that I know of."

"He said he was lonely and wanted to marry again," Emma shares.

"I just bet he does," Lee grumbles.

"He left with Sarah to go get drinks. That was the last I saw of him," Anna shares.

"Thank you," I tell them all. Unfortunately, now we have nothing to talk about. Which is abundantly obvious as we're all pushing our food around on our plates.

"You have to talk to me, Emma," Lee voices his frustration, his voice low but again carrying around the table.

"No, I don't," she snaps. "And leave me alone."

"I can't, Em," he pleads. "You know why. Don't ask me to. Anything but that."

"Oh, look at the time," Anna says. "I have to get home and feed my cat," she says as she jumps up and tosses a bunch of bills on the table before rushing out the door.

"Are you fucking happy now?" Emma snaps.

"Yes! Because now at least you're fucking talking to me," Lee yells.

"Don't get used to it," she fires back tossing bills on the table and storming off.

"Fuck!" he thunders.

"You have to back off, Lee," I say.

"Claire—" Wes tries to stop me.

"You're hurting them," I push. "Can't you see that?"

"I can't, Claire," Lee pleads. "I need her."

"At whose expense? Anna's?" I question.

"Claire—" Wes tries again only to be cut off yet again as well.

"I never promised her anything," Lee explains.

"And that makes it right?" I can't help but ask.

"I don't know," Lee says softly.

"She's important to Emma, Lee," I tell him something he already knows.

"I know that," he lets out a breath in anger? In frustration? I don't know what and I don't care because this, all of this is his fucking fault. I'm so angry that I feel my face burn with it. This is absolutely ridiculous. The whole thing is driving me mad.

"Emma will never do anything to hurt her," I say softly, not letting any of that anger bubble over the surface.

"She'll get over it," Lee presses on. I can see by the look on his face that he's determined to have his way. I just can't help but feel that it's all about to blow up in our faces. I'm not sure who will survive it, if anyone.

"She's not getting over it, Lee." I say softly. "I don't see this working out for you."

"Claire—" Wes tries one more time.

"I'm in love with her," Lee says dropping his bomb one more time in my lap.

"Shit," I bite out.

I'm not sure if I thought the situation was ever going to change or if I thought he would lose interest or what. But Lee's decisions, his actions, are affecting more than just him and he is being so narrow minded that he can't seem to understand that.

"Yeah," Lee agrees.

Leave it to Wes to break the silence as he raises a hand in the air and calls out, "Check please!"

chapter 21
blood

I'M LOST IN THOUGHT.
I brood the entire car ride home from dinner. Just when I think I have my life on track everything falls to shit. For years, I fought tooth and nail for every scrap. Every case that could possibly make my career, take me to the next level. To say I was driven would be a major understatement.

And now I'm stuck on a high-profile case that I don't even want.

And why don't I want it? Because it could cost me greatly. It could cost me Wes. Because I might have been near to strangled by a deranged serial killer a couple months ago, but it was Wes who found me. It was Wes who saved my life. I might be traumatized, and it might have changed me, but that day changed him too. I can't blame him for that.

And on top of all that, my brother is being a Grade A asshole and I am powerless to stop it. He is so lost to Emma that he can't see that he's turning everyone else's life upside down in the process. And poor Anna is never going to be the same. Hell, neither is Emma. The whole thing is tearing her apart. My stomach burns as my thoughts tumble around in my brain like a load of wash in the dryer.

And on top of everything, I have another serial killer to find. Because what kind of person hacks up people and carves an initial into their bodies? A psycho. I don't even need Anna to spell that one out for me.

Because we arrived at the scene separately, we had both of our vehicles out and about, no cozy carpooling for Wes and me. Although, I think we could use the time to ourselves to think about all that has happened in the last couple of days. At least, I know I can.

I pull into the driveway beside Wes as he waits for me. He doesn't go on ahead to open the door or go on into the house, he waits for me in the driveway and walks up with me. That's the kind of thing that sticks in my mind. Wes cares for me in a way that no one ever has before. He genuinely wants to spend every minute he can with me, making up for time we had lost.

"A penny for your thoughts, babe," he says softly as he opens the front door.

"What?" I ask.

"Honey, it doesn't take a crystal ball to see that you're a million miles away."

"I'm sorry," I tell him genuinely.

"It's going to be okay, Claire," Wes reassures me.

"Are you so sure of that?" I ask. "Because I can't help but feel like nothing is ever going to be the same again." Wes wraps me up in his arms, holding me tight.

"Then let's go to bed, baby. Maybe everything will seem better in the morning."

"Okay," I tell him.

I let Wes lead me up the stairs. I let him slowly undress me, piece by piece, before tucking me into bed. I watch with rapt attention as he strips off his fed suit, button by tiny little button. Wes has an amazing body that he obviously works hard at keeping when I'm not paying attention. I, on the other hand, nourish mine with butter and pizza. Different strokes for different folks, I guess.

"What's that look for?" he asks as he shucks his pants to the floor.

"I was just admiring your beautiful body," I tell him honestly and watch him preen at the compliment, so I can't help but poke him a bit. "It's obvious you work hard at it despite your advanced age."

"Advanced . . . advanced age!" he blusters. "I'll show you advanced age!" he shouts as he pounces on me.

I let out an undignified squeak and roll to the side trying to make a quick exit, but he grabs me by the waist and flips me to my belly. His broad palm lands hard on my ass and I yelp.

"Wes!" I complain but we both know that it's halfhearted because even I can hear the laughter in my voice.

"So, you think I'm an old man, do you?" he asks as he pulls me to my hands and knees.

"I don't think, I know that you're an old man," I say with wide eyes as positions himself behind me. "Do you know that they say that forty is the beginning of the end? I should start shopping for your convalescent home tomorrow."

"We'll just see about that," he says as he thrusts his cock deep inside me and I can't stop the moan that falls from my lips as he hits that magic spot deep inside.

"Wes," I pant as I drop down to my forearms and brace.

I know that this will be a wild ride, so I brace myself and Wes does not disappoint as he powers deep. Neither of us will last long like this and I don't care. I love Wes best when he is wild and free. After the last couple of days we both need this release, this moment away from everything else.

Here we are just Wes and Claire, the rest of the world can wait.

"I need you to get there, baby," Wes growls as he plunges deep in a hard and fast rhythm. "Touch yourself. I need you to get there."

I balance myself on my left arm and shoulders, gripping the sheet in my fist for purchase as I slide my other arm between my body and the bed down, down, down until I can feel the side of his cock where his body enters mine and it's a heady feeling to touch the very place where we join together with my fingertips grazing him as I go.

"Claire—" he warns his fingers digging into my hips and I move my own fingers to my clit and circle.

I gasp when my finger hit my heated flesh. "Yes."

"I want it," I says as he plunges in again and again and I'm helpless to do anything but to give him what he wants. As my climax washes over me I hear him call out my name as he follows me over the edge.

Wes and I fall in a sweaty, breathless pile and he rolls us to the side, my back to his front and he curls around me pulling the blankets up over us. He buries his face in that crook between my neck and shoulder, a place he focuses on most of the time, and chuckles in my ear. His voice gravel smooth and still rough with sex, "Advanced age, my ass."

And then we both drifted off to sleep. Too bad it would prove to be a restless one and in the coming days I would look back and wish I had trusted my gut when it warned me otherwise. Nothing here is as it seems. And even though

I let Wes feel like he convinced me differently, I still can't help but feel like something very bad is about to happen. If I hadn't pretended to agree, maybe things could have turned out differently. But then again, I guess we'll never know.

• • •

Run!

I'm running as fast as my little feet will take me through the woods behind my parents' house. I have to get away from the bad man. If he catches me now, I'll never get away. I have to be free.

Run! I have to run faster.

I see the blue gray light as it spills through the trees. Mommy always told me this was her favorite part of the day—looking at the sun as it comes up in the morning. I ran away late in the night when the bad man was sleeping. It was my only chance. After he broke the lock on the closet door I knew that I had a chance to get out. I wasn't trapped anymore with nothing to stop me.

I had to get home. I push the door to the outside open and take my first breath of fresh air. The air inside was dusty and gross. I didn't like the smell of it at all. But now I'm outside and free. But I have to run or else the bad man will catch me.

Free.

I'm free. That's the words in my head as the trees break and I see Wes standing at the edge of the backyard. I'm free. I'm finally free. Wes looks up and he sees me.

"I've got her!" he shouts to someone.

My heart is beating so hard in my chest and it hurts to breathe but I try to suck in as much as I can. I'm so tired but I have to keep running. I can see Wes standing on the edge of the woods looking back at me. I can tell just by looking at his face that he'll protect me. Wes always protects me. He will keep me safe. He will keep me free. Forever.

I push my feet just a little harder, I run just a little faster. I'm almost there. I'm almost free when he reaches for me and I collapse in Wes's arms. But when I look down, I'm covered in blood. There's so much blood that it's everywhere. All over my clothes and Wes's. There is blood all over the trees and it soaks the moss and dirt of the forest floor. It's clogging my lungs and I can't breathe. It's smeared across his face and matted in my hair. It's in my mouth and all over my hands.

I look up into Wes's dead eyes. I always knew the bad man would kill me I just didn't know he would get Wes too. There's a pain in my chest where my heart used to be. I know for sure that it's broken because my sweet Wes is dead and it's all my fault.

I open my mouth and scream . . .

• • •

Earthqake.

My body is being thrown about so bad that it must be an earthquake. No, it's hands on my body, shaking me. For a second, I'm still gripped in my dream and think that the bad man has me again until I hear Wes's deep voice.

"Claire, you're safe," he says as he shakes me again. "Wake up, baby. You have to wake up."

"Wes?" I ask gulping in as much air as I can and choking because my lungs still sear with panic. I blink my eyes open several times to clear the sleep and the lasting effects of my nightmare. "You're alright?"

"No, I'm not fucking alright, baby," he growls.

"What's wrong?" I ask feeling alarm trill through my body.

"Your nightmares."

For a minute I flash back to the time when I was so deep in my puppy love for Wes that I gave him my virginity at eighteen and he threw it back in my face because he had witness my having a night terror so bad he knew that he couldn't save me. I didn't know it then, but Wes had thought he was doing what was best for me by pushing me away. He had no way of knowing that I wouldn't tell anyone about my nightmares and how they torture me through all hours of the night. He had thought that my family would get me help and one day everything would be hunky dory.

Lately, he swears he'll follow me into my own person hell to pull me back out again, but I have always wondered if there would come a time that he can't handle it and now I can't help but wonder if that's the case. My heart stutters before it speeds up and my face feels hot. He must see the look of alarm cross my face because he speaks quickly.

"It's not that, baby. I'm not going anywhere," Wes reassures me. "But they're coming more often."

"I know." But I don't know. In the back of my mind, I am always wondering when Wes will leave me because he can't take it anymore.

"We have to do something about them, honey," he says softly.

"I don't know how." And it's true. If I did know how to fix them, to fix me, I would.

"You can't go on like this," Wes tells me something that I already know, and I do know. I know that I can't survive like this forever. But I also haven't been willing to really dive deep and get to the root of the problem. Anna has been after me for forever to do some deep hypnosis therapy mumbo jumbo and I have been avoiding the task for a long time. Maybe now it's time to stop running. But still, I don't really want to . . .

"You think I don't know that?" I try to push away from him but his arms close tight around me, holding me to him.

"We'll get through it."

"You're tired of it." I feel the tears sting the backs of my eyes before the wet hits my cheeks. "I knew you would get tired of having to deal with it."

He sighs. "I'm tired of seeing you hurt, baby. I don't want to see you suffer anymore. But I'm not fucking going anywhere."

"Yeah, but for how long?" I can't help but ask. As soon as the words leave my mouth I instantly want to pull them back in.

"Forever."

"You can't mean that," I say. How can he promise me everything when so much is still hanging in the balance? "You can't say that."

"I just did."

"Wes—" I start but he interrupts me. Again.

"I'll promise you the moon and mean it because I love you. If these nightmares never stop I'll still be by your side because I love you that much. But I want you to live a life of peace and beauty because you deserve it but also because I love you and also selfishly, I want to be the one to give you that."

"Wes," I whisper this time with my heart in my throat. "I love you too."

"I know it," he says smugly. "Now, go back to sleep. Tomorrow is going to be a long day." And I did. I curled up in the safety of Wes's strong arms and went to sleep. It would be later that I would realize that I should have stayed awake and basked in the beauty of my life the way that it was because very soon, everything would change.

chapter 22
the missing piece

*B*EEP... BEEP... BEEP...
I wake to the sound of Wes's alarm on the nightstand and his arms still heavy around my body. The early morning light is just starting to sift through the bedroom windows and I can't help but feel like his words from the middle of the night will ring true. It's going to be a long fucking day.

"Are you still a million miles away?" Wes asks me as he brushes my hair back from my face to behind my ear.

"Yes and no," I answer.

"What's bothering you, baby?" Wes asks me.

"Something's wrong," I pause in answering his question. "I just can't put my finger on what. It's like a bad omen or something, but something is really wrong."

"It's your brother," he guesses on a sigh.

"Maybe a little," I say and when he raises a brow questioning the veracity of my comment I continue. "Okay that's part of it . . . a *big* part of it."

"You interfered after I told you not to and didn't like the answers you found." Wes sighs before tracing a finger down my cheek. "I knew you would be disappointed. As cheesy as it sounds I hate seeing you anything but happy. I know that it has to happen, that's life, right? But I still hate it."

"No! Yes. I don't know." I sigh. "Emma keeps hooking up with Lee behind Anna's back. Then talking shit about him in front of her face. It's so weird and twisted and stupidly reckless but that's not it."

"That's their business, baby," he says in response when really I was thinking he would say something like "That's crazy! What's gotten into those assholes?" Wes's lack of shock hits me like a sack of bricks and it dawns on me the missing piece to my puzzle.

"You knew!" I demand. "You filthy lying bastard! You knew that my brother was wrecking lives with his dick and didn't tell me so that I could try and stop it."

"Yes."

"And you didn't tell me!" I cry out in all my anger.

"No, I didn't," Wes says calmly.

"Well, why the hell not?" I demand getting all worked up over it.

"Because it's none of our business and Lee confided in me as his oldest friend," he explains calmly. "Also, because there's nothing you can do about it."

"You don't know that!" I yell. And he doesn't know for sure. Who's to say that I couldn't have talked some sense into Emma or even Lee before hearts became involved and they all got too deep in the bullshit to wade their way out? Maybe I could have stopped them all from falling in love with the wrong someone.

"I do," he says. "They have to figure this out on their own."

"But they're going to fuck it up!" I complain and Wes laughs.

"Yeah, honey, they are but so did we and look where it got us," he says squeezing his arms around me. "Now, let's go to work and fight crime like the badasses we are. Then tonight we'll pray our closest friends pull their heads out of their asses. Sound good?"

"That's probably as much as I can ask for," I sigh.

"Great!" he says smacking my ass. "Let's go." And then he throws the bedding back and knifes out of the bed taking me with him.

• • •

"It's the exact same," Emma informs me from her desk when I step out of the elevator in her dungeon—I mean basement morgue.

"It can't be," I respond.

Wes and I had showered together. Then actually took the time to have breakfast in our kitchen together since we weren't carpooling today before he kissed me goodbye in the driveway.

"I'll see you later, babe. Call me if anything comes up in the case."

"Will do, bossy man." I shot him a mock salute. Wes stops his descent into his car and narrows his eyes on me over the roof of his Fed-mobile. "What?"

Wes stalked back around to where I was standing next to my Tahoe. "Don't be cute and make me want to fuck you when I need to go to work."

"Who's being cute?" I asked. I shrugged my shoulders. "This is just me."

"I know it's you, but you are anything but just," he said as he pulled my body into his. "Everything you do is cute and everything you do makes me hard."

"I can tell," I laughed because the proof of his statement was pressing into my belly.

"Claire—" he warns just before he crushed his mouth to mine and I was lost in a swirling storm of teeth and tongues and bodies pressed tight, to heat and lust. Suddenly the predicament isn't so funny.

"Have a good day at the station, baby," Wes said before walking away from me to jump in his car and head off to work with a pretty fucking smug expression on his stupid handsome face. All while I was left standing in our driveway wondering what had just happened. I shook my head like a etch-a-sketch and then hopped in my Tahoe to head to the station.

About a nanosecond after I had pushed through the glass doors Emma called for me to head down to the morgue because she was finished with the autopsy of Dennis Boyd. Now I'm standing here with her in her creepy basement morgue wondering what wrongs I had done in my life to land two serial killer cases back to back.

"Did you hear me?" she asked.

"Yeah." I swallow past the lump in my throat. "I heard you."

"From the bump on the head to the ligature marks on the wrists, it's all the same."

"Walk me through it one more time, now that I know that there are two of them. Tell me step by step, how they are the same," I ask as I pull my notebook out of my back pocket and snatch a pen off the top of her desk.

"You better return that when you're done!" she snaps. Our Emma is a wee bit of a Nazi when it comes to her stationary and office supplies.

"Yes, Mistress," I say on a mock bow.

"That's better." She preens in a haughty manner.

"Can we move along now?" I ask. "I would hate for Lee to figure out where we are and wander down here. He'd only get in the way." I hate to use their issues against them, but I have shit to do so I need her to focus.

"Uhh . . . yeah . . . he'd only . . . uhh, get in the way." I take one look at her splotchy face and realize what she's saying without words.

"Dude, you banged him again?"

"I can't help myself where he's concerned." She throws her arms up in the air before bringing them back down to cover her red fucking face. "I hate him, and I don't want anything to do with him. But then he crooks his finger at me and before I know it, I fall on his magical penis and come to when the orgasm settles."

"There is so much wrong with that entire statement," I stare at her with what has to be a horrified expression on my face. "I'm going to need you to refrain from using phrases like, magic penis and orgasm around me when referencing my brother. That's just gross, yo."

She sighs. "I know."

"So back to the autopsy . . ."

"Oh, right," she begins. I can see Emma mentally shake off her own personal woes. "Both victims have large contusions on their heads. I would guess that that is how they were subdued."

"That makes sense. Kerrigan Adams was a petite woman, but Dennis Boyd was fit and about six feet tall."

"Yes, exactly," she says. "They both also have abrasions on their wrists from being bound."

"There was no rope or cuffs at either crime scene," I remind her.

"Yes, but the skin doesn't lie," she says. "I did some impressions and it matches a standard jute cord you can buy just about anywhere so that was probably a wasted effort." She shrugs.

"You never know." And it's true. Even the most obscure piece of evidence or fact can be what brings the whole case together. You just never know until it's right in front of your face.

"Also, both victims were stabbed to death but the way the stab wounds bled suggests the first wound was to the heart and death would have been quick. The initial A was also carved into the skin in the chest area postmortem on both victims."

"Still gross," I say off hand.

"That it is, my friend. That it is." She's got a weird sense of humor, this one, but then again, when you work in our field and see how cruel people can be, you kind of have to have one to survive.

"Thanks, chick. I'll see you later," I say as I make my way over to the elevator.

When the doors open back upstairs—or really, above ground—I head back to my desk and pull out every note, every stitch of paper, every piece of evidence in the case no matter how small or trivial and place it on top of my desk. Sometimes, seeing the clutter all laid out can help me spot a connection I had otherwise missed.

I need to follow up some leads on Dennis Boyd. There are too many pieces of the puzzle missing where he is concerned. I need to make some phone calls. He's not from around here so there aren't many connections to be made but still there's something.

I pick up the phone and dial the number I have for his ex-wife in Connecticut.

"Hello?" she answers.

"Adrienne Boyd?" I ask.

"It's Mrs. Michaels now, who's calling?" she asks.

"My apologies, Mrs. Michaels, I'm Detective Claire Goodnite from the George Washington Township PD, can I ask you some questions about your ex-husband?"

"Dennis?" she asks me. "I can't see why you would be asking me about Dennis but go ahead, Detective."

"Was there any tension in your marriage?" I ask.

"Not really, no," she answers. "Really, we just grew apart."

"Was your divorce amicable?"

"Why are you asking me these questions?" she asks. I can hear the frustration in her voice.

"Mrs. Michaels, Dennis Boyd is dead."

"What?" she asks. "You have to be mistaken."

"I'm not, ma'am, we have a positive ID," I inform her. "So, I'll ask again, was your divorce particularly ugly?"

"Not at all," she says quietly. "We were both mostly just over it. We were young. Dennis wasn't ready to be anyone's husband let alone mine. We're still friends today."

"Can you think of anyone who would want to harm Dennis?" I ask.

"Not at all. You can't think someone did this on purpose . . ." she lets the thought hang in the air because I can't answer it the way she wants me to before I continue with my questioning.

"Dennis Boyd was murdered, Mrs. Michaels. I'm so sorry," I say when I hear her sob over the line.

"Was there anyone or anything new in his life that you noted?" I ask.

"He was going to a new church," she answers. "Said that he was going to a singles group and that he was ready to meet someone special. My husband and I are—*were*—happy for him."

"Thank you for your time, Mrs. Michaels," I tell her. "If you think of anything else, don't hesitate to call me."

"I will," she says softly. "Just find who did this."

"I will," I promise her just before ending the call.

I place the phone in its cradle on my desk and look down at all the shit that I have accumulated one more time. Kerrigan Adams and Dennis Boyd. Their lives shouldn't have anything in common with one another and yet they do. It seems so simple that I can't believe I didn't see it sooner.

"That can't be it," I say to myself. "It can't be that simple."

But it is.

It's a tiny little detail, one that seems so silly that there is no way that could be the connection. I scan everything again three more times just to be sure. And again, there it is. I can't believe we missed this.

I pick up the phone and dial the extension for Wes's desk. If he's not in the office I'll track his ass down because this is the break we have been looking for. He picks up on the third ring.

"Special Agent O'Connell," he answers.

"Well, aren't you all fancy and shit," I droll.

"Hello to you too, Darling," he laughs. *"Is there a reason your calling me at work or was it just to harass me?"*

"Harassing you is a valid reason particularly because you have a nice ass," I tell him forcing my voice to sound as serious as possible even though I can barely get through the words and have to bite down on my lip to keep from laughing. I'm pretty sure Wes can tell too. Silly bastard.

"Despite my advanced age?"

"Yes, exactly." I'm nodding my head, but he can't see me. "But alas, there is a reason."

"And what pray tell, would that be?" he asks me.

"Tragically, we have to go back to marriage classes tonight." I let out a heavy sigh.

"I'm glad we're over our last drama and all," he says after a very pregnant pause. "But I thought we agreed that wasn't for us?"

"Oh, it's not," I reply. "But I was looking at the case notes for Dennis Boyd's murder and comparing them to those of the Kerrigan Adams case. You'll never guess what I found."

"And what exactly would that be?"

"That our two victims were not only parishioners of the very church we attended marriage classes at, but they were both members of the very same singles group that our dearest friends just recently joined." I can't help sounding smug, but I do. I love that I'm the one that cracked this case wide open. I can just feel it in my bones. This is the missing piece to the puzzle.

"You're kidding," he says with all seriousness, the playfulness of earlier is long gone.

"I wish I were," I tell Wes. "Someone is killing off church singles and we're going to find out why."

"Well, I guess I don't have to worry about you getting caught in the crosshairs this time," he mumbles.

"And why is that?" I ask.

"Because you're not fucking single and you're never going to be single again," he says with finality.

"There *is* another bright side to this," I purr. "We get to send Lee back to the singles group."

"That's mean," he laughs. "But I won't say the fucker doesn't deserve it."

"Agreed," I say with an extra sweet tone of voice.

"You know? You're scary when you plot against family members," he tells me.

"Why thank you, Wes, that's the sweetest thing you've ever said to me."

• • •

I spend the rest of the work day making phone inquiries to try and prove my theory. Every person I have talked to so far has told me what good people they thought both Dennis and Kerrigan were—*good, church going, people.*

As it turns out both victims had been looking for love in all the *right* places before their untimely deaths this week. Which makes me wonder what's really going on here? Not to mention, both were active members of Father Matthew's very successful singles group. So when the clock strikes five o'clock, I jump in my Tahoe and head out to our favorite family church for marriage classes.

Hopefully, after the other day, they will still take Wes and me.

I'm running a little behind schedule, so I take the first available spot in the parking lot and jump out, palming my keys as I go. When I make it to the steps of the church just before the doors open for the evening Lee, Emma, and Anna are all standing there with their arms crossed over their chests staring daggers at me. Wes, on the other hand, is grinning from ear to ear like a loon and is clearly enjoying himself.

"So glad I made it in time," I say running up the steps.

"I hate you," Emma snaps.

"Yeah, what she said," Anna adds glaring at me.

I choke back a laugh, unsuccessfully I might add, when their eyes narrow on me. "This is going to be fun."

"I'm not sure I care for your definition of fun, sister dear," Lee drolls.

"Then you should have handed the Adams case off to someone else," I reply.

"Yeah, someone less sadistic than a Goodnite," Emma gripes.

"Yeah . . ." I agree wistfully.

"Good evening ladies and gentlemen," Father Matthew says as he pulls open the massive front doors of the church. Then as he takes in Wes and me, "Well, I have to admit that I am surprised to see you two here tonight."

"We're so happy to be here," I say in my best impression of a happy soon-to-be-misses.

"I take it you settled your disagreement?" he asks on a raised brow.

"Of course," I answer.

"Well, then, welcome back," he says as he waves us in.

"Thank you, Father," Wes says buttering him up.

"Father Thomas will fill in for me with the single group again tonight." A collective groan goes up around the room.

"Did I miss something?" Wes asks.

"Father Thomas can be a bit . . . *serious* from time to time," Father Matthew explains.

"I thought he was the hip, young guy everyone was all excited about?" I ask.

"He is. He's just very passionate about certain things and shall we say . . . *long winded*."

"Oh, okay." I laugh.

"Well, shall we head into the office?" Father Matthew asks.

"Sure thing," Wes says and we all head down the short hall.

He motions for us to sit in the chairs again and we do. This time Wes keeps a hold of me placing our linked hands in his lap. The priest looks taken aback by this show of tenderness and intimacy.

"So, you resolved your tiff, did you now?" he asks.

"Yes," I answer.

"It was just a misunderstanding," Wes answers.

"So, you chose your intended over your career? That's not very modern of you," he muses.

"It's not, but I also had the choice taken away from me." I shrug my shoulder.

"So, you're still working the case?" he asks me.

"Yes," I answer him honestly not willing to expound on the subject.

"And how does that make you feel, Wesley?" Father Matthew asks him.

"Not too bad," he answers.

"What brought about the change of heart? You were pretty upset about it the other day." Father Matthew is trying to point out that we haven't really solved anything, but he doesn't know that Wes and I have talked everything out and are excited to move forward with our marriage. He also doesn't know that we're excited to catch a killer too. We just have to figure out who it is first.

"Well, for one, I understand that Claire was put in a tight spot, and two, we're working together now," Wes answers honestly.

"You're both working the investigation now?" he asks, and I can't help but wonder about his sudden interest in policing or if it has anything to do with the murders of two of his parishioners.

"Yes, we're collaborating on this case," Wes repeats.

"You know what they say?" I ask casually. "Two heads are better than one!"

chapter 23

i really hate serial killers

I'M FEELING MORE CONFUSED than ever when we walk out of the office with Father Matthew. But I stumble over a step when I walk into the main room and see the singles group also breaking up for the evening. Anna looks sick and Emma look absolutely furious. My brother, Lee, on the other hand is surrounded by a gaggle of women that I have never seen before.

"Oh shit," Wes mumbles when he comes up behind me.

"Looks that way," I reply.

"Why is he so stupid?" Wes asks me.

"I'm pretty sure they dropped him on his head a bunch as a baby," I explain.

"Well, I'm duty bound as his best friend to go bail his ass out of a sling. Care to come help?"

"No, thank you," I say sweetly. "I prefer to watch his impending doom from afar."

"Thank you so much for your compassion. It's astounding," Wes kisses me on the cheek. He laughs as he walks over to Lee.

"A bunch of us are going to that new bistro over on Cicada. I'd love it if you joined us," a petite brunette purrs as she leans into Lee's arm.

"What do you know," he answers. "My friends and I were going to dinner too. Maybe we'll see you there."

"That would be great," she says before trotting off.

I walk over to my friends eyeing the warily as I go.

"I'm never coming back here again," Emma declares upon my arrival.

"Okay," I say.

"I think it would be best if I did not come back either," Anna shares.

"Yeah, we thought it would be fun, kind of a good joke while you and Wes had your classes . . ." Emma adds before looking over at Lee and his harem. "But it's not funny anymore."

"Let's just go to dinner and talk about what you guys saw tonight. Then we'll never talk about this moment again," I plead

"Agreed," they both say at the same time.

"Ready to go, ladies?" Wes asks when he and Lee walk up to our little parlay.

"Yep, dinner," Emma says looking anywhere but at Lee's face.

"I'm thinking I'd like to try that new bistro over on Cicada," Lee says.

"Brother—" Wes warns under his breath, but I can hear it.

"I hear good things about it," Anna says.

"You're playing with fire, Lee," I warn.

"Maybe that's a good thing," he says.

"Or maybe you'll get burned."

• • •

"'It is God's will that you should be sanctified: that you should avoid sexual immorality; that each of you should learn to control your own body in a way that is holy and honorable, Or learn to live with your own wife; or learn to acquire a wife.' I told you but you did not listen. You never listen."

But she doesn't listen. This one lusts for a husband of her own so badly that she doesn't care where he comes from. She is free with her touches and flirts unashamed! She is so unclean I have to purge her. She will understand when it is all over.

"Don't," she begs just like the common whore that she is. "Please don't do this. I won't tell anyone, I swear it."

"I know you won't tell anyone because you will be dead," *I inform her.* "Are you ready to meet your maker?"

"No," she says as she pulls on her bindings, but it is too late.

I pull the knife from its sheath and grip the hilt firmly in both hands high over my head. I bring the blade down swiftly plunging it into her wicked heart. I repeat the process over and over again, pulling the knife from her warm skin only to plunge it in again the way she lusts for a man's body to enter hers again and again. It is that sin that she must atone for and I am helping her. For I do the Lord's work.

I pull the blade free one more time hating every second that I have to hurry this time for fear of being discovered too soon. I dip the pointed tip into the flesh of her chest that she chose to expose with her wanton ways and carve an A for adulterer.

I slide the blade back into its sheath hidden in my clothing and with one look back at her I see that she is at peace and I know that she is with our Lord answering for her sins of the flesh.

And then I walk to the sink and wash my hands carefully letting all of the blood run free down the drain and then I dry my hands carefully on a paper towel before walking out the door and never looking back.

• • •

Regardless of whether or not it was a good idea, we all pile in our separate cars and head to the new little bistro over on Cicada. The room is dimly light with a darwood bar and cozy little tables to provide an intimate atmosphere. I can see why the singles would want to meet here to take their conversations to a more personal level.

When I walk in Lee is at the bar with the brunette and Emma is in a state. I'm kind of afraid. Judging by the look on her face that she might just set the whole building on fire. If I'm crazy she's crazier. Anna was always our voice of reason and calming influence but even she looks like she could commit murder at this particular junction. I only hope Lee is ready to reap what he sows.

When he sees me he leaves the brunette and walks over to us with a beer in his hand. The hostess takes us all to a dark booth in the back where things deteriorate further. Anna takes one look at the tight seating and pretends to take a call from a patient and leaves.

"You don't need me here anyways," she says sadly when I walk her out.

"Of course we do. Please stay," I plead but we both know that it's only a recipe for disaster. I hate Lee for breaking up our group of five.

"Nah, I don't really fit in anyways. I never did." She shrugs. I'll talk to you later."

I walk back into the bar to find that things haven't gotten any better. Lee is still an asshole and Emma is still pretending to hate him. I honestly don't know how much more of this bullshit I can take before I lose it completely. Something has to give and soon.

"I hate you more and more," I hear Emma say when I get back to the table where Lee has her wedged against the wall in the far side of the booth.

"But you love my cock, baby," he responds.

"Thank Christ you're back," Wes shouts when he sees me. "I can't take more of the *Days of Our Lives* shit happening over here." Then he downs a large portion of his beer. Yikes! It looks like I missed a lot.

"Neither can I," Emma snaps.

"How about we talk about what happened during the singles group tonight," I press. "Anything interesting happen?"

"Father Thomas preached the entire time about sins of the flesh and fornication," Lee says. "He seems pretty fixated on adultery." As soon as the words are out of his mouth my eyes fly to Emma and the blood rushes in my ears.

"What did you just say?" I ask.

"That Father Thomas preached the whole time—" Lee starts.

"No," I cut him off. "The last part."

"He seems pretty fixated on adultery?"

"Holy fuck," Wes says under his breath.

"What am I missing?" Lee asks.

"Adultery—" Emma says.

"A scarlet letter."

"A is for adultery," Wes says a little stunned. "We know where their lives overlapped, now I think we know what's linking them."

"Who was the woman that went out with Dennis after the last meeting?" I ask quickly hoping to God that there won't be any more victims.

"Sarah Holt," Emma says. "What would you want with that tramp?"

"Jealousy is an interesting look on you, honey. I can work with that," Lee winks.

"God you're disgusting," she says brushing his arm off of her shoulder.

"Wait, who is Sarah Holt," Wes asks.

"The brunette that was pawing all over Wes earlier," Emma answers. I look back to where the group is having dinner, but I don't see the brunette anywhere.

"Where is she?" I demand.

"Over with the rest of the group," Lee answers.

"No, she's not. Where is she?" I ask again.

"I-I-I thought I saw her go to the restroom about when you walked Anna out," Emma stutters.

I jump up and race for the bathrooms with Emma hot on my heels. That was at least thirty minutes ago, she could be long gone by now and no one would know until her body surfaces a day or two later.

Unfortunately, when I push opened the restroom door I realize we won't have to wait to recover Sarah Holt's body because she's dead on the bathroom floor with her wrists bound with rope and a large, bloody A carved into her chest.

"It looks the same," Emma whispers as she leans in to check for a pulse. "She has no pulse." But I already knew that by the vacant, faraway look in her glassy eyes.

"God damnit, not another serial killer. I really fucking hate serial killers,"

I say. "You stay here with her while I shut down this restaurant and get Lee and Wes started canvassing for witnesses."

"Okay," she says softly. I look back at her.

"You didn't cause this."

"I know that," she says but she won't look me in the eye, so I seriously doubt her truthfulness.

"Do you?" I ask Emma.

"Yes . . . *Mostly*."

"It's not your fault, Emma. You have a right to live your life and have human emotions like love and jealousy."

"I know," she says quietly.

"I hope you do. I'm going to go find the guys. Call it in!"

chapter 24

work, work, work

"YOU WON'T BELIEVE WHAT happened!" I practically shout when I get back to the table.

"She's dead in the bathroom," Lee says looking a little devastated.

"She is," I answer Lee. "Emma is calling it in now, you two go canvas the area while I get the bar shut down for the night."

Both Wes and Lee jump out of the booth and take off at a run. Lee for the table at the front of the restaurant where all of the singles group members are sitting and Wes for the back side of the bar to see if anyone say anything that they shouldn't.

I see the manager heading towards the bar and I move as quickly as possible, so I can head him off at the pass. He's quicker than he looks and I end up chasing him down the hallway towards his office.

"Excuse me! Excuse me!" I shout.

"What?" he barks when he turns around.

"My name is Detective Claire Goodnite and I need you to shut this building down," I demand in my take no bullshit voice.

"Excuse me but I do not think so," he growls.

"Sir, with all due respect—" I start but he cuts me off.

"No. If you had any respect at all you would respect the fact that I'm trying to run an honest business here and I don't have time for any pigs—no matter how pretty—coming in here and trying to shut me down for no reason," he huffs and I instantly don't like him.

"I wouldn't call a woman being brutally murdered by a deranged killer in your ladies room 'no reason' but who am I to judge?" I shrug. "Regardless, I don't need your permission to lock down and active crime scene."

I hear the sirens of the units Emma called coming in. I love the sound of back up. I head back down the hallway in time to hear Lee shout, "I am Captain Goodnite with the George Washington Township PD, please remain where you are and we will get to you shortly."

Several uniformed officers rush in and I have never been more excited to see them in my life. "Officers, I need you to lock this site down. Crime Scene Unit should be here shortly.

"Detective Goodnite!" Someone shouts to me. "I'm Gloria James with the George Washington Township Post, what can you tell me about this event?"

Just my luck that there would be press freaking dining here when I'm trying to handle a crime scene. But I've heard good things about Gloria so here's hoping. I've also heard Gloria—who looks to be an extremely well kept forty-five—has the hots for Lee. Worst case scenario, I'll press that for an advantage.

"Not one fucking thing, Gloria. You know the rules."

"Oh, come on! I'm locked in here and you're not going to give me anything?" She demands.

"I might give you an exclusive when this is all said and done," I warn. "Or I might not. That depends on you."

"Excellent!" she cheers. "Am I allowed to get up and make myself another martini?"

"I'm not answering that. I'm also not looking . . ."

"I got you," she laughs as she hops up and grabs a martini shaker like a pro.

I turn to walk to the door when I see the ambulance and the Crime Scene techs pull up in the body mover. I need to help them out and get them all to Emma and under her command.

"Not so fast, you fucking bitch!" I turn around just in time to dodge the fist of a very irate manager.

"I wouldn't do that if I were you," Wes growls as he grabs the manager and flips him around pinning his arms behind his back.

"And who the hell are you to get in my way?" the manager snarls.

"Her husband," Wes says point blank and I have to admit it is a tiny bit premature, but I like it. So I smile brightly at him.

"And I should care because?" the manager sneers.

"You should care because assault on a police officer and preventing them from carrying out their duties are both crimes," he informs the bar manager letting in all sink in before continuing. "And because I'm a Federal Agent."

"You've got to be fucking kidding me," the manager groans.

"I wish I were," Wes sighs before turning to a uniformed officer and saying, "I need a pair of cuffs and an escort for my dear friend here down to lock up."

"Roger that, sir," someone says.

"I have to admit that it's never a dull moment with you, Sunshine," Wes says to me with a saucy wink.

"Ha!" I laugh. "You don't know the half of it!"

"Now that this place is all sorted out, we have to go talk question Father Thomas and Father Matthew," Wes tells me.

"I know," I sigh. "I'm just having a hard time thinking that a priest could be a cold-blooded killer."

"I know that you are," he looks away, his gaze taking on a far-off quality before turning back to meet mine. "But after the weird conversation we had with Father Matthew about Father Thomas this evening and his singles group sermon on Sins of the Flesh, fornication, and all of that adultery shit we have to."

"I know it. Let's check in with Lee and Emma. Just to make sure they have everything under control and then we can head out," I tell Wes.

I take off looking for Emma and find her still in the women's restroom overseeing the loading of Sarah Holt's body on a gurney for transport. She's in her element, a force to be reckoned with, as she commands her team. I can see why Lee is so taken with her. Hell, if I were into chicks, I'd probably do her too. Emma is beautiful in a wild and windblown way as she takes command of her team ordering everyone about.

"Emma, Wes and I need to go track down a lead, do you have everything under control on this end?" I ask.

"Of course," she says as she waves me off. She doesn't even bother to look at me as she shoos me away. "I'll call you tomorrow with the autopsy results."

"Thank you!" I call out as I head back out of the bathrooms.

When I catch up to Wes he's in a hushed conversation with Lee. When I near, they both look up at me and stop all talking. That I do not care for at all.

"What's going on guys?" I ask.

"Not much, I was just telling Lee that we're about to head out to the church. He is officially in charge of wrapping up this crime scene," Wes says with a straight face and I smell bullshit. Sometimes, I'm fairly sure he uses his SERE training to evade my questions. I do not like it, I do not like it at all.

"Is that all?" I ask narrowing my eyes. I'm not sure what they're talking about, but secrets have no friends and all that.

"Of course." He smiles sweetly at me and I don't trust it for a minute.

"And these secrets have nothing to do with the current caseload?" I question.

"What secrets?" Lee asks with his own blank face.

"Don't you two use your navy ninja skills on me!" I bark. "I know what you're doing."

"We're not doing anything," Lee says innocently.

"Nothing, my ass," I grumble under my breath.

"Ready to go, Pumpkin?" Wes asks sweetly.

"Do not ever call me Pumpkin again unless you want to get punched in yours," I snap. Wes barks out a laugh before grabbing my hand and leading me out the door before I can punch him right in his pumpkins with all thoughts of Wes and Lee and they're stupid secrets long forgotten. *For now.*

"Sure thing, Cupcake."

chapter 25

in prayer

WES KNOCKS ON THE side door, the one that leads to the living quarters for the priests just after ten o'clock. We stand on the small, dimly lit, concrete stoop for what seems like ages. In fact, we wait so long that Wes has to knock one more time.

When the door opens, Father Matthew stands there in a pair of old fashioned men's pajamas with the pants and matching button down top in a light blue with a darker blue pinstripe and piping all along the edges. The color sets off his blue eyes and shock of gray hair quite handsomely.

"Claire? Wesley? What are you doing here so late?" he questions.

"Can we come in for a second, Father?" Wes asks.

"Are you in crisis?" he asks. "Did you call off the wedding? We can pray together for guidance. Come on in."

"No nothing like that," I hedge as we make out way inside the modest apartment.

"Father Matthew, who's there?" I hear Father Thomas ask.

"Claire and Wesley," he answers as the young priest makes his way down the hallway and into the communal living area.

"Maybe we should sit down," Wes says politely.

"Yes." Father Matthews says. "Where are my manners?"

"It's fine," Wes answers.

"Can I get you all something to drink?" Father Thomas asks. "Coffee? Tea? Water?"

Since I like to make an effort not to eat or drink anything in front of anyone who might be a serial killer—especially after being poisoned by a murderer and then subdued and almost strangled by a psycho earlier this year—I decline.

"No, thank you. I'm fine," I say.

"I'm fine as well," Wes says politely.

It's times like this that I really appreciate how well trained he was by his crazy, fancy assed parents. I guess it doesn't do well to have your handsome son drinking from the finger bowl at state dinner when you're an elected official of any capacity. But whatever, he's polite when I'm tired and a little punchy and incapable of being so.

Although, it's also times like these that show me how different we can be. While Wes was being raised with a silver spoon in his mouth, Lee and I were raised to have a foam finger in one hand and a loaded hot dog in the other while screaming for the home team. Maybe his parents were right and I'm bound to embarrass them all on the campaign trail next year. Who knows? But I still don't care. Wes and I are meant to be. If I can come to terms with it, so can his parents.

"What is this all about?" Father Matthews asks.

"Kerrigan Adams," I say softly.

"Yes," he says. "I had heard the tragic news."

"Do you know who did it?" Father Thomas asks. I narrow my eyes and tip my head to the side studying him before I voice my answer.

"Not quite yet, but we're closing in," I say confidently. He visibly swallows and looks nervous. I know it's him, in my gut I know, but I have nothing to pin it on him. "Did you know her?" I ask him.

"Of course," he says. "Kerrigan was a regular parishioner in this church. I knew her well."

"Did you now?" I ask.

"Was there anyone who paid too much attention to Kerrigan?" Wes asks the room.

"Not that I know of," answers Father Matthew. "What about you, Father Thomas?"

"Not that I know of. She was well liked all around," the other priest answers.

"She was a good girl from a good family," Father Matthews adds.

"She was," I tell him. "I've had many conversations with her parents and they're broken up about what happened."

"As I can imagine," Father Matthews says.

"And what about Dennis Boyd?" Wes asks changing the subject quickly so that we can better discover what makes the priests nervous and what does not.

"Dennis was fairly new to the church. He didn't grow up in this one like the rest of you did," Father Thomas answers.

"He only came here after a messy divorce. Infidelity and sin make for bad bedmates in a marriage," Father Thomas says.

"Who cheated?" I ask. "Dennis or his ex?"

"I believe he did," Father Matthews answers.

"And did any of the singles group, to your knowledge, have harsh feelings towards Dennis because of his messy divorce?" Wes asks.

"No. I don't think any of them knew what had happened in his past," Father Matthew said.

"Did either of you have strong feelings about the Boyd's divorce or Dennis's infidelity?"

"Of course we have strong feelings!" Father Thomas snapped. "We're in charge of cleansing the souls of hundreds of people. We're tasked with their spiritual purity and that's nothing to be taken lightly."

"And how do you feel about Sarah Holt?" Wes asks as we both watch them closely for their reactions.

Father Matthew's eyes go wide in shock. "You can't mean?" he asks.

"Yes, Sir," Wes responds. "Sarah Holt was murdered this evening. The same way as Kerrigan Adams and Dennis Boyd."

"No," he says. "I can't believe it." Father Thomas stays quiet but pensive.

"What can you tell me about Sarah Holt?" I ask.

"She was a parishioner here and a member of our singles group," Father Matthew says.

"Had she been single long?" Wes asks.

"Yes, her last beau didn't want to get married and she hadn't found anyone in a while," Father Matthew says.

"But it wasn't for a lack of trying," Father Thomas adds not quite under his breath.

"Did you disapprove of her dating?" I ask.

"No, of course not," Father Thomas answers. "The church frowns on promiscuity."

"What Father Thomas means is that we are a bit old fashioned and like to see couples settled together for a long time, not bouncing from one mate to another. Am I right, Father Thomas," Father Matthew asks.

"Yes, Father Matthew," he responds.

"Did you know that a letter A was carved into their chests after they were murdered?" I watch Father Thomas flinch. It's subtle, almost undetected, but it was there.

"How barbaric," Father Matthew, says. "Why would someone do such a thing?"

"It is our belief that someone was branding these victims as adulterers," Wes says softly.

"And you think it was someone from this church?" Father Matthew asks incredulously.

"It's not a far reach," Wes says. "They were all members of this church, specifically the singles group."

"Do you think someone was trying to purify their spirits when they were murdered?" I press on.

"I couldn't say as I was not the one who did it," Father Thomas said.

"Where were you tonight?" I ask.

"I was here," he answers. "I spend every evening in prayer before I turn in early every night after indulging in a light supper and some evening news."

"Did you leave the church property this evening?" Wes asks.

"No, I did not."

"How about you, Father Matthews?" Wes asks.

"I was here with Father Thomas," he answers before adding, "Also in prayer."

"Thank you," I say standing up. "We'll be in touch soon."

"Please do keep us updated," Father Matthews asks.

"We will," Wes assures him before leading me to the door.

We walk quietly through the dark parking lot with my hand held tightly in Wes's. When we climb in his car I turn to him unsure of how to express the conflicting feelings I am having.

"He's guilty," I say.

"We don't know that yet," Wes says. He's always playing Devil's Advocate and right now I'm not sure I appreciate it.

"They're not in this car, Wes. You can put away the good cop act," I say snottily.

"I'm not playing good cop," he tells me seriously. "We don't know for sure that Father Thomas is guilty. We can't go off halfcocked."

"I just . . ." I pause taking a deep breath. "I just have this feeling that something isn't right. You know?"

"I know," he tells me. "And it's important to trust your gut. I can't tell you how many times a little intuition saved mine or Lee's life in the desert. But we have to be sure before we do anything drastic."

"Yeah, I guess," I say.

"Let's go home," he says to me.

"What about my Tahoe?" I ask.

"I lifted your keys when I realized it was going to be a long night and handed them off to an agent of mine. It's probably already in the driveway." He shrugs his shoulders unrepentantly.

"That is kind of scary, Wes," I say slapping his shoulder. "I'm so impressed!"

"That's what it takes to impress you?" he asks. "Petty theft?"

"That's grand theft auto of a government vehicle, you crazy! Who does that?" I demand as he starts the car.

"You mean like when you hotwired this very government vehicle a year ago?" he asks with a raised brow.

"Uhh . . . whoops," I say cautiously. "I forgot about the time I stole the Fed-mobile."

"Yeah, whoops," he says sarcastically as he drives through town.

"In my defense, I had a good excuse," I defend my actions.

"What excuse?" he practically shouts in the dark car.

"You were about to get Lee to fire me!" I shout right back.

"So, committing a fairly serious crime was how you combated almost getting fired?" he laughs. "I'm not sure I am ever going to understand your logic and reasoning no matter how long we'll be married," Wes says as he pulls into the driveway next to my department SUV.

"That's wild," I say getting out of the car.

"Keys should be in the mailbox," he says. I walk out to the curb and open the mailbox and sure enough, there they are.

"Well, I'll be damned," I muse.

"Come on," he says. "It's been a long day and an even longer night. I think a hot shower and then as much sleep as we can pack into an hour or two is in store."

"It's barely midnight and we don't have to be up until six," I remind him. "How did you get only an hour or two of sleep?"

"Easy," he smiles that slow lazy grin that has always turned my belly to mush and usually means exciting things. "I'm going to walk you upstairs to our bedroom and strip you down, that might take ten minutes, then I'm going to fuck you in the shower, that might take an hour. After that we'll actually need to shower so that's another thirty minutes. And then I'm going to take you to bed and make love to you until we both forget how awful life can be. Then we'll sleep. You good with that?"

"I'm good with that," I answer on a nod which makes his gorgeous smile flash that much wider.

"Fantastic," he says before touching his mouth to mine in a hard, quick kiss. That's actually one of my favorite of his kisses, the quick lip touch that means so much more and usually proceeds fantastic things.

Wes takes me by the hand and leads me up the walk to the front door. Without dropping his grip on my hand, he shuffles his keys in his free hand and gracefully unlocks the door, pushing it open for me to walk inside. After he passes through the entryway behind me, he shuts and locks the door before leading me up the stairs.

When we hit our room at the end of the hall, we each slide our sidearms out of our holsters—his hidden, mine not—and lock them up for the night before as previously promised, Wes pulls my t-shirt over my head.

He takes my hand again and walks us into the bathroom where he reaches in the shower and turns the water on to warm up. His coat is long gone but he pulls the knot in his tie loose before letting it slip through his fingers. He takes my hand in his and gently wraps the blue striped silk around my wrist, not tying it tight, but letting it slip free.

"One day I'm going to bind you with my ties—naked to the bed," he tells me in his whiskey smooth voice. "And then I'll eat you until you beg me to stop and then I'll fuck you until we both can't take it anymore. What do you have to say about that?"

"Okay," I whisper. His smirk is ridiculous as he unbuttons his crisp white shirt. I often wonder of it's in a handbook somewhere that the Fed suit can only be equipped with a white button-down shirt because they all wear the same one. Only Wes makes it look oh so good.

"I thought you'd be onboard," he says as he pops the button on my jeans. The zipper rasps loudly in contrast to the running water through the otherwise quiet room.

Wes does not push my jeans and panties down but instead slides his palm flat inside my panties and down my mound. He runs the tip of his index finger through my slit and I practically come out of my skin.

"You're always so fucking wet for me," he growls circling my clit with his finger.

"Yes," I say as he slides two fingers deep inside me and pumps them in and out until I'm arching against him and clawing at his shoulders.

Only then does he slide his hand free to the sound of my whimpers and pushes my jeans and panties to the floor. Wes unsnaps my bra and tosses it to the ground leaving me there to stand totally naked as I watch him pull the belt free from his slacks and drop it to the ground before lowering his zipper and letting the dark material fall to the floor unceremoniously. His amber eyes never leave mine as he hooks his fingertips into the waistband of his dark gray boxer briefs and shoves them to the ground letting his heavy cock spring free.

"Come here, baby," he says with his voice gruff and I do not hesitate to jump in his arms in time for him to lower his mouth to mine. I open underneath his and he licks in.

He does not move his mouth from mine as he backs into the shower dragging me along with him in the very best of ways. I gasp when the warm water hits my skin and Wes glides his rough hands up and down my sides, warming me up from the inside out.

Slowly, Wes turns me around to face away from him. I tip my head back and enjoy the way the warm water sprays on my skin and loosens my muscles. I hear the cap on the body wash bottle pop open as he squirts some in his hands and then I feel his heavy palms land gently on top of my shoulders as he works the lather into my skin in small, slow circles.

Inch by inch, Wes moves his hands across my shoulders and down my arms working every kink in my body out. And then he presses the length of his hard body against my back. He works his hands slowly up the sides of my waist needing and massaging as he goes until he reaches my full breasts. Wes cups one in each hand, circling my nipples with his thumbs and I arch my back pushing further into his hands when he pinches them hard in between his thumbs and index fingers.

Wes wraps one arm around my belly pulling me tight against him while he slides his other palm down, down, down until he circles my clit with his index finger. I try to wiggle against him for more friction, more anything, but he's holding me so tight that I can't move. I can only take what Wes will give me and he's giving me everything.

I look down and watch as Wes pushes his hand down even further and slides two fingers deep inside me, his thumb taking over on my clit. My body is on fire and I'm burning up from the inside out. I desperately try to grind against his hand as he pumps his fingers in and out.

"Wes—" I cry out.

"That's it, baby. It's mine and I want it. All you have to do is give it to me," he rumbles in my ear as he uses his hand to push me over the edge.

Wes loosens his hold on me so that I can catch my breath and I turn around to face him. He looks into my eyes, watching me watch him as he slowly raises his fingers to his mouth and sucks them in deep. When he slips them from his lips he tangles his fingers in my hair at the back of my head and crushes his mouth to mine. I open up underneath him and he plunges his tongue inside. The taste of the heady combination of him and me and my body heats again.

Wes presses me back into the shower wall and the stone tiles are cool on my skin. He wraps his hand firmly down my thigh and lifts it to press high on his hip. My muscles burn as they stretch and the movement opens me up to feel his hard length rub against my most intimate places.

He slides his other hand out of my hair and down my side to my other thigh lifting me up high on the wall. I let out an undignified squeak until the noise is abruptly cut short by the feeling of the tip of his cock at my entrance.

And then he makes good on his earlier promise to fuck me in the shower as he thrusts deep inside me. I gasp at the fast intrusion. Wes doesn't give me time to adjust before he's moving hard and fast in and out of my body.

This is one of my favorite things about being with Wes—like this—together. That he can be sweet and tender or dirty and a little wild, either way there is a connection that is made between us in the moment and I revel in the feeling of the slip and slide of his cock inside me.

Wes plunges in and out of my body harder and harder as he takes my mouth and the feeling is overwhelming. I have to break my mouth away from his to try and catch my breath, crying out. I feel my body clench around him as his movements become more frantic. We're both riding the knife's edge right now, so close to falling over and we both know it.

"Claire—" he groans as he moves within me, over me.

"Yes," I call out as he pushes me over the edge right along with him.

After a moment, Wes pulls out and then lowers my shaky legs to the shower floor. Otherwise we stay wrapped up completely in each other. My heart is still pounding when he pushes my wet hair out of my face so gently, tenderly even, with his rough hands.

Wes lowers his mouth to mine again, but this time it's sweet, tender, and short. When he leans back he pulls the hair tie holding my long hair up in a messy bun out, letting it fall around my shoulders like a wet mop. I must have made a face when it fell because Wes laughs.

"This is one of the things I love about you," he says so softly that I almost don't hear it.

"That I look like a drowned rat in the shower?"

"That this has never changed in some ways. You've always had this massive amount of long, black hair. Paired with those eyes, and baby you take my breath away." My heart fills. I know that he loves me, but Wes isn't a man of many words. For him to speak like this I know that he not only means it, but that it's important for him that I know how he feels.

"Wes—" I say, my emotions clogging my throat.

"And that ass doesn't hurt either," he says, and I laugh. Message received. Wes thinks I'm special, but we don't need to wax poetic about it for all time. That's just not his style.

Wes reaches for the shampoo bottle and pours some into his palm. He works a lather between his hands before working the soap into my hair. His strong fingers massage my scalp and I can't help but let out a little growl making him chuckle. Wes tips my head back into the water to rinse the suds free before washing his own hair. When he ducks his head into the running water, Wes pops out and shakes his head like a dog making me scream.

"Wes!"

"What, baby," he laughs.

"Nothing, you mutt," I laugh too. "I just love you."

"I love you too, Claire," he pauses soaping up his body to say before shutting of the water.

Wes trails a towel over every inch of my body, even squeezing the water out of my hair before quickly drying himself off. He neatly hangs the towel back on the rack before scooping me up in his arms like a bride and carrying me to our bed.

Where he drops me like a rock.

"Wes!" I shout but he covers me with his hard body and then smiling, he covers my mouth with his.

He kisses his way down my body stopping to nip and then suck on the side of my neck before soothing the hurt with soft open-mouthed kisses. He trails his lips, slightly parted down my throat and over my chest and down to my breast. He licks my nipple and I arch into him as he sucks it in deep into his mouth. He circles my other nipple with the tip of his index finger, his nail scraping lightly. And then he lets my nipple got with a pop.

He slides back up my body and kisses me hungrily before I press on his shoulders to have him sit down in the middle of the bed. I climb on his lap, straddling him. I like being this way with Wes, face to face, nose to nose, because I can see everything he's feeling, every emotion as it flashes across his face.

I rise up on my knees before sliding down his cock. I slip my legs out from underneath me and wrap them around Wes's waist. He pulls his knees up to better balance and we sit like that wrapped around each other touching and kissing. Here, like this, there is no rough fucking but gently rocking together. His cock deep inside me as his body rubs against my clit.

Here Wes fulfills his last promise to me, to make love to me until we both forget that anything exists outside of him and me.

When at last we come together like a wave gently cresting over my skin, Wes rolls us to lie down in our bed. He pulls the blankets over us and just as gently he whispers, "I love you," before we drift off to sleep.

• • •

Run!

I'm running as fast as my little feet will take me through the woods behind my parents' house. I have to get away from the bad man. If he catches me now, I'll never get away. I have to be free.

Run! I have to run faster.

I see the blue gray light as it spills through the trees. Mommy always told me this was her favorite part of the day—looking at the sun as it comes up in the morning. I ran away late in the night when the bad man was sleeping. It was my only chance. After he broke the lock on the closet door I knew that I had a chance to get out.

Free.

I'm free. That's the words in my head as the trees break and I see Wes standing at the edge of the backyard. I'm free. I'm finally free. Wes looks up and he sees me.

"I've got her!" he shouts to someone.

My heart is beating so hard in my chest and it hurts to breathe. I'm so tired but I have to keep running. I see Wes, his face, I know that he'll protect me. Wes always protects me. He will keep me safe. He will keep me free.

I push my feet just a little harder, I run just a little faster. I'm almost there. I'm almost free when I get to the clearing where I saw Wes standing just up ahead, only he's not there anymore. Or he is. Wes isn't standing, he's lying on the ground covered with blood.

There is blood all around the ground and the trees drip with the sticky stuff. I have never seen so much blood and I want to be sick. But when I look to Wes for help, his eyes are open on his beautiful face but he doesn't see anything because my beautiful Wes is dead and it's all my fault.

"No!" I scream.

And I know that I'll never be free. Not ever again.

• • •

No! Not Wes. Not now. I scam. The tears burn hot down my cheeks and my heart is breaking, no, it's not broken, it's shattered into a million pieces that will never be put back together again.

"Shh," someone whispers. "You're alright, honey."

"Wes?" I ask but that's not quite right, he's dead. I saw him die.

"It was a dream, baby," he explains, and I force open my eyes.

"You're here?" I ask, and I hate that my voice sounds so small.

"Yeah, honey. It was just a dream," he tells me. "Do you want to talk about it?"

I stop and think about it, I have never told Wes about any of my dreams before, only Anna. I do not ever tell anyone else about them. I can tell he's holding his breath too—probably thinking he's about to be turned down. Again. But I'm not, this time is different because it feels so different to me.

"Yeah," I say softly. "I do."

"I dream this same dream all the time," I explain. "It's back when I'm running away. I'm running through the woods and I have to go faster and faster because I don't want the bad man to catch me. I can't go back to the closet—"

"Wait," he says. "You're remembering?"

"Anna thinks it might be memories, but they come differently every time, so I don't know."

"What do you mean?" he asks. "Explain please."

"Well, like this one—" I start.

"Wait, are there more than one?" he asks me.

"Yes, I dream about being taken, a closet, I'm assuming I was kept in one, running away, and when you rescued me," I finish softly.

"Anything else?"

"I dream about the . . . *abuse.*"

Wes is quiet for a long moment and I wonder if he doesn't really want to know which I'm not afraid to admit kind of stings. He has been badgering me for months to tell him what my nightmares are about and now that he has a tiny glimpse at my hell, he doesn't want to know. That makes me feel small and unimportant and I don't like it at all. I brush those feelings off and stuff them away for a really bad day.

"You said they change?" he asks. "How so?"

"Like I was saying, this one is the one where I'm running away and you save me. I see you through the trees just up ahead and I hear you call out to Lee that you've got me."

"Yeah," he says. "That really happened."

"Usually I dream that you grab me and I pass out, that's when I wake up," I explain.

"That's what really happened, honey," he says softly. "I really think you're remembering. You're working through something and it's just out of reach."

"Yes!" I shout. I'm getting excited that Wes seems to understand. "It's like the answers are just under the icy top of a frozen lake. I know that they're there but I still can't get to them."

"What else do you dream about that day?" he asks me.

"Sometimes, I dream that the bad man catches up to me and I never make it back to you," I whisper into the dark.

"I'm so sorry," he says. "But you should know that there is nothing I wouldn't do to find you, to get you back. There is no distance too far. I love you too much. I will always find you, honey."

"This time, I dreamed that when I got to you, you were dead and lying in a pool of blood," I say as fast as I possibly can. I hate the taste of the words in my mouth.

"I'm right here, Claire," he says as he takes my hand and places my palm to lay flat on his chest. "I'm alive and right here and I'm not going anywhere," he says resolutely.

"I know that," I explain. "And I really do, but I can't help but feel like something is wrong."

"What do you mean?"

"Maybe it's a bad omen or something, but I can't help but feel like something really bad is about to happen," I explain.

"You can't think like that," he tells me. "This case is really bad. It's ugly and it's messy, but you can't go through life waiting for the other shoe to drop."

"I know that." And I do, I really do, but still. I can't help how I feel.

"Do you?" Wes questions.

"Yes," I tell him. "But you need to listen to me, Wes. Something is really wrong here. I can feel it in my bones."

"I think it's been a really long week and you're overworked and tired. I think you're really worried about your friends and your bonehead brother is being an idiot so you have a lot on your plate. Let's just go back to sleep and when we wake up in the morning, everything will seem better."

"Okay," I say quietly like the kid who just got a dressing down from the principal, but I can't help but feel like agreeing with Wes is making a huge fucking mistake. It's too bad that later would prove how wrong we really were. Only then it would be too late.

chapter 26
the results are in

*B*EEP... BEEP... BEEP...
Wes's alarm sounds on his nightstand and this morning I can't help but feel like everything is about to change. He reaches over and shuts the alarm off before turning to me.

"You okay, baby?" he asks me.

"I don't think so," I say hesitantly. More than anything, I don't want to go back to the days where Lee and Wes think I'm incapable of handling my duties. And even more than that I don't want him to know that I am visited by nightmares almost every night now. That I tossed and turned all night after I told him about my dreams that seem to be turning into memories.

"Everything is fine," he says. "Nothing is going to go wrong today."

"You can't say that!" I shout jumping up from the bed.

"Claire, be rational," he says firmly.

"Excuse me?" I ask. Wes couldn't possibly be insinuating that I am acting crazy.

"Claire—" he starts.

"I'm not crazy!" I shout sounding even to myself like anything but sane or rational.

"I never said that you were," he snaps.

"You didn't seem to be implying that I'm not either," I tell him as I fold my arms across my chest.

"I'm sorry," he says. "I just don't want you upset." I sigh. That makes sense. I'm not sleeping well and that coupled with the stress of this case is making me a little frazzled.

"I'm sorry too," I say softly.

"Come here, baby," he says, and I walk over to him letting him pull me into his arms. "Everything is going to be okay." I just nod, but as we get ready for work I can't help but feel like there is a dark cloud hanging overhead. I still feel like something is really, really wrong.

• • •

I drive to work thinking dark thoughts so it's incredibly fitting that it rains.

This morning, Wes and I did not touch or fool around as we got dressed. The intimacy between us was lost, not for forever, but for the moment. He thinks I'm worried about nothing, but I can't help but think I have everything to worry about.

I showered by myself, waiting until after he was done with his own shower to step in and then dressed silently by myself. I have no doubt that he waited for me to join him in the shower like we do every morning because he took the world's longest shower for a man. But I just couldn't even though my heart ached to join him, to have him hold me in his arms. I know it makes me sound weak, but I needed him to hear me, to hear my worries and my fears, and to help me through them, not just brush them aside. Shit, I've been friends with Anna for so long that now I need to be a sharer. I can't wait to tell her, I bet she's going to love the shit out of that.

I can't top the sinking feeling in my stomach that something is very wrong. That I'm missing something. I have to stop Father Thomas before he hurts anymore people, but how?

As I pull into the parking lot the ringing of my phone breaks me out of my head.

"Goodnite," I answer as I pull into my spot in the back.

"Hey," Anna says when I answer. "It's me."

"Hey, yourself." I smile glad to hear my friend's voice this morning.

"I . . . I just wanted to call and check in," she says softly.

"Is everything okay?" I ask.

"Yeah," she sighs. "I'm just feeling a little silly after I freaked out and bailed last night," she explains. I can hear in her voice that she is uneasy with the situation, maybe even unsure and that is the exact opposite of how I would usually describe Anna. That simple fact makes me mad at my dipshit brother all over again.

"Well, you missed all the fun," I tell her.

"Oh yea?" she asks. "How so?"

"Well, Sarah Holt was murdered by the killer. Probably right after you left."

"You're kidding?" she asks shedding her weird feelings from the previous night and in an instant assuming her professional role.

"I wish I were. Same MO as Dennis Boyd and Kerrigan Adams."

"That's awful," she says, and I can hear her shudder. I do too because it *is* awful.

"We had to shut down the bar. The manager was a real asshole and tried to take a swing at me."

"How did that make you feel?" she asks me, falling into shrink mode and I realize that I have missed our chats. As I've been letting Wes in more it doesn't mean I can't talk to Anna too. I can have them both.

"It pissed me off, but Wes grabbed him before he could and arrested him. It was awesome!" I cheer, and she laughs.

"That is awesome," she laughs. "Go Wes!"

"Then Wes and I went to the church to talk to Father Thomas. I know it's him I just can't get anything that will stick," I can hear the frustration in my own voice. After a slight pause, Anna speaks.

"What makes you so sure that it's Father Thomas?" she asks me.

"Well, everyone said he preached about sins of the flesh and all that. Plus, he talked about Dennis Boyd's divorce and all that," I explain. "I just do, damn it."

"But I'm not sure that makes him guilty," Anna says softly.

I sigh. "Fuck. I know it. I'm losing sight of what's important, but I can't help but feel like something bad is about to happen."

"I'm sure it'll be fine," she says.

"Yeah," I say. "You're right. Wes said the same thing this morning." And isn't that really the crux of the problem? Everyone keeps saying everything will be fine and no one is listening to me say I have a very bad feeling.

"I'll call and check in later, maybe we'll go to dinner. Just us?" she asks me.

"Sure, I'd like that," I tell her before she hangs up and I sigh again. There seems to be a lot of sigh worthy moments this morning. Maybe Wes is right, it's not a bad omen, but a culmination of a shit case, a wedding to plan, and my brother tearing apart our social group with his wayward dick.

But even as I think it, I know that's not it.

• • •

"We have a winner!" Emma shouts when the metal elevator doors ding open and I can't help but laugh. "Come on down!"

"You're ridiculous," I tell her.

"You already know this," she says.

"So, you called me down here because…?" I ask.

• • •

I was sitting at my desk with my umpteenth cup of coffee of the morning and an ulcer that is most definitely developing in my gut looking over all of my case notes and trying to find anything I can on Father Thomas when the phone on my desk rang.

"Goodnite," I answered.

"The results are in," Emma barks into the phone. "Get your ass down here." And then she hangs up.

I sighed in frustration for the millionth time this morning when the dots wouldn't connect. I can't help but feel like a Sword of Damocles is hanging over my head. Like a clock is ticking down the seconds and I'm running out of time. So, I push back from my rickety desk and head for the elevator to be greeted by Emma who is obviously feeling the strain as well. She's not a big fan of serial killers either.

• • •

"What do you got?" I ask her.

"Autopsy results," she says taking on a more serious demeanor.

"Anything unusual?" I ask her.

She sighs. "I really wish there were. Should I just run the highlights for you and email you the report?"

"Yeah," I say. I hate this shit.

"Alright, highlight reel: Sarah Holt was struck on the side of the head but that is not what killed her. More than likely it subdued them so that the killer could bind them with the jute. Fibers were found in the wounds on her wrists confirm it is jute."

"I don't understand why Father Thomas is beating the victims over the head to subdue them," I muse aloud. "He seems young and pretty fit."

"He does," Emma adds. "But what if it's not him? What if it's one of the members of the singles group? That probably fits the profile better anyways although you'd have to check with Anna for that."

"True."

"So back to the highlights?" she asks me.

"Yeah, sorry," I murmur.

"Sarah Holt was stabbed through the heart and then repeatedly several times before the letter A was carved into her chest. She was still warm but dead when we got to her so that was shortly before we found her, I'd say ten minutes or so."

"Thanks, Emma," I tell her before heading back upstairs to my desk.

I call the bar and ask for their security camera footage. Emma is right, Sarah Holt had to have been murdered just before we found her, so the killer would be on those tapes.

"*Cicada Bar and Grill*," someone answers.

"Yes, I'm Detective Goodnite with the George Washington Township PD," I say. "I'd like to speak to the owner."

"This is the owner and we don't talk to cops here," he says in a gruff voice.

Unfortunately, it seems, that the bar owner shares the same sentiments about law enforcement that the manager does.

"There was a murder at your restaurant last night, I need to see the security camera footage," I tell him.

"Well, then you can bring me a God damned Search Warrant or you ain't getting shit, lady," he barks into the phone. *"And let me tell you, you and your Fed aren't welcomed here either."* And then he hangs up.

"God damnit!" I shout as I slam down the receiver. Doesn't anyone care that there is a serial killer on the loose. You would think more people would be willing to do something as trivial as hand over some stupid security tapes to help out.

My phone rings again. I sigh and answer it, "Goodnite."

And then everything goes to shit just like I knew it would.

chapter 27
sanctuary

"*I* KNOW IT'S YOU!" she says as she chases me through the sanctuary. I just smile at her.

"You have everyone looking at Father but it's you." I shake my head and smile indulgently at the petite brunette like she's a small child. "You killed Kerrigan and you killed Dennis and you killed Sarah."

"Is that so?" I ask as I inch closer to her.

"Yes, it is and I can prove it!"

"And how is that?" I ask.

"I'm a psychologist for the police department, I put together profiles," she says triumphantly. "And I checked around, I can prove that your alibis are nothing but lies."

"Like what?" I ask as I edge closer to her still. She doesn't seem to realize how near to each other we are, and I revel in the hunt.

"You were at the bistro the other night. I saw you on my way out and I didn't realize it at the time because you were dressed in street clothes, but it was you. I realize that now . . . What are you doing? She asks but it's too late. I swing my arm out clipping her across the face with an ornate gold cross.

The woman falls in a heap and I love the poetic justice of this sacrifice being made at the Lord's altar. I pull her body up to the steps at the front and pull the piece of jute out of my pocket. I carry it with me everywhere. It's the very same one that I used to bind everyone's wrists together so that I could do the work that I set out to do.

"'The woman was dressed in purple and scarlet, and was glittering with gold, precious stones and pearls. She held a golden cup in her hand, filled with abominable things and the filth of her adulteries.' You could have been many things but instead you chose to be a whore just like them," I whisper into her ear the words of Revelations as she begins to wake.

I hear a noise near the doors and I know that this will have to be quick. I won't be able to savor this sacrifice like I did the others. This will be my last act in the service of our Lord and I take my blade in both hands one last time raising it up over my head

"Police!" Claire. "Don't move!

But I do move without hesitation. The knife arcs through the air and plunges into Anna's heart. I watch her face as every emotion flits across her face. I hope *she's happy now. She looks of panic, of desperation, and then as it changed into resignation. She knows now that she is dying. My work is finished. My mission has been fulfilled.*

And then I hear the gunshots blast through the sanctuary . . .

chapter 28

man to man

Wes

A BAD OMEN. That's what the superstitious guys on the old teams would call what Claire described this morning.

When she woke up in my arms this morning screaming at the top of her lungs still gripped in the clutches of one of those fucking awful nightmares, she said something felt off, *wrong even*. I didn't tell her at the time, but I felt it too. Something is wrong, I just don't know what.

I'm standing at the window in my office trying to wrap my mind around the demons that chase my girl at night, the ones I can't see. I would give anything, *do anything*, to spare her from those nightmares which are coming more and more often.

There's a knock on my office door.

"Come in," I bark out and in walks Lee. He looks like shit, but then I guess if I were in his shoes, I probably would too.

"Well if it isn't Deputy Dipshit," I greet him in a man hug and slap him on the back. "What's up, brother? You look like hammered horse shit," I laugh.

"Thanks." He rolls his eyes. "I really appreciate your undying loyalty."

"Anytime," I respond. "So, what brings you to my neck of the woods?"

"I need advice," he says and by the look on his face, he would rather eat a bag of nails and be anywhere else in the world than here having this conversation with me.

And again, I can't blame him.

"What's going on?" I ask.

"I'm in love with her." he says. "I'm in love with Emma and she hates me."

"It definitely seems like that's the case." I tell him.

"Thanks for sugar coating that for me, man. It really helps." he snarks before asking, "What do I do?"

"I wish I knew, Lee. I really do. But I kind of agree with your sister, I'm not sure you can overcome this love triangle situation. It might be best to just walk away," I tell Lee honestly. I know it's not what he wants to hear but maybe it's what he needs to hear. Things are in pretty sore shape right now and we have a murderer to catch.

"No!" he shouts. "That's out of the question."

"Then you have to make things right with Anna before you continue to pursue things with Emma. But I would be upfront with her and tell her that you're trying to right those wrongs and be a better man," I tell him. At least that's what I would do if I were in his shoes.

"That's a good plan," he says. "Did my sister make you this touchy feely?"

he asks me.

"Hell no!" I laugh. "Claire would hand me my balls in a paper cup first."

"She's a tough cookie but underneath it all she's just a big softy," he tells me.

"I know." I smile at my best friend. "She's the best thing that ever happened to me."

"Don't worry," he says. "She knows." I throw my head back and laugh.

"So, you think talking it out will work?" he asks me looking—for the first time in any that I can remember—worried. Not even when we were dodging enemy fire or hunting down the baddest of the bad in some far off, war torn nation, did I ever see Lee look worried. In fact, he was eerily calm before, during, and after those missions.

"I don't know," I tell him honestly. "But with women, the one you love in particular, full transparency is usually best."

"So you tell Claire everything?" he asks.

"Everything that matters," I tell him seriously when my phone rings. "Yeah?" I say when I pick up the phone. "*Anna's at the church. She says she knows who the killer is*," Claire's panicked voice comes through the line. Jesus this doesn't sound good.

"Lee's here. We're on our way." I end the call abruptly and jump up from my seat.

"What's up?" Lee asks instantly alert.

"Claire just called," I tell him as I grab my keys. "Anna's at the church she says she knows who the killer is. We gotta roll." I'm running out the door but he's right behind me. Just like old times.

We jump in my car and I'm peeling out of the parking lot. We're probably the closest to the church from everyone else. Here's hoping we can stop Anna from doing something stupid. At least that's what I'm praying for anyways.

"This is all my fault," Lee says from my passenger seat.

"Brother. Now is not the time to freak out," I warn.

"You're right. She's smart. She'll be smart," he chants but I can't help but feel like Claire's nightmare was right, in that everything is about to go to straight to shit. I had a sixth sense overseas when an op was about to go tits up, we all did really. It was the only way to stay alive and it hasn't left me since. I feel the same tingling along the back of my neck when a case is not what it seems, and I have to fight against scratching at the back of my neck now.

I cannot believe that Anna would try and solve this herself. This killer is dangerous. But she was so sure she could show Lee that she is his equal, that she's good enough for him. The truth is she was always better than him. I love Lee like a brother but he's been a real ass where these two women are concerned.

Unfortunately, she couldn't see that somewhere along the way, while she was falling in love with Lee, he was falling for Emma. What a cluster fuck. I pull into the parking lot of the church on two wheels and throw it in park before Lee and I are out and running. Hell, Lee bailed out and was running before the car had stopped. That's how urgent the situation is, or SNAFU, Situation Now All Fucked Up, as we would say. I see Claire heading for the church from the other end of the parking lot. We are running full out, but nothing would prepare us for what we would encounter when we entered the sanctuary.

And then Claire screams . . .

chapter 29

Anna

I'M RUNNING.
"Goodnite," I answer."*I'm at the church. I know who it is come quick,*" Anna whispers into the phone when I answer the phone just before the click sounds telling me that she ended the call abruptly. I pick up my phone and dial Wes, "*Yeah,*" he says when he picks up. "Anna's at the church. She says she knows who the killer is."

"*Lee's here. We're on our way.*" And then he ends the connection.I pick up my phone one more time and dial Emma. "Anna's at the church. She says she knows who it is. I'm on my way there now," I say when she picks up the phone."*Fuck!*" she bites out. "*I'm on my way.*"I'm running to my SUV by the time I hang up with Emma I'm climbing in and turning the key. I am probably the farthest away from the church. Praying I get there in time and so fucking angry that Anna would try and solve this herself. This killer is dangerous. But she was so sure she could show my dumb fucking brother that she's a contemporary.

She couldn't see that somewhere along the way, while she was falling in love with Lee, he was falling for Emma. Or she didn't *want* to see it.This is just a big fucking mess.I pull into the parking lot of the church and barely have the Tahoe in park before I'm running for the church doors with the car door hanging open. Lee and Wes are heading for the church from the other end of the lot. Somehow, I made it here before them but then again, I did break land speed records to do it. We all are in hot pursuit, but nothing would prepare us for what we would encounter when we entered the sanctuary.

I'm running as fast as I can, pushing my body as hard as I can. From the minute I hung up the phone from talking to Anna, I knew that she was going to do something stupid. How could she? The answer is simple, she wants to belong that badly, to be worthy of someone like Lee whether he was in love with her or not.

"You take the front, I'll go around back," Emma says. She has her gun pulled as well. We are a small township but even the Medical Examiner is trained to handle an intense situation.

"Got it," I say. "Wes and Lee should be here any minute, they were right behind us."

As I run up the steps, I pull my sidearm from its holster and steady my arms. I breathe in three times and out one to center my focus. It's some SEAL trick Lee taught me ages ago and it helps. I push open the big double door and enter the sanctuary. I draw my sidearm when I hear Anna's scream.

Nothing could prepare me for what I was about to see.

"What have you done?" I hear Father Thomas scream from the side but I can't look at him now.

"Police!" I shout. "Don't move!

But Father Matthew does with a maniacal look on his face. The knife arcs through the air and plunges into Anna's heart. Until the day I die, I will never forget the look of panic, of desperation on her face as it changed into resignation. She knows. And then I pull the trigger over and over again. I empty my magazine into Father Matthew's body until he falls limp to the side. I never would have guessed that the calm and quiet priest who told Wes and I we were a lost cause, who practically pointed every finger at Father Thomas, had killed four people in the name of God.

Pain.

What a stupid little word to describe what I am feeling right now—just four fucking letters—such a mundane word to explain the white-hot lightning rips through my torso in the vicinity of where my heart used to be. It sears so acutely that my breath catches in my throat.

"No!" someone screams. I think it was me. It might have been me, but I don't know.

Hands grab me from behind to stop me from closing the gap between me and the bloody body on the altar steps of my family church. These slabs of muscle, bone, joint, and tendons restrain me, they hold me back from the jarring loss. But the cold truth of what has come to pass is front and center for all to see. They pull the now empty, wasted piece of steel and lead from my hands and toss it behind them.

Lee pushes Father Mathew's body away to the side. Emma rushes in from the back and drops to her knees by Anna's side and unties her hands. Emma is leaning over a prone Anna on the steps to the altar.

Blood covers them both. "Anna! God damnit stay with me," Emma shrieks as she tries to stop the blood flowing so freely from slices and holes places all over her petite body. I drop to my knees beside her. "What can I do? Tell me what to do!""Just stop the bleeding."*Anguish.*

This is anguish. This severe pain. A wound licked raw that I know will never heal. This is a wound that will only fester and turn putrid.

Before I had looked at victims and thought why can't I save them? Or it should have been me. But looking at the shell of what had been as it's splayed on the plush carpet of the altar steps I know without a doubt that I would trade places in a heartbeat. If only it was my blood that was spilled and not hers.

"Emma," Anna rasps. There's a rattling behind her voice and everyone in this room know what that means. *A death rattle.*"Save your energy, babe," Emma tells her sweetly."I see it now," she says. "It was wrong of me to want him. He was always yours."

"No," Emma denies as the tears stream down her beautiful face. "Don't say that."

"Love him for me." My breath seizes in my lungs and my own tears burn behind my eyes.

"No. You do it because I won't!" Emma sobs.

"He loves you," Anna rattles.

"I don't care," Emma lies.

"He's going to . . . to need someone to . . . to love him." I can see that it's taking all of her energy to get her last wishes out.

"No, Anna," Emma pleads. "Anything but that."

"Just . . . love him." And then her eyes dip closed never to open again as the last of her breath rattles out of her body. "Anna!" Emma cries. I'm stunned. I'm in shock. And I don't know what to do. "Emma, honey," Liam says as he reaches for her. "No!" she screams as she pulls away. "Don't touch me!""Emma," I call out unsure of what to do. "No, Lee. This is all your fault." Liam looks as if he has been struck. "Emma, you can't mean that," he pleads.

"She wanted so badly to belong to you, to fit into your world and that pushed her straight to this moment," Emma says with an eerie coldness in her voice.

"Emma," Lee calls out again. "Do me a favor, Lee and just stay the fuck away from me." And then she storms outside.

Wes grabs me from behind again and pulls me away from my friend. The only person I would turn to when the road turned dark. How many nights did she talk me through a terror I couldn't see myself through alone? Too many to count.

"Let me go!" I wail. My voice is harsh and raw. The words are ripped from my chest leaving a raw wound in its wake.

"No," someone says. I don't know who. I don't care either, but I think it may be Wes. I can't stop staring at the broken remains of someone I had loved above all else. Someone who managed to do the unthinkable, to break down my walls and invade my heart.

Grief.

If this is what grief feels like I don't want it. I want to go back to this morning when my life was normal. I had had the world at my feet, and my family was whole. I feel raw... *exposed*... I'm a wound that's been flayed open down to the bone. But it cannot be stitched or cauterized.

Maybe this is shock. I don't know. All I do know is that the world is a darker place tonight. This is not a loss that I or anyone else will get over. Not now, not ever.

Everything has changed.

epilogue
end of watch

COLD.
    I walk into the Civic Center feeling cold and empty. I flash my badge to the officer guarding the door, but everyone here knows who I am and why I'm here. The seats are all empty but one. Lee sits in the corner in neither the front nor the back. Not wanting to bother him in his grief or willing to talk to anyone, I sit in the back.

Anna's flag draped coffin sits at the front on a wooden stand with a uniformed officer standing guard on either side. While Anna may have felt like she didn't belong to us, that she was never a part of the department since she acted only as a contractor, but in the end the department was there for her, insisting on full burial honors, which for someone without a badge is almost unheard of.

Lee needed no persuading having agreed wholeheartedly. His guilt at casting her aside is riding him hard.

I don't even know why I am here, I guess I just needed to be near her one last time to get my head on straight before her funeral in the morning. At home I was restless. I couldn't sleep. I didn't even know how to try.

The last week has been a nightmare of a media circus. Not to mention coming to terms with the fact that the priest who baptized Lee and I turned out to be a psychopath on a murderous rage. I was right when I said Father Thomas didn't have to subdue his victims to tie them up. I was also wrong because he wasn't the killer. To which I owed him a huge apology that he accepted graciously. He really is a nice guy.

It turns out after we spoke on the phone, Anna realized that she recognized Father Matthew in plain clothes walking into the Cicada Street Bar and Grill as she was leaving. Instead of telling Wes, Lee, or myself, she decided to prove once and for all that she was part of the team. But having no training, she didn't know that rule number fucking one is never go in unarmed and without backup.

Anna made a fatal mistake that day and for it we're all suffering the consequences. Lee and Emma in particular. After being unable to stay away from Lee despite her friendship with Anna, Emma is now torn up with grief and blames Lee for everything. To my knowledge, she has not spoken to him since the day Anna died. Lee, who is so in love with Emma that he pushed and pushed her regardless of Anna's feelings is now back to square one. Where before he had Emma in secret in his bed, now he has absolutely nothing and according Wes, is unraveling at an alarming pace.

As for me, I don't know where to start. I can't make heads or tails of my feelings. I have cried more in the last week than I have in years. The worst part is, the nightmares aren't a maybe anymore but happen like clockwork every night, sometimes several a night. I can't help but think that without being able to talk them through with Anna I won't be able to overcome them. Three years ago, a visit with a department shrink was the last thing I needed or wanted. Yet somehow, she had become one of the most important people in my life and now there is an empty spot in my heart that can never be filled or repaired.

I don't know how long I have sat here when Wes slides into the seat next to mine. I turn into his arms and smell the spicy scent that is inherently Wes. I bury my face in his t-shirt and just breathe it in finding comfort in him.

"I thought I would find you here," he says to me. Wes looks adorably rumpled in a pair of gray sweatpants that say *NAVY* on the leg in big blue letters and a t-shirt. I on the other hand, look like shit in a pair of black leggings and an oversized sweatshirt. Ironically, the one that matches the pants Wes is wearing.

"Yeah," I whisper. "I just didn't know where else to go."

"To me," he says. "When in doubt, you always come home to me and I promise I'll be there to help you sort through it."

"Okay," I agree because that sounds really nice. Wes is my partner in all things and I needed that reminder.

"Let's go home."

Wes wraps his arm around my shoulder and leads me out to my car in the parking lot leaving Lee to sit with Anna in silence. He deposits me into the driver's seat and then I follow him home. Like always, he's waiting in the driveway for me to climb down and then he pulls me gently into the safety of his arms. Wes walks me into the house and up the stairs, down the hall and to our bedroom where he pulls down the covers and tucks me into bed where I fall asleep as best as I can until I need to get up and dress for my best friend's funeral.

What we did not see was Lee sitting with Anna's casket all night until the wee hours of the morning when he left only to shower, shave, and don his dress uniform signifying himself as the Department Captain.

• • •

"'Blessed are the Peacemakers for they shall be called the children of God,'" the Pastor invokes the service with after we take our places in the congregation of the Civic Center. The church felt wrong to be the place that we honor Anna's sacrifice at. "While Dr. Anna Garner was not an officer of the law she tended to them. Dr. Garner, I am told, was more a member of this team than she ever realized while here on Earth."

I stand next to Emma, she looks both regal and sad in her simple black wrap dress with lace cap sleeves and heels. Sad, she looks so abundantly sad. My dress uniform is stiff from lack of use. Usually it hangs wrapped in cellophane in the very back of my closet and is only pulled out for tragic events just like this one. Only usually, I stand in the back of the crowd and think what a tragic loss of life or how sad it is to lose a fallen comrade. I'm not sitting in the front section with the other mourners.

For years, I lived fast and loose chasing one case after another with zero regard for my safety. I always thought it would be me who would fall in the line of duty and my parents would stand sad but proud of my bravery. I never once imagined that I would lose someone so integral to my life.

Wes stands beside me looking devastatingly handsome in his black fed suit with a crisp white shirt and black tie. Last night he shined his shoes for hours. Just polishing them over and over again, as though he could never get them shiny enough. Anna would say that was his own way to deal with his grief, so I left him to it but kept a watchful eye just in case he needed me to bring him back from the edge.

"Let us bow our heads and pray," the pastor leads. "Dear Heavenly Father, help us to find solace in you during these dark times. Please guide these officers as they carry their grief for their fallen comrade, their sister in arms." I take the time to listen to his words and think there is nothing that will bring that solace he speaks of. Right now, everything seems so bleak that I can't even fathom a way out of this grief.

After the pastor finishes speaking, Lee dressed immaculately in his uniform, every piece meticulously laid out, steps up to the podium and while he looks perfect, I can see that he is anything but. His lips are pulled tight just so and I can see the whiteness in the corners from strain. His hand shakes just a bit, it's subtle so no one would notice it but me. Or Emma as she stiffens beside me.

"Thank you all for coming," he says. "Anna Garner was an integral part of our Department and while she was not out on patrol tending to the community, she was in the station tending to its officers. This job is not an easy one and she took it on with compassion and grace. It takes a strong person to hear about the things officers see every day and she did with kindness in her heart wanting to ease those burdens and we are all better for having known her."

"Fucking ass," Emma says under her breath.

"Emma," I whisper grabbing her hand in mine. She does not turn to look at me, but she does nod once and then squeeze my hand before dropping our connection.

When Lee steps down from the podium he is replaced on the stage with a choir who sings *Eternal Father*, a staple at all Police and Military funerals.

When the pastor steps up again, "'Blessed are the Peacemakers,' Matthew said," he begins to expound on the passage we all know so well but I can't help but flinch at the name. "Fortunate are we to have those who watch over our community and we are all so fortunate to have them. Jesus knew that those who put their lives on the line for their communities are so special and I would like to touch on that for a moment in the readings of Matthew."

"God, I hate that name," Emma whispers as a shudder wracks through her body causing Lee's attention to focus solely on Emma even though his body does not move and he remains facing forward, I can tell that he is acutely tuned into her.

"I was just thinking the same thing," I whisper back.

When the Mayor steps up to speak I do everything in my power not to roll my eyes. In fact, I'm pretty sure every officer in this building feels the same way. This particular Mayor has never been a big supporter of law enforcement and it shows in his recent budget cuts towards safety equipment like flak jackets and life vests.

"Pompous windbag," I hear Lee mutter under his breath and have to bite my lip to keep from laughing. Laughing at a funeral would be highly inappropriate or so I have been previously told.

All possible outbursts of hilarity are muted when two women from the choir to sing *For Good* from the *Wicked* Soundtrack. It's fitting, and I can't help but cry again. I hate fucking funerals. It's so stupid but as they sing about never seeing one another again and parting ways I can't help but feel like my heart shatters just a little bit more.

"Please welcome, FBI Special Agent in Charge Wesley O'Connell for the tolling of the bells." When Wes is called to the podium to lead the bell ceremony a sob caught in my throat. He looks so handsome in his custom tailored black suit.

"In the Navy, we ring a bell to signify a ship or a sailor lost at sea or in battle. I think it's only fitting that we honor Dr. Anna Garner this way," he explains. "Please join me in a moment of silence as Officer Jones rings the bell twenty-one times in honor of Dr. Anna Parker who I had the extreme pleasure of calling my friend. She will be sorely missed." A sob bubbles up from my throat and Emma reaches for me again.

The bell rings once.

The tears that have burned behind my eyes all morning run freely down my cheeks. I have cried so much that there shouldn't be any tears left to cry.

The bell rings twice.

I'm so fucking angry. How could Anna have been so stupid? Why would she take a risk like that? The gambled with everything and lost.

The bell rings a third time. And then again and again and again until they have rung twenty-one times. Each one like a bullet to my heart.

Wes looks to me and in that moment I mouth the words "Thank you," to him. Thank you for loving me, thank you for this beautiful tribute to our friend, thank you for understanding. He nods once and then exits the stage.

"Color Guard, retire colors," the funeral commander calls out and the uniformed men assigned to the duty pick up their flags and stand in formation at the head of the aisle just in front of Anna's flag cover coffin.

A bagpiper plays *Amazing Grace* as the Color Guard steps forward to make room for the pallbearers. Six more uniformed officers lift up Anna's casket high on their shoulders. We stand in stunned silence as Anna is led out of the Civic Center by the bagpiper followed by the Color Guard and then our own sweet, Anna.

We all file out behind them. Her casket is loaded into a shiny black hearse escorted in the front by three motorcycle patrol and two black and white units in the back with lights flashing. Together she is driven off to the cemetery where she will be buried in a private service in an hour.

We all file into our vehicles marked with bright orange FUNERAL tags and follow soberly behind them. Wes holds my hand as he drives.

We park on the side of the road as Anna's casket is loaded into a horse drawn caisson. And then quietly, our small group walks behind it to end at Anna's final resting place where the pallbearers once again carry her casket from the caisson and then place it on the racks that will eventually lower her into the ground. Every step I take is a step towards the end. Towards goodbye and I feel like there are lead weights in my legs but somehow, I keep moving forward.

"'The Lord is my Shepherd . . .'" the pastor begins to recite Psalm 23 and Wes holds me tight in his arms as I cry freely. There is no stopping them now. Anna is gone, and this is it.

"Please retire colors," the Funeral Commander calls out and I sob as the uniformed officers fold up the flag that had covered the glossy casket and present it to Liam. Lee then turns on his heel and kneels to present the flag to Anna's parents.

"It is with my deepest condolences that I present to you this flag," he says handing it off before stepping back to the side. "And the knowledge that your daughter died bravely in the line of duty."

This is the part that I hate. I know it's coming, we talked about it and everyone felt like it was a fitting final send off to Anna, our one last tradition for a fallen officer but I can already feel myself losing it as Lee turns the dial on the radio that he holds in his hand. Lee clicks the button on the side of the radio three times in quick succession to signify the time was now.

"Dr. Anna Garner . . . this is dispatch paging Dr. Anna Garner . . . Dr. Anna Garner . . ." the radio crackles and another sob bubbles up.

Lee picks up the radio and presses the button on the side. "This is Captain Liam Goodnite of the George Washington Township Police Department. Dr. Anna Garner is officially relieved of duty. End of Watch on this day, the sixth of August."

"Dispatch copies, Captain Goodnite," the voice crackles and I can hear the tears in her voice too. "Dr. Anna Garner is relieved of duty. End of Watch August 6, 2018."

"That concludes our service today," the pastor says. "Immediate friends and family are welcome to stay."

The bulk of this little group peels off, walking back to where the cars were left. There will be a small luncheon provided at the station for all that took duty today and the rest that head back there to go to work. I won't be going. I'm not ready. After this I have a date with my old boyfriends, Jack and Johnny. After that I have no plans.

Together, Wes, Emma, Lee, and I watch as they lower Anna into the ground. It's over. Anna is gone. I wrap my arms around Wes's middle and hold tight until I feel like I can curb the tears.

"You ready to go, baby?" he asks me softly.

"No," I answer. "But I don't think I ever will be."

"Emma—" I hear Lee start.

"Don't," she commands in voice filled with nothing but ice. "Don't you dare."

"Emma, you have to talk to me," he demands.

"No, Lee," she snaps a little wild. "What you don't seem to understand—so I'll say it again louder for the kids in the back—is that I don't have to do anything. The least of which will involve you."

"Emma, I love you," he pleads and it's hard to watch him in this moment of desperation.

"Save it for someone else. You've ruined enough lives here," she spits out with so much venom even I flinch.

"You can't mean that," he says stunned looking like someone hit him.

"I do." And then she walks off never looking back. After she marches out of sight, Lee seems to shake off his shock and chases after her.

"What do we do now?" I turn and ask Wes who is standing just slightly behind me.

He takes my hand and says, "Starting today we put one foot in front of the other and we just go from there. But baby?"

"Yeah?" I answer.

"We go together."

And as we walk out of the cemetery hand in hand I realize that it looks like Emma is falling apart more than I realized. I'm going to have to keep an eye on her and Lee both. But now I feel like I can handle it because I have Wes at my side.

One thing is certain, I was right when I had said everything has changed because it has.

the end... for now.

VOLUME 4 OF THE claire goodnite SERIES

kiss me goodnight

dedication

For Sean
Thank you for being my very on HEA. a thousand years with you won't ever be enough.
It was only every you.

*"I was a boat stuck in a bottle,
Never got the chance to touch the sea.
Just forgot on the shelf,
No Wind in the sails,
Going nowhere with no one but me.
I was one in one-hundred billion.
A burned out star in a galaxy.
Just lost in the sky wondering why
Everyone else shines out but me.
But I came alive when I first kissed you,
The best me has his arms around you.
You make me better than I was before.
Thank God I'm yours."*

-Russell Dickerson

prologue

it's you

THERE IS A MARCHING band pounding away in my brain.
I must have had too much to drink at the rehearsal dinner last night, I think. I can get my ass ready for today—my wedding day—because if I don't, my bestie, Emma, will have my ass.

I pry my eyes open, only then do I realize that I am not in our hotel room on the coast. I'm not in the luxury king sized bed full of fluffy euro pillows and down comforters near a window looking out at the Atlantic Ocean. I'm not where I should be. It takes my brain a minute, still feeling as fuzzy as it is, that I'm not . . . *safe*.

The light shines through the wooden slats of the doors.

I'm here. I am right back where I started. Where I thought I would die when I was so small, just a baby really. I'm where I once escaped and had naively thought I would never be back. I scoot back on the worn, torn carpet floor of the closet that I was locked in once before, until my back hits the wall. I try to make myself as small as possible hoping against all hope that he won't see me but as I hear the footsteps growing louder and louder, I know that there is no hope to be found at all.

The closet door swings opened and I realize how stupid I have been. All this time that I struggled, that I suffered from those terrible nightmares and prayed that they would either end or I would finally remember just who had tried to harm me when I was just six years old. All those times I thought I was safe, that I was free, were really nothing but lies because looking down at me with a sinister smile on his face in this little house of horrors from my haunted past is the last person I ever would have thought would be capable of this kind of thing.

I was never free, I was living under the watchful eye of a monster, a wolf in sheep's clothing just waiting for their chance to pounce. His smile broadens and his eyes glimmer with excitement in the knowledge that he's won. It's finally over, this game of cat and mouse that we have been silently engaged in for twenty four years.

He pulls his leather belt free from his pants and loops it around my neck. I look up into his warm eyes, ones that I had always trusted as he tightens the leather around my neck.

"It's you. It was always you," I say as suddenly every memory finally clicks into place. Anna would be so proud.

I gasp as the air is squeezed out of my lungs. I struggle to pull more in even though in my brain I know that it isn't possible. Maybe this is how it was always supposed to be. Maybe this is how my story was always supposed to end. My name is Detective Claire Goodnite and I'm about to die.

You know what they say, every story has its ending, I just wish I was prepared for this one.
I can already tell that this one's gonna sting . . .

chapter 1
shots fired

One week earlier...

MY ENGAGEMENT RING glitters in the late afternoon sunlight as my hand sits on top of the steering wheel. I had just wrapped up support interviews to help out a fellow detective with their case. There seems to finally be a lull in the excitement here in George Washington Township and I, for one, am glad for it.

Truthfully, after this year, I'm not sure I could handle anymore excitement. One more surprise and the men with the big butterfly nets and funny jackets might come and take me away (Ha ha!) to the padded rooms with full service horse tranquilizers.

It's time from my own *Happily Ever After* and I am going to take it.

I have no active cases as Wes and I are about to get married in a handful of days. The hall down at the shore has been booked and paid for. It didn't feel right to get married in the church where Anna died. She had thought a beach wedding where bridesmaids wore frothy, light pink dresses sounded delicious and in her honor, that exactly what we'll have. Down to the letter. Wes and I are going to make Anna's dream wedding come true. It feels like the perfect way to honor her and her sacrifice, one that I still don't fully understand, and thankfully Wes agrees.

We are getting married for us, this is our time, finally! But the way in which we're doing the deed is all class and romance, it's all Anna.

I can't help the burn in my heart when I think about Anna.

It's been months since she died and I still cry every night. Lucky for me, Wes is there to hold me through the night, through it all. Emma hasn't been the same either. I know that she blames herself for what happened and while she didn't make the best decisions, she didn't send Anna careening with her gruesome end at that church. That rests solely on her own shoulders. And the sick bastard who murdered her.

Emma blames Lee too.

My poor brother has been struggling to find an inroad with Emma and she isn't budging an inch. He is so desperate to make any progress with her that it's becoming painful to watch him crash and burn every day. I have to wonder, will there come a day when he gives up and moves on? And if so, will Emma regret it when he does?

I just don't know.

I turn left past the old church on my way back to the station. The ticking of my turn signal beats as fast as my heart when I see the steeple. My palms sweat and my stomach turns. The new department shrink told me this kind of reaction is normal after a traumatic event. I told him to fuck off.

So did Emma and Lee even did too.

It's not his fault. I know that and the shrink, if he's worth his salt, probably does too. I let one department shrink into my life five years ago in order to make detective and to be totally honest, after everything that happened to Anna, I just don't have it in me to let anyone else in. It hurts too much when they go.

It was part of my brother, Lee's edicts before I could sit the exam. Lee is the Captain of our humble little department which is all well and good when he's kicking crime's ass and taking names, not so great when he's threatening to fire me every other day. And because he is both my brother and my boss he was well aware that I was kidnapped from our family home when I was six years old. Lee felt that I might have some spectacular amounts of baggage—and I do—that might keep me from doing my job. It doesn't but he had know way of knowing.

Lee made me start seeing Anna—only back then she was Dr. Garner—for weekly sessions. I had no way of knowing that she would become family, the sister I never knew that I needed, my ride or die chick, my best friend for life, well at least for the duration of *her life*. That is until she fell in love with my brother, *Deputy Dipshit* as I like to call him, and he fell in love with someone else. It damn near killed Anna, and then when she decided that she had to prove her worth in our little law enforcement community, to Lee and to everyone else, it finally did kill her when she crossed paths with a psycho.

When I was up for detective, Lee was sure that I would never pass the psych eval because of my personal history. I like to think it's nice to know that he had the utmost confidence in his baby sister and he still does to this day. He made me start sessions with Anna to uncover my past and balance out the heavy shit we have to wade through every day on the job. Somewhere along the way she became my friend.

When I was taken, there were never any ransom demands made, in fact the kidnapper never made contact any with my parents. My dad was the Captain of the department Lee and I work for now. At the time, they had theorized that it had to be someone my dad put away. I can only assume that they never meant to let me go. I guess we'll never really know. And that thought keeps me awake for far more nights than I care to admit.

Fortunately, I was a badass even at six. I broke free and ran away. Unfortunately, I was so malnourished and sleep deprived that I have little to no memories include who my attacker was. I know that he was a man, but his face—*or lack there of*—still haunt me every night. It's like someone took an eraser to his face. I can see so much of the closet where he kept me and the dirty pallet on the floor that was my bed, I hear every heavy footfall of that bastard as he stomped his way to my hiding spot and the way that he would pant a little in excitement when he told me to call him daddy, I can even feel the toes of his boots in my ribs as he kicks me in my dreams, but I can never see his face.

He left me with a handful of memories wrapped up in nightmares that terrorize me every night. Ever since Anna was murdered, I have several most nights, starting with one and rolling right into the next and then the next after that until I get out of bed and pace, giving up on peace and a sound night's sleep. It's getting to the point that I'm afraid to fall asleep at night. And worst of all, Wes is starting to notice how bad it's getting. I can't deny it any longer and truthfully, I don't want to. It's time to let Wes in.

But what haunts me the most, is never knowing who he was. I can only assume that to this day, he is still living free. There is even a chance that I know him in some capacity. Maybe he's the guy who delivers my mail or the man who changes the oil in my car.

Maybe I will never know . . .

• • •

I sight my scope taking the wind speed and direction into account like any marksmen worth his salt would.

This is really is the perfect spot.

There are fat, greedy businessmen meeting over lunch in a restaurant across the way. It looks like most of them are drinking their lunch. From here I can see people out enjoying their sunny afternoon in the Indian Summer sunshine. A mother with a baby carriage . . . But the icing on the cake is the school group on a field trip to the museum.

Soon they will all learn that no one is safe from me. I am not a man to be messed with! Soon they will all learn that they cannot play games with me because I am the gamemaker.

"Ahh . . . and there is the man of the hour," I say to myself as a police officer walk around the corner.

I fire the first round into the crown and watch as the scream and scurry like ants out of an ant hill. I laugh silently to myself as they look around to see where the shots are coming from but I have chosen this spot perfectly after hours of meticulous consideration.

This is the perfect blind.

I fire another shot and then another.

"There you are, my queen," I coo when I finally see my prize in the crowd.

I knew that she couldn't help herself, she would have to be here at a scene like this. We're not very different here and I. She is the prey and I am the hunter. We are two sides of the same coin really. A Yin and a Yang. She doesn't know it yet, but we belong together.

I watch her move trying to protect the people, she thinks that she is so good. But really, this is all her fault. This blood shed is on her hands. And soon she will learn the hardest lesson of all, that I always win.

And then I set my sights on the male police officer and pull the trigger . . .

• • •

My radio crackles to life . . .

"Code 30! Code 30!" It's not everyday that an emergency call for assistance comes over the radio like that and my heart starts pumping.

I pick up the radio and click the button. "This is Detective Goodnite, what is your position?"

"Twenty-third and Main."

"I'm on my way," I reply as I flip on the lights and sirens on my tahoe.

"Code 30! Code 30! Shots fired . . . officer needs assistance."

"This is dispatch," my radio crackles again. *"All available officers please respond. Be advised this is a hot scene."*

"Officer is advised," I respond.

"Oh Jesus . . . he's shooting at us! He's just shooting everywhere at everyone. It's madness!"

I recognize that voice over the radio. It's Officer Rodriguez. I've known him for years and our cases intersect often as he's out of the same station. He has a wife named Alma and a little girl named Angelina. He told me three weeks ago that Alma is expecting again when he RSVP'd to my wedding.

My stomach somersaults again and again and I'm sure that I might puke. My hands are sweating on the steering wheel. I remind myself that this is nothing like Anna. Everything is going to be just fine. But when I park my car a block over from the scene, nothing is fine.

A sniper is on top of one of the buildings raining open fire on absolutely anyone who happens to be down below. It's insanity and I have never seen anything like it. It only take me a second to know that the bad man of my past will have some competition in my nightmares tonight.

I unsnap the strap on my holster and pull my sidearm free and hug the walls of the buildings taking cover where I can as I weave my way over to the scene.

There are civilians everywhere just trying to get out. I have to stop and take a deep breath to focus on anything. Once again, I rely on the SEAL breathing exercise my brother had taught me long ago. I breathe in deeply, holding it there, only to take in even more air, and then one more time. When I meditate at home, I imagine and three story building and filling that building up with air one floor at a time before slowly emptying the building but there is no time for that here.

When I slowly expel the air from my lungs, my focus snaps into place just as I was trained to do. I see a young mother with a baby in her arms. She's pinned against the side of the building. Her baby stroller sits abandoned and over turned on the curb not far from where she's hiding now. All of her baby items are spilled out of the discarded bag.

When I look up her eyes so full of fear for her and the tiny pink bundle in her arms hits me full blast. "Please help me," she mouths.

I nod to her as I hold up my index finger to my mouth signalling to be quiet. I still don't know where the shooter is and I don't want her to get caught in the crosshairs on my command.

Other officers and detectives are arriving on the scene. People are running everywhere. It's pandemonium.

There seems to be a lull in the gunfire. I can only hope that the shooter is out of ammunition and they either have no more or need time to reload. Either way, this woman and I aren't going to stick around to find out. I have to get her and their baby out.

I see Jones across the way and I motion to him that I'm going to get these two out of here. He nods that he understands. I make my way over to her and push them towards the wall as I keep my back to her.

"Hold on to my belt," I instruct her. "We're getting you out of here."

"Thank you," she whispers.

I start to move them along the wall using my body to shield them. I'm determined that they get out of here as quickly as possible so I can get back in there and help some more. But right now, this little baby and her mom are my number one priority.

A quick look around me shows that other officers—some I know and some I don't recognize—are involved in similar tasks. Jones has a couple of frustrated business men and Rodriguez has kids from a school group that was just leaving the museum a couple of doors down.

And then everything happens all at once . . .

The gunfire resumes, from where I can't see, but I pause in my shuffling of the young mother and her baby down the side of the building to try and decipher. No luck. I have to keep moving them. I look at her pale face from over my shoulder.

"You do exactly as I say," I command her in a harsh whisper. "No matter what."

"Okay." I can hear in her voice that she is holding in a sob. This woman is a tough one but any normal human being would be scared in this situation.

"You stay low and as close to the wall as possible," I order her.

"Okay," she whispers.

"Stay behind me if you can. If something happens to me you keep moving. Stay low, move fast, and watch your surroundings. Do you understand me?" I ask her. I need to hear this woman agree to follow my directions. This is the only way that I can insure her safety to the best of my abilities.

"Yes," she agrees.

"There are police officers and paramedics waiting just past the building after this one. We just have to get there," I tell her.

"Okay." I can see her nod her head out of my peripheral.

"Just get there," I demand.

I pick up the pace when I notice one of the businessmen, who look like they had most likely drunk their lunch at their afternoon meetings takes a swing at Jones. God dammit! Why can't they just let us evacuate them to safety? Frustration burns in my guy because I know that I can't stop to help him because I have to get this woman and her baby out of here. Fucking assholes.

Jones slugs the businessman, laying him out flat. He catches the drunk ass and throws him over his shoulder in a fireman hold. The rest of the party follow without so much as a snide remark or eye roll as Jones leads them down a different alley than I'm pushing the mom and her baby down. Good for Jones. If he gets reprimanded over that move, I will make sure to go to bat for him. I heard he's sitting for the Detective's Exam next month and I don't want to see anything get in the way of that. Jones is going to be a damn good detective.

"Keep moving," I say just under my breath. "It's just a little bit further. We just have to keep moving."

I hear the report of the rifle just before a wild shot hits the brick above my head raining chunks of brick and mortar down on us. A sharp piece must have hit me on the forehead by my hairline because I feel a sharp stinging sensation before blood trickles down my face and into my eye and mouth.

The young mother lets out a little scream.

"Hush, we just have to keep moving," I demand. She doesn't answer but just nods as I keep pushing her down the wall.

If she alerts the shooter to our position we are nothing but sitting ducks and I can't let that happen. If anyone is getting out of here alive, it's this woman and her baby. I'll see to it myself if it's the last thing I do, I just hope it's not.

We're almost there when a child's scream rings out. I look back just in time to see Rodriguez, who was corralling the school group from the museum look up at me. He's bleeding from his shoulder and his eyes are wide with fear. No. No no no no no no. No fucking way. I know the look on his face. He knows that he's done. I have seen this look one too many times and I don't want to see it now. I shake my head no.

"Keep moving," I mouth to him.

Rodriguez doesn't acknowledge that I have spoken to him. He just stands there frozen and opens his mouth. When he speaks his voice sends chills down my spine with one word.

"Run."

And then a bullet from some rooftop around us pierces right through his heart cutting his life short.

"Move!" I shout to the mom.

Jones turns around and starts running towards the kids corralling them against the building. I push her faster down the wall. The sooner that I can deposit her with the paramedics, the fast I can get back here to cover Jones and anyone else who may have show up. I feel so torn. I want to cry over my friend.

I want to help Jones get all of those kids out and I want to find that fucking shooter. But I can't because I will not abandon this one woman and her child when we're so close to safety.

"Keep going," I order again.

"Okay," she whimpers.

"We're almost there. I can see the end of the building," I tell her. "There's going to be a break in the coverage where we are out in the open. Do not look back, just run for the police blockade. I'll be right behind you."

"But—" she starts. She is going to panic. I can see it in her eyes and I can't let that happen. If she loses it now, this woman won't make it out of here alive.

"No matter what," I reassure her. "I'll be right behind you."

"Okay," she whispers.

"Here it comes," I tell her. "On three, two, one, go!"

We take off. She clutches her baby girl tightly in her arms as she runs for the police blockade. An officer that I don't recognize sees us and motions for us to run in like a third base coach telling his batter to run home. "Go! Go! Go!"

She just passes through the blockade when another shot rings out. It feels like a linebacker hits me from behind and I stumble. No, scratch that. It feels like I'm being run over by an African elephant. I'm pretty sure those are the bigger ones. Although I don't know and I really don't care right now.

The impact lifts me from my feet for a second and it's like I'm running through the air. Maybe it's the blood loss, maybe if the hit to the head that I took, but for a second, my mind flashes that I'm just like Michael Jordan in Space Jams. I don't even know if that's who was in that movie but it seems right. And then my toes touch the ground again and I keep going.

I don't lose my footing even though I stumble. The blood from my forehead is still stinging my eye and blurring my vision.

I just make it through the blockade when my feet stop working. My brain feels like it's full of cotton and everything feels so cold even though it's a warm fall—an Indian summer.

"Detective Goodnite!" someone shouts but I'm not sure who or from where because the edges of my vision are creeping in.

"We made it," I say just before everything goes black.

chapter 2

stitches

LIGHTS. THE LIGHTS are so bright.
I blink my eyes open against the rows and rows of large, round spot lights overhead. No, not spotlights, surgical lights.

Something jostles me like an earthquake and I groan.

"Well, it looks like Sleeping Beauty is finally ready to join us," someone says from behind me. I look over and there sits one of my favorite paramedics in the area.

"Hey, Bill," I smile weakly at him. "What happened?"

"You got shot," he tells me.

"Ouch," I cringe. "Well, that sucks."

"That it does, my dear. That it does." I roll my eyes and wince. Ouch. That hurt.

"Well, I say it was only a matter of time the way you Goodnites cowboy around," Bill's partner, Dan, says from his spot in front of me in the driver's seat.

"Hard-de-har-har, asshole," I grumble.

"I try," he chuckles.

"Bill?" I ask.

"Yeah, Claire?" he answers me.

"Do I still have my gun?" I ask sweetly.

Bill opens his mouth to answer me but Dan beats him to the punch. "Per regulations, the sidearm of an unconscious officer is to be removed and stowed in a locked compartment and then turned over to a high ranking officer in the chain of command," he sites. I let out a frustrated sigh. Damn.

"Can I have it back now?" I ask sweetly.

"Are you going to shoot Dan?" Bill asks me.

"Maybe." I shrug my shoulders.

"Then no!" Dan shouts from the front of the truck.

"You have to give it back eventually!" I snap. I hate being without it. And it's my very favorite one.

"I'll give it to Wes or Lee," he crows. "They're much nicer."

"Were you always this much of a baby?" I ask Dan.

"No!" he shouts.

"Yes!" Bill corrects at the same time. I bark out a laugh that turns into a yelp as a sharp pain rips through my shoulder.

"Ouch!" I shout. "Mother fucker that hurts."

"Sit back!" Bill orders. "And no sudden movements. You were shot for fucks sake."

"Fucker," I mumble under my breath.

"What was that?" Bill asks.

"Nothing," I mutter petulantly like a child who was caught being naughty not that I have any reason why. I was the one who was shot. A little sympathy would be nice but apparently that's not coming.

"Anyways, sit back and relax," Bill says with an evil smile in his voice. "Because you know O'Connell is going to shit kittens when he finds out you were shot."

"Oh shit."

"So true!" Dan cackles. "Hey, I bet he already knows."

"What?" I ask feeling all of the blood drain from my face.

"It went out over the radio when you were hit," Bill answers.

Shit, shit, shit. I have to call Wes. I have to let him know that I'm alright. I bite my lip and fight past the pain searing through my shoulder as I reach for my jeans pockets only to com up empty.

"Where's my phone?" I demand.

"I have no idea," Bill shrugs. "You must have dropped it somewhere out there."

"Fantastic," I say just as the ambulance pulls to a stop at the Emergency Room entrance to the hospital where I seem to have spent so much of my time over the last year.

"Well, this is where your ride ends," Bill says as Dan pops open the back doors and they unload the gurney that I am strapped to, bouncing me as much as possible. I grit my teeth to keep from crying or screaming or both.

I just know that those assholes are doing it on purpose.

The glass doors of the Emergency Room slide open and a triage nurse runs up to us. Her eyes go wide when she realizes it's me.

"Hey, Josie," I greet her.

"Are you fucking kidding me?" Josie snaps.

"Was it something I said?"

"I don't know what's going to be worse," she answers. "Your man up in here tearing the place apart to get to you or your nutbag family tearing this place apart to get to you."

"I'm sorry?" I shrug sheepishly.

"Just do me a favor."

"What's that, Josie?" I ask.

"Next time you get hurt do it in another hospital's zone and not mine." The snickers and cackles of both Dan and Bill can be heard throughout the hospitals. I shot them both a withering glare but it's Josie who gets those two apes to stop.

"What do we have?" she asks them as they hand of their clipboard for discharge.

"GSW to the upper left shoulder," Bill says.

"Through and through?" Josie asks.

"Looks to be a deep graze," Dan answers.

"And a head trauma and laceration," Bill finishes.

"Well, aren't you just a fun bag of tricks today?" she asks as she looks me over.

"I do like to keep it interesting," I droll. I try to look at my fingernails casually but it turns awkward when I realize that my arms are strapped into the gurney. I let out a heavy sigh.

"Take her to Bay five," Josie orders.

The boys wheel me through the open corridor of the ER, past the central nurse's station, and through the drab blue curtain of what I can only assume is Bay five. Fantastic.

"On three," Bill says.

"Wait, guys—" I start but they don't listen as they unbuckle the straps of the gurney and the blood begins to flow back to my uninjured arm.

"One . . ." I try to scramble to get my bearings but with one arm I am fairly unbalanced. "Two . . ."

"Guys, really," I plead.

"Three . . ." And then they hoist me up and onto the bed in Bay five. Even though I knew it was coming, it still catches me by surprise and I let out an undignified squeak which I know will be making the rounds of the station by the time I get back there because both Bill and Dan don't even bother to hide their mirth at my expense.

My cell phone falls out of my pocket as they move me and I fall on it like an alcoholic falls onto a bottle they forgot they had. Thank God! I need to call Wes and tell him that I'm alright so he doesn't freak out but when I go to hit the home button the screen won't light up, the battery is dead as a doornail. Fuck!

"Goddamnit," I gripe.

"Don't laugh," Josie says as she makes her way into the bay. "You all are just as bad patients as she is. It's a hazard of the trade, I guess."

"Not true," Dan gripes.

"So true. Now get out," she commands with a smile on her face.

"We're not back in service until we can release her firearm to her department lead," Bill says with a wicked smirk.

"You could just release it back to me," I tell them.

"That's not true and you know it," Josie reprimands me.

"I know but it was worth a try."

"Not in my hospital it's not."

"Ugh, fine," I concede.

"Now, you two out of the bay so the doctor can get in her and stitch her pretty ass back up," Josie says as she shoos them out just in time for a tall woman with brown hair twisted up into a bun with streaks of silver shot through it. She's beautiful.

"Hello, I'm Dr. Emory," she tells me with a smile on her face. "You must be Detective Goodnite. I've heard so much about you."

"Call me Claire," I tell her.

"Claire it is," she says before turning to Josie. "What do we have here?"

"GSW in the upper left shoulder and a head wound and laceration," Josie answers.

"Let's irrigate the wound and see what we have," the doctor tells Josie as she snaps on a pair of latex gloves after scrubbing her hands in the sink.

The doctor peels away the bandage on my forehead and begins cleaning it.

"What happened here?" she asks me.

"Sniper shot the brick wall behind me and I got hit with a chunk. It's not so bad," I answer.

"I heard about the sniper on the radio," she says.

"Yep," I answer because I can't talk about it until I have been debriefed.

"It appears that it isn't that bad. Head wounds to bleed a lot though," she says thoughtfully as she tends to the wound. "I don't think it need stitches though."

"Fantastic." The doctor places steristrips on my forehead and then covers it with a clean bandage.

"I can't say the same for the shoulder though," she tells me as she moves on and undresses the bandage that Bill put on to stop the bleeding in the truck.

"Damn."

"Yeah," she says. "By the look of it, you're luck it was just a graze. Anything lower and you'd probably be dead." At the words coming out of her mouth my blood runs cold. It could happen to any of us on any day. But today I was on a bullshit assignment and never thought the day would end like this—a day where I watched another friend die right before my eyes.

"This is probably going to sting a little," the doctor says as she injects something to numb the pain while she stitches me back up.

"Yeah," I answer a little lost in my own thoughts. "It already does."

"I'll be as quick as I can." And she does. I have never had a doctor stitch me up as fast as she does before placing another bandage over her handiwork to keep it clean.

"Thanks," I say.

"Don't thank me yet," she says shining a small flashlight in my eyes. "I'd say you have a mild concussion and need rest. The nurse is going to give you an antibiotic injection to stave off infection and those hurt like a bitch." I can't help but laugh at her cursing. She was all prim and proper and class right up until now.

"Okay," I laugh until Josie hits me with a mother of all shots that does, in fact, burn like a bitch but it was nothing in comparison to actually being shot. "Argh! Shit shit shit!"

"I told you," the nurse says.

The doctor opens her mouth to say something to me but then a commotion breaks out in the ER just outside those ugly blue curtains.

"I knew I should have bet money on your man," Josie says.

"Oh shit," I mumble as the curtain is roughly shoved back and Wes, with a wild look in his eyes steps into the bay.

" 'Oh shit' is right," the doctor mumbles. "I'll just get your discharge orders ready."

"I'm gonna fucking kill you!" he roars as the doctor races around him.

"Not in my hospital you won't because then I'd just have to put her back together again," Josie tells Wes on a raised eyebrow. "You heard me!"

Wes just sighs and rolls his eyes.

"It's not that bad," I defend holding up my good arm before Wes can get a word in. He narrows his eyes. "Well . . . I guess it kind of is. My dress is strapless and the good doctor tells me this is going to leave a scar."

"That's not fucking funny, Claire!" Wes thunders into the room.

"I'm sorry," I tell him. "You're right it's not funny. I don't have a dress at all yet."

"How could you, Claire?" he asks his voice no eerily calm. It's when he's calm that worries me the most. When his voice is controlled and steady is when Wes is his most emotional.

"I had to help them," I defend myself. He sighs and runs a hand through his hair. "I couldn't just leave those people there and I couldn't just let everyone else work to protect those people while I sat back and took it easy and you know that."

"I know," he tells me. And he does. Wes wouldn't want me to be the kind of person who doesn't stop to help someone in need, but that conflicts with his need to have me safe and accounted for.

"I'm okay," I tell him.

"Okay," he says making his way over to me. I scoot over so that he can sit next to me on the hospital bed and he wraps an arm around me, gently holding me. I can hear Wes's frantic heartbeat under my ear.

"Can I have my gun back?" I ask into the stillness of the room.

"No fucking way," he says quietly into my hair.

I sigh. "I thought as much."

chapter 3

we'll just see about that

"ALRIGHT, GIRL, YOU'RE all set," Josie says as she pushes the drab blue curtain aside and walks back into the bay with my discharge papers. "Don't do anything crazy, lots of rest, but not too much rest because of the concussion."

"So I need to wake her up every hour?" Wes asks with an evil glint in his eyes that I don't quite trust.

"It couldn't hurt, but it's not a bad concussion. She needs to keep her stitches dry and she has an prescription for antibiotics. You can fill it at the pharmacy here or have it filled anywhere," she explains.

"Thanks," Wes says pocketing the little blue square of paper.

"Well, I'll just leave you guys to it. Here are some spare scrubs and a pair of flip flops from the gift shop so you can leave because, well, you look like total shit and those clothes need to go in the garbage," Josie informs me before turning on her heels and walking out of the bay. Wes doesn't laugh because he's still too mad at me, at the situation, at everything to let himself but the corner of his mouth does lift in an interesting twitch that leaves me hopeful.

"Ready?" he asks me once we are alone.

"Yeah," I answer softly. I know that I scared him, hell, I scared me too. I think it's best to just let Wes have a little quiet to sort his thoughts and maybe I just might need a moment too.

Carefully, I push up off of the hospital bed and move to stand. I start to try and pull my tattered shirt over my head but even with one shoulder cut away I still can't manage it. I'm sure that a frown mars my face between my brows as I struggle.

Wes steps forward and gently brushes my hand away. He gently pulls my top over my head and then down around my injured arm to avoid jostling it. He scowls when he notices the bandage on my shoulder after he uncovers it. I feel bare—vulnerable—standing in front of him in nothing but my lace bra with all of my wounds exposed.

Wes raises his hand and with a gentle tenderness he brushes back the wisps of hair that fell from my ponytail. What a mess I must look like and yet, when I raise my face to meet his eyes, I see nothing but love and worry. Wes looks at me like I am the most beautiful woman in the world even when I am at my worst and it reminds me that even after one of the worst days imaginable, I have Wes to go home to.

As long as I have Wes, I can survive anything else that come my way.

Wes places a soft kiss on the top of my head before pulling back just enough to unsnap my jeans and push them down my thighs only to become tangled up in my favorite boots. I let out a heavy sigh. Wes guides me back to sit on the edge of the hospital bed so that he can pull my tall, gray boots from my feet one by one.

"Don't throw those out!" I panic at the thought. I love those damn boots.

Wes smirks. "I wouldn't dare."

"Thank you."

Wes doesn't respond other than a quick nod before pulling my jeans the rest of the way down my legs and then sliding the scrub pants up. He offers me a hand to help me up and I take it placing my good hand in his. Wes pulls me up to stand and then rolls the scrub top in his hands and slides it over my head and my good arm through the arm hole.

"Umm . . ." he hums as he clearly realizes we should have out my injured arm in first. "Lets try that again."

Wes pulls the oversized top back over my head and straightens it out before gingerly guiding my injured arm through the armhole and then pulling it over my head then I can slide my good arm through. Wes pops the tags off of the flip flops before dropping to one knee in front of me. Wes slides his hand down my calf before lifting my foot and placing the sandal on it before carefully lowering my foot back to the ground. He repeats the process making me feel a little like Cinderella and not like the walking disaster that I am.

Wes rises to his feet again and turns me around. He gently pulls the rubber band from my hair shaking out my haphazard ponytail and massaging my scalp in the process. I lean back into his hands and let out a little whimper. His hands feel so good and I feel like I was in a car crash. Before I'm ready, Wes pulls his hands from my hair and then quickly plaits my hair in a loose braid, just the way he did when I was a little girl, just the way he did when I was last in the hospital.

This tendre side of Wes always makes my heart skip a beat.

"Lets go," he says to me as he holds out his hand. I take it without hesitation like always.

Wes scoops up my boots and pockets my dead cell phone before leading me out the door and down the hallway. I smile at Josie as Wes pulls me through the ER and back out of the sliding glass doors. In fact, Wes pulls me through the parking lot and over to his Fedmobile. He beeps the locks on the key fob and drops my hand to pull open the passenger door for me. Once I climb in, he slams my door shut before pulling open the back passenger door and dumping my boots in the back unceremoniously.

Wes stomps around the hood of the car. He's clearly not over his anger yet. I know that I scared him pretty bad, but still, I was the one that got shot and it's not like I did it on purpose. He's acting like this was my plan all along. Ugh!

I hope he thaws out some on the drive home but as he drives through town it seems that he isn't calming down any. Actually, by the time Wes pulls into the driveway, he seems more mad that when he arrived at the hospital in the first place. This doesn't bode well for the rest I'm supposed to be getting.

Wes puts the car in park and turns it off. He steps from the car and slams his door before stomping around to the passenger side before wrenching the door open.

"Wes?" I ask but he just holds out a hand to help me from the car which I take.

He says nothing as he pulls me up the walk to the front door. I stand there in silence and Wes fumes while he unlocks the front door. He pulls me through the threshold before slamming the door shut. The lock sounds like a gunshot in the quiet house and I can't help but jump. It's been a long fucking day and I'm all nerves and frayed edges. My jumpiness seems to make Wes even more angry and he utters and oath under his breath making me cringe a little.

"Wes?" I ask again but he just takes my hand and leads me through the house.

Wes turns on no lights leaving our space awash in the glow of late afternoon sunset. He leads me up the stairs and down the hall straight to our bedroom. He pushes open the door and I follow him through where he stops and turns to me.

Carefully, Wes slides the scrub top from my body tossing it to the floor. He reaches behind me, unhooking my bra and sliding it from my shoulders letting my breast hang free. He unties the waistband of the scrub pants and pushes them down my legs, taking my panties with them. I step out of them and my flip flops. Wes thrusts his hands into my braid and drops his forehead to mine leaning to the side, careful of my bandage.

"I can't lose you, Claire," his painful whisper echoes through the late afternoon.

"You're not going to lose me." I place my free hand on his cheek, holding him to me while I reassure my man that I'm here, that I'm alright.

"I can't lose you," he repeats.

"I'm right here, Wes, and I'm just fine."

"You're not fine!"

"It's nothing that a few stitches and some antibiotics can't cure," I tell him, pulling his face down to kiss me.

"We'll see," he pouts before taking over the kiss.

"I'm right here, Wes. Feel me," I plead with him as I grab his hand in mine and place it over my chest so that he can feel the beat of my heart for himself. "Feel me."

The pain in Wes's eyes turns feral.

"I don't want to hurt you."

"Then don't," I push him. "But you should know by now that I'm made of tougher stuff than glass."

"Claire, I don't think—" he starts but I stop him.

"Maybe this is exactly what you need," I tell him. "Maybe this is exactly what I need," I say as I push his hand over a few inches to cover my breast.

He squeezes it gently letting his thumb glide over my nipple. I wait in unsure silence for him to make his decision, but it's when Wes opens his mouth to give me my answer that I know that I have won this round.

"You better lay down," he orders and I am happy to comply.

I can't help the smile that plays on my lips as he begins to strip off his suit starting with his tie before unbuttoning his shirt. I watch with rapt attention as piece by piece his clothing hits the floor. This is my Wes. This is us. I knew he couldn't stay mad for too long. A wicked smirk tugs at the corner of his sexy mouth as he moves the pillows from the head of the bed to the middle motioning for me to lay down crosswise with my legs hanging off od the side of the bed.

"You think you won this round, don't you?" he asks me as I settle back into the pillows. I look up into his eyes as I answer him.

"Well, yeah." I slow blink. I mean we are naked so yeah, I did win.

"We'll just see about that," he says as he drops to his knees in front of me and tosses my legs over his shoulders.

Wes does not give me a chance to prepare of catch my breath before sliding his strong hands underneath me, gripping my ass in a firm hold and spreading me open before him. I bite my lip as he licks my pussy completely, rolling his tongue over my clit again and again. Not letting up for even a second. I'll never last like this, but then again, that's exactly what Wes wants.

I thrust my fingers into his hair, holding him tight to me. It's my only anchor in the storm that he's raging over my body between Wes hold my hips down and my injured arm hanging limply at my side.

"Wes," I call out as he gives me no relief from his torture as he hurdles me closer and closer to the edge. "I-I-I'm going to come."

"Let it happen," he rumbles against my core.

Wes continues to suck and bite and lick with the sole purpose to drive me to the brink and I am helpless to do anything but take it and oh how I want to take it. If this is my punishment for scaring the hell out of Wes I will gladly take it with a smile on my face.

"Wes, Wes, Wes," I chant over and over.

I lose my grip on his hair and tear at the bedding underneath me with my good hand. Wes doesn't just eat me, he devours me with abandon and I am lost. My whole body seizes. I close my eyes tight and arch my back as best as I can and come.

Wes releases me from his hold and stands to his full height, towering over me as I lay sprawled on the bed. I feel him line the tip of his cock up with my entrance but still he waits.

"Look at me," he commands. "Open your eyes and look at me."

The second my eyes flutter open and lock with his he thrusts deep letting me take all of him. I feel a twinge in my shoulder but it's so worth it. I school my face as best I can so that he won't notice.

Wes pushes my legs open wide and grips my upper things in his powerful hold as he slowly glides his cock in and out, in and out. From this angle I can see how slick he is from me as he sinks his cock in over and over. It's mesmerizing.

"Wes," I whisper lost in the moment.

"This," he says sliding his fingers through my wetness where his cock joins with my body again and again. "This is all mine. Do you see this?"

"Yes," I breathe.

"This is for me and me alone," Wes tells me something I already know as he thrusts deep inside me.

"Yes," I whisper as he pumps his cock again.

"I'm the one that makes you this wet." He slides out only to drive back in to the hilt.

"Yes, yes, only you," I chant. At this moment I would promise him anything.

"I'm the one that gets to eat this pussy," Wes growls as he powers deep again and again.

"Yes, yes."

"And it's my cock that gets to sink deep inside you," he growls as he does just that again and again, so slowly it's maddening.

"Yes, Wes."

"And it's me who gets to make you come," he says as he circles my opening around his length. "With my mouth, with my fingers, and definitely with my cock."

"Yes," I pant as he moves his thumb to my clit pressing down as he circles in time with his hips.

"Do it now," he commands as he plunges deep. "Come for me."

I call out his name and then I do.

Wes leans over me and drives deep. He pushes my hip down in his hand to meet his hard thrusts which are fast and faster now although he is still careful not to jar my arm. I wrap my good arm around him and hold on tight.

"Again!" he shouts.

"I-I don't know. I don't think I can," I whimper.

"You can," he says as he plunges in over and over again hitting all the right spots.

"Wes," I plead.

"You can!"

And then I do exactly as he says, digging my nails in his back as I do. Wes thrusts once, twice, before roaring his release as he follows me over the edge.

He frames my face in his hands as he slowly glides in and out sending shivers up my spine. I love Wes like this, when he's tender after. He places his forehead to mine and looks deep in my eyes.

"I can't lose you, Claire."

I cover his hand with my own. "You won't lose me."

"I can't, Claire. I won't survive it."

"You won't," I promise him. "For better or worse, I'm right here and I'm not going anywhere."

"You're right here," he repeats my words back to me.

"With you," I promise. "I'm always here with you."

"With me," he repeats.

"I think we're even taking vows proclaiming such in a week." I smile at this man that I love more than anything in this world.

He swats my thigh gently in retaliation. "I'm serious, Claire."

"So am I. I'm fine, Wes," I say pressing my mouth to his.

Wes quickly takes over the kiss obviously needing to reassure himself that I am still here. That I really am just fine. Alive. And it breaks my heart a little that he needs to but I love him and I'll give him this moment and then together, we'll put the pieces back together.

Wes lifts me up in his arms like a bride as he puts the pillows back where they were at the head of the bed and pulls back the covers. He deposits me in the middle like a queen before heading into the bathroom. I hear the water run for a second before he comes back to me carrying a washcloth. I blush as I he tends to me which only makes him roll his eyes and laugh.

"I'll be taking care of you for the rest of my life, beautiful, you might as well get used to it now." He winks at me before heading back into the bathroom.

"And I'll be taking care of you for the rest of mine!" I shout to his retreating back.

"I wouldn't have it any other way," he says softly as he climbs into bed beside me and pulls the covers over us.

Wes wraps himself protectively around my as he drifts off to sleep. I let the soft sound of his even breathing lull me into a gentle sleep that would stay anything but because when I'm asleep, even Wes can't keep the monsters at bay.

chapter 4
familiar

*W*ES AND LIAM *are so mean! I can't believe they won't let me hangout with them. I bet they're just afraid that I'll tell mom and Mrs. O'Connell about the magazines they're hiding with the girls in bikinis in them.*

I'm stomping through the woods behind our house. I don't need those gross boys to have some fun. And those boys are gross! They smell weird and put on too much stinky spray stuff when they think I'm not looking.

I just make it to the street on the other side of the trees from our house when a white van pulls up next to me. I hear my mom in my head telling me not to talk to strangers. I feel my eyes going wide as he steps out of the van.

"Claire!" he says and I wonder how he knows my name. "There you are. I need your help!"

"What do you need help with?" I ask.

"I'm so glad you asked, Claire," he says my name again like he says it all the time. It's weird but I don't think too much about it. "My puppy, Millie, got out. She's missing. Can you help me find her?"

"I don't know. I should probably go back home . . ." I say.

"No!" he shouts and it startles me and I jump a little. His eyes widen when he notices my reaction. "I need you to look for her while I drive around. I'll give you this candy bar if you help me . . ." he offers, holding up my most favorite kind. I instantly grab for it, but he pulls it back.

"Okay, what does she look like?" I ask.

He smiles a creepy smile showing all of his teeth, but I open the front door and get in the van. He hands me the candy bar and I realize that I don't even know what his name is . . .

"She's little and fluffy and white . . ." he trails off as I dig into the sweets my mom never lets me eat before dinner. Ever!

All of a sudden my head feels funny and my ears feel full of cotton like last summer when I got an infection from swimming too much. I open my mouth to tell him something is wrong, but my words don't work. They won't come out! I turn my head to look at him, a scream stuck in my broken mouth. He just smiles his big, creepy smile and everything goes black . . .

When I wake up I'm on an old, yucky blanket on the floor of a dark, smelly house. It's not my house. I know that. I rub the side of my head, it hurts so much. When I look up, the strange man is leaning back in an old torn chair, his feet spread wide and there's a strange bump in the front of his pants that he keeps rubbing his hands on. He smiles when he notices that I'm awake and for the first time ever, I'm scared.

"Hello, Claire, I'm glad that you're awake," he says to me in a scary voice. I just sit there staring with my eyes big. "You may call me daddy."

• • •

My breath seizes in my lungs and I wake with a start. I bolt straight up in the bed clutching the sheets and blankets to my chest.

"Claire?" Wes calls from behind me. I can hear the sleep in his voice and know that I woke him from a sound sleep. A deep sleep that he undoubtedly needed.

"Yeah, Wes?"

"Are you okay, honey?" he asks me.

"I'm fine, baby. Go back to sleep," I tell him softly but he doesn't go back to sleep. Wes sits up in bed behind me curling a long leg up next to me on either side. Wes wraps his arms tight around me from behind.

"Bad dream?" he asks me.

"Yeah," I answer taking a deep breath. There is something about this dream that is bothering me more than they usually do. I just can't put my finger on it.

"You wanna talk about it?" Wes asks and truthfully I don't . . . but also I do. I know that if I don't share this part of my life—for worse or for better—with Wes I will one day lose him to it. He's either all in or he's out and I am not going to keep secrets from him. I know he's waiting out my silence for an answer . . . for anything really and I'm going to give it to him.

"Actually, I do," I answer as bravely as I can be.

Wes squeezes me briefly before saying, "Tell me what happened."

"It was the day I was taken," I tell him.

"What happened that day?" he asks. I know that he has read the transcripts from after I was found. At first I was angry with Wes, this was an invasion of my privacy, but the closer we became, I realized how deeply those day affected Wes as well. I'm not the only one who had their life changed forever that day.

I can tell by the way that he leans into me and rub my shoulder gently that he also wants to know if this was a nightmare or am I actually remembering. For the first time ever after I had a nightmare, I'm actually excited to see how close to the truth my brain is staying.

"I remember . . ." I start. Wes just holds me while he waits for me to collect my thoughts. I feel like it'll feel better to just get it out faster like vomit, it's better not to let it linger, so I open my mouth and let it all spill out in all of it's ugly little details. "I remember I was so mad at you and Lee because you wouldn't let me hangout with you. I know now how silly that was."

I feel him tense behind me but he has to know. Wes has to hear it all.

"I went walking through the woods even though I wasn't supposed to but I was so mad that I just didn't care—I was so mad that it made me reckless. It's all my fault," I admit my frustration out loud which is something I have never done before.

"Honey, you were just a little girl," Wes says softly.

"I know that, I do, but still, if only I was more careful . . . I don't know . . . something!" I hate how frustrated it makes me. I feel so stupid.

"We can't go back, baby, only forward and we go together," Wes says softly.

I take a deep breath. "I know."

"So then what happened?" he asks me.

"I guess I had walked farther into the woods than I had realized because when I hit a road I knew I was in trouble."

"What road?" Wes asks me.

"I don't know," I admit. "I know I got there from my house but I was so mad at you guys that I wasn't paying very good attention."

"That's okay," he reassures me. "We don't need that now. Lets keep going."

"Okay," I agree. I can't go back, only forward.

"What happened next?"

"I realized that I was farther away from home than I had thought I was when I hit the road and I knew I needed to turn around and go back home but then a man in a white panel van pulled up and asked me for help finding his dog. So stupid, right?"

"Not stupid, Claire, you were just a little girl," he tells me what I already know for the umpteenth time.

"I know, I know." I hold my hands up. I scrub them down my face before pressing on. "I knew I shouldn't go with him, but, Wes?"

"Yeah, baby?"

"He knew my name. He knew who I was when he stopped for me. I-I-I don't think it was random," I tell Wes what I know in my heart.

"I don't think it was random either," Wes agrees.

"Okay." I take a deep breath trying to slow my racing heart.

"Then what happened?" he asks me.

"I climbed into the van and he gave me my favorite candy bar. It was before dinner and everything and I wanted it so I unwrapped it and ate it right there in the front seat."

"And then what?" he says softly rubbing my back as he talks me through one of the worst days of my life.

"And then I felt funny. Like my tongue wouldn't work anymore. I felt like I was at the far end of a really long and dark tunnel. And I felt so so sleepy."

"And then what happened, Claire?"

"And then everything goes blank and when I wake up I was in a dirty room on an old blanket and the man was sitting on the sofa . . . he was just sitting there, Wes, just watching me."

"What did he do when he noticed you were awake?" Wes aks.

"He told me I could never go home and that I was to call him daddy from now on. That's when I usually wake up." A shudder wracks my body. I hate that part of the dream. I hate how filthy it makes me feel.

"And did you wake up then this time?" he asks me.

"Yeah," I answer.

"What did he look like? Did you recognize him?" Wes asks.

"I can't ever see his face," I explain. "It's just . . . blurry or out of focus. But . . ."

"But what?" Wes asks. He's clearly holding back his frustration that I can't remember. That we both need to know who it is once and for all so we can lay these demons to rest and move on with our lives.

"But I think something was different this time," I say.

"Like what? What was different?" Wes asks.

"There was something about his voice that sounded almost . . ." I trail off.

"Almost what?" Wes asks hanging onto every word of my description.

"Familiar," I finish. "I think I know whoever took me. Not that I recognize them, but that they are familiar to me."

"Shit," Wes bites out.

"Yeah," I agree.

"Do you feel a little better?" he asks and I can hear the hopefulness in his voice.

"Yeah, I do," I answer as I hold onto his arms wrapped around me.

"Wanna try and go back to sleep now?" Wes asks me.

"Yeah, I do."

We lay back down in our bed and Wes pulls me into his arms. I turn at the last second to that I'm face to face with him. I want him to see how much I appreciate him and how much I love him for helping me through this moment.

"When are you going to stop saving me?" I ask him my voice sounding so small.

"Probably never." He shrugs. "I kinda like it plus you've got a great ass."

"I love you, Wesley O'Connell."

"And I love you, Claire."

He pulls his arms tighter around me, grounding me to the here and now more surely than I could ever have done myself. But even though he makes me feel safe and protected, I hear Anna's voice in my head telling me I need to find out the truth or I will never truly know peace again. And as I drift off to sleep I know that that is exactly what I'm going to do. I will uncover all of the secrets of my past even if it kills me. Too bad I would find out later that it probably would.

chapter 5

stay put

*B*EEP... BEEP... BEEP...
  Wes uncurls his arm from around me to silence the alarm on his phone that sits on the nightstand. As much as I don't want to leave this bed, I know that we have to face the day. Officer Rodriguez and his wife and child deserve our full attention. The mother and her baby, the school group, even those asshole businessmen deserve to have my full focus on this investigation.
  So it's not really about me and what I want or don't want. It's about settling a score. It's about righting a wrong. I can't bring Rodriguez back, but I can find him justice.
  I pull the covers back on my side of the bed and roll over to push myself up to get up out of bed when an arm snakes around my waist from behind, hauling me back into the bed.
  "Where do you think that you're going?" Wes asks me, his deep voice gruff with sleep.
  "To work?" I ask.
  "No," he says with finality. "Try again."
  "To the station to catch up on paperwork?"
  Wes just shakes his head. "Un-uh. Try again."
  "To your office to hang out with you?"
  "Absolutely not," he says crossing his arms over his chest.
  "Oh come on!" I shout throwing my hands up in the air. "You have to let me into the bat cave some time." Wes just raises an eyebrow as he stares me down. "Please?"
  "No," he says shaking his head. "You, my gorgeous girl, are going to stay put."
  "Says who?" I demand.
  "Guess."
  "You can't make me." I say crossing my own arms across my chest mirroring his stance as I sit in the bed.
  "You were shot yesterday, Claire," he says his voice low.
  "It was a flesh wound!"
  "Claire—"
  "I'm fine, Wes!"
  "You have a concussion," he tells me something that I already know and also something I cannot dispute.
  "Sort of..." I hedge.
  "No, baby, there is no 'sort of' about head trauma."
  "I'm—" I start only to be cut off by Wes again.
  "Baby, if you say that you are fine one more time I am seriously going to

lose it."

"Okay," I say softly.

"Just stay in the bed," he smiles before standing to head to the shower.

"But what if I don't want to?" I ask as he starts to move away from the bed. Wes turns back to look at me with a wicked gleam in his eyes.

"I'll call Lee," Wes volleys back as he turns around and prowls back towards where I'm laying in the bed.

"Lee wants Rodriguez's killer found and bad," I tell him something he already knows is true.

"I'll call you dad," Wes tells me as be sits back down on the edge of the bed next to me. "In fact, that sounds like a great idea . . ."

I shrug as if it doesn't bother me one way or another. "I could always bribe you . . ."

"Ahh, now bribing a Federal Agent is a pretty serious offense," Wes says his voice low and rough. "What did you have in mind, baby?"

And then I lean into him, pressing him back into the bed on his back with my good side before shimmying down his body. I balance myself on my knees between Wes's spread legs and look him directly in the eyes as I lean over and take his hard cock into my mouth.

"That'll do," he says after clearing his throat. "For now."

I widen my stance just a little bit for better balance and tentatively reach for him with my injured arm. It doesn't hurt so wrap my fingers around his base and stroke. Wes groans a little in the back of his throat and he clenches his fists at his sides.

I swirl my tongue around the tip of his cock and lean forward just a little more, bracing myself on his muscular thigh. I bob, sliding my mouth up and down his hard length triggering another groan or growl to escape Wes's sexy mouth.

He squirms on the bed, tipping his hips ever so slightly as if he can't help himself. Wes is barely holding himself back from thrusting up into my waiting mouth. The fact that Wes is so turned on that he can hardly contain himself has my body heating up.

It turns me on the that I turn him on.

I clench my thighs together as I swirl my tongue around the tip of his cock again and again. I run them together like a cricket seeking some kind of relief but it's no use. I can't help myself. As I push Wes closer and closer to the edge, I let go of my grip on his thigh and slide my hand down, down, down, to in between my own legs. I slide my fingertips through my own wetness and gasp around Wes's hard length causing it to slide deeper into my mouth. I swirl my finger around my cit faster and faster in time to the way that I slid his cock in and out of my mouth. I'm almost there . . .

"Are you touching yourself?" Wes asks just before he knifes forward to grab me under my arms dislodging him from my lips, and pull me up up up until he can twist at the waist and gently toss me back against the pillows.

"No?" I ask just a little bit breathless.

"I'll ask again," he says looming over me. Wes uses his knee to nudge my legs wider so that he can settle in between my thighs. "Were you touching yourself?"

"Uh huh," I answer honestly with my chin to my chest so that I can look him in the eyes.

And then Wes slides in deep.

"Wes," I breath.

"Maybe." He pulls back and drives in deep. "If I fuck you hard enough, you won't be able to walk."

"Wes." I roll my hips trying to take him deeper.

"Let alone try and leave this fucking house." He plunges in again.

"Yes." I need him so much. I need him hard and deep and fast but he's only giving me so much. Wes is teasing me. And I *just need* so much.

"So you'll stay put."

"Oh God," I moan as I clench around him.

"That's it, baby," he says as he thrusts again and again.

"Wes," I plead.

"Give it to me," he forces out through his gritted teeth. "It's mine and I want it." And then I do. I throw my head back and scream his name as I come.

I dig my nails into his shoulders and clench my thighs around his hips as he powers deep into my body again and again. I love the way his body moves over and into mine, sweat dripping down his muscular body, one that I am more than happy to get to spend the rest of my life worshipping.

Sex with Wes has never been bad and it's only gotten better with time. He was good at twenty-six, but he's life changing at thirty-eight. A religious experience between the sheets and a real man that loves me unconditionally during the day. Wes is the whole package and then some.

I feel it building again as Wes drives forward with so much power that the headboard rocks against the wall with the same electric force that he rocks my body and once again, I am powerless to stop it.

I hold him tighter with my whole body, with everything that I have as if I could pull him deeper into me and keep him there. My body is burning with the embers of a fire that only Wes could light and keep burning. He drives forward again and I am lost to the flames, calling out to him as I come. Wes tips his head back exposing the column of his throat and growls his release as he follows me over the edge.

We lay together for what feels like hours, but couldn't be more than a few stolen moments while our breaths even out and the sweat cools. My arm burns like a little bitch but it was so worth it. Wes kisses the corner of my mouth touching the very tip of his tongue to my lip before taking it away. He leans back to look at me with a smug look on his face that is wholly deserved.

"There," he says as he climbs from the bed. "Now you'll stay put."

"Asshole," I make a half-hearted attempt to shout at him as he saunters off to the shower. I could be pissed at him but . . . well . . . *he's not wrong.*

chapter 6

playing hooky

I LAY BACK letting my body sink down into the mattress and take a deep breath. It feels like the down will swallow me up if I let it and I'm half tempted to do just that. Wes was right to be so confident because my entire body is like an over cooked spaghetti noodle.

I feel nothing but the slight burn in my shoulder and the echoes of an ache in my temple. But that's it. Nothing more.

I let myself shut my eyes and just float adrift in my afterglow—not quite asleep but not fully awake either—just letting the early morning sun slither through the curtains and across my skin and over the backs of my eyelids while listening to the birds outside. Something I have never done before. I guess it takes being shot to stop and smell the roses.

I crack an eyelid when I hear footsteps and a swishing sound. Wes is standing there, peeking around the corner from the bathroom with nothing but a towel slung low across his hips. So low that I can see that tantalizing vee that leads down to the promise land.

"Just checking," he mumbles before turning tail and heading back to the closet to dress.

"Just checking what?" I manage to ask but by the time I get the words out of my sleepy mouth, he had already gone so I let myself drift back to my morning catnap among my downy clouds.

I'm not sure how long I had laid there in my absent thoughts when strong hands pulled me up and out of my cocoon. I find myself cradled in Wes's muscular arms. He gently crashes his lips to mine and kisses the hell out of me. And I let him. I let his tongue stroke the seam of my lips for entry and I give him that too. But it's doesn't last long. Before I know it, Wes is depositing me back into my fluffy nest and I am powerless to do anything but blink as he kisses my forehead.

"Be good," he orders softly as he walks out the door. I can't help but think how good his ass looks in his Fed suit before I drift back to sleep.

• • •

"Come out of the closet, baby."

"No," I whisper, tears hot on my face and snot stuffing up my nose.

Liam and Wes were right. I'm just a baby. A big kid wouldn't be crying in the dark corner of a closet hoping it'll all go away if you just wish hard enough. I bet Wes never cries. I know Lee doesn't.

"Come out now, Claire. Playtime is over."

"No," I cry louder. "Please don't make me."
"Now!" He growls as the closet door rattles. I gasp.
"Leave me alone!"
"Get out of the fucking closet, Claire!" He roars.
"Please no," I cry harder, my body shaking with each sob.
"When," he kicks his hard boots against the closet door and it shudders.
"Please."
"Are you," he kicks it again.

The doors are the kind with the slats that fold sideways. We have them at home and mama says I always pinch my fingers in the accordion. Whatever that is.

"I just wanna go home," I whisper.
"Gonna," he kicks again.
"I just want my mommy," I sob. "Please. I just want my mommy."
"Fucking," the boards snaps and I scream.
"I just wanna go home, please," I beg.
"Learn!" he shouts as he kicks the broken boards out of the way. He leans down and grabs me by my upper arms.

"Please," I wheeze but my words are cut short when he slaps my face hard. So hard I taste blood in my mouth and it's so yucky I feel sick. I'm going to throw up from the yucky taste. I try as hard as I can not to. I know that if I do, he'll punish me again. I don't want that. Anything but that.

"You are home, baby," he coos right before he slaps me again. I cry out again, falling to the floor with his last hit. It's so strong he knocks me down with it. "And I thought I told you to call me daddy," he says as he lands a hard kick to my back.

"You're not my daddy, you'll never be my daddy," I whisper. "My daddy is a nice man. He would never hurt me. You'll never be my daddy," I say again but the bad man can't hear me, he already walked away. I have nowhere to go,

but one thing is for sure, I have to escape.

• • •

"Claire!" someoe shouts.

I wake up with a scream lodged in my throat, my heart is pounding with the need to run and the burn in my shoulder is telling me that I won't get anywhere fast.

"Claire!" someone shouts and I realize it's Emma.

Emma is standing before me in my bedroom. What happened? I was asleep, I think. I look at the clock and realize that it's ten in the morning. I look back up at her and she the worry for me that she's projecting out.

"I'm fine," I tell her.

"Okay," he says after she audibly swallows like a cartoon character and I realize that Emma knows me and Wes and Lee now, but she didn't know us then. She didn't know us when I was a kid lost and scared in the woods. She didn't know the guys as scared teens feeling guilty for not watching a little girl as closely as they should have. And now I can't help but think that Emma now knows maybe a little too much.

"So . . ." I start awkwardly. "What brings you by?"

"I heard you cut class so I came to have a little fun too," she says. She's still shaken by what she walked in on but she's trying her best to bury it. I can appreciate that so I'm going to go along with it.

"I'm not cutting class, I was shot." I roll my eyes.

"Semantics." Emma shrugs.

"Won't Lee be pissed?" I ask.

"Who gives a shit what Captain Goodnite wants?" she snaps. "I don't. And I don't work for him. I work for the county at the discretion of the Mayor."

"Well then," I say thinking we could both use a day off. "I guess we're cutting class. What should we do?"

"Well, I was thinking that it's high time we finish planning this wedding," she says looking a little unsure of herself. Neither Emma nor I gave a shit about wedding planning, it was always Anna who wanted it to be a special day. Emma even once went so far as to say she would never get married. Also words I had previously spoken.

"Are you feeling alright?" I can't help but ask. Emma raises a brow in response to the question and the irony is not lost on me. But still . . .

"I'm fine," she shoots back my previous answer. "The place is booked and invitations have been sent but you don't even have a dress. Or flowers. Or a cake." She ticks off on her fingers.

"We're kind of in poor shape when you put it like that."

"Exactly," she agrees obviously picking up steam to her cause.

"So where do we start?" I ask.

"The shore." The Jersey Shore. I haven't been there in years. This could be fun after all.

"Let me just get dressed and I'll be right down," I say drawing her attention to the fact that I am obviously naked under the sheets. I pull them up to my neck and embarrassment burns hot across my cheeks.

"Nice," she smirks. I just roll my eyes. It's on the tip of my tongue to ask her when was the last time she's seen Lee. I know they still hook up and it's even more traumatic than before so I refuse to take the bait and throw it in her face. "I'll just go make some coffee."

I wait until after she leaves the room to jump up and hurry through my morning routine. I'm eager to start out on what might be my first fun day in ages. And with a friend too. I'm eager to shake off this cloak of death and sadness. Look at me attempting to be normal and shit!

We'll just overlook the recovering from a gunshot wound business . . .

chapter 7

the shore

I RUN INTO my closet and stand there for a moment unsure of what to wear. It's been a long time since I didn't have to get up and get ready for a day at work. The last time, I didn't have to head to the station for any length of time was the last time I was injured. I pretty much lived in leggings and t-shirts. In fact, that's exactly what I was wearing the night Wes proposed.

He was so handsome, standing there on the deck in the backyard, surrounded by twinkle lights and flowers. Soft music played and he had a feast laid out for us on the patio table. Wes had on worn jeans and a button down shirt with the sleeves rolled back. *Hello, arm porn!* His feet were bare as he stood there before me and told me he loved me, he had always loved me, and he always would.

We danced to Ed Sheeran soft and slow in the grass as he slowly sank down onto one knee and asked me to marry him. He wants to be my partner and lover, my light in the darkness and while I know that it is unfair to bring him into my own personal hell, I also couldn't imagine then and I can't imagine now a time when I wouldn't love Wes with all of my heart. So I looked into his whiskey colored eyes and said yes.

Wes slipped the mother of all diamond rings on my finger—the one that I have worn every day since—and then he made love to me right there in the backyard under the late afternoon sky. It is by far one of my favorite memories. I let my right hand drift over to my left to touch the center stone on my ring like a lodestone. It guides me back to center. I don't need the ring or the fanfair, I just need Wes.

Emma was wearing jean shorts and a ribbed tank top when she blasted into my bedroom this morning so that is exactly what I will wear. I pull on light jeans shorts over my bra and panties, but instead of a fitted tank, I opt for a loose fitting vee neck tank in white. I slide a pancake holster into the back of my shorts before checking the magazine on my side arm. I load a round into the chamber before locking it into my holster.

Yesterday might have been a one off, but on the chance that it wasn't, I'd rather be safe than sorry.

I slide my feet into a pair of converse sneakers and pick up my badge. I realize that I don't have anywhere to stick my shit so I dig through the back of my closet for a small designer bag that Anna had gifted me years ago and stuff my badge, my wallet, and cellphone. I look at all the extra space in there and toss in a few hair ties and my drop gun for good measure before slinging its long strap across my body.

I take the stairs slower than usual because the concussion, while mild as it may be, has me singing the national anthem in my head to keep from puking while the room spins. I want to go back to work as soon as possible and falling down the stairs in my own home won't exactly tell Wes and Lee that I'm ready for battle.

Emma is furiously texting someone on her phone but pauses to look up at me when she sees me. I feel her appraising look and know that she is taking stock of everything wrong with me, probably to report back to Wes.

"A purse?" she asks me on a raised eyebrow.

"What?" I ask mildly offended. "I can't carry one?"

"No," she answers. "You can't. How many guns do you have in there anyways?"

I'm a little wounded that she sees through me so thoroughly. I kind of don't want to answer her. She'll be unbearable, really.

"Just one," I say with my head held high.

"And in total?" she asks me as she scans my carefully chosen outfit. "How many do you have on you over all?"

I let out a heavy sigh. "Just the usual two," I answer.

"Oh good." She smiles a wicked smile. "Me too. Let's roll!"

I laugh and shake my head at her. "You're ridiculous," I tell her.

"But I'm your ridiculous."

"This is true." I sigh. When Emma is like this, when her sense of humor and her uniqueness shine through, I know exactly why my brother fell in love with her. I just hope one day they figure it all out because life is so short.

"Whatever." She rolls her eyes. "You love me. Now let's go get you married!"

"Alright."

We walk through the front door and I push the button to lock it behind us before climbing into her white jeep cherokee. Emma turns the key in the ignition and fires her up. Taylor Swift singing about someone making you do something that you shouldn't blasts through the speakers. I look at Emma through the corner of my eye. She is full of surprises these days.

She reaches over to the dashboard to turn the volume down.

"What?" She shrugs a shoulder. "I love me some T-Swift."

"I don't doubt that," I tell her as she cranks up the volume and pulls out of my neighborhood on two wheels.

"That's alright," she says when the song ends. "I have prepared a prenuptial planning musical snack for you."

"Should I even ask?" I shoot her the side eye.

"Of course," she laughs before switching playlists.

I can't help but laugh as I hear the opening chords to Blondie. Emma and I sing the entire *Bridesmaids* soundtrack all the way down to the shore. There is a lightness in my chest that hasn't been there in a longtime and I have Emma to thank for that. She's truly a wonderful friend.

• • •

By the time Emma pulls into one of the paid parking lots by Seaside Heights my chest hurts from laughing so hard and my eyes are wet from crying, not from sadness but laughter. Finally. After all this time, my heart still hurts so very much.

"Here's our first stop," she says as she turns the ignition off.

"Where are we?" I ask as I look around.

"I figured, we'd get the shit part over first," Emma says as she looks around. She audibly swallows down what looks like . . . fear before finishing on a whisper. "You know? Rip it off like a bandaid."

When I look at the big marquee sign over the shop that we are parked directly across from I can't help but throw my head back and laugh. Emma looks to me quickly and a scowl pulls at her brow.

"Come on." I laugh. "It can't be that bad."

"You don't know that!" she shouts.

"Do you have any colors in mind?" I ask as we push open our doors and step down from her jeep.

"Emma wanted pink," she says softly as we head into the bridal shop. So that's how it's going to be? Alright, I can handle that. Pink it is.

Bells tinkle as we push open the door and a young woman, probably in her early twenties, dressed in slacks and a sweater twinset. She has a tiny bit of a manichal gleam in her eyes but I probably would look like a sociopath if I had to work in wedding hell all day every day too.

"Hello and welcome to fairytale brides!" she greets us enthusiastically. "My name is Destiny and I like to think that makes me pretty darn qualified to help you plan your magical day. Now who is the lucky bride?"

"She is," Emma says catching me off guard as she shoves me into the slightly desperate clutches of bridal barbie.

"But she is my maid of honor," I rally trying to turn the attention away from me. "Her name is Emma and she loves the color pink!" How is this girl allowed in the state of New Jersey? She is was too perky for any self-respecting Jersey girl.

"Yes!" Destiny fist pumps the air. "I just knew I was going to love you girls. Pink. Is. Awesome!"

Emma drags her index finger across her neck in a throat cutting motion as Destiny grabs her by the hand and drags her down an aisle of racks completely covered in pink dresses and mouths to me, "You're dead. Sleep with one eye open, Goodnite."

"Bring it."

"So were we thinking long or short?"

"Fancy," Emma answers. "We're doing this up right."

"Awesome!" Destiny squeals. "Where is the ceremony?"

"On the beach here at the shore," Emma answers as we watch with twin horrified expressions as she loads up her arms with what has to be a bare minimum of twenty pink dresses.

"Right this way, Moe," Destiny calls over her shoulder.

"No," Emma says looking a little pissed. "My name is Emma. Not Moe."

Destiny just laughs before explaining, "No silly. Not Moe, MOH—Maid of Honor."

"Ohhh," Emma and I both say at the same time. We are so out of our league here.

"Let's just get you in a fitting room," Destiny says as she pulls open a mirrored door.

"I'll . . . uhh . . . I'll just wait for you out here," I stammer as the mirrored door slams in my face, blocking out the disgruntled frown of my very best friend.

"Benedict Arnold," I hear her gripe from the other side of the door.

I sit on a beautiful, yet grotesquely uncomfortable upholstered chair just outside of the fitting rooms. I hear a rustling and then a groan come from within the dressing room.

"Everything . . . okay," I call out hesitantly.

"Oh just peachy," Emma responds.

"No, this is really more of a cotton candy than a peach," I hear Destiny correct Emma and I can't help the snicker that escapes my mouth.

"I heard that!" Emma snaps.

"Oh, come on out," I say. "It can't be that bad."

"Oh, it can," Emma says.

"Come out and let me see."

"Un uh."

"Please . . ." I beg.

"No."

"It's my wedding," I challenge.

"I hate you," she says before she opens the door. I am willing to admit that I am wholly unprepared for the sight that greets me is my dear friend in a bright pink strapless monstrosity. I want to laugh but I know Emma is also armed so I rein it in.

"That's . . ." I start. "Not that one."

"Thank God," Emma mumbles before heading back into the fitting room.

I lean back in my seat thinking that this day might not be so much fun after all. That dress was truly terrible and by the horrified expression on Emma's beautiful face and the stack of pink that I had seen Destiny drape over her arms, I'm not thinking such good things about the rest of this dress search.

The mirrored door opens again and I look up. Emma is wearing a hot pink strapless dress with a knee length hemline and enough tulle underneath to make rockabilly dreams come true. It has a wide black belt around her narrow waist. The dress is awful but apparently, my bff has a banging body. No wonder she brings all the boys to the yard.

"No," I say before she even steps out of the dressing room.

"God bless you," she sighs as she turns on her heel.

The next hour is spent in more of the same. One terrible dress after another when my phone chimes with a text in my purse.

WES: How goes the day of rest?

Huh? How is my day off going? I can't say that I'm resting because I'm not. I should be truthful but the truth often gets me into hot waters where Wes is concerned. I am just about to fabricate the truth with a little white lie when I realize that big bastard has probably already tracked my phone. Damn find my friends app.

ME: Not resting? I'm dress shopping with Emma.

The little typing bubbles pop up right away so I know that he was waiting for my response.

WES: I know, I already tracked your phone and called Emma.

That sneaky bastard! I just knew it! My fingers fly over the keys on the screen of my phone.

ME: I knew it! That's a little shady even for you, Fed.

The little bubbles pop up immediately again.

WES: It is and I'm sorry. I'll make it up to you tonight.

Color me curious. My interest is peaked.

ME: How?

WES: You can sit on my face tonight.

Yep, that'll do it. That's the ball game, folks.

ME: Apology accepted.

WES: Seriously, what are you doing?

ME: Planning our wedding and carrying a purse!!!

The text bubble pop up again and then disappear only to pop up again. They vanish again before showing one more time. Wes must be confused by my response because it would seem that he is typing, deleting, typing, deleting over and over again.

WES: Wonders never cease with you.

I roll my eyes at the screen. It makes the light throbbing in my temple gain some momentum.

ME: Ha Ha. *Slow clap*

WES: Plan us a good wedding day, baby.

I can see the smile on his face in my head. Wes loves the idea of us finally getting our happily ever after. And if I'm being totally honest, so do I.

ME: Okay.

WES: See you tonight.

I am just putting my phone back into my bag when I hear the door click open one more time and there stands Emma looking like a fairy princess . . . no a queen. Emma looks like a grecian goddess with her strawberry curls piled up loosely on top of her head. The dress she's wearing is gathered high on her clavicle with a narrow cut exposing her muscular shoulders. The dress skims her lush curves and falls at her feet. When she does a little pirouette before me I can see that the entire back is open. It's pink but such a soft whisper of the hue that it's almost silvery setting off her pale skin.

"Well . . ." she says unsure of herself. "What do you think?"

"You're gorgeous," I whisper while staring at her. Emma tucks a lock of hair behind her ear in an unusual show of vulnerability.

"Don't joke," she says quietly.

"I'm not kidding. This is the dress."

"Are you sure?" she asks me hesitantly.

"Yeah," I answer her. "Do you like it?"

"I feel . . . pretty."

"Then this is the one," I tell her.

"I had a feeling . . ." Destiny says peeking around Emma. "Let me just get these castoffs out of the way and you can change back when you're ready, MOH."

"Yeah, Moe," I tease. "I just want to look at you for a bit."

"Me too."

Emma and I stand there—her on the carpeted platform and me behind her—just staring at her in the mirror lost in all the beauty that is Emma. And she is beautiful. Medium height and curvy with strawberry blonde hair and green eyes that hold a little bit of sadness just beyond their surface, but then again, don't we all.

I startle when an avalanche rolls towards us in the bridal shop. I don't realize that it's Destiny until the avalanche starts talking.

"It's your turn next, bride!" she cheers enthusiastically.

I can help the groan that slips out from between my lips. Emma throws her head back and laughs.

"I'll just change real quick," she says as she hops down from the platform and hurries into her dressing room clutching her long skirt in her hands. "I wouldn't want to miss this."

"I heard that!" I shout as a now empty handed Destiny heards me into another room that's hidden beyond the mirrored door.

As soon as the latch clicks closed she is pulling my clothes off and I'm a little alarmed at how fast she does it.

"Oh dear," she says when she uncovers my holster.

"I'm a police officer," I say quietly not wanting to startle anyone else in the bridal salon.

"It's okay," she says. "I'll just let you handle that real quick." And I do, stuffing it down into my purse.

I turn back and she's holding open a dress for me to step into and when I do, Destiny is pulling it up to cover my body and fastening it closed at my back.

"Oh boy," I mumble not sure what I'm looking at.

"Come out, bitch!" Emma calls from the other side of the door.

"Uhh . . ." I stammer.

"Oh no," she barks from outside. "I did it now you have to. That's the deal."

"I was shot!" I bargain.

"I don't care. Get your happy ass out here."

"I can't wait until you get married," I snap.

"Well don't hold your breath, sister, because it will be a cold day in hell before that happens."

"You don't know that," I sigh as I push open the door and step out. Emma has her mouth hanging open. This dress really must be that bad.

She pulls her phone out of her purse and snaps a quick picture.

"Hey!" I shout.

"Now go take that off, it's awful," she orders. I catch Destiny biting her lip to keep from laughing at Emma and I. Maybe she's not so bad after all.

We head back into the dressing room and after a huge stack of dresses that was one bad one after another, I am just about to quit.

"This is hopeless," I whine to Destiny. My shoulder is starting to burn and I'm tired and cranky. Emma looks gorgeous in her dress and I look stupid in every single dress. I want to cry and I *never* cry! And I'm starving. I need tacos and I need them now.

"I have one more I want you to try," she says to me.

"I don't know . . ." I hedge.

"These were terrible, I admit," she says taking a deep breath. "But this one will be the right one. I can feel it. Trust me one more time?"

"Just one more," I tell her. "Then I'm getting tacos. This has been a taco kind of day."

Destiny laughs before grabbing the last dress off of the hanger and holding it open for me to step into it. She pulls it up as soon as I step into it. I slide my arms in and she quickly does up the hidden zipper. I turn and look at myself in the mirror and freeze. I'm not looking at me, but someone beautiful. She's soft and feminine—*delicate*—and everything I want to be. At least on my wedding day.

"Well," Emma calls. "Don't keep me waiting."

"Trust me," Destiny says on a smile as she pushes open the dressing room door for me to step through. "It was well worth the wait."

"Fuck me," Emma mumbles as I climb up onto the platform and look over my shoulder at her. "She's right. You're beautiful."

"I feel beautiful."

I turn and look back at myself in the mirror. The dress has a deep vee in the front and sleeveless. The nude illusion fabric covers the bandage on my shoulder. White, gauzy fabric is delicately wrapped over my breasts making me look like I have a generous amount of cleavage but in a tasteful way. The skirt is miles and miles of soft, filmy layers of sheer, white fabric that flows out around me in the prettiest way. The back is a vee cut down to just about my ass and a spray of tiny, white flowers from from over my left shoulder and down across my waist and again down the back to add just the right amount of decoration.

"This is it," Emma says softly. "This is the one."

"It is," I agree before turning back to Destiny. "I'm afraid to ask how much it is though."

"It's actually paid for," she tells me making my own jaw drop down.

"What?" I ask. "That can't be right."

"It is," she assures me. "I checked your file when Emma called to schedule this appointment this morning. It's all be prepaid by a Dr. Anna Garner."

I feel my throat tighten and a burn behind my eyes. Anna.

"She paid for your dress, veil, MOH's dress and two more bridesmaids dresses and a flower girl," she tells us. "It's been paid for for months."

I'm sure it has been. The last thing Anna did before she left this world was buy me my fucking wedding dress. A friend to the end and always a champion of my relationship with Wes. I look to Emma in the mirror and she her swallow the lump in her throat. He eyes are red rimmed and glassy just like I'm sure mine are.

"How did you find this place again?" I ask her.

"Anna chose it."

"Anna," I whisper.

"Yeah."

"Okay," I say shoring up my strength. "We'll take it all," I tell Destiny.

"Wonderful!" she cheers.

I look to Emma. "I need tacos . . . and tequila."

"Here, here," she responds softly. "Although we still have to pick out a cake."

"Chocolate," I tell her. "Wes loves chocolate cake."

"Chocolate cake it is then," Emma agrees. "Now let's see about those tacos."

Emma and I chose flowers over tacos and margaritas that I probably shouldn't have mixed with the tramadol the ER doc prescribed—or as I like to call it, fuck it all, because it knocks me on my ass and then some—but who's looking?

• • •

After lunch, she took my to buy the most ridiculous pair of heels known to man and I hate them instantly.

"You can't wear those big clunky boots on your big day," Emma reminds me.

"I'm not," I inform her kicking out a sneaker clad foot. "Today, I'm wearing sneakers."

"You can't wear those ratty assed shoes either."

"They're not ratty!" I defend my favorite off duty shoe.

"Half of the heel is missing on your left foot!"

"Oh . . . whoops."

"Yeah, whoops," she mimics me with her arms folded across her chest. "Now walk!"

I scrape my feet across the floor in the shoe department of this high end department store. I stumble a little. The stilettos on these heels are impossibly high.

"I'll never be able to walk in these," I cry.

"That's why you have to practice," Emma says to me the way that one would scold a whiny child.

I let out a sigh and begin walking again. Lost in my own thoughts of impending doom when Emma breaks the silence on my trek across the floor once more.

"You have to admit the shoes are really sexy."

"They are," I agree on a sigh. They are ornately beaded swirls of silver beads over nude pointed toe pumps with mile high stilettos.

"I imagine Wes will have a field day with them," she tosses out filling my head of images of Wes's face when he strips off my gorgeous gown to find my wedding lingerie and these heels underneath.

Or maybe he won't even peel my dress down . . . maybe Wes will just fuck me dress and all. The imagery sends a shiver up my spine and I pick up my pace suddenly able to master these shoes like Tyra on a catwalk.

"That's what I thought," she says. "We'll take them."

chapter 8
safe and warm

I'M SITTING ON the old recliner that Wes loves in the darkening living room as the sun goes down beyond the windows. I have an afghan my gran knitted across my legs and an ipad in my hands. I'm reading a trashy historical romance that my mom swore would heal me from the inside out.

"This highlander wields his penis like he wields his claymore," she had said this afternoon when she called me to tell me that she had sent her favorite book to my account. Although she whispered the word *penis*. "If that doesn't heal you, I don't know what will."

"Mom," I had laughed into the phone. "I'll check it out. Thanks for thinking of me."

"Of course," she had said before continuing. "Wes will thank me. I find them . . . inspiring."

"Mom." I laugh. "I'm not sure I need to know these thing."

"What?" she had asked with the air of innocence in her voice that she lacked in real life. "It's true and you're almost a married woman. You're going to have to learn to keep things spicy."

"Trust me. Wes doesn't have any trouble keeping things spicy," I had mumbled.

"Well," she had laughed. "Good to know. I'm glad you're feeling better, baby girl. I'll talk to you real soon."

"Alright, mom. I love you."

"And I love you," she had said before she rang off.

That was over and hour ago. I downloaded the book right away and have been lost in it ever since. She was right, our highlander does wield both his penis and his claymore with excellent precision. I had no idea that historical romances could be so . . . steamy.

The lock on the door clicks and I immediately look around like I am guilty. I guess I'm embarrassed to be caught reading a sexy romance novel.

"What's going on here?" Wes asks immediately taking the temperature of the room. My eyes are so wide that it feels like one of my eyeballs might pop out.

"Nothing."

"What were you doing?" he asks me.

"Oh, just reading."

"Sure," he says shutting the front door behind him and twisting the lock. "What were you reading?"

"Just a book."

"I gathered that," Wes says with a raised eyebrow. "Mind if I take a look?"

I let out an eep: "No, don't do that."

He watches me for a moment rolling up his cuffs as he moves deeper into the room. "Have you eaten?"

"No. I waited for you," I say nervously. "I'm sorry. I didn't start anything. I wasn't sure when you would be home." Why am I so nervous?

"Don't apologize," he says before planting a soft kiss on my forehead. "You were supposed to be resting today. Want to come talk to me while I fix something quick?"

"Sure."

I follow Wes into the kitchen and watch as he pulls chicken breasts out of the fridge along with vegetables. He pulls oil and a skillet from the cabinet.

"Can I do anything to help?" I ask.

"Sure thing," he says before picking me up and setting me to sit on the island next to the cutting board where he laid out the vegetables.

Wes heats up the oil in the skillet before placing the chicken breasts into the pan. He moves over to the island and picks up a knife cutting salad vegetables while he stands next to me. His elbow brushes my thigh every so often sending tingle up my spine and heat to other places.

Mom was right about the book. I'm feeling inspired.

"So what were you reading?" he asks me softly.

"Oh this and that," I answer as vaguely as possible while feeling the blush heat my cheeks and travel down my neck.

Wes dumps the vegetables into a big, blue glass bowl. He sets the salad over on the other counter before dumping the cutting board and knife into the sink.

"So pretty," he rumbles as he traces a fingertip down my neck and over my chest just skirting my cleavage. "I love it when you blush."

"I'm not blushing," I lie.

"What were you reading?" he asks me again, crowding me in.

"It was nothing . . . really."

"Tell me," he whispers. "Please."

"It was a romance that my mom sent me," I admit.

"That doesn't sound too bad," Wes says as he steps between my legs. "What was it about?"

"A highlander." Wes smiles wicked.

"And what did this highlander do?"

"He wields a sword."

"Anything else?" Wes rumbles as he places open mouth kisses against the side of my neck. His beard scraping my skin in delicious ways.

"He also wields a pretty powerful penis," I admit when Wes scrambles my brain with his mouth.

"Is that so?"

"Yeah," I breathe as he moves his hand up underneath my blousy tank top to burn against the bare skin of my belly.

"I bet we can do better than that," he says with confidence.

"Oh yeah?"

"Yeah, baby," he says as he unsnaps the button on my shorts. "Lay back."

I do as Wes asks laying back on the cool stone of the kitchen island. He pushes my tank up exposing the skin of my belly and places soft kisses there as he unzips my shorts and pulls them from my body.

"So wet," he tells me as he touches his fingertips to the gusset of my panties before pulling them down my legs. "Is this for the highlander or for me?"

"You," I tell him as he traces my opening with the tip of his index finger.

"That's fucking right." He sinks that finger deep into my pussy and I want it and so much more.

"Wes." My breath catches in my throat as he pulls his finger from between my legs and sucks it deep into his mouth, keeping his deep whiskey eyes locked on mine. Wes says nothing as he pops that finger free and then unbuttons the buttons down the front of his Fed dress shirt before letting it fall to the floor. "Please."

But that's the last coherent thing I say as he leans over, putting his mouth on me. He licks me like a starving man. All the air is sucked out of my lunges as he flicks my clit with his tongue over and over never letting up, never letting me catch my breath. Wes's scruff abraids my inner thighs

I arch my back against the stone countertop, the cool marble a harsh contrast to the way that Wes is heating my body from the center out.

Wes drags his lips down my thigh as he thrusts two fingers deep into my center but it's just not enough.

"I-I need," I pant.

"I know what you need, baby," Wes says as he pushes to his feet to stand over me.

Wes unbuckles his belt and unhooks his pants. The sound of his zipper wrapping down is drowned out by the pops of the chicken as it sizzles in the pan but when he pushes his pants and boxers briefs down, letting his hard cock springfree to bob between us thick and heavy, I could care less about the chicken.

"Wes." I roll my bottom lip into my mouth and nip at it as I watch Wes pump his hard length in his fist.

"Do you want my cock or a highlander's?" he asks me as he notches the tip to my opening.

"Yours," I pant desperately. "Only yours."

My correct answer is rewarded when Wes drives home in one long, hard thrust. I let out a groan release my lip from my teeth.

Wes leans forwards on his elbows on either side of me. He grinds his hips into me as he drives froward. Each slow thrust is accentuated by a swivel of his hips.

"Your highlander might turn you on, baby," he says as he slides in again.

"Yes," I pant.

"But it's my cock that makes you come."

"Yes."

Wes slides his hand up the side of my body and pinches my nipple between his fingers as he palms my breast before leaning down to take it in his mouth. I arch my back and let him take it as he slides deep, hitting a secret spot deep inside.

Wes lets his teeth scrape against my nipple as he lets it slide free from his mouth. He slides his arms underneath my back spearing me deeper onto his cock, pulling us upwards so that I'm sitting on the edge of the counter as he powers into me again and again.

I wrap my arms around his shoulders and hang on tight as he drives faster and faster.

"I love you so much," he says against my mouth.

"I-I love you," I pant.

As he drives his cock faster and faster, harder and harder into me I know that I'm close, so so close. It won't take much to push me over the edge.

"I-I'm going to—" I start

"Come now. Give it to me."

Wes presses his mouth to mine absorbing the noises that are coming from my mouth as I fly over the edge. Wes is right behind me thrusting one more time before planting himself deep as he lets go and comes inside me.

Wes places soft kisses to the corner of my mouth and then the other, over each of my eyelids, and then finally over my mouth. I open underneath him and let him lick in. Wes breaks out kiss to drop his forehead to mine.

"Thank the highlander for me." He laughs.

"I think . . ."

"Yeah, baby?"

"I think I'm going to buy you a kilt for a wedding present." At that, Wes throws his head back and laughs. The chicken mostly burned to the pan behind us.

WEs kisses me—quickly but passionately—one more time before sliding free from my body and doing up his pants letting his belt hang open.

"I'm just going to lay here and die," I inform him while I'm spread out like a starfish on the large island in the kitchen.

To that, the love of my life just smirks, smug bastard that he is and all.

"Well this doesn't look so good," Wes says from somewhere behind me. I tip my head back and to the side to see that he is poking at the chicken breasts in the pan with a spatula.

"I'm sorry to say it," I tell him. "But those look like a done deal."

"I'm sorry." Wes sighs.

"No, don't apologize. It was worth the sacrifice. I mean . . . I enjoyed myself."

"I know." Wes smirks at me again. I roll my eyes.

"You are truly ridiculous."

"I know that too," he tells me. "But I'm your ridiculous."

"That is true."

"Still planning on laying the naked?" Wes asks me.

"Yeah, pretty much," I answer. "Why?"

"Because this chicken is raw on one side and charcoal on the other. The whole thing is going in the trash."

"Ok," I start to respond feeling confused. "What does that have to do with my lack of clothing?"

"Because I'm calling in a pizza and I didn't know if you wanted the kid who delivers to see you in the all together. I mean, on the one hand, I won't have to tip him because you'll be the tip, but on the other hand, I'll have to kill him because he's going to want to give you more than just the tip and he's not giving you anything."

"That was the most convoluted diatribe I have ever heard."

"Are you going to put on pants or does little Jimmy have to die tonight," Wes says on a raised eyebrow.

"His name isn't even Jimmy!" I shout throwing my hands out to my sides as I sit up on the counter.

"Well, then what is it?" Wes challenges me.

"How the hell should I know?"

"Pants or death?"

I shoot Wes a death glare. "I guess I should go find some pants . . ."

"That's what I thought," he chuckles as he swats me on the ass when I bend over to snatch his dress shirt up off of the floor.

"I'm freaking going!" I shout as I hop off of the counter and head for the door.

"Hey Claire," he calls after me. I stop walking out of the room and turn to look at him.

"What is it, Wes?"

"But I'm not wrong, baby."

I just turn back around and start walking again and mumble, "I better get extra pepperoni and sausage out of this."

"I'll get you your extra pepperoni, baby," his sex rough voice rumbles over my skin even from across the room. "But I've got all the sausage you could need right here."

And he's right. He does.

I quickly make my way down the hall to the bathroom. I slip my arms into Wes's shirt and button a few buttons but that's it. He's so tall that it falls to my knees. I'm covered in case the pizza delivery kid catches a glance. I pull a hair band that I have stashed in the drawer out and toss my hair up in a messy bun on top of my head. I look in the mirror and see dark tendrils of my hair hang soft and loose around my flushed cheeks. Apparently good sex agrees with me.

I walk back out of the bathroom and Wes freezes in his tracks when he sees me. Good. He deserves to be teased a little.

"That's not quite what I had in mind," he tells me on a raised brow.

I shrug. "It's good enough."

"Good enough to get poor Jimmy maimed or killed?"

"That's up to you, dear. You know I'd never stand in the way of your evil plans . . ." I let the twinkle in my eyes show him that I'm teasing.

"Dangerous game, darling," he says following my lead.

I shrug again letting the game slip away. "I just like your shirts."

Wes's face goes soft before he answers me. "Far be it from me that I should ever deny you anything."

I just nod once.

"But I will take it back whenever I want," Wes warns me.

"Or you could just leave it on," I whisper. "There's nothing stopping you underneath."

Wes takes an instinctual step towards me when the doorbell rings. He clenches his fists at his side only to open them and then clench them again.

"We don't need pizza do we?" he asks me on a strangled voice.

"I'm starving," I say while shooting him my most innocent smile. "I can't survive alone on rabbit food."

"Of course you can't," he mumbles under his breath before turning on his heel and answering the door.

I walk back into the kitchen and pull open the fridge. There is a bottle of wine in the back and tonight feels like a good wine night. I pour two glasses and place them on the counter shooting interested glances at the island countertop.

I dress the salad and am serving it onto plates when Wes walks back in carrying a giant pizza.

"My hero!" I cry draping the back of my hand across my forehead as if I might swoon.

"Hilarious," Wes drolls.

"I try." I bat my eyes making Wes smile and his whole face softens making him look younger.

"No pizza for you," he says as he lifts the box up over my head and out of my reach.

"What?!" I shout. "I didn't mean it. Give me my pizz back."

"Now tell me you love me . . ."

"I love you!"

"Now tell me I'm better than any highlander."

"You're so much better!"

"Here's your pizza," he says as he places the box on the island, pausing to look at where we were thirty minutes earlier. He slow blinks before turning back to me. "You know? I don't think I ever really appreciated this kitchen before . . ."

"Me either," I say before stuffing a giant bite into my mouth.

• • •

"What's on your mind, baby?" Wes asks me as I towel off my body. My skin is still bright pink from the hot water of my shower.

"It was just a long day."

"I thought it was a good day?" he asks me as he wraps his arms around me pulling me in close as he rests his chin on top of my head. I love when he does this. I'm fairly tall for a woman so the fact that he is tall enough to make me feel small and delicate is kind of nice.

"It was," I begin to explain. "We found out Anna prepaid for all of the dresses right before she died. That was tough on us both."

"Did you pick out a dress?"

"Yeah," I say softly knowing that there is a wistful quality to my voice.

"Is it pretty?" he asks me. His voice is quiet in the still evening of our bathroom.

"Yeah," I sigh. "And kind of sexy too."

"Sexy?" Wes asks me. "Tell me about it."

"Unh uh," I decline.

"No?" I can hear the smile in his voice.

"No. I want you to be surprised."

"Okay, honey," he says toying with a lock of my wet hair. "I'll be surprised."

"Okay."

"Anything else bothering you?" he asks me.

"I can't stop thinking about Rodriguez," I admit.

"Yeah," he agrees. "Me too."

"Any new information?" I ask grasping at anything Wes might be willing to give me. I have to know what happened. I have this driving need inside of me to find the answer and solve the puzzle.

Wes studies me for a moment before letting out a heavy sigh. I know in that instant that he is about to give me the truth, whatever that might be.

"We have nothing," he says and the vein at his temple pulses. I can tell how angry that makes him. It makes me angry too. "There are no tapes, no notes, no faces. We have nothing."

"I hate this," I whisper.

"Me too, honey."

Wes pulls the towel from around my body and places it on the bathroom counter before rolling up one of his t-shirts and dropping it over my head. I push my arms through the armholes as he lets the faded fabric drop around my thighs.

"Let's go to bed," he tells me holding out his hand for me to take it and I do without hesitation.

Wes walks me towards our bed and drops my hand only to pull the bedding back so that we can climb in. Wes pulls me into the safety of his arms after pulling the blankets back over us. I feel warm, and safe, and sleepy so I let myself drift off.

It wouldn't be until days later that I would realize that I was never safe.

chapter 9

go gray

"COME OUT OF the closet, baby."
"No," I whisper, tears hot on my face and snot stuffing up my nose. Liam and Wes were right, I'm just a baby. A big kid wouldn't be crying in the dark corner of a closet hoping it'll all go away if you just wish hard enough. I bet Wes never cries. I know Lee doesn't.
"Come out now, Claire. Playtime is over."
"No," I cry louder. "Please don't make me."
"Now!" He growls as the closet door rattles. I gasp.
"Leave me alone!"
"Get out of the fucking closet, Claire!" He roars.
"Please no," I cry harder, my body shaking with each sob.
"When," he kicks his hard boots against the closet door and it shudders.
"Please."
"Are you," he kicks it again.
The doors are the kind with the slats that fold sideways. We have them at home and mama says I always pinch my fingers in the accordion. Whatever that is.
"I just wanna go home," I whisper.
"Gonna," he kicks again.
"I just want my mommy," I sob. "Please. I just want my mommy."
"Fucking," the boards snaps and I scream.
"I just wanna go home, please," I beg.
"Learn!" he shouts as he kicks the broken boards out of the way. He leans down and grabs me by my upper arms.
"Please," I wheeze but my words are cut short when he slaps my face hard. So hard I taste blood in my mouth and it's so yucky I feel sick. I'm going to throw up from the yucky taste. I try as hard as I can not to. I know that if I do, he'll punish me again. I don't want that. Anything but that.
"You are home, baby," he coos right before he slaps me again. I cry out again, falling to the floor with his last hit. It's so strong he knocks me down with it. "And I thought I told you to call me daddy," he says as he lands a hard kick to my back.
"You're not my daddy, you'll never be my daddy," I whisper. "My daddy is a nice man. He would never hurt me. You'll never be my daddy," I say again.
"I am your daddy!" he roars as the wooden slat splinter inward.

I'm stuck, trapped under the broken pieces of wood and chips of paint from the closet door. I scream when the pieces of wood go flying towards my face and reach up to cover my head with my arms. Maybe it will save me from the sound beating I'm about to get but I know that it won't.

I have nowhere to go, but one thing is for sure, I have to escape.

• • •

I scream again.

"Claire!" he's shouting my name.

"No," I cry. "I won't come out. You can't make me."

"Claire."

"Please, I'll be good, I promise. I just want to go home," I plead as hot tears pour down my cheeks, my eyes are still firmly closed to the bad man.

I know when I open my eyes that I will see his mean face and I don't want to. No! I have to. I have to know who the bad man is.

"Claire."

I open my eyes and I look up at him expecting to see his mean face but all I see is a blur. No! I have to know who the bad man is.

"Claire, please come back to me," Wes's rough voice pleads. It cracks on emotion.

I blink my eyes trying to clear my mind whether it's a waking nightmare or the truth is left to be determined.

"Wes?" I ask hesitantly. I'm wrapped safely in the cocoon of his arms.

"Thank God," he rumbles before answering me. "Yeah, baby. It's me."

"Okay," I whisper. "I think I had a nightmare."

"I know, honey," he says as he brushes the sweat dampened hair back from my forehead and around my face. "Can you tell me about it?"

This is what I love about Wes. He doesn't push me for more in these moments. He does not demand that I give him the information that I don't have or can't bare to give him. He just asks patiently and then sits back and waits for me to offer up anything or everything or even nothing at all.

"I-I think . . ."

"Yeah?" he asks.

"I think I remember dark hair," I tell him hesitantly. "I think he had dark hair. The man who took me had dark hair."

"That's great, honey."

"But that's all I remember. When I look up into his face all that I see is a blur."

"But that's something. You're remembering and that's huge. The information will come, it just depends on when," Wes reassures me.

"But what if I never remember who he is or was?" I ask admitting one of my biggest fears.

"Then so what?" Wes shrugs his shoulders.

"What?" I ask unsure that I heard Wes correctly.

"So what? Who cares if you never remember the details," Wes says. His voice growing in volume and determination to get his point across. "I don't care. I mean I do. I want you to have what you need to heal, but at the end of the day, I just want you."

"Wes—" I start but he interrupts me still on his mission to make me see how much he really loves me.

"I want you in whatever package you might come in. So grow old, gain fifty pounds, let all that hair that drives me wild go gray. It'll still drive me wild when I'm eighty. My point is that none of that matters. I'm still going to love you like crazy and I'm still going to want to fuck you every night."

"Wes?"

"Yeah, baby?"

"I'm pretty sure that was sweet wrapped up in all of that vulgarity," I answer.

"It was," he answers me. "Remember, don't remember, it doesn't matter. What matters is at the end of the day it's you and it's me. The rest is just details."

And he's right. Wes is so very right. All of the bullshit is just that, bullshit, because at the end of the day, it's going to be just Wes and me and that is everything I will ever need to make it though.

"I love you, Wes." I reach up and place a soft kiss on his lips.

"I love you too," Wes tells me, his voice rumbling deep and rough in the still night. "How's the shoulder feeling?"

"Pretty good, why?" I ask.

"Because now I'm going to fuck you."

"Oh," I stammer.

"Yeah, 'oh.'"

And then Wes rolls me to my back covering my body with his. He covers my mouth with his and I happily open underneath his expert lips as he wedges his hips between my thighs and I readily accept him. Wes licks into my mouth as he rocks his hips to slide his cock back and forth through my wetness but never penetrating. His teasing drives me crazy and I arch my hips in an attempt to take him into my body.

"Not yet, greedy girl," he says after he tears his mouth away from mine. I let out a low whine at his opposition to what I currently want—what I need.

"Wes," I breathe.

He pushes the hem of his t-shirt up uncovering my thighs as he goes and then my hips. I hear his breath catch in his throat when he uncovers the juncture of my thighs where his slick cock pressed against my folds is there for us both to see.

"Wes, please," I plead.

"Not yet," he pants as he rocks his hips sliding the slick length of him against my clit. The motion sends sparks shooting off of my skin and I shudder at the contact causing Wes so stop moving again. "Soon."

Wes continues to push the hem of the t-shirt up and up and up exposing my belly button. He leans over and kisses and nips at the soft flesh that he uncovers. Wes glides his lips up and up following the trail that the t-shirt leaves in its wake until he reveals my breasts.

Wes scoops the t-shirt up and over my head in the same quick fashion that he had dropped it down around me for me to sleep in only a few hours earlier before tossing it over his shoulder to the floor. And then he places a soft kiss to my breast before teasing the nipple with a quick swipe of his tongue. I feel the sensation everywhere including where his cock is nestled to me.

Wes caresses my other breast with his heavy palm, running his thumb in maddening circles around my nipple as he sucks its twin into his mouth. He scrapes his teeth over the sensitive bud before soothing it with his tongue.

He lets my nipple slip from his mouth with a pop before kissing his way up my neck. All the while rocking his hips against mine. My breath seizes in my lungs when he scrapes his teeth against the side of my throat as he notches the tip of his cock to my opening.

"Wes," I pant as he slides in side.

"Yeah, baby," he answers my call in a rough rumble.

I arch my hips to make him go faster but as is always with Wes he does things on his own time in his own way. I'm shaking, desperate for him to give me more. The slow and steady push and pull of his body and mine is slowly driving me mad.

"Wes—" I call out but he doesn't hear me as he pumps inside me in his unhurried pace. "Wes, I-I need—"

"I know what you need," he says as he drives his cock in with a little more force.

"I need you," I answer as the head board rocks against the wall with an audible thump.

"Yeah," he rumbles again as he drives home this time a little faster but not by much. And yet, it's all I need. "You do and I need you."

"You do?" I ask as I cling to his back my nails digging in as I hold on.

"With every breath I breath, baby, I need you."

His words are all I need to send me over the edge. I tip my head back and call out as I do. This time Wes is right with me, coming with me. He drops his mouth to mine as he does and I happily drink in his groan.

After a moment, Wes pulls out and rolls to the side taking me with him. He wraps me up in his arms.

"Tink you can sleep now?" he asks me as he brushes my hair back from my face. I look up into his eyes and wonder what he must see when he sees me. I'm most likely a mess right now as I take stock of myself. I'm a little battered and bruised and now thoroughly fucked, but I'm okay.

"Yeah," I say softly. "I do."

"Good," he says as he tucks us back into bed not reaching for my discarded shirt.

I settle in and close my eyes. I let every muscle in my body relax one by one and every vertebrae loosen in the same fashion. I am almost ready to drift off when Wes speaks to me one last time.

"Claire?" he asks, his voice soft in the midnight quiet.

"Yeah, Wes?"

"I won't pretend to know what's going on in your head with these nightmares . . . these memories . . . but baby?"

"Yeah?" I answer.

"You're safe with me."

"Okay, Wes."

"I mean it, Claire. You're safe with me and you're always going to be safe with me. Don't ever doubt it."

"I won't, Wes," I promise into the night.

"And baby?"

"Yeah?" I answer.

"I'm right where I want to be." His voice rings true with so much emotion packing it's punch. With so much feeling that my heart pounds in my chest. "So don't ever doubt that either."

"I won't."

"You're safe with me."

Those were the last words I heard before we both drifted off to sleep and I believed them with my whole heart. I believe in Wes and his strength and smarts and I believe in his heart that he loves me and he would do anything to protect me. Even willing to lay down his own life for me.

But even Wes can't protect me from some monsters in the dark . . .

chapter 10

hamburger

*B*EEP... BEEP... BEEP...
Wes's alarm blares from the bedside table on his side of the bed. If it were mine, I would hit the snooze, but it's not, it sits like a sentry on his side of the table with the full knowledge that Wesley O'Connell who is everything that is good and right and dependable will not hit snooze and will shut it off.

I let out a weary sigh. Will I ever be as good as Wes? That's a question with an answer that will only come with time . . . and maybe some bourbon. Maybe I should go on one of those soul searching adventures in a yurt in New Mexico . . . nah, Wes would never be on board to smoke some peyote and wait for the spirit animals of our ancestors to tell us the meaning of life.

I wonder what it's like to have sex in a yurt . . .

I rub the sand from my eyes as Wes reaches over to silence his alarm after not nearly enough sleep. I feel the bed shift underneath us as he rolls to face me.

"A penny for your thoughts," Wes asks me as he brushes a lock of hair out of my eyes.

"I was wondering what it would be like to have you make love to me in a yurt."

Wes pauses for a moment appearing for all intents and purposes to be stunned. That's it, I finally broke him.

"What?" he laughs as he rolls me to my back with him on top of me settled between my thighs.

"I was thinking that this has been a tough year," I admit.

"Yeah, honey," he says, his face softening.

"So I was wondering if maybe I should go on one of those spirit guide things in New Mexico," I continue.

"Okay?" Wes says waiting for me to finish my train of thought for the full story.

"But then I realized you probably aren't the kind of guy to smoke a bunch of peyote and then sweat in a yurt while we wait for the spirit animals of our ancestors to tell us what we're doing wrong."

"I don't think that's exactly how it goes on those trips," Wes says biting the inside of his cheek to keep from laughing.

"So you do what to smoke peyote and sit in a yurt?" I ask him.

"Uhh . . . not exactly."

"That's what I thought. But then it got me to thinking what it would be like to have sex in a yurt . . ."

Wes pulls the sheets up over our heads.

"I can probably answer some of your questions for you right now," he says to me. I see the heat in his eyes and like a moth to a flame I am drawn to him over and over again.

"Oh yeah?" I ask as I wiggle my hips underneath him. "I do have a few questions . . ." I trail off.

"Well let me see what I can do to set your mind at ease," Wes says as he rocks his hips sliding the length of his cock through my slit.

"Yes," I breathe.

"My beautiful Claire," he says as he rocks his hips again against me. "Always so wet for me."

"Yes."

"And only me," he says as the look on his face turns feral.

"Yes, only you." I moan as he thrusts inside.

I wrap my arms around his back and pull my knees up to my sides so that his strokes his deeper than before. We both moan at the new angle.

Wes places soft kisses all around my face and he gently glines in and out of my body and I rock my hips against his. It's soft and sweet and gently and yet we need more.

"Wes?" I ask between shallow plunges of his cock

"Yeah, baby?" he asks as he slowly rocks back and forth between my legs.

"It was a flesh wound, honey," I tell him gently as he slows his pace to lie still with his hard cock still inside me. "I won't break."

"I know that," he says on closed eyes.

"Do you?" I ask him.

He sighs. "Yeah, I do." Slowly, he withdraws his length from me before slamming all the way in. "My girl needs to be fucked this morning."

He pulls almost all the way out before driving back in hard and fast.

"Yes," I pant.

Wes pulls all the way out before gripping my face in his hand so I can't look away from him. His fingers digging into the flesh of my cheek and his thumb between my lower lip and chin. "You will tell me if anything hurts and we will stop immediately."

"Yes, Sir," I respond cheekily.

Wes lets go of my face before grabbing me by the hips and flipping me over onto my hands and knees. He shoves my upper body down into the mattress so only my ass is in the air.

The swat he lands to my backside rings out in the quiet room and I bite my lip as a rush of wetness floods my pussy.

"Don't give me any ideas that you aren't willing to follow through on, baby," he says, his voice raspy with sex and need. "I like it too much."

"Maybe I like it too," I admit as I look over my shoulder.

Wes dips two fingers into my pussy spreading my wetness around on his fingers before circling my asshole. "Yeah, I see that you do like it," he says as he sinks in a finger. "I wonder what else you might like?"

"Wes," I moan.

"I know, baby," he coos. "You need my cock."

"Yes."

He notches the tip of his cock to my pussy and slowly slides in. From this angle, with his finger in uncharted territory, I feel full. So full that it won't take much for me to come. Wes circles his hips as he slides back in and curls his finger.

"Oh, God."

"That's right, baby," Wes says as he pulls out and pumps back in, this time a little faster. "Soon I'm going to own this ass like I own this pussy and it's going to be so good."

But I can't think of the words coming out of his mouth while every brain cell I ever had is scrambling and rearranging. It's all that I can do to hang on to the edge of the mattress while Wes masters my body. This is exactly what I wanted and so much more.

"You're so close. I can feel it. The way your pussy grips my dick in all that wetness that's just for me. The way your body flushes and the way that you bite your lip. And those sexy as fuck noises that you make when you're about to give it all to me." He pumps his cock again and again, his other hand squeezing my ass cheek in his large palm the bite of it is almost enough to send me over.

"Yes."

"Let go, baby," he says as he thrust a little harder. "I'll catch you when you fall."

And I do.

"Wes!" I cry out as wave after wave crashes over me and I come harder than ever.

Wes pull his finger free and grips my ass cheeks in both hands. Hard.

"Yes!" he shouts. "That's it, baby." As he plunges in again and again harder and harder as my orgasm rolls over into another.

"Wes," I cry out.

"That's it," he growls as he pumps harder and faster. "Oh fuck, fuck, fuck, you feel so fucking good the way that you squeeze my dick." There is something about Wes's dirty talk that drives me absolutely wild.

"Yes."

"Yes! Again!" he demands.

"I-I don't know if I can," I cry out.

"You can!" Wes shouts as he powers his cock faster and faster, his fingertips biting so hard no doubt they'll leave bruises. Give it to me."

"Yes," I moan but I'm not sure if any words come out as he drive his cock deep and I scream as I come.

"Fuck fuck fuck, that's it, that's it, oh fuck, Claire!" he shouts as he plants his cock deep inside me and follows me over the edge.

Wes collapses on top of me and I love the feel of his weight pressing me into the mattress. The breath in our lungs sawing in and out of us in tandem.

After a moment he pushes up a little so that all of his weight isn't on me any more but in truth, I never mind.

"Well," he rumbles after placing a tender open mouth kiss to the side of my neck making me smile. "Life with you will never be boring."

"I aim to please, Mr. O'Connell," I whisper.

"As do I, Mrs. O'Connell." He takes my earlobe into his mouth and nips just a little before letting is go and pulling out of me. "But now I really do need a shower and so do you."

"I do?" I ask.

"You do," Wes agrees. "I'm all for staking my claim on you, but even I wouldn't make you go into the station with sex hair and my cum drying on your thighs."

"I do appreciate the lack of caveman this morning," I tell him.

"Oh, I'm still a caveman for you, baby," he says as he skates his fingernail down my crack and over his new found territory making my breath seize in my lungs. "But there is a time and place for it."

He reaches for me to help me up and I stand on shaky legs like a newborn giraffe. There's a smug twinkle in his eye that says he knows that he fucked me proper this morning. And, well, he did so I guess that smug look is earned.

"Let me shower you and then I'll drive you to work," he says. I sigh. Wes is really going to be unbearable to live with now.

"Okay," I say and then let him do just that.

• • •

It would seem that some lessons take longer to be absorbed. I guess I am going to have to make myself more clear—crystal fucking clear.

I hate that she drives me to this level of anger but that's on her not on me. She could have been mine all along, but no, she made a poor choice and now we all have to live with the consequences.

So instead of fucking my prize in my soft, warm bed this morning, I was out stealing a car. That's so . . . pedestrian. Such petty crimes are beneath a man like me, and yet here I am. I hate that she brings me down to this level.

I slowly drive past the side street where I know that the police are stopped for lunch. A fucking hamburger. I shudder at the thought of such common food. I would never eat anything like that.

I circle back and drive again. I'm trying to get her attention. When I circle back again and pass her one more time, I know that I have. I wink as I watch her pick up her radio.

It's showtime!

I park this car on a side street. I won't be needing it anymore.

I head out on foot and walk directly up to the driver's side of the police car. There are two of them in the front seat eating lunch. Their styrofoam cartons in their laps and used napkins litter the dashboard. It's so filthy. Unsanitary.

She rolls down her window.

"Sir, can I help you?"

I smile wide and nod but don't answer her verbally. I casually paid a friend of a friend of a friend on the force with a coke problem to make sure that their body cameras didn't work this morning. But don't worry, he won't be in the way for long.

He looks up at me nervously, he knows what is about to happen because I explained everything to him this morning, but I don't acknowledge him.

"Sir, what can I do to help you?" she asks but it's already too late.

I pull the forty-five from the back of my pants and shoot her between the eyes. Before her partner can get a word out of his mouth I fire two rounds into his chest and one into his head. I neatly tuck the gun into the back of my pants and pull my jacket down low to cover it.

I mile at a small shopkeeper as I walk past and then head down the stairs to the subway. Just like any other anonymous man in America.

But soon, my queen, you'll know it's me because I'm coming for you . . .

• • •

Today sucks I'm so fucking bored.

I twirl in my rickety desk chair one more time. This morning when Wes dropped me off he made Liam, my fucking boss, promise not to let me do anything more strenuous than paperwork.

"You have got to be mother fucking kidding me!" I had shouted.

"Do you kiss her with that mouth?" Lee had asked Wes who had laughed, that big bastard.

"I do," he smiled and I rolled my eyes. "But she's got other places I prefer to kiss."

"That's my sister and that's also disgusting," Lee groaned.

"Hey man, you started it," Wes said holding his arms out.

"Still gross," Lee said. "Now get out of my station."

"Gladly," Wes had said. "We have a deal?"

"Yep, it's like 1993 again and I'm babysitting my little sister," Lee rolled his eyes.

"Yep, that's pretty much it."

"Don't I get a say at all here?" I asked.

"No!" They had both shouted.

"I hate you both," I had pouted as I crossed my arms across my chest.

"No you don't," Wes said as he pulled me into his arms for a quick kiss. "You love me."

"Unfortunately," I sighed.

"Try and be good, babe," he laughed. The fucker. But I was too busy pouting. "I'll pick you up at five."

That was four freaking hours ago . . .

Now, I have completed every fucking page of busy work Lee had placed on my desk with a pat on my head and a thoroughly patronizing round of "Be good," with a pat on my head.

I absolutely hate busy work. I get that the reports need to be filed, but no cop worth their weight wants to actually slow down and do the work to fill them out. We thrive off of being in the field and exist in a constant state of motion.

Filling out reports are neither of those.

I twirl in my chair one more time when the tones alert to another distress call. After the mass shooting the other day, the department captains got together and decided that all distress calls will automatically be patched in to all stations and all radios and cars.

What I hear next would chill me to my bones . . .

"Did you see that?" Officer Jasmine Alexander asks who I'm assuming is her partner, Matt Jerome. I have never gotten that warm and fuzzy feeling from him.

"See what, Jazzy?" he asks you can hear the frustration in his voice. *"You're imagining things."*

Officer Alexander must have hit the distress code without alerting her partner which never means good things.

"I'm not imagining things," she says. *"That car has driven by three times already. It's weird."*

"Just eat your burger, Jazzy."

"Hey, Matt—" she starts but he cuts her off.

"Save it," he orders. *"Just eat your lunch so we can go back in service."*

She clicks her microphone as if she is just relaying a call. *"Dispatch, a white, middle age male is approaching the vehicle."*

"Dispatch copies, respond with caution."

"Sir, can I help you?" she asks the unidentified male. After a pause where we can't hear him say anything Jasmine asks again. *"Sir, is there anything I can help you with?"*

There is nothing but silence followed by a loud *pop* that can only mean one thing. The room is silent. And then another *pop, pop, pop* sounds.

"Officer Alexander, do you copy?" the dispatch officer shouts. "Officer Alexander, Officer Jerome, DO YOU COPY?"

Nothing. There is nothing. We all know that can only mean one thing.

"All responding officers in the area, this is dispatch, please respond to shots fired on the corner of Main and seventeenth. Car is no longer in service

for dinner."

The room freezes before expanding, like a glass windshield in a car crash. Officers and Detectives alike run at top speed out of the room. I jump out of my chair and catch Lee as he races out of his office palming his car keys. I grab him by the back of his arm and he whirls around on me.

"Take me with you," I demand.

"No."

"I'm not kidding, Lee!" I shout. I have to go with him, I have to be there because Jasmine was my friend.

"This isn't a game, Claire!" he shouts.

"You know I don't think this is a fucking game!" How dare he say such awful things. "You know that she was my friend!"

"You're injured," he argues with me.

"I've been cleared for duty and you're wasting time!" He is and he knows it, I see the indecision warring on his face. Thank God my brother makes the right decision.

"Get in the car and don't fucking do anything stupid," he orders.

"I won't," I promise hoping that it isn't a lie.

I follow Lee out to his truck that looks identical to mine but it's new and the radio works. Unfortunately, he uses that to listen to a shit ton of Garth Brooks on the normal day, but today is anything but normal.

The car stays eerily silent as we drive across town. Silent as a tomb.

"We're going to have to walk in," he says to me. The scene has already been blocked off and all of the responding officers vehicles are lining the available roadway.

"I'm up to it," I say as I catch a glimpse of the black and white as we drive up a cross street and I feel the egg sandwich that I had for breakfast in the car on the way to the station this morning churning in my stomach. It's been a long time since I was sick at a crime scene.

But I guess today is a day of revisiting.

As we walk up the side street after Lee parks his department vehicle, I can't help but to remember the case that Jasmine and I worked on. My sister's murder, although at the time, I had no idea that Bonnie Bradley, a down and out forty-something single mother of three by day and down and out stripper by night was my half sister, but now I do.

When we responded to the scene that night, she handled all of the dancers with extreme care and a protectiveness that rivaled a mama bear. The young police officer impressed me right from the beginning. I was sure that her future was so bright and now it has been snuffed out, extinguished, forever.

It's incredibly unfair and if it's the last thing I do, I'm going to find out who did it.

chapter 11
bedlam

IT'S PANDEMONIUM.
When Lee and I turn the corner and approach the scene it's complete bedlam. People are screaming. While this neighborhood is not an affluent one, it is a relatively safe one. The people who have gathered on the street behind the yellow crime scene tape wears masks of shock and fear.

You can smell that fear in the street.

Police officers, firefighters, and paramedics alike wear their grief and sadness like a cloak. We've lost more of our own. Again. And this time not just one, but two.

All while eating a fucking hamburger.

I will probably never be able to stomach another one after today.

As I approach the yellow tape I hear someone calling my name. "Claire!" But I don't pay any attention. It's like I'm at the far end of a tunnel and that tunnel is underwater. The voice is foggy or faint. It sounds so far away.

"Claire!" it sounds again. "Get back!" But I keep walking towards the tape.

Each step I take feels as if it's encased in concrete. But I force myself to keep pushing forward. I have to see with my own two eyes before I can believe that this really happened. That our small township is under siege. But from who? From where? I don't know. I just don't know.

"God dammit, Lee!" the voice shouts again and I pause in my steps to look over my shoulder. Wes is running towards me from far away. "What the fuck is she doing here?"

I turn back towards my goal.

"She made me," Lee says to Wes.

"When does anyone make you do anything, Lee?" Wes roars. "God dammit, Lee, don't be such a pussy!"

"I swear it," Lee says.

"Dammit, Claire!" Wes shouts. "Get back!"

"No," I say. "I can't. I have to do this. I have to be here. For her."

"Please, baby. I'm begging you," he says. I look up and notice that Wes is right next to me although he doesn't make a move to pull me back. "Don't do it."

"I have to," I whisper. The look in his eyes is desolate. He knows I have to do this and he also knows it's not going to be good. Shit it must be bad. "Come with me?"

"Always," he vows to me.

"I want to be strong," I admit my voice low for Wes's ears only. "I don't want to fall apart before I have a chance to find who did this. Don't let me fall apart. Make me be strong."

"You *are* strong," Wes reassures me.

"Okay," I say for lack of anything else.

Wes wraps his arm around my waist and I let his strength seep into my bones. We approach the crime scene tape and I see the carnage for the first time. I feel the bile rise up in my throat but I beat it back.

"She was eating a fucking hamburger on her dinner break," I say hearing the anger reverberate through my voice.

"Yes," he confirms the facts.

"A fucking hamburger." I grind my teeth together to keep from screaming.

"I know, honey," Wes says as he rubs my back. I dig my fingers into his hip.

"We're going to find the man who did this and we're going to make him pay," I say my voice low.

"Yeah," Wes agrees. "We fucking are. And we're going to do it together."

"Okay." I take a deep breath for the first time this afternoon. "Where do we start?"

"Let's review everything that's visible from right here and then go forward from there," he orders. And I can do that.

I move my gaze towards the asphalt. "I see shell casings outside of the vehicle."

"Good," Wes says. "He stood outside the vehicle. That matches what we know from the distress call."

"There are one . . . two . . . three . . . four. I count four casings. That matches what we heard over the call," I confirm.

"It looks like Jasmine was down with one," he says his voice soft. "Matt looks like a double tap. Emma will confirm."

"Yes," I say forcing myself to take another deep breath and look up. That's when I see it. "They're wearing body cams."

"It's standard practice now," Wes says before realizing what I'm saying. He turns to several other suits in the area. "I want this body cam footage yesterday!"

"Yes, Sir!" someone says as they jump to get him what he wants. Police and FBI alike will do anything to bring this guy down. We tend to band together when one of our own is murdered.

"Good work, Detective," he says.

"Thanks."

I watch Wes look around at all of the businesses on this street.

"I want all of the security footage from every shop or restaurant. Anyone who has one, get it!" Lee commands the officers.

I thought the scene on this street was bad until I heard the *pop . . . pop . . . pop* of a high velocity rifle report. After the mass shooting the other day, the entire law enforcement community responded to this shooting, the cold blooded murder of two police officers while sitting in their squad car on their dinner break.

"It's a trap!" Lee shouts.

"Everyone take cover!" Wes yells over the roar of the blood in my ears.

We all dropped what we were doing a ran straight here in order to do our part to find justice for Jasmine and Matt. What we didn't know at the time was that it was a trap and we are all sitting ducks.

It's a sight to behold to watch the two of them take over as they issue commands to keep everyone safe. I can see how they worked so well together in their SEAL days.

"I want eyes on that building now!" Lee demands.

"He's gone, Captain," Officer Jones replies.

"Let's secure this scene and get the fuck out of here," Wes says.

"Captain the ME is here with her team and the body mover," Jones says.

"Abso-fucking-lutely not!" Lee yells. "She does not set foot in here until I have a three click radius cleared. Do you hear me?"

"Copy that, Captain. Dr. Parker is going to be pissed though," Jones tells him something we all know.

"Let her be fucking pissed. Pissed is better than dead," Lee answers, his voice eerily calm.

"I hear that," Jones says before breaking out into a jog to tell Emma and her team that they have to sit and wait.

After what seems like forever, Emma and her team are finally allowed in when the area is secure and the sniper is long gone. And as predicted, Emma is fuming mad.

"You don't get to make decisions for me and my team, Captain," she spits out my brother's title as if it's the most disgusting thing on the tip of her tongue.

"Yes, I fucking do," he snarls back. "I am the Captain of this department."

"And I don't fucking answer to you," she snarls.

"Yes, you do. This is my fucking crime scene," Lee practically growls. "And even if it wasn't I would never let you put yourself in harms way."

"Fortunately for you, I don't care about that either," she spits out.

"When are you going to cut me some fucking slack, Emma?" Lee asks as he runs a hand through his hair. "Can't you see that I care?"

"Can't you see that I don't?" she barks.

"If I believed that bullshit for a minute, I would walk away right now, but we both know that's not true, don't we?" he snaps.

"I don't know what you're implying?" she pouts but it's fake the look on her face is worried and I can't help but stand here and watch them implode for the eightieth time this month.

"Don't you?" he asks taking a predatory step closer to her. Lowering his voice so only we can hear, Lee says, "You know that I love you like I know that you love me even though you like to pretend that you don't. Just like I know that tonight, like every other night, even though you don't want to admit that either, it'll be my cock that you ride and my name that you call out into the dark."

Emma audibly swallows past the lump in her throat.

"What's wrong, Angel? Cat got your tongue?" Lee presses into her personal space. They always seem to rise to the challenge with each other and never in a good way.

"I need to get to work," she says her voice unsteady and Emma, as a whole, appears to be off kilter. God they're a fucking mess. I wish they would just figure their shit out already but I'm not that lucky.

"That's what I thought," he replies, a smug expression playing on his face.

After Emma and her team unload their supplies and begin to catalogue and collect every piece of evidence, Liam and Wes go back to directing the investigation. If anyone can track this mother fucker down, it's Liam and Wes. If he hadn't have just murdered two good cops, I would almost feel sorry for him. But that's not the case. He took a bright light from this world and now? Now I will happily greet him at the gates of hell.

chapter 12

this just in

"LET'S GO HOME."
 By the time Wes tells me we're done for the day, the sun is going down, Emma had moved the bodies hours ago, and there is absolutely no evidence of the guy that murdered two police officers in cold blood.

I'm tired and frustrated. I'm hungry and sad. But most of all, I just want this nightmare to be over.

"We're done here for the night," Wes says as he reaches out to take my hand. I had been interviewing shopkeepers all afternoon but at this point I was just comforting them.

"If you think of anything else," I say to the older gentleman who owned the small grocery store. I hand him one of my cards. "Give me a call."

"I will," he says.

"Excuse me," I say politely as I let Wes lead me away.

We climb in his Fed-mobile without speaking a word to each other. It's not that we're mad or upset with each other, in fact, just the opposite. But in moments like this, during cases like this, Wes and I both need a moment of quiet. The stillness helps me collect my thoughts and begin to process them. I have long since believed that Wes operates in the same fashion.

Wes pulls into the driveway and we climb out of the car. He meets me at the hood with a scowl pulling between his brows. When we are at work, I am my own person, but when we're after hours, Wes likes to be a gentleman, opening doors for me and such. He gets frustrated when I don't let him. I grab his hands and squeeze his fingers gently so he knows I didn't mean it as a slight to him.

He punches in the code and unlocks the front door, holding it open for me to pass through and I do. The house feels dark and ominous after the day that we have had so I switch on every light that I pass on my way to the kitchen and some that are out of my way too.

Wes trails behind me into the kitchen. He picks up the remote and starts clicking buttons while I pull last night's cold pizza out of the fridge. The screen lights up adding more false brightness to a dreary night.

"Hot or cold?" I ask but Wes isn't listening to me. He's turning up the volume on the television while I open the box.

I freeze when I hear the words coming out of the TV.

"This just in . . ." the female news anchor says. "Station KVXY has received an anonymous note that we believe to be from the killer . . ."

"That's correct, Marcy . . ." the male anchor says. "This station received a letter late this afternoon. As you all know, we have been covering the case of the police murders since mid-day . . ."

"*That is correct, Steve,*" she says as she turns her smile to him. I hate her. She's annoying, she wants Wes, and someone invited her to our wedding, but in this moment, I hate her most of all. "*We are going to read that letter to you now.*"

"*The letter reads as follows,*" Steve the news anchor says holding up a sheet of white paper.

"That better not be the actual note," Wes growls as he pulls out his phone and starts texting someone—probably either Lee or someone in his own chain of command—while watching the news. My eyes are glued to the screen and I can't make myself look away. "So much for fucking evidence."

" '*Dear Citizens of George Washington Township and the surrounding areas, You have probably noticed some events of recent are not the usual for our sleep little township. I can assure you that they will eventually stop and the place we call home will be safe once again. But not quite yet. You see someone has to pay for their transgressions . . .*"

Oh God, I feel the bile rise up in my throat. I don't know who this guy is but I have a sinking feeling what's coming. My luck has held steady at bad all year and it can't have magically flipped the dial to good all of a sudden.

"*Detective Claire Goodnite has been a very bad girl and until she is willing to right those wrongs . . .*"

"What the actual fuck?!" Wes roars.

"Wes," I whimper.

"*The shooting last week and the one today were all my handiwork. And such events will continue until I have the apology that I so rightly deserve. Until then . . .*' " the news anchor reads. "And it's signed 'the hunter.' "

"I don't like this at fucking all," Wes snaps.

"I-I . . ." I start but I don't know how to finish it. I don't know what words should come out of my mouth. But most importantly, I don't know what I have done or to who that would cause this kind of retaliation.

Wes's phone rings and he pulls it back out of his pocket having only placed it there moments before.

"Yeah?" he answers. "We saw it . . . Not good, brother . . . right . . ." and then he hangs up.

My whole body is shaking. I'm not hungry and a I don't know what to do. Wes pockets his phone and opens his mouth to tell me what whoever that was on the other end of the phone—probably my brother—had to say but when he looks at me and sees my face, what has to be the terror that I'm feeling telegraphed across my face and the way that my body shakes he turns to me quickly. His legs eating up the ground between us in quick strides.

"Claire, fuck, baby," he starts but I don't have anything to say. "Come here."

Wes pulls me into his arms and holds me tight but even he can't stop the shaking that quakes my body. He lifts me up into his arms and carries me upstairs to our bedroom.

"What do you need, baby?" he asks me when he sets me back on my feet.

"I d-d-don't know," I answer and I don't I have no idea what could right what is so obviously wrong in my life right now.

"A shower? Tea? Bed?" he asks as I shake my head no. Nothing sounds good right now.

"Shower," I answer. "I have to scrub clean."

"Okay," Wes says as he marches us into the bathroom.

He flips on the lights before turning on the shower to heat up. Wes backs out of the shower and begins stripping off our clothes but what is usually fun and seduction is replaced with economical movements that serve a purpose.

When we're both naked, he takes my hand and pulls me into the shower stall and directly under the steaming water. I let the scalding spray sting my skin in hopes that I will snap out of what has me twisted in knots so that I can make heads or tails of what is going on.

Wes pulls a bottle of shampoo off of the shelf and pours some in his hands before massaging it into my hair. He tips my head back under the spray and rinses the suds out gently like you would a child.

He hands me the tube of my face soap to wash up as he quickly showers himself clean and I scrub my face until it feels raw but I still don't feel clean. The way Wes looks at me with concern in his eyes says I might have actually scrubbed my skin raw.

Wes picks up a bar of soap that he just scrubbed his body with and carefully washes every inch of my skin but not in the harsh way that I had just washed my face. He rinses the soap from my skin and shuts off the taps, grabbing a towel as he steps out. He dries his body quickly before touching the soft terry cloth to my skin chasing the droplets away.

"What do you need, baby?" he asks me. "Food?"

"No," I answer honestly. I couldn't eat even if I wanted to.

"Bed?" he asks. That's probably the only thing that I can handle. I need to sleep the rest of this day away. I only hope that when I close my eyes, it's not Jasmine and Matt's lifeless bodies that I see.

"Bed."

"You got it," he says as he walks me over the the bed and pulls the blanket and sheet back for me to climb in.

Wes climbs in behind me and pulls the covers over us cocooning us from the outside world. But it's when he pulls me into his arms that I bury my face in his chest and finally lose it.

"I-i-i-it's all my fault," I cry.

"No, baby, it's not," he tells me but in my head over and over again, I hear that bitch on the news tell me that it is.

"It is!" I sob. "He said so."

"This is the working of a madman," Wes says quietly just letting me cry. "Normal people don't go on shooting rampages because they are mad about some transgression."

"But he blames me!" The tears are flowing free down my cheeks and I can't seem to catch my breath.

"Claire—" Wes starts but I don't let him finish.

"Rodriguez and Matt are dead because of me," I sob. "Jasmine is dead because of me!"

Wes wisely does not interrupt my meltdown, he just holds me through the storm. And while what he said is true, only madmen harm others as punishments for whatever slights they perceive happened but that fact of the matter is, this guy blames me—not anyone else but me.

When my tears have run dry and the sobs that wrack my chest are echoes of the ones that came before them, I finally close my eyes. My fingers till clinging to Wes as he holds me and I succumb to my exhaustion and fall into sleep.

• • •

Run!

I'm running as fast as my little feet will take me through the woods behind my parents house. I have to get away from the bad man. If he catches me now, I'll never get away. I have to be free.

Run! I have to run faster.

I see the blue gray light as it spills through the trees. Mommy always told me this was her favorite part of the day—Looking at the sun as it comes up in the morning. I ran away late in the night when the bad man was sleeping. It was my only chance. After he broke the lock on the closet door I knew that I had a chance to get out.

Free.

I'm free. That's the words in my head as the tree break and I see Wes standing at the edge of the backyard. I'm free. I'm finally free. Wes looks up and he sees me.

"I've got her!" he shouts to someone.

My heart is beating so hard in my chest and it hurts to breathe. I'm so tired but I have to keep running. I see Wes, his face, I know that he'll protect me. Wes always protects me. He will keep me safe. He will keep me free.

I push my feet just a little harder, I run just a little faster. I'm almost there. But when I push through the trees, Wes isn't reaching for me. He is standing over a pile of bodies—the bodies of Officer Rodriguez, Officer Jerome, and Officer Alexander. Their mangled corpses are littered at his feet.

When Wes finally turns to me his face is not full of hope and of love for me, but one of anger and disgust. I know in that moment tht Wes hates me even before he opens his mouth to talk.

"This is all your fault, Claire."

• • •

"No!" I scream. It's not my fault but in my heart of hearts, I know that it really is. "No! Don't hate me, please."

"Claire," someone says my name.

"Don't hate me! I need you," I beg.

"Claire, baby," someone says as they shake me awake.

"Please! I'm so sorry. I didn't mean to!" I wail.

"God dammit! Wake up, Claire!" Wes roars and I gasp as I come fully awake.

The realization that it was another nightmare has rocked me.

"Wes," I plead.

"I'm right here, baby," he reassures me.

I push up out of the bed. I have to move. My body is restless and I don't know what od do other than to pace but Wes has other ideas.

"What's wrong?" he asks me as he hauls me back into the bed and back against his body.

"I have to move!" I shout. "Let me go! Can't you see I have to move?"

"You're restless?" he asks. "Your nightmare rattled you and you're restless."

"Yes," I say through gritted teeth.

"Tell me about it," he demands.

"No, please," I plead.

"Get it out," Wes orders. "It's a poison and you have to cut it out."

"Yes," I agree before I begin to explain. "I was running. I had escaped and I could see you through the trees in the clearing. You saw me . . ."

"Yes, that happened," he tells me. "What else?"

"But when I got there you weren't reaching for me." He frowns at me looking confused. This is clearly the part of the story that goes off script. "When

I get the the bodies of all the cops are at your feet and when you look at me I know that you hate me."

"Claire—" he tries to interrupt but I don't let him. He is right. The truth is like a poison and I have to get it out.

"You tell me that it's all my fault and it is!" I shout into the dark room.

"No." He shakes his head vehemently.

"It is!" I argue. "Ow do you see what I can't sit still? That I have to move?"

"Run or fuck?" he asks me.

"What?"

"You said that you need to move," he explains. "So we'll do it together. Do you want to run or fuck?" It only take me a minute to decide.

"Fuck."

"Hard and fast. That's the only way to fight out what you need to," he tells me.

"Yes." I feel my body heating against his.

"It won't be sweet."

"No," I tell him. "I don't want that."

Wes nods once before rolling me to my back and sliding in hard and fast at the same time. I cling to his back, my nails digging in as he pumps into my body hard and fast, just as he had promised me.

It is not sweet and loving nor is it romantic and meaningful. It's sweaty and dirty, it's teeth and nails, and it's exactly what I needed in the moment.

After my orgasm washes through me I finally feel a glimmer of the calm that I had been craving. Wes holds me, his cock still deep inside me as the sweat cools and we can finally catch our breath.

"I can't be without you, Wes," I say softly before the moment is over and I lose my chance to speak my feelings and my fears.

"You won't, baby."

"You can't promise me that, Wes," I sigh. "We don't know what the future will hold."

"I can," he says his voice ringing strong and true in the bedroom.

"How?" I ask my voice sounding small and unsure but in this moment, I will take whatever reassurances that Wes can give me.

"Because I'm just that fucking good," he says. "Can you sleep now?"

"Yeah, I think I can," I tell him.

"Alright, honey," he says as he rolls and curls me into him, settling us back into the bed.

As I drift off again the wisps of calm in the storm that Wes had given me start to drift away and I'm left with the gut deep feeling that nothing will ever be okay again. And in a few short days, I would come to realize how very right I was . . .

chapter 13
officially official

"I NEED YOU on this case," Lee says to me when I walk into his office the next morning.

When Wes and I had gotten up this morning we were more somber than usual. There was nothing about this morning that called for our usual morning hanky panky so we quietly showered and dressed and then he drove me to the station.

Wes had kissed me softly on the lips with a quiet, "I'll see you later." And then he was gone.

I had walked to my desk and fired up my computer so that I could go over everything I knew about both shootings. I was lost in case notes when my brother had called me into his office with a hollard "Goodnite!"

That was ten minutes ago and now Lee had just said that he needed me on this case. For years I have been waiting for him to so those very words. Years!

"What was that?" I ask feeling a little petty.

"The department needs all hands on deck for this asshole. As much as I hate to admit it, you're the best." Lee sighs and runs a hand through his hair. A gesture I have come to know as one of frustration.

"Awe, thanks big brother." I smile an I-just-won-Ms.-America smile.

"Yeah . . . well, don't get used to it," Lee barks.

"Sure thing, boss." I wink at him

"I'm setting up a task force. Say hello to you new partner." Lee explains to me. I had a feeling who I would see before I even turned around.

"Hey, Fed. What's up?" I ask on another wink. Fake good humor can take a gal a long way. Fake it till you make it and all that . . .

"That's Special Agent O'Connell to you." He winks at me.

"Yes, Special Agent O'Connell." I mock salute. "Yeah, I'm not sure how I feel about that."

"We'll try it again tonight when I pull your hair and fuck you from behind," he rumbles for my ears only. Forgetting for a moment that we were in Lee's office. Whoops.

"That does hold some merit."

"Yeah, I'm going to need the assurance of a little decorum in front of the rest of the task force…"

"Aye aye, Captain," I say. Lee sighs.

"You two are officially investigating the hunter case," he says. Gone is the joking and ridiculousness. This case calls for nothing but seriousness and focus.

"You got it." I tell him.

"Yeah, I think that I do," Lee says softly after giving me an appraising look. "See that I don't regret this."

"You won't."

"You need to prepare a press conference," Lee orders.

"Roger that," Wes says.

"Keep me in the loop," Lee tells us. "Now get out of my office."

As Wes and I head out of Lee's office my cell phone chimes from my back pocket.

"Goodnite," I answer.

"Hey, it's me," Emma says. "Come down to my lair." And then she hangs up.

"What was that?" Wes asks me.

"We've been summoned to Emma's domain," I explain on a shrug.

"Well then let's hop to it." Wes claps his hands.

We follow the path through the bullpen to the elevator and I lean forward and push the call button. Wes and I stand side by side as we wait for the elevator to take us down to the basement morgue where Emma calls her home away from home.

The bell chimes as the steel doors slide open and Wes follow me into the metal box. He pushes the button for the bottom and we ride down.

"What the hell took you so long?" Emma shouts when the doors slide open.

"The elevator?" I droll.

"Funny, funny," she snaps before turning to Wes. "What's shaking hot Fed?"

"A task force to find the hunter," he explains.

"I heard about that," she says as she looks me over. I can't help but feel like these two see all of my secrets on the surface. "How are you doing?"

"About as good as expected," I answer.

"So not actually good at all," Emma reads between the lines.

"Exactly."

"So what do you have?" Wes effectively changes the subject.

"My buddy ballistics," she answers on a bright smile. Emma is kind of an odd duck. The same high velocity rifle was used in both shootings."

"What was it?" I ask.

"Looks to be a springfield, smooth bore," she answers.

"Registered?" Wes asks.

"Nope." She pops the p sound which always drives me bonkers mad.

"It was probably bought in pieces and assembled at home," I say thinking allowed.

"That's true," Wes agrees.

"Now here's where things get interesting," Emma begins. "Jerome and Alexander were done with a forty-five at close range. That doesn't fit the mass shooting profile."

"That was the bait," I say. "To get us all there so that he could shoot at us."

"I thought so too," she says. "But after last night's news broadcast, I can't help but wonder if it was more personal since you and Jasmine were friends."

"If that's the case," Wes says. "Then you better watch your back, Emma."

"My thoughts exactly, Fed-Man."

"You got anything else for us?" I ask Emma.

"That was it," she says. "Watch your back, sister. The enemy is close."

"You too," I say softly. Emma winks at me just before Wes and I turn for the elevator.

"Let's go show those reporters whose boss." Wes winks at me as we climb into the elevator.

"And which reporters do you suppose will be at this press conference?" I ask as casually as I can. Wes rolls his eyes telling me that he's onto my ulterior motives.

"You know that Marcy and Steve will be there. They broke the story and they will want to follow it through," he tells me with his voice soft and thoughtful and I absolutely hate it.

"Yippee," I say without the enthusiasm the word implies.

"Claire," Wes chastises. "Be nice."

"It's hard to be nice when everytime she sees you she's practically humping your leg," I complain.

"She does not." Wes looks me in the eye with all seriousness and I just stare right back.

"She does too."

"Okay, she does but that's not the point. I'm with you," he says to me.

"You better be with me or they will never find your body," I growl under my breath. Wes just throws his head back and laughs before crowding me into the corner of the elevator.

"Baby, you know that I am exactly where I want to be or I wouldn't be there," Wes says his voice low and full of sex and something more. "I did not just chase you for years. Years, Claire! Watching you with other guys, waiting for you to clue in that I was here and waiting. Only to finally get my ring on your finger and your glorious ass in my bed every night only to turn around and chase after someone like Marcy."

"Well," I say for lack of anything better.

"Now, you should probably push the button if you want this elevator to actually go anywhere. Or we could take the stairs. Your call, baby. But whichever you choose, I'll be right behind you."

I roll my eyes and push the button in the elevator to the tune of Wes's low laughter.

"Ugh, fine," I groan as I push the button in the elevator. "Let's go show everyone how officially official we are so that we can catch this asshole and solve the damn case."

"And then we'll get married."

"Yes, Wes." I sigh. He's lucky I find him cute when he's persistent. "Then we'll get married."

Silently I add the *I hope* to the end. One thing I would learn in the coming days was that hope was all we had left and even that was about to be sorely tested . . .

chapter 14

marcy, marcy, marcy...

SPECIAL TASK FORCE, my ass. Who do they think they are dealing with? I am clearly the superior competitor and they never stood a chance. They will never catch me before I catch them I think it's time I left a little reminder.

When is she going to learn? While I find myself becoming frustrated with Claire I have to remind myself that she will be some much fun when I bring her to heel. That is what I have been waiting for all this time. What I have been working for.

She needs to learn that she chose wrong. All of this is on her head, not mine. The blood spilled in on Claire's hands, I am just the tool which which to serve her punishment.

And soon I will be the master of her universe when I bring her world crumbling down. Yes, my queen need to learn to kneel at the feet of her king and beg for mercy. Of which I am not sure I will give.

But first I have to send my queen a message...

• • •

"Do you feel Detective Goodnite is fit for duty?"

That question came about ten minutes after Wes and I walked into the press room at the station on the heels of Liam to answer questions about the hunter case. And that disgusting question came dripping from none other than the over inflated lips of Marcy the news anchor. Yay!

"Good afternoon ladies and gentleman of the press. My name is Liam Goodnite and I am the Captain of this department," Lee had said when he walked up to the podium.

"Is this about the hunter case?" Marcy had asked.

"Yes, it is," He confirmed.

"I would be happy to work Agent O'Connell," she said her voice full of victory. God, I hate her. "The hunter reached out to me, after all."

"The hunter allegedly reached out to the news station KVXY," Lee said. "We have yet to confirm it."

"Don't be ridiculous," she snapped. "I have proof."

"I will be needing all evidence turned over to the joint task force between the George Washington Township PD and the FBI. They are now tasked with bringing this killer to justice."

"I will be happy to turn them over to Special Agent O'Connell personally," she had purred.

And as much as I love Wes in this moment and I know that he meant well, but here is where he fucked up. "You can turn them over to my partner on the joint task force, Detective Goodnite."

"Do you feel Detective Goodnite is fit for duty?" she asks now as I stand here a little dumbfounded that this press conference went down hill so fast.

"I do," Wes confirms.

"You can't mean that," Marcy snapped.

"I do," Wes repeats.

"Could that be because she offers you special perks to the job?" Marcy asks her voice turning vicious.

"If you're referring to the fact that Detective Goodnite and I are engaged to be married, then yes, we are, but as we are professionals in our fields we are able to separate our work from home lives," Wes warns.

"Engaged?" she gasps.

"Yes," I answer holding up the back side of my hand to show off my glittering ring. "Now if we could get back to the task force . . ."

"Excellent idea, Detective Goodnite," Lee says.

"Captain Goodnite, don't you think it's a conflict of interest to have Detective Goodnite on this task force?"

"No," he says his voice firm.

"But the hunter made it clear that this is all her fault."

I don't move my mouth but I do gasp. Her words sting. I know that I blame myself and the hunter definitely blames me but for other people to blame me hurts. I feel the burn of my own shame creep across my face.

"That is ridiculous," Wes snaps. "Only a madman blames his cruel actions on someone else. Detective Goodnite has never been responsible for this person."

"I'm just saying," Marcy starts. "That there is no place for her here."

"Detective Goodnite was born in George Washington Township and has worked in one capacity or another for the department for over ten years. If anyone has a place here, it's her," says Lee making me smile. "I think that's about all we have time for today, folks. Marcy, I expect you to turn over all evidence in your possession or I will get a court order."

"Then get a court order," she snarls. "I'm not giving her shit."

"I could arrest you for obstructing justice," Lee warns.

"Go ahead and try my," she snaps back. "That is unless it's Agent O'Connell with the handcuffs . . . then I'm available."

"Don't count on it," I say under my breath.

"You know your mom called me last week and offered to give me your number but I told her that I already had it. Come on, Wes, you know how good we are together. How . . . electric."

I think I'm going to hurl.

"That's enough, Marcy," Wes warns.

"Call me when you get bored of her. I know how to keep you happy." She winks and then she's out the door.

"Claire—" Wes starts but I just hold out my palm to silence him.

"I'm not judging you by your past lovers . . . but yeah, I'm judging you by your past lovers." I force out a sigh barely holding in a laugh. "Thank God you found me when you did." I finally laugh. Wes and Lee join in too.

"I thank God every day I found you."

chapter 15

call it in

"READY TO GET out of here?" Wes asks me after we wrapped up the press conference that was an epic shit show and closed up shop for the night.

"Yeah," I sigh.

"I'll catch you kids later," Lee says as he palms his keys and heads for the door.

"You know he's going to go see Emma, right?" I ask Wes.

"Claire," Wes says, his voice full of warning. "Stay out of it."

"I think it's time we stop lying to each other, Wes, and start this marriage with honesty, don't you?" I ask him.

"Yes . . ." he says hesitantly.

"I agree," I say on a nod. "So let's be real here. I think we both know I'm not going to stay out of it so I'm going to stop pretending like I am."

Wes laughs. "You are ridiculous sometimes, you know that?" he asks me.

"But I'm your ridiculous and that's really what's important here."

"Yeah, baby," he says on a smile. "You are."

Wes takes my hand in his and walks me out of the station. He beeps the locks on his Fed-mobile and opens the passenger door for me. This car is truly ridiculous. Even if I didn't know he was a federal agent, the dark maroon Crown Vic with government plates sure cleared that up for me.

"Don't look at me like that," Wes laughs.

"Like what?" I ask.

"Like you're silently judging my company wheels," he elaborates.

"Oh yeah, I totally am." I laugh.

"I know you are." Wes says as he drives us through town.

I hate this part of cases like this. Where you hurry up and wait. There is no quick moving casework, there are no miraculous discoveries like you see on TV. Real police work is slow moving. The cases don't magically solve themselves and it takes sheer will and determination to find that tiny little needle in a haystack to solve them most times.

This is one of those cases.

So while we've had busy days it feels like we're getting nowhere fast and I hate it. It drive me crazy especially when it's someone like Jasmine. I want to solve every case, but it sticks in my craw when it's such a heartless crime in cold blood. For Christ's sake she was eating a fucking hamburger. It wasn't even a fair fight.

My mind is wandering when Wes finally pulls into our driveway otherwise I would have noticed the surprise waiting for me.

"Call it in," Wes snaps gathering my attention.
"Call what in?" I ask as I look up. "Oh."
"Yeah, 'oh.'"
Painted across the garage door—which was a really nice one made to look like an old carriage door and I really liked it—in blood red paint, which really, is not very original is "This is all your fault, Claire."
I sigh. "I really hate surprises."
"Yeah," Wes says. "When it comes to you and this house, I really hate surprises too."
"Hey," I rally. "Look on the bright side, it's not a snake."
"Not funny, Claire," Wes warns.
"What?" I ask feigning my innocence.
"You know what? Never mind." He sighs running his hand through his brown hair. "I have to call this in."
"I'll call Lee," I offer. "You call in the Feds."
"Claire . . ."
"What?" I ask again.
"Can you even say 'FBI'?" he asks me.
"No, it's tastes funny on my tongue," I say making a face.
"You know the FBI pays for this house you live in," he informs me.
"Whatever." I roll my eyes making Wes smile. Damn, I love his smile. It always makes me feel better and still manages to give me butterflies. "I could always go back to my old apartment . . ."
"The hell you could," he barks.
"That's what I thought," I mumble feeling a little smug.
"Just call Lee, would you?" he sighs.
"Okay," I mumble. "So touchy."
"I can hear you!"
"I'm calling Lee now," I say loudly as I fish my phone out of my pocket and dial my brother. "I'm not talking to you."
It rings three times . . . four . . . Jesus, Lee. This is fucking important. Five rings . . . Wes is talking to his office and I'm feeling a little like a dickwad standing here calling my brother only to have it ring six . . . no, seven times before he finally answers sounding a little out of breath.
"What could you possibly want right now?" he barks into his phone.
"Wow, good talking to you too, asshole. Never fucking mind," I snap feeling a little irritated and under loved.
He sighs. "I'm sorry, was it important?" he asks me.
"No, not at all," I reply blandly.
"Good tell me about it in the morning," he says.
"Nah," I say wanting to reach into the phone and slap the shit out of my brother for preferring to get laid instead of answering the phone when I have a goddamned emergency. "I'll just tell the FBI agents when they get here. Have a nice night!"
"Wait! Claire—" he shouts but I hang up. He might call back or maybe even show up but he deserves this for being an asshole. Am I acting like a child right now? Yes. Will I take it back? Hell no.
I see the red and blue lights heading up the hill towards the house and I let out a weary sigh. Wes moves to stand next to me and puts his arm around me in a mix of protecting and comforting and I greatly appreciate it
"Did you get ahold of Lee?" he asks me.
"Something like that," I say.
"Uh-oh. What happened?"
"He's an asshole and said I should call him in the morning to tell him what-

ever was bothering me," I explain.

"What?!" Wes roars. "You did tell him what happened, right?"

"Well, he didn't really give me a chance so I just hung up on him. He sounded . . . preoccupied."

Wes hangs his head. "Really?"

"Kind of . . . out of breath," I say. I have to bite my lip to keep from laughing at the scenario, at the look on Wes's face right now, at everything.

"I kind of want to say way to go, buddy, I kind of want to punch his face in," Wes says on a sigh. "I'm so torn."

"I know. Me too."

A couple of black and white's and a couple of Fed-mobiles pull up to block the driveway and the curb in front of the house. Jones steps out of the first car and shakes his head when he sees me.

"We really have to stop meeting like this, Goody," he laughs.

"Hey, at least it's not a snake," I say in good humor trying my luck at my joke one more time.

"Claire—" Jones starts.

"What?" I ask. "Too soon?"

"Just a little," he laughs.

"That's what I said!" Wes joins in.

"I guess everyone's a critic tonight!" I harumph.

"So what do we have here?" one of the Feds asks.

"Someone painted a lovely note for my wife-to-be on our garage door—" Wes starts.

"I loved that garage door," I pout. "Why would someone do that?"

"Maybe because they are a deranged sociopath?" Wes asks.

"That's probably true," I agree with him.

"May I proceed?" he asks.

"Yes," I smile sweetly at him. "You may."

"Thank you," Wes says to me before moving on. "As you can see, we saw it when we pulled into the driveway this evening."

"Has anything been moved or touched?" the Fed asks. I narrow my eyes. This isn't my first rodeo. Wes squeezes my hip so I stay quiet.

"No," he answers. "We called it in as soon as we could." That was mostly true.

"Let's get Crime Scene in here," the agent shouts to the group when Lee pulls up to the curb looking worse for the wear.

Lee and Emma, also looking pretty bedraggled, jump out of Lee's tahoe and I'm feeling pretty pleased by the sight of them so unkept.

"Don't—" Wes starts.

"Well, I guess we know who Lee was entertaining," I mumble.

"Comment," he finishes.

"Too late."

"I see that." Wes sighs. His lot in life is really rough sometimes.

"What the hell is going on here?" Lee roars.

"Well so nice of you to finally make it, Captain," Jones smirks. "Dr. Parker."

"Shut it," Lee snaps. "Will someone tell me why I am just now finding out that one of my officers was threatened by the hunter?"

"I'm thinking you don't want to open this line of dialogue right now, brother," Wes says subtly.

"Oh, I think I do."

"It's your funeral," Wes shrugs like its not sweat off of his back.

"Maybe if you weren't so busy thinking with your dick you would know that when I called you an hour ago, I was trying to tell you about this," I snap. "But instead I was told to report to your office in the morning. So you can either pitch in and figure this out so I can go to bed or you can get your happy ass back in your truck and go home."

"Claire—" Emma starts.

"You decide," I order not taking my eyes off of my wayward brother.

"Agent Cortez," he says breaking eye contact. "Tell me what we've got."

And just like that, my brother decided to be a grown up. Well how about that?

chapter 16

missing something

BY THE TIME the Crime Scene unit rolls out Wes and I are beyond exhausted.

I have big plans to climbs the stairs and flop into bed. Hopefully, all of this happens before I fall asleep. Wes, on the other hand, has other plans.

He shuts and locks the door behind us before he scoops me up in his arms like a bride and carries me up the stairs. Wes takes his time, he's not in any hurry because he knows that I am right where I want to be—held in his arms like I am all that truly matters in the world. I put my head on his shoulder and relax.

When we reach our bedroom, Wes sets me on my feet while he pulls his side arm and holster from his shoulder. I pull my from my waist and boot, handing them to him to lock up for the night.

I stand there patiently and wait for him to return from the closet. Wes doesn't keep me waiting long. When he returns to me he is wearing his suit pants and belt but he lost his button down shirt and Government issued tie in the closet along with his shoes and socks. The sight of his bare feet always did do me in.

Wes steps up behind me and pulls my t-shirt over my head letting it fall to the floor. My breath catches in my throat when he places a soft kiss to my bare shoulder as he unhooks my bra. I let the ribbon and lace fall to the floor. Wes cups my breasts in his palms and I lean back against his bare chest.

His thumbs skate over my nipples as he nibbles at the spot between my shoulder and my neck and I am gone. Wes glides one heavy palm down my belly to the front of my jeans where pops the button and pulls down the zipper one handed.

"Wes," I gasp when he slides that hand down the front of my jeans and under my panties.

His fingertips immediately find my entrance. Wes swirls his fingertip through my wetness before bringing it up to circle my clit over and over again.

I whimper at the loss of his fingers when he pulls them free from my pussy and then shoves my jeans and panties down my legs. I step out of them and kick them away.

Wes takes my hand and leads me over to the bed. I lay back into the middle of the bed as Wes follows me down. He covers me with his body, his mouth on mine but it's soft and sweet not harsh and desperate.

When he slides into my body it's like coming home. Wes is my home. He brings me back to center when I feel lost and out of control. He is my north star that guides me home in the dark and I should have known all along. I can live without him, but now that I have lived with him, I don't even want to try.

Wes pumps his cock into my waiting body and my climax washes over me like waves in the ocean, not all consuming and out of control but steady waves, one after the other. He drinks in my moans and whimpers as he places soft kisses of the corners of my mouth and my eyes, my cheeks and my chin.

And then finally, when the last of the waves crashes and I begin to surface, only then does Wes plant himself to the root and come inside me.

"I love you so much," he says softly.

"I love you too, Wes."

He rolls us to the side and holds me as we fall asleep.

• • •

It's dark. So dark.

At night my mommy leaves a nightlight on for me and my favorite piggy stuffed animal that I've had for ages to help me sleep. I hate the dark. Monsters only lurk in the dark. I want my mommy but I can't cry. If I cry, the bad man will come and he will hurt me again. He always hurts me. Even though I don't want him to, I know, he always comes, but this time I will be ready.

I was digging in the closet when I knew that he was asleep. I found a pile of old junk. He must have been too lazy to clean out the closet that has been my prison for I don't know how long. But his laziness is my win. In the corner under the pile of old stuff, I found a baseball and then a glove, and in the very bottom of the pile, I found an old metal bat. Just like the kind Liam and Wes used when they were my age.

Sometimes it pays to be the little sister. My whole life I've been following Wes and Liam around hoping that they would play with me. I even told Wes that one day he would marry me. He just laughed and said, "I'm not so sure about that, squirt." That's what he calls me. Squirt.

So all the times, I followed them around when they played ball or walked in the woods finally is going to pay off even if Wes never wants to marry me because I learned how to swing a baseball bat watching them. I learned to run through the woods following them. I am going to run away from the bad man because of all that I watched them do.

So I wait. And I wait and I wait and I wait. I almost fall asleep. Almost. I feel my eyelids getting heavy but then I hear footsteps and I know that he's coming. He always comes.

So I sit quietly and try not to make any noise. I hurry to my feet and grab my bat. I crouch in the corner with the bat over my shoulder just like Liam showed me how to do. When I hear the lock that he keeps on the closet door open I know that it's time.

My hands sweat and I feel shaky all over.

"Wake up, Claire, it's time," he says as he pulls open the closet door. "What are you doing?" He asks when he sees me but I don't answer. I swing the bat as hard as I can, hitting him in his big belly.

When the bad man falls forward, I swing one more time, hitting the side of his head just like Liam and Wes taught me to hit a baseball when I finally got them to include me. And then I run.

"Claire!" he shouts. "You better get back here right this minute."

I run out of the closet while the bad man screams my name. I run out of the ugly house that smells funny and then I run out into the woods.

I run and I run and I run. But I know he's going to catch me. A mean hand grabs me by my arm from behind and I scream . . .

• • •

I scream.
 I scream and I scream and I scream. I try to shake off the hand that has me but his grip is too strong. He is too strong.
 "Claire, baby, wake up," Wes says as he shakes my arm. "Baby, it's me."
 "Wes?" I ask.
 "Yeah, honey," he says softly.
 "I'm okay," I say trying to reassure myself.
 "You're okay," Wes tells me.
 I sit up in bed and the sheets stick to my sweaty skin. My stomach pitches back and forth and my head is pounding. I bring my knees up to my chest and rest my forehead on them while I try and catch my breath.
 Wes sits up in the bed next to me letting the sheets pool around his trim hips. He puts his arm around me just holding me. Offering me comfort but not seeking or demanding anything from me. God, I love this man.
 "So you want to talk about it?" he asks me. Wes's whiskey smooth voice sounds in the dark room.
 "I think . . ." I begin and then tail off.
 "Yeah, baby?" Wes asks me.
 "I think that I'm missing something," I admit.
 "You're missing something in your memories or in the hunter case?" Wes asks me.
 "Both," I answer.
 "Okay," he says softly. "What do we need to do to figure it out?" And I love that. He is not telling me that I need to figure it out or demanding that I move on, but instead, Wes is asking me what we can do together because we are a team, because Wes and I are a we, not a me or a him, but a we. Together we can figure it all out. I hope.
 "I don't know yet," I admit.
 "Well, when you do, let me know, okay?"
 "Okay," I tell him.
 I only hope that when I figure it all out that it won't be too late.
 Famous last words . . .

chapter 17

sitting duck

BEEP... BEEP... BEEP...

When Wes's alarm sounds in the morning I'm both groggy and restless. My lack of sleep from the night before has me fuzzy and feeling like my head is full of cotton and my eyes are gritty and full of sand.

But it is the overwhelming feeling that I am missing something vital that has me throwing the sheets back and leaping out of bed on the second beep of Wes's phone.

All night long I tossed and turned after talking my nightmare out with Wes. I can't help but feel like maybe it really is all my fault. I know that sounds crazy, but at this point, I have to look at every angle and for whatever reason, this guy has decided to focus on me. I can't say that I'm thrilled about that but if it gets me the answers that I need then who cares.

It's a sacrifice that I am more than willing to make. But the lives of my officers are most definitely not.

"Where's the fire, babe?" Wes asks as I'm halfway across the floor to the closet already.

"The station!" I shout over my shoulder. "I'm missing something. I just know it!"

I pull a bra and panties from my drawers at random and haphazardly pull them on my body not caring if they match or not. I grab a t-shirt and pull it over my head when Wes follows me into the closet and starts donning his Fed suit. I have to admit that It's an interesting progression from every day guy to super fed.

"I know," he tells me as he wraps his tie around his neck. "I know we're missing something too, but what?"

"I don't know," I answer as I pull on my jeans.

"For whatever reason," Wes says as he pulls on his dress shoes. "He's fixated on you."

"I know." I pull on my sneakers and drop a pancake holster into the back of my pants instead of my usual side holster. Today I feel the need to be invisible.

"Who would have a beef with you?" Wes asks me as he pulls his shoulder holster on.

"Other than Marcy?" I ask.

"Babe, you have to let Marcy go." He rolls his eyes.

"I know."

Wes grabs our side arms out of the safe and hands me mine. I drop my badge in my pocket along with my phone.

"Also, we know that the hunter is a man," Wes adds. "And as much as I hate to ask this, but I have to. Any scorned lovers in your past?"

"No," I answer right away. "I barely stopped to collect a first name. I didn't actually date anyone."

"The thought of you with any other man makes me want to vomit," Wes says looking a little green around the gills.

"Well, we couldn't all be as discerning as you were in your single days . . ." I roll my eyes.

"You know I wasn't a monk while I was waiting for you to either grow up or give me the time of day, babe."

"I know," I sigh. "But now you know how I feel about all of the Marcys of the world that pop up and flaunt their extensive knowledge of your penis in my face."

"Touche."

"Ready," I say as Wes palms his car keys.

"Let's roll."

The ride to the station is a silent one. Wes and I are both lost in our own thoughts. There is a connection somewhere and I'm missing it. I just know it. What Wes said this morning in the closet has been playing in my head over and over again.

Could I have spurned a lover in my past?

I thought I had left a trail of me happy with an orgasm and no strings but . . . what if I was wrong?

Wes pulls into the backlot of the police station where I work. He parks his car but doesn't shut of the engine.

"I have to go into my office for a little bit and settle some stuff," he says turning to face me.

"Okay," I say. "I'll meet up with you later. I think I want to go walk some of the crime scenes and see if anything clicks."

"Take Jones with you," he orders.

"You do know that I am a very capable police detective, right?" I roll my eyes. "I mean I know I have one of those pesky vaginas and all but I do a pretty good job of getting the job done."

"And you know that I love you and for whatever reason, this guy is gunning for you. Is it so bad that I just want you in one piece?" he asks softly.

"No." I sigh. "I'll be careful."

"Somehow, I doubt that. But I'll let you get to it."

"Hey Wes?"

"Yeah, honey?" he answers me.

"I love you too," I tell him. "I mean I really love you."

"I really love you." He smiles that panty dropper smile at me.

"It was only ever you, Wes," I say softly as I climb out of his car and shut the door behind me. I know that it was a chicken shit move to drop and emotional bomb on him and bail but I'm not overly comfortable with laying myself bare like that.

I push my sunglasses up on top of my head as I walk through the glass door of the station and scan the room for my man of the hour. And there he is now pouring himself a cup of coffee.

"Jones!" I shout as I head towards the kitchenette.

"What's up, Goody?" he asks me.

"I want to walk the past crime scenes today," I explain. "What do you say you come with me for a second set of eyes?"

"I have to clear it with the Captain, but if he signs off on it, sure. Sounds good to me," he smiles.

"Great!" I tell him. "Let's go talk to the dragon now."

"Maybe don't call him that to his face," Jones suggests.

"Now where is the fun in that?" I laugh.

Jones nervously follows me into Lee's office.

"And what can I do for you two this morning?" he asks Jones and I.

"I would like to go walk the crime scenes again and I want to take Jones with me for a second set of eyes," I explain.

"But I'm on patrol tonight," Jones adds.

"Consider it done. I'll call Marcusen in," Lee says. "He's been asking for extra hours."

"Thank you," Jones says to Lee.

"Anytime," Lee says. "And guys?"

"Yeah," I answer.

"Yes, Sir," Jones says standing up.

"Watch your sixes. I don't like what's going on here."

"Yes, Sir," Jones repeats. I just nod before following him out of Lee's office.

"Your wheels or mine?" I ask.

"Mine," he laughs. "Yours are terrible."

I sigh. He's not wrong.

I follow Jones back out into the back lot of the police station and into the passenger seat of his cruiser. It's been awhile since I was in a patrol car. It brings back fond memories.

"Do you miss it?" he asks me.

"Sometimes," I answer. "But not the drunks. God they always puke in the backseat."

"Always," he laughs.

"I heard your sitting the Detective's Exam next month," I say softly.

"Yeah," he answers me.

"You got this."

"You think?" he asks looking up at me nervously.

"I think you'll make a great detective, Jones," I tell him honestly.

"Thanks, Goody."

Jones pulls up at the scene of the downtown shooting and parks his cruiser. We climb out and begin walking what we know happened.

"I was here," he says pointing to where he was arguing with the drunk businessmen.

"I was over here with the young mother and her baby," I tell him.

"There were bodies here, here, and here," Jones blocks out in the street.

"And Rodriguez was with the school group over here . . ." I point out.

"So," Jones begins. "If I was the shooter, where would I be?"

• • •

That bitch.

I knew, I just knew that she would be back. In fact, I was counting on it. She thinks she can outsmart me, but she can't and I'm here to prove it to her.

She thinks she can walk away from me like that. Like I mean nothing. I am fucking everything! And I will be her everything, she just doesn't know it yet. It's frustrating to know that she should have been mine for over a year. A year, I waited for her to realize the mistake she made, but nothing.

Unacceptable.

And she thinks that she can flaunt someone else's ring in my face? On television no less? Absolutely not.

Oh no, my queen. It's time to pay for your sins. It's time to come home to me.

I watch her move through the scope of my rifle. Her long black waves flowing down her back and her violet eyes bright. She's so beautiful. Her curves hidden under a baggy sweatshirt and jeans. A body that I am intimately acquainted with.

I could shoot her right now and be done with it . . . but that's too quick. I have earned this reparation. She needs to atone for her year of transgressions and I am going to watch her squirm while she pays, and only then will I finally take what has been mine all along.

No, I won't kill her now . . . but soon, my queen. Soon . . .

I turn ever so slightly, and let my finger fall from the trigger guard and squeeze just enough. The report echoes along with her scream—a sound that makes my heart beat and my cock hard. It takes a powerful man to control a rifle like this and not let it control then man. That is why I am such a skilled hunter.

Now it's time to let my prey dangle for a bit . . .

• • •

"So, if I was the shooter, where would I be?" Jones asks softly as he scans the surrounding rooftops.

"I don't know," I tell him. "Now would definitely be a good time to have one of those SEALs around though."

"That's true," Jones laughs before stopping the noise abruptly. "Did you see that?"

"See what?" I ask. His words have me instantly alert.

"Maybe nothing," Jones says. "But I thought . . ." he trails off.

"You thought what?" I ask just as he shouts to me.

"Get down!" and he shoves me to the ground.

The rifle report cracks through the air. I open my eyes in time to see Jones take a hit to his shoulder and throw him backwards.

"No!" I scream. "No, no, no, no, no. Jones."

I crawl over to him and place my fingertips to his throat. He has a pulse. It's thready but it's there. Thank God! "You stay with me, Jones. Do you hear me?" I order.

I pull my phone out of my pocket and dial the emergency line.

"9-1-1 dispatch," she answers.

"This is Detective Goodnite and I need an ambulance downtown in front of the museum," I yell. My voice is frantic.

"Tell me what's happening, Detective," she says. "I have an ambulance in route."

"Officer Jones was shot from a rooftop," I answer her.

"Can you see the shooter?"

"No," I answer.

"Are you in pursuit of the shooter?" she asks me.

"No," I answer again. "I'm with Officer Jones."

"I'm dispatching a unit as well," she tells me.

"Thank you."

"Do you have cover?" she asks me what had been bouncing around in my head from the moment Jones had told me to get down.

"No, we're sitting ducks."

I hear the sirens in the distance and send up a silent prayer of thanks. A touch to Jones's neck tells me he's hanging in there, but barely. He's still unconscious.

"You hear that, Jonesy?" I ask him softly. "Here comes the cavalry."

The paramedics come running in with a gurney and as soon as they have him stabilized and strapped to the board, They are off and running not wasting any time that could be critical to Jones's survival.

I take off after them, refusing to leave Jones alone. After all, this is all my fault.

"Wait," I shout as I jump onto the ambulance behind Jones and the medic. "I'm coming too."

The ride to the hospital is nothing but the sporadic squawks of the driver's radio in the silent ambulance. I am used to that kind of background noise and can usually tune out what I know isn't important. But tonight is anything but a usual scenario.

"Here you go, ma'am," the paramedic in the back says to me. I don't even realize that I'm crying until he handed me a tissue.

"Thank you," I say as I grab the tissue from his outstretched hand.

"He's made it this far and he has a pulse," he says to me. "That's better than most GSW's we see."

"I know," I say nodding my head.

When the ambulance pulls into the hospital the quiet of the ride over is replaced by loud noises and chaos as they pull Jones off the ambulance and whisk him through the hospital doors. I'm hot on their heels until he hits the magic steel doors of the Operating Room and the nurse turns to me to tell me I am no longer allowed to follow, stopping me dead in my tracks.

"You're going to have to wait over there," she says as she points to some terrible chairs in a small room. "Someone will come for you when we know more."

I do as I'm told and go and sit in the uncomfortable chairs for who knows how long. I wait and I wait and I wait. I change my position. I cross my legs and uncross them, I lean forward bracing on my knees and then I lean back with my legs outstretched in front of me.

Then I get up and walk to the other side of the room where there is a coffee vending machine and fish a bunch of quarters out of my pockets. I know that the coffee is probably terrible and yet I don't care I need something to hold in my hands to keep them busy. I need to put something hot in my body to maybe warm me—just a little—from the inside out because I am overwhelmingly cold on a typical hot Indian Summer day.

I'm not just cold, I'm frozen from the inside out. I'm numb.

The machine finally stops wheezing and spits out my coffee. I slide the little door back and pick up the paper cup letting out a little yelp as I do because holy shit it's fucking hot and some just splashed on my hand and it burns.

I walk the length of the room while I alternate blowing on my coffee and sipping it. I turn on my heels and pace the length of the room while drinking my coffee and then I do it again and again until me coffee is gone.

I walk the length of the room one more time and toss my cup into the trashcan like Lebron freaking James but my lucky is holding out today—meaning I have no luck at all—and it hits the edge of the trash can before changing its trajectory and falling to the ground.

"Shit," I bark out as I walk over and scoop up my cup this time tossing it gently into the trash can.

"Hey," a vaguely familiar man's voice sounds from behind me and I turn around. "Hey, it is you."

Shit! I know him but where do I know him from?

"Hey," I say lamely while I search for his name. Oh my God, why can't I remember where I know this guy from.

"I never saw you back at the bar after that night," he says and it all slams back. Funny how for years I have been trying to remember three days of my life that are lost to the ether and here I am remembering with an unfair clarity the night I slept with this guy to get back at Wes when he crashed into my life almost a year ago and demanded his place there.

Fuck me running I cannot catch a break today.

"Matt?" I ask. "No, Mike, it's Mike, right?"

"Mark, actually." And I swear it was there for a split second but an anger like I have never seen before flashes across his face. Mark is pissed, no, Mark loathes me? His intense dislike for me or this situation is gone before I can ever really put a name to it.

"I'm so sorry," I explain. "It's been a really bad week but that doesn't excuse my rudeness."

"It's fine," he says.

"It's not but thank you for being gracious. So how have you been?" I ask.

"Good, I'm getting married soon," he tells me and that makes my smile which was forced to start spread wide across my face.

"That's awesome," I congratulate him. "Me too."

"What a coincidence," he says looking over his shoulder. "Well, it was nice seeing you but I better get going."

"Sure, have a good night."

After he walks out the hospital doors, I sit down and place my face in my hands. God my life was such a mess a year ago. I can't believe that I used and discarded that nice guy and so many more just like him while I was in such a bad place. I can't help feeling like a total asshole.

"Claire," I hear my name and look up. Wes is rushing through the glass doors.

"Wes," I run and jump into his arms. Oh how I need him right now.

"I got here as soon as I could," he tells me.

"It's okay, you're here now and that's all that matters."

"What's going on?" he asks me. "Any word."

"No word," I tell him. "I don't even know what time it is."

"It's about seven o'clock."

"Shit," I say.

"Baby, what happened?" he asks me.

I take a deep breath and roll my shoulders back to shore up my courage before explaining. "Jones and I went to the downtown site to block out what happened and bounce ideas off of each other."

"Yeah, we talked about that this morning."

"H-h-he was there," I barely get the words out.

"Who was there?" Wes asks me.

"The hunter," I answer.

"Fuck!" Wes bites out.

"I know," I say as the tears I thought I had under control begin rolling down my cheeks again. "He was on top of one of the buildings just waiting for us. I think Jones saw him because he yelled at me to get down. H-h-he saved me, Wes."

"He's a good man and a good cop, Claire," Wes explains.

In my mind I know that Wes is right. Jones is a great man and an even better cop. If he gets the chance to sit the Detective's Exam I know that he'll blow it out of the water, but that's a big if right now. And I think the part that sticks with me the most is that none of this would be happening right now if he wasn't with me today. He would be fine and healthy and having dinner with his wife,

Linda right now if he wasn't my friend.

Because at the end of the day, we all know that this is my fault. Sure not directly, but some how, some way, I was the catalyst for a madman to become a mass murderer.

Wes sits with me for I don't know how long, just holding me and gently rubbing my back. What he doesn't do is promise me that everything will be all okay in the morning, because that's a promise we both know he couldn't keep. I'm not sure anything will be okay in the morning.

"I need to go wrap up a few more things before I head home. Do you want me to come get you?" he asks me.

"No, I think I need to be here," I tell him.

"Okay," Wes says softly. "Do you want me to come back and stay here with you?" Wes ask me.

"No, it's okay," I answer him. "There's no reason for both of us to be miserable."

"But I'm miserable without you," he says as he tucks my hair behind my ear.

"Then, yeah, come back for me." I smile at him.

"I will," Wes promises me. "I'll always come back for you."

And then he kisses me on the forehead and walk out the door. Too bad I would find out later, I should have asked Wes to stay with me and not go back to the office because I would find out later that it would be the difference between life and death.

Sometime after Wes leaves, Lee walks in with Linda and I immediately jump to my feet when I see them. Linda's face is red and splotchy with tears stains down her cheeks. She looks terrible as she leans on Lee for support. It's then that it dawns on me, that if something like this every happened to Wes, I wouldn't survive it. I know that now.

"Come sit down," I say as I help usher Linda to the seat next to the one I was sitting in.

"Thanks," she says.

"Can I get you a coffee or anything?" I ask.

"No, I'm okay," she says. "Has there been any word?"

"No," I answer as I shake my head. Linda's face crumples as she sobs into the wad of tattered tissue she has clenched in her fist.

"Linda," I start. I have to swallow past the lump in my throat a couple of times before I can say what I need to say. "I am so sorry. This is all my fault."

"No!" she shouts. I deserve her anger and now we both know it.

"Yes, this killer is punishing me for something, I don't know what, but it's my fault Jones was hit," I explain.

"No!" she snaps again taking my hind and sandwiching it tight between her two. "Don't you dare take responsibility for that monster. My husband would be furious if he could hear you right now. You're no more responsible for his being shot than I am and I don't want to hear you suggest otherwise."

"Okay," I say softly for lack of anything better to say.

"Good," she says firmly. "It's done now."

"Mrs. Jones," the Dr. in the doorway calls out.

"That's me," Linda says as she jumps to her feet. "I-i-is my husband alright?"

"He's out of surgery and stable but he's not out of the woods yet," the surgeon tells her.

"Is he awake? Can I see him?" she asks the hope in her voice ringing out for all to hear.

"You may go and see him now, but know that your husband is in a coma."

Her face falls again.

"Is he going to wake up?" she asks.

"My hope is that he will when his body has healed some. Right now he just needs rest so that's what his body is doing," he tells her.

"Okay. We can do that," she says as she rolls her shoulders back. "Now take me to my husband please."

Linda looks back to where Lee and I are standing. My brother seems to read her mind when he tells her, "We'll be right here, Linda. Don't worry, we're here for you."

"Thanks, Captain, Claire," she says before following the surgeon through the big metal doors.

• • •

It's time. It's finally time to take what is mine, but first I have to make her pay. She thinks she can be with that FBI agent on the news. That he is better than me, well I will show her.

What better way to make my queen come to me then to remove her king from the board? When she realizes what I have done I bet she comes running. Then I will show her who the real king is once and for all.

Oh, here he comes now . . .

"Excuse me!" I shout to get his attention. He looks tired and frustrated. Good. Now it's time to play . . .

chapter 18

well, fuck.

Wes

THIS CASE IS driving me fucking nuts.

It's always a fun fucking day when you realize that you are hunting a freaking psycho who has decided he has an unhealthy fixation on your woman. Also, it's never a good freaking day when you realize that this exact scenario has happened more than once. This year.

I swear on all that's holy that when we solve this fucking nightmare of a case and Claire and I finally—fucking finally—get married I am going to take her on a vacation to end all vacations and make us both transfer to outstanding parking tickets because this is ridiculous.

And speaking of nightmares . . . it is killing me slowly to wake up to another one of her devastation half memories. I pray to God every night that she either remembers or forgets for once and for all. But I will tough it out and keep my trap shut because whatever those nightmares may do to me is nothing in comparison to the hell that my girl has been living in for twenty-four fucking years.

I let out a heavy sigh and run my hands through my hair as I push through the automatic glass doors of the hospital. My frustration is boiling too close to the surface and I hate that. I prefer to stay cool, calm, and collected.

"Hey man," I hear someone call out. I look over my shoulder and see a man that looks vaguely familiar.

"Can I help you?" I ask the man.

"Oh my God, thank you," he says. "I didn't know who else to ask but my car won't start. Can you take a look at it for me?"

I want to tell this guy no because it's been a long fucking day and I have a metric shit ton of stuff to do before I can get back here to be with Claire while we wait for news on Jones. But that's not why I do what I do and this guy is in the hospital parking lot so he was obviously visiting someone too so his day is probably just as shitty as mine so I turn to him and do what I always knew I would do. Too bad it will turn out to be a big fucking mistake.

"Sure man," I tell him. "Pop the hood."

I hear the click of the latch on the hood of a suburban that looks brand fucking new and wonder why it's having problems but I don't really know now do I?

I raise the hood and prop it with the post to hold it open and lean down to take a look.

"I don't really see anything out of the ordinary," I tell him. "Why don't you try and start it so I can hear what it sounds like?"

But he doesn't do that.

Instead, I feel something hard and heavy hit the back of my head and my knees give out. I crumple to the floor as my vision waivers and it's like watching the tuner going out on an old television.

"Thanks ever so much for your assistance," the man says as he smiles down at me. "Please allow me to introduce myself. I'm the hunter."

And then everything goes black . . .

Well, fuck.

chapter 19

not okay

Claire

"HE'S GOING TO be okay, right?" I ask.

"I don't know," Lee tells me and I let out a heavy sigh. I just feel so defeated.

"You okay, kid?" Lee asks me when we sit back down.

"Not really," I admit.

"You don't say," he drolls and I roll my eyes.

"You know you're kind of a mess yourself," I tell him something I'm sure he already knows.

"This isn't about me, kid," Lee says trying to change the subject again. "This is about you."

"I know," I answer him and also don't. "And also, it's really not. Tonight is about Jones."

"Yeah," my brother says.

"He told me today that he was going to sit the Detective's Exam," I tell Lee.

"He is," my brother confirms. "He's going to make a damn fine detective."

"Better than my," I say trying to lighten the mood.

"Everyone is a better detective than you," Lee laughs.

"Thanks, asshole."

"I'll be here all night."

"While, we're playing group therapy session," I wade in.

"Claire—" he starts to cut me off but I don't let him finish.

"For real, Lee," I push back. "Right now it's just you and me so tell me the truth. What's going on with you and Emma?"

"I still love her," he says.

"Well, that sounds promising."

"And she still blames me for Anna's death and hates my guts."

"That doesn't sound so good," I tell him.

"But every night she shows up at my house to ride my dick and then leave us both feeling empty in a room full of self loathing."

"Wow, I'm sorry I asked," I tell him.

"Yeah, it's not great." He shrugs.

"What are you going to do?" I ask him.

"What can I do?"

"I don't know," I admit.

"I need her so much that I will take whatever she gives me and be happy. It's less than I deserve so I'll take it. If she can't ever love me back or forgive me, then that's okay. If all she wants is my cock, than that's fine too."

"It's not fine," I sigh.

"No, it's not, but it's what I have."

"Also, don't ever say 'cock' in front of me again either."

"You brought that on yourself," he says on a smug smile.

"Did I ever tell you about the time Wes tied me up and spanked me?"

"Stop!" Lee shouts. "You win! I quit!"

I laugh. "Never mess with the master!"

"Let's just try and get a little shut eye, alright?" Lee suggests.

"Sure," I say as I tip my head back against the while and try not to imagine all the hospital germs crawling around all over this room and close my eyes.

Before I know it, it works and I'm asleep.

• • •

Run!

I'm running as fast as my little feet will take me through the woods behind my parents house. I have to get away from the bad man. If he catches me now, I'll never get away. I have to be free.

Run! I have to run faster.

I see the blue gray light as it spills through the trees. Mommy always told me this was her favorite part of the day—Looking at the sun as it comes up in the morning. I ran away late in the night when the bad man was sleeping. It was my only chance. After he broke the lock on the closet door I knew that I had a chance to get out.

Free.

I'm free. That's the words in my head as the tree break and I see Wes standing at the edge of the backyard. I'm free. I'm finally free. Wes looks up and he sees me.

"I've got her!" he shouts to someone.

My heart is beating so hard in my chest and it hurts to breathe. I'm so tired but I have to keep running. I see Wes, his face, I know that he'll protect me. Wes always protects me. He will keep me safe. He will keep me free.

I push my feet just a little harder, I run just a little faster. I'm almost there. I'm almost free when a strong hand wraps around my arm so hard that it hurts, pulling me around to face him, not Wes, the bad man. Wes is gone and the only person near me is the man I would do anything to get away from.

"No!" I scream.

"You're mine, Claire. You'll never be free."

• • •

"Jesus Christ!" Lee shouts as I bolt upright in my seat. "What the fuck was that?"

"Nothing, Lee," I tell him. "Just go back to sleep."

"I can't go back to sleep," he practically shouts. "You were fucking screaming."

"I wasn't screaming," I deny. In all truth, I was probably screaming but my brother doesn't need to know that.

"Yes, you were," he tells me. "Is it always like this?"

I let out a sigh before admitting, "Mostly."

"Jesus," he mutters. "You need to get help, Claire."

"Thanks, asshole," I growl. "I was but my therapist died so excuse me if I don't want to run out and get another one."

"Claire—" he starts but I won't let him finish.

"Just let it go."

"Does Wes know about this?" he asks me on a low voice.

"Of course Wes knows," I tell him. "He's with me every night."

A frown pulls at my brow and I look at the time on the lock screen of my phone. It's after three in the morning and Wes isn't back yet. He said he was coming back.

"What's wrong?" Lee asks, accurately assessing the change in my mood.

"It's after three in the morning and Wes isn't here," I explain.

"I don't understand," Lee says.

"Before you guys got here, Wes was leaving," I explain. "He said that he had some more stuff to wrap up at the office and then he was going to grab a change of clothes and come back here to be with me."

"But he's not here now," Lee states the obvious that has acid burning in my stomach.

"No, he's not."

"Try calling him," Lee suggests.

I pick up my phone and dial Wes's phone number. It rings several times before going to voicemail, "Hi. You've reached Wes, leave me a message at the beep."

"Well?" he asks.

"Voicemail."

"Let me try," he says. I watch my brother pull his phone out of his pocket and dial his best friend before frowning at his phone and then hitting the button to end the call.

"Well?" I ask.

"It rang three times and then went to voicemail," he tells me.

"Shit!" I bite out.

"Wes always answers his phone."

"Let me try him again," I say but I don't get the chance because my phone dings with a text message from Wes's phone.

WES: this is the hunter meet me at this address or you'll never see your beau again.

"I think I know where Wes is," I whisper.

"Where?" Lee asks.

I hold up my phone to show him the text. "I think he's with the hunter."

"God damnit!"

I furiously text him back asking the question I know that I don't want the answer to but for Wes, I have to. I love Wes that much. I would do anything for him.

ME: What do you want?

WES: You. It's time to pay for your crimes.

"What are you doing?" Lee asks when I grab my phone and jump out of my seat.

"I have to go get him."

"Not on your fucking own, Claire," he shouts. "That's suicide. Let me get a team together."

"I can't wait, Lee," I tell him. "You get a team together, I have to leave now."

"No," he says standing there between me and the door, unmoving. Like a stone in the middle of a riverbed. I'll just have to go around him and I know exactly how to do it.

"What if it was Emm?" I ask quietly.

"That's not fair," he says.

"I'll never play fair where Wes is concerned, brother mine," I tell him gently. "I love him so much that I know that I would not survive this world without him."

"We're right behind you," he sighs. "This is going against everything that I know is right."

"I know, me too."

"Then don't do it," Lee pleads.

"I have to."

"Claire—"

"If I don't make it," I start.

"Don't talk like that," he orders.

"If I don't make it," I tell him. "Name your first kid after me!"

"What if it's a boy?" he shouts as I'm running out the door.

"Then that sucks for him!" I shout as I race to my car.

Shit! I don't have a car. I see a cab stopped at the curb just down the way and I take off running for it. "Taxi! Taxi!" I shout.

• • •

Stupid bitch!

I am so disappointed in her. She thinks she can come here and save her precious boyfriend. As if I would ever let her! She needs to learn some manners and I am just the man to teach them to her.

She is not the winner of this game. She can't be because I am the game maker! I make the rules and I am the true victor here.

I pull the ropes just a little tighter around the big idiot in the chair. This bar has been closed for awhile now. I bought the building and wouldn't let them renew their lease because I have been waiting for almost a year just for this moment.

She chose me over him that night and now it's time to remind her why I am the superior candidate. Not him.

I bet she's almost here. Showtime!

chapter 20

what took you so long?

"WHAT THE HELL?"
This can't be it. The taxi pulls over at what is the old bar I used to frequent from time to time when I was looking for guys to hookup with in a no strings attached kind of a situation.
But this place is boarded up and run down.
In the year that Wes and I have tap danced around each other to finally get our shit together and be an us, this place has gone to shit. I let my mind wander back to the last time that I was here . . .

• • •

"The usual?" Joe, my favorite bartender asks as I walk in.

"Yeah," I smile and take a seat at the end of the bar where I can watch the people who move around the establishment and pick my next victim.

Joe slides the seven and seven on a cocktail napkin in front of me. I smile my thanks as I pick up my drink and take a sip. I swivel around on my barstool and watch the crowd absentmindedly. There's a couple of cute guys, but nobody peaks my interest.

I feel someone sit down next to me and I look up. He's about five eleven or six foot with a mop a sandy blonde hair and brown eyes. He has an easy smile and he immediately turns it my way. I look back at Joe who winks and shakes his head. He knows my drill.

He looks at me and smiles. "I'll have what she's having," he says to Joe and I think he might do. But I'm just not that into it. I'll see how it goes.

Joe slides the drink in front of him and he happily sips his drink while waiting for me to say something. I finally decide to help him out.

"Well, what do you think?" I ask.

"I think it's not bad. Is it your signature drink?"

"I don't have a signature . . ." But I'm stopped by Joe.

"She does and it is."

"I'm Mark," he smiles at me and holds out his hand for me to shake. As I take his hand in mine and notice a firm grip on a smooth hand with no calluses and clean trimmed fingernails. The callous on my index finger grazes his knuckles and he bites his lip.

"I'm Claire," I say smiling.

"So Claire, do you live around here?" he asks. "Wow, was that as bad as

it sounded?" I laugh.

I feel eyes on me and I start to scan the room but come up short when I see Wes scowling from a table in the corner. A waitress with a trim waist and balloons for boobs grazes his elbow with her rock hard nipple as she delivers his drink, a cold beer in the bottle, but his gaze stays locked on me. I roll my eyes and turn back to Mark.

"No, it wasn't that bad," I lie.

"So what do you do, Claire?" Mark asks.

Joe groans.

I bite my lip and shake my head no. I'm not going to tell him. It will end all the fun. There's no way Mr. Businessman or Mr. Lawyer wants to go home with a police detective. I look over at his polo shirt and jeans and think he's cute in a very country club sort of way.

"Oh, you want me to guess do you?"

I smile wider because he'll never guess and nod my head. I sip my drink and wait for him to guess. This could be fun. And I need fun. The missing boy, Anthony, and Wes and our fucked up past have my emotions too close to the surface.

"A dental hygienist."

"Ew, gross. I would never stick my hands in people's mouths." I laugh. Although I have stuck them in a dead body so what does that say about me.

"A librarian."

"Do I look like a librarian to you?" I laugh.

"Only in my dreams," he laughs. "That was cheesy too, right?"

"Yeah, kind of. What about you? What do you do?" I ask. I feel eyes on me again and I look over my shoulder. The waitress with the flotation devices and the huge hair is sitting in his lap, his ear is caught between her teeth. They're crooked, I notice uncharitably. I'll drop an extra twenty in the offerings tray on sunday and ask for forgiveness. It was worth it.

"You know that guy?" Mark asks.

I look back at him and see him looking at Wes and the hooker. "No," I say as I look at him. He's handsome and nice. I should choose a guy like him. I toss the remainder of my drink back and ask, "You want to get out of here?"

"Hell, yes."

"Your place, I'll follow you out," I tell him as I stand. Mark throws some money on the bar top for Joe and I see him tip his imaginary hat at me behind Mark's back as thanks for the huge tip. Or maybe it's my ability to leave with a guy in less than an hour. I mentally shrug, who knows.

As I found out following his nondescript sedan home, Mark lives around the corner from my local bar. That's going to be awkward later. I pull into the visitor spot closest to where he parked his car. He waits for me by the door like a gentleman and then leads me up the stairs to his second floor apartment.

Mark holds the door open for me but as soon as it closes behind me I grab him by the shirt and pull him against my body, breast to chest, and kiss him deeply. Not bad. Not great, but not bad. Mr. Country Club is not an aggressive lover.

He breaks away from my body to push my jacket over my shoulders. I pull his polo over his head and toss it to the ground. Mark sees to it that my t-shirt and bra go the same way. He smiles his coy smile at me again before taking my *hand and leading me to his bedroom where I make my second major mistake of the night.*

• • •

And it snaps back into place like a rubberband.

I know exactly who has Wes. My skin crawls at the idea that so many people had died because of someone I hooked up with the better part of a year ago. I think of Rodriguez, of Matt and JAsmine cut down in their prime and then I think of Jones fighting for his life in a hospital bed.

How stupid I was. I bet he laughed when he left there. He saw me in the waiting room and pretended to give a shit but really he was there to bask in how low he brought me.

That son of a bitch!

"Thanks, man," I say as I hand the cab driver a bunch of bills. And watch him peel out from the curb like his pants were on fire.

I don't even blame him. This neighborhood doesn't look so good anymore.

I don't have anything left to lose but Wes and I'm not willing to wait for the cavalry to get here before going in. I need to know that Wes is alright, that he's even still alive. Although, I feel like in my soul I would know. That on a cellular level, we are connected enough that if something really happened to Wes, I would know. As hokey as it sounds, it's true.

I push open the door to the bar and I step inside. When I do, I see the reason for the mug smile on his sadistic fucking face, and there he sits, happy as you please, with Wes in the chair on the other side of the table and a gun pointed directly at the love of my life. Wes, the one man I could ever love is tied to a fucking chair with a gun pointed at his head.

"Hello, Claire," he greets me.

"Hello, Mark."

"I'm so glad you could join me tonight," he says like he has invited me out to the opera or a fancy dinner party.. So not creepy at all . . .

"And where exactly am I?" I ask him. I want him to tell me what's going on even though I'm pretty sure I can read between the lines, even here in crazy town.

"We're where it all began," he says as he waves his gun arm around. "I bought this place for you."

"Charming, I love what you've done with the place," I snark.

"Don't be cruel," he snaps. "You are the one that made me play all of these silly games."

"Silly games?" I question as shock rolls over my body one inch at a time. "You call killing tons of innocent people and good cops silly games?"

"Of course," he waves his gun hand again. Those people don't mean anything to me."

"You're crazy," I whisper. "Abso-fucking-lutely stark raving mad, bat shit crazy. Bonkers."

"Don't be rude!" he snaps. "It's time now."

"Time for what?" I ask suddenly feeling nervous. I need to stall. I need everyone else to get here and save the day now that I know that Wes is alive.

"This is it, Claire," he tells me.

"What is it?" I ask again. I'm still standing in the entryway to the old bar.

"This is when you lose," he says cryptically. "Why don't you come in and take your coat off."

"Did you think I would let you have him? Did you think that I didn't see you look at each other all night?" he demands and I have no idea who he is or what he's talking about.

"What?"

"You're mine, Claire! And now you have to pay. You thought I'd let you leave me for him, that you could use me as a pawn in your slut games, but I am the ultimate hunter."

And then it all snaps into place. I thought he was a random, someone I could use and forget way back when I was avoiding Wes and all commitments. I left this guy in his apartment one night and never looked back. How could I have been so stupid? And the worst part is, I never even remembered his name until I saw him again at the hospital last night while I was waiting on word on Jones.

"I grew up hunting in the woods with my grandfather. He was one mean bastard too. He believed to be accurate the first shot not the second so a bunch of stupid cops was nothing to me. But like I said before, you had to pay."

"Stupid," I snap. "Jasmin was not stupid. She was good and she was kind but she was not stupid. She was on her dinner break eating a fucking hamburger you monster!"

"Soon you'll be screaming my name, Claire, but I'm okay if you like to call out monster too. I just want to hear you scream."

"In your dreams, pal."

"No, Claire, in yours. How's that going by the way?" He's too young to be my kidnapper so I know that he's baiting me but still the idea that he knows my inner thoughts and terrors rankles.

"Just peachy," I snark.

"You think you're so smart. So tough and strong. Brave even. I wonder what you'll be like when I really hit you where it hurts. How will you feel when you watch pretty boy here die at my hands."

"I'll be just fine because you aren't going to hurt him," I say bold as you please while inside I am shaking in my converse sneakers.

"Say goodbye, Claire," he says as he pulls back the hammer but he never gets the chance. I pull my side arm from the back of my pants just the way Wes and I joked about earlier that morning and fire center mass just like I was taught.

"Goodbye, asshole." And then I empty the rest of my magazine into the center of his chest for good measure.

"What took you so long?" Wes demands.

"I'm sorry." I wink at Wes. "It's been a long night."

"Well, try not to have it happen again," he says with laughter in his voice. "Seriously, it's good to see you. That dude was bananas."

"I kind of got that impression."

"Funny," he rolls his eyes.

"I'm not gonna lie, I'm kind of enjoying being the one to do the saving this time," I tell him as I start to untie the ropes around him. "You can be the hero next time though. I wouldn't want to wound your precious male pride."

"This time?!" Wes yells and then winces like his head is killing him. "There isn't going to be a next time, Claire."

"Sure, baby. Whatever you say."

chapter 21

rehearsal

One week later...

I FUSS WITH the white eyelet sundress that I have just slipped over my head in front of a large oval mirror in my suite at the shore.

Three hours ago, Emma pulled up to the house in a convertible she had rented for the weekend.

"What's all this?" I had asked her.

"We need to live a little," she had explained. "It's been a rough couple of months."

"No kidding."

So we had loaded up my dress and my suitcase into the backseat and headed down the coast singing to the radio with our hair blowing in the wind. It was the best time I had had in a long time. The stress of this case and the guilt that I carry have been riding me hard lately. While Jones pulled out of his coma a few days ago, he's still holed up at the hospital while they make sure he has everything he needs for a full recovery with his wife, Linda, at his side. and I'm sure next month he's going to kick the Detective's Exam's ass.

Emma had pulled into the circle in front of the resort and let the bellhop unload our bags with a quick, "Be careful with that one," she had said point to my dress bag. "It's precious cargo." and a fifty dollar bill for his trouble.

"You just made that kid's day," I had told her.

"Shh," Emma had stage whispered. "I don't want people to think I have a heart."

"I think you have the biggest heart of all."

We checked into the hotel and settled into the honeymoon suite where Emma and I will spend tonight and get dressed for the wedding in tomorrow and then Wes and I will spend our wedding night here.

"So this is where the magic is going to happen," Emma had joked as she flopped down on her back on the big, fluffy bed with all of its down pillows and duvet.

"But of course," I had laughed. She had swatted me with a pillow until we both laughed until we cried.

"I guess we should get ready for this big dinner that Wes's stuffy parents are holding in your honor tonight," she had said without even trying to pretend to be excited.

"I be nice," I had warned her.

"Yeah, yeah, yeah."

I had brushed out my windswept hair into thick, beachy waves and applied a little makeup to my face. I want to be pretty but I don't want to look like I'm trying to hard. Tomorrow, though, I'm going to knock Wes's socks off with my wedding day glitz and glam.

I took my dress on its hanger into the bathroom and changed into it, slipping the delicate material over my head and pulling up the side zipper.

When I stepped out of the bathroom I was greeted by the sight of Emma in a soft pink sundress and sandals looking absolutely beautiful and surprisingly sweet and delicate.

"More pink?" I had asked her.

"It felt right at the time," she had said nervously. "But now I'm not so sure."

"You look beautiful," I had told her before turning to the mirror to fuss at my dress.

I, too, don't feel overly comfortable in girly clothing. What a pair, Emma and I must be.

Now, we stand here side by side looking bewildered and frightened which is ridiculous considering we're both kind of badass bitches.

I trace a finger over the scar on my shoulder. It's a reminder that I will have for the rest of my life that some mistakes stay with you for eternity and have very lasting consequences. Jasmine is one of those consequences. So is Jones, but he's getting there. He also told me yesterday that if I apologize one more time he's going to kick my ass when he gets back to work.

I told him he's on and that I can't wait.

I trace the silvery line on my shoulder one more time before Emma sighs and swats my hand away.

"Stop that!"

"I can't help it," I admit.

"I have it on good authority, that men dig scars, so let it go," she tells me.

"I know," I sigh. "I just feel so . . . guilty."

"Well, you have to stop that," she admonishes.

"Hello pot, paging kettle," I laugh. Emma is one to talk about guilt the way she's hanging on to hers after Anna's death.

"I know." She sighs. "Let's just try and enjoy this weekend and get you hitched, okay?"

"I'll make a deal with you," I offer up.

"I'm not sure I want to know."

"I'll relax and enjoy the weekend if you do too."

She lets out another heavy sigh. I'm clearly trying her patience this weekend. "Okay, fine. I'll relax and enjoy the weekend too."

"Good. Now let's go and get this rehearsal show on the road before we're late for dinner."

Emma and I walked down to the wedding venue arm in arm like the opening scene of Laverne and Shirley. Just two independent women, ready to take on the world, or in this case, a wedding weekend for the society pages.

"There you are!" the wedding planner shouts just a little too loud. It makes me wonder if she thought I wouldn't show or something.

Wes walks up to me and kisses me sweetly on the lips. "You look beautiful."

"Thanks," I say suddenly feeling shy.

"Glad you could make it," he smiles at me and I can't help but to smile back.

"Were you afraid I wouldn't come?" I ask.

His eyes heat and he leans down to whisper in my ear, "Oh, I know you'll come. I just wasn't one hundred percent sure you would turn up for this dog and pony show."

"Thanks for the glowing vote of confidence," I snark. "Maybe I changed my mind."

I start to pull away from Wes but he laughs as he grabs my hand and pulls me back against him. "Not so fast."

"Ugh. Fine. I guess you're stuck with me."

"Happily," tells me.

"Places, people!" the wedding planner calls out.

Wes and his mom are in the front of the line up. He is supposed to walk her to her seat next to his dad and then stand at the altar and wait for me. I'm hoping she doesn't start slinging her shit this weekend but really, we all know it's just a matter of time. While she's my mom's best friend, she has never thought that I was good enough for her son. It's been getting worse the closer Wes and I grew to each other.

My late sister, Bonnie's children line up next to each other and then Lee and Emma behind them. I feel bad for making them walk down the aisle together but Emma is my Maid of Honor and Lee is Wes's Best Man. They don't have a choice. Also, I'm secretly hoping forcing them together for the weekend will make them finally work their shit out once and for all because they clearly are miserable without each other and if anything the last year has taught us, it's that life is infinitely too short.

My parents and I are in the back. I have chosen to have both my parents walk me down the aisle and honor my mom. It's a break from tradition but she's been the best mom I could have asked for and this moment is all about celebrating our family so it just felt right.

"Okay, here's what we're going to do," the wedding planner instructs everyone to their places and I love watching her order everyone around. It's kind of fun.

Wes winks at me from his place at the altar and I have this overwhelming sense that, this is it. This is where I am meant to be. The road here was not an easy one, but life with Wes will be totally worth it. To be loved by this man, so wholly and completely is more than I deserve but I am unwilling to live without him.

My parents and I are halfway up the aisle before the wedding planner turns around and gasps in horror. Well, it looks like my run of shitty luck is holding after all . . .

"What are you doing?" she yells.

"Umm . . . rehearsing?" I ask confused.

"The bride does not walk up the aisle any other time than when she walks to her groom for real. It's bad luck. Like really really bad luck."

"Whoops." I shrug.

I see Wes behind her laughing and shaking his head at me. He looks carfree and unconcerned so I figure we'll be alright but I can't help the feeling of doom that just hit the pit of my stomach.

After thoroughly horrifying the wedding planner with my epic run of bad luck, she walks everyone through their duties for the big day. The whole time Wes smiles at me like I am the most important person in the world.

"Alright, everyone," the wedding planner claps her hands. "That's a wrap! Go enjoy dinner and don't get drunk!"

"I'm totally getting drunk," Lee mumbles as he walks by. It will be an acto of God if Emma doesn't act like she's been touched by a leper everytime she has to take Lee's arm. Every one winced when she would flinch when he reached for her.

"Me too," Emma mumbles as the head for the restaurant where our rehearsal dinner is being hosted by Wes's parents.

I kind of want to get drunk too. Those two are going to take then years off of my life they way they keep going on and on.

"Well," my dad breaks into my thoughts. "I have been looking forward to this day for your entire life."

"Dad," I whisper smiling at him.

"You picked a good guy," he tells me. "But then again, I never doubted you."

"I love you, Dad." I hug him tight.

"And I love you, baby. Now let's go watch Emma and Lee makes asses of themselves." I through my head back and laugh.

"Sounds good, Dad," I tell him and let him escort me into the restaurant where everyone is waiting.

When we sit down at the tables that are pre-arranged for our party, I see that the beer and champagne is already flowing. And along with the rest of our families, the SEALs are in attendance. This should be interesting.

I look to their table, and everyone is laughing and smiling but surfer. He has a dark longing on his face that I can't put a finger on. I bet there's a story there.

"Don't go there," Wes warns low for my ears only when he joins me at my side.

"Go where?" I ask innocently.

"Leave surfer alone."

"He's across the room, how can I possibly bother him?"

"Just leave him alone. IF you have to meddle, meddle with Lee and Emma, but surfer has his own demons to expunge."

"That sounds mysterious."

"Just leave it alone."

"Yes, Sir," I snap.

"Mmm, you have no idea what those words from your lips do to me, baby," Wes says as he bites his bottom lip. "Let's try that tomorrow night."

My cheeks heat at his dirty suggestion and the table of SEALs clearly don't miss it as they start hooting and hollering and making their own lewd suggestions. Wes just laughs. And Lee shakes his head covering his ears which makes me laugh too.

The dinner service is my favorite meal of beef wellington, mashed potatoes, and cooked spinach. Wes planned this dinner all by himself and he clearly thought of me when he planned the menu. It warms my heart to know that he knows me so thoroughly.

Wes clinks his dessert spoon against his wine glass as he stands up from his seat beside me at the table.

"If I could have your attention," he says as the room quiets down. "As you all know, Claire and I have had a long road to get to this moment right now and you all have been part of that, so thank you for helping u get here.

"Claire, you are by far, the greatest thing to come into my life and I would be lost without you."

"Wes," I says smiling up at him. "I love you."

"So I got you a little something to show you what an honor it is to be chosen by you," he says as he hands me a light blue bag.

I open the bag to reveal to light blue boxes under the white tissue paper. The first one that I open, a small square box, holds to glittering diamond solitaires twinkling at me from the white satin pad and I immediately put them on. It is exactly what I would have chosen for myself.

"Thank you so much," I tell him.

"Keep going," he says on a smile.

The next blue box is long and rectangular and holds a matching diamond tennis bracelet on its satin bed. It's stunning and while I wouldn't wear it every day, I will wear it on every special occasion and think of Wes in this moment.

I hold out my wrist for him to slip it on and after he buckles the clasp, Wes kisses my pulse point under my wrist.

"Thank you," I mouth to him.

"My pleasure," he rumbles.

"Yes, I think it will be," I whisper. Wes's eyes heat and twinkle at my blatant suggestion in front of our closest friends and family.

"And lastly," he tells the room. "Long ago, I gave Claire my most prized possession when she was just a little girl. I have no idea where it went and I bet she doesn't either, but it was way back then that she stole my heart along with my favorite baseball cap so in honor of her finally making me the happiest man in the world, I bought her her own."

Wes pulls from behind his back a Yankees ball cap. It's brand new with tags still on it and the dark navy of the hat is stark and unmarred against the white stitching of the NY on the front. I look at him and this hat a little confused. I don't remember Wes ever giving me a hat and that makes me sad.

"I forgot about that hat," my dad says. "Whatever happened to it, Claire?"

"I have no idea," I say honestly.

"You wound me, baby." Wes laughs.

"Thank heaven," my mother says, her voice full of laughter. "She wore that thing everywhere. Backwards too with her long hair hanging down. I finally had a girl to dress in ribbons and lace and you heathens taught her to spit and pitch a ball instead."

"Man she had an awesome swing though," Lee says, his voice ringing with pride for his little sister.

Wes places the cap on my head, backwards and tucks my hair behind my ears and it all comes rushing back.

I was six years old, and the boys had just taught me how to hit a baseball.

"Damn, she's good," Wes had said his voice ringing with pride.

"Did you think my sister would be anything but?" Lee asked.

"Well, she is your sister." Wes had laughed.

"Yeah, and she's perfect."

"She is," Wes had agreed. "So perfect, I think she's earned a prize." He pulled the worn and battered and obviously well loved Yankees cap off of his head and placed it on mine, tucking my hair back behind my ears just as he did now.

Three weeks after that beautiful moment in my parents backyard with my brother and his best friend, the man I would eventually marry, I was wearing that ball cap when I made my escape attempt. I must have left it behind in that closet. My stomach pitches at the thought. That something so beautiful could be tainted by something so dirty, so foul.

"Thank you, Wes," I tell him. "I love it."

"And I love you," he tells me as he places a soft kiss on my mouth.

The night moves on with more laughter and stories of Wes and I growing up. His parents do not join in the merriment.

"Will you excuse me for a moment?" I ask him. "I'm just going to run to the ladies room for a minute."

"Sure, baby," he says with a touch of concern in his eyes. "Everything alright?"

"Yeah, I think all the wine just got to me," I lie. I'm going to be sick. My stomach pitches and somersaults all over the place.

"Just don't be too long," he says and I watch the heat flare in his eyes one more time. How this man can love me so much after all that we have been through still amazes me more and more every day.

He kisses me again, this time a little deeper and the SEALs go wild. I roll my eyes and push away from the table. I head towards the restroom and pause halfway across the room to look over my shoulder at Wes who has his sole focus on me. If only I have paid more attention to the rest of the occupants of the room, I would have noticed that someone else paid me too much attention as well.

When I enter the ladies room I walk into the stall and drop to my knees before losing the entire contents of my stomach into the toilet. As I heave, I think of that dark closet, where I left behind Wes's most prised possession and I hate whoever took me with my entire being. Why can't I remember?

I flush the toilet and move to the sink to wash my hands. I cup water to my mouth to rinse the vomit out and grab a paper towel from the holder to try and repair the mascara that ran when I puked.

It's pretty good. I don't look great, but I'll just blame it on the wine when I get back to the table. When I push the door open, I never see him coming, I only feel a hand cover my nose and mouth. A cloying scent fills my lungs and then it's lights out . . .

chapter 22
left behind

*I*T'S DARK. SO DARK. At night my mommy leaves a nightlight on for me and my favorite piggy stuffed animal that I've had for ages to help me sleep. I hate the dark. Monsters only lurk in the dark. I want my mommy but I can't cry. If I cry, the bad man will come and he will hurt me again. He always hurts me. Even though I don't want him to, I know, he always comes, but this time I will be ready.

I was digging in the closet when I knew that he was asleep. I found a pile of old junk. He must have been too lazy to clean out the closet that has been my prison for I don't know how long. But his laziness is my win. In the corner under the pile of old stuff, I found a baseball and then a glove, and in the very bottom of the pile, I found an old metal bat. Just like the kind Liam and Wes used when they were my age.

Sometimes it pays to be the little sister. My whole life I've been following Wes and Liam around hoping that they would play with me. I even told Wes that one day he would marry me. He just laughed and said, "I'm not so sure about that, squirt." That's what he calls me. Squirt.

So all the times, I followed them around when they played ball or walked in the woods finally is going to pay off even if Wes never wants to marry me because I learned how to swing a baseball bat watching them. I learned to run through the woods following them. I am going to run away from the bad man because of all that I watched them do.

So I wait. And I wait and I wait and I wait. I almost fall asleep. Almost. I feel my eyelids getting heavy but then I hear footsteps and I know that he's coming. He always comes.

So I sit quietly and try not to make any noise. I hurry to my feet and grab my bat. I crouch in the corner with the bat over my shoulder just like Liam showed me how to do. When I hear the lock that he keeps on the closet door open I know that it's time.

My hands sweat and I feel shaky all over.

"Wake up, Claire, it's time," he says as he pulls open the closet door. "What are you doing?" He asks when he sees me but I don't answer. I swing the bat as hard as I can, hitting him in his big belly.

When the bad man falls forward, I swing one more time, hitting the side of his head just like Liam and Wes taught me to hit a baseball when I finally got them to include me. And then I run, my favorite ball cap tumbling to the floor *but I don't stop for it. I can't stop for it. I just have to run and run and run and I keep running.*

I run out of the closet while the bad man screams my name. I run out of the ugly house that smells funny and then I run out into the woods.

I run and I run and I run. But I know he's going to catch me. A mean hand grabs me by my arm from behind and I scream . . .

chapter 23

she's gone

Wes

"SOMETHING'S WRONG," I say quietly. "What's taking her so long?"

Lee laughs."Nothing is wrong. Chill out, man. Nothing is going to go wrong."

"I mean it, Lee," I say looking to my best friend since birth. I feel an edginess that only comes with years of honing a great gut instinct that has kept us both alive on more than one occasion.

After a moment, he looks at his watch again. "It has been awhile. I'll just go check on her . . ." he says before taking off down the hall.

He's taking too long. I feel it in my bones, something's wrong with Claire. I realize I was standing from the table when he calls out my name.

"Wes! Down here!" he shouts from back down the all by the bathrooms.

Just like fucking *Cinderella*, one of her shoes, those ridiculous heels that I told her turned me one, is laying on its side. She must have dropped it on her way out.

Part of me thinks she ran, but I know that's not it. Claire wouldn't run from this, from us, she's in it one hundred percent and then some.

"She's gone." Lee echoes my thoughts. Someone took my Claire. Again. And that burns in my gut. I know deep down in my soul that whoever took her this time won't let her escape. Have her demons really come back to haunt us like this? When we are finally so close to having everything we ever wanted?

"Find anyone who saw something. Talk to everyone here. No one leaves," I demand.

"I pull my phone out of my pocket to call her but it goes straight to voicemail. I kick myself for my stupidity. Her little green clutch with the peacock on it is still sitting by her place at the head table next to my seat with my jacket over it. I know with certainty that she didn't leave of her own accord now, but then, who took her? Only family and friends and here tonight. Who do we know that would betray us like this? That could have betrayed her twenty four years ago?

"We're going to find her," Lee tries to reassure me and him both.

"We better, or it's going to kill me . . . Lee, there's something you don't know . . ." I start to tell him what I have suspected for a week or two now but never brought up to Claire. I never had the courage to ask her.

"What's that?" he asks me, but I can't share my deepest thoughts and hopes with him. Not yet.

"Nothing, let's just find her," I tell him.

We head back to the dining room but the scene is wrong. Something is different.

"Who's missing?" Lee asks.

"Holy shit," I whisper. "No." Just in time to see Lee's dad race from the building. He wouldn't betray me like this. He couldn't. The blood is rushing in my ears and my heart is about to beat out of my chest because I cannot rationalize a world where he would betray me like this. But in my head, I know that he did.

"Where were you standing in the yard the night that Claire came home?" Lee asks me.

"Facing the woods to the east," I tell him as all the pieces to our fucked up puzzle start to fit together. The answer was right in front of my face all along. I think I'm going to be sick,

"I think I know who took Claire," Lee says like he's about to brace me for bad news.

"Me too."

chapter 24

it's you

Claire

THERE IS A MARCHING band pounding away in my brain. I must have had too much to drink at the rehearsal dinner last night, I think. I better be able to get my ass ready for today—my wedding day—because if I don't, my bestie, Emma, will have my ass.

I pry my eyes open, only then do I realize that I am not in our hotel room on the coast. I'm not in the luxury king sized bed full of fluffy euro pillows and down comforters near a window looking out at the Atlantic Ocean. I'm not where I should be. It takes my brain a minute, still feeling as fuzzy as it is, that I'm not . . . *safe*.

The light shines through the wooden slats of the doors.

I'm here. I am right back where I started. Where I thought I would die when I was so small, just a baby really. I'm where I once escaped and had naively thought I would never be back. I scoot back on the worn, torn carpet floor of the closet that I was locked in once before, until my back hits the wall. I try to make myself as small as possible hoping against all hope that he won't see me but as I hear the footsteps growing louder and louder, I know that there is no hope to be found at all.

The closet door swings opened and I realize how stupid I have been. All this time that I struggled, that I suffered from those terrible nightmares and prayed that they would either end or I would finally remember just who had tried to harm me when I was just six years old. All those times I thought I was safe, that I was free, were really nothing but lies because looking down at me with a sinister smile on his face in this little house of horrors from my haunted past is the last person I ever would have thought would be capable of this kind of thing.

I was never free, I was living under the watchful eye of a monster, a wolf in sheep's clothing just waiting for their chance to pounce. His smile broadens and his eyes glimmer with excitement in the knowledge that he's won. It's finally over, this game of cat and mouse that we have been silently engaged in for twenty four years.

How stupid I was. How many times did I go to dinner at their house? How many times did I think he was the one in my corner? For fucks sake I even fell in love with his son.

He pulls his leather belt free from his pants and loops it around my neck. I look up into his warm eyes, ones that I had always trusted as he tightens the leather around my neck.

"It's you. It was always you." I say as look into the eyes so much like the ones on the face I see every night before I got to sleep. Judge O'Connell looks down at me with triumph in his brown eyes and suddenly every memory finally clicks into place.

Anna would be so proud.

I gasp as the air is squeezed out of my lungs. I struggle to pull more in even though in my brain I know that it isn't possible. Maybe this is how it was always supposed to be. Maybe this is how my story was always supposed to end. I was never supposed to get the guy. I was never supposed to get the happily ever after. I was never supposed to live . . .

Spots start to dance in front of my eyes. I keep fighting even though I don't know why. I should just relax and let destiny take me, maybe? When the door to the cabin swings open with a thud and there stand my dad, my first hero, come to save me.

"Let my daughter go, you sick fuck!" he demands and Judge O'Connell looks nervous for a minute when my dad raises his gun. A small *smith & wesson* thirty-eight and loosens his hold on the belt around my neck. I can finally take a breath, shallow as it might be. "I trusted you!"

My dad pulls the hammer back and the barrel spins but before he has a chance to pull the trigger a loud boom erupts in the room and red blood blooms out around my dad's chest. His face a mask of surprise and disbelief as he crumples to the floor.

"No!" I scream. "No, no, no, no. Dad!"

"I couldn't let you win," my future mother-in-law says as she steps out of the shadows with a small pearl handled revolver in her hand. I remember the year Wes bought it for her for Christmas because he wanted her to feel safe in her own home while her husband was busy sending the bad guys to prison. And now she used it to murder my dad. What a joke.

"You couldn't let me win?" I snap. "When did I ever win?"

"You stole my husband!" she screams at me. "Did you want me to just sit back and watch while he became obsessed with you? Your dark hair and your pretty purple eyes. The pink of your mouth and the way it turned him on. I couldn't take it anymore!"

"I didn't steal your husband!" I scream right back not caring one fuck that my hands are still bound and I'm about to die too. "Your husband kidnapped me and molested me!"

"You made him do it. He couldn't help himself the way you called to him like a siren," she argues her crazy delusions and her husbands.

"I was six years old!" I yell. "I was just a baby and you took everything away from me."

"You were going to ruin everything!" she says. "My life, my husband's career, everything that we had worked so hard for was all going to fall down like a house of cards because he could not stay away from you."

"You're sick." I spit.

"So he took you and was going to do whatever he needed to with you to get it out of his system," she says like it's no big deal.

"He was never going to let me go, was he?" I ask her.

"Of course not," she says looking at me like I was always a disappointment. "We couldn't have any loose ends walking around and talking now could we? And then somehow you managed to escape him but you didn't remember anything so I thought, what's the harm?"

"So why now?" I ask her.

"Because you can't take both of my boys from me!" she screams losing the tight grip on her control again. "You can't have both my husband and my son."

"I just want Wes. I'm in love with Wes," I say strongly.

"Yes, and they are both in love with you," she sneers. "But with you back in Wes's like he will never run for office like we expect him to, like we need him to in order to carry on the family tradition."

"Wes doesn't want that," I tell her.

"No, you don't want that. This is what Wesley was bred for. But with you hanging around, his father can't seem to get a rein on his . . . appetites." Oh gross, I think I'm going to barf. "We watched the hunter chase you and I thought, for once luck has smiled on me and someone else will handle my dirty work, but alas, no."

"Why are you doing this?" I ask her.

"So that my husband and my son can move on, with me at their sides, of course," she answers cooly.

"Of course."

"Now, can I have her?" Judge O'Connell asks as he digs his fingers into my hair pulling some stands from my scalp when I try to flinch away. He caresses my lip with his thumb and the vomit burns in my throat and I know that I'm seconds away from puking again.

"You have one hour to play," she tells her husband. "And then I'll be back to finish the job once and for all."

Mrs. O'Connell turns to walk away but the door swings open again this time Wes is there and his face is wrenched with pain and betrayal. I want to reach out and comfort him but I can't. His dad is holding me by my hair and my hands are still bound.

"What the actual fuck is happening here?" he roars as takes in the room.

"Wesley, leave right now," he mother orders. "And I will have all of this cleaned up like it never happened. And then we can move on together, as a family."

"Are you fucking crazy?" he thunders. "You think I'll just sit back and let you murder my wife?"

"She's not your wife yet," she snaps. "And she never should be. She ruins everything. Now step back, Wesley, before I have to shoot you too."

"You would really shoot me?" he asks dumbstruck.

"I would do anything to protect your father," she says. Poor Wes, That has to hurt. "Now, let's move past this."

"No," Wes says breaking my heart. "Dad, let her go."

"I can't, Wesley," he admits. "I need her more than you could ever understand."

"No, Dad," Wes says. "Because I need her so much that I can't live without her."

"I'm sorry, Wesley," he says not even looking up to his son as he answers. Instead he's watching my eyes as he slowly pulls on the tail of his belt and squeezes the air out of my body.

"No!" he shouts as the room explodes.

Liam and Surfer push through the door and into the room. They both fire guns in their hands. Who shot who, I still can't tell. But Judge and Mrs. O'Connell are gone and for that I am truly grateful and also heart broken for Wes. I'm not sure we can move on from this. If my kidnapper was anyone else, I think we would be fine, but a betrayal like that from his parents, will cut deep.

"I knew you'd get here in time, Son," my dad's voice wraps in the room.

"Dad!" Lee and I both shout.

"I'm not out yet," he says. "I have too much life to live still." And thank God for that.

Wes comes over and pulls a folding knife out of his pocket and without saying a word, he cuts the ties that bind my hands together and pulls his father's belt from around my neck. And then he turns and walks outside without saying another word.

The sirens sing in the distance and I know that the police are on the way. It's a huge relief but at the same time, I am worried about Wes. My heart breaks for him.

My dad was whisked away in an ambulance but this time the medics said he looked good and that it was good that he was talking so I didn't go running after him into the night like I did with Jones, plus I knew I had to stay and give all the statements.

It's hard to lay my soul bare and put all my demons on display for my fellow officers to see but I do. I give my statement and I tell them everything. Lee and Surfer give statements as well because they discharged weapons but we all know that the shoots will be clean upon review. And then in an interesting plot twist, some men in black show up and whisk Surfer away after demanding that his entire statement be redacted because he was never here.

"Whoa," I say after they leave.

"You have no idea," Lee says his eyes wide. "I had heard, but, yeah, whoa sums it up."

"I have no idea what just happened," I tell my brother.

"I think for both our sakes we should pretend it didn't," he tells me. "You going to be okay, kiddo?"

"I think so," I say. "I'm not sure though the jury is still out."

"I think you'll be alright," he says after a minute. "But that one needs you bad."

My eyes follow Lee's down the gravel drive to where Wes is standing with his shoulder slumped and his head hanging low.

"He hasn't said a word to me, Lee," I admit. "I'm worried he can't look at me anymore."

"He feels guilty," Lee tells me. "Like it's all his fault that you got hurt. Then and now."

"But it's not," I say.

"Don't tell me that." Lee shrugs. "Tell him.

"I think I'll do just that," I say as I push up from where Lee and I were sitting and walk over to Wes.

I press my front to his back and wrap myself around his waist. His arms wrap around mine locking me to him.

"I am so very fucking sorry, baby," he starts.

"You have nothing to be sorry for," I say with all honestly. "You saved me, then and now."

"I didn't," he says shaking his head. "Surfer shot my dad although we can never tell anyone that."

"I know," I tell him. "Lee and I got the shake down from the men in black too. It was wild."

"I told you to leave him alone," he says softly.

"Lee said he'd heard a rumor . . ." I trail off.

"I know more than Lee," he tells me and when I open my mouth, he stops me. "But I still won't tell you."

"Damn it, Wes!" I pout.

"Do you think you can still love me?" he asks me quietly. Wes's vulnerability cuts me to the quick.

"I have loved you since I was six years old and you gave me your ball cap," I tell him honestly. "And I have never stopped and I never will."

Wes pulls me around to face him and crushes his lips down on mine in a soul searing kiss. Wes and I might have a rocky road in front of us, but it's nothing we can't handle because life with Wes is always worth it.

"Wanna get married?" I ask him.

"Probably right after you get checked out at the hospital," he tells me.

"I'm fine," I deny any injury.

"About that," he says as he runs his finger tip across the bruises on my neck that have been purpling deeper and deeper over the last hour. "I think there are some things we should have checked out."

chapter 25

the one

One Week Later...

"ARE YOU READY for your forever?" Emma asks me as she pulls my simple veil over my head.

"Yeah," I smile. "I was born ready."

"Then let's do this!" she cheers making me laugh.

Emma kisses my cheek through the thin material before herding my nieces out through the french doors on the patio. I hear the first strings of the song that they are walking down the aisle to and I know that this is it. There are no more hurdles to jump. I can finally be with Wes.

This is the first day of the rest of our lives.

The music changes and it *The Longer the Wait, The Sweeter the Kiss* by Josh Turner and it couldn't be more fitting. Wes and I have literally waited our whole lives to get here.

This is my cue. The french doors open one more time and I step out to look up into the face of my brother, Liam, who is smiling sweetly at me and looking very handsome in his Navy dress blues. A uniform that I haven't seen in a very long time and still holds a special spot in my heart.

"Wes and I got permission to wear them." he says noticing what has my attention. I smile at him.

"What are you doing here?" I ask him. He is supposed to be standing at the altar with Wes as his best man but instead he's here, surprising me.

"What?" he asks on a wink. "Can't a guy give his only sister away to his best friend?"

"I guess a guy could if that guy is you," I say softly feeling a little choked up.

Lee walks me through the courtyard garden path that winds its way down to the sea where Wes and everyone else are waiting for us. At the front of the aisle waits my dad.

Lee hands me over to my dad who turns to Lee and says, "I've got it from here."

"I know you do, Dad," Lee says. "But mind if I tag along?"

"Sounds great, Son," my dad says to Lee before turning to me. "Sorry about the sling, your mother wouldn't let me skip it."

I can't help but bark out a laugh. We are all so much alike. That Goodnite stubbornness is a sight to behold.

"I'm sure it's fine, Dad," I tell him. "Hey, we've got matching father daughter gunshot wounds."

"That's not funny." Dad and Lee growl at the same time making me smile even brighter.

"I always knew that Wes was the one," Dad says to me and emotion clogs my throat. "Treat each other with kindness and love."

"I will," I promise my dad.

"I know you will."

When we reach the altar, Wes is waiting with a smile on his face like I have never seen before and if I'm not mistaken, a shimmer in his eye that matches mine. I'm barely holding on to my emotions. I'm going to cry like a little baby and we all know it.

"Remember what I said, Wesley," my dad says to him as he passes my hand from hi to Wes's.

"Yes, Sir, I do," Wes answers and Lee smirks.

"Who gives this woman away?" the minister asks.

"Her mother and I do," my dad answers.

"Thank you. You may be seated."

"I wouldn't give her to anyone but you, Brother," Lee says to Wes as he takes his place beside him and pats him on the shoulder like men do.

"I know," Wes answers and the emotion in his voice is telling.

"What did my dad say to you that was so important?" I whisper to Wes as the minister begins the ceremony.

"No take backs," he whispers back. I can't help the smile that spreads across my face and I barely restrain my laughter.

That is so like my dad to welcome Wes to the family officially and then tell him no take backs. I come from a family of weirdos and I wouldn't have it any other way. And at the same time, Dad is providing Wes with the family that he always deserved and didn't get.

"Marriage is not a shelter for the faint of heart," the minister begins. "But I believe you two already know that one."

He is an older man with a kind smile and white hair. His stature is small but his presence is huge. When we explained our situation to him last week and why would couldn't have a priest or a judge, he said he would be happy to perform our marriage ceremony.

"At this time, the best man will perform a Navy tradition, and ring a ships bell for each of the important people in the Bride and Groom's lives that are no longer with us and could not be here today," he says before calling out each name.

"Officer Luis Rodriguez." Lee rings the big brace bell once.

"Officer Matt Jerome." Lee rings the bell twice.

"Officer Jasmine Alexander." Lee rings the bell a third time.

"The bride's sister, Bonnie." Lee rings the bell a fourth time and I know what's coming so I take a deep breath a steel myself. Wes takes my hand in his giving me a gentle squeeze of support.

"And their dear friend, Anna Parker." Lee rings the bell a fifth time and I look over my shoulder to the chair on the aisle that was left open for her with her bouquet sitting on top of it and offer up a silent prayer that wherever Anna is, that she is happy.

"At this time, Wesley and Claire, have chosen to recite their own vows."

"Wes, I promise to make you feel loved and cherished every day. I promise not to drive you too crazy, only a little crazy. I'll be your shelter in the storm as you have been mine. I will not stop making fun of your Fed suits or your Fed-mobile because we both know you secretly like it. I won't promise to be perfect, but I promise to love you with all that I am until the day that I die. This is my vow," I say softly.

"Claire, I have always loved you. In fact, I can't remember a time when I didn't in one way or another. I promise to be your lover and protector. I promise to be your shelter in the storm the way that you have been mine. I promise not to overly judge your disgusting love of junk food, but will continue to appreciate the ass that it provides you."

"Wes!"

"I will love you and honor you faithfully until the day I die. This is my vow," he continues his voice ringing loud and true.

"I now pronounce you husband and wife. You may kiss the bride," the minister finishes loudly to the shouts and whistles and catcalls of all the SEALs including Surfer.

I look to Wes and smile as he flips my veil over my face and pulls me into his arms. Wes kisses my socks off, that is if I was wearing socks and not these ridiculous heels Emma made me get.

"Ready?" he asks me.

"To be with you?"

"Yeah," smiles at me.

"I was born ready." And then he takes my hand and we get started on the first day of the rest of our lives.

• • •

By the time we walk into the reception hall my cheeks hurt from smiling by I am ecstatic at the idea that when Wes and I get back from our honeymoon in Italy that we will have a stack of pictures to put up in our house and one day show our children.

The room is filled with all of our friends and family who cheer ridiculously loud when Wes and I are introduced as Mr and Mrs. O'Connell. I'm pretty sure it was the SEALs. They are a pretty rowdy bunch even in their early forties.

Mr. and Mrs. O'Connell.

I have to admit. I love the sound of it. I'll probably always be Goody or Detective Goodnite at work, but in real life, I am Claire O'Connell. I know that Wes thinks that after everything that happened that I wouldn't want to take his family name, but in truth I want to be tied to Wes in as many ways as possible.

My love for him is that big.

Wes leads me out into the middle of the dance floor and twirls me into his arms. We dance under the lights to the words to Yours by Russell Dickerson and they couldn't be more true. Wes expertly twirls me around the dance floor.

I have lived many years before Wes came back into my life, but with him I can accomplish anything, I can survive whatever life throws at me because I have him by my side. He truly makes my life better in every way.

"Thank God I'm yours," Wes repeats the song lyrics in my ear as the song ends.

"I thank God I'm yours too, Wes." The tears still shimmer in his eyes. Mine too. I knew today would be full of feeling but I love it. My heart is full to bursting for him.

My love for him is that big.

• • •

"It's time," Wes says to me later that evening.

There is one last thing to do and I am dreading it, but it needs to be done. It's time to say goodbye to my friend.

Emma, Lee, Wes and I quietly leave the party and walk out to the beach in our barefeet. We carry nothing with us but Anna's bouquet.

Side by side we stand in the dark with the waves crashing over our feet as we silently offer each other support as we say goodbye one last time.

"Thank you for a beautiful day, Anna. I miss you," I say out loud.

"Thank you for being my friend. I miss you," Emma says. Her tears leave tracks down her face.

"I wish you peace, Anna," Wes says.

"Be free," Lee adds last before I toss her bouquet into the ocean,

"Goodbye, Fancy Pants," I say. "Until we meet again."

"Emma, can we talk?" Lee asks as she turns to walk away.

"Has hell frozen over yet?" she snaps back. Her emotions are obviously riding her hard right now as she wars between wanting Lee and her guilt over Anna.

"It doesn't have to be like this," he says softly. She looks like she waivers for a split second before walking off.

"It does," she calls over her shoulder.

"This is ridiculous," he barks as he trails off after her.

"She feels guilty," Wes says wrapping me up in his arms. "Don't worry, Lee's a tenacious guy. He'll figure it out."

"That's what I'm worried about," I tell him.

We stand there looking out at the sea with me cradled protectively in his arms. Wes silently giving me me the comfort that I need to know that everything is going to be alright.

Because his love for me is that big.

• • •

"It's time to cut the cake," the wedding planner tells us after we return to the reception.

She herds us toward a massive cake that is as tall as I am sitting on the table. On top of the cake is a small statue of the VJ day kiss couple and I love it. It's a little scandalous and I just know that this was Emma's contribution. The rest of the cake starts in a deep pink at the bottom and fades up to white at the top in the most beautiful ombre. It's very classy.

I place my hand on top of Wes's on the cake knife and together, we slide out a small piece. I scoop it up with the server and put it on a plate to hand to Wes.

"It's chocolate," he says surprised to she the rich color of the actual cake.

"Yeah, I know," I tell him. "It's your favorite."

"You got my favorite cake for our wedding cake?" he asks me.

"Well, yeah," I answer his question. "I wanted you to have special things today too."

I don't get a chance to finish that train of though because Wes, so moved with love and the spirit of today, that he pulls me into his body and crushes his mouth to mine in a kiss even better than out wedding kiss. As his tongue sweeps into my mouth the rest of the room falls away and I am lost to Wes.

That is until the room erupts with cheers and whistles and I have to duck my head to hide the embarrassment stinging my cheeks. Wes just laughs.

"Maybe we should put a pin in that thought," I say for his ears only making Wes laugh even harder.

"Sure, baby. Whatever you say."

He scoops up a small bite on one of thos forks and offers it to me. I keep my eyes on his as I open my mouth and take his offer. I hold a bite out for Wes and he just shakes his head no. I roll my eyes letting him know that this isn't part of the agenda.

He just laughs and kisses me again.

"I prefer my cake from your lips," he says wiping the corner of his mouth.

"You are incorrigible," I tell him on a laugh.

"Better get used to it, baby." But I hope I never get used to it. I hope I wake up every day for the rest of my life with the overwhelming feeling that I am incredibly blessed. That I am the luckiest woman in the world because Wes makes me feel that way every day.

Because his love for me is just that big.

• • •

Emma

A little dutch courage is going to be my downfall.

I could see the toasts coming a mile away like a bad car crash on the turnpike. I knew that Lee was going to be charming when he gave his. I also knew that I was sorely unprepared to see him in his old Navy dress blues. Dear baby jesus in a trench coat it should be illegal for a man to look that good in a uniform.

So I was nervous and all through dinner the champagne was free flowing so I partook of that champagne. And then I realized shortly after I gave my toast—one that was free of all the delightful stories of Wes's penis because my bestie, Claire, can be a little dull from time to time—that I had perhaps imbibed too much.

My face felt flushed, my body felt hot, and I knew that I needed some fresh air. So after I wished my bestie and her groom a long and happy life of blissful joy and boning—and real talk, I killed it in there—I excused myself from the party to go back to the water's edge to catch my breath and cook down. What I didn't plan on was a very sexy police Captain, one I can't seem to keep my hands off of, had followed me.

"You can't avoid me forever," he says softly from just behind me.

"It would be a lot easier if you played along," I whine just a little bit. God damnit, I am a strong and independent woman, I do not like how needed I am around this one man.

"I can't do that, baby," he says. "I need you too much."

"No," I deny.

"And I think you need me too," his sexy voice rumbles and I feel it in a lot of interesting places, but then again, with Lee I always do.

"No," I whisper.

"And I think you're scared to fall," he says softly as he puts his hands on my shoulders and gently turns me around to face him. "But I'll catch you, I promise."

"What if you don't?" I ask ashamed to admit how scared I am.

"You have to trust me," he says.

"I can't."

"Just for tonight," Lee pleads. "Just trust me for tonight and we'll go from there."

"Okay," I say softly.

"Okay?" he asks unsure of what to do now that I have agreed.

"Okay," I repeat.

He looks so happy and I'm half afraid that it's the champagne that's making me agree to be his even if it's only for a night. No, that's a lie. Truth be told, I am in love with Liam Goodnite, and just as much as I know that he is it for me, I also know that I could never hold him. A man like Lee would get tired of being with one woman after a while, especially if that woman is me and I know that it hurts like hell to walk away now, but it would kill me to see him walking away after six months or a year of loving him the way that I would if I could bring myself to let down my guard.

I look up and realise that we have slowly moved out of the light shining from the reception and down to just under the pier. It's dark here and a little secluded. The music from the party can be heard just barely.

And in that moment, I want Lee like I have never wanted anything in my life.

"Don't look at me like that, Emma," he says his voice strained. "I can't walk away like a gentleman when you look at me like that."

"Like what?" I ask.

"Like you want me. Like you need my cock like you need air to breath. Like you want me to make that pretty pink pussy of yours come," he says his voice low and rumbly.

"Yes," I breathe as I back up and my shoulders hit one of the wooden posts of the pier. "I want that. All of it."

"Emma," he pleads as he says my name like a prayer.

"I want that," I say letting the wine make me bolder than I normally would be. "I want your cock and I want you to make me come. And I want you."

"Fuck," he bites out before crashing his mouth down on mine.

Lee kisses me like a drowning man in a hurricane, his kiss is fierce and powerful and all consuming. I let out a whimper and he takes that opportunity to sweep his tongue inside my mouth and I suck it deep letting it brush over mine as he plunges it in and out of my mouth.

He breaks his mouth away from mine and I miss it immediately.

"Lee," I plead. What for, I'm not sure, I just know that I need more. More of hiss kisses, more of his touch on my skin, his cock. I don't know. I just need more.

Slowly, so painfully slowly, Lee slides the skirt of my dress up bunching it in his large hand as he goes. When it's up above my hips, exposing my delicate pink panties, Lee slides the damp material aside and plunges two fingers into my pussy.

"So wet for me," he says softly.

"Yes," I agree. I lean my weight back on the post as my knees begin to buckle.

"Are you going to come for me like this or do you want my cock in that pretty pussy of yours?" he asks me. And I will con on his hand if he keeps it up, but tonight I'm giving into all the vices that are bad for my health: wine, Lee, and if he fucks my brains out I'll go bum a smoke from one of the valet guys.

"I want your cock," I say honestly. I watch captivated as he unbuttons the front of his trousers. His hard length springs free and I want it. I want all of it. Everything that Lee has to give me. In this moment, I will take whatever that may be. No regrets, I will YOLO the fuck out of him.

"That's my girl." Oh how I wish I were his girl. God what would it be like to be loved by him like that. "Lift your leg around my hip. That's it."

He pulls the gusset of my panties to the side and slides his cock all the way in. Lee lifts me up, bracing his hands under my as so that he can lift me up and the drive me down on his cock over and over again.

"Oh God," I moan as he slides me up so that only the tip is inside me and then powers me back down again.

"That's it," he says as I clench around him as he slides me up and then drives me down on him again.

"I-I'm going to—" I gasp as my orgasm rolls over me like a steamrollers.

"Lee!"

He pins me to the post and pumps once, twice more before calling out my name into the night as he follows me over the edge. "Emma!"

Lee holds me in his arms against the wooden post as we both struggle to catch our breaths. He leans his forehead against mine.

"So what are you doing for the rest of tonight?" he asks me.

"I had grand plans to go bum a smoke from one of the valet guys," I admit and feel Lee's smile against my mouth.

"Well, seeing as how they have all gone home for the night, how about you come back to my room with me instead?"

"I suppose I could do that instead," I say hesitantly.

"Excellent," he whispers.

Lee sets me on my feet and waits for me to regain my balance and then hand in hand we walk down the beach and back up to the resort where Lee will let us in his room and we'll spend another night together.

What could one more night hurt?

• • •

Claire

Fireworks of all colors burst bright over head.

It's midnight and one of the last fireworks displays of the season. Most of our guests have gone home or to their rooms in the resort and only a few stragglers are left. Wes and I wanted to enjoy the entire night instead of rushing out to be alone. This wedding felt like a long time in the making and we wanted to enjoy all of it.

"Look at that one!" I point to a big purple firework that glitters in the sky. "It's so pretty."

"Not as pretty as you," he whispers.

"Wes," I smile feeling a little shy at all of the attention today.

Wes wraps his arms around me and I lean my back to his front and enjoy the rest of the fireworks show, that is until he presses his erection into my ass and it's hard enough that I can feel it through the miles and miles of froth fabric that my dress consist of.

"Have I told you yet how much I love this dress?" Wes leans down and rumbles in my ear.

"No, I don't believe you have yet," I tell him.

"Well, I do believe it's about time that I sing its praises."

"As you should," I agree.

"You ready to get out of her, Mrs. O'Connell?" he asks me.

"For life with you?" I answer him with a big smile on my face. "I was born ready."

And then Wes and I sneak out and head up to our honeymoon suite that overlooks the ocean to get started on the rest of our forever. One thing I'm sure of, life with Wes will never be boring. I can't wait.

epic epilogue
the best day of my life

Claire
6 weeks later...

"ARE YOU READY for this?" I ask Wes as we walk out of the doctor's office and jump in his car. As always, Wes holds the door open for me, ever the gentleman.

"Of course," he answers smoothly. "Why would you think I wouldn't be?"

"Well, you were looking a little green around the gills there. I thought we might be puking together for a second there."

"I never puke," my husband says with all seriousness.

All this talk of vomit has my stomach turning. Long gone are the days of my waking up to be sick because of the lasting effects of a nightmare that wouldn't let me go, and now I puke regularly for a whole new reason. A great reason. I'm pregnant.

Wes and I are having a baby.

"Let's stop talking about puking, please," I say my voice a little high and uncomfortable. Wes gives me a knowing smirk, but fortunately changes the subject.

We are on our way to meet Emma and Lee for lunch to tell them the good news and to officially move me to desk duty and filing. Yay! Not really, while I know that I will be bored off of my ass for the next six months, I know that it is what I need to do, so I'm finally okay with being benched.

Tonight at dinner, we're going to tell my mom and dad.

Wes had started suspecting that big changes were on the horizon the week before I was taken again and he had even planned to talk to me that night about it. It turns out my husband is a very perceptive man because he was right.

The directions we forgot to read after I was shot by the hunter had neglected to inform us that the antibiotic shot that I was given in the hospital and the the prescription that I was give for oral antibiotics after I was discharged had rendered my birth control shot completely ineffective. I had no idea and now I'm glad for it because I couldn't be happier.

Wes pulls into the parking lot of the diner around the corner from the station. Neither Lee or Emma's cars are here. And I'm sad to admit that they are not together after our wedding. I had high hopes that they would finally work their problems out but I guess it just isn't meant to be.

Wes holds the shiny glass door open for me and holds up his hands to ask for a four top. The hostess grabs four menus before walking us to a table just around the corner from the dessert counter and suddenly I am ravenous.

I open my menu and everything looks good but I home in on the double bacon cheeseburger. When I look up, Emma and Lee are headed our way.

"Hey!" I say jumping up to hug my best friend and my big brother.

"So, how was the honeymoon?" Lee asks.

"Italy was amazing," Wes says with a smug smirk on his face.

"Oh, gross," Lee says making a gagging noise. "That's my sister, asshole."

"No, that is my very sexy wife."

"Ok, that was kind of gross, Wes," I tell him.

"Too far?" he asks playfully.

"Just a smidge," I say holding up my thumb and index fingers about an inch apart.

"My apologies," he says on a not at all feeling guilty smile.

The waitress comes and takes our order and I settle on the double cheeseburger and extra fries. Emma asks for chicken noodle soup but she just pushes it around in her bowl. Come to think of it she's not looking that great. I feel bad, but I also don't want to catch anything if it's contagious.

"Are you feeling alright?" I ask her softly for her ears only but then Lee homes in on what I've said.

"Are you sick?" he asks.

"I'm fine," she answers but the look on her face says she's anything but.

"So what did you call us down here to tell us?"

I lean back in my seat and look at Wes before answering. "I'm pregnant."

"No shit," Lee laughs. "I thought you were just fat."

"You asshole," I grumble while Wes laughs. "Why do I like you again?"

"Because I'm your favorite big brother," he explains.

"You are my only big brother," I correct him.

"And I'm really happy for you, kiddo," he tells me. "But for real, you are looking kind of fat."

"Nice knowing you," Wes mumbles but I choose to ignore that.

"I'm not fat, you nut sack! I'm having twins," I shout.

Emma looks around a little uncomfortable before seizing her opportunity to escape. "I guess I'm not feeling well after all, I should go," she says before tossing a twenty on the table and practically running for the door.

"What was that all about?" I ask Lee.

He lets out a heavy sigh. "I just don't know. We were fine until about a week ago and then she just stopped calling and started looking really sad again. I can't get her to talk to me."

"Well, I'm sure you'll figure it out," I try to reassure my brother.

"I will," he tells me. "Don't worry about me. I'm happy for you guys."

"Thanks, Lee," Ws says shaking his hand as my brother stands and drops a twenty on the table. He walks out of the diner and I have a funny feeling he's going to go after Emma. Again.

"Ready to get out of here?" Wes asks me throwing some more chas on the pile on the table.

"Yes, but first I need pie," I tell him.

"One celebratory piece of pie to go," he tells me as he stands to make his way over to the dessert counter.

"Better make it two if you want any because I'm not sharing," I inform my better half.

"This pregnancy has only made your eating habits worse," he tells me. "At some point in time you are going to have to eat a vegetable."

"Bite your tongue!" I laugh.

"Pie coming right up," he says as he returns with my pie.

Wes leads me out to the car where he drives me back to our house.

"Do you want your pie now or later, baby?" he asks me as he lets us into the house.

"Later," I tell him. "Now I kind of just want to hang out with you."

"Sure," he says. "What do you want to do?"

"Watch a movie with me?" I shrug. We almost never have down time but I got used to just being lazy with Wes in Italy.

"Sure," he says as we snuggle up on the sofa with a big throw blanket. "Maybe we'll find a sexy highlander for you."

"Oh, you're so funny," I play swat him. Wes still teases me about the romance novels my mom gave when when I was recovering from being shot and they still lead to some pretty steamy moments with my guy.

"I'm just teasing," he tells me as he brushes a lock of my hair back from my face. "I love you, Claire."

"And I love you," I tell him.

"Never stop saying it," he says softly. "I need the words."

"I'll always love you."

We sit on the couch and watch some spy movie that we have both seen a thousand times. It will probably always remind me of the night that the men in black came for one of my husband's friends. But as we promised each other that night, we have never spoke of it again.

We also haven't seen Surfer since.

After awhile I ask, "Are you really happy?"

"Of course," Wes says turning to face me. "Why wouldn't I be?"

"I don't know," say fidgeting suddenly feeling a little insecure. Fucking hormones. "It happened so fast. I just don't want you to regret anything."

"Look at me, baby," Wes says lifting my chin to meet his eyes. "I have not one regret when it comes to be married to you. I want this baby with every fiber of my being and I love you just as much. So don't be nervous. Be happy and enjoy this time with me before we're a four."

"Okay," I say finally letting myself feel truly happy.

"And baby," he says.

"Yeah?"

"One more thing. This is by far, the best day of my life.

• • •

Wes

6 months later . . .

"I'm here!" I shout as I race through the hospital. "I'm here. I'm here!"

"Right this way, Mr. O'Connell. They're waiting on you," the nurse tells me. "Put on these scrubs and then come with me." She shoves me into a changing room and I dress as fast as I can.

When I jump out of the room she's standing there waiting for me and she has a look on her face like I'm the biggest screw up she's ever seen.

The nurse leads me down a long hallway and pulls me into an Operating Room that looks like it's something out of an Alien Abduction Sci-Fi movie. There are huge circular lights overhead and the love of my life is draped over a steel table in the middle of the room. She's surrounded by people in scrubs and rubber gloves and surgical masks. The nurse hands me a mask and a hat and shoves me in the room.

"I'm here, baby," I say as I head over to where her face is because as they are setting up a big blue paper tent, I am sure that I do not want to see my wife turned inside out.

"Glad you could make it, Dad," the surgeon says. He's a funny guy and by funny I mean he's a raging asshole but everyone says he's the best at delivering babies so here we are and by we I mean me as I am the one that eats all the shit he shovels my way.

"Sorry," I say eating up a little more shit. Yum! Yum! "We had a huge break on a human trafficking ring and I didn't know my wife's water was going to break while eating some Mu Shu Chicken when I was in an interrogation room." Whoops guess I'm not eating as much shit as I thought today.

"It's okay," my sweet wife says. "You're here now, that's all that matters."

"You can sit here by me," the Anesthesiologist says so me.

I think I may have impressed him by accidentally mouthing off to the doctor. But in all fairness this case is riding me pretty hard and my favorite partner has been benched for a few months. Not to mention Lee is an absolute disaster these days. But who can blame him what with everything going on in his life and all.

"Thank you," I tell him as I sit on the tiniest stool known to man. This shit wasn't made for a man of my size.

"I'm ready to meet the babies," Claire says to me. "How about you?"

"You know I have been ready for months," I tell her on a smile she can't see because it's hidden by a mask.

"We're ready to begin," the doctor says. "You're going to feel a little tugging."

"Oh," she says. "I s-s-see what you mean."

"Would you like to see your son be born?" the doctor asks and even though I know what it means I'm about to see I nod my head. "Well, stand up and say hello."

I stand and my knees feel weak as I watch this tiny little creature all covered in crap be pulled out of my wife. It's actually kind of creepy and not at all magical but this is my boy so I feel a burning in my nose and I know that I'm going to cry.

"We need suction," the nurse says.

"Suction."

"Take him to the NICU now!" someone shouts.

"No," I say not fully understanding what's going on. "He's supposed to come here. My wife wants the blue sheet picture. She's been saying that for months."

"Sir, your son isn't breathing we have to take him." I'm numb. I just nod and sit down on the stool.

"Wes," Claire asks. "What's going on?"

"Everything is going to be just fine," I lie. I'm not sure of anything right now. I just know that I'm numb.

"Here comes baby number two," the doctor says and I pop up to watch a little girl with jet black hair be pulled from her mother.

Again the nurse says, "We need suction." And my heart sinks.

"Suction."

"Be ready to transport to NICU now!" Someone shouts.

"My wife didn't even get to see them," I say as the nurses in the room gather up my baby girl and start running out of the room with her in their arms when they hear me, they *Lion King* her over their heads like that damn monkey so we can see her on the way out the door.

"Wes?" Claire says.

"Yeah, baby, I'm right here."

"I don't feel so good," she says and when I look at her she doesn't look good at all. "I think I'm going to be sick."

"Wow," the doctor says. "That is a lot of blood."

"Suction," someone calls. There's that fucking word again. I don't think I'm ever going to be able to hear it again after today.

"Sir," a nurse says. "You need to come with me to the nursery."

"No, my in-laws are there to be with the babies. I'm going to stay with my wife," I explain our plan for this delivery that they should fucking know by now because we have had it in place the entire time.

"No, Sir," she says firmly. "You have to come with me now." She starts pulling on me and I don't know what to do.

"Wes," Claire says groggily. It sounds like she's drunk. "Where are you going? What's happening?"

An alarm starts to sound in the room and the anesthesiologist says, "She's crashing."

"Sir, we have to go now!"

And I blindly follow her out of the operating room and wonder if on what would have been the happiest day of my life, did I just lose everything.

I go to the nursery and watch my beauftiful little babies all cleaned up and looking so much like their mother with black hair and violet eyes. My boy's chest sucks all the way down to his spine with every breath he struggles to take and watching him guts me with every breath but how much time will I have with him? I just don't know.

My father-in-law comes in the room and pats me on the shoulder. Lee isn't here anymore but I'm not sure where he's gone off to. He's got a lot going on though so this is the norm for him lately.

"How are you holding up?" Claire's dad asks me.

"Not so good," I mumble.

"I have to believe that it's all going to be okay," he says to me. "Our family has lost too much."

"I thought when I got the call from Lee that today, I would leave here a married father of two and there was a minute there that I wasn't sure I would be going home a widower," I admit.

"I know," he says. "They scared the shit out of me too today. But everything will be okay, you just wait."

"I can't lose her," I voice my biggest fears.

"You won't," he reassures me. "You just have to have a little faith."

"Okay," I tell him.

"Mr. O'Connell you can see your wife in recovery now," a nurse says the sweetest words that I have ever heard to me and I jump ready to run.

"We'll just head out," he tells me as he signals to his wife that it's time to leave.

"See you in the morning," I say to them on a smile for the first time in hours

The nurse hold open a door for me and I walk into an open room with lots of beds in it, but I only have eyes for the dark haired angel staring at me like she's never seen me before.

"You don't look so good, Wes," she says and her voice is rough. The must have tubed her when she was sedated.

"You scared me, baby," I tell her.

"I scared myself."

"Don't ever do that to me again," i beg. I'm not afraid to be a pussy in this moment because I can't live without her. I love my wife just that much.

"I won't. How are the babies?"

"Beautiful," I tell her. "A girl and a boy."

"I'd like to name the girl Anna," she says softly.

"I like that," I tell her. "How about Faith for a middle name?"

"I like that," Claire says on a smile. "How did you come up with that?"

"Upstairs I was scared and your dad told me I just had to have a little faith," I tell her. "Is that too cheesy?"

"Not at all. I love it. Anna Faith O'Connell," she says testing it out.

"I'd kind of like to name the boy after Lee and your dad," I tell her.

"I think they would love that," she tells me.

"But not a first name so when Lee has a kid there aren't seventy five Liam's in the family."

"How about a middle name then?" she asks me.

"Sounds good to me."

"Wesley Liam O'Connell sounds good to me too." She kisses me sweetly. Tears clog my throat.

"You want to name our son after me?" I ask her.

"Of course," she says like it's not big deal. "You're the greatest guy I know."

"I love you," I tell her.

"And I love you," she says. "Are you happy?"

"Of course," I tell her. "Today is by far the best day of my life." To that she just smiles.

• • •

Wes

Nine months later . . .

"Beer?" my father-in-law asks me.

"Thank you, Sir," I tell him as I except the bottle he brought over to me.

We are standing on the edges of the party while my wife and her mother are fawning over their grandchildren. Claire is sitting in an armchair with Anna Faith bouncing on her lap and I swear to Christ she has never looked more beautiful.

Her long black hair is swept up in a bun on top of her head because my son loves to cling to it and these days those bright purple eyes shine with laughter and a genuine happiness not because of shadows that lurk in the corners of her mind.

We're at her parents' home surrounded by their friends and family because it is their fortieth anniversary. I look at them and they are so happy and still so in love and I want that. Even though I know that I don't deserve it.

I always wonder when I'm surrounded by all of the Goodnites if they hate me because I'm the product of monsters. The very same ones that lurked around every corner for their daughter.

"Thank you for letting me be part of your family," I tell him. I swallow past the lump in my throat.

"You were always part of this family, Wes." He pulls his brows together in though.

"Thank you for showing me what a normal one looks like anyways," I say letting my guard down. "I needed it more than I thought I did."

"I always knew."

"You did?" I ask him. I have to admit, that stings a little bit to know that my father-in-law always knew that my family was a colossal shit show. That I needed the Goodnites because I was being raised by wolves in sheep's clothing.

"I always knew what kind of man you'd be," he says continuing to turn my world upside down. "You and Claire have this. One day you'll look back, surrounded by grown children and grandbabies and you'll know exactly what this feels like and let me tell you, Son, it's so much more than great. It's a heat in your chest and a burning in your gut. It's the knowledge that you are the luckiest man alive and that God has seen fit to grant you so much more than you ever asked for, so much more than you ever thought you deserved."

"I know that feeling, Sir," I tell him honestly. "I feel it every morning when I look at your daughter and our children."

"Like I said before," he winks at me. "I always knew what kind of man you are." And the he walks over to Claire to claim his granddaughter out of her arms.

Claire walks over to me with a smile on her gorgeous face. "What were you and Dad talking about?" she asks me.

"How important family is," I tell her.

"I'm sorry," she says. "This kind of stuff must be hard for you."

"Not at all, baby," I smile at here. "Every day with you is easy."

"So you're happy today?" she asks me and as I think on today with my wife and our children while we celebrate her parents life long happiness, her dad making sure that I knew that I already was part of this family for a long time and always would be, but more importantly, that he thinks Claire and I have this kind of love, that all this beauty is my future ignites that warmth in my chest that he spoke about. I know that I already have a life of beauty with Claire as my partner so I answer her the only way I can.

"Of course," I tell her. "Today was the best day of my life."

• • •

Wes

Christmas, six years later . . .

"Santa came! Santa came!" my beautiful kids shout as the run through the house in a whirlwind of wrapping paper and bows leaving the detritus in their wake.

"I see that!" I tell them. "Merry Christmas, kiddos."

"Merry Christmas, Wes," Claire says from beside me. We've been sipping our morning coffee while we watch the kids revel in Christmas joy.

"Merry Christmas, baby." I lean down and I kiss her lips. Claire gets more beautiful every day and I am the lucky bastard that gets to love her.

This year the kids have grown by leaps and bounds. We've both cut back at work so that we can be at all the class parties and field trips. This year, I even coached a baseball team and it was awesome.

I couldn't ask for more.

"Looks like he brought something for daddy too," she says softly with a happy twinkle in her eyes. What could my girl be up to now? She and the kids already gave me a new baseball glove to play catch with the kids and I gave her a swing for the porch so we can sit out there and watch the kids play together.

What could be left?

"Oh he did, did he?" I ask on a raised brow. She loves when I do that.

Claire hands me a small decorate box with a big bow on it that I definitely did not see under the tree this morning. That means she must have been hiding it somewhere to save it for last. I know then that this must be special. And when I pull the lid off the box I know that I'm right.

"Again?" I ask her feeling my heart rate pick up. In the small box was a long white stick with a big purple plus sign right in the middle and a glossy grainy picture no bigger than the palm of my hand but it holds a key component that my heart didn't know that I was missing all along.

"It's just one this time," she assures me but it doesn't matter if it's one or five I'm still going to worry and I'm still the happiest man alive. "Are you happy?"

"Of course, baby. This is the best day of my life."

• • •

Claire

Nineteen years later . . .

"Happy Anniversary, baby," Wes says as he wraps his arms around me from behind. "What are you doing over here?"

"Just taking it all in," I answer.

Today is our twenty fifth wedding anniversary and Wes insisted we hosted all of our family and friends for a big dinner party so our home is filled with all the people we love, Jones and his family, Lee and his. Our sister, Bonnie's kids who aren't kids anymore and their families. Hell, even our kids aren't babies anymore and the proof of that is the baby boy with black hair and violet eyes that our daughter, Anna Faith, is bouncing in her lap.

"I am a grandmother. When did that happen?" I ask my still handsome husband. His dark hair is mostly silver now and I love it. His whiskey eyes smile almost every day now.

"About six months ago," he says.

"You know what?" he asks me.

"No, what?" I laugh.

"Your dad was right all those years ago."

"How so?" I ask Wes.

"He told me he knew what kind of man I was from the beginning and that I would always love you. He said that you and I would have what they had."

I look around the room filled with all of the people we love so much and our home filled with love and happiness. "Because we do."

"Yes, we do," he tells me.

"Are you happy?" I ask him.

"Of course," Wes answers me. "This is the best day of my life."

What he hopefully knows by now, and I have done my very best to show him, is that every day with Wes has been the very best day of my life and each one is just a little better than the last.

the End

(For real this time. Mostly. Sort of.)

hush little baby

a liam goodnite novel

Life in George Washington Township and the surrounding areas has once again been shaken up. Young, unwed mothers are turning up hacked to pieces after crude caesareans and their babies are nowhere to be found.

While overseeing the investigation, Captain Liam Goodnite receives some surprising news that just might give him the push that he needs to make the sexy Medical Examiner, Emma Parker, his once and for all.

Only Emma isn't one to forgive and forget.

Good thing life has taught Lee some tough lessons and now he's willing to do whatever it takes.

about jennifer rebecca

Jennifer is the *USA Today* Bestselling Author of the Claire Goodnite series and the Presidential Affair. She is a native of San Diego, California. She credits her love of books and reading to her mother and her knowledge that real heroes do exist to her dad.

Jennifer is a graduate of California State University San Marcos where she studied Criminology and Justice Studies. She is also a member of Alpha Xi Delta.

She currently lives in East Texas with her husband, Sean, and their three children along with an entire menagerie of lovable but sofa eating animals. She can often be found on the soccer or baseball fields, reading, or wondering what the hell her senior citizens have gotten up to now. Jennifer is convinced that if she puts her apple watch on one of the dogs, she might finally make her step goals.

She loves a great romance, an alpha hero, and lots and lots of laughter.

stalk her

Website
JenniferRebeccaAuthor.com

Newsletter
JenniferRebeccaAuthor.com/Newsletter

Facebook
facebook.com/JenniferRebeccaAuthor

Instagram
@jenniferrebeccaauthor

TikTok
@jennirlreads

BookBub
bookbub.com/authors/jennifer-rebecca

Dangerous Dames Facebook Group
facebook.com/groups/JRDangerousDames

also by jennifer rebecca

The Alaskan Wildflowers
Wildfllower

Accidental Hex Series
Birthday Hex

Royal Secrets and Lies
King of Lies

A Presidental Affair
The Senators Secret
Caught by the Chief of Staff
The Press Secretary's Passion

The Claire Goodnite Series
Tell Me A Story
Tuck Me In Tight
Say A Sweet Prayer
Kiss Me Goodnight

The Funerals and Obituaries Mysteries
Dead and Buried
Dead and Gone
Dead and Deceived

Liam Goodnite
Hush Little Baby
Don't Say a Word

The Murder on Ice Mysteries
Attack Zone
Layback

The Southern Heartbeats Series
Stand (Vol. 1)
Whiskey Lullabye (Vol. 2)
Mercy

Sunnyville Series
(co-written with Alyssa Kale)
Ready to Run